Abigail's Wedding

(The Curio Chronicles)

Robin John Morgan

First published (Paperback) in the UK in 2023 by Violet Circle Publishing.

Manchester, England, UK.

Print ISBN: 978-1-910299-42-5
Digital ISBN: 978-1-910299-43-2

British Library Cataloguing in Publication Data.
A catalogue record for this book is available from the British Library.

All paper used in the production of this book are sourced only from wood grown in sustainable forests.

www.violetcirclepublishing.co.uk

Also by Robin John Morgan.

Heirs to the Kingdom.

Book One, The Bowman of Loxley.
Book Two, The Lost Sword of Carnac.
Book Three, The Darkness of Dunnottar.
Book Four, Queen of the Violet Isle.
Book Five, Crystals of the Mirrored Waters.
Book Six, Last Arrow of the Woodland Realm.
Book Seven, Bridge Of Sequana.
Book Eight, The Circle of Darkness.

The Curio Chronicles.

Part One, Abigail's Summer.
Part Two, Curio's Summer.
Part Three, Curio's Christmas.
Part Four, Abigail's Wedding

Other works.

Rise of the Raven.
The Countess of Darkness

Han's Cottage

Life can be, and should be spontaneous.
Every second should be lived, and savoured.

Be you, and go live.

I had come so far away from then, and not just in my life, but the life of all the Curio's had changed so much from those days when we were just getting to really know each other, sat in my dad's guest house across the road from my current home.

We had been gelled as a group, because none of us felt we belonged. The truth was, there was no place in Wotton life for us at that time, we were shamed and shunned, and tried to avoid facing those who wronged us. Our lives had changed so much, some of it was luck, and some hard work, but the one thing in common we all shared, was our love for one person.

(Abigail Jennifer Watson)

Chapter 1

Curio Live.

The camera blinked, ready for live broadcast, as the crew checked makeup, and lighting. Notes were on the desk in order, and the producer wearing his head set, cleared the floor, and River Cable TV, was almost ready in the studio. The floor manager looked at Amy, and lifted his hand ready, and the camera light turned green, the floor manager counted down, three, two, one, he pointed at Amy.

"Good Afternoon, I am Amy Walker, coming to you live from the studio of River Cable TV News, and welcome to what is being billed as one of the most important events, for the mental health of young people, in the last decade. For the next three days, we will be carrying a joint live stream with the charity web site Curio Life, transmitting to fifty countries all across the globe. We have such a packed program of guest speakers, and special surprise guests, and some exclusive behind the scenes interviews all lined up. So, stay tuned, as it is almost time, and we are now going live to London, and the event, where we have Brett Eton. Hi Brett, tell us what is the atmosphere like there today, we are hearing that there is not a single seat empty?"

Brett Eton, stood at the front of the loud arena filled with excited voices, his back to one side of the dark stage, he smiled into the camera.

"Hi Amy, it is almost time, and I must say, the atmosphere in the arena is electric, as everyone has packed into every single seat, and is eagerly awaiting the start of what we have been promised, will be an event that will shake up the mental health world for years to come. We have such a wide range of people here, from the mental health profession, celebrity guests, bands, to Curio supporters, and a very obvious amount of Abigail Jennifer Watson fans. We have been told there is only seconds left to go, and the excitement is at fever pitch, so I will hand back over to you, and let's see what the Curio's have in store for us."

The house lights slowly dimmed, and the hum of conversation lowered, all eyes were on the stage, the two huge screens either side flickered into life, the stage lights brightened, to reveal a heavy red back curtain, with a large white screen, and to one side of the stage, a lectern from which to speak. The air was filled with anticipation, as a tall woman with long brown hair, wearing a white dress, walked onto the stage with a smile, she walked up to the lectern, and looked at the camera.

On both sides of the stage, the large screens came to life, and a close up of her stood smiling, came into view. She stood silently waiting for a few moments, and then leaned into the microphone.

"Good evening, my name is Alison Williams, and when I was in my twenties, I used to have a flourishing acting career, until I was singled out by a bully, who made it their business to try and destroy me, because I was different. You see, I did not buy into all the glitz of show business, I lived a quiet life, away from the cameras and media. I hardly ever spoke to the press, and one reporter did not like that, and so he began a campaign to smear my character, and as a result, that dream I had as a child to appear on stage, and in front of the camera, was taken away from me."

Alison stood still and looked out into the audience, there was utter silence, such was the power of her statement.

"Many of you will look at me and say, well so what, for a time you got a six figure pay packet, you did alright. I cannot deny, I invested wisely, and I live a comfortable life, but let me assure you, at 3am when you are alone in a dark house, with the curtains drawn to hide you from press camera's, and every dream you had, has been crushed, you are drunk, and staring at a bottle of anti depressant pills, no amount of money can make you feel better. The effects of being bullied, go beyond money and status, and they hurt in ways deep down inside that tears your soul apart."

Behind her, the screen in the centre of the stage turned a soft pale blue. She turned and looked back to it, and lifted her hand, and bright letters appeared on the screen, she turned and looked at the audience, and smiled.

"Welcome to Curio Live."

Suddenly the audience erupted into applause, and she gave a chuckle. She waited for a good few moments, and then lifted her hand, for the audience to quieten. The place was packed to the rafters, she looked back at the screen and lifted her hand, she pressed a small black controller in her hand, and a row of boxes appeared on the bottom of the screen, with a large phone number and text information above it, she turned back to the audience.

"Today we start the first of what will be a three day fundraising event, as we hope to take the charity Curio Life up to another level. For four years, the Curio Life site has been visited from young people all over the globe, and it has been a platform that has given young people aged 18 to 30 a voice. A chance to tell their story, and get vital help and support. It was started by just six young 24 and 25 year olds, who understood what it was like to be shunned and shamed for being different, their voices were stifled."

She took a breath as behind her, pictures started to appear that had the face of every person who had ever uploaded a video, which moved in a stream of sad, lonely, and painful faces.

"No one would listen, and so they did something very brave, they all filmed their story and put them up online for the world to see. The result of those brave six, were seen by others, who felt as desperate and isolated as they did, and discovered they were not alone, for possibly the first time in their lives, they had a voice. Shunned by society, they chose not to be labelled as society would deem, they were all different kinds of people, with different sexualities, and with different understandings of the world. They shared one thing in common, all of them were curious about the world, about life, about themselves, and none of them understood why they could not just be left, to be who they wanted to be, and so they rejected the society they lived in, and named themselves Curio's."

The audience applauded, and Alison gave a large smile, and waited a moment for it to quieten.

"This event, which will run for the next three days, will be live streamed all over the globe. On this stage, you will see a great many motivational speakers, health professionals, celebrities from all over the world, and get to watch workshops on self help. We have live streams from across the globe, as others show us the reality of their world, and we also have some amazing live bands. All of the people involved in this event, are donating their time for free, and we are all asking simply for you to watch and learn, but most importantly, help. The boxes behind me will show how much has been raised, for what we hope will become the first of many Curio help centres, which will provide residential support, for many young people struggling to find their way, in a world that has turned its back on them. We have a lot of special events, and seminars planned all over this complex, for visitors to attend, and we have a lot of surprises for you. So, to begin tonight, and start the weekend, let's have our first surprise. I am delighted to welcome to the stage someone very special, and one of the inspirations and main driving forces behind this project, please welcome Miss Abigail Jennifer Watson."

I stood in the wings and Birch smiled.
"Sweetie, you will be wonderful." I looked at her bright eyes as they sparkled, and took a deep breath.
"Birch, I want to puke." She kissed my cheek.
"Sweetie, the back screen is twenty feet high, no one wants to see that, trust me, you are cute, but throwing up at that size, is just too unsettling. Now get out there and make me proud." She spun me round and patted my bum.

The stage was as big as the village green, it was huge, and I felt small and insignificant, as I took my first few paces with my stomach churning. As I came out from behind the curtain, to the music of Avril, the noise was insane, Alison applauded and smiled at me.
Hiding my inner terror, I walked slowly to the centre of the stage, and the microphone, and I stood smiling as the audience went crazy. The spotlight was on me, and either side of the stage were two huge close ups of me on the screens, with my red eye makeup and my red tipped fringe, and my long black hair with the red tips.
Today I wore boot cut satin pants, and a black flowing gothic top. I waited longer than I expected for the applause to quell.

I looked round the huge arena, not really seeing everyone, but seeing enough. I took a deep breath, swallowed hard, and leaned into the mic.

"Hi, I am Abby, and I am a Curio."

The audience went wild again, and I gave a giggle, it really was terrifying, and yet unbelievable, thousands of people were all packed in to see this. I had no idea how Birch, Roni and Katie, had managed to pull this off. I waited for a few moments, doing my best not to have a panic attack. I took a deep breath, and leaned forward, and felt my legs trembling.

"Four years ago, my friends and I all made a video each, we were only around 24 years old, but we had all suffered rude comments, unkind words, and some blatant in our face hostility. The crazy thing is, the reason was, I left for university to study English Literature, and I was a blonde, blue eyed country girl. When I came home, I looked pretty much like I do tonight, you see, this is me, it is who I am, my fiancé calls me her dark little beastie, and in a way, I am, because I am a writer of gothic fiction and horror. When I came home, because I looked like this, I was called slut, whore, transient, and a great deal more, and the place where I had grown up, the place I called home, and was supposed to be a place I was safe, became my idea of hell. Five years after returning home, having endured so much hate, I slid into depression, I sat alone one night on my bed, with a bottle of tequila, and a bottle of sleeping pills, and I wanted to end my life, such was the pain I felt. Luckily, I passed out, and I never did it. I woke the following day, feeling at the most wretched I had ever felt, and feeling like the biggest failure on the planet. I had hit rock bottom, and that was my turning point, my wake up call, and the day I decided to really fight back."

Behind me on the screen a picture appeared, and the audience gasped, I looked back at it, and shuddered, even now I go cold if I see it. I took a deep breath, and felt a tear in my eye as I looked at it, I lifted my arm and pointed at the screen. I swallowed hard and wiped my eyes.

"That is the selfie I took that night; it is not pretty is it? That is me, me at my absolute worst moment in my life. Today I am a pretty well known writer, I am classed as a public figure, and yet like Alison, I shy away from the media, not because I am arrogant or stuck up, but because they look at my work, see my hair, and my eye makeup, and they simply assume I am a slut, a whore, a transient, and they write things like that about me. Even now, after all these years, I am not free of the public gaze, I am different, I am me, and society does not like me, and so I have opted out of it. I live a quiet life with my own lifestyle, surrounded by the most amazing people who are not just my friends, they are my family. Oddly enough, they are all Curio's too." I smiled, and the audience applauded, and cheered.

 "Ladies and gentlemen, and viewers who are on live stream all over the world, my friends and I told our story, and in doing so we managed to bring together people from all over the planet, who shared our feelings, and understood our troubles. There are so many out there suffering, because this world can be very cruel. Young people are feeling confused, lost, unable to cope, and in many extreme cases, they are taking their own lives. Recently my fiancé informed me, that the odds of being born, are actually trillions to one, can you imagine that? Everyone of us here today, is literally a living miracle, and yet the number of young people taking their own lives, is rising on an annual basis, and I am not sure about you, but I feel very strongly we should do something to at least try to stop it?

 The Curio Life Project has reached out to over two hundred organisations with vital funds that they needed, and we now want to bring all those people, who have such large hearts and have helped so many of us, together, by providing them with resource centres. Even though an online presence has helped, there are still a lot of young people out there who do not have friends or support, they are struggling alone, and we want to give them a place they can go to, where they are supported, and safe. A place where we can give them aid, support and education about who they are, and in doing so, help them improve their lives. The lines are about to open, and we desperately need donations, our Curio site has merchandise for sale, and you will find for the next three days a whole host of things created for this event, only available this weekend. Every penny we raise, helps someone who looks like I did on that dreadful night, and so we are asking, please help them. Thank you, all of you, for being here today to support us, and for being a part of Curio Live."

The whole arena exploded with applause, and it was deafening, I stood and smiled and waved, and then turned slowly, and walked off the stage back towards Birch, waiting in the wings, Alison continued with the rest of the program, I reached Birch, who wore a huge smile.

"Sweetie, you were wonderful." I was trembling.

"Birch, I am going to puke." She turned and yelled.

"Katie, we need a bucket." I have no idea where it came from, but one appeared, and I grabbed it, and leaned in to it and!?

"YERK!" Birch stepped back looking disgusted, and screwed up her face.

"Oh Sweetie, that is messed up, I was going to kiss you, but I think I will wait." Chloe appeared in her dungarees and handed me a bottled water.

"Here, rinse your mouth out, and when that is done, I have vodka in the dressing room." She smiled as I took it.

"I saw the picture you put up; how come we have never seen it?"

I took a large swig of the bottle and swilled out my mouth and spat it into the bucket, it was most un-lady like, my mouth felt instantly better, and I handed the bucket back to Birch, she looked inside and gave a shudder.

"Oh, Sweetie, I do love you, but this is the single most unattractive thing you have ever done to me." She handed the bucket to one of the crew.

"Be a Sweetie, and empty this for me." He looked appalled, but took it, she smiled a sweet smile.

"Thank you, you are a treasure." Chloe looked back at the guy walking away.

"You know if you freeze dry that, you can put it on Ebay and make a fortune?" Birch gave another shudder.

"Chloe Sweetie, you are screwed up too." I giggled; Birch pulled me into a hug.

"You were really wonderful out there, you looked great on the big screens, you can relax a bit, you are not on stage again until Sunday." She looked at my mouth.

"Sweetie, I love you, but honestly, at the moment, your breath smells like Satan's sewer, go with Chloe, and drink vodka, actually, drink lots of vodka, you need to kill whatever is lurking around your tonsils." She kissed my cheek and fondled my bum, and gave a cheeky giggle.

"I will see you in a little bit, how about later we try out that huge bath in our room, just you and me, lots of hot water, white wine and naughtiness?"

"Yeah, I would like that, don't work too hard, you have mum and Katie to help out, I know you, do not exhaust yourself, I want some of that energy used on pampering me later." She gave an excited giggle.

"Oh, Sweetie, I want to go straight to the room now, but don't worry, I am saving something up for you later." I kissed her cheek, and she held her breath.

"Yuk!"

I started to laugh, as I walked off with my bad breath from puking, and Chloe, maybe I did need something stronger to cleanse my mouth? As I walked away from the stage I felt better, I think it was sheer relief. I was getting better on stage, in the last few years I have done a lot more TV and live interviews, and my nerves were not as bad, although there was always a bucket on standby.

This place was huge, and had at least ten times the amount of people I was used to, and my nerves got the better of me, but as I headed for the dressing room, my stomach calmed down, and I felt better. I headed for the gin; I needed a large one to steady my nerves.

The next three hours of my life were pretty much planned, Shoots of Summer, the follow up to my first book, of my group of teenagers living a wild life, had come out and was yet another hit, and for the next three hours, I would be sat in one of this Hotel Arena's many rooms, with a huge pile of books, signing copies, and meeting the readers. I actually enjoyed it, for me it was the best part of being a writer, I got to spend a few minutes with all the people that loved my books, and it always felt special.

Chloe was to be my chaperone for the event, Katie insisted all the Curio's stayed in pairs when out in public, and we had two very large guys with us. Katie called them protection officers, but they were basically hired muscle, today we had Derek and Roy. They were actually nice guys, and good fun, we misbehaved, and they covered for us, which for Chloe and me, left to our own devices, with alcohol, was probably a good thing.

Is it strange that I am becoming used to screaming fans? I still struggle with the cameras and their flashes, and so I always have at least three pairs of round mirrored sunglasses in my bag.

These things ran pretty smoothly, I would walk in, usually behind a long table covered with a cloth, and the wall behind me would be covered in posters of the book cover. The table would have stacks of books, and Chloe would sit at my side, and as each person approached, Chloe would open the book to the title page, and place it in front of me to sign as I spoke to the reader. It was crazy really, but she had really come to love doing them with me, and so whenever Birch was not available, I took her along.

There were always assistants, to provide liquid, and cater to our needs, and as always security. I did have one guy ask to hug me, and he tried to cop a feel of my boob, so they were always on watch, and any funny business, and the offending idiot would be thrown out, but for the most, it all ran well. My hand ached after; I could sign a good few hundred books at a big event like this one.

After over three hours, I was tired, in the main arena guests were on stage talking and showing slide and video presentations. Birch was going to be one of them, but I just wanted some silence, and headed up to my room, escorted by Roy. I assured him I would not be leaving the room again until meal time, and would inform him if I did, so he could collect me, he was very sweet, and for such a big guy, actually very gentle.

I entered the room, on the floor was a suitcase with clothes thrown all around it, from where Birch was looking for a sock. I smiled, even here in a high class hotel, she was no different from the guest house four years ago on her return.

I flopped on the bed, and undid my pants and slid them off, it felt wonderful to feel my skin free from the restriction of my clothing. I picked them up and threw them to the chair, and then lay back, flexing the fingers of my writing hand, it was so nice to be in a room that was silent, I closed my eyes and just relaxed.

The Curio Live event had taken two years from Birch first talking to her mum and me, in our kitchen at home. She had worked hard, and all of us had joined in to support her, after all, this was an important cause. Our soul aim was to provide care facilities, for those many names and faces we had all spoken to on the Curio site, who were trapped, isolated and alone, with no support, and had no one to hold their hand, and no one to comfort them.

As I lay with my eyes closed, I thought of those days alone in the guest house, those nights in tears and in pain, after yet another public humiliation that day from Marjorie and her group of hateful friends. Just like now, I would lie on the bed in silence, but unlike now, I was filled with internal pain, that tore deeply at me. It robbed me of my dignity, and my confidence, to the point where I lost my faith in living. I cannot deny, I have read hundreds of stories like mine on Curio Life, I have cried hundreds of times reading them, and spent days and weeks, answering every single one.

Some of those people have had weeks and months of correspondence with me, some of them have become well known faces and friends online to me, and I have seen their journey from a cry for help on the site, to a resolution as the site directed them to the care they needed.

I knew that it was just a simple space to tell our story, but against all the odds, it has become a place for thousands all over the world to tell their story, and in a strange way, I felt proud that I had played a small part in it. Our task, which is headed by Birch, is to raise the funds, we have sites, we have a developer, and we have the people to staff them, what we lack is the funds. For the next three days, we will hopefully show the world our aim, and they will rise to help us, and if not, we will all go home, and carry on as we were, talking to strangers, and giving them reasons to continue.

On the TV, which was tuned to the live stream, the writer Christian Besson was talking about his work with young people who have tried to kill themselves with Birch. As much as I wanted to watch, I was simply too tired, and I slipped into a dream, and just drifted quietly in the silence of my room, as I rested. I had arrived yesterday, and unpacked ready, and then done several walk throughs and pissed around a lot with Chloe, and we all got really drunk last night. It had been a long day, rising at six with a hangover, for one last run through, and then all the hustle and bustle of the sound checks, and scripts, then heading to the stage to prepare for my introduction speech. I must admit three hours of book signing on top of all that, was a little too much and I felt wasted.

Birch has been here for two weeks, I spent a few days at the end of last week, and the weekend, but returned home to link up with Amy from River, and the rest of the River TV group at home. It has been a long exhausting week, and if I am honest, I am feeling the strain a little. I never sleep well when Birch is not with me. Hotels used to feel like treats, now they feel like prisons, especially here, as we are all isolated from each other, to avoid the press. Katie wants to keep us apart until the end of the event, for last minute impact, but I cannot deny, I have felt a little lonely at times this week.

It was three hours later when I woke, Birch was sat on the bed, straddled over me smiling, and stroking the hair from my face.

"Hi sweetie, it is time for a meal, you have not eaten all day, and we have a VIP table ready for us." I yawned, and stretched out my arms.

"I would rather stay here in bed with you, do I absolutely have to go?" She leaned over me.

"I would love to stay here alone with you too, but we are expected, we have thirty minutes to get ready." I gave a sigh, and she leaned down towards me.

"We have some time though."

She came close and started to kiss me, it was warm and soft, and I closed my eyes and just enjoyed the moment, smelling her scent and feeling her lips. Her warm hand slid up inside my top, and I gave a happy little moan, she moved down and started to kiss my neck, I moaned a little louder, and felt my top lift up, and she moved downwards more.

"Oh Baby, yes, oh god that is so nice."

Her hand slid down towards between my thighs, I moaned again, this was all I needed, I had no need of glitz and pomp, I breathed out a happy sigh.

"Oh Birch... OH BABY YES!"

It is strange how life changes. Nine years ago, I yearned to touch her and be touched by her, but I was terrified of the things people would say if I did, and so I went out of my way to sleep with men. Four years ago, in the midst of breaking down, I told her I loved her, and wanted her, and a few days later, she made love to me for the first time, and yet I still had sex with men, sometimes in front of her, but for the last few years there have been less men, as I drifted into only Birch.

Two years ago, we renewed our oath to each other, and we presented each other rings and made the promise of marriage, and I will not deny, there has been a few wild threesomes with a guy on occasion, but our love making has become even more frequent. I was eighteen when I met her, and she was nineteen, today I am twenty eight, and she is twenty nine, and yet in the last six months, I have felt my levels of lust and desire grow in significant ways. Am I becoming a paler version of Chloe, because just being around Birch gets me wet and horny, is this some rite of passage, as I head towards being thirty?

I have no idea, I just know if I see her, I want her, we have been going at it like teenagers recently, and at times it is like madness. I had her on the cellar table last week, we were supposed to be sorting out the wine, two nights ago we got up at two am and had sex in the pool, before that we were going at it in the hot tub.

We have done it recently on both balconies to our room, in the attic, on the stairs at four in the morning, on the kitchen island, we even snuck into the garage and did it on the roof of Petal. I have no idea why I feel like this, I mean, I love her, I have for a long time, and I have to consider it, is this all my hormones fault? Honestly, at times, I am exhausted because of it.

This is probably why I write and sleep, I am always in bed, which is a nightmare, because if she comes in and I am in bed, I drag her in with me, and I have worried I am becoming a nymphomaniac. Well not worrying, I mean, I am getting laid at least four times a day, why would that worry anyone? I have even started to work out and take vitamins just to keep my metabolism boosted enough to cope with my desire.

Birch gets lots of psychology magazines, and I have started to read those in my search for answers, I even typed into my search engine 'why am I always horny?' but all I got was articles on sex addiction, and I am sorry, but if I was screwing the whole village,

I would accept that, but I am not, my focus is solely on one person.

My climax was hard, and I made a lot of noise, as I arched up on the bed, Birch chuckled as she crawled back over me with a smile, and flopped on top of me, I wrapped my arms round her, and held her close, feeling happy and dreamy, she kissed the side of my neck.

"Sweetie, I am still hungry." I looked down at her.

"For food or for me?" She looked up.

"I need food Sweetie, come eat with me and the others." I gave a sigh.

"My legs are shaking, I need a moment, and then yes I will join all of you, I want my strength, because when we get back here later, you are mine for the night." She gave a giggle, and looked at me with those gorgeous green eyes.

"Oh Sweetie, I am going to eat really fast now."

Roni and Katie picked the venue, I should have known, with Katie, everything was high class. At the far end of our hotel restaurant, a VIP area was roped off, and it was here we were to be seated, as usual Birch and myself were running behind. As I walked through the hotel with Birch on my arm and our two minders, people stopped, smiled, and whispered to each other, I was not a lover of being in London, far too many people recognised me.

We arrived at the table and sat down, the waitress handed Birch and myself the menus, and I looked at the vegetarian options. Recently I have been getting a little bit health conscious, and I have cut out some of my meals of meat. To be honest, I was getting a bit of a belly, and one night Birch gave it a tug, and I saw a huge mound rise in her hand, which freaked me out a little.

Just seeing that made me realise, even though a party life is wonderful, and boy have we partied, it was getting to me a little, and so I started to exercise more and eat better, we have even installed a gym in the attic. Three times a week, I eat veggie, and luckily Chloe and Edwina were on board with it, and joined me, Birch has always eaten far healthier than any of us, and just slid into it.

It was nice to sit with the group, but what was nicer was all of us were targets for the cameras, not just press, but guests. I was used to it, but this for them was their first experience, and finally they got a taste of my life.

The food was excellent, the wine flowed, but with hundreds of people with cameras, it was not long before we called it a night, and Birch and myself had a bath and bed night planned. Tomorrow was press day, it would be all hands on deck, as we each took turns talking to the press, and to be really honest, I was not looking forward to it at all.

Chapter 2

Wotton Life.

It was early morning and the sun was up, and I sat beside the large patio window, which was open, high above London. I wanted the fresh air, but my fear of heights kept me several feet away, so I sat back and sipped my coffee, as I made notes in my journal.

Katie did not want any of us to do an interview with the press in more than two's, her aim was to keep us separate as a group, until the end of the event, which is why we were all paired up throughout the whole event. Birch was off this morning with Anthony, and Deb's who was at home with Jimmy, had not arrived yet.

It felt strange that with the sun up and the warmth of the day starting, I was missing home, which considering it was a place I once feared, it felt strange. Wotton had changed so much in the last nine years, hell in the last two years alone, I have seen so much change. We all still lived in the house, at number three Waterside Lane, but there were a few additions, Luke was a permanent part of life, Edwina and him had at some point become a very serious item, and for that matter, so had Anthony and Michael.

Both the guys made a good contribution to home life, Terry was a very frequent visitor, and we just accepted that he was part of us, although Chloe still had a lot of action on the side with some of her models. The biggest change to our homelife, was Edwina's business was growing, and for a while she had considered renting offices, as she needed to bring in new staff, but she was working out of the house.

The problem was solved, when Birch suggested we build a new bigger garage on the side of the house. To her it was logical, firstly we have the space for a bigger garage, and behind that level with Chloe's studio, because the garage went right back, we were able to build a store room, for book stock.

It was basically a large empty room with lots of shelves and boxes. Secondly it brought the outer cellar door inside the house. It had been a worry ever since the vicar used it to get his club things, and thirdly, the old garage was very large, so by replacing the large garage door, with a glass front and a new glass door, it instantly became an office. G5 fitted blinds, like they had in Chloe's studio, to keep the sun out. Michael did the rewire, the walls were insulated, and carpets were fitted. Now, the door in the kitchen, led into a corridor, with two doors, one to the garage at the end, and one into Edwina's office, where Samantha, a very talented twenty five year old, computer whiz worked.

It is so strange looking back to Christmas two years ago, we had so many trials as we strove to do something as simple as a normal family Christmas. I often sit and think back, and can see how much it bonded us together as a huge family. I have often heard that sometimes family is not who you are related to, but who chooses to stay at your side in tough times, and I think that Christmas really taught me the importance of what it means to be surrounded by the love and support of these amazing talented and quirky people.

It sounds odd, but something as simple as trekking up above the manor on March first, which we did as a group, and planting a cherry tree above Wotton in memory of May, who had died the previous December, really showed the love and support we all had for Birch. By just being there as she shed a few tears, she knew she had us always to stand by her side in sadness. God, I love my Curio family.

The biggest news of our year was Deb's was pregnant, she was actually five to six weeks away from birth, and we were all very excited about the prospect of becoming aunties, and uncles. She always had big boobs, but recently, they had grown huge, I was convinced they were bigger than my head, which fascinated Chloe and me. We had a good banter going, and when I fondled them for fun, Deb's who turned beetroot, got mad, and so we have all been banned from touching them.

Is it weird, that when people encounter a pregnant woman, they always touch their belly, and tell them how happy and proud of them they are? Chloe and me discussed it, and we still cannot work it out, although Chloe did point out, no one rubs the guys balls and tells them, 'Well Done!' I laughed my ass off when she told me, but I do think she had a point, which if you think about it, it is sort of odd. It is yet another of the strange rituals that surround having babies, which as you know, I try to avoid.

Things between her and Jimmy were better than ever, after his last Christmas Day booking in Japan, where she discovered he had taken up the groupies again, Deb's played him at his own game and slept with Creamy. Jimmy knew about it, and did not appear too concerned, until he saw Creamy modelling for Chloe in the buff. One look at Creamy's junk, and Jimmy was a reformed citizen, such was his fear of losing her to a bigger man.

Battered Taco were on an indefinite break, so Jimmy was home a lot more, he had fallen out with Floyd, and as much as I hate that scumbag Kyle, he was actually right. Floyd did not like the fact that Jimmy was a really good guitarist, and on their last tour Floyd had got so out of it, Jimmy played lead and sang, and the band did the gig one band member down. Jimmy is currently working at home, in a new studio he has built, and is working on some solo material. Deb's thinks he has done it to prove a point, and show Floyd he is acting like a big baby.

Speaking of babies, Claudette had a little girl, and shortly after the birth, her and Alberta separated, apparently Alberta did not like that she got less attention. I cannot deny, I always felt she hated me, and she gave off a bad vibe, I thought she was too controlling, so was not surprised when Bev told us. Jon Claude is supporting Claudette, his relationship with Claire fizzled out as he struggled to perform sexually with her, after the impregnation. Chloe is convinced the baby looks like Luke, honestly, I just think it is unattractive, and it is really long, it has legs like stilts.

Bev, bless her, is still having trouble with her mum, but her and Bridgette seem to be doing well, she has just started a new course on green keeping, I know, how hard is it to grow grass? But she is happy and enjoying it, and as she puts it.

"When I tell folks, I grow grass for a living, they seem to really respect me." Bless her, she really is wonderful.

Somewhere in the midst of this huge event, Aden is around,

he is site manager for the Curio Site, and is handling the live stream under the supervision of Edwina. Gill should be here, as Sweetie's Retreat is closed at the weekends. Aden and Gill are still together and are engaged, they plan to marry next year, we were all amazed to learn that Aden finally plucked up the courage to ask her.

Marriage appears to have been in the air for a while. Marion married her long term man friend, Sydney, earlier in the year, and against the odds, Amanda the florist married Andrew at the end of last year. The best love story of the village has to be that of Hatty and Clive, they are still going strong after four years, and Hatty is still her usual radical self, but when you see them together, you can see how much she adores him. He is a quiet thoughtful man, not the fastest snail in the race, and yet his laid back approach to life, is perfect for her, he spends hours, just sat watching her paint.

During our first Christmas at home, mum partnered up with Ellen, when she left the care home after the death of May, her favourite resident, and they opened up Waterside Galleries, in the old antique shop, in the village. It has gone really well, mum has sold six of her paintings, well actually one was to Birch and the other Hatty. Chloe has sold eight to date, and she is delighted, especially when you consider they were all erotic and sexually explicit, and they were not cheap, her paintings go for several thousands of pounds, but she still will not sell the one in her room of Birch and myself sun bathing, trust me I have tried.

My mum has done really well for herself, and has become a strong independent woman, she spends most Saturdays and the occasional Sunday, with Patrick, he dotes on her, but she is adamant there will be no marriage. She is happier than I have ever seen her, and I love that, she deserves it after years of dad and his dullness.

Speaking of, he is still with Angela, I am still convinced it was only because he liquidated a lot of his assets after the scandal, which saw his partner Graham, get ten years in prison. I am not convinced he is completely okay with the idea of his daughter marrying a woman, but in all fairness, I think Angela has played a behind the scenes role in things, and to date, he has said nothing to offend Birch or myself.

In a weird twisted way, I am grateful to her, I don't want Birch to be hurt again by him, and in a show of good faith, I have ceased hostilities with Angela. On the few occasions we have met for lunch, I have been nice and polite, even friendly.

She is still nervous around Birch, which is silly, Birch told me, she would not have beaten her senseless with the ash tray, her objective had she done it, would have been to make her ugly, and that would have only taken two smacks in the face. Birch assured me, she would have ensured all her senses remained intact, I do love her northern attitude at times, but let's be honest, Birch would never have hurt her... I think?

Dad and I get on, we are cordial, and we do not fight as much, but our relationship is still very lacking, especially when you compare it to what I have with Will. I have really grown to love Birch's dad, we get on so well, and he spoils both Birch and myself rotten, and I cannot deny, I love it. Roni is Roni, I have had a special bond with her since the first time I met her. I talk to Roni a lot, she gives me great advice, not just for life, but she is great at helping me understand characters. She really knows how to get inside the bad guy's heads, and Birch often sits and laughs, as we talk and explore, the deranged minds of some of the new characters I am working on.

Wotton has not changed much to look at it, the green is still kept immaculate by Ronald, who always drives past on his mower, and tips his hat to Edwina, much to Chloe and my amusement. The Tea Rooms has had a complete overhaul, and been redecorated, it is funny, I still get unsettled when I go in. Celia and Lillian are still huge perverts, and Birch always loves to tease them, as she points out new young hot girls in the village to them. Izzy was wrong though, Stacy is just a fan, it was Louise who turned out to be the lesbian.

Peter and Mary have two younger assistants in the Post Office/ Village Store, both apparently Sun Club members. I see a lot of Paula from the Sun Club, she is often at our house sprawled out with Chloe on the lawn, and I visit her at the club when I need somewhere quiet, to chill out whilst Birch is at work. I joined the club, and I bought Birch a subscription, she does not go as often as I do, but we do love to walk alone naked in the woodland there, those are very special days to me, because the true love of life radiates from her on those days.

Izzy is still a bit of a mystery to me, she spends a lot of time at her club, which we know is at number seven, two doors up from us. She spends a lot of time with the owner Malcolm Forbes Benedict, but none of us know if she is actually dating him, we have tried asking, but she just laughs at us. Chloe is convinced, and so is Deb's, but the truth is, we just don't know.

The thing that Birch finds the most unsettling, is the fact that Prude Prim has had a baby boy, which she has named Rupert after her grandfather. We looked it up on social media one night for a giggle, and Birch was so appalled at its ugliness, it put her off her pizza. It is not a pretty baby, but hey high five to Nigel, he finally made it out of the virginity club.

I cannot mention Nigel without mentioning our nemesis, and yes, she is alive and well, and is still rude to us all. I cannot deny, I was greatly shocked in the new year after our first Christmas together, when Marjorie bought Birch and myself a coffee and a cream bun, in the Tea Rooms. I was very polite, and I thanked her, Birch explained it was her way of showing her gratitude, for helping to protect her, and save her life, so I took it in the spirit it was given, although I am not sure she is aware it was Bev who gave her CPR.

The Shrew Crew is aging, which basically means they are nastier than ever, and their favourite pastime these days, is quoting bible passages at the engaged lesbians. I think I know every passage off by heart now, so in a way it has been good bible study into my lack of morality.

Speaking of the immoral, Norman and Daisy have gone from strength to strength, although Daisy has let slip, she had Norman snipped, three children is enough, on top of running what has become a thriving business. The Nursery has expanded, much to the distaste of Marjorie, who still refers to Norman as a cultural luddite, for destroying what she considered to be a heritage garden.

Sweeties Retreat has gone from strength to strength, although there was a little stir in the village a few months back, when one of the patients went into the Post Office and started sniffing all the women. Pat was called in, and Birch and Izzy handled the damage limitation with the women in the Post Office, and Bobby the sniffer has been banned from ever going in there again. I must admit, both Chloe and myself thought it was hilarious that Pat, a seasoned therapist, told all the women that Bobby had sniffed, 'he is quite harmless, just sniff him back, he really likes that.' Hence, Birch and Izzy were required.

I still avoid Thursdays at the retreat, it bothers me that I start to hum and shake my legs, when I am around what Chloe lovingly calls, 'The Wank Group.' She did actually attend one session, but was asked not to come again, because she gave herself a public orgasm, and screamed Deb's name through the walls, which sent Deb's running out of her shop in complete melt down. In abject terror, she ran up to the Tea Rooms, to be later calmed down by Birch. Deb's was really angry with me, for telling Chloe about the group in the first place, it took her a week before she would talk to me again.

After the incident with Martin, and almost losing Birch, I started to have some pretty scary nightmares. It is hard to hide them when you sleep with a therapist, and as promised, Birch set me up some sessions with her new therapist Suzanna Richmond, who had been Chloe's trauma therapist. I actually really like her, and to date I am still seeing her, mainly because she has given me a space to really thrash things out.

I talk about Martin, and Nigel, and how his stalking affected me, and I also talk about my dad, and my feelings towards him, and I have really started to understand myself a lot better. Birch thinks it has made a huge difference to me, I am not sure, but I do feel a lot happier in life.

Our naked lifestyle has grown a great deal, hardly any of us wear clothing at home, most people who visit have got used to it, and now consider it normal to find a group of happy naked women in the kitchen laughing, joking and cooking. Samantha found it a little hard to adjust when she first started working with Edwina, because she has to come into the house to wash cups or use the toilet. We have had her in a skimpy bikini out in the garden on the sunnier days, but as yet, she has not taken the plunge, but she has grown quite accustomed to jiggling boobs, and shaved chuffs, and now she just does not notice.

The Curio family, as we all refer to ourselves, has grown a little, and we have all grown even closer, we are like brothers and sisters, and we look out for each other and take care of each other. We are not as outcast now, the village I do not think it has accepted us fully, but they have grown accustomed to us, especially considering we have been involved in, and supported every event the village has organised.

It is normal to see all of us in steward vests helping out, carrying and lifting, or directing people around events, with a happy smile. We still act like kids and piss about, and somehow, we always get caught by the Shrew Crew. To be honest, it is quite fun, seeing them scowl at us, and we always end up with our heads down sniggering, as we are reprimanded by them.

I think that maybe because I chose to live my life as a writer, I have learned to sit back and take stock. When Birch first came home with me and we talked in my mum's kitchen that first day, I told her, that in this village, how it looked on the outside, was far more important than how it was on the inside.

As I have grown older, and sat in thought, I can see that today, it is still as true as it was then. Behind closed doors things are very different than the image this small village portrays, with its perfect Village Green, and its moral figured head of the Church stood at the top of the hill. The village is beautiful and quaint, I love to sit, and just take it all in, and really absorb its idyllic rural beauty, but the truth of it all really is it is fake, the picture it paints is of a time long since passed.

The reality of life is that behind closed doors things are very different, the quaint moral picture painted by this village does not exist. There are naturists, swingers, wife abusers, sexual deviants, dope smokers, alcoholics, rapists, narcissists, manipulators, con men, liars and cheats, just like anywhere else in this country or the world. People have become as fake as their social media account profiles, and maybe in some way that is to blame.

Everyone knows it is easy to hide on the internet, and create a false identity. Hell, there are so many filters and apps, you can add to an account, you can change your whole appearance. Maybe that is the problem, all of us are being guided away from our true selves towards living a lie. Do people still talk honestly and openly? I don't think so, but it is easy to see why, when we have politicians, like Walter Parkinson, a man who took bribes to close down the hall to stop Deb's wedding, or put his own mother in a care home, to stop her from telling the truth about her own son.

The Peter Ford's of this world, benefit from the lies they spin, and the under handed methods they use. I have no trust of the media, I have seen the way they have lied about me, or sensationalised stories about me, to the point where the only honest thing they say is my name. Every day, people go on the internet, and get spoon fed the lies and bullshit, and so it does not surprise me that people have become what they are. Birch has often told me, a person will only ever accuse you of doing something they are quite prepared to do themselves, and in that you can read their character, and after many years of watching, I have come to agree with her.

I really love my friends, I love Birch so deeply, and I feel very close and connected to all of them, and I do often wonder why. If you think about it, I am a sinical bitch at times, and yet I never doubt those who I live with, my trust in them is implicit. Is it because we are all perfect? No, we are not, we are all flawed as hell, and we screw up just like everyone else, and so, I ask myself, why these people?

My answer is always the same, which is, simply put, they are not fake. None of them hide who they are, call them out on their flaws and they will agree with you, and I love that. The Curio's are open, what you see is what you get, and they do not make excuses or try to paint over it, they are there right in front of you, and they are real. Maybe that is why we are hated equally as much as we are loved by others. So many people today have bought into the idea of fake is real, which when they are actually confronted by real, they are offended by it. I really do think this is at the heart of all the heartache and pain we have endured in the last nine years here in Wotton.

I came out of my thoughts and felt the sun on my body, and it was nice, I cannot deny, the feeling of the sun on my naked skin still makes me feel alive and vibrant. I put my journal and pen down, I picked up my coffee cup, I drank the last half, it was not that hot. I had again, spent more time than expected day dreaming with my thoughts.

The knock at the door announced Edwina was here, we had phone lines to man, and a press meeting to attend, I gave a sigh, as I got up and headed for the door. I yawned as I opened it, Roy saw me and turned around quickly to avert his eyes. Edwina gave a sigh.

"Why aren't you ready, Abby we have phones and interviews to do?" I turned, and walked into the room.

"Way to depress me much Edwina, Christ, I hate these things as an author, why does Katie force me to do them as a Curio?" She closed the door behind her.

"Abby please behave, this is our big weekend remember, and by the way, you need to shave, things are looking a little bit fluffy downstairs." I looked down and giggled, and gave it a stroke, Edwina looked at me.

"Okay that is a little unsettling, please only do that when you are alone." I looked up and smiled as I ran my fingers over it.

"It's really soft, Birch really likes it, she calls them my kissy prickles." Edwina picked up my pants.

"Yeah well, that is for her, it is not something I want to consider." I shrugged.

"She says she likes the way it feels on her lips." Edwina held out my black faded jeans.

"Again Abby, I don't want to talk about your vagina, if you were any other woman, I would be baited, but you are an engaged lady and off the market." I smiled at her.

"You know you want me, just say it?" She giggled.

"Honestly, I would screw you in a heartbeat, but not with a ring on your finger." I felt the ego stroke.

"Wow, am I that hot?" She held my jeans and shook them at me.

"To be honest, you have gorgeous eyes, and a killer body, and I have heard how loud you moan, you tick all my boxes, but it will never happen, and you know why?" I grabbed the jeans.

"I get it, and yes, you know you are beautiful, you really are, but as much as I love you, and I really do, I have never wanted to sleep with any other woman. If I lost Birch, I would probably end up as big a slut as Chloe, and screw every guy I met, I would never go back to a woman." She threw a vest top at me.

"I have always known that Abby, and I actually really respect it. Now come on, and hustle that round little ass of yours, we have callers and the press to please." I slid my leg into my jeans, and pulled, and then looked up.

"This is all being done here in the hotel, isn't it?" She nodded at me.

"Yeah, why do you ask?" I slipped my other leg into my jeans and pulled them up.

"I really do not want to wear shoes; I am going bare foot." Edwina gave another frustrated sigh, as she handed me an Avril t shirt, to wear over my vest.

"Honestly, Chloe and you are hard work, I had to fight her this morning just to get a bikini top on her under her dungarees, so her tits didn't fall out in front of the cameras. You two will be the death of me, right come on, you need make up, let's give the press their dark little beastie." I sat down in front of the mirror.

"I bloody hate doing public shit, I want to go home and chill in bed." She giggled as she held my face, and prepared my eyes. It was time to shine for the public.

The phones were actually fun, people got such a shock when I spoke and told them they were through to me, Aden was convinced it made them donate more. I talked to people who had posted to the site, as I sat in a room with another fifty phone operatives. Edwina sat at my side, and she was really good, and again when those calling found out they were talking to a Curio, their donations went up. I felt really good sat there wearing my head set, it is strange really, but it made me so happy talking with everyone, knowing they too wanted to help us all. I really wanted this to be a success for Birch, she had worked so hard to organise this, but like all things wonderful, my time on the line came to an end, and with Edwina at my side, I gave a sigh, now it was time to face the press.

Ten minutes later, after a quick coffee, Katie stood with us by the door that led into the interview room.

"Abby, I have made it clear to all the press, this is not publicity for the book, I know the book is about all you guys, but this weekend is about Curio Life, not Shoots of Summer or your gothic novels. If they ask, ignore them."

I nodded, I understood, my biggest concern all along is that my presence would distract people from the whole point of the event, I took a deep breath.

"I understand Katie, honestly I don't even want to talk to them, so avoiding questions for me is perfect." She gave a smile, and patted my cheek.

"I love you Abby, you know that right, go in, stay chilled out, and just let them know about the Curio project from your point of view, and don't forget, we need donations."

She opened the door ready, and I looked at Edwina, turned and walked in, I had on my mirrored glasses, and as the flash cameras went off, I was relieved. They have no idea how bright those things are, and they have loads, which really hurts my eyes.

We had a long table with mics on, and a row of seats, the fast action shutters of the camera's clattered as we walked in, and we headed for the middle two seats, as Katie had instructed us and sat down. Katie sat just to our left, as I looked out at the rows of seats, and the tripods at the back, which housed TV cameras, and press cameras. I noticed Thomas Jennings sat on the end of the second row, he was probably the only person in the room I trusted. More cameras flashed, making me blink, even with glasses on. Katie directed the event, she looked at the press.

"Good morning, ladies and gentlemen, please wait for your turn, and direct your questions to either Miss Pemberton, or Miss Watson, but please keep everything strictly to the Curio event." She pointed at John St James. He looked at both of us.

"Ladies if I may get a response from both of you, considering your status, and your income, why should people fund this project, isn't it possible that all of the Curio's as a collective could pay for this themselves?" I sat back, and Edwina leaned into the mic, she gave a chuckle.

"This project requires at least forty million, I am not sure where you get your information from, but as a collective, we could not possibly finance that ourselves." He looked at me, and I leaned forward into the microphone, inside I felt a laugh, wow, this guy was a real piss taker.

"Mr St James, I will not deny, my books sales in the last few years have improved my life, and if I could finance this, do you think I would honestly be sat talking to a friend of Peter Ford? Last night I made the speech that launched this weekend, if you replay that speech, and watch the background, you would have noticed that all the boxes on the screen were empty, and the second I said the lines are open, the figure of one hundred thousand appeared. Just play it back and watch, as I walked towards the side of the stage, it jumped to two hundred thousand. That was my fiancé with my phone, and her phone in the wings, both of us made the first donations to launch this event. Once I had left the stage, I did a three hour meet and greet book signing, and every penny from every book sold went into this project's funds. Now if you do not want to contribute, I am fine with that, but there are a lot of people out there that do, why do you have a problem with that?" I sat back, Katie smiled, as did quite a few of the reporters. Katie pointed. The hand held mic was handed to a female reporter.

"Janet Banks, Lifestyle Magazine. Ladies you have put on your website that you are all Curio's, and you reject societies labels, but it is a matter of record that Miss Pemberton, you are a bisexual, and Miss Watson you are a lesbian, why are societies titles not good enough for you two?" Edwina twitched, she had never openly spoken of her sexuality, I sat up, and leaned into the mic.

"Miss Banks, what is your sexuality, do you fuck women or are you strictly missionary with men, could you provide me with a list of references from satisfied men please?" The whole room sniggered, she looked embarrassed, I stared at her.

"Not pleasant, is it? You see, what you are missing is that firstly, under the labels of your society, I am not a lesbian, I have had sex with guys too. Curio is a label we all chose to use, because we are all tired of people like you, who judge us for who we sleep with, and label us for only that aspect of our lives. We picked our own label, because we are all much more than that. Our sex life or sexuality is just one of many parts that make up who we are, and yes, it is important to us, but is who I or any of us sleep with any of your business? Look at the web site, and how many people agree with us, a Curio is so much more than who we sleep with.

A Curio is a complete person, who is curious about all things, like life, the world, nature, ourselves, and who we find attractive. We are all so much more than who we sleep with, so why have you got the right to label us for just one aspect of the life we live?" Thomas smiled and gave a nod, Edwina leaned into the mic.

"All of you should watch the videos on the site, and really understand what all those persecuted people are dealing with, you are so quick to label people for who they sleep with, or what they look like, or dress like, but the Curios are much more. We have an amazingly talented hair stylist, an incredibly talented artist, one of the most sought after therapists in the south of England, a highly qualified biochemist, an IT specialist, and a very talented writer. All of us have a private life, read books, read blogs, and talk about everything we encounter, we are curious about who we are, and where we can fit in, and yet once again, the press just focus on, and sensationalise our sex lives. Honestly, it appears to be far more important to you and our critics, than it actually is to us, and frankly it is insulting to degrade any of us to the level of our bed partners, even you have still not told us what your sexuality is?"

She sat back and smiled, Katie was very pleased so far, I leaned back towards the mic.

"Miss Banks, I have read your magazine, and some of your articles are really good, if I am honest, I was hopeful for an intelligent question from you. All of you are obsessed with the same sensationalism that we see in all the media, and that is a really big part of the problem. Look at the camera, this is going out live to the world, and out there, young people are sat watching, hoping that this will give them a vital life line that is the one reason they need, not to kill themselves today. We need a massive amount of donations, so we can give those young people that help and support, so please all of you, take this seriously, because we are deadly serious about this, it is not a stunt. I have spoken to every single person that uploaded a video, and the six of us are the most regular members of that site's forum. Why don't all of you go back to your rooms, read those threads on the forum, and then come back and talk to us properly."

Edwina looked down, and the room was silent, they had no idea just how much I was shitting myself, thank God the table had a long cloth to hide my shaking legs. Katie had a very big smile, she pointed to Thomas.

"Thomas Jenkins, Daily Informer. Ladies I have spent a lot of time on your site, and it is clear that there is a gap into which young people are falling. The Curio's group I know have fought hard to build their life, so I would ask you both, how can people really help these lost young people out?" I smiled at him, finally something that would help us, and he knew it. Edwina leaned into the mic.

"The best way today is to support Curio Live, make a donation, buy some merchandise, if you cannot do that, go to the site and talk to these people, give them advice, ask them how they are doing, and if you know of a charity that supports young people, give them a link or phone number to use." I nodded agreeing.

"Thomas, nice to have a good question, so thanks for that. Look, a lot of young people are sensitive and insecure, and older people sit in judgement of them, because they have a different look or a different attitude, but they never ask why? Not all of us like the same kinds of sex, or foods, or cars etc. Instead of sitting in judgement, because you either do not agree or do not understand, try having a conversation with them and learn something. You know, I have never met a person yet that does not like being asked, how are you today, or are you going to be fine, it is common sense, just be respectful and try to understand. You know what the biggest crime I ever committed in my home village is? I dyed my hair black, when I was nineteen that is it, and it got so bad, I considered killing myself, how many of you have dyed or restyled your hair, was it so bad for you that you wanted to kill yourself?" I shook my head.

"No, because you are all above thirty, and people do not look down on you, and that is the only reason. Our young people do not deserve to be treated this way, it is shameful, and it should stop. So, appease your guilt, pick up the phone, and send these kids some hope in the form of a small donation." Katie pointed to another reporter.

"Mary Wilkinson, The Mail Today. Miss Watson, don't you think a lot of the people you talk to, just need to get real, and pull themselves together, and instead of looking for free handouts, just get a job and knuckle down, like the rest of us. I understand you were bullied for dying your hair, but be honest, if you had not of dyed it your life would have been easier. Being young is not a right to a free ride?"

Edwina looked at me, she knew exactly where I was going with this one, and she wanted nothing to do with it. I stared at her, as I sat back in my seat, and looked at her, she was late forties, early fifties with dark red dyed hair.

"Miss Wilkinson, I like your hair, I really love the colour." She gave a smile, as the other reporters at the front turned to look at her.

"Tell me Miss Wilkinson, how many times a day do you get told you look like a slut, or a whore with that hair?" She looked shocked, and the reporters gasped, I smiled.

"Not nice is it… I have had that pretty much every day since I was nineteen, and maybe not dying it is the answer in your eyes. As for my life being easier, I am sorry but I cannot agree with you, because when I was blonde, which is my natural colour, and I was at home in my village where I was supposed to be safe, a man still tried to rape me, because he said I looked like a slut. So, it appeared to me, blonde or black, made no difference, tell me, does dying it red get you laid more, or less times?" She looked horrified as the cameras turned to her. I stood up, and leaned over to the mic.

"Go look at the site, read it, and then talk to Katie, and if you drop your self righteous bullshit, and trash talk, I will talk to you one on one, but you better come up with some serious questions, because these kids are suffering, and we are trying to help them, because they dammed well need it. So stop wasting our time on your petty sensational, and judgemental bullshit, and when all of you grow the hell up, I will talk real help and real support with all of you, because that is why me and all the Curio's are here, not to have our time wasted by a group of patronising, self serving bigots."

I turned and walked towards the door, and the cameras exploded with flashes, Edwina jumped up, and followed me quickly through the door, she grabbed my hand.

"Abby, I get it, she was fucking offensive, but why did you not just ignore her? I am not sure that is good PR for the Curio's." I turned and looked at her as Katie came through the door.

"Edwina, all they wanted was to find a way to hang us, screw good PR, I am not here to kiss the ass of the press, I am here to get the funds Birch and Roni need to do this, and apart from Thomas, not one of those shits are serious about this, and I have no intention of pandering to them. I would rather be out there meeting the people who bought tickets, and thanking them for their donations." Katie walked up and put her arm round me.

"God, I love working with you, that was perfect, do you know that from the moment you started talking, the numbers started to rocket, Abby, that little outburst, just banked us two mill more." She kissed my head, Edwina gasped, Katie leaned over and kissed her cheek. I smiled.

"Can we go now?" Katie giggled.

"Roy, go and hang out with them and keep them safe, and watch the one with no shoes, she is real trouble." I winked at Roy, and he chuckled.

Chapter 3

Code Pop Tart.

The audience applauded, as the speakers left the stage, and the stage lights lowered to black. The audience sat in their seats, and there was a hum all around the arena, as people started conversations. On the dark stage, the back screen lit up, and then the two screens either side came to life and a roughly filmed video appeared, it was the very first video that was ever uploaded to the Curio site.

"Hi, I am Chloe, I am an artist, and I am 24 years old. It is so tough being a young artist, I live for painting, and er... Well, sex too, it inspires my work. I have been skint for ages, really trying to stay afloat, and I can tell you guys, God, it has been so hard, and that was when I ran into my group of friends, who we call the Curio's." She gave a really sweet smile.

"You see guys, the problem is, here in my village I want to belong, but there are some here who hate me, because I don't really fit in. I like life and modern stuff, I don't wear clothes a lot, yeah, I really dig the nudist thing, but if I have to wear clothes, I want them to reflect me, not some old bores idea of what I should like, and for that I get called slut, trash, and whore. I laugh it all off, but I can tell you all, alone, in secret, I have done a lot of breaking down, and shed a lot of tears." She stopped for a second, and her face clouded over, almost as if remembering something painful.

"I am young, so I'll ask all of you out there, why is it wrong to just want to be me? I know you guys really get it, so hey, why not make me a video, and let me see your story. I think that would really be brilliant, come on don't be shy, I shit myself filming this, but you know what, I am glad I have done it."

The audience applauded as the screen froze on Chloe's smiling face. A spot light hit the floor near the side of the stage. A small figure dressed in dungarees, with her hands in her pockets sauntered onto the stage. She stopped, turned to the screen, and looked at it, over the speakers there was a giggle.

"Hell, was I ever that young?"

She turned, and walked to the front of the stage, and stood there with her hands in her pockets. She was wearing a head mic.

"Hi… I am Chloe, and I am a Curio, how are you all doing?" She gave a huge smile.

The audience went crazy, stood up and cheered, and she giggled. I stood at the side of the stage with Birch.

"Christ she is brave."

Birch smiled watching the small screen on the mixing desk, where Chloe stood giggling at the loud applause, and I have to admit, it was deafening.

"She is so sweet Deads, look at her, she has no idea how loved she is for all the people she has talked to on the site." Edwina looked worried.

"She is so vulnerable up there, I just hope no one shouts anything at her, I know how easily she could be crushed."

Chloe stood there on the huge stage, stood in the spotlight, waiting for the crowd to settle down. It took time, and then everyone sat back, she turned and looked back at the screen behind her.

"Wow, I really need to make a better video." The audience giggled, she turned back and walked along the edge of the stage.

"I was the first person to make a video, I sat in my studio late at night, and I looked at the camera, and I said to myself, if there was another me out there, what would they want to know about me? That is what I filmed, I did not edit it, looking at it tonight, maybe I should have." She stopped, turned, and looked at the audience.

"I am not good with speeches, to be honest, I am winging it tonight, they needed a surprise guest to fill in, and guess who got the short straw?" She giggled, and the audience giggled with her.

"Okay so that is not completely true, I wanted to be up here, I have never done this before, and I have seen how much Abby gets scared by it. You know what, I gave it some thought, and it occurred to me that there must be a lot of people here, who use Curio Life. So, I figured what the hey, I have already talked to these people, so out there, I have loads of friends." She looked out at the audience.

"Guys, I am nervous, so if you have been on the site, and uploaded a video, or you have commented on the forum, do me a favour, just clap your hands. Just you, it's okay if you have not been on yet, there is time, so please just clap so I know I am with mates." The noise from the audience was deafening, Edwina turned, and smiled at us.

"Wow, she is brilliant, just look what she has done, she has shown the world how many people have used it." Chloe took her hand out of her pocket, and waved.

"Hey there my mates." She giggled, as she waved, making sure she waved to every aspect of the audience, even the ones high up.

"I knew you guys would come and give us some support, because you guys know how important it is." She wandered across the stage, stopping and smiling as she looked down into the audience.

"Look guys, if you have seen all the talks, and workshops we have shown on the live feed, then you know what we are about, you know how desperately needed the help we want to provide is. I bet all you guys have sent us a pound or two already, so I am not going to stand up here and tell you this is a good cause, you already know how important it is." She stopped and smiled.

"I thought tonight, I would talk about the people behind the site, I figured what the hell, I get so many messages from all of you about who the Curio's are, and as you saw earlier with Abby, all the press really care about is looking for dirt and blowing everything out of proportion, about our sex lives. The press are like the high street version of the Shrew Crew, and we all know what we think of them don't we?" The audience gave a loud boo! and she started to laugh, as she walked back to the middle of the stage. Chloe stopped in the centre of the stage.

"I live with the Curio's, we all share the same huge house, now the press say it is a den of decadence and depravity, hell, I wish it was, we all get sick of reading that shit, because it is not true. Okay so we are a group of six, and shock news, we all have relationships, and hey guess what, we are liberated, so we actually have sex lives. The press call that depravity, I call it normal, I don't know anyone who is in a relationship, and not having some sort of sex."

She stood for a second and smiled. I could not help but smile as I saw the close up of her, as the cameras panned in on her. She had such an infectious smile, and kind eyes, and I knew, everyone in the audience was fixed on her. She took a breath.

"I love living with Abby, she is the most amazing friend. Every morning our house is crazy, I mean, we have three women running round getting ready for work, slapping on makeup, looking for clean knickers, and trying to eat breakfast. Anthony is always so calm and efficient, and he never comes down to breakfast not looking immaculate, but Abby and me, well, we are a mess. We sit still and say little, and just drink our coffee, Abby does not talk, until she has had a few coffees. Everyone heads off to work and that is my favourite time, because it is just Abby and me, sat alone drinking coffee, and talking." She smiled.

"She is stood just off stage, and she will be hating this, Birch is probably holding her back to stop her coming on a dragging me off." She chuckled, and the audience giggled.

"Abby is a writer, and because of that she really looks at things, and out of all the Curio's, she is the one I always ask first for advice. She always tells me something that really helps me, she is like a sister to me. I have a big sister as well, but you know that, Edwina, has been there for me so many times in my life, she has never let me down once, and I love her so much for that. I am hoping her current boyfriend man's the frig up soon, and asks her to marry him, because he will get the best wife ever." She giggled and looked at the camera.

"Oops, sorry Weena."

The audience all gave a giggle. Birch hugged Edwina who was sat in the control seat turning purple.

"How could she on live TV?" I sniggered.

"Be honest, he needs a push, and what are sisters for?" Chloe giggled and looked out into the darkened audience.

"Birch is a maniac, she really is the authentic free spirit, and I think the kindest person I have ever met, and all of us adore her. She is like a mum and a sister all rolled into one, and she is so clever, I mean look at all this. This event is her baby, she thought of it, and she planned it, and she made it happen, how unbelievably brilliant is that? I bet you won't read that in the papers. Debs is a great friend, she only lives with us part time, because she married a rock star." The audience whistled and applauded, she chuckled, as she looked out, into the audience.

"When Jimmy is on tour, she stays with us, I hang out with her a lot, especially in the studio, and we talk a lot. I bet most of you don't know, but she is a biochemist, she really is incredibly brainy. You probably read that trash piece recently about is the baby Jimmy's, where they assassinated her, saying it was probably another guy's child. Probably, hell, they did not even know, she sat in my room that night and cried for hours. Trust me, its Jimmy's, those two make an amazing couple, and they are so excited they are going to be parents, the Curio's are all going to be aunties and an uncle soon, and we are pretty excited about it. Deb's is really into family, and we are lucky because she includes us in that." She stopped and smiled.

"Last but not least we have Anthony. Do you like my hair? He does it, just like he does Abby's and Edwina's, he is really good, but you know that, because let's be honest, Birch's hair is inspiring, isn't it? Anthony was really bullied at school, he had a terrible time of it, he was forced to live a life that was a lie to hide who he really was, and it made him so unhappy. We all know, because we were the ones that gave him the space to be himself, and wow, what a wonderful guy he is. Like Birch, he is caring and compassionate and really supportive, we have all had bad days, and he just knows and appears, and he makes such a difference. He is really witty and funny as well, we can be in a mad panic and in the middle of chaos, and he will say something, and we will all crack up laughing, he really is the nicest guy I know."

I stood watching the screen and just smiling, she was so at ease, so simplistic, and so lovely, her honesty just flowed out of her. She walked to the back of the stage and looked up at her frozen picture, I could see her, stood with her hands in her pockets as she stared at it. She turned and smiled, and lifted her hand out of her pocket and waved.

"Hi Abby, Hi Birch, oh dear, Edwina is scowling at me." The audience giggled, she turned and walked back to the front of the stage, and stood still.

"A few weeks ago, a news article called me privileged, and you know what they were right, today I am very privileged, and I am not going to argue with them. I was just glad they actually printed something that was right for once." She chuckled.

"I don't need to be lectured by a reporter who has no idea of truth, I am, I will always hold my hand up and admit it. You know why?" Chloe just stood there in silence watching the audience, and she waited.

"Shall I tell you? I am privileged, because I used to live in a shit hole, and I was really suffering. My landlord hated me, because I would not sleep with him, so he kept on putting the rent up. I was working my ass off, and it was never enough, and so I had to cut the only thing I could, I bought less food. He made it quite clear, all I had to do was screw him every Friday, and he would fix the heating, and lower the rent. That was my life four years ago, four years before that, I was called a whore, because I had make up on and wore false nails, and got my eyebrows done. I was labelled as one of the village sluts, and a maniac thought that would make it okay to try and rape me in the church. Yes, I am privileged, or at least I am today." She took a deep breath and Edwina stiffened in her seat, I looked at her.

"What is wrong?" She stared at the screen.

"She is getting upset, be ready just in case."

I looked at the screen, and saw the tears in her eyes. Chloe swallowed hard and wiped her eyes and gave a sniffle, the audience was so quiet you could hear a pin drop. Chloe shook her head.

"Sorry, it still gets to me at times, I do try to smile more, but every now and again, I feel it." A voice shouted from the darkness.

"We love you Chloe." She gave a giggle.

"I love you guys too."

She smiled and Edwina relaxed. Chloe wiped her eyes. From behind her, Birch appeared, and the audience roared into life, she smiled, walked up to Chloe, and handed her a tissue.

"Here Sweetie, you are doing brilliant."

Chloe gave a chuckle as Birch waved, turned and walked back off the stage, Chloe looked back and watched her, and wiped her eyes. Cheers rose up from the audience, she turned back to them with a smile.

"See, she is always there when you need her." She took a deep breath.

"Okay, where was I? Oh yeah, privilege. As I said, the reporter was right, because even though I have had my time in hell, as you have seen today, I have the privilege of living with some amazingly loving and caring people. I know how lucky I am, we all do, and that is why all of us are here this weekend doing this, because what Curio Live is about, is finding places, where everyone who goes there, gets to have what I have. I lived alone in fear, and one day Birch appeared, and she said, hey come live with Abby and me, and suddenly I was surrounded with support and encouragement. I was broke, I had nothing, I had lost loads of weight, and I had lost all hope, and my friends came looking, found me, and encouraged me to move forward again. Today I am very privileged, because I am a full time artist, and I have an outlet to sell my pictures, so for the first time since I was nineteen, I have a little money, I have food, and I have a safe place to live, just think of that for a minute, it is not a lot really to ask is it?" Edwina sat back in her seat.

"Holy shit she is amazing, wow, I have never been prouder of my sister than at this moment." Chloe looked out into the audience.

"Every day, I talk to people who do not have what I have, and that is why if you look at the forum stats, I have more hits than anyone else, because I talk to these people and I tell them my story. Every one of us, Birch, Abby, Edwina, Deb's and Anthony, have a similar story from some point in our life. It is why we are here, it is why we set up Curio Life, and why we have organised Curio Live. We want to provide that level of comfort and support, that the press call us for having. We want help centres, which have the right people to give the right advice and offer the right help, so that everyone who has ever felt like we did, can be lifted up, as we have been. I want everyone on Curio Life, to have my privilege of friends, of support and of encouragement, so get out your phones, and start calling, because there is a hell of a lot of people out there in need, and we want to help them." She stood still and took a deep breath.

"I just want to say to all of you here today, thank you for listening, and we really thank you for being here to support us. I am Chloe, and I am a Curio."

She bowed, and the whole arena exploded into cheers, screams, and wild applause. Edwina turned to the guy at her side.

"Turn the house lights up, let her see this."

Chloe stood at the front of the stage, and the lights came up, so she could see just how many people were there, everyone was stood up, and smiling, she could not believe her eyes, she stepped back from the edge of the stage, and just stood smiling, like a rabbit caught in the headlights. I looked at Edwina.

"Give me a mic."

Chloe was frozen to the spot, she was happy, and she was also terrified, behind her I walked on to the stage. I walked towards her as the cheers intensified, and I thought to myself, why the hell am I doing this? I came up to her side smiling, and held up the mic as I slid my arm round her waist.

"Ladies and gentlemen, Miss Chloe Pemberton, isn't she absolutely lovely?"

As the audience applauded, I pulled her close and she took a breath. I slid my hand down to her hand, and gripped it. She was stood smiling with tears in her eyes, I am not sure her brain could handle just how many people she had addressed. I gave her a slight tug, and she turned and smiled at me, and wiped her eyes, and followed me. We walked to the back of the stage, turned and waved, and then walked off, I grabbed her mic pack, and switched it off. Chloe was shaking, and looked shocked, she looked at Edwina.

"Why the fuck didn't you tell me there was that many, when the lights came up, I almost pulled a Rosie, and shit myself?" Birch pulled her into a hug.

"Chloe Sweetie, you blew them all away, you were utterly captivating, and the audience loved you. That was the best advert for supporting us, we could have ever asked for, and the numbers are soaring." She looked a little white, I smiled at her.

"Chloe are you alright, do you need a bucket?" She looked at me.

"I am not you, I do not need it, but I could really use a drink, that terrified me, I was fine until someone hit the light switch."

Alison Williams headed onto the stage, and we moved out of the way, as the next guest speaker got ready. Roni was in charge of this section of the event, and she appeared, and pulled Chloe into her arms.

"Chloe you were an absolute natural, they lapped you up, and as a result, the phone lines are red hot, cash is flowing in." Chloe smiled.

"I was okay, all I did was tell the truth, I didn't lie, honestly Mrs D." She chuckled, and kissed her cheek.

"I think you are marvellous Miss P." Chloe sniggered.

"That sounds like I piss myself." Edwina turned round in her seat.

"Well, you did in the cellar, and the attic, so she is not wrong really is she Miss P?"

We all giggled and moved out of the way, we were finally on free time. Accompanied by our minder, we broke the rules, I mean, after all that is what we do at times. There were three of us, and we all had the bar in mind, Katie had warned us that the Press had ways of sneaking in, but we needed a drink, and we had Roy, and a guy called Tony with us.

The main bar was a large spacious place decked out in cedar, we headed for a secluded corner, and the waitress came over, I ordered three double rums with cola, no ice. We sat back and relaxed, Chloe slipped her shoes off and wiggled her toes, bare feet and carpet is so nice, and she joined me. Our minders sat just down a couple of tables from us, so we had limited privacy, but should we get hassled, help was at hand.

We sat back, and Chloe took a big swig of her drink and sat back with a long outward flow of breath. Birch patted her leg.

"Is that better Sweetie?" She nodded.

"Yeah, I will be fine now, when the lights came up, it freaked me out." She looked at me.

"Abby, how the hell do you do this, I have watched you loads of times, how do you sit in front of so many, and come over as relaxed?" I shrugged at her.

"I have the house lights down, and the spotlights on me are so bright, I cannot see who is out there. To be honest Chloe you were the same, it was only when the lights went up you were aware of everyone." She took a sip of her drink.

"I am so glad you came on to get me, honestly, I thought I

was going to piss my pants I got so freaked out." I sat back and relaxed, and I chuckled.

"Now you know why I prefer to be at home, and also why I feel sick, honestly it is terrifying. Hey you only have the stage to fear, I cannot walk freely in some places without being followed, and photographed, and then there is all the press articles. At home with you guys, is the only peace I get."

They both appeared to finally understand, and I sat back watching, as other people in the bar would casually turn to look at us, or point us out to others. This was the reality I had to live with, because I loved writing, and it came at the cost of losing my privacy, which was not easy for me, as I was at heart, a very private person.

I love when a genuine fan stops me, and asked for me to sign something, and I will never say no to them. But when you have cameras pointed at you all the time, even if you are just walking round the supermarket looking for bread. That picture appears in a tabloid paper the following day, with some snide comment, that is when it becomes annoying. I have come to understand that what the press do to me today, is no different from that first summer home, because I am still being scrutinised, and judged exactly the same way as I was by Marjorie and her Shrew Crew, nothing at all has changed.

My home is the only place I feel safe, the ten foot wall around the back garden, and all the trees we have, are the only thing that shield me from them. It is the only place I can let my guard down and just be me, and just like that summer nine years ago, I hide away and stay under their radar.

Birch nudged me, and I snapped out of my dreams, Katie was stood staring at me with her hands on her hips.

"I said, I thought I told you that you must only stay in pairs?" I blinked up at her, behind her Roy had a smirk.

"I am in a pair, those two are a pair, and I am not with them. I am just sat here minding my own business, looking for someone else." Birch sniggered; Chloe looked at the table, she gave a snort.

"Look Abby, I know you hate these things, but can you please try to understand why I am keeping you all separate, just for once play nice?" I frowned at her.

"Why is this my fault, how do you know they did not kidnap me, and drag me here for drinks?" Birch bit her lip, and her eyes twinkled, I looked at her.

"Why is she not picking on you, it is always you that gets us into mischief?" She smiled, and leaned in and kissed me.

"I thought you liked me getting you into trouble?" I giggled.

"I do, you always make the trouble more fun." Katie gave a huff.

"Look you three, I need you all back in your rooms until the meal, and please stay the hell away from the press." Chloe gave a sigh and drained her glass, I lifted mine, and huffed.

"God, you're the worse mum ever." She looked at Birch, and rolled her eyes.

"You should know better, you know why I keep her at arms length, there are press all over the public lounges, one slip up and she will be all over the papers tomorrow, now come on." She turned to Roy.

"Use the back stairs, and don't let her talk to anyone without my permission." I slid off the seat to make room for Birch to exit.

"God this is worse than school, it is like Hatty's class all over again." Chloe nodded, as she smirked at me.

Birch linked my arm and we followed Roy away from the people, and out of the public areas. I really just wanted to go home, if this was going to be my life away from the house, what was the point of even leaving it?

By the time we got back to the room, I was miserable, being cooped up in a hotel with nothing to do, and not being able to hang out with the others was getting to me. I sat on the bed as Birch poured a couple more drinks, thank God for her big bag, she was always well stocked for emergency's. She sat at my side and handed me a glass.

"It is only for one more day Sweetie." I leaned forward, and held my glass in front as I rested my elbows on my knees.

"I am sick of it, what is the point of doing all this if nothing changes? I am a prisoner here, or at home, no matter where I go or what I do, at home I hide in my room or the garden. In the village I am always on my guard, and now here finally away from home, I have to sit in my room and be a good little girl. The only joy I have these days is when we are alone." I glanced back and looked at her.

"Do you remember that new year when we came to London to see dad? I loved that time, he paid for a room and the following day, we walked arm in arm through London, just chilled out and talking." She smiled and gave a gentle nod.

"I remember it, the sun was out even though it was freezing, and we went shopping and then walked to the station." I looked at my glass and the clear liquid inside.

"I really loved that day, we were miles away from the village, and the press did not know we were here in London, and we were just like a normal couple. I was so in love with you, because you had asked me to marry you, and I was filled with happiness. Now it sounds stupid and silly, but just walking with no hassle, with just you, Birch, it was the best feeling ever. I don't think I have felt that normal since. Ever since I signed the new contract and the second book of the summer series came out, I have been caged. I cannot even walk down the hallway, or hang out with the others in their room, without having to request permission, and have a minder pick me up." I felt tears forming.

"Birch, I just want to go home; I just want to be able to sit in the sun and walk freely around our house alone."

"Hey Sweetie, come on this is not like you." I started to sob, and saw my tears drop into my glass. I wiped my eyes and tried to swallow the rest of the tears.

"I am sorry, I am trying not to be selfish, but I thought with all of us here it would be fun, but the red haired Nazi won't even let us have that." Birch slipped her arm around me, and pulled me close.

"I am so sorry; this is not fair on you." She kissed the side of my head.

"Deads Sweetie, I am not surprised, and to be honest, I thought something like this would happen. If it is really that bad, then I have no choice, but to release the Pop Tarts."

She stood up, and I looked up at her and frowned. She walked to the dresser and picked up her phone. I was confused as I watched, she gave me a cheeky smile, as she looked at her phone and dialled, then held it to her ear, she blew me a kiss, and the phone on the other end obviously picked up.

"Go to Code Pop Tart, we are going for action." I stared at her like she was bonkers.

"Birch, what the hell, are you a Bond villain now, what the hell is code Pop Tart?"

She gave me another cheeky smile, I sat on the bed and watched as she walked to the door, there was a gentle tap, she opened the door a jar, and a hand appeared holding a rucksack. She took it with a giggle and closed the door.

"What the hell is going on Birch?" I saw her eyes, and she had the wicked mischievous look; she gave an excited giggle.

"I really wanted to do this, I am so glad I can, oh, this is going to be so much fun."

She came over to the bed and put the rucksack down, and opened it, and pulled out a pair of black skin tight leggings, I recoiled.

"Holy Shit, fashion attack or what, why the hell did you buy them?" She handed them to me and grinned.

"Put these on." She handed me an old sweat shirt, with a picture of Madonna on it, I stepped back.

"Yikes... Holy shit Birch, I would not be seen dead wearing that." She glanced at me as she pulled out a Taylor Swift sweat shirt.

"Would you rather wear this one?" I shuddered.

"Screw you Birch, I am not wearing either, I am a rock chick through and through, I would not be seen dead in either of those." She smiled, and pulled out a long coppery wig.

"That is kind of the point Sweetie, if you look like you, then you have to stay here, but if you look nothing like you, well you can go where you please." She smiled and stood up.

"Deads, five years ago we would have broken every rule in the book, so what I am saying is, be a red little bad taste beastie, and come out for a walk with me." She pulled out a pair of bright red canvass capri pants, I dropped the leggings and snatched them out of her hand.

"Madonna would defo wear tacky shit like those." Birch giggled, and picked up the leggings. I looked at her and pulled her into me.

"Baby, you have no idea how much I love you at this moment in time." I gave her a long slow kiss, and she shuddered.

"Oh shit Sweetie, I am not sure I want to go out now." I giggled and undid my pants.

"I will screw you later, and it will be long slow, naughty and disgraceful, and you will love it." She got excited and jumped on the spot.

"I am so excited now; we are going to have such a good night."

I pulled my top off and threw it on the floor, and pulled on a vest, followed by my capri pants and my trainers, I then pulled the baggy sweatshirt over my head, with a smile, I looked in the mirror and cringed.

"Oh Christ, I look like Nigel's wet dream." Birch came up and stood at my side, and shuddered.

"Oh Christ, this must be what they wear in hell." I giggled.

"You look frigging rancid." She smirked.

"Says the girl in a frigging Madonna sweat."

I felt so excited it was stupid, I sat down, and Birch did my makeup, she did my eyes in pale blue, and it looked bloody awful. I looked in the mirror at myself.

"Holy shit, I look like I ran away with Twisted Sister on tour."

Birch pulled my hair up, and brushed it all to the top of my head. She then slid a stocking sort of cap over it, it was pink and made me look bauld, I gave a violent shudder and then sniggered.

"Oh Christ, that looks really messed up."

She giggled as she lifted the wig and straightened it up, then slipped it over my head, and suddenly I had long flowing coppery red hair, and with the blue eyes, I looked like Katie's younger hooker sister. I stared in disbelief at myself, Birch gave an approving nod, I turned to her.

"Would you shag this woman?" I could see her fighting to be tactful, I smiled.

"Be honest, would you?" She looked upset.

"Frig no, you are an ugly bitch."

I burst out laughing, and she smirked. Birch did her eyes in a ghastly purple, and then pulled on a long chestnut brown curly wig, I took one look at her, and pissed myself laughing.

"Holy shit Birch, looking like that, you belong in a brothel." She smiled.

"Sweetie, if I was, I would make double what everyone else does, I mean, look at my ass in these horrific leggings, thank god for good tone."

She giggled, but oh my god we looked a right sight, and nothing at all like Curio's. We were finally ready, and Birch sent a text, a few moments later there was a soft tap on the door. Birch had a glittery shoulder bag, she opened the door and Edwina burst out laughing.

"Holy shit!" We stepped out, and she fought to keep her face straight.

"Okay bitches, I get ten percent of everything you earn." She pointed to the far end of the corridor.

"Chloe is waiting to let you out, go have fun." I smiled at Edwina.

"Thanks for this, I really need to get away from here, even if just for an hour." She smiled.

"Don't try buttering me up Bitch, my cut doesn't fall." She giggled.

"Go have fun, now hurry whilst the coast is clear." We hurried giggling down the hall and onto the staircase, at the bottom, Chloe stood holding two coats.

"Holy fuck, if a guy asks you out, he is pissed, or he wants to pay you."

She handed me a green canvas jacket, and gave Birch a long black one, I recognised them as Edwina's.

"You will need these, it is going to rain, well drizzle a bit." I kissed her cheek.

"Fifty quid and I am yours for an hour." She sniggered.

"Fuck, you got high expectations."

Birch took my hand, and we opened the door, and stepped out into a side plaza garden. I smelt the air and it felt glorious, I took a long deep breath, and Birch squeezed my hand.

"Come on Sweetie, let's go explore."

We made our way through the gardens towards the side gate that led to the main road, just hearing the sound of traffic, and looking up at the cloudy sky was delightful. How sad is that, I was getting off on pollution and clouds? As we approached the gate, Birch squeezed my hand.

"Put your head down."

I looked ahead, and my heart skipped several beats, Roni stood smoking a cigarette, we leaned in together and walked with our heads down. I felt naughty and panicky, and my heart beat a little bit quicker, but it was a real rush. I felt like an escaped convict on the run from the law and dodging the sheriff. We made it passed her, and I breathed a long sigh of relief, as we hit the pavement, and turned sharply into the street. I felt a grip on my arm and looked down.

"And just where do you two think you are going?" I gave a long sigh, crap, she recognised us, I looked at Birch, and she was laughing.

"Oh, Mum for god's sake!"

Chapter 4

M.I.A.

Roni stood laughing as we faced her, somewhat pissed off for getting caught. I had just felt my first taste of real freedom, and now I was busted, she shook her head.

"I knew it... Why am I not surprised at all, is there no level you two will not stoop to in order to misbehave?" Birch sniggered

"Pretty much no... Mum we are grownups, what is wrong with a little life outside all the publicity." She started to giggle.

"Sorry darling, I don't want to laugh, but Jesus Christ, you make a right pair of ugly buggers. You call yourself grown up dressed like that, what the hell were you both thinking?" I gave a snort, and started to giggle; Birch sniggered.

"We thought if we were ugly no one would want to look at us." Roni held her hand to her mouth and gave a squeak of a cackle.

"Well, you won that badge." Her shoulders shook.

"Hell, you two are brave, don't stand in one place for too long, you will get arrested." She gave another squeak, and leaned forward as an almighty cackle came out of her.

I was pissed off I had been caught, but I had never seen Roni laugh so much. Birch was giggling as her mum looked up, she shook her head and burst out laughing again, she held her hand to her mouth, as the strangest squeaks I have ever heard came out of her. Birch looked down at her.

"I am glad you are enjoying this mum, so are you going to snitch on us?" She took a deep breath in, and stood up straight, she had tears in her eyes, she looked at me and gave a snort. And pulled me into her arms, and hugged me.

"Oh you poor sweet girl, what has my daughter done to you?" She giggled in my ear.

"I have seen it all now." She wiped her eyes, and tried not to look at us, as she tried to compose herself, she looked at us and tried to keep a straight face.

"Jemi, sweetheart." She sniggered, and shook her head.

"I should have named you Gloria." She gave another almighty cackle of a laugh. I was trying not to laugh, but Roni was really funny. Birch looked pissed off and impatient.

"Mum, just tell us." Roni turned to her side, and took deep breaths to calm down.

"I will make you both a deal." I nodded, that sounded pretty good. Birch eyed her suspiciously.

"What kind of a deal?" Roni turned and looked at her, and bit down on her lip, she took another deep breath.

"I want a picture." Birch shook her head.

"Holy shit no, I will never hear the end of it." She looked at me and sniggered.

"Abby one picture and I will pretend I never saw you." I was up for it, it seemed reasonable, I looked at Birch, she shook her head.

"Deads, do not fall for it, she will put it on next year's Christmas cards, she is not to be trusted." I shrugged.

"Baby, I need to get out of that cage, all I want is one day alone, unrecognised, with the woman I am going to marry. I just want to have a walk without being stalked by the press." Birch gave a sigh, she looked at her mum.

"If I even see it at the wedding, I will release that picture, you know which one, on the internet." She shrugged.

"I am a sex therapist, it can only enhance my reputation, but alright, you have a deal."

She held up her phone, we stood together as she sniggered again, and then 'Click' She took the picture with a smile.

"You have your phones I take it?" I nodded.

"Alright girls, go have fun, and if you get any problems, call me, not Katie. I will do what I can to cover your asses, after the skate board incident, I take it Chloe is involved in this?" I nodded.

"And Edwina." She chuckled and gave a sigh.

"Alright I will know who to talk to if Katie finds out, go on, go and have fun, and enjoy your freedom Abby, and please do not get arrested." I gave her a big smile.

"Thanks Roni." She smiled.

"Any time sweetheart, Jemi, take good care of her. Oh and by the way, it was the ring." I frowned, she pointed at Birch's hand.

"Her ring gave you away, it is so utterly unique." She smiled.

"Go on, scoot."

We turned with smiles, and hurried off before she changed her mind. Roni watched and shook her head, she lifted her phone and looked at the picture then started to giggle. Roni opened her message app, and attached the picture to it, with the comment 'Guess who,' and then addressed it to Will and pressed send. She walked back towards the garden and started to giggle, her phone pinged, and she looked at the message, and burst out laughing again.

Birch took my hand, and we hurried away from the hotel. Inside I was feeling rebellious and excited, and happy. Birch looked back at me and smiled; I was wearing a wide smile. We headed towards the river, and slowed down a little, we were both far enough away from the hotel, I stopped and leaned on the wall to look out over the river.

"Oh god, this is so nice, just to be out in the open and breathe." Birch turned me around and smiled.

"Here, let me fix this."

She slid her hand in her bag, and pulled out a small packet of wipes, she took one out and cleaned the heavy makeup off my eyes. She smiled as she looked at me, and pulled out an eyeliner, and carefully redid my eyes. Birch leaned back and took a look.

"That is my Deads."

She leaned in and pulled me close, and kissed me, it was so nice, and gentle, I gave a happy little moan, and slipped my arms round her. She finished the kiss, and moved her head back, she was still very close and her green eyes sparkled.

She broke apart and leaned on the wall at the side of me, as we both faced the river; she took out another wipe and cleaned her eyes. I took her eyeliner, and she faced me with a smile, I watched her eyes carefully as I redid the lines, and her eyes really came to life, she always looks gorgeous with her eyes done.

We just leaned on the wall watching the boats, it was cloudy and dull, but just being able to breathe in a wide open space was amazing.

"Is it mad that I am loving this so much, you know just us out here alone?" She smiled at me, and lifted her hand to my face, and stroked the red hair from it.

"I like that you love the simple things." She looked out at the boats.

"Some of my happiest times have been like this, watching you at dawn in the snow, walking on the canal, and even walking in the woodlands to pick out a Christmas tree, I loved that woodland, even though we had to kill a tree to be there." I slid my arm into hers.

"Let's walk, just walk and talk, and that way I can enjoy only being looked at by you."

She smiled and turned with me, and we started to walk, the trees were huge and beautiful, I loved the peeling bark. Birch talked softly about how they were plane trees, and well known for their tolerance of pollution.

The thing I love about being alone with her, is she does not resist life, Birch just goes with the flow, and follows her instincts. She is one of those people who easily picks up on the vibes of others, she can be the rowdiest person you could know, but she also has a quiet somewhat shy side, and it is that part of her that really does attract me.

Everyone knows she is crazy, but on the rare occasions I get her alone, and go quiet, she just slips into it, and oh god it is so sexy. She is thoughtful, and considerate, and has the cutest chuckle ever. I have had so many long conversations with her in the past when she was like this, and I honestly think it was those times alone in Uni, that really made me start to think about her in a different way.

All my life I had dreamed of my perfect man, and I knew he had to have a quiet, caring side. For me it was a really important aspect, and as I walk with her listening to her, I am convinced it is probably the biggest aspect of her that attracted me to her. Her voice can be so soft and soothing, when she talks about herself, and I always felt this was the real Birch, the part she hid from almost everyone. This was the Birch her mother talked about, and here I was being given exclusive access to it.

For over two hours we sipped take out coffee, as we walked along the river, and crossed over towards shops, and bought a few things. We got something to eat, and had more coffee, and just relaxed and destressed. It was the best time I had experienced in ages. No one will understand the wonder of normal and boring, unless of course, like me, it has been taken away.

It was cloudy but warm, and I unzipped my coat, Birch leaned back against the wall and took a picture, she gave me a giggle, I took out my phone and took one back of her, and then we stood together for a selfie. It was amazing, because people were just passing us by, not looking, staring, or pointing us out, it was almost like we were invisible. I turned to her and moved up close, she slid her hands inside my jacket, and pulled me closer to her, I smiled.

"Thanks for this, I really needed it." She smiled, and pulled me a little closer.

"I want this time too, you know Deads? There are times I just want to grab you and run. I hate the way the press treats you, and I have to watch that you know? There is a part of me that just wants to punch them, but I cannot, because even I have to protect your reputation. Sweetie, I really love our time alone, today has felt so special, just us alone walking, and talking, it has felt so nice, I am glad we did it."

She pulled me close, and I felt her hands under my sweat shirt, I gave a giggle as she slid them up over my vest, her eyes twinkled and she ran her fingers over my small mounds, and played around. I breathed in as I felt the tingles, she smiled, as she saw my reaction.

"Birch, we are on the street, oh god, I really wish we were alone." She gave a chuckle and tweaked me, I drew a breath, and bit my lip.

"Birch, don't tease me it's not fair, I am getting way too turned on." She leaned into me and started to kiss my neck, she breathed in my ear as she tweaked, and then softly spoke as the goosebumps ran all over my body.

"Have you ever done it in a public convenience?" I gasped.

"Huh?" She gave a soft giggle in my ear.

"There is one over there."

Katie looked at Edwina, she was really pissed off.

"Well, where the hell are they, the Curio's are the guests of honour tonight?" Chloe sat on her bed.

"Don't you think you are being too hard on Abby? So were them at the press conference, she needs a break, she has more pressure on her than any of us, and she is doing her best. I don't blame her if she has disappeared." Katie stared at her.

"Chloe, have you any idea what has gone into this event behind the scenes? Jemi should know better, she knows how important the guests at the gala are tonight, they could donate some serious money?" Edwina gave a sigh.

"Katie, you need to chill out, Birch pretty much planned and organised all of this long before she brought Roni and you in. I know, because I worked on this with her for over a year and a half, before you got involved. Abby is her greatest priority here, so if she needs to have her here, she will do." Katie looked at them both, her eyes glared at them.

"I know you two know more, fucking Curio's, the whole bloody lot of you are too God dammed close, you are all bloody mischief makers. You better get hold of Jemi and let her know, I want their asses back here, dressed and looking the part before that meal starts." She turned and walked out slamming the door; Chloe looked worried.

"Fuck, she is really pissed off, should we get hold of them, and warn them?" Edwina lay back on her bed.

"Chloe, Birch knows what she is doing, both of them will be back in time. Look, ignore Katie, she likes to throw her weight about, but at the end of the day, she needs Abby far more than Abby needs her. If Abby wanted to, she could just take over that aspect of Roni's business, she could literally run the publishing aspect of the Dixon Corp single handedly. Chloe, you forget what she did at Uni, Abby is more qualified for that aspect of the Dixon group than anyone else." Chloe was really surprised.

"I knew she did books and stuff, I didn't know she was that qualified, shit, I just got an art degree, I feel pathetic now." Edwina giggled.

I will not deny, when Birch pulled me into a toilet cubical, and started to touch and kiss me, I was a little freaked out. If you have never done this, I can tell you, it is a little bit terrifying. I became so turned on, before I knew it, I was tearing at her clothes like a pervert. Is it messed up that having sex, and hearing other people outside, is scary as hell, but the hugest turn on ever?

I gasped, biting my lip as I tried not to scream out in ecstasy, I leaned back against the wall panting, Birch slid up from between my legs and kissed my tummy. She made her way slowly up, kissing me softly, as my legs trembled, and I gasped more air into my lungs. She moved over my boobs, and I shuddered, as more tingles shot through me. Her face came level with mine and she smiled, and kissed me, I could taste myself on her lips. I pulled her close, and felt her naked body against mine, and I felt very happy. Birch leaned back and looked at me, I smiled.

"God, I love you, you are wild and crazy, and you turn me on more than you will ever know." She giggled.

"We will have to go back soon; will you be alright now?" I nodded.

"I have loved every second of today." She kissed me again.

"We need to get dressed, and then grab a cab."

Twenty minutes later, we arrived outside in a cab, the press looked, but did nothing, neither of us fitted the bill. Birch sent me ahead, as she paid, so I jumped out with my head down and walked quickly inside, she was right behind me. We walked up the lobby towards the lifts, Roy looked at us.

"Sorry Ladies, this lift is VIP only." I gave a giggle and leaned in.

"Roy it's me, I am wearing a wig, and shitty clothes, you know, a disguise." Birch took our ID badges out of her bag, he looked at me confused, and then smirked, and shook his head.

"Miss Watson?" I smiled at him; he gave a long sigh.

"The boss is going mental; she has been looking everywhere for you two." I giggled.

"We needed some sexy alone time away from here." He shook his head again, turned, and put his key in the door and they opened.

"Go straight to your room, we all got screamed at for letting you slip out, I will give you ten minutes, and then I will have to tell her." I chuckled as I walked in.

"Thanks Roy, you are a real pal." He smiled as the doors closed, and Birch pressed the button for our floor.

We got back to the room, and I took off my wig, and shook out my hair. I stripped and headed for the shower. Birch stuffed all our stuff into the bag, and put it in the wardrobe out of sight, she followed me into the shower and grabbed the soap, lathered it up, and started to rub me all over. It tickled and I giggled, she moved in close and kissed the back of my neck, I reached out, and pushed my hands onto the wall, as her soapy hands moved all over me.

"WERE THE FUCK HAVE YOU TWO BEEN!?" I jerked, spun around and slid behind Birch

"Katie, we are in the frigging shower." She stood glaring at us, as I slid behind Birch to hide myself.

"I don't give a fuck, I have been worried stupid all day, and sent people out looking for you, now where the fuck were you?" I glared at her.

"GET THE HELL OUT OF THIS ROOM, I AM IN THE FRIGGING SHOWER, NOW GET OUT!" She stared at me, and folded her hands.

"Just who the fuck do you think you are talking to Abigail?" I stared at her with anger in my eyes.

"Oh, I don't know, my ex manager maybe, how frigging dare you just walk in here when I am showering. Now get the hell out, or I am out, and in the next cab home." She looked at Birch.

"Are you going to stand there and let her speak to me like that Jemi? I have an event to run, she is supposed to be the highlight of it." Birch gave a sigh.

"Katie, we are in the shower, it's supposed to be private, go in the other room and do as she asked, we will be in shortly." She looked shocked.

"Fucking seriously, you are taking her side over mine, you know how important this event is, you know what is riding on it, how can you just let her run amuck? What if the press saw you, do you honestly think you could keep her safe from that pack of hounds out there?" Birch pushed me further behind her as I nuzzled into her back out of sight.

"Katie, I am not taking her side, Abby is naked and showering, you have no right being in here, just go and wait for us. This is improper conduct of a manager, this is her privacy, now respect it." Katie gave a snort, turned, and marched out of the bathroom, slamming the door.

"Fine! Fucking princess, as if I have not had enough shit today already, cocky arse fucking Curio's. I am not working with all you fuckers again; you are all a fucking nightmare." Birch turned, and pulled me close, and wrapped her arms round me.

"Are you alright?" I nodded.

"Sorry I shouted, I don't want her near me when I am naked, I just freaked out to see someone in here." She kissed my forehead.

"Finish your shower, I will go sort this out."

Birch got out, and I turned and leaned on the wall and let the hot water run onto me, she pulled on a robe, and left the room, closing the door behind her. Katie was sat on the bed, she looked really angry and fiery.

"You are out of fucking order Jemi, I am technical manager of this event, and I need to know at all times where the main players are. You promised me you would keep them in check, you said no parties and no wild behaviour, and yet first chance you get, you just piss off without a word." Birch poured a drink.

"None of this was Abby's doing it was mine, so if you want to sling mud, do it at me. Abby is twenty eight years old, and you sent her to her room like a naughty child, what the hell Katie, are you her mum now? She was feeling the pressure and getting upset, she wanted to leave and go home, so I took her out in a way no one would recognise her. I didn't tell you, because I knew you would be just like your being now, so I told my mum instead. As for barging into a private bathroom, that is definitely out of order, and she was right to tell you to leave." She turned and looked at Katie, who was looking even more pissed off.

"Okay, so if you told your mother, why did she deny any knowledge of your whereabouts." Birch shrugged.

"She knew we were out; she did not know where, which is kind of the point of being alone. Abby needed a couple of hours away from this madness, and so I let her have it, we were back in good time, and we will be there tonight. Your outburst was unnecessary, and actually worked against you. I agree you are managing this event, but that does not give you the right to dominate your main actors. She suffers a lot from the press, just being here makes her a target, and one I may add, you are happy to put her up as. I saw the press coverage, why didn't you step in, and stop them?"

"What do you mean, she handled herself perfectly?" Birch nodded.

"Yes, she did, but she should not have had to. Katie she is not me, she hates being insulted and gets upset, I can hack it, Abby can't, never put her in a position like that again, jump in and cut the press off." She stood up, looking outraged.

"I am sorry the CEO's daughter does not like the way I run things, I am sure a quick chat with mummy will get me fixed. I have an event to run, just get her to the dinner."

She walked out, and closed the door. I came out of the bathroom; Birch was sat on the bed sipping her drink. I felt really guilty, I had heard everything from the bathroom.

"Birch, I am really sorry, if I had known it would cause this much trouble, I would have stayed here." She looked up at me with those beautiful bright green eyes, her hair hung wet round her shoulders.

"It's not just you Sweetie, I wanted to get out too, and honestly, I don't regret it. I really enjoyed it; we need to get out more together." I sat on the bed, and took her glass out of her hand and took a sip.

"Wow that is strong... It would be nice to get out more, at least we have a good disguise kit now, although that sweatshirt smelt weird." Birch gave a chuckle.

"It did a bit, it was really unsettling kissing your boobs and smelling that strange odour, it was like kissing a bag lady." She started to chuckle, as I looked down and sniffed my chest, just to make sure.

"Bobby would love that." I gave a smirk and took her hand in mine.

"Birch, I don't want to be seen as a problem, because I won't be, but I do not want her near me if I am naked. I am really sorry, because I know she is a friend, but I feel creepy around her, when I am not dressed. For the last year and a half, she has been great, I have no problems with her, she calls me Abby, and she does not make all the sex jokes, but I still feel weird if I am changing around her." She gave my hand a squeeze.

"Deads, it's fine, you have a right to be private in a bathroom, Katie should not have come in, she should have waited. Look don't worry about this, she will be fine tonight, she understands the bigger picture now."

I hoped so, it kind of brought the whole day down. I thought about our time alone walking down the Thames, as I dried Birch's hair lost in thought, and I remembered her soft voice as she talked and giggled with me, and the excitement of making love in the toilets. I still could not believe I had done that; quiet sex is so hard to do, it made me smile thinking about it, and my spirits lifted a little.

Tonight, was a formal fund raising event, and a lot of VIP's had been invited who were interested in making donations. We all had nice little dresses for us to wear, to accentuate our feminine charms, mine was the usual screw me, little black dress. Birch had a screw me harder little dark green dress, she wore her matching necklace and bracelet I had bought her for Christmas just over a year ago. With her hair done, and her eyes redone, not as heavy as they normally are, she really did look stunning.

I went with the full on Avril eyes, which with my black hair with red tips, made me look chic gothic, I looked very vampire like, which pleased me. Tonight, would be a social, with food and drinks, and sadly enough, there was a red carpet entrance, which once again meant press and cameras. I had a small black handbag, and so decided to go with my darkest mirror glasses, which I could remove, and put back in my bag once inside the hall.

Katie bought us both thongs, which I immediately rejected, I cannot deny, I hate the things. If I absolutely have to, I wear panties, but seeing as it has been years since I last wore any, I decided to go commando. I knew there was no way Birch would wear any, and the odds of Chloe wearing any in a room full of men, was pretty slim.

The good news was, Deb's would be joining us, for the last month she had been at her home with Jimmy, and the house felt strange without her. I had really missed her, and so I was really looking forward to seeing her.

I slid on my new high heels; I had not worn a pair in ages. I walked up and down the room, I was a little unstable, I wobbled as I looked at Birch.

"I thought you said it was like riding a bike?" She blinked.

"Sorry Sweetie, I was distracted, you do look very lovely, and my mind slipped a little." I gave a sigh.

"Stop being perverted, and tell me how the hell I walk in these?" She shrugged.

"It's just like riding a bike Sweetie, it will come back."

I gave up, she was not listening, I wobbled up the room again. I was not convinced I would last the night, so thought it would be prudent to put some flat shoes in my handbag.

Birch looked at her watch and gave a sigh, it was almost time, and Roy would be back to ensure we made it to the lounge on the first floor, where we would all gather. It would be the first time all weekend, where we could be in one place together. Roy arrived and we headed down, well, Birch walked like an amazon goddess, and I wobbled, although I was getting better by the minute.

I was glad when Roy arrived, not because it meant going to the event, but because I just wanted to be around everybody again. It was hard to be separated, we lived together in the same house and spent all day crossing paths, so here it had been strange. We headed towards the lift and down to the first floor, where we entered what was called the lounge, which was basically a meeting room, with comfy chairs.

I went straight to Deb's and pulled her into a hug, her hair was up and beautiful, and she had on a long dark blue gown. Her tummy was really big, and just seeing her got me all excited. I touched her tummy and smiled, as she watched me.

"You know Abby, for someone who has said she will never have children, you seem to be really into the idea." I looked up at her.

"Deb's, I think the idea of growing a person inside yourself is amazing, and I am excited, but it is not for me, it is because it is you. Deb's you are my oldest friend, and watching you grow and mature and get married, has been so nice to be a part of, and now I can also be a part of this too. I really am so excited for Jimmy and you, and yes, I cannot wait to see this little person who is half you."

Katie and Roni arrived to organise us, Katie was clearly a little stand offish with me, I just avoided her, and tried not to push it. Roni was in charge and we all sat down, it was nice to see

Luke, Michael and Terry dressed in suits. Chloe and Edwina had similar dresses to me, except Chloe was wearing a dark purple, and Edwina had a deep burgundy red. Roni instructed us in the approach to the evening.

We were on the first floor, and so we would have to walk down the public staircase, which was a wide open carpeted stair. We would then walk towards the dining room, and in between was a red carpeted walkway, on which one side had press and TV, who would want to talk to us and take pictures. I was very nervous about the press, I always appeared to get mauled by them, Katie stepped up and looked at me across the room.

"Everyone, if the press asks you anything that is not about this weekend's event, just ignore their question, and talk about Curio Live, that way they get the info that we need them to have, and it will be up to them to either write about it or ignore it." I nodded at her, just so she knew I understood.

We were going down in pairs, which I was very relieved about. The thought of going alone terrified me, it is crazy, I take my clothes off at a club and walk around naked in front of strangers without a worry, and yet the idea of walking up a walkway, fully dressed, with a line of press was so much of a terror for me.

Deb's was going first with Jimmy, she would go in the lift, as it was easier for her. Then it would be Anthony and Michael, then Birch and myself, followed by Chloe with Terry, and then Edwina with Luke. Roni and Will would also be there with Gill and Aden. Katie had a date for the night, who was in the room with us, but mainly had her back to us, as she helped organise everything, and there was a whole host of rich and famous guests, all of which would have a chance to offer extra support if they wished too. Katie looked at her watch.

"Right, everyone, get yourself ready, Debbie, Jimmy, you are up, Roy will guide you to the line." Birch slid her hand into mine, and I turned to her, she smiled.

"Deads, you will be fine; I will be with you." I nodded feeling my throat go dry.

I was so glad she was going to be there with me, and I felt the nerves in my stomach, Deb's winked as she walked toward the door, Katie opened it, and I saw Roy, he lifted his arm to direct them. This was it, this was a big moment, I took a deep breath, and tried to compose myself. I lifted my glasses, and slipped them on, I was as ready as I was going to be, because to be honest, if there was a backdoor, I probably would have bolted for it.

Chapter 5

Selling Ourselves.

I stood at the top of the stairs, and Birch took my hand, and threaded it through her arm.

"Tonight Sweetie, you are my wife, and I am your escort."

We took a step forward into the view, I looked down the stairs to the bottom, and the red rope that marked the line the press could not cross. Behind it they were all lined up, waiting with their cameras, I took a deep breath, Birch patted my hand as I linked her, and we both stepped onto the top step, and suddenly there was an onslaught of flashes.

We walked down the stairs slowly; I was in high heels and terrified of falling. As we got closer to the bottom, I noticed Alison Williams with her husband talking to the press. We hit the bottom and Roy stepped up, and walked slightly behind us, we crossed the space, and stepped onto the red section of carpet, with a wall filled with Curio Live pictures, and suddenly, my name was being shouted out by just about everyone.

Birch kept me close, as reporters asked us to stop for pictures, I came to a halt and smiled, it felt good to have her at my side, they yelled for us to separate, but I was not letting go. Birch spoke through her smile as we stood there.

"What the hell do they need so many pictures for, hell, I bet half these guys have more pictures of you than their wives?"

I smiled for the camera, reporters were shouting from the middle, and back of the line, along the front, there were a lot of TV cameras. I stopped and spoke to quite a few, and it felt like forever as we moved really slowly along. I had rehearsed my lines and stuck rigidly to the script, and surprisingly, a lot of them were happy with that. I spotted Mark and Brett from River TV News, and walked over towards them. Mark smiled as I approached him, it was so loud with all the shouting, it was hard to hear anything, I leaned forward as he lifted the mic, journalists either side leaned in with their mic's.

"Miss Watson, lovely to see you, how do you think this event is going?" I leaned into the mic, as another TV reporter started asking Birch questions.

"I have not seen the full totals yet, but when I last looked, we were well on our way, and all of us are keeping our fingers crossed, we can reach the goal." He smiled.

"Your opening was really powerful, and there have been a lot of comments, especially about how the media treat you, which was evident today at your press conference. Chloe's comments about the lies the press print, has also really stirred up a lot of public commentary. There is quite a debate going on about press intrusion, do you think it will make much of a difference?" I smiled as I shook my head.

"They had the same debate two years ago when the Peter Ford story hit, and nothing changed, they just replaced him with a dozen more, so I am not holding my breath. All I want, which is why I am here doing this, is for them to take this event seriously, and just report the facts, because we can do so much good with this event. There are people in a bad place out there, really hoping we get these centres built." He nodded.

"All of us at River TV are right there with you guys, and we are all hoping you do it." I smiled at him and the camera.

"All of us are here, working really hard on this. We have been involved as surprise guests in other people's presentations, we have all been on the phone lines, and out on the floor of the arena helping out at the workshops. And yes, we have been delighted to see River was there with us, you guys have been wonderful, and we are very grateful for all your support." He gave a beaming smile and nod of appreciation.

"What did you think of Chloe's presentation, she gave a few Curio secrets away, and you guard your privacy, was it worrying to watch?" I chuckled.

"Chloe is amazing, I love her to bits, she is a great friend, and she did not really say anything people do not already know. Wasn't she fantastic? For her this was a big step, and it was scary for her, but she did it. She is such a caring and genuine person, and out of all of us, she spends more time on the site talking to people than any of us." He smiled.

"She is pretty good looking as well." I laughed.

"I only have eyes for my Fiancé, but I do know guys who would love to date her." He looked to the side.

"She is here, so please tell her to come talk to us." I nodded, and looked at her with Terry, and waved her over. Mark thanked me, and I stepped back to make room for Chloe, as she came over with a beaming smile.

We moved up the line, stopped a few times to talk, and I noticed a few people who had trashed me in the past, and ignored them, even though they shouted me. I looked back and saw Chloe enjoying the attention, I smiled at her, and leaned into Birch, she turned to me.

"Are you alright, you know there are a lot of people who want to talk to you?"

I was aware, they were all shouting my name, I recognised a face in the group and moved towards her, I had spoken to her several times on my tour of the states. She waved excitedly as I got closer.

"Abigail, long time no see, how are you doing?" I smiled, but could not for the life of me remember her name.

"I am doing really well, living the quiet life and writing, and just being me." She nodded.

"This is a great idea, and the word is you may bring this states side, hey we could really use something like this, what are the odds of you guys doing that?" Birch moved in closer to listen.

"We would love to come states side, we have a lot of young people on our site, from the US, but we need to get off the floor here first. We are hoping we hit our target here this weekend, and then maybe we can look to other set ups. We would love to get more funds in so we can work quicker, because these services are really needed." She looked at Birch, and held out her hand.

"Doctor Dixon, we have heard a lot about you in the states from Abigail when she was over, will we be seeing you with her in the future?" Birch leaned in to her.

"I think after her last visit, we were separated longer than we wanted to be, so the odds are I will probably be with her next time she visits. I hope so, it is after all up to her publisher." Katie appeared, at our side.

"Sorry guys, we need to get you all in, as it is about to start." I nodded and the reporter handed me her card.

"I am in the UK for two months, and we would love to update all your fans across the pond, would you call me?"

I smiled and took the card, I looked at it, her name was Jessie, and I gave her a nod as Birch pulled me away, I waved that I would, and she smiled. I felt good, as I knew she had done some good coverage on me. Cameras were going off all over and I blinked as they caught my eyes.

We were guided through the double doors, into one of the banquet rooms, and it was huge. Down the left side of the room was a long table with white cloths, and a line of Chefs, who were organising food as waitresses carried it off on trays to serve. At the far end and down the right side were clusters of tables and seating. Each table sat eight people, to my right was a long bar and there were a dozen waitress's taking orders to the guests. Important and immaculately groomed people were either sat at tables, or stood in groups talking to each other, and I assumed it was about the event.

There were far more guests than I thought there would be, some I recognised and some I had no idea who they were. I spotted Aden and Gill, Alex and Morty, and even Megan was here with Bongo. I was delighted when I saw a group talking, one of which was Gordon Stimes, who had interviewed me for his TV talk show on books. He waved whilst stood with a very attractive woman, I smiled and gave a little wave back to him, the woman glanced at me, as he leaned in to her and said something.

There was a small temporary stage, and Katie walked up on to it as the others arrived in the room, and began her speech on the importance of this event. Birch saw the bar, and gave a yank on my arm, we walked over towards it, as Katie delivered her speel. A waitress came up to us, and asked what we would like, I looked at her, she smiled.

"Give me your order and take a seat, and I will bring it to you Miss Watson." Birch ordered our drinks, and we turned to view the room, as all the guests who had been watching applauded. She swanned off the stage like a queen, as every one of the guests got back into their conversations.

We walked up the room towards a table, I saw Deb's sat down, and headed for her, she grinned as we sat down with her, she had a plate piled high with food, and a tall drink of orange. She looked really healthy, her skin was flawless and she had rosy cheeks, she looked at her plate.

"Abby, I cannot stop eating, honestly I am going to be huge by the time the baby comes."

"You look really healthy, Deb's stop worrying about it, we can go to the gym, or jog together like we used to, and get you fit and lean again." Birch sipped her drink.

"You are young and this is your first, the odds are you will lose a lot of it very quickly, it's the second and third that bugger your body up." A shadow crossed the table.

"Good evening, ladies." We all looked up, at a grey haired guy, who to me looked about mid to late fifties.

"Would you mind if I sit a while and talk about your project?" Birch gave a smile.

"Please, take a chair, I am Jemima, this is Abigail, and that is Debbie, and you are?" He sat down and looked at us.

"I am Andrew McAnderson." I knew the name, but was not sure why, I looked at him.

"Aren't you something to do with the car industry?" He smiled.

"You are very insightful Miss Watson, yes I am, I import high performance vehicles for wealthy clients." Deb's nodded at him.

"You are the sports car guy, my dad looked at your site a while back." He appeared impressed. I was impressed because I suddenly remembered my dad talking about him, and how he would kill to get his account, the guy was a billionaire, he sat back and smiled.

"I like your group, you are obviously very on the ball, I cannot deny, I am very interested in your project, but I would like to know more about it." I looked at Birch.

"This is Jemi's baby, she has planned pretty much all of it, any questions you have, she is the one to talk to." He looked at her and nodded.

"So, you are the brains behind the project, I should have known this was the work of a doctor, so Jemima, tell me what you have in mind?" A guy leaned over my shoulder and made me jump; it was Gordon Stimes.

"Abby, could I steal you a moment?" I looked at Birch, she smiled and nodded, and so I stood up.

"Would you excuse me a moment?" He smiled as Gordon led me away to meet a young guy, who was immaculately groomed.

"Abby, there is a man here who is interested in investing, he manages a large app design company, and he is pretty loaded, and wants to speak to you."

I was okay with that; it was at the end of the day the reason we were here. I noticed Chloe and Edwina were both talking to groups, as was Anthony, so I felt I better do my bit.

Colin Richmond was from money, his family was well known in London, my dad had done some business with them, and handled some investments. I remember him being happy and telling mum about them. Colin was the youngest son of three children, and from what I had heard, had a bit of a reputation, he was often in the paper for his lifestyle choices. Gordon introduced me, and he looked me up and down and smiled, and then offered his hand.

"Delightful to meet you Miss Watson, may I call you Abby?"

He was blonde, blue eyed, tall, and very well dressed in a perfectly tailored suit. He had a lot of gold on his wrists and fingers, and the obligatory expensive Swiss watch. Colin was polished, well educated, and very smooth, he also had a lot of confidence, but there again, he had the money to back it up. I kept eye contact.

"I am okay with Abby; I assume I may call you Colin?" He smirked, he lifted a hand, and a waitress appeared, he did not even look at her.

"Bring Abby a vodka and cola." He smiled.

"I have an interest in your little project, and I am considering a donation, and so naturally felt I should get more intel from the source, I find you curiously interesting."

He kept waving to people in the room and giving a conceited smirk to them. I watched him carefully, he was confident, and I would say a tad too in love with himself. The waitress appeared with my drink, I took it, looked her in the eye, and thanked her, I turned back to Colin.

"I am not that interesting really, and looking at the pack we put together, I am pretty sure you know just about everything about our aim this weekend. There really is nothing to be curious about, I live a boring life, and I am at my happiest alone writing." He smirked.

"Nevertheless, I am prepared to throw some cash in the pot, the question is, how much of my curiosity can you quell, because the more you quell, the higher the donation will be?"

Well it did not take him very long, I understood that perfectly and smiled, dodged the issue, and launched into my rehearsed script of how many young people would benefit from the project. How if he did donate his money, we would use it to its absolute best to prevent suicide, house homeless or abused young people, and provide much needed mental health services.

He listened carefully, but I felt he was not really that serious about anything I had to say, but there again, why would he be? He had never gone without or suffered in his life. He had everything he had ever wanted, served to him on a plate. I noticed his eyes wandering as I spoke, and began to feel like I was wasting my time. He took a sip of his drink.

"I am very interested, but I am not convinced this is the cause for me, I am quite sure it will take something far more persuasive to quell my current curiosity."

There it was, I was surprised it had taken him so long, I knew the moment we met what he really wanted. He wanted to screw me, that was the only reason he was here, and it was very clear to see. I thought for a second to see how far he was prepared to go.

"I am unsure as to how to quell your curiosity, although, I would be interested to know what your starting figure would be?" He took another sip of his drink, his eyes never leaving me, he was clearly thinking he had a shot.

"Well, let's just say I am happy to start at a hundred grand, so how about you quell my curious side, and we shall see where we can get to." I smiled and took a sip of my drink.

"So, tell me, if I quell your supposed curiosity, just how much is that worth? I mean, at the end of the day, this is a fund raiser with a target, and I am considered one of its most valued assets." He gave a chuckle, and his eyes wandered down and across my figure again.

"Your dress is very smooth, I see no lines, I like that, so, oh

I don't know, I am sure I could squeeze out two mil, although, throw in your friend, and maybe I could double that." His eyes moved to across the room for a second, and I turned and looked across at Chloe.

"Really, that is quite an offer, but seeing as this is a charity event, and considering we are the main attraction, your price falls low of the mark for both of us. If I was to offer us up, I am sure we would be worth more." I looked back at him.

"And yes, we are that good." He gave a laugh.

"I like a girl who understands her place, and its value, so if I am to raise my bar, name your price." I caught Chloe's attention, and nodded for her to join me, she excused herself and headed over to us, I looked at him.

"We are worth at least six." He gave a chuckle.

"You drive a hard bargain, I am in the royal penthouse at the very top of this place, and I like to enjoy myself, so I expect you until at least the evening tomorrow." Chloe arrived at my side and smiled, I looked at her.

"What do you think of this guy, because he just offered me six mil to take us upstairs and screw us until tomorrow evening?" She frowned at me.

"Seriously?" I nodded at her, he looked her up and down and smiled.

"I did indeed, I always pay for the best, I except nothing less." Chloe looked at me and shook her head.

"Not interested, I don't do ownership, and I don't fuck posh wankers." I smiled at her.

"Yeah, that was my thought too, I just wanted a second opinion, cheers Chloe."

He looked instantly annoyed, I am sure no was a word he had probably never known, I shrugged at him.

"Win some, lose some, but let me give you a little advice, when it comes to women of quality, your curiosity means shit. You were supposed to make me curious, that way you may have had a chance. As my friend so casually pointed out in less than two seconds, you came across as a complete wanker, and that is just not sexy." I turned to walk away, and he grabbed my arm.

"No one turns me down, have you any idea of who I am and what I can do?" William who was a few feet away, saw what was happening and walked over towards us.

"I will tell you what you can do, you can unhand my daughter in law. Is there a problem Abby?" I shook my head.

"He assumed I would screw him for a large donation, but as he has just discovered, living on assumption is not the road to fulfilment." William looked at him, and he looked really pissed off.

"I am sorry Mr Richmond, but this is a respectable event, not a place for your eye to shop, I will have to ask you to leave?" He let go of my arm, and turned on Will.

"Seriously, you are throwing me out, have you any idea of who my family are?" Will gave him a nod.

"I am well aware of your parents, and I am sure they have no wish to pay to make yet another sexual harassment case go away, now please leave quietly. You are aware the press are just outside the door, it would be a shame for you to appear in another paper being evicted by two somewhat large security guards."

He handed his glass to Will, and then walked towards the doors, Will watched him go, Birch was at my side and I had not noticed.

"Are you alright Sweetie?" I turned, and looked at her, and nodded my head.

"Yeah, Dad is watching over me, I think I just found another friend for Kyle to hang out with." She gave a giggle.

"He was that bad?" I watched as he stormed through the door. Everyone who had stopped and was watching, turned back to their conversations, I gave a sigh.

"He wanted Chloe and me for six mil, if he had wanted you instead of Chloe, I may have considered it." I giggled, and Birch smirked.

"Deads Sweetie, for us two, it would have had to be at least ten." I giggled; I love the fact she saw herself as valuable.

"I would defo pay ten mil to sleep with you." She turned to me, and laughed out.

"Oh, Sweetie, I will always do you for free." I smiled as she walked back to the table to talk with Andrew. I thanked Will, and then wandered around smiling and saying hello, Gordon approached me.

"Sorry about that, I know he has a reputation, but he assured me he was here on business." I shook my head.

"Honestly Gordon, we get it all the time. I dyed my hair, so I am seen as a slut, or some guys just feel the challenge of converting a lesbian back to the proper ways. They think they have some magical parts, and they will just instantly turn us all back to men drooling sluts, it is kind of sad. They never understand that, just because I write that sort of thing, does not mean I live that way." He nodded, but looked a little guilty.

"I felt I should apologise." I smiled.

"And that is why I come on your show. I like a man who has manners, and is respectful, you are a dying breed Gordon. And may I say, that you have a stunningly beautiful wife, and I should know." I winked, and he laughed.

"Your fiancé is equally as stunning, if I may say so. You know, I have never forgotten that first interview you did, she had her eyes fixed on you for the whole time, and she looked at you so adoringly, you both make a very lovely couple." I turned and looked across the room at her.

"She is the love of my life Gordon, and I am well aware of how deep her love is for me." He looked round the room.

"How is it going tonight?"

"I do not know, the funds are rising, all we can do is wait until tomorrow and hope we make it, but to be honest no matter what happens, we have made a good start towards doing something really good for a lot of people, which is all that really matters." He nodded, and saw he was being signalled by his wife.

"If you will excuse me Abby, I am needed, but if it is possible, I would love all of you on the show, tell Katie to call me."

I nodded, and smiled as I watched him walk away, and then continued around the room. I stopped, talked to guests, and answered questions, and gave explanations of how we would achieve our goals, and what we had planned for the future. I posed for pictures with people, we took a few group Curio shots, and we all smiled.

I talked to Aden and Gill, they look so good together, Alex was really enjoying the event, she was not used to this level of quality and style. She told me of some of the people she had spoken to, she had felt a little out of her depth, but Morty had backed her up, and between them, they hoped they had swung a few people into donating. It was fun to see her having a good time, I watched the room, there was a lot of long conversations and laughter in the room.

I noticed the very well dressed blonde lean in and give Katie a kiss on the cheek, Katie smiled, and slid her hand across her bum, that was interesting. Edwina appeared at my side and handed me a drink and smiled.

"You noticed then, talk about a Birch lookalike." I watched how she watched the blonde cross the room to talk with a group.

"Who is she, I saw her briefly earlier, do we know?" Edwina smiled.

"She is called Anita, she is apparently Katie's new assistant, the word on the ground is she goes through a lot of them, and all of them are glamourous, and blonde with green eyes. Just watch, every time Katie goes near Birch, Anita looks pissed off, she is a smart girl with a good record. She has already worked out she is just a pale substitute, which is why Katie goes through so many. Be careful Abby, she may look like she has given up, but if you ask me, or I would say Roni, it is clear, Katie will do anything to get Birch in her bed." I shook my head.

"It will never happen, Birch knows the score, she is not interested." Although, I thought it was interesting that even Edwina had noticed, Luke waved he looked panicked, I smiled.

"I believe your man is in need of rescue." Edwina chuckled, and patted my shoulder.

"It is ridiculous, he is a really smart hacker, but shove him with people, and it's like he has no idea what keys to press." I chuckled.

"I think he just hit, Ctrl-Alt-Delete." She giggled as she walked off to save him.

I must admit I had to wonder, it was well known that those who piss Katie off, encounter her wrath, was that why she had been so controlling, was she having a go at me to show Birch she was the better of us? I was well aware I needed to be wary of her.

Katie appeared to be natural in this situation, she was calm and elegant, she really did look beautiful, with her long red hair. I watched as she introduced Birch to a couple to talk, and noted the way her hand on Birch's back was a little lower than expected.

She never missed a chance to show her desire, even if it was only subtle. I had worked with Katie for four years, and when we first started working together, I really liked her, I saw her not just as a manager and a promoter, but also a friend. I admired how driven she was, I loved her strength, and her ability to stand tall, and fight for what she thought was best for me, and as a manager, I have no complaints.

In the last couple of years, since Birch talked to her, and told her to cut out all the sexual advances, I have seen a different side of her. She loves this sort of life style, she fits in perfectly with the rich and the elite, to her, everything is designer and first class all the way. As I have seen so many times around these kinds of people, they are uncaring and unfeeling, and very selfish. Today, everything is about Katie and what she wants, it is always what she thinks, and there is never room for compromise, and it feels cold, cruel, and cut throat.

Watching her with Birch, I could see that she was no different than Colin Richmond, she would gladly pay to sleep with Birch, and it would be nothing more than a meaningless shag to her, except it would be her way of getting even with me.

She once told me this was my life now, this was who I was, but as I looked around at the people in this room, flaunting their wealth, and pretending to be something they were not, I knew this was not who I am. I am never going to fit in with these people, yes, I can throw on a posh dress, and wear false eyelashes, and walk around smiling and being nice, but in truth, I hated how cold inside the rich were. I hated their ruthless need for attention, for no other reason than their bank accounts contained more than most. I can understand why my dad fits in with these people, he had always strutted around in his fitted suits, with his fake smile, and the smell of money in his nose.

I saw how mum suffered, and also how she was just a token in his life, the model wife, with the model child, both seen but never heard, it made me feel sick to the stomach. I did not belong here, I wanted nothing to do with it, I was only here to pimp my smile because a lot of unfortunate people would benefit from all of us kissing their rich ass, and didn't they just love it?

Deb's waddled up and slipped her arm round my waist, she looked down the room, and saw I was watching Birch, stood talking as Katie stood at her side with her arm round her.

"You do not like her Abby, do you?" I glanced at her, and smiled.

"Is it that obvious?"

"I think the stare of death is probably giving it away a little, but considering what she is doing right now, I don't blame you. That is disrespectful to you, especially here in public, and to be honest, she is also doing it right in front of her Birch copy girlfriend. If I am honest, it pisses me off, it should you."

"Deb's, I have never been a jealous person, not ever, so why am I angry she is touching Birch, I mean, there is no way Birch would ever do anything with her?"

"Abby, she is just using a powerplay on you, Birch told me what happened in your room. You stood up to her, and showed her that she is not as powerful as she thinks. Honestly, she needed to be put in her place. Abby, you worry too much, Birch would never do anything with her or any other woman." I gave a sigh.

"Yeah, I know that, and you know that, the question is, does Katie?" Deb's understood me.

"What are you going to do about it?"

"I am not sure, Birch is not someone who will take kindly to me acting territorial, but I have got to tell you Deb's, Katie aims to bed her, and she will use whatever means she can. I need to prevent that, because if she does, Birch and me are done." Deb's gave a gasp, and looked at me.

"Abby, you don't mean that, you and her have overcome so much in the past? Hell, all of us have seen how strong you are, seriously, there is nothing you two cannot get past." I shook my head.

"Deb's, everything has a limit, hell, you saw that with Jimmy, he had no problems with you fooling around while he was on tour. Yet the moment he saw Creamy, he knew that was as far as he was prepared to go, that was his limit, and as a result he changed his habits. Katie is my limit, if Birch goes there, there will be no coming back for me." Deb's gasped.

"Holy shit... You know being pregnant makes me hormonal and a little emotional and a tad insane at times, do you want me to beat the shit out of her with one of Jimmy's guitars?" I sniggered, and turned to her, she looked really serious, which was a bit scary.

"You know I love you right?" She gave a little giggle.

"I love you too, I love Birch too."

I watched down the room, and Birch slid her hand round, and lifted Katie's hand off her bum, I smiled, and in my mind, I heard myself say, 'good girl.'

It was getting late, and Deb's was tired, Jimmy arrived to take her back to her room, I gave him a huge hug as Deb's smiled at me. He was so different these days, more relaxed, and always smiling, I honestly thought being off the road was the best thing for him and Deb's. He winked at me.

"You looking real tasty tonight Abbs, if these old shits don't cough up just for those big blues, there ain't no hope for blokes left in this world." I giggled.

"I saw you doing your bit for us, I also heard you had done your bit manning the phone lines. We are all really grateful, thanks Jimmy, now go on, go take care of my best friend in the world, and her precious cargo." He leaned in and kissed my cheek.

"Abbs, don't you go worrying bout that red haired slapper, I saw you looking, she ain't got a patch on you, and we all know it." I nodded.

"Thanks Jimmy, I think I needed to hear that tonight."

"Anytime Abbs, you're a real babe, and almost as pretty as my Goggle Bear."

He laughed and I gave a giggle, Deb's took his hand giggling, and walked off down the room with him. Wow, she had come so far since our school days. It was nice to see her so happy, she had such a dreadful time at school, it was nice to see her married, and so in love with a really good guy. Roni walked up holding a glass and smiled at me.

"How are you holding up, I would say this place is writer hell for you?"

"I am okay, I have talked to a lot of people tonight, I hope it has helped."

She stood at the side of me, and watched. People were leaving and the crowd was thinning, some were going on to other places, some just home. All of us had done our best, all we could do now was cross our fingers. Roni took a sip of her drink; she saw me watching Birch.

"I heard you and Katie had a spat, and you laid down the law on her, good, it took you long enough?" I was a little surprised and I turned to her.

"I don't like her just walking in, I was showering, and she just barged in and started lecturing me, so I told her to leave. I will admit I was not particularly eloquent." Roni gave a shrug.

"I would have done the same Abby; I think you were in the right." I was relieved to hear it, Roni moved slightly forward and turned.

"Abby, you are going to be a part of this company, and so it is right that you ensure that people understand who you are. I know you well enough to know that you are always polite and respectful, but if I may say so, you also have a big heart, and at times, people try to take advantage of that." I gave a sigh.

"I do not like being nasty, if I can avoid it, I will, but to be honest Roni, I have been pushed around and called too much. I don't have an issue with Katie, but when it comes to my private life, she needs to know there is a line she must not cross. Today she crossed it." Roni understood me perfectly and she gave a slight smile.

"Abby, Katie, has worked hard to be where she is, this for her is a dream come true, but she has been influenced by the people she chooses to socialise with, and as a result, she is a little too comfortable with getting her own way. There will be occasions where she needs to be put straight, never fear doing it, stand your ground, and face her out. Trust me, I know her well enough to know that she will handle it. She won't like it, and she will sulk for a while, but she is no fool, she wants this gravy train to keep running, and she will not derail it for anything."

I nodded, I understood what she was saying, I just hated having to do it. Roni smiled.

"It is time we wound this thing up, we have done our best, no doubt tomorrow we will see if we have done enough." I gave a sigh.

"I just want to curl up with Birch, and snuggle, I am really tired." She gave a smile.

"Not much longer, and then you can run away and hide for a while."

I giggled; she knew me so well. I walked down the room and slipped my arm round Birch, her and Katie were talking to her dad. He smiled as I leaned on Birch's shoulder.

"You look tired Abby."

"I am, and a little drunk, I am hoping this hot daughter of yours is going to take me to bed soon, and act disgracefully." He laughed, and Birch gave a giggle.

"Sweetie, you know being disgraceful is my star quality." She kissed me softly.

"Come on then, we shall brave the press one more time, and head to bed." I had forgotten they were all outside, I had hoped they had got bored and gone home.

We finally said goodnight to everyone, and I put my glasses back on, and we walked out into the barrage of flashes. Wow, they were persistent, I had no intention of stopping as we walked arm in arm. Reporters called out, but I just ignored them, and headed for the lift with Gavin and Roy, to keep everyone at arms length.

Ten minutes later, I was naked in bed as Birch cleaned her teeth, I heard her spit and then the water stopped. The sheets were cool, and the bed firm, and I lay back and just relaxed. Birch walked in and climbed into bed, she turned and looked at me, I was gone, she smiled and snuggled down, and curled round me.

"Night Sweetie." She kissed my cheek softly.

Chapter 6

Last Day.

I woke to the smell of coffee, Birch giggled, as she held a cup in front of my face.

"Sweetie, we are having breakfast in bed." I blinked, and took another long sniff, and I felt my mouth start to water. I sat up and yawned, my head hurt.

"What time is it?" She handed me the coffee.

"It is gone eleven."

I lifted the cup to my lips and sipped it, the taste exploded in my mouth waking it up. Birch slid into bed at the side of me and handed me a plate of toast, and some bacon. I lifted the toast, and could see her watching me, I stopped chewing and looked at her.

"What?" She smiled.

"Deads, I will never be unfaithful, you do know that don't you?" I lifted my cup and sipped at it.

"What has brought this on all of a sudden?" She chuckled.

"Those eyes of yours are insanely beautiful, honestly, I drown in them, and yet last night, they looked like you wanted to kill Katie. I noticed, and just so you know, I told her to stop." I looked at my plate, and I suddenly was not hungry, I handed it to her, she loved bacon. I got out of bed and walked up the room

"I am going to run a bath and soak, if you are going to join me, lock the door when you come in." She looked at me.

"Deads, talk to me." I stopped, and looked back at her.

"You are a free spirit, and I do not want to stop that, but if you think I am okay with her rubbing your ass in front of everyone, I am sorry, I am not. Honestly, if it was anyone else, it would not bother me. Look, I know she is your friend, and I have no issue with it, but do not ask me to trust her, she has you still in her sights, and the one thing I know for sure, is Katie gets what Katie wants." I grabbed the handle to the bathroom.

"Actually, I am locking the door, I think I will bathe alone today,

I also have a banging head, and need some peace."

I walked into the bathroom and closed the door, clicked the lock, and pushed my head against it. What the hell was I doing, why was I being like this, it made no sense to me? I moved to the bath and put the plug in, and turned on the hot water. She tapped on the door.

"Deads, this makes no sense, please let me in and talk to me."

I sat on the edge of the bath with my head in my hands, I know it makes no sense, but I had this huge ball inside me, and I felt it tighten every time I saw Katie touch her. The lock clicked and the door opened, she stepped in, I looked up. Birch stood holding a coin.

"It's a safety lock, it can be opened in case of emergency. So, we need to talk, so you tell me what is going on in your head, because I am confused." I gave a long sigh.

"I don't know what the hell is wrong with me. I just know, I have all these crazy feelings at the moment, oh crap... I am sorry, I am so sorry." I looked at her, and shook my head, which I regretted.

"Honestly, I am not normally like this, but Birch, I am afraid... I just cannot help thinking she will move heaven and earth to prevent the wedding, and take you away from me. I know it's not rational, honestly, I do, but that is how I feel." Birch sat on the toilet and looked at me.

"Deads, I don't want her, I never have, I don't want any other woman, do you not think I have not had offers, I have? To be honest, it is messed up that women know about us, and yet still hit on me. Sweetie, if we ever broke up, which we won't, I will go right back to guys." I put my head down, and closed my eyes.

"Do you not think I do not know all this already; I do? I cannot explain it, I wish I could. When I saw her pawing at your ass like that last night, I cannot believe I am saying this, but I got jealous, and I frigging hate people like that."

"But why Deads, you know I would never touch her?"

"Birch, I watched her, and you. I saw you push back on her hand; you were enjoying it." Birch gave a giggle, and looked embarrassed, her voice went quiet.

"Actually... About that... I am not sure I should tell you; it is sort of embarrassing... But... Well, the truth is, she started rubbing, and I had been trying to hold a fart in all night, and when she did that, it just sort of leaked out." She put her head down and sniggered, I was a little shocked, and opened my eyes and looked up at her.

"You farted on her hand?" She nodded, and kept her head down, and sniggered again, I felt a jolt in my tummy, and it came up inside me, and I snorted a giggle.

"Holy shit, I hope she did not smell her hand later, actually she probably fingered Anita with it." Birch gave a snort and started to laugh. I felt my tummy wobble, as I giggled. She shook her head.

"Don't laugh, it was awful of me, I really did not mean it, but it just came out, I was so glad it was a silent one." I laughed out loud, and she gave another snort, and giggled.

"It is not funny Deads, I felt awful after, I was just so glad it did not smell." I started to laugh.

"Well, any thoughts I had of shaking hands and making up, have gone right out of the frigging window."

She looked at me and gave a cackle of a laugh. I leaned back and turned off the tap, she slid off the toilet on to her knees and put her arms around me. I still had the giggles. Birch looked up from just under my boobs.

"Don't talk about us splitting up, it frightens me, I asked you to marry me because I don't want us apart." I looked down at her, and smiled, as I stroked her hair back from her face.

"I am sorry, I didn't mean too." I gave a sigh.

"I don't know what is wrong with me at the moment, I think I need to just get home, and have normal again. I find all this hotel and rich people talk gets to me, and I get scared about it all." She kissed my tummy and smiled.

"Will you let me in the bath with you, I want to get soapy with you?" I smiled.

"Of course you can... But no fart bubbles." She giggled, knelt up, and kissed my nipple, I felt a tingle shoot through me, and shuddered.

It was the last day, thank God, and we had been told by Katie to look our best for the end of the event. We were all rebellious Curio's, so we put on our ripped jeans, old vests and I wore a chequered scruffy shirt, which was open, and I had the sleeves rolled up. I also had on my round mirror glasses, and an Avril base ball cap backwards. Birch slipped on a pair of boot cuts, with a rip in the ass, and an old faded Zep t shirt, she wore a denim shirt decorated with embroidered flowers.

Today we would all appear together on stage, and we were going to appear as the Curio's really were in real life, scruffy, comfortable, and just us. Chloe was back in her dungarees, Deb's had big baggy dungarees on, and Edwina was in a scruffy pair of jeans and an old Atari t shirt. Anthony looked clean and tidy, but he did wear jeans and a long sleeved sweat shirt. We looked like a right bunch of trouble causers. When we arrived in the wings of the stage, Katie had a fit, Chloe shrugged.

"You want the Curio's, well this is who we are, all those people on the web site dress just like us, and that is why they identify with us."

Aden was sat watching the monitor with a head set on, smiling, Roni was on stage finishing off her presentation, which had involved a lot of people talking about the help they had got from Curio Life, Katie let out a long flowing breath.

"Honestly, this thing cannot end quick enough, you lot are a fucking nightmare. I need a two week holiday after this just to recover."

The audience burst into applause, and I saw Roni smiling to the camera. Alison Williams grabbed the mic, and walked onto the stage with a smile, she shook Roni by the hand, as she came off, and walked towards us. Alison stood in the centre of the stage.

"Ladies and gentlemen, we have something very special for you today. Behind the scenes, there has been another very special project running, which the Curio's do not know about. This will be as much a surprise for them, as it will be for all of you, and so here to introduce it, is someone I know you all know, and he will tell you all about it. Please welcome to the stage, from the band Battered Taco, vocalist Mr Jimmy Blazer."

The audience went crazy, as Jimmy walked on from the far side of the stage with a guitar and a tall stool, I looked at Deb's.

"Do you know about this?" She gave a smile.

"I might do." She giggled, and I laughed, and looked at the

monitor, where the others were now closely huddled.

Jimmy set his stool down, and stood next to the mic, as the audience roared, he gave a chuckle, and waited for calmness to descend, he looked back at the big screen and it came to life. Aden was busy on the computer control, and talking into his head set. Jimmy looked round the arena.

"Wow, it has been a bit of a while since I stood on the boards, and looked out. As you know, the band are taking a bit of a break, to be honest, we were all pretty knackered after the states, and with the new album doing well, we thought, fuck it, let's chill for a bit." The audience chuckled.

"Right guys, with me being on my lonesome at home with the missus, and waiting for our new little band member, I figured I would write a few tunes not quite like the band do. You know, dip my toe into other ponds, and stretch me legs and all that?" He adjusted the mic stand a little and pulled the stool closer.

"As you all know, my missus is a Curio." The audience applauded with whistles and cheers, and he laughed.

"Fuck me, if she ain't more famous than I am now? So, the thing is, all those guys are amazing, honestly, they is the coolest people I know, and I am in a bloody rock band." He giggled, and was really enjoying being back on stage.

"Look guys, what they are trying to do here is brilliant, I see all of you on the web site, because I sit with me missus whilst she writes to you all. Well then, it got me thinking, because these guys really need this cash, and we all have given a few quid to help. Every one of the band has lobbed something in the pot, but you know, I am a rock musician, so one night in me studio, I looked at me missus and I says, hey Goggle Bear." He giggled.

"That's what I call her, it's my little nick name like, I say, is there anything I can do to help? Well, we sat down and we did a little brain storming, well she is the brainy one, I just looked dumb and twanged on me guitar, and between us, we wrote a tune, she did the lyrics, and I put all the rest together. So right now, on the website, you can download the tune for just three quid, it's a video, which was actually put together by a group of really cool guys, called, Aden, Luke, and Bongo. I am going to play the tune for you now, and the pictures for the video will run behind me, on the screen, would that be okay with you lot?"

He smiled as he got comfy on his stool, and put an ear plug in so he could here Aden at the control desk. Deb's was giggling as we all stared at her.

"You sneaky bitch." Aden chuckled, as he keyed everything up. Jimmy organised his guitar and ran his fingers down the strings.

"This tune is dedicated to a really amazing person, I love her to bits and she is me missus's best mate, this one is for Abby." I felt a jolt inside me.

He began to play, a soft rhythmic tune, and behind him the screen came to life, as pictures from the website came to life. 'Hi I am Chloe, Hi I am Anthony. Hello, my name is Birch, you know, it's the hair thing. Hey everyone, I am Edwina, Hi I am Debbie, and I am a Curio.' The pictures showed me, I turned and laughed. 'Guys I messed up again, I keep hitting the wrong buttons, oops, shit! Hi all, my name is Abigail, I am twenty four, my life is shit, and I am most definitely a Curio, actually I am very curious as to how the hell this camera works.' The audience laughed as Jimmy played on, as the pictures turned to all the outtakes, we had with us hugging and crying and just giving long sighs. Jimmy leaned into the microphone, and started to softly sing.

"Don't look at me that way.
Don't say those things you say.
Why don't you treat me right?
You won't see me cry tonight."

I stared at the screen and watched, and listened to his words, and I felt Deb's put her arm around my waist.

"Someone take this pain away.
Stop saying the things you say.
Can't you see that I am in pain.
Stood here crying in the rain."

I watched the video behind him, and I saw my emails to Debs, printed out on the floor, and lines were highlighted in bright yellow pen, and I suddenly realised what Deb's and Jimmy had done. I felt the tears well in my eyes, and Deb's squeezed my waist a little harder.

"These are all lines from your emails to me when you were alone, and I was stuck in Cambridge, it is alright we used them isn't it Abby?" I nodded lost for words, Birch gave a sob and took my hand in hers.

"I keep asking myself why, am I living a big lie.

I just cannot take this pain; I need to just be me again.

Tell me why, let me go, give me a reason, so I know.

Understand its now too late, I cannot handle much more hate."

I turned and pushed my face into Birch, and she wrapped her arms around me, it was the darkest time in my life, and I just sobbed into her shoulder, as it all came back. Birch held me sniffling with tears running down her cheeks. Deb's smiled and wiped her eyes. I could not help crying, and I sobbed, and suddenly Jimmy came towards the end of the song; I had missed the last couple of verses.

I looked at the monitor to see that awful picture of the selfie I took just before passing out, as the words came up the screen quoting the figures of how many young people killed themselves, and how many suffered from depression. He struck the last note as I wiped my eyes, and the audience erupted from their seats into applause. He smiled and waited for it to settle down which actually took a long time. He gave a sad smile and nodded to the audience.

"Listen guys, long before the Curio's built their site, me missus and Abby would write to each other, and Abby was having a really tough time. I mean life ain't that great for any of us at times, but she suffered, and it was because of that the Curio's came together and set up all of this. Every line of that song, was something Abby wrote in her letters to Deb's, we just lifted them and did a bit of rearranging. There are thousands of people like Abby and the rest of the gang suffering, and that is why, you need to download that video, because every penny, will help someone in need."

He put his hand to his ear, as he listened to Aden, and then ran his finger down the strings.

"It looks like I made all the Curio's cry, they are all back there bawling their brains out." He laughed as he looked back.

"So, it appears, I can play another tune. So, all my lovelies, what are we going to play?" He laughed as the audience all yelled out one particular Taco tune, he leaned into the mic.

"I think I would need another stool to do that one."

Back stage, Roy appeared with a stool, and Aden handed Deb's Jimmy's top hat, she gave a massive laugh, as Roy took her arm, and walked her onto the stage, wearing his hat. The crowd roared with appreciation, and Jimmy looked back and chuckled, Deb's in her big baggy dungarees beamed with delight, As Roy set up her stool, and helped her up onto it, facing him. Jimmy winked at her.

"This brings back memories, which reminds me, have you seen my hat?"

He started to play, and I stood and watched, wiping my eyes, as for the second time, Deb's sat front and centre, with a huge beaming smile, and Jimmy played the song he hoped would find her for him five years ago. The crowd sang along with him, screaming out the words, 'I want the girl in my hat back.' It was such a lovely moment to see, knowing that there inside her, was their child, who must have been listening to every lyric. Birch stood behind me and hugged me, she gave a sniffle.

"Doesn't she look happy?" I nodded watching her face.

"She knew the moment she met him, she would love him forever, and so did he. They belong together forever, I really hope they make the distance, Deb's deserves that."

When Jimmy finished and the crowd roared with applause, he leaned over and kissed her softly, and I smiled as I watched them on the monitor. Birch watched from my shoulder.

"I really love those two." I leaned my head on to hers, and smiled.

Jimmy slid off his stool and took Deb's by the hand, he bowed to the audience, and she slid off her stool carefully, behind them the picture of me, was frozen on the screen with the words 'Download Now from Curio Life.'

Behind Jimmy, two guys, dressed in all black, wheeled a couple of red sofas onto the stage. Jimmy took Deb's by the hand and led her off the stage, Jimmy was all smiles, he put his guitar down, and pulled me into a hug.

"I had to record it, those lines are the truth, and a great song should always be the truth. I hope you forgive me for not asking, and I hope you forgive me if it made you remember things you shouldn't?" I held him close.

"It is alright Jimmy, it is a really beautiful song, I hope it does a lot of good. And by the way, I love you, both of you." Behind us,

Alison Williams walked back onto the stage, and she smiled, and dabbed her eyes.

"That was pretty special, wasn't it? Wow such a powerful song, and it is available from the Curio Life website for download now."

The screen behind her changed and the Curio Live logo came up, with the large totals box, but it was blank. She looked back behind her, and looked at the large screen.

"Shortly we will know what this event has managed to raise, but before all of that, I think I have been given the best job in all of this event, because right now, on this stage, I want all of you to welcome the Curio's. Chloe Pemberton, Edwina Pemberton, Debbie Ford Battersby, Anthony Parker, Jemima Dixon, and Abigail Jennifer Watson."

We all took a deep breath, and walked onto the stage, and the crowd went wild, and roared as they saw all of us together for the first time. Holding hands, we all walked up to the front of the stage. We were wearing face mics, and all of us smiled, and waved to the audience and the cameras. Alison was all smiles as she walked to us, the crowd were on their feet applauding, and it looked like there was not going to be an end to it any time soon. Roni stood back stage with Katie watching the monitor, she shook her head.

"Honestly Katie, when Jemi first brought this to me, I had my doubts, but hell she has pulled it off, just look at them, they are like rock stars." Katie smiled.

"They are a fucking pain in the arse, but you know what, I am glad they did it. I think Jemi needed this the most, she needs to understand that she can take her work on the road."

On stage, the crowd were finally settling, and Alison guided us to the two large sofas, we all walked over and sat down. Alison had an armchair between the two sofas, and we all settled down, and Alison looked round.

"That was quite the welcome guys, what was that like for you?" Edwina looked at the crowd and waved.

"It was pretty mind blowing, I don't think any of us expected that, but I must admit, it is heart warming." Alison looked at me.

"Abby, you have had more stage time than any of the others, how are you feeling?" I was blown away, and just getting used to all of this.

"I am pretty emotional right now, Jimmy completely threw me, and then to see so much love, just so openly shared like this, I must admit, I have a lot going on inside at the moment." Birch took my hand and gave it a squeeze, Alison smiled.

"The new track from Jimmy is now live on the website for download, it must have really hit you hard to see that actually, Debbie took lines from your messages to her, and turned them into lyrics, and created such a beautiful if not, very powerful song?"

I swallowed hard as I remembered the song, I looked at Deb's and smiled, and the tears filled my eyes. Deb's smiled at me.

"I think Abby does not need to say the words, I was at her side when Jimmy sung, and it touched her deeply. We did not tell her we used her words, she realised when she saw the video, with all her messages on our studio floor, and to be honest Abby, your words were already a song, we just did a little arranging."

I wiped my eyes on my sleeve as Birch slid her arm round me, and tried to smile, Anthony took hold of my hand and gave it a squeeze. Alison could see the effects, and moved on.

"Birch, all of this came about through Abby, and all of you suffering some pretty nasty stuff. The Curio housemates' section is pretty intense, but I think that is why all of you became so relatable to those on the site, would you agree?" She smiled, and looked out at the crowd.

"Abby wrote an incredible blog, I read it all again a few weeks back when we were preparing, I suppose to have a writer in our midst has helped a lot, because as everything happened, she took on the task of writing it up. She also does such a wonderful job of really capturing the truth of how we all felt at that time. I think those who visit the site, read it and it really talks to them, and they get it, they understand it, because they too feel exactly the same. I have always felt the blog was the driving force of the site, and through that, our message to everyone was heard loud and clear by those who needed to hear it." Alison smiled, and gave a nod as she looked at me.

"What do you think Abby?" I took a breath and felt Birch squeeze my hand.

"It has always been a team effort, I love writing the blog, but to be honest, it is seeing what the guys have gone through and listening to them talk that was the inspiration for me writing it. We were always clear, it had to be precise and accurate, and I feel that what I wrote is. The whole site and all of Curio Life is a team effort, and everyone who uploads a video is also a part of that. We have sort of created a community for those left behind, and I don't really know, but maybe the site is their way of catching up and getting their lives back on track as we did. I think it is something we are all very proud of." Alison looked around as everyone gave a nod.

"One big team, that does come across very strongly being around you guys. Anthony, you have not done the stage before, but have been whizzing around the complex joining in everything. You have been in interviews, on the demonstration and workshops, and been on the phone lines. If that was not enough and from what I hear, you are somewhat of a behind the scenes genius with the girl's hair, and I have to say, what you have done for Jemi, is inspired?" He looked proud.

"Oh Darling, just so you all know, it is a nightmare, and I have pledged to only do it for Jemi, and honestly, I am happy about that. I should have known she would test me with something so out there, I had to develop a whole new technique to do it." Birch giggled.

"You know you love it; I have made you a ninja of the salon trade, admit it?" Alison laughed.

"Could you just stand up and let us really look at it?" Birch stood up and spun slowly around, Alison was really impressed, the crowd roared with appreciation.

"Now I have heard the idea was to make it look like birch bark, and Anthony, I have got to say, that you are a truly amazing stylist, it really does look like the birch tree." Birch sat down, and Alison turned to face the others.

"Chloe, this was your very first time on the stage, and to be honest, I was watching and thinking, wow, this woman is a natural. You were so relaxed, what was that like for you?" Chloe gave a huge smile.

"I really loved it, I talk every day on the site, every morning after my breakfast, I have a chat with Abby, and then I go to the studio and log in on my laptop. When I got on stage, I just thought I have already talked to these guys, and so I just imagined I was in my studio talking to everyone on the site. I could not see that far out, because the spotlights are pretty bright, it was only at the end when the lights came up that I got terrified. Honestly, if Abby had not come out, I am sure I would still be stood there now."

She giggled and I smiled at her, Alison sat back in her chair so she could look either side of her and get a look at us all.

"I am quite lucky, because I see you all behind the scenes, and watch how you interact with each other, and you really are very close to each other, is that from living together in the same house?" I looked at Birch.

"You are kind of the glue with all of us, what do you think?" She shrugged.

"I am not sure it is all me. I think Abby and myself, are a little like the parents, we do own the house, so I suppose we are looked to if there is a problem. To be honest, if there are any things we need to sort out, we have a house meet and talk everything through. We are very honest with each other, and we don't hide our feelings, so after four years of living that way, we have just naturally bonded deeply. It's a matter of trust, we all have each others back." I nodded.

"We are more like a family, I see them as my brothers and sisters, they are beyond friends to me." Chloe giggled.

"I hate you two really, I just stay because the rent is cheap." The audience and Alison started to laugh, I blew her a kiss, as all of us giggled. Alison chuckled.

"Okay, speaking of family, we have a marriage, and a birth on the horizon, so mum to be, how are things going?" Debbie gave a big smile, and her eyes twinkled.

"I am doing great, I have about five weeks to go. I don't have any worries at all, I have a brilliant husband, and five impending aunties and uncles, so if I have any problems, there is always someone on hand." Alison smiled and nodded.

"You are lucky, I think most women would love a back up team of five, if they needed it, do you know what you are having yet?" Debbie shook her head.

"No, we decided to be surprised, but honestly we do not care, Jimmy and me just really want a little Curio." She smiled at Alison, who gave a beaming smile and turned to face Birch and myself.

"So, Jemi and Abby, you two are about to tie the knot, any nerves yet?" I took a deep breath.

"We are fine at the moment, I am sure I will be nervous, but I am really looking forward to it. To be honest we made a vow to each other at Deb's wedding, the first picture taken of us kissing, was actually as we made the vow. It got splashed all over the press, so in a way, we have been committed for four years, so this is more us having that time, to make it stronger and recommitting to each other." Birch gave a nod of agreement, and squeezed my hand.

"We really don't have to get married, but we want to, and that really is the difference, there is no other woman alive I want in my life. Abby is my whole universe, and I want everyone to know that." Behind the scenes Roni smiled.

"Listen to her Katie, because after watching you last night, I think you need to get the message. If you want my advice, you will back off, because if you don't, you will lose two really good friends." She stared at the screen, and the happy look on Birch's face.

"I am aware of them Roni, she turned me down once before remember?" Roni gave a smirk.

"You have been playing a dangerous game, do not underestimate the power of Abby. If you want my opinion, you will meet more than your match if you take her on."

On stage we were all laughing, Alison had the giggles, as we talked about skateboarding in the hotel car park, and getting told off. Alison turned and looked at Edwina.

"Edwina, you are technical genius on this one, I believe you have a team behind you, and all the graphics for the event have been your responsibility? That must be a hell of a lot of work, just the video's we have all watched alone must have been a mammoth task?" She nodded and looked at Birch.

"Two years ago, Birch brought this to me to ask if it was possible, and since that time I have been filming and editing. To be honest, none of us expected Curio Life to get as big as it has, which says a great deal about today. It has been a big job, but Birch has such great insight, and explained it all in such detail, to be honest, the team I have working with me really had the best plan to work. We are really happy with how it turned out, and it has been fun to expand into a large production like this has been." Alison smiled as she looked around at us all.

"I cannot deny, this really has been an inspiring event, I think every country involved has done something to contribute to the three days, it really is a credit to all of you." She smiled as the audience applauded, and then turned to look back at the big screen.

"Alright, we have learned a little more about you guys, so let's look at the event. You guys have worked really hard for two years to make this happen, and this weekend, you have all popped up everywhere, joining in and supporting all the guests and activities, and your aim is three centres. One in the south, one in the north west, and one in Scotland. That is an expensive project, which is going to cost at least forty million, that is a big target, and it is expected that funds will flow for at least another week after this finishes today."

We all nodded, I was feeling really nervous, it had taken so much to get here, and I knew if it flopped, the press would hang us. Alison watched us carefully; she could see how nervous we had become. I clung to Birch's hand, and felt my heart beating faster.

"All of you have done a lot at this event, you have been seen at workshops, on stage, in press interviews, all of you have made videos that have been played on the River TV broadcasts, who are streaming this live. Last night you hosted a VIP event, and Abby, you did a big book event which donated all the sales to this event, so you have all put in the time. After all of this how have you done, are you ready to see?"

We all took a deep breath, and nodded at her, we turned, and looked at the screen where the blank boxes were highlighted. Birch gripped my hand and took a deep breath; I could feel my heart beating even faster, and I was really nervous. My stomach twisted as Alison lifted her mic.

"Can we see the total to date please?"

The screen flashed, and there was a drum roll through the speakers, and the then the boxes lit up, and I could not believe my eyes, as I read £66,345,792. I was stunned as I looked at Birch, my voice was weak.

"You did it." I started to laugh.

"Holy shit, you did it." She had tears in her eyes as she stared at the numbers, she turned and pushed her head into me, to hide her face, and cried. The audience went wild, and it was so loud.

Chloe and Edwina were bouncing with joy, Anthony was smiling like an idiot, and I held Birch as she wept, she had worked so hard, and put so much effort in. I had tears in my own eyes and she shook. Alison smiled, and the noise level of the audience faded.

"Wow you guys are amazing, congratulations, would any of you like to make a comment. We all looked to Birch, who pulled her head out of my shoulder, and Anthony handed her a handkerchief, her eyeliner had run, and she dried her eyes, I took it off her and wiped under her eyes and smiled.

"This is your baby Birch; we were just the backing singers on this one." She smiled and gave a sniffle; she looked back at the screen.

"I am so happy, and so surprised, and I am so very grateful to everyone who has supported this. I watch every video, and answer every comment I can, and this money will give Curio Life, the means to open its arms wider, and help even more young people. Thank you so much everyone, you have done so much good with this money, it will change lives." Alison waved her hand out to the front of the stage.

"All of you, the cameras are yours, and you have the crowd, go talk to them."

We all stood up and walked to the stage edge, the house lights came up and everyone was on their feet applauding and yelling out to us, we all waved and said thank you, and we all smiled. Birch had tears in her eyes, but was wearing a huge smile, Edwina wiped her eyes, and I felt amazingly emotional. Deb's was all smiles and waving madly. I slid my arm round Birch, and pulled her close. Alison walked up to the side of the stage, and held up her hand, as the audience roared, looking like they were not going to stop any time soon.

"Ladies and Gentlemen, this was Curio Live, and we thank you for tuning in and making this the resounding success it has been.

Thank you to everyone on the live stream, and good night."

The crowd just roared even more, and all we could do was stand and smile and wave, as behind us the screen flashed the total. I was so thrilled for Birch, I had woken up so many nights to see her sat at her own little desk working, and that was all I wanted, for her to see it was all worthwhile. I turned to her smiling face, and in front of everyone, I pulled her close and kissed her. The cameras flashed like crazy, and I just did not care.

Chapter 07

Prude Party.

Until you have really missed it, you will never understand the joy, of waking up at almost nine in the morning, in your own bed? I love hotel beds, they are firm and snug, and I will not deny, there is something really nice about hotel sheets.

My biggest problem had been that I live with a group of people, and my day was spent crossing paths with them, which led to fun and spontaneous conversations. For most of the last ten days, I had been kept separated for most of the time from them. Waking at home, in my own bed, knowing all my friends would be around, was just wonderful for me.

I lay back and just enjoyed the moment. It is bank holiday Monday, and also Mayday, and in the village, Mum had organised a May pole for the children. The shops that were open had stands out for extra sales. The Book Shop was closed, which gave Denise, a day off, as she had worked the shop alone over the weekend, although her long time boy friend John, had mucked in.

Deb's was still working in the shop, but that was more her sitting at a small desk on a computer that had been installed, so she could keep her feet up and rest. Jimmy did help out, but recently he had been doing a lot of recording.

Birch was off today, although she was not in bed when I woke up, I just enjoyed laying back and stretching. We had arrived home last night, around nine, and once I had a coffee, and dragged my stuff up to my room, I hit bed, and was asleep before ten, and it appears that I have slept for most of the last twelve hours. I turned, and looked out of the window, the sun was out, and the little forever tree, which had grown somewhat, appeared to be really enjoying the dry weather. It has rained for weeks, and so to finally have three days of dry weather, lifted most people's hopes.

Luke, Edwina, Chloe and Terry, had stayed in London, there

was a lot of our technical equipment to pack up, and remove at the arena, and Katie and her company were still there packing things up. Edwina and Chloe also were doing a live broadcast from the hotel with Amy of River TV talking about the event and the success it had been. Roni and Will were still in the hotel, they had planned a few days touring the sites. Deb's was back home with Jimmy, and Izzy was enjoying a day off. I didn't really want to get up, but I felt guilty, because I was the only one in bed.

I made my way downstairs to the kitchen, the sun was really bright as it streamed in through the two sets of large patio doors, which were open. I walked towards the kettle, and lifted it to check the water level, I yawned as I put it down and clicked it on, and reached for my mug.

While the kettle boiled, I stood near the doors and looked out, Birch and Izzy were in the pool swimming. I felt a little guilty, I had not been running since last Tuesday, I should at least get some exercise, the problem was, I did not want to, the kettle clicked and I returned to making my first coffee of the day.

A few minutes later, I walked onto the patio with my sun glasses on, and sat on a lounger with my knees up. I sipped my coffee, and felt the warmth of the sun on my body. It had felt like ages since I had been naked outdoors, and I relaxed enjoying the soft breeze brush my skin. It was so peaceful, no screaming fans, no reporters, and no Katie ordering me about, this was the life I loved the best.

Birch saw me, pulled herself out of the pool, she gave me a big smile, grabbed a towel, and walked across the grass drying herself.

"Hi Sweetie, did you sleep well?" She came up to me, and sat on the end of the lounger, wrapped in her towel, and leaned onto my knees.

"You look a lot better, I was worried last night, you really looked pale and tired." I smiled at her.

"I am okay, I was just tired, I was so happy you got the success you did, but I just wanted to get home and sleep." She placed her head on my knees, and watched me with those huge green eyes, she smiled.

"Sweetie, the weather is gorgeous today, I really want to plant things, and I need a bigger pot for my forever tree.”

I sipped at my cup, she loved plants and the green world, but we had a fully landscaped garden, which Norman had assured us was low maintenance, so there really was little to do. She smiled a sweet smile, and I chuckled.

“So, what do you have in mind?” She kissed my knees.

“I want a normal sort of day, just you and me, nothing fancy. I thought a trip to the nursery in Petal, and just have a look to see what is pretty. I want to get dirty and plant something. I need to touch the earth, and this is the only day off I am going to get, but I want to do something alone with you too.” I gave her a nod.

“I need more coffee, but yeah, that would be nice.” She smiled and kissed my knees again, then slipped off the lounger and headed inside.

Thirty minutes later I was sat on the toilet, and Birch sat on the bath filing one of her nails. It is strange how much we change as people when we become settled in a relationship. There I was happily enjoying the release of my flow, with Birch literally a few feet away, there was time in our lives when we would have turned our backs, or closed the door. Now it did not matter, we were so at ease, it was normal to just sit and go, although I will admit, I never want to take a dump in front of her, I think that would be just too weird for me.

Actually, thinking back, there was that one time when I was in the bath relaxing, and Birch ran in looking panicked, looked at me for a second, bit her lip, then cracked, and went. We had been to an Indian curry house in Oxendale, the night before, and she suffered terribly. It was awful, I felt for her, she told me it was like shitting liquid fire. It ruined my bath, as she stunk the whole of the upstairs of the house out. Let me just say, I fled with horror, left her to dissolve, and ran soaking wet for the patio, and copious amounts of fresh air, gagging. I cannot deny, I never thought for one minute, that perfect little round cute bum, could be so sodding toxic.

Curry is a dangerous thing when not respected, many hours later I rubbed cold cream on her cute, if not burning hot, red little rosebud. That was the day Chloe showed us the benefit of sitting on a frozen sausage, which apparently, she had done a few times in her life at home with her parents, experimenting with the recipe. Wow, she is really messed up, although when I wedged one in Birch's butt cheeks, she gave a happy moan of relief, so go figure?

Feeling relieved, with an empty bladder, I dressed ready for the nursery, it was really warm, so I pulled on jean shorts and a vest, I grabbed my black denim jacket. Birch tossed me the keys as she loaded several plastic crates into the back of Petal. We had taken to using crates for everything these days, as it cut down on bags, and although Norman viewed them suspiciously, he did commend us, as we could use them over and over for a lot of different things, and they cut out the need for single use bags.

Once loaded, the gates opened and we set off, Birch was in high spirits, she loved plants, and her natural side was showing, as we drove up the main street of the village, and turned right onto Station Road. Like all bank holidays, the tourists and the locals were all out in force, as the village put on side attractions and events, Ronald had erected the huge May Pole, and as we drove up, I could see mum and Peter supervising the children dancing around it holding ribbons, as a medieval looking band played.

The nursery was busier than expected, and the car park, which had been expanded a few times was almost full. Norman and Daisy have worked really hard to build up the business, and against popular belief, a lot of the stately gardens are still in tip top condition. The staff has grown a great deal, much to Chloe's delight, as there is a solid workforce of strapping young men, and on her visits, she rarely leaves with a plant, but never leaves empty handed.

Norman chose to expand the nursery into the open fields at the side of the property, although the thing I love the most, is he left the wild flower meadow right in the centre of the nursery, and mowed pathways through it. To get from one part to the other, you have to walk through a large field of the most beautiful colour, and it is always awash with butterflies, it is one of my favourite places in the village.

When we entered the nursery, we always walk past the site of the old shed, it is now a row of large glazed greenhouses, but I love to walk the path, and remember that day when Birch first saw the hunk of junk that we now drive.

That has always been such a special day in my life, for not only was it the day we got Petal, but that was the day, Chloe made peace with us all. In a way, I think I have always seen it as the first real day of the Curio's. In my mind, that was the day we started as a group, and Hatty took a picture, which she painted, and it hangs above my bed as it has no matter where I lived, I even took it to Uni for a year.

It is funny really, because I cannot remember what my life was like before Chloe became a part of it? It feels at times like we have all been together forever, we have seen and done so much together, I cannot imagine not seeing Chloe every day, or not hearing Edwina yell at her for using a wrong flash drive, or leaving Percy somewhere inappropriate.

Birch was all smiles as she skipped along, letting the long grass brush against her hand, as she marvelled at all the butterflies. Ten minutes ago, we were driving and talking about life, and now she was just like a child, marvelling at the wonder of the natural world.

We reached the area marked with a large sign as Herbaceous Perennials, and Birch got really excited, she ran along the bench picking up plants and admiring them, and showing them to me with a big happy smile. I watched giggling, and I thought I have seen this before, it was like watching a ten year old with a two pound coin, in the sweet shop. I pointed behind me, as I saw a bench filled with really brightly coloured plants in trays.

"What about them, they are pretty?" Birch turned, and shook her head.

"Oh no Sweetie. Planting them feels like murder, they are only annuals, and the frost will kill them, I want plants that will live forever."

I shrugged, in all honesty I had helped my mum a thousand times, but I never really knew what I was doing. Mum would place plants on the flower bed, and I would put them in the soil as she showed me how to, I never really bothered learning their names. Birch appeared to know all about plants, to be honest I have always thought she had some sort of psychic connection with them, she is weird like that.

I admit I know little about these things, but I cannot deny, I loved the names. Birch walked along naming them, 'Coreopsis, Rudbeckia, Geranium, Potentilla, and my favourite Heliopsis.' She walked around talking to herself, handing plants to me as she called them 'her lovelies,' and 'precious dear thing.' I staggered under the weight of the basket.

"Birch where are we going to plant all these?" She turned with bright happy sparkling eyes and a big smile.

"I want to create something new, and beautiful, and all these are needed."

By the time we were done, I realised I had finally met someone who was more insane than my mother when it came to plants. When we reached Petal, I could hardly walk we had so much stuff. I started to crate the plants up whilst Birch returned for more, she reappeared, and put down another arm full, and then went back to pick up the rest. I filled each crate and put it in the back, and Petal was starting to fill up, when she turned up with a huge pot, I looked at her like she was insane.

"Birch what the hell are you going to do with that, live in it?" She giggled, as she put it down and panted.

"I want my forever tree to have plenty of room to grow." I looked at the pot unsure if it would fit in Petal.

"Birch how big are you going to let this tree grow, because if it gets too big, we will never get it off the balcony, you saw how big they grow when we were in the forest?" She smiled.

"I love my tree; I want it to grow into a big happy tree." I lifted the pot up, and wedged it into Petal.

"Birch, baby I get that, but if you want it to get full size, you may have to plant it in the garden." She gave a sigh and looked sad.

"I know, just not yet, I am not ready to see an empty balcony." I shook my head and gave a slight smile, I cannot deny, it is the best present I have ever bought her, and I really loved how much she loved it.

Driving away felt like we had a mobile meadow, although I must admit, it smelt really earthy and wonderful as I sat in the driving seat. We decided we would visit the village, and possibly go for a coffee, it had been two weeks since I had last been, as Curio Live had taken all of our time up. We drove up Station Road, and into the centre of the village, we saw a parking place outside the dress shop, and pulled in.

Birch took my hand, as we walked up the street towards the hardware store, it was strange seeing the salon closed, but Anthony deserved the day off, he had done a lot of guest spots around the event, helping out many of the side attractions. He had signed t shirts, and given little talks, and like all of us, had done a lot of press interviews, all in all we all felt he had been a perfect ambassador for the event.

Green Street had a row of burger vans set up on it, the Deli was closed and the Church Hall was open and hosting side events. The May Pole dancing was over, yet the pole looked really beautiful with all the ribbons plaited around it. Children were running around all over the place, and one vendor was serving up giant pink and yellow candy floss, which was a huge hit with all the children.

We approached the Tea Rooms, which was as always very busy, inside was full, so I grabbed a table outside, the sun was out and it was warm, and with my shades on, it was nice to just sit and enjoy it.

Birch went inside, I gave her the cash, I knew how much she loved to chat up and tease the ladies, so I just sat back, and chilled out. I had not noticed that a few feet away to my side, Primula and her friends had arrived, and were sitting themselves down. I was lost in space when I felt a soft tap on my arm, and I jumped with surprise coming out of my day dream. I turned to see a face I recognised from school, she smiled.

"I am sorry Abigail; I did not mean to startle you." It was Fidelity Hannigan; I blinked, and slid my dark glasses down.

"Fidelity... Hi, it has been a long time, wow, I have not seen you since school, how are you?" She smiled.

"I am good thanks, I wanted to say congrats, I think what you and your friends have done is really wonderful." I smiled.

"Yeah, we are all delighted, we had no idea going in if we would raise anything, but we have more than we need to really help people."

I liked Fidelity when I was at school, we were not really good friends, so much as friendly, we had worked together a few times on group projects in science. She had her group, which was the popular girls, of which Molly was one, and I had mine, which was basically seen as all the losers, like Deb's and Ben Shepperton.

The thing I had always liked about her, was she would always acknowledge me and smile, she was never snooty or stuck up like the rest of her friends, and I often wondered why she hung out with them. I was starting to wonder about that again when I saw her friends, who included Prim, Molly and Sofia, and surprisingly Marion. Fidelity smiled and gave me a nod.

"I really hope the cash helps, it is really needed, it is nice to see you, and see how well you are doing."

She sat back, and the others on her table whispered, I figured Fidelity was about to be briefed about the social protocol of the village, and made aware that one should not talk to the likes of me. I was surprised to see Molly, she had moved out of the village two years ago, but apparently, she was back, although it was a bank holiday, so there was a chance she was visiting. I hope so, God, the thought of her living here and teaming up with Prim, was very unsettling.

Just sat watching them, it was almost like a young Marjorie, formulating the roots of the Shrew Crew, now there is a scary thought, were these the future of Marjorie's legacy? I lifted my glasses, back over my eyes, sat back, and hoped they would not stay long. I also wished Birch would hurry up, I felt exposed and alone with a group of future Marjorie's scrutinising me.

For the last few years, Marion had been a little less critical of me. She had become a regular of the bookshop, and I had run into her a few times. A couple of times I had heard her talking to Denise, and I had recommended a few book suggestions to her, and a few months later she stopped me in the shop and thanked me. It seems since that time, when she was in the shop, she was polite and cordial with me, I have often wondered if it was the effects of Sydney on her, or did it have something to do with the huge row she had with Henrietta on the green a year back?

Either way, it did not matter, as she was hanging out with Prim, and as I had seen many times, she was as bad as Marjorie, so I kept things low key around all of them. Molly had changed little, her hair was longer and she looked like she had put on some weight, but apart from that, she was very good at quoting scriptures whenever she saw me, and pointing out how my relationship was unnatural, and against God.

Molly had told me many times in the past, that Birch would drag me down into hell. When I considered my morbid curiosity with demons and demonic possession, I pretty much figured if Birch did, and combined with my hatred of cold weather, I felt Hell would if anything, provide me with good research material for another good Hands of Death story. To be honest the thought of rolling naked through the fires of hell, embraced in Birch's naked arms, actually turned me on a little, I know, Chloe thinks I am messed up too?

A shadow crossed my eyes, and I opened them, and there she was, my alabaster Amazonian temptress, with those sexy green eyes and that amazingly long white hair, with patches, that curled in a flick across her face, and now hung level with the base of her butt cheeks. I smiled as I looked at her, as she sat and glanced at our table neighbours, her eyes twinkled, as she whispered to me.

"I see they opened the crypt doors again, and let the biblical zombies out?" I gave a slight titter, as I pulled my cup towards me.

"Yeah, I thought the sun destroyed the undead, I was obviously wrong."

She chuckled and slid her chair to my side, and leaned into me, she slid her hand onto my thigh, and stroked it softly. Prim noticed and gave a scowl, which was the drawback of glass outside tables, she gave a tut.

"Some people have no shame, flaunting their sin in public." Molly looked over, and gave another disgusted tut.

"What do you expect, when you throw God out of your life, and worship the minions of Satan?" I turned to see her looking right at me, I smiled.

"Molly, you know that husband you married, Kenneth, he is a God fearing man, isn't he?" She looked at me like I was filth.

"My Kenny is a moral and righteous man, so why Abigail Watson, has it got anything to do with you?" I shrugged.

"I was just wondering Molly, because you know on those occasions, when you are alone in bed with him, and he touches you, and you feel all those wonderful little tingles ripple through your body?" Her cheeks turned pink, and she looked shocked.

"Abigail Watson! You should wash out your potty mouth." I smiled.

"All those wonderful feelings that make you filled with desire and lust, well Molly, that is the work of Satan. Those are the feelings of the pull of demons, and even you can fall prey to them. That is why I write about them; I am fascinated by how the devil can take over you puritans so easily."

Birch giggled and put her head down, even Fidelity looked away, Primula looked horrified, and Molly turned beetroot. I smiled at her.

"Birch and I do that to each other every day, we are weak, and we like the ways of Satan."

Primula almost dropped her cup and gave a gasp, Fidelity gave a snort, and pretended to reach for her hankie, and even Marion smirked. Although, I knew the kind of books she like to read, so she enjoyed the touch of Satan as much as we did. I felt smug and lifted my cup, I think that is the first time I have ever known Molly lost for words. Molly scowled at us with hate.

"You two are crude, ignorant and disgusting, it clearly shows how vile you have become Abigail Watson. Cavorting with the likes of her, it says in the bible, God will strike down the unrighteous." Birch leaned forward and smiled, as she looked at Molly.

"I am glad to hear you read your bible, I have read it a few times, and it says a lot of interesting things. I take it you read the King James bible, Molly, is it?" She looked offended as if Birch saying her name would somehow infect her.

"Of course I have, no self respecting person of faith would read any other bible, what is it to a harlot like you?"

Birch gave a nod, I had no idea where she was going with this, I did not even know she had read the bible. Birch looked at the group of women all staring at her scornfully.

"There is one word, and if you read the King James, which was printed in 1611, and don't even get me going about why it was printed, but there is one word, and it is a word you will find nowhere on its pages, do you know what it is?" Primula turned her lip up, and leaned back in her seat.

"I doubt you will be correct, but do tell miss know it all." Birch looked at me, and her eyes danced in her face, she was clearly enjoying it.

"The word ladies is homosexual, it is nowhere to be found, it was added to the bible in 1946, by a church that wanted to persecute gay people. Look it up, you will find that is correct."

I smirked, God she was amazing, even I did not know that, and I thought I was a master bookworm. I have read it a few times, I had to for bible study when I was younger. Birch lifted her cup, her eyes sparkling and fixed on the group of women. Fidelity appeared interested.

"Really, is that true, it is not in the James?" Birch nodded at her.

"Yeah, I know far more than these ladies realise, I also worked with a client in Manchester, her case was terrible, she was a lesbian, and her vicar found out. He took it upon himself to cure her of sin, he quoted Leviticus 8 at her endlessly, and then one night, as part of his cure for her gayness, he raped her, so she understood the value of a good hard penis." The group gasped in disgust; I looked around at them.

"Well girls there is a relief, that is the one thing our vicar does not have, but I am sure your husbands have already given you that lesson, and you all now understand. After all it is the one choice you have made isn't it that separates you from us, you prefer a good hard penis?" Birch sniggered, and sat back in her seat. Prim stood up looking appalled.

"Abigail Watson, you are vile, crude and disgusting." Birch looked at me and smiled, she leaned forward and looked at the scowl on Prim's face.

"Primula, you know, you are possibly correct; however, I seem to remember a live stream many years back, and it appeared at the time, that as vile as she was, Nigel appeared to really enjoy that about her." She smiled.

"Tell me, was he like that the night you conceived?" She gave a horrified gasp, and took two steps back, she looked at the others.

"I cannot stay here a moment longer with such filth, I am leaving, are you coming?"

Molly and Sophia stood up, and it appeared that Marion and Fidelity had no other choice. The group marched off across the green as Birch sniggered.

"Self righteous bitches, they annoy the shit out of me, they screw just like the rest of us, and they enjoy it just as much." I watched as Prim looked back, she was talking at high speed, and I assumed slagging us off as normal, I smiled.

"Poor Kenneth, the next time he gets horny, Molly will probably make him pray at the side of the bed instead." I chuckled, Birch ran her hand up my leg, and I jumped, she giggled.

"The devil is upon me, save me oh revered writer of the demon realm." I started to laugh.

"I shall rip off your clothes, and start the exorcism as soon as we are home." She leaned into me.

"Are we going home soon?" I gave a giggle, and slid my arm over her.

"We are now... Although you know Birch, Prim will go out of her way to attack us now, we have enough problems with Madge and the Shrew Crew, I am not sure we need the Prude Party as well?" Birch shrugged.

"I think for now Sweetie, she is too bothered about going home and slapping Nigel. I did hit what must be a very raw nerve for her, after all, you are gorgeous, successful, and sexy as hell. I am sure she feels she could never live up to that, and she knows it, just like all of us. Nigel got caught wanking off to your pictures, for now, she has other things to deal with."

I watched as she reached the bottom of the green and crossed the road, she was visibly upset. I think I actually feel a little sorry for Nigel, at the end of the day it had taken me a long time to get over what he did, and I suppose in a similar way, he was also haunted by it. It was a strange feeling to understand that the backlash was as hard on him as it had been on me, and yet he was still friendly and polite with me. I find that surprising, and also feel it is actually a redeeming feature of his.

Birch took my hand, and pulled me up from my seat, she slid her arm round my waist, and we walked towards Petal.

"Deads Sweetie, I can almost hear your thoughts, Nigel chose to marry her." I understood that, and I took a long breath.

"I know it sounds strange, but I feel a little sorry for him. Do you honestly think it was his choice to marry, I don't think it was,

I think his mother arranged and organised all of it, and she put the thumb screws on him?”

I stopped and turned my head to her, wow, her eyes were bright green, and sparkled, I felt a jolt in my tummy.

“I really think he is unhappy; I know it sounds crazy, but before he married her, he always stopped or waved, and he always had a big smile. I know how he feels, he told me a million times, and I always felt bad telling him I could not feel like that for him. I guess I always thought he would become obsessed with another girl at some point, and then hopefully she would feel the same, and he would end up happy, but he hasn’t.” We arrived at Petal, and Birch slid her hand out from my waist, she turned to me and smiled.

“This is why I love you so much Sweetie, no matter what happens, you always find the good. I have told you, life is about the choices we make, and if you do not like your life, make different choices. I love that you see the injustice in this, but at the end of the day, he chose this Deads, the way I see it, he has two choices, which is stand up to her, or leave her.”

I unlocked the door, and climbed in to the passenger seat, Birch got in the driver’s seat, I clipped on my belt, and looked at her.

“He should leave her.” Birch shrugged, and swept her long patchy hair over her shoulder, so she could fasten her belt.

“I doubt he will, look at Milton, he ended up in a BDSM club just to get some attention and love.”

It was a startling thing to think of, and yet I remembered that horrible day sat in the hospital waiting room, when he told me that Marjorie was not always like she is now. In a way, I felt a little happy for him, because he at least had some memories of happy times. Nigel did not have those, he was starting where his parents already were, and he was only twenty eight, in my mind, it felt wrong.

Birch started the engine, and I felt the lurch, as I was pushed back into my seat. In her usual psychotic manner, Birch swung Petal round and shot down the road at speed, I pushed my feet against the car floor just in case. We drove at break neck speed back to the house, and as always, I was greatly relieved when Birch parked, and turned off the engine, and regretted getting carried away with my thoughts, because had I been more focused,

I would have grabbed the driving seat.

Petal smelt great, the problem was she was filled with plants, and we had to unload, and then carry everything into the back, and it was hot. The crates were heavy, and felt a lot heavier once we carried them up the side of the house, and down past the far end of the pool. It felt it took forever, and I wiped my brow as I panted, and my arms ached really badly. I could not understand why, as I had really been exercising, and working out, of which my flatter little belly was proof.

I looked at the pool, and it looked cool and refreshing, and my mind was made up, I stripped and dived in, and felt instantly relieved. The water was heated, but it was not as hot as being under the sun and working, and I felt the joy ripple through me as I stroked down the length of it, and arrived at the other end. Birch was right behind me, and came swimming up to me, she swam in front of me and put her arms round me, I smiled as I felt her push against me.

"Hi Sweetie."

She leaned in and kissed me, I slid my hands down to her round bum and gave it a squeeze, and pulled it closer as she wiggled and ground into me. I gave a little moan as she kissed me with passion, I slid my hand up her side, to the side of her boob, and she moved slightly to let me slide in my hand and play.

"Nope... Nope... Nope... No cumming in the pool, I have to swim in there too."

Birch broke away from our kiss, and looked up to see Chloe, who looked red faced and hot, and was pointing her finger at us.

"You told me you would not fuck in the pool, so if you are going to do that, go do it on the grass. I want to swim, I would prefer no lady juices in the water, just in case I swallow some." I started to laugh.

"Chloe, there is hundreds of gallons of water in here, even if I do cum, it is not that much, I would say less than a turkey." Birch looked at me.

"Seriously, remember when you washed my hair?" Chloe gave a frown.

"Really... You actually came that hard Abby?" Birch nodded at Chloe with a big smile.

"She was as dry as a little husk when she finished." Chloe

shuddered.

"You guys are fucked up; you know that right?" I chuckled, as I slipped out from Birch's arms, and swam to the side of the pool, and the steps.

"It's all yours Chloe, I am taking my wife to be upstairs, and going to find out if I can make her match me."

I giggled as Birch happily swam towards me, Chloe shook her head, as Birch followed me up the steps and took my hand. Dripping and smiling, we walked up the lawn, and Birch got excited.

It had been a strange day, and I was ready to just hold onto Birch and snuggle in with her, I felt a little cooler, and a little more at ease, and yet somewhere in the back of my mind, I could not help but think, Primula would at some point come at me.

When Marjorie moved into the old Suttons Farm house, four years ago, she was unhappy with having it named after someone else. She complained it did not sound like her home, so after some discussion with Milton, and taking note of the fields that surrounded it, she renamed the property 'Meadow Cottage's.'

The fact it was a large five bedroomed farm house with a three bedroom barn conversion next door, and the fact it looked nothing like cottages appeared irrelevant to her. Name plates were made, and the council were informed, as well as the post office, and from that time, the name stuck, and she felt happier. In truth, it was a beautiful house, Bradley's company had completely restored it before the sale, and brought it up to all modern codes.

No one would deny, it was actually a much nicer house than the vicarage, and was set in some very beautiful gardens. Once everyone saw it and told her how glorious it was, any feeling of opposition to living there, which she had made very clear many times to Milton in the weeks running up to her moving in, faded away. Marjorie now boasted about how it was the jewel in the crown of Upper Waterside Lane.

The strange thing was, as I have told Birch many times, Nigel is actually a really clever guy. He aced his exams, and went to work for a really large laboratory over near Millington, and he is rumoured to have worked on several high security projects for the military. He has published several papers on some of his genetic research, and is well regarded in the Science Community.

I have always felt that he was so pampered and spoilt by Marjorie, that he really did not get exposed enough to the real world, and as a result, he really never learned the ways of social living. I have never thought he was a bad person; I saw how he was bullied and victimised at school. If anything, he was soft and caring, and actually an innocent and kind person. Birch calls it me seeing the good in others, and maybe I am a little guilty of it.

Okay, so he took a lot of pictures of me, which he used to masturbate, and yeah, when I found out about it, I really was disturbed and creeped out by it. I will not deny apart from that, I have never actually heard of him saying anything bad about another person, he has never hit or beat someone up, and he is just not capable of being a bully. If he dropped the stary eyes gaze, and hid his attraction to me, I really would not have an issue with him, because the truth is, he is the most harmless person in the village.

I do feel sorry for him, honestly, he should have disobeyed his mother, and worked as far from home as possible, and that way, he may have had a chance of really starting to understand the world, and if that had happened, maybe he would have ended up with someone who was not Primula.

At number 1A Meadow Cottage, Primula stood with her hands on her hips, and with a face of thunder, as she stared with fiery eyes at Nigel.

"How could you, how could you even like that slut, have you any idea how humiliated I was when that blonde haired harlot said that?" Nigel stood looking very nervous and guilty, he had his head down in utter shame.

"It was a long time ago, and I got in trouble, why are you bringing that all up again? I told you; she was just a slut I wanted to bed, nothing more, and Mummy said I could."

"So, you did want to sleep with her, you thought she was attractive?" He shook in his shoes, and lifted his head up and looked at her with frightened eyes, her face was furious, and red with her anger, and he was really scared.

"I did not touch her, I asked her out and she said no, I liked her, she was kind to me at school, and I thought because she had sex with my friend James, she might have sex with me. I was the only one who had not done it, and they all made fun of me, all I wanted was to have sex with someone, and I thought she would. I was wrong, she was really a lesbian."

Primula walked across the room and slapped him hard, her temper exploded out of her, as she yelled at him, he ducked and whimpered, as she lashed out again and again, slapping him around the head time after time.

"I am so sick and tired of having to clean up after you, have you any idea how humiliated I am? You are supposed to be a real man, and you are useless and pathetic."

He squealed, as she hit and battered him, her temper raging out of control, so much so the baby woke up and started crying. Nigel fell to his knees under the onslaught of her slaps and whimpered, as his tears fell on the rug. She stood back gasping for air, a look of hate on her face.

"I will never forgive you for what you did, now get out of my sight."

Nigel got up with his head down, and ran out of the room, he opened the front door and left, and walked quickly down the path on to the road weeping. Sadly, this had been a normal part of Nigel's life in the last year. Since the birth of his son, Primula had become more and more violent, and it did not really matter what he did, she was never happy.

He had a good wage coming in, his position was very highly paid, he had a good number of investments, and on paper he was actually a wealthy man, and Primula had expensive tastes, and a very handsome allowance. Her life had been one of luxury and prestige, Nigel had simple tastes, he spent little, and his money had simply piled up. Primula put an end to that, and her home was filled with antiques and fine things, she may despise him, but she enjoyed his bank account, and the benefits it gave her lifestyle.

The saddest thing was, Nigel understood the Curio's better than anyone. He walked in tears down the lane, and took the path down towards the canal, which was where he went to cry, and wait until Primula calmed down, and let him back into the house. Unknown to any, his life had turned into a living hell, of shame and fear.

Chapter 8

Facing the past.

It was two forty five in the afternoon, I lay back on the bed and relaxed, it had been a long day, we went shopping for plants, had an encounter with Prim, came home, unloaded Petal, snuck off for loud and exhausting sex, and I have answered a zillion questions on Curio Life, while Birch went out to plan out her new ideas for the garden, and finally I collapsed on the bed, stretched my legs, and just lay there looking at the ceiling feeling loved up.

My phone beeped and I turned my head, I reached out my hand and picked it up off the duvet and lifted it up in front of me. It was a message from Edwina, I opened it to read it. 'We have leakage again.' I gave a sigh and sat up. I got up off the bed, and headed downstairs, Edwina was waiting at the bottom of the stairs, and pointed into the living room, I nodded and headed in.

Birch was sat on the sofa, all around her on the floor there were crumpled tissues, at least thirty. She was curled up with her book, bawling her eyes out... AGAIN! She looked up with red eyes, and saw me, and just bawled even louder, I looked at her and gave a long sigh.

"Birch, you have read it about forty times, how can you still get so upset, you know the story backwards?" She grabbed another tissue and blew her nose, her eyes were red and swollen, as she looked up at me. Her face screwed up again, and her voice went high pitched.

"It's so beautiful, I cannot help it." She bawled her brains out even more. I just shook my head.

Leakage alerts had become a regular part of our life. For well over a year now, whenever Birch decided to read her favourite book, she would end up bawling her brains out in a corner somewhere. The Snow Queen, my love letter to Birch, had meant to be a source of inspiration for her, to show her the true depths of my feelings, which apparently, it did. The problem was, it reduced Birch to an emotional pile of tears and wails.

In the early days, all the Curio's had been very curious about the strange large book she carried all over the place, but after a few bouts of an uncontrollably devastating weeping Birch, they had started to fear it. Things had got so bad, that if Chloe even saw it, she would run to her bedroom, lock the door and refuse to come out until it had been put away.

Deb's once asked if she could read it, and everyone screamed at the same time 'DON'T!' Such was the fear it had instilled in them all. I was starting to think the frigging book was cursed. What I did not understand was Birch had read it over and over, and yet somehow, each time she read it, she became even more broken than the time before.

Anthony was convinced, we would find her dead from dehydration, holding the book in a corner one day, and to be honest, I was starting to think he could have a point. It had got so bad recently, we had started buying boxes of tissues in bulk, she was using that many, as was evident from the floor surrounding the sofa today, which was surrounded by the discarded damp things. Edwina referred to it as Birch's ring. If we were out and she opened it, when we returned, we would find wide rings of white surrounding anywhere she had been sat, as it always ended the same way.

Birch would reach maximum emotional velocity, and then hugging the book to her chest, she would run upstairs to her room, and launch herself onto the bed, and cry into her pillows until she was utterly spent, and pass out. I was so glad I had decided to never publish it, I am sure there would be loyal Abigail J W readers, tossing themselves out of windows, and off tall buildings all over the place.

I walked over and sat by Birch as she blubbered, I handed her a fresh tissue as her nose ran, she took it and blew hard, it sounded like a knackered trumpet, she tossed it into the circle on the floor. I grabbed her hand.

"Birch, Baby, if it is making you this upset, maybe it is better if you just close the book." She turned with heavy red eyes.

"I don't want to; I really love reading it." I could not help but smile.

"Baby, you are close to a breakdown, reading is making you cry,

I did not write it to upset you, I want to cheer you up." I handed her another tissue, she took it and wiped all the running mascara off her eyes, and sniffled.

"Deads, this book makes me so happy; I am not sad, I cry because it is so unbelievably beautiful."

"Birch Baby, your eyes are so swollen and puffy, they look like just shagged vagina's, I mean seriously, I am not sure you can handle much more of the joy in that book today, you are an emotional wreck." She snorted in, and blinked.

"I love this book, I want to read it a million times, Deads Sweetie, you have no idea how precious it is to me, this is your love, and it is all mine." Her face screwed up.

"AND IT SO BEAUTIFUL, AND MAKES ME SO HAPPY!" She looked at me, and bawled her brains out again.

"I LOVE YOU SO MUCH DEADS." I gave a frustrated sigh.

"Baby, maybe you should read it in your room, you are scaring the girls again." She nodded.

"Okay."

Birch put the ribbon page marker in the book and closed it, and then grabbed two boxes of tissues, stood up, and walked slowly, sniffling out of the room, and up the stairs. I followed her to the bottom of the stairs and watched her, as she headed to her room.

"It's all clear guys." Chloe popped her head around the library door.

"Has it been put away?" I nodded.

"Yep, you are safe to come out now." She breathed a sigh of relief, as she walked slowly into the hallway.

"I have to ask Abby, are you sure it is a book of love, I mean, are you absolutely sure you did not go into some sort of satanic trance when you were writing it, and locked a demon in it, weirder things have happened you know?" I sniggered and looked at her.

"What, like Gwenda in the walls?" Chloe stiffened.

"Hey, be careful what you say, I am still not fully convinced it was all Milton that night." I shook my head.

"Chloe, I have told you a thousand times, what I wrote was very special, those were really deep private feelings that were meant just for Birch, it is why I did not publish it." She checked the stairs out again and nodded, just to make sure.

"I am telling you Abby, if you publish that book, you will go broke, everyone who reads it, will end up sitting in a bath and slitting their wrists, and you will have no more readers left to buy books. That thing should be sealed in a crypt, and surrounded with a circle of salt, it's that dangerous." I started to giggle; she watches way too many horror films.

It felt like my life was meant to be harder than everybody else's. I wandered through to the kitchen following Chloe, who made a dash for her studio whilst the coast was clear. I clicked on the kettle, and grabbed my cup, and the coffee beans, and took the lid off the grinder.

Two minutes later the kettle clicked, and I filled my cup, then headed for the fridge, I opened the door, and felt my heart sink.

"Guys, we have got no milk." Chloe looked round the door and frowned, as I opened the top cupboard door to see the shopping list, which was pretty long.

"Seriously... Oh fuck, we have to shop." I looked at my watch.

"It's bank holiday, we will have to rush they close early."

It was a mad scramble, as we dressed and grabbed Petal, and then headed to the edge of Oxendale to the large Mesco supermarket, which was the only one left, Chloe had not been banned from. Chloe grabbed a trolley, and we headed inside. I used to hate shopping with mum, I hated it more with dad. My mum was a very efficient shopper, she had her list, knew where everything on the list was, and bought precisely what she needed, she was in, around, and out in minutes. Chloe and myself were more the saunter round, and piss about sort of shoppers, hence her ban from the other supermarkets.

We wandered down the aisles, I have no idea how people remember where everything is, even with huge signs above the aisles, I still always end up going four aisles to find something. I once saw a diagram on social media, that showed a map of the store, and it had a red line drawn round the aisles, to show the most efficient way to shop. I remember at the time thinking, if that was me, it would just look like someone scribbled on it with red crayon. We stopped at the spices, it was one of our favourite places, I picked a jar, and giggled, I looked at Chloe.

"Psst... Oh, oh, oh, Chloe I am!"

I held up the jar with a label that read 'Cumin' she giggled, a woman a little further down the aisle looking at cooking sauces scowled at me as I giggled. We loved the herbs and spice section, as it had loads of jars, and they all had a large letter on the front of each one. We always pulled a few out and rearranged them to spell naughty words, our word for today, which involved, two basil and two oreganos, and a saffron, spelled 'BOOBS'. We both sniggered like teenagers as we walked away.

The trolley started to fill with all the items on the list, and a lot of items not on the list, like gummy bears, biscuits, trifles, and jellies, as well as more alcohol, oh, and five huge bags of various crisps, and a big box of cream donuts. You know how it goes, supermarkets pray on the weak, and Chloe and me were the weakest when it came to treats. I did buy Birch some socks, with little flowers on them, in various bright shades, and a low fat selection of yoghurt.

With a trolley filled with extra meat, six loaves for the freezer and eight bags of crinkle cut chips, we headed into the cosmetics section, for eyeliner. I was busy looking which is not always easy, as there is always a row of young teenagers huddled around blocking the whole stand. I waited as they preened themselves in the mirror, I gave a sigh stood behind my trolley filled with goods. Chloe appeared a few feet down, and held up two bottles, and in a loud voice she called me.

"Hey Abby… Which one of these lubes is best for anal?" I sniggered. One of the young girls turned and looked at me, I shrugged.

"Not sure Chloe, maybe one of these kind young ladies might know?" I smiled. They moved, and faster than I thought they would, Chloe chuckled as they passed her, going pink. She came up at my side laughing, it worked every time, bless her.

Selecting eyeliner and mascara is an art form, and there are rules that must be adhered to. It is a long process of elimination, that takes careful scrutiny and time, Chloe lifted one up.

"Wow these are only a quid." I held out my hand.

"Give me three."

Job done. I threw them in the trolley, and we moved on towards the organic shampoo. Birch has a very detailed list of brands. I learned early on in our relationship, that one never ever changes her brand, which suited me fine, as I just walked up and grabbed exactly what she needed. For me it was a different story, my specialist taste in shampoo and conditioner started at 'What's Cheap?' and did not progress further, which is why I never shop with Anthony.

We came up the toy aisle giggling, having put all the dolls in sexually compromising positions, with the teddy bears, and turned towards the check out, when I heard my name, I stopped and turned, and felt a cold tingle run down my back. I was looking at a tall dark haired guy wearing a designer fitted suit, he had a neatly clipped beard, which to be honest, did not make him look any more mature for his age, which was the same as mine. This was something I had never expected, especially in a supermarket, I swallowed hard.

"James!"

Chloe looked at him, not really understanding the significance of the moment, and I had to admit, this was the one occasion I wished I had not left Birch at home. He smiled; he did not appear to have changed that much.

"It's been a long time; you look really good." I suddenly felt angry, as I looked at him.

How could he just be so calm and cool, he screwed me, took my virginity, and then dumped me? He also told Nigel, who told Martin, and not an hour after losing my virginity, Martin tried to rape me. I just stared at him, Chloe picked up on it and looked at him, I wanted to scream, but chose not to.

"Yeah, no thanks to you, what do you want, as I remember you got what you were after, and then dumped me?" He gave a sigh.

"I have always regretted that Abigail." Yeah, I bet he had, as I remember he was on the tail of Wendy Patterson within days.

"Which part James, screwing me, or telling that worm Nigel he could have me now?" He looked at the floor.

"It was not like that." I shrugged.

"Well, that was pretty much how it looked, especially since Nigel told Martin Hinkley, and within the hour he tried to rape me, and he did that because your cum was still inside me. Maybe now, ten years later, you can tell me why you lied about wearing a condom and stealth screwed me? You didn't even walk me home, you just pissed off and left me, half naked lay on a hay bale."

He looked really uncomfortable, and honestly the way Chloe was looking at him, I was not certain he would be leaving the store alive. He took a step forward and lowered his voice as he looked around and noticed people were watching.

"Look Abigail, we were young and stupid, I regret a lot of things I did back then, I never wanted to hurt you." I gave a snort, and could not believe how angry that made me, I stared at him just hating his entire being, where was all this emotion I was feeling coming from?

"No, you just wanted to take my virginity to notch your headboard with, and then run towards Wendy's bed. You know what the sad thing is, I really cared about you? I actually thought we would make a great pair, I told you I was not on the pill, you came in me anyhow." He looked from side to side trying to keep his voice low, Chloe looked like she wanted to kill him.

"Look, it was not deliberate, I was inexperienced, I did not have the sort of control..." I snapped in.

"What, you have now, well, how reassuring, it's good to know you learned self control?" He looked around at those watching, and gave a sigh, he turned back to me and held his hands up.

"You know what this was probably a bad idea, but I have a friend who is in trouble, and out of all the people I know, you and your friends are the best I know who could help them? I have followed all your Curio stuff, and I got my company to donate. Abigail they are in a really bad place, and I do not know how I can help them, they need help. Look, I am sorry, I really am, I was a fucking idiot, but you know what, if I had known that arse was going to do that, I would have stopped him. I get it, I am shit in your eyes, but I would never have let anyone hurt you, I hope you know that?" Chloe stared at him.

"You don't sound very sorry, what is it James, now she is famous you are interested again?" He looked at her, and shook his head.

"Why would you care, you fucked enough of my friends back then?" He looked at me.

"I still have your number, have you changed it, if not, can I ring you and talk about my friend, I want nothing for me Abigail, I just want to help them?"

I felt caught in a trap, he knew me well enough to know, I would not turn my back on someone in trouble, I gritted my teeth.

"You can call me, or text, my number has not changed." He nodded and looked relieved.

"Thanks, for what it is worth, I really am sorry, I read in the paper what happened with Martin. Honestly, I never realised it was that night, as I said, if I had known, I would have protected you. I get it, in your eyes I am utter shit, and I deserve that. I will call you and give you the details, and I hope you can help them, apart from that I will not bother you anymore." I nodded.

"We will do what we can for your friend if we can." He turned, put down his basket with his shopping still in it, and walked away, I watched him go as Chloe moved to my side, she put her arm round me.

"Are you alright, you are shaking?" I swallowed and gave a nod.

"Yeah, thanks Chloe... I am fine, a little pissed off, but I will be alright. Come on, I just want to pay and get home."

We paid, and grabbed as many boxes as possible, because all our crates still had plants in them. We loaded up Petal, and I jumped in and started the engine, Chloe reached over and put her hand on mine, I turned and looked at her, she looked upset.

"Abby, I am so sorry about that day when I pushed you about losing your virginity. If I had known that was the night, you know, he tried to rape you, and also how James treated you, I never would have asked, and I am really sorry you felt bad that day." I smiled.

"Chloe, there was no way you could have known, the only person I have ever told is Birch, it was not your fault." I could see she was trying to hold back her tears.

"Birch told me to shut up, I should have realised it was a horrible time for you, and I am really sorry, I love you Abby, I would never hurt you like that." I nodded and understood.

"To be honest Chloe, forget you ever heard what I said, god knows, I have been trying since that night, we are good, and I love you too." She smiled and swallowed back her tears.

"Let's go home unload, and I will try and find yet another hiding place for the frigging book." She giggled.

"Yeah, I think you will be needing Birch a little more stable tonight."

I was glad to get home and head up to my room, Chloe told me she would get Edwina to help put the shopping away, and I was grateful. I looked in on Birch, she was flat out, lay face down hugging her book, the floor was covered with tissues. I left her to it and headed into my room, and lay back on the bed, my mind awash with memories I did not really want.

The sad thing was, I was so into James, oh God, I was obsessed with him back then. I was so in love, and the daft thing was, when he asked, I wanted to have sex with him, I was over the moon to lose my virginity to him, because I honestly thought he really cared.

Today, brought a lot back, like I had made it so clear I was not on the pill, and the crazy thing was I saw him put the condom on, he must have slipped it off without me knowing, who the hell does that? I will never understand that, I have often wondered what would have happened if I got pregnant that night, would he have stayed with me, or would he have denied it?

It is so strange, because since coming home, I have been shamed for being sexual. Marjorie, and the press, are both obsessed with my sex life, and yet as I think about it, if I was a male writer, would I really have all this trouble? It appears to me, guys can do pretty much anything they want, no one has attacked James for his sexual life. He screwed half the school, and I will add, did whilst treating the girls like shit, and yet no one said a word. Even today, he had a go at Chloe because she screwed a good few of his friends, and it was like his male friend's part in that was irrelevant. It was Chloe's part in it that was shameful, and I have to ask why?

James looked at Chloe like dirt as he had a dig at her, like she was in the wrong, and yet wasn't his behaviour worse? James appeared to me to be just the same, and from where I was stood, it appeared to me, at least Chloe was more honest about her sex life than he was, so who was in the wrong really? Chloe has never hidden her sex life, she has always been honest and up front about it, which is a hell of a lot more than I can say for James. It appears to me, that there is no social stigma for James, and honestly, it pisses me off. Why can woman not embrace their own sexual desires without shame, after all, don't we live in a modern society of equality?

It appears to me, little has changed since my school days, the hypocrisy of life is unchanged no matter how much liberation has been achieved, and how it looks, is still more important than how it actually is, and I for one am sick of it.

It became very apparent a few years ago, I have a shitty taste in men, one way or another my whole life has been filled with men who let me down. No wonder I picked Birch, she has been the only person in my life who has not shafted me, well not yet. I slid off my pants, and slid under the duvet, once again I felt like curling up, and hiding from the world, as my past came back to haunt me again, would I ever be free of it?

I must have fallen asleep, because the next thing I knew, I opened my eyes, and Birch was smiling and staring at me, her voice was soft.

"Hi Sweetie." I smiled.

"Chloe has a big mouth." She chuckled and gave out a sigh.

"Yep, she does, but she has a huge heart, and she loves you." I sat up.

"Honestly I am fine." She lifted the duvet and slid in at my side.

"People who are fine don't miss meals, Deads Sweetie, it was James, and there is a lot associated with that. Pretend all you like, but that was a big deal Deads, and I know you, just how much anger did you hide?" I gave a long sigh, did I not have any secrets at all, this is what comes of living with a therapist?

"I was in the supermarket, so I held everything in, which is probably better, but I was really angry." I turned and looked at her.

"He just walked up and said my name like I was just some random girl he once knew; it pissed me off. I mean, the only reason he even acknowledged me, is because some friend of his has got themselves in some sort of trouble, and he needs our help." Birch winced.

"Ouch!" I nodded.

"I know right, he took my virginity, and even though I told him not to cum in me, he did, and then he just pissed off and picked up with another girl. Birch if I had not hung around to wipe his cum out of my panties, I would not have been in that room when

Martin came in." She understood.

"You think James is responsible?" I frowned.

"What, you don't?" Birch took my hand.

"Sweetie, I really do understand you, honestly, I do, but as bad as you feel, I don't think you can put all the blame on James. Martin is a rapist, and he had his eyes on you, just like he did Julia and Chloe and all the others, if not that night, he would have come at you another night. What James did was shitty, and you finally got to say all the things you wanted to say, and could not back then. I am proud of you, because you kept it calm and held your nerve, and finally got to face him, and point out his shitty behaviour. He had that coming, but only for his behaviour, not someone else's." I flopped back in the pillows.

"I know, and I understand what you are saying, I was just so angry at him. Birch the only reason he remembers me, is because I am famous for being an author and a Curio. If I wasn't, he would not even know me now, I was just another shag to him, and according to society, that is fine, he is male, and he can do that." She squeezed my hand.

"Sweetie, you loved him, you thought you could trust him, he proved you couldn't and that is really shitty, you know, we have all been there, even me." I looked at her, feeling really surprised.

"What, even you?" She nodded, and looked a little sad.

"He was called Benny, and I was just sixteen, I was really into him, God, I adored him. My mum hated him, which made it worse, the more she disapproved, the more I wanted to be with him. Deads, he promised me the world, and foolishly I believed him, he took me to a party and I got pissed, and to cut a long story short, he promised me to a threesome, and when I said no, he hit me. I was lucky, I managed to climb out of a window and run off."

My eyes almost popped out of my head, I could not believe what I was hearing, I was actually shocked.

"Seriously, holy shit Birch, why have you never told me this?"

"Like you, I was so angry and so hurt, I buried it, because I was too stupid to see I was being groomed by his lies. I was ashamed of myself, because I should have listened to my mum, it took me a long time to get over it. I suppose, it is why I was so afraid when you first told me you loved me, I wanted so desperately to believe it, and I know it took me a long time, and I am sorry about that."

I did not know what to say, she had always appeared so stable, all of us looked up to her, because she was the one that always appeared to be one step ahead of us, and so street smart. I guess now I understood why, she had learned the hard way. I gave her hand a squeeze.

"You know, you did not have to tell me this, so why did you?" She smiled.

"Two reasons really, the first, your book to me, because you showed me things you have hidden and kept secret in it. I knew you loved me Deads, I just never realised how deep it actually was, which is why I keep reading it, because it blows my mind and makes me so happy." I smiled.

"Even though it makes you cry so much?" She giggled.

"I cry because it contains all your beauty, and it is so rich and so stunning, I feel a huge privilege, knowing those words are written for me. Honestly, you have no idea how important those words are to me, and every time I read it, and even though I bawl my brains out, I love you more." She looked so sincere and so beautiful, her eyes sparkled more when she talked about the book, and I felt overwhelmed knowing something I wrote was so highly regarded.

"Birch, you said two things, what was the other?" She lay back on the pillow and smiled a big smile.

"Chloe... When she told me about today, she told me she felt bad, because she knew it was something you had only ever told me. She showed me how special I was that you trusted me with that knowledge. She saw how hurt you were, and how hard you fought to hide your emotions to hold it all in, and she was honoured that you revealed that in front of her. I think the other aspect was during the live event when she gave that talk on stage. Deads, I did not know the reasons the rent was being put up was because her landlord was black mailing her into sex, none of us knew until that moment, and it took my breath away when she said it. Chloe told the world and I had not had the courage to tell my future wife, and it revealed a flaw in me, because you should know, and you should also be the only person I have ever told." I frowned.

"What, you have not told your mum?" She shook her head.

"Only you, and it is right that I have told you. Deads, that day at the arch you trusted me with a huge secret, tonight I have trusted you with mine, and it has taken me a long time to get here, but I want you to see, that this is not a book, but it means just as much to me, and that is why I have shared it with you."

My mind was blown away, I turned on the bed and put my hand on her face and turned it towards me, leaned in and kissed her. I love her there is no doubt, but in that one special moment, I could see just how much she truly loved me.

I lay back lost in thought, Birch rolled on her side and snuggled into me, but my mind wandered. How many women had been tricked and fooled in their younger days, but saying that, having seen how Marjorie had treated Milton, I had to wonder how many men had suffered at the hands of women? In my mind, all I could see was the cruelty and the cold selfishness of people today, it was frightening to see how close to home it got, just seeing how my mum had suffered for years.

Martin's way of justifying his crimes by blaming me, or how Peter Ford had attacked innocent people for no other reason than he did not get his own way, so he exploited and destroyed them to keep the cash flowing in. All of it was shameful, and I began to see Birch was right, I had never had the right to respond, but today I had. I had looked James in the eye and called him out on his bad behaviour, and I hoped he would remember that and think about it. What a shame all those girls he used have never had the right to tell him. I hoped I spoke out for all of them, and I hoped it stayed in his thoughts, and made him see himself as he truly was.

Birch was so right, once again she opened my eyes, and as I lay in bed with her curled around me, just staring at the ceiling, I felt my anger leave me, because finally I felt I had some sort of closure on all of it. She was so amazing, because finally I knew I could let go of all of it, and move forward and focus on my future without the past constantly dragging me back, and surprisingly, it felt good.

Chapter 9

Sudden Nerves.

At some point last night, I had fallen asleep, fully dressed sat on top of the bed, being cuddled by Birch. When the alarm went off, I was naked, in bed being cuddled by Birch, and I was for a moment a little confused. In the past I had been drunk, so was oblivious to it, but last night I was sober as a judge when I flaked out. Birch has ninja skills I am still unaware of, and that is for certain.

I finally managed to wake Birch up, and she tore out of bed complaining about how warm and snug she was, and how she wanted to hold my boob all day. Then she saw the time, and morphed into warp speed, as she flew around the house getting ready for work. Breakfast was the usual craziness, as everyone got ready, and the thing that has always got me, was why do they have to do their hair and makeup in the kitchen?

It makes far more sense to do it in their rooms first, but nope, it is eyeliner and lipstick, pony tails and bobbles, all whilst moving at speed, and grabbing bites of toast and slurps of coffee in between. As always, I sat quietly saying nothing and waiting for the caffeine to kick in, as Chloe wittered on to everyone passing. Finally, by half eight, the house descended into silence after a kiss from Birch, and a bang of the front door, and I gave a long happy sigh revelling in the peace. Chloe giggled.

"It's nice being home again, I love my life here."

She refilled my cup knowing words from my lips were not far away. I looked over my cup at her with a beaming smile, she was just itching to talk. I put my cup down.

"You look way too excited for eight thirty, what are you cooking up?" She looked fit to burst.

"I am excited, aren't you?" I frowned.

"Why should I be?" She looked astonished, as I lifted my cup back to my lips.

"Abby, you get your first fitting today, come on, if it was me, you know, if I ever get there, I would be exploding all over the place." I put my cup down.

"Chloe, I won't see it, because it is supposed to be a surprise." She nodded.

"Well yeah, I know that, but you must be a little excited, I mean, there is nothing saying you cannot feel it?" I chuckled; she made a good point.

Just to flip back to eight months ago, Birch and I had been starting the preparations for the wedding, and even though we had pretty much everything in hand, we still had not decided what we would wear. Both of us were torn between wearing a suit, or going a little further and wearing a dress. Birch was flapping in her usual way trying to decide, and to be honest, just talking with her about it, got me all excited and indecisive, and we both hit the dead end of not really knowing what to do.

The solution came when Anthony stepped in, and he asked us both the same question. He looked at us both, and he told us.

"If you can, just imagine each other walking up to you at an altar, and what your love would look like, then you don't have a problem. The solution is simple darlings, both of you design the perfect attire for each other, that way it does not matter, you both get to see the love of your life dressed exactly as you have dreamed."

I have to admit, it was a perfect idea, and Chloe, Deb's and Edwina jumped in and added to it. The solution we had come to was, I would dress Birch exactly as I wanted to see her, in something that would reflect her perfectly, and she would do the same. Deb's was maid of honour, and so would have to coordinate everything else to match, because there is some unwritten rules of females, that you cannot see your bride in her dress before the wedding.

Anthony would act as a wedding attire supervisor, because it had been Chloe who said, we should not see each other's design until the day, which meant today, I would be trying on my clothing for my wedding, blind folded, as would Birch. I cannot deny, my friends are weird, but I am going along with it.

As you could possibly imagine, Birch loved how unconventional it was, and got amazingly excited. So, we now had a scenario where by, we would not see each other's attire until the actual day, but we would also, not see our own attire until the day, it was sort of a double whammy, and actually at the time it made sense and seemed fun. Today I suddenly felt very nervous. Chloe was to be my eyes, and Edwina Birch's eyes, both would take a picture and send it to Deb's, and Anthony would oversee that we both did not break the rules.

I was about to have clothing fitted that Birch had designed as her ideal of who she saw me as, and I was a little bit nervous. After all, this was Birch, and she does have some strange ideas. In a tiny panic a few weeks ago, I got Birch to agree that our mums would be able to be involved.

They would see what she had come up with for me, after all, my mum was the voice of reason, and if it was bonkers, she was the only person I trusted to tell me the truth. Chloe loved all of this of course, I worried she had been around Birch too long, as she was way too excited about all of this.

The fitting was at two, Birch had a couple of sessions before that, and would come home early, hence her panic this morning. Mum would be here just before, and Roni was coming down from London, where she was enjoying a few days of sight seeing with Will. I felt calm when I got out of bed, but just the mention of it from Chloe, and suddenly I was terrified, I felt my heart rate increase, as I looked at her.

"I am shitting myself Chloe." She smiled.

"Why? Abby, you guys are so in love, I think Birch will make you look beautiful, remember, this is how she wants to see you." I swallowed my coffee.

"Yeah, but what if it is all fairy's and unicorns, cupids and shit like that?" She sighed.

"That is what you are worried about, God, if it was me, I would be more worried it was not crotchless knickers and a Satan t shirt." I felt my heart jump, and alarm ripped through my system.

"Oh shit... You don't think she would do that do you? Chloe, you know what she is like for pranks and slutty stuff? Oh Christ, I really hope she has not gone rogue on me, I will never live it down." The panic flooded into me, and Chloe gave a smirk.

"Jesus Abby, chill out, I think Birch will surprise you, she knows you so well, I think whatever she has designed, you will adore it." I gave a sigh of relief.

"Honestly?"

My heart was suddenly pounding, and my stomach had turned to a swirling mush, I thought about it as I looked at her, and then my eyes narrowed.

"What do you know, has Edwina said anything?" She shook her head, and looked disappointed.

"She won't tell me anything, trust me I have tried, but she said I was shit at keeping secrets, and so has stayed tight lipped. It's a bugger when your own sister does not trust you."

It did not help, I had hoped to crack Chloe, but Birch and Edwina had outsmarted me, and I got the short straw, I drew Chloe, the most likely to crumble under pressure.

I was trying really hard to hide my insecurity and fear, don't get me wrong I love Birch with all my heart, but I also know her so well, and I know how she can have a crazy idea and go off on a tangent, and get completely carried away. It is as they say, a Birch thing, and I had spent the last two months, trying to imagine every possibility she could have looked at, when it came to her idea of what reflected me best, but Satan's Slut had not crossed my mind, oh god, my brain was starting to unravel.

The worst part of it all was, everything depended on what she was thinking that day, if she was all bubbles and exuberant, I was basically screwed, because knowing her, I would probably have a suit of printed hearts, with wings on the back, and a cupid's arrow stuck in my hair. I had been praying she was in a business state of mind, it was her most rationale and stable side, and if she was, I knew she would come up with something classy and sociably acceptable.

I had never once thought about her sexually deviant side, oh my god, would I walk out in front of my friends looking like a stripper? The problem was, I would not know until my actual day of the wedding. Oh God, I think I am going to have a panic attack.

Chloe appeared to be able to read my thoughts, she reached across the counter and grabbed my hand, I was starting to breathe rapidly.

"Abby calm down, look, we will see it today, well I will and you won't, but honestly, if I think it will embarrass you, I will tell you, and we will talk to Birch… Although, I have to ask, just how sexually deviant have you been with Birch?"

I shrugged, I mean we had tried stuff, I had no idea, we made love the only way we knew how, was it messed up, I really needed to find out?

"Chloe, I don't know how lesbians screw, I have never asked what is, and what is not screwed up, Birch is a sex therapist I just figured she kne…" My words died in my throat, and reality crashed into me, I gave a gasp.

"Oh shit… Chloe, she really knows a lot about weird messed up stuff, am I some sort of deranged screwed up lesbian pervert, and not even aware of it?"

I felt panicked as hell, I really had no idea, I just tried stuff, and hoped it worked, is that why she would cum so hard, was I into really messed up shit? I put my hand on my heart, and felt it pounding inside me.

"Oh Christ Chloe, I think I am having a heart attack." The sweat rolled off my forehead, and down my face. She squeezed my hand.

"Abby, for fuck's sake just calm down and breathe, you are panicking over nothing." I nodded at her, my eyes wide open in a fixed stare at her, she smiled.

"Wow, you talk about Birch getting carried away, Abby relax, you are blowing everything out of proportion and over thinking it. Come on, just breathe and calm down."

I took deep breaths, as she held my hand, and tried to regulate myself. Chloe was right, I was just nervous, nothing more, and I was getting carried away. Birch loves me, she would never knowingly humiliate me, I took a huge breath, and blew it slowly out through my mouth, Chloe smiled.

"Feeling better?"

I nodded, as I took another breath, this was just pre-marital nerves, nothing more, everything was going to be fine, after all, Deb's was involved, and she would never let anyone make fun of me. I took another giant breath, and felt my heart rate regulating, I was fine, everything was going to be just perfect. I looked at Chloe.

"Let's just not talk about it, it's freaking me the hell out." She gave a giggle.

"Wow, I never thought I would ever see you this much in love, but you know what Abby? I think it is so lovely, it is nice to see you like this, it really is, because that means this is absolutely right for you." I gave a long slow breath out.

"Honestly, you think this is definitely the right thing to be doing?" Her dark eyes were filled with such care and compassion, as she looked at me.

"Abby, how could you doubt it, look what you two have achieved together? I love you guys so much; I am totally going to bawl my brains out at your wedding." I gave a little giggle.

"I think we will all need a lot of tissues that day." I felt better, a little calmer and less panicked.

"Thanks Chloe, I am so glad I have you." She lifted my hand and kissed it.

"That was so not a gay kiss, it was so straight it's unbelievable." I giggled and she smiled at me.

"I love you Abby, I am so glad we are friends."

"Yeah, me too."

It was time to make a move, I needed to clean my room and organise the washing, I had clothes all over the place. I refilled my cup and headed upstairs as Chloe made her way into her studio, my room was a tip. I put my cup on my mat on the desk, gave a sigh, and got stuck in. I filled my laundry basket to briming over, and I had not got all my clothes off Birch's floor yet. I lifted it up and staggered down the stairs, and waddled into the kitchen, and dropped it on the floor in front of the washer, I hate washing!

For the rest of the morning, I cleaned Birch's and my room, we would be doing the fitting in them, and it was a nice day, so I opened the balcony doors, hoovered and polished, and got everything neat and tidy. Once everything was put away and neat, I sat at my desk and logged into the Curio site.

It was unbelievable to see how well it had done, Aden set up a special Curio Live area, and had added all the videos from the event, and at the top of the site, the boxes showed that the total was still rising, it gave me a butterfly feeling, knowing the new team assembled by Birch would be able to start working on the first of our centres.

The download tab showed Jimmy's song had seen one hundred and thirty thousand downloads. I smiled, he must be really happy, this was after all his first track that would appear off his solo album. There was a soft tap on the door and Roni popped her head round and smiled.

"Hi, is it okay to come in, I am not disturbing you, am I?" I twisted in my chair, and smiled.

"Daft question, you are always welcome."

She slipped in through the door and came in, she had a good look round, noting the pictures of Birch in the small frames on the wall above my bed, and the large painting of us, she smiled.

"Hatty is good... I was quite jealous when you got that, I would love a picture of all of you by her." She turned and sat on the bed.

"I know I am early; I wanted a chat before everyone else got here, how are you feeling now you are back home?"

The thing I love about Roni, is she does not hide anything, she just gets straight down to business, and from the moment she stepped in, I knew she had an agenda. I smiled as I swung round in my chair.

"I am happy to be home, where there are no rules or restrictions, or press." She nodded and gave a chuckle.

"Will noticed how much it was getting to you, he was concerned, which is why we covered for you when you snuck out. Katie was quite unhappy with the behaviour of the Curio's, she thinks you are all a nightmare to work with." I could see her watching my reaction carefully, I just smiled.

"Katie is a control freak, and we cannot be controlled. To be honest Roni, it did not have to be that way, her stupid rule of pairing up was the problem. We could not even visit each other in our rooms, she treated us like little children, so we rebelled. If I am honest, we were fine, it was her attitude that needed adjusting, which we did." Roni gave a chuckle and swept her long white hair behind her ear, her intense green eyes twinkled like Birch's.

"It was obvious between you and Katie there were issues, especially at the fund raising dinner, there was a distinct icy blast between both of you." I shrugged.

"As long as she keeps her mucky hands off my future wife's ass, I don't have a problem with her. I found it very unprofessional of her, I am sure her girlfriend felt the same."

"You met Anita then?" I looked at her, and giggled.

"You mean the Birch lookalike, I saw her, she gave me a wide birth, I think she was warned off." Roni's eyes twinkled.

"Anita is actually very nice; I think you two would like each other under different circumstances." I shrugged.

"I don't have an issue with her, I mean, I don't really know her. As long as Katie keeps stuffing her tongue in Anita, and keeps it well away from Birch, I don't honestly mind, as I said, she gave me a wide birth so I do not know her."

Roni had a habit of biting her lip when she was thinking, I have seen Birch do it a million times, she looked up at me with those sparkling green eyes, God Birch was so like her, it was scary, I smiled.

"You might as well say it Roni, I live with Birch, and she has all your traits, go on let me have it." She gave a loud chuckle.

"Hmm, I see some of her has rubbed off on you too... Abby, I am looking at doing a little reshaping of the organisation, especially the publishing wing, so I want to float something at you." I nodded; I was with her so far.

"I am looking at bringing in more people under Katie, and farming out her clients..." I smiled, as I cut in.

"And you want me to work with Anita?" She looked at me impressed.

"To be honest yes, Katie will still organise everything, but Anita will handle you at all events." I shook my head.

"No." Roni stopped and leaned back a little.

"You did not even give me time to fully explain." I shook my head.

"Sorry Roni, but I am not playing Katie's games. I am tired of them, get me someone else, a person who Katie is not sleeping with, and I will be fine. If you cannot do that, let me find my own. I will advertise, and Birch and myself will interview them before they report to Katie." Roni smiled, she leaned forward, her eyes fixed on me.

"God you are so perfect for Jemi, wow, you are her absolute ideal. I have no issue with that, but I will need you to explain why you will not work with someone you do not even know."

I sat back as my chair spun slightly from side to side, I put my foot down and it stopped, my eyes locked on Roni's.

"I may be paranoid, I am not sure, but my gut says this is a set up, it is some sort of political power game of Katie's. As soon as I saw her in that room with Katie, I spotted it, and I do not believe I am wrong, call it a writer's hunch. Katie puts me with a Birch lookalike in hope of me being tempted by her likeness to Birch. She packs us off somewhere, and then hopes nature will take its course, but it won't, because I will never cheat on Birch."

Roni gave a knowing smile. "And?"

"This is Katie's way of trapping me, to free up Birch, but she has miscalculated, because she just assumes, we think like her. I noticed that when she put us up in the hotel in London a couple of years back, and she told me, this is who you are now Abby. She was wrong, yes, we have cash, and a really nice house, but neither Birch or myself are like her, and we do not play games and use people. Anita probably is a really nice person, but even so, she is pale in comparison to Birch, and that is Katie's biggest mistake." Roni appeared impressed.

"So how is this Katie's biggest mistake, Anita is very professional, I think she would work well with you, Katie does to?" I pointed to the pictures on my wall above my bed.

"The way I feel about Birch has nothing to do with how she looks, I mean yes, she is gorgeous and sexy and very feminine, but that is not the reason I fell in love with her. God, Birch is vastly more than great boobs and a killer ass, and that is Katie's mistake, because that is how she looks at women, but that is not who I am. Anita is a pale imitation, because she does not have Birch's heart and soul, that was quite clear the other night. Birch's personality radiates out of her like a beacon." Roni breathed in.

"Good... I am happy to hear this, you have seen this exactly the way I have. Abby, I have known Katie a long time, she is not a bad person, and she is extremely good at her job. As you have seen, she is not infallible, her weakness is her jealousy. Katie likes to get her own way, and when she does, she is all smiles, but I have found on occasion she needs to get her wings clipped. I am happy you are reading this situation well, because it is clear you have your finger on the pulse, and I needed to see that." I gave a sigh.

"To be honest, it pisses me off that I have to put up with all this shit, just to promote a book. All I have ever wanted was to just write, and show up when needed, and in between all that, just be left alone to work here, she does make it harder than it needs to be." She agreed.

"If I am honest with you Abby, this is a really good experience for you, because this is exactly what business is like today, it is all power plays and politics. I cannot tell you the kinds of ego's I have to deal with in all of my ventures. I know you have been trained in business, but you also need to understand the people. Just knowing you have a good handle on it, is a relief, because Jemi has a big heart, but with your sound advice, she will be more careful, and will not be played as easily."

I understood that, I really did, and I had seen and heard a lot in the last two years, about how this business worked, most people think I am a push over, but I am not.

"Roni, I do not like being nasty, I really do not like upsetting people, but never think for a moment I will not step up if needed. I can promise you, if people try to use or manipulate Birch, I will be the first to speak out. Birch already knows how I feel about Katie, I spoke with her at the hotel and aired my views. If you want to replace Katie with an assistant to manage the day to day events, I will be happier with that, considering recent events."

"Leave it with me Abby, I will sort all this out for you, focus on your wedding, and Jemi, and just live as you choose and be happy... Right, coffee, Jemi will be home soon, and judging by her call earlier, she is becoming very excited." She giggled as she walked towards the door.

"You know she is going to be impossible to control today, don't you?" I slid off my chair.

"That is what makes her special, to be honest Roni, this really is the biggest thing she has ever done, I mean, tell me honestly, did you ever think she would propose, because I live with her, and I didn't?" She slipped her arm around me as we walked down the hall.

"All I will say is I lived in hope, and I am so glad she did." I felt the smile on my lips, and the little burst of happiness that lit up inside me.

"Yeah, me too, I really want this Roni, more than I think Birch realises." We headed down the stairs.

"To be honest, you are hiding it well, but it does show a little. Abby, we all get one go at life, make the most of it and just live it."

We hit the kitchen, where Chloe was making coffee, her ass was covered in yellow paint, Roni shook her head and chuckled, Chloe looked embarrassed.

"I slid back on the floor to get a better perspective, and I didn't see the paint tube. It's not wasted, I sat on a few canvases and got some ace bum and vagina prints, not sure what I will do with them, but I will come up with something."

She was golden, there was no doubt, but she was lovely, she made us both a coffee and headed for the shower. Roni sat opposite me spinning her cup slowly on the counter, she looked nervous, she looked up at me and smiled.

"Would it be cheeky to ask what you have designed for her?" I could see the excitement in her eyes.

"If I asked you to describe your daughter, what would you say?" She tilted her head slightly and smirked.

"That is a question loaded with traps… If I had to describe her, I would say that I think she is very beautiful outside and inside. She can be clumsy, and yet she has a very refined elegance at times, she is bright, happy and at times very loud, but she is also deeply caring and loving. I am very proud of the woman she has become." I gave a nod and smiled a very wide smile.

"That is what I have designed for her, because it will show all those qualities. To be honest, the hardest thing about today, is that I will not be able to see her in it, because that is all I want, to see her, dressed in my design, and stood at my side. You are lucky Roni, very shortly, you will actually get to see her as I do, but I will have to wait another six weeks."

The front door banged, and Birch appeared looking very excited, her eyes were wide and shining, and sparkled brightly, she gave me a huge smile.

"Hi Sweetie."

She ran around the island, and pulled her mum into her arms and gave her a massive hug. She was so excited, and Roni appeared to pick up on it, and giggled as she hugged her. I gave her time to take off her coat, and hang it up, and poured her a coffee, she came over to me and pulled me into her arms.

"Sweetie, I am so excited, are you?" Her eyes were dancing in her face, I felt a pang in my stomach, I looked into her eyes.
"Birch, can we talk privately just for a minute?" She frowned.
"Are you alright?"

I took her hand and walked up the hallway, and pulled her into the library, I felt really nervous. She looked at me as I closed the doors and leaned onto them, Birch suddenly looked serious.
"Deads, please be honest, please tell me you are not going to back out, because your face is scaring me?" I took a deep breath, and shook my head.
"Birch, I am never going to back out, honestly baby, I want this more than even you realise it. I will not deny, I am literally terrified, and I am freaking out a little, because everyone is making a huge deal and its weeks away." She grabbed my hands and breathed out.
"Shit Deads, I just panicked like crazy, I thought you were going to tell me it's over." I shook my head and I grabbed her waist and pulled her close, her arms came around me, as she squeezed me tight.
"Okay, we are staying together, so what has got you so freaked out, that you almost gave me a heart attack?"
I felt my stomach twist, and I slipped out of her arms, and walked down to my desk. I had to be careful, her voice went calm, and she walked round the desks towards me.
"Deads, it is obvious something is eating at you, so just say it, I mean, how bad can it be?"
I put my head down, I could feel myself slightly trembling, I looked up at her, her eyes were fixed on me and bright happy green, I tried to smile, my voice was a little strained.
"Baby, I want to marry you, oh god, you have no idea how much I want this, to be honest, knowing how badly I want it scares the shit out of me." She smiled and nodded.
"Me too... But?" I gave a sigh, and knew I just had to say it.
"Birch, I cannot help panicking, and I really hate myself for asking, I do honestly. Just tell me, that on the day when I put on the clothes you have designed, it will not make me look slutty, or make me feel embarrassed. Oh God, I sound like a real twat, please Birch, understand me, this is not a naughty elf costume or

anything like that, this is my wedding?”

I stood looking at her feeling wretched, I was a complete shit, and I knew it. She stood up and I swallowed hard as I looked at her, I felt so awful inside, and I looked away, I could not look at her.

“I am sorry, I am such a horrible person, I do not deserve you.” I heard her sigh, and then felt her arms slide around me, I kept my face turned away, her words were very soft.

“Deads, Sweetie, if you must know, when this was suggested, I was not completely happy about it, because I thought it was unfair, I could not see my outfit before I was married. Every girl has that moment when they get to choose, their dress or suit or whatever it is they want. Then I sat back, and I thought about it, and I changed my mind.” I turned my head and looked at her, her eyes were really close, and looked massive, and I felt my heart flutter a little, God, she is so beautiful, she smiled.

“I cannot deny, I am really excited today, because I will at least get to see the reaction of others, and I know you Sweetie, I know how much you will want what is best for me. I am so excited because this more than anything, will show the real truth of who you think I am. Oh god Deads, I am going to be terrified when we get married, not because I am afraid to, but because I want it so badly, I am afraid I may lose it at the last second.” I shook my head.

“Birch, you will never lose me, I want this so badly, because finally, in front of everyone I will be able to be who I am, the real Abigail Watson, with no apologies, no excuses, showing the world what I want, which is you.” She smiled, and small tears appeared in her eyes.

“I want that too Sweetie.”

She slid her hands down and grabbed my hands, and pulled me over to my chair, I sat down, and she grabbed her chair and pulled it towards her. Birch sat in front of me and took my hands, she flicked her long white hair behind her, and gave a long breath out.

“Deads... I sat with a pad for four days making a list of everything I felt, and everything I saw in you. I thought about all the aspects of your body, that I find thrilling, I considered how you treat others, and I made a list of all those moments I have stopped and been captivated by just watching you do something. The more I thought about it, the more I understood your value to me. Another very important part of you, especially through my eyes, was all those times where we have been alone, and all those crazy little conversations we have had, and after great thought, and I mean serious thought, I came up with what you will wear today. I hope it will show you how much I love you." I breathed out and nodded my head, to show she understood me.

She leaned forward and kissed me softly, and I melted into her lips, we broke apart and she smiled.

"You will look perfect, and beautiful, and you will see yourself through my eyes, and if I am honest, the sexy side of you, the way I see you in that respect, I am not prepared to share that. That side of you is just for me, and I would never embarrass or shame you, you have had enough of that." Yeah, I felt like a complete shit.

"I am sorry, I got frightened, you know, you do have a tendency to go off on a crazy rail, I started overthinking and I should not have done it. Just knowing it is not a Satan shirt and crotchless panties is a huge relief." She sat back and looked at me.

"Have you been talking to Edwina?" I felt a pulse of terror run through me, and stared at her.

"WHAT!?" She burst into laughter and snatched me into her arms, and she gave a huge cackle of a laugh.

"Oh Sweetie, did that frighten you? I am sorry I could not resist, oh my God, your face was so funny. Oh Deads, I do love you." I breathed a huge sigh of relief into her shoulder as she laughed.

Chapter 10

Dressing Blindfolded.

Panic averted, and feeling a little relieved, I came out of the library with Birch. Mum and Edwina were in the kitchen, Chloe had not appeared yet. The buzzer went and Birch grabbed my hand, with a squeal.

"They are here."

I looked at her wild face, oh God, she was about to explode, she gave a wild excited giggle as she turned to the door, yep, she was going off the scale, and this was just a fitting, God knows what the actual day was going to be like.

Birch pulled open the door, and the woman behind it jumped back with a shriek, and then chuckled, I walked up to the door, and to the side of Birch.

"Ella, excuse Birch, she is way too excited, and is moving towards madness at a fast pace." She smiled, and leaned in and kissed me on the cheek, and then Birch.

"It is lovely to be back, if I am honest, I am a little excited myself." I held the door back and she walked in, behind her in the old van, two young girls were preparing the clothing to be brought inside.

I have never really been into designer labels that much, I shopped at some pretty big stores, but I always bought off the peg clothing, most of which were gothic orientated. Katie constantly bombarded me with emails about this designer and that designer, and I have always refused them, and gone out and bought my own clothes.

After we had decided that we would design each others clothes, I sat with a pad and sketched my thoughts. I am no artist, but with the help of some tracing paper, and my laptop screen, I got a pretty good picture of Birch naked, on to which I could roughly draw the shape of what I felt, would portray her best.

My problem was that when I closed my eyes and imagined how Birch would look, I simply had no idea how to make that possible in reality. I decided to enlist the help of a local designer, and whilst going down a long list on the internet, I came across a reasonably new and struggling designer, and suddenly realised that I knew her older sister. Ella was the younger sister of Hailee Grantham, who was in my history class at school.

I found her number and gave her a call, and asked if I could see her, she was delighted, and jumped at the chance. I wanted to meet her and talk, and asked if there was somewhere private, we could meet, her studio was her spare room in her flat in Oxendale. When I arrived, she had a mannequin, with a black dress on it, and I loved it, and over the visit I saw how she drew her designs, then bought the fabric, and then sewed them herself on her machine in her studio. Ella was struggling, and working really hard, and she reminded me very much of Chloe.

I showed her the pictures, and then tried to explain my strange imagination, of what I wanted, and she just got it. She sat at her computer, and started to show me fabric and video clips, and I knew then, Ella was the perfect choice. Her biggest problem was the cost, what I wanted would not be cheap, so I told her, I wanted her, and was happy to pay up front, and I saw such an amazing smile and I was sold. That night I sent her two thousand to cover costs, which was far more than she needed, and I was so happy I told Birch.

Birch was so delighted with my enthusiasm, she decided to go with her too, so in a very short period of time, Ella went from struggling designer, to two huge well known clients, and much needed funds. I really loved the fact that we could once again, help a new young business, and because of who I was, give her a lot of exposure.

Coffee, fast talk, and excited giggles, and twenty minutes later, I was stood in my room, wearing a pair of very flowery panties for the first time in ages, under my robe, as Roni, Chloe, and mum sat on the bed. Ella, who had Alice and Carol to help her, prepared me. Ella took a long black blind fold, and carefully placed it across my eyes, she tied it in a way it would not slip, and suddenly I was locked in darkness, with only my hearing to guide me. Ella spoke quietly.

"Abby, I am going to take off your robe, so do not panic."

I nodded, and felt the soft silk slide off my shoulders. I stood still, knowing I was stood there in front of two girls I did not know, with my boobs on display, thank God I am a naturist, and so felt relaxed. I had no idea what Birch had designed, I heard the zip on a bag, and figured it was the bag that they had temporarily hidden in my wardrobe, I felt my breathing slightly increase, I was nervous, but also a little excited.

There was movement all around me, and I heard a gasp, I moved my head slightly, I was not aware my mum had covered her mouth, Ella spoke quietly.

"Abby, I need you to raise your right leg, and then when I tell you, lower it, raise your left."

I will not deny, I felt a pang of disappointment, Ella was going to put pants on me, I figured I would be wearing a suit, and my heart sank. I know it sounds silly, but I was hoping Birch would want me more girlie, although, I do remember when we went to court to fight Marjorie, and she leant me one of her suits, and that night she was so turned on by it, she almost ripped it off me, so maybe that was her ideal of me.

Ella tapped my right leg and I lifted it, I felt something cool touch the side on my left, she guided my leg down, and then tapped my left, and I lifted it up, I heard a slight rustle, and I gave a gasp.

"Please, just tell me it is a dress." I heard Ella chuckle.

"Girls help me... You tell me Abby, are you ready?"

I nodded, and suddenly felt the material on my legs, I waited as I felt it, and it went past my waist, and I smiled, and felt tears in my eyes.

"She made me a dress! Oh mum, I will be wearing a wedding dress, she really wants to show my feminine side."

Ella guided my arm into a sleeve, I felt the huge joy rising, as what I now knew to be a dress lifted over my breast and into place. Tears rolled out of my eyes soaking the blindfold. I know it sounds so silly, but deep down inside, I had really hoped she would want to see me this way. I gave a sniffle, as I felt the straps come up to my shoulders, and I heard Ella giving instructions to the two girls.

It felt impossible for me to stand still, and I had to lock my legs, as I sniffled, it felt like torture to not be able to see it, I really wanted to know what Birch had in mind. I felt a yank behind me, and gasped, Ella was close to me.

"Is that alright, it is not too tight is it Abby?" I shook my head, as I felt the front of the top tighten closer to my small breasts.

"Abby sorry, I have to do this."

I frowned under the blind fold, and then felt a small warm hand cup my right boob and move it up slightly, she giggled and then cupped my left.

"It is not everyday someone can say they fondled Abigail Jennifer Watson's boobs and got paid for it."

All around the room there was chuckles. I felt the dress lace up at the back, as the two girls tightened it, and then there was a lot of movement behind me, I could not resist, I lifted my hand and placed it against my bust, and I smiled. I could feel gemstones or beads, and they formed patterns, my imagination ran wild. The front was cut to the top of my breasts, so it was not low cut, and the shoulder straps were not too thick, and it felt like the beads ran onto them. I slid my hand down towards what would be the dress part, I felt a hand gently grip it.

"Abby, no cheating." I giggled.

"Ella, is this what you expected, you know, are you happy with it?" She was quiet for a second.

"Abby, if I may take a small liberty." I felt a soft kiss on my cheek, and her whispered words.

"I cannot tell you what it means to see you in my work, you have a stunning figure, and I am so delighted with the finished article, thank you." I smiled.

"It looks good then?" Roni spoke.

"Abby, you look stunning, your mum is in tears at the moment, and so is Chloe." I turned slightly, hoping I was facing Roni.

"This is how Birch sees me, is it what you imagined?" My mum gave a sniffle.

"Oh Abby, this is absolutely you, she is so right, and you look beautiful, so elegant, I am overwhelmed." I smiled and felt the tears start again.

"Looking at this, how much does she love me Chloe?" She blew her nose.

"I am not going to tell you Abby, but I will stand at your side on your wedding day, and once you see it, I will enjoy watching you truly understand how she sees you, but trust me, you will not be disappointed."

Ella stepped back and viewed her work, Mum and Roni lifted their phones to take a picture, even Chloe took a sneaky one. I stood blindfolded in front of my wardrobe, in a long dress that hit the floor, and had quite a long trail behind me, which I could not feel as I was stood still. It fitted my figure perfectly, the front split just above my breasts into one inch straps, there were no sleeves. The front of the top was patterned with hundreds of black beads.

What I could not see, and everyone else could, was the dress itself was the exact red of my hair tips, and flared out from my hips, but it was covered in a layer of black voile material, which gathered at the bottom in a wide frill, and it gave the whole dress a rich deep red, gothic, classy look. The back was really low cut, and was laced up with wide red ribbon, it was vampiric, and definitely what a dark little beastie would wear. Just feeling everyone's reaction made me feel happy, I knew Birch had been true to her word, and I really do not know why I was so worried, I just wished I could see it. I moved my leg, and could feel the soft fabric.

"How long is it, what shoes will I need?" Ella replied.

"Jemi has taken care of it Abby, so do not worry, everything is taken care of, on the day you will have everything ready." I nodded.

"Right Abby, it is time to get you out of this, until the day."

The truth was, even though I could not see it, I did not want to take it off. I felt the back loosen, and the dress slipped, and I felt sorry to feel it slide off me. I stepped out and gave a sigh, and felt my mum hug me.

"Oh Abby, I am so excited, I cannot wait to see what you have done for Birch, you looked so beautiful, I just cannot wait for June to get here."

It took about ten minutes to pack everything away. Ella slipped my kimono back on, and the girls took the dress out to the van, so there was no trace at all in my room. Finally, the blindfold came off and I blinked as the light flooded into my eyes. I looked around the room and smiled, Roni, Chloe, and my mum had red puffy eyes.

My time was done, and so I had to swap with Birch, who had been held captive in the library by Edwina. Roni unlocked the partition door, and walked through with Ella and her two girls, closely followed by mum, I heard Birch's lock click, Chloe guided me out of the room, and we headed for the kitchen.

As we passed the library, Chloe tapped on the door, and Birch gave an excited squeal, the door opened and her happy face appeared. I stopped as she looked at me, and I walked back and pulled her into my arms.

"I want to see it so badly; oh, Baby, I am so happy you want me in a dress." I kissed her softly, I noticed her eyes on Chloe, she smiled, and Chloe nodded.

"Birch, she looked so beautiful, I am straight, and I was blown away, it is perfect." Birch looked at me.

"I want to see it too, I spent a long time planning it with Ella, Sweetie, I am so excited, so what have you done for me?" I gave a happy chuckle, as her bright eyes looked at me with hope.

"Just like me, you will have to wait and see." She pouted her lip.

"Go on, give me a little clue." Edwina yanked her arm.

"I knew you would be trouble, come on, you will feel it soon enough."

Birch gave a happy little squeak, kissed me quickly, and got dragged off up the stairs by Edwina. I headed for the kitchen under the watchful eye of Chloe. I sat at the island, and Chloe handed me a gin to celebrate, she sat down and looked at me.

"You know Abby, I live with you and I see you every day. For a girl, you do have a great body, and a really nice figure. Honestly, I have seen you dressed and seen you naked, but when you put that dress on, I saw you in a completely different way." I gave a slight frown.

"How so?" She smiled.

"I think I saw something in you only Birch has ever noticed, I do not know quite how to say it without sounding like I am as gay as fuck, but you had a sort of deep sensual, elegant, and really feminine aura around you. I am not saying this very well, but as I looked at you, I got really emotional, because I suddenly saw why Birch fell so hopelessly in love with you. I know it sounds weird, but it felt like for the first time, I was seeing the real you, a part of you I had never noticed before. Does this make sense or am I sounding fucked up?”

“You sound like you want to screw me.” I giggled.

“No, I get it, you make complete sense to me.” She nodded and smiled.

“You looked so pretty, I want to paint you in that dress, I want to try and capture that feeling one day.”

I was so happy that Birch wanted me in a dress. I guess as much as we all want to be different, and we want to be unique, there is a part of us that still falls into the old stereo typical rules of life. There is a part of me that once dreamed of being a fairy tale bride. I had no idea what my dress looked like, all I knew was it had some sort of bead work on it, but it was enough just to know, that I would in some way have my fairy tale.

I had done the same for Birch, I had sat for a long time thinking of what I would really want to see before me as I gave my vows, and I made my design based on that. Birch stood shaking with anticipation wearing her blindfold, her hair was now so long, that Ella had carefully rolled it up and pinned it at the back of her head, she unzipped the bag that was hanging on the wardrobe door, and carefully lifted it out, and Roni gave a gasp.

She covered her mouth, and as Edwina lifted a hand to her mouth, it revealed the dress was white, decorated with the palest of green, but what caught their attention, was the millions of small sequins, that flashed and sparkled like the sunlight glinting off the frozen snow. Ella smiled she lifted the dress and gave it a shake, and suddenly the whole room was lit with the tiny glints and flashes of rainbows, as every sequin flashed a spectrum of colour. Birch stood dithering, her head looking around.

“What... What... Come on tell me, I need to know, is it a dress, is it a suit, I know you can see it, Mum, Edwina, tell me?” Roni sat on the bed with Felicity, both of them had tears in their eyes, and were lost for words, Ella smiled.

“Jemi, be patient and wait, Abby was as excited as you are, but she was well behaved, okay, I want you to lift your right leg.” Ella bent down as Birch raised her leg.

"Is it pants, do I have a cool suit… Oh come on, someone say something, I want to know a little bit, this is Deads dream." Edwina sniggered.

"You get nothing, live with it, now behave and do as Ella tells you."

Birch gave a long sigh, and lifted her left leg, and Ella with the help from her girls slowly lifted the dress up Birch's legs. Alice guided her arms into the small capped sleeves, and Ella arranged the dress ensuring Birch's breasts were fitted snuggly. Birch smiled.

"I have a wedding dress; she wants me in a dress, Mum."

Ella smiled, as she stood back, and looked at the dress, that ran from the capped sleeves on the shoulder in a v shaped plunging neck line, that ran down to just above her navel. Either side of the dress was heavily embroidered with a very pale green coloured pattern of interwoven birch tree leaves. The whole dress which fitted tightly at the waist, flooded out to the floor and a long train, which was sparkling like fresh snow, it was stunning. Ella looked at Roni, who was completely overcome and wiping her eyes, Flick was the same.

"Well mum's, what do you think?" Roni swallowed hard; her voice was much higher than normal.

"Jemi, it is stunning, it is perfectly you." Birch smiled, and her hands lifted to the dress as she ran her fingers over it, Edwina wiped her eyes.

"Birch, you look absolutely beautiful, Abby has created something so amazingly special, honestly the only way I can describe it, is by saying, there really is no other dress you could wear, it is completely you." Flick nodded.

"I am lost for words Birch, I truly am, it is elegant, and stylish, and absolutely you." She smiled.

"It feels really nice to wear, it is so soft, what colour is it?" Roni smiled, and shook her head.

"Never you mind, do not try pulling a fast one on us, you will see it on your wedding day. Jemi darling, trust me, you will not be disappointed, my God, she really loves you Jemi, it is absolutely and perfectly you."

Even stood still, the fabric sparkled, and the slightest

movement, sent the whole dress into twinkles that cast rainbows everywhere. Ella held her hand and slowly turned her round, the back plunged down to her waist, and was covered like the front in small birch leaves, it looked truly stunning. Ella turned her back round, as everyone lifted their cameras, and the whole dress exploded as her hips twisted with flashes of white and rainbow colours. Roni just sat and smiled, the dress did exactly what Birch did, it lit the whole room up, she turned to Flick and took her hand.

"Flick, your daughter is amazing, I think she knows Jemi, in ways I never will." Birch gave a titter.

"Well yeah mum, we sleep together, we do things you cannot be a part of, and not only that, she loves me Mum, more than anyone else realises." Edwina nodded.

"Looking at your dress, it shows Birch." Birch gave a shy smile.

"Edwina, what does she look like in her dress?" Edwina shook her head.

"I do not know, I am not allowed to see, it is part of the pact." Flick smiled.

"Birch, she looked so beautiful, and it is perfectly her. I do not think anyone would have thought of making her a dress like that, only you, and if I may say so, it shows how deeply you care about her. Jemi it is everything she is, and she will be so happy when she sees it." Birch nodded and gave a smile.

"I want her to be my dark little beastie, the girl who found herself for the first time with me at Uni. I know it sounds daft, but when she walks out, I want everyone to feel the way I did, when she first came out of the bathroom at Uni having done her hair black for the first time. If I am really honest, I think that was the moment I fell in love with her, just seeing her, with those bright blue eyes and that amazing hair, that is how I will always see her." Flick smiled, and then burst back into tears, as did Roni, then Birch. Edwina smiled at Ella.

"Get used to this, if you do more of these, you will see a lot of tears." Ella giggled as she slowly slid down Birch's dress, Birch pouted.

"I want to wear it longer, oh Sweetie, can I not just stand here for a little while?" Ella shook her head.

"My God you two are as bad as each other, Abby did not want to take it off either." Birch gave a giggle.

"That is because she knows I designed it." Ella smirked, as Birch stepped out, and she handed the dress over to Alice and Carol.

"Get this out of sight as quickly as possible, I don't trust either of these two."

I was sat in the kitchen talking with Chloe, when Edwina appeared, she smiled and pulled me into a hug.

"It is stunning and fits her like a glove, God Abby, she looked absolutely gorgeous. I am telling you, I wanted her there and then on the floor. You have no idea, I am taking a bat to your wedding, I will be batting off lesbians left right and centre when they see her in that." I giggled into her ear.

"I am happy Edwina; I want her to look the best she ever has." Edwina leaned back and smiled.

"I want that book, somehow I feel the two are connected, I want to read it." Chloe stood up, and stepped back from the island, her eyes were wide as she shook her head.

"What the fuck is wrong with you Weena, no one should read that book? I've told you; it needs locking in a chest of bricks, and lobbing off a ship into the ocean. That book is fucked up, have you learned nothing from Birch?" I could not help but laugh, and looked at Chloe.

"Chloe, I have told you, it is just a story about Birch and me, and actually it is a very beautiful story." Chloe nodded.

"Yeah, fuck that, it's full of all your crazy girlie feelings and stuff, and it makes everyone heart broken and mushy, that book is not to be trusted. Birch was rationale until she read that, and look at her now, she is crazier than she has ever been. I am telling you, that book should be locked up and the key thrown away for the sake of all of us." She wiped her brow, and showed me her hand.

"See, I am sweating just talking about it, that book is fucked up." I just shook my head and giggled, I looked at Edwina.

"The book is Birch's, you can ask her, but I doubt she will let it out of her sight."

I find it strange, how much power emotions have, I put my heart in my story for Birch, and also in my design for her. I have no idea what my wedding dress looks like, but just from mum's and Roni's reaction, I think it is clear that Birch has really considered all of her feelings within the design of the dress.

Both of us have obviously taken a lot of time to sit and think very clearly about what we represent to each other, and it has drawn a lot of fascination from those around us. I must admit, it makes me wonder, is this how we all learn from each other? I know babies and young children learn by mimicking their parents, but this has made me wonder if it is something we do not lose as we grow up?

I have never really understood why so many people in the village have looked down on me and called me. Seeing everyone's reactions today, I must admit, if I take the example of Marjorie, who is a forceful person, it is easy to see how people look to her and copy her, and I cannot help but wonder, if she was to be replaced with someone nicer, would everyone change their views?

Birch often talks of what she calls the 'Sheeple.' Those people who appear unable to form an opinion of their own. Today, Birch showed great love in her choice of dress design, as did I, and everyone is feeling the love, and in a way, their happiness has increased with our excitement.

My mind moved to Primula, I feel she sees me as an enemy, I certainly think she is a threat to me, because from where I am sat, she is rising to replace Marjorie, which means it will just go on and on, and that bothers me more than you would think.

Shrieks and screams, alerted me to an incoming crazy person, and yep, she swept through the doorway, and her boobs pushed into me as she wrapped her arms around me and squeezed me to death.

"I LOVE MY DRESS!"

I tried to talk, but that is not easy when you have a face full of boobs, I waited for her to finally released me, and I looked at her bright happy smiling face.

"How do you love something you have not seen?" She just stood with her fixed happy smile.

"Deads Sweetie, it's a dress, don't get me wrong I would have worn anything you did for me, but Deads... It's a dress." Her eyes danced with happiness, and I giggled.

It is crazy really, she has been so adamant about not getting married for as long as I have known her, and yet the moment she considers it, even with a free spirit like Birch, all those stereo typical dreams every girl has, come flooding back.

I will not deny, when I was younger, I had the same dream, of a big church wedding and long flowing dress and bridesmaids and flowers, and the full nine yards. Deb's wedding was probably more in tune with how I once thought, and I am thrilled we both picked dresses, because I want to look nice for her, but honestly, I would stand naked in a field and be just as happy to marry her.

Chloe handed her a drink, I am not sure filling Birch with happy juice at this point in her craziness is wise, but either way, it was looking like an all girls together day, with laughter and joy. This is the thing I love about living here, Chloe sells a picture, it's party time, I finish a book, and it's party time, and today we tried on dresses, so it's party time, and Roni and Mum were getting in on the action.

I took Ella by the hand and walked her into the library.

"Let me settle up with you now, Birch is so happy and she has not even seen it yet, give me the bill." She looked at me, a little surprised.

"Abby, you gave me two grand, honestly that is enough, it covered everything."

I looked up at her, she had the nicest dark eyes, and such lovely long brown hair, but her face was pale and under her eyes were dark, she reminded me so much of Chloe when she first moved in.

"Ella if you want to be a serious designer, do not sell yourself short. I am going to promote the hell out of you, so set a good price, people are not paying for your materials. They are paying for all those books you read, and all those clothes you ruined learning. A designer is paid for her creative talent, and you are worth double, and so I am paying for your true worth, and so will Birch, it will help you get going." She stood looking at me, and tears filled her eyes.

"Honestly, I would do both the dresses for free, it has been such a thrill." I smiled at her.

"We are weird, but we are lovely." I wrote the cheque, stood up and handed it to her, she pulled me into a big hug.

"Thanks for believing in me Abby, it means everything to me." I put my arms round her, and gave her a big squeeze.

"We will work together again; you can be sure of it." She wiped her eyes, as she put the cheque away, I took her hand.

"Come and have a drink with us, we are celebrating, it is something else we do a lot, any excuse for a party." She giggled. I walked back into the kitchen, and Birch was sat on the kitchen unit looking very happy.

"Hi Sweetie." I walked up with a smile, and she opened her legs to let me slip closer to her. She lifted her hand and stroked the hair from my eyes.

"Your fringe has really grown, are you happy Deads?" I nodded and slid my arms round her waist.

"I am very happy, are you?" She smiled.

"Oh Sweetie, you have no idea how much." She folded her arms round my shoulders, and pulled me close, and I snuggled into her, she looked down at me.

"What are we doing about hen parties, I mean, are we having one, or are we just going to get pissed here?" I looked up at her.

"Won't Deb's be doing that for us?" She smiled.

"Probably, but I was thinking something a little more different, a little more us." I was interested.

"Like what?" Birch leaned down, and pulled my face to her, and kissed me softly.

"For now, it's a surprise, but I have a treat in mind, and oh Sweetie, it will be perfect for you."

I smiled, yep, I was definitely intrigued, she had that I am planning something naughty look on her face, and I knew her so well, and knew whatever it was, it would be big.

Chapter 11

Gut Fears.

Like all things in my life, inspiration trumps everything else. I can be washing clothes, helping Birch in the garden, or just stood on the drive vacuuming out Petal, and suddenly boom, my brain explodes. It is at times like this, hermit Abby kicks in, and I run to my desk, put on my ear phones, and get lost in the words, as I start the ritual of writing another book.

I always feel guilty, but this is who I am, and yes, for a while Birch feels neglected, but I always work hard afterwards to make it up to her, by spoiling her rotten. She is really busy at the moment, as she is working with Aden, and four new people to begin the preparations for our new Curio Centre, which all of us are excited about. The problem is I have this great story forming in my brain, and as much as I want to be involved, at the moment I have to write, it's like an illness, and I have it, and the only cure is words on a page.

Recently I read the finished manuscript of Sanctuary Arch, I like to read a finished book long after it is out, just to keep things fresh in my mind. Since writing it, as ideas came, I wrote small pieces, and have been filing them in a folder on my computer, so I have a pretty good amount of the story, but what is missing is the detail, and a good lead character. As I sat at my desk, day dreaming, I remembered the really sweet girl called Karen Braydon, who just appeared at my side in the restaurant, and she was so sweet, and so lovely, I promised her, I would put her in a story.

For a couple of weeks, an idea was starting to formulate, I had been distracted by the Curio event and the dress, but time was freeing up, and I had the space to let my imagination run wild. At the end of Sanctuary Arch, Willis was suffering in the only place he could live in peace, which left him permanently separated from Gabrielle, who had been dragged by her father into a monastery, where she was being held captive on sacred ground.

For a long time, I had thought how to get Willis into a monastery, so he could rescue her, and it was at this point Karen popped into my head. I had a character that would in my mind, be the daughter of a local pastor, who was bitten, and was transformed into a vampire.

Because of her father's work to rid the world of vampires, she knows about the Arch, and so travels there to speak with Willis, where she tells him about a legendary sword, that may allow him to walk in the light, and on sacred ground, and so their journey begins.

I write in the dark, with just a few scribbled notes, which basically means, I make it up as I go along, and I never know what the next chapter contains. Birch thinks I am bonkers, but I love surprising myself, it makes the writing fresh and vibrant. I had worked out the characters, well, the basic ones, and I knew I would invent more as I wrote, which was fun, and I had an idea of the sword, so all I had to do, was fill in the gaps, and my writing began, and it flowed.

I sat back and felt good, my chair swung from side to side, as I rocked it, I had done some cutting and pasting, and my first chapter was written, and I felt wonderful. There was a tap at the door, and Chloe popped her head round, she made a tense smile sort of face.

"I hate disturbing you Abby, but there is a woman here who wants to see you." I swung round in the chair.

"Who is it?"

Chloe pushed the door open, to reveal Anita. Okay, that was unexpected, she walked in, and stood in front of me, with her long tanned legs, her long bleached white hair and pale greenish, blue eyes. I have never seen her this close, and as I looked at her, it was clear to me, she was nothing like Birch. I pointed to the bed.

"Anita... Sit down, I am a little surprised to see you here, so what is on your mind?"

She looked a little nervous as she crossed the room and sat down, I spun round in my chair and looked at her, she breathed out a long sigh.

"Can I just say Abigail, you are huge, famous, and naked, so I am a little intimidated." I frowned.

"Why, I have done nothing to you? If I am honest, I vaguely know of you. I mean, I know you are Katie's girlfriend, and her assistant, but that is pretty much all, so why would you feel that way?"

"Abigail, I am not with Katie anymore, I guess your refusal to work with me, screwed up everything, so she kicked me into touch. I was going to leave the company, but Roni rang me, and we talked... Look, all I can say is that ring on your finger, for me that means something, it is a no go zone. Abby, I am really good at my job, I obviously suck at picking girlfriends, and so if I am going to put my all into promoting an author in this company, and honestly, I love your books the most, I want it to be you."

Okay, so that sort of crept up on me and slapped me in the face, she looked terrified. She was around Birch's build, her boobs were more my size than Birch's, from what I could tell, she had a reasonably nice ass. Her hair was naturally blondish, so I assumed bleached it whiter. She wore a pale yellow blouse, which did not really hide her black lace bra, and a short skirt, of grey cotton, with a business jacket to match. Her legs were long, although it was clearly fake tan, and her high heel shoes, which were actually nice, looked a little worn on the heel. I thought for a second, choosing my words carefully.

"Anita, I don't really know you, I know Roni believes in you, and so I am assuming you have what it takes. I have got to tell you, I am uneasy about working with you, as Katie is a very real threat to me, and you have a history with her." She nodded; it did not take much to understand she knew that before she arrived.

"Look Abigail, just give me a chance, let me prove my worth, you have an event and a press conference coming up, so let me take you through it, and if I do not please you, then I will walk away completely from the organisation. Abigail, I love your books, I really do believe in your books, let me prove myself and show you, I am better than anyone you may be looking for." Roni had clearly told her the score.

I must admit, this was so out of left field, it took me by surprise, and to be honest, I wanted to talk with Birch and get her views on this, although, I was aware that Birch did not see Katie as I did.

"Anita, can I think about this, will you give me a day or two to mull it over?" She did not look very hopeful but she nodded, and stood up.

"That is fine, and is better than I expected. I have done my homework, and so talk to Jemi, and see how she feels about this. I have an envelope here, it contains the names of four other people, they are the best. Well almost, but just to prove I am on the level, check them out, and you will see. If Jemi is against me, I know enough to know I am done, so the other four will be suitable for you." She handed me the envelope, and smiled.

"Just for the record Abigail, your hunch about Katie, is right, trust me, because I am a casualty of it. Alright, my details are inside, so I will wait for your answer."

Anita turned and walked out of my room, and I was left staring at the envelope feeling a little speechless. I threw it on the desk, it seemed pointless to read it, and my mind was now distracted, there was no way I could write and focus now.

I grabbed my cup and headed downstairs, Edwina and Samantha were sat in the kitchen, Edwina smiled as I walked in.

"There is a fresh pot ready, I thought you would be down soon, so what did the fake Birch want?" Sam reached over and grabbed the pot; she smiled as she poured the coffee. I lifted the cup.

"She is nothing like Birch, firstly, her eyes are too pale, and secondly, she is far too business like, and I think she is frightened of me. She wants the job of promoting me." Edwina gave a nod.

"I figured as much, and she should be scared of you, after all, you faced out Katie, and put her in her place. So, what did you decide, or are you delayed until Birch is back?" I chuckled, was I really so predictable?

"I want to talk to Birch first, she has told me, her and Katie are no longer an item." Sam looked at me.

"Okay, I know nothing of how you girls do things, but I have been caught in relationship traps in the past, so I have to ask, do you believe her, it is okay I ask you isn't it, if I am butting in just say so?" I laughed.

"Sam, around the kitchen island is open forum, if you are in here when we are talking, you are part of it. In regard to her and Katie breaking up, I am not sure, Katie has not really been very talkative since I blew her out. Although, she warned me, that my hunch about Katie is right, so maybe she is playing with a straight hand."

The problem was I just did not know, my feeling whilst I listened was a good one, I did feel she was being straight with me, but I really did not trust Katie. I know she could be malicious, and vindictive, and my big concern was that she would apply pressure to Anita, and ultimately, I would end up caught in a trap. Edwina lifted her cup.

"You know Abby, there is more than one way to skin a cat. She must be good, because Roni has faith in her, and so the way I see it, Katie has taught you a lot, so take what you have learned and use it to tie Anita's hands." I frowned, not quite understanding, it was clear Sam didn't either, I looked at her as she sipped her drink.

"You will have to explain that, I am not sure I get you."

"Get her to sign a contract. Look, Katie is good at organising, but let's be honest, her people skills suck, because there is always a simmering sexual agenda with her. So, if you want this Anita to represent you, get her to sign an agreement, and any improper conduct, and she is out. Put a privacy clause in it, and map out your expectations, if she breaks the contract, she is out with no arguments. If she signs it, she is on the level, if she kicks up a stink, then she is still aligned with Katie, either way, you will know." Now that made good sense.

"You know what, you are a God send, are you sure you don't want the job?" She chuckled.

"Sorry, as much as it would be fun, I am happy with what I have, I have no wish to expand just yet. Me, Sam, and Aden have a lot on our plates at the moment."

I had asked Edwina twice now; I knew she would be great and I would have no issues with her. The simple truth was, promoting me, would take her away from Luke, and she did not want that, she was enjoying being close to home, and close to Luke, and I did not blame her.

"Yeah, I get it, you have enough on your plate. I think I am going to meet Birch at work and walk home, and then talk. I want to know what she thinks, you know, talk it all out and see what her crazy brain makes of it all?" Edwina smiled.

"I think that is the best, let her talk it through, if something is not right, you know she will see it Abby, and let her know how you feel, and I mean really feel. Tell her Abby, tell her how threatened you feel, be open and honest, and have a real conversation with her."

Edwina knew me so well, I wish she did have time, I loved that she could just spot how I was feeling and go with it, she would be better than anyone to work with me. I sent a text to Birch, and told her I wanted to walk after work and would meet her. I got a, 'Oh Sweetie, I would love that so much' back, and smiled, it would be nice to be all alone out of the house.

Two hours later, I arrived at the reception at Sweetie's Retreat. Susana came through the door and saw me, she looked at me.

"We are tomorrow, aren't we?" I nodded.

"Yeah, I am here to pinch the boss lady, I am going to drag her out for a walk." Meg winked, and I giggled. Susana gave me a smile as she picked up a green file.

"You can tell me all about it tomorrow, I am heading up there now, I will let her know you are here." She looked at the row of waiting patients.

"Kelly, you can come through now." A girl with long red hair got out of her seat, and walked through the barrier, and followed Susana up the stairs.

Birch came tramping down the stairs and peeped round the corner, it was impossible for her to hide, her long white hair swung out, I looked and saw her and she smiled a big smile.

"Hi Sweetie… I won't be a minute." I leaned over and saw her nip into the office and drop off some files, and then she came grinning towards me, leaned in and kissed me.

Birch linked my arm, and we headed across the green towards the Hardware Shop and the passage down the side to the fields, and woodland behind the church, Birch looked round, I had never taken her this way before.

"Where are we going Sweetie?" I leaned onto her, as we walked onto the wide sandy path, that led through Dursley Woods.

"I need to talk; Anita came to see me today." She stopped, and looked at me.

"Why would she come to see you, what did she want?" She actually looked worried, I smiled and moved, and she started walking with me.

"Katie is taking more of an organisational managerial role in the organisation, and that means each author will be handled by someone else. Anita told me she wants to take on the role of promoter for me, she said that her and Katie have split up." Birch gave a slight nod, as we walked towards the woodland path.

"Well, that does sound like Katie, she is not one for sticking with one girl, for as long as I have known her, she has always had three or four on the go. Dead's, you said that you thought this Anita was brought in to cause us problems, so has all that changed now?" This felt awkward, and I was really not enjoying this at all.

"That is why I wanted to talk to you, honestly Birch, I do not know what to believe. She sounded sincere, but I do not know if I can trust her, she asked me to give her a chance at the next event."

We walked under the trees, just ahead of us the small stream bubbled over the stones, as it swept to the culvert that would take it down under the village to the canal. We stopped as the path turned, and I watched the water skipping over a large stone, and falling a foot down towards the mass of rock and leaves, gathered in a small pool, before heading on towards the culvert. Birch gave a sigh, and her bright green eyes locked with mine.

"Sweetie, I trust you; I hope you know that? I have no worries about you working with her, because I know nothing will happen, even if she does have a slight look of me. The way I see it, you either give her a chance, or walk away, but I know what you think about why Katie dated her, and I still am not completely convinced about that. We are about to be married, that will put Katie off. The question is, what do you want to do?" I shrugged.

"Your mum thinks she is the best, and I trust your mum, but the thing is, what if she is still close to Katie, do you think she will try to cause trouble, because that is the last thing I want? To be honest, I have worked hard to get the reputation I have, so I know anything I write has a chance of selling, I have my issues with Katie, but let's be honest, she got me off the floor. Katie will still be involved, she will be at all the events, she will still be organising them, and Anita will take care of my day to day dealings." Birch slipped her arms around me, and smiled.

"Sweetie, I trust you completely, if you want to work with her try it. Look, I know you are not into other women, I know nothing will happen. The way I see it, if you really are right about Katie's motives, it makes no difference, because nothing is going to happen, even if this Anita does look like me, so I think you must do what you feel is right for you, and your future as a writer."

"She isn't." Birch frowned.

"Isn't what?" I gave her a squeeze.

"She is nothing like you, I mean, she has white hair, and kind of a similar figure, but her boobs are more my size, and her eyes are a pale watery greenish blue, and she has nowhere near your personality. I did not fall in love with you because you have great tits and a killer ass you know?" She giggled, as she looked into my eyes.

"Don't tell me, you love me for my brain?" She started to laugh, I snuggled into her.

"I love you for all you are, you look out for me, you love me, and you have the most amazing way of looking at me. You see me like no other person ever has, and to be honest, you are freaking amazing in bed." I giggled, and she leaned in and kissed me.

"See, how can anyone rival that?"

She took my hand, and we started to walk again, it was nice to be out in the countryside, it felt freeing and spacious, and Birch breathed deeply taking in the air and enjoying being under the trees. We walked for about ten minutes, holding hands, silently in thought. We came out at the top of Manor Road, and crossed over onto the old track, that took us up the hill behind the manor, I stopped to look down on our house in the distance. Birch slipped her arm round me.

"So, do you know what you are going to do yet?" I nodded, as I looked across the fields and trees, seeing the roof of our home.

"Edwina told me I should make her sign a contract, with a none sexual conduct clause, so if she suggests or tries anything, she will be terminated." Birch appeared impressed.

"It is good advice; it will also ease your mind. If as you think, Katie is up to something, it will head her off at the pass, and prevent her from using Anita. I think it's worth trying, a lot of companies today have a none fraternisation policy, would you like me to help you draft it?" I turned and looked at her, she smiled and lifted her hand to my face.

"Deads, Sweetie, you cannot work if you have all these doubts. If this puts your mind at rest, then I will help you sort this out." I could see the concern in her eyes.

"Birch, am I being paranoid, if I am, you will tell me, won't you?" She just looked at me with a soft smile.

"Sweetie, this is obviously bothering you. Look, I do not see Katie as the big threat you do, because I know how to handle her. Honestly, I have told you, if she starts anything, I will stop it. I understand her, I know how her mind works, so if a signed agreement helps you work with Anita, with no issues, then do that. All I want for you is to be happy, so do what it takes to sort this out, I am behind you all the way." I nodded, I mean, I know that anyhow, it is why I am marrying her.

"Thanks... I am sorry Birch, I know she is your friend, and I don't want to make waves, honestly, I don't, but some of the things she does scares me. Birch, I don't want to lose you."

She pulled me into her arms and squeezed me, I put my head on her shoulder, and wrapped my arms round her.

"I could not handle us breaking up Birch." She squeezed harder.

"We won't Sweetie, stop worrying about it." I gave a sigh, and just stood feeling insecure in her arms, I felt bad for bringing it up, but I could not help it, I just felt that Katie was a threat, and a very dangerous one.

I stood just enjoying the closeness for a few moments and then slipped back, she smiled at me, and I leaned in and kissed her, it felt close and intimate, and I really needed to feel it. She pulled back and her eyes shone and sparkled.

"So, what does my dress look like?" I smiled, and then started to giggle.

"I am not telling you, it's a surprise, and you need to stop asking me." She pouted.

"What, not even a little clue, Deads, I am so excited, you do know I am going to wear it all week don't you?" I shook my head.

"What, will you be wearing it for work?" She shrugged.

"I might, after all, a wedding dress is formal wear, I could get away with it." I took her hand and started to walk.

"You do know you are bonkers, don't you?" She squeezed my hand.

"I am really excited, to be honest, I did not think I would be this excited, but I just cannot wait, I actually want to be married as soon as possible, I really want to be Mrs Sweetie." I chuckled.

"Is that what we will be, the Sweeties?" She gave a loud cackle of a laugh, she looked at me with a huge smile.

"Do you remember at Uni, when we used to sit in the bar and make fun of people's names, by turning them in to rude words?" I nodded, and she sniggered.

"I wrote Watson Dixon on a pad the other day, and then realised, if we applied the rules of the game, it would be What Dicks?" She gave a huge cackle of a laugh.

"Deads, it,s perfect... You know, two girls married and no men in sight." She gave another loud cackle.

We stepped onto Waterside Lane, Birch looked around, understanding where she was. Just up from us on the other side of the road, to our right, was Deb's house, it was a large estate, on which not only was her home, but also her parents and Bradley's business offices. We turned left to head back home, and walked hand in hand down the lane, as we approached our own gates, she looked at me.

"Do you feel better now, are you happy to move forward?"

"Yeah, I know what I want to do now, thanks, it has helped." The gates opened, and we walked up the drive to the door.

"I enjoyed this Deads, I like walking and talking, we should do it more often." I put my key in the door and turned, she stood waiting, her long white hair blowing in the breeze, and lifting off her shoulder.

"I love you baby." She smiled, and stepped closer.

"I love you too." The door swung open as Edwina walked down the hall, she looked at us kissing like teenagers, on the door step.

"God, you guys make my life look sad and pathetic, take it to the bedroom, where even though we will hear it, we won't have to watch, and then we will all feel better about our own pathetic lives." I pulled away from her kiss, and looked at Edwina and smiled, she gave me a big grin, winked, and walked into the library.

Birch had work on the computer to do, her and Edwina had things to sort out for the new centre, so I headed upstairs and sat at my desk, and tried to think of how I would word a legal document. My attempt was pretty miserable, I knew I needed help, and there was only one person who I thought could help me, and so I hit the button, and the video link connected, she smiled when she saw me.

"Abby my dear, I expected this." She gave a giggle.

"How are you?" I shrugged and gave a long sigh.

"Roni, I have a problem, and I need some advice." She sat back in her chair.

"Is it mad that I am so happy you called me for advice, so I am assuming it has something to do with Anita?" There is no hiding around Roni, so I just dived right in.

"Anita came to see me, she wants me to agree to her representing me, but I am not sure... Well, I spoke to Birch, and she told me it is up to me, I have been thinking, I want to write an agreement, you know, like a none fraternisation thing, but I am not sure how to do it."

Roni appeared to be impressed, she had a slight smile, as she considered my point. She looked at me with that same Birch like quality, and pushed her white hair behind her ear, as she leaned forward into the camera.

"Abby, I think it is a smart move, I think it shows shrewd judgement, we already have a document on file you can use." She gave a chuckle.

"We have never implemented one, but Richard worked one up a few years back after your talk with Jemi about Katie. Take a look at it, it may need a little rewording, but the bones are there." I felt relieved.

"Roni you are an angel, thanks I owe you big time. I hated talking to Birch about this, I feel really guilty because she is Katie's friend, but I looked Anita up and looked at her work history, and she does appear to be really good, especially with press, and at the moment, I think I need that." Roni gave a big smile.

"Abby you are a large asset to this company, you can talk to me anytime, although it is good you and Jemi have talked about this. You know, don't think Jemi is not aware of Katie, she is. I know it does not always look that way, but trust me, she knows her better than I do, and she is not stupid. Abby, she loves you, and she has spent more time talking about her wedding in the last week than she has with me in the last year, she wants this far more than you realise. Trust me, if Katie tries anything, she will answer to Jemi."

The problem was, I was trying to avoid all that, I did not want this just exploding so close to my wedding. I was trying to diffuse this before it got out of hand, I gave Roni a smile, I was secretly thrilled Birch was so excited.

"I am as excited as she is Roni, honestly, I want to scream from the balcony, but I am feeling really unsettled, because I just have this feeling inside that I need to protect her, but I am afraid, because I do not want her to think I am curbing her freedom. Roni, I feel so trapped at the moment, is it me, am I just over reacting to all this, is it wedding jitters?" I felt tears in my eyes and my emotions surge, as I looked at the screen. Roni leaned into the screen.

"Abby sweetheart, take a moment and just breathe, calm yourself, and try to relax a little, then listen to me very carefully."

Birch was typing when her phone beeped, she glanced at it and saw 'Dad', she stopped typing and picked it up. It was a message and she opened it up and read it. 'Jemi, you need to go upstairs and hold Abby, she is upset, go now.'

She stood up and hurried upstairs, walked into her bedroom, Abby sat on her chair sniffling as Roni spoke to her.

"Sweetie what is wrong?" I jumped in my chair, she came over and knelt down and put her arms around me, I gave a sniffle, Roni spoke.

"Jemi, Abby needs some quality time, she is feeling very insecure, and she needs to feel safe at the moment, so take this time." Birch held me close, and looked at her mum.

"I am on this Mum." Roni smiled and waved.

"Night you two, take care of each other, and I will talk soon." The screen went blank. Birch lifted my face, and smiled.

"Okay Sweetie, sit calm, take a breath, and then I want you to start talking, if you were talking to mum, then this must be about Katie and Anita, and there is more to this than you are telling me, so tell me all about it."

I wiped my eyes and looked at her, God, she was so beautiful, and yet she looked worried. I took a deep breath, and started to talk.

Chapter 12

Clashing.

Birch sat on my bed, and held my hand for three hours, and we talked, and kissed, and then made love. It made a difference, and I was surprised at myself, because I told her everything, and did not hold back.

The following day I met up with Susana early in the morning, and did a one hour session with her, and talked through everything with her, and it really helped me. I think just saying my thoughts out loud, helped me to understand what was going on inside me. It gave me a chance to really understand my fear, and work through it, even if it did sound a little paranoid. I left with a much better idea in my mind of what I was going to do, which in itself, was a calming experience.

Later that morning, I opened the email Roni had sent me, and downloaded the file, and read through it. It appeared to be a bog standard agreement, but it was well worded, and really suited the purpose, I felt this would be a good start.

It was a small step forward and the start of what I hoped would clear the air and settle everything down, and give me peace of mind. The way I saw it, if she refused, then nothing changed, and if she agreed, it would bring about a positive change of direction for me.

I printed out three copies as Roni had advised, one for Anita, one for Roni's file, and one for me. I emailed Anita, and asked her if she could free up some time to talk, and asked her if she would like to meet for a coffee.

Talking with Birch gave me a lot more confidence, and so when Anita responded, I felt happier about talking to her, and arranged to meet her in the Tea Rooms, when she was free. It sounds odd, but I did not want to meet her at the house, and the Tea Rooms felt like neutral turf.

The email response came an hour later, she had moved a meeting to create time, and could meet me at two in the afternoon, and sent me her phone number. It was warm but cloudy, so I dressed in black boot cut pants, a long black top, and grabbed my denim jacket, and my shoulder bag, and walked down the lane towards the village. Edwina was with Birch in the practice, Deb's was in her shop, and Chloe was out shopping with her mum. Anthony was as always working on hair, it had been quiet at home, actually it was even too quiet for me, which is new.

I smiled to myself, as I remembered my mum talking to me a few days before I moved out, and how she told me that the house might appear too quiet one day, and she was right, she amazes me at times. I reached the bottom of the high street and stopped for a moment, and watched everyone going about their day, nothing ever changes in Wotton Dursley, no matter what happens, it just stays the same.

I took a deep breath, and walked up the street, people nodded as they passed. It felt like that with age, people saw me as more stable, although there were still those who would never accept me. I noted the Shrew Crew outside the dress shop all scowling at me. I gave a smirk, I really was a new younger version of Hatty, tolerated but not to be completely accepted.

The blinds were open in Sweetie's Retreat, and I tapped on the glass and waved to Gill, Alex and Meg, as I walked past. They all smiled and waved, and I felt a light bounce to my step, as I approached the Post Office, and crossed the road for the Tea Rooms.

I walked in, and was greeted with a smile from Celia, I looked around for an empty table, there was one towards the back. I ordered a coffee and explained to Celia I was expecting a guest, and paid in advance for her coffee. I noticed Lillian was not there, and looked back around, this must be the first time in my entire life, I had not seen her in the place.

"Celia, where is Lillian?" She gave a sad smile.

"She has been poorly recently, so I have told her to stay at home." It felt weird, I did actually love seeing her reaction to Birch.

"Give her our love, and tell her to get well and hurry back, we will miss her." Celia smiled.

"I will, she will love hearing you said that." I winked.

"I know I am her secret crush; I just keep quiet about it."

Celia giggled at me, as I walked over towards the table and sat down. Louise delivered my coffee with a smile. As she turned, I saw Anita walk in, she was wearing jeans, and a long denim shirt with a t-shirt underneath, and plimsoles. I lifted my hand and waved, she smiled and came over and sat down, she looked happy, but still nervous.

"Hi Abby, thanks for seeing me." She shuffled in her seat to get comfortable.

"I am glad you could make it; I ordered you a coffee, I hope that is alright?" Louise arrived, and looked Anita up and down, she appeared to approve, she put her cup down with a smile. Anita turned to me.

"I take it you have thought about what I said the other day, it probably sounds odd, but if you are not going to go through with it, say now. I prefer fast and ruthless; it is easier to deal with?" I smiled, as I noted she suddenly became a little nervous.

"I do have a proposition, I have given what you said a lot of thought, and I have taken some advice. So, I want to propose that considering certain behaviour from Katie, and how she played you in order to create problems in my relationship, I want to know if you would be prepared to sign a disclaimer?" She nodded understanding what I was saying.

"If I sign this, does that mean I get to be your promoter?" I opened my bag, and slid out the paperwork, I lay it face down on the table.

"I have looked into you, and checked out your resume, and you have a lot of skills. If you sign it, and you can explain how you will benefit me more than Katie, I will give you the job." She looked at the documents.

"Can I read them first?" I nodded at them.

"I think you should, although, it is just a basic none fraternisation agreement."

Anita pulled out her silver pen and clicked it, I slid the paperwork over to her, and she turned it over to read it, I lifted my coffee and watched as I sipped it. She scanned over them, pursed her lips, gave a slight nod and signed it; she then signed the other two copies.

"I take it you will be signing too? I will be straight up front with you Abby, I am bisexual, there is no shortage of bed partners should I require one, you are cute, of that there is no doubt, but I am sure I can contain my wild sexual desires around you." She smiled.

I chuckled as I slipped out my biro, and signed the papers, and handed her one copy, and put the other two back in my bag.

"Okay Anita, tell me why you are better than Katie, and how will that positively benefit me?" She sat back in her chair and lifted her cup.

"I know what it is like to work with Katie, and how her endless inuendo is irritating, so there will be none of that. I would hope in time we will be friends, because that will improve our working relationship. I do not like the way your press conferences have gone; I will step in and protect you better. I think Katie hung you out to dry during the Curio event, and I think the rest of the country should actually get to see you. Abby, you have never gone further than London, but your fans are right across this nation." I had to admit, she was saying things that Birch had actually told me, I was impressed.

"You think I should go on the road?" She nodded.

"Why not Abby? I have watched all the footage of you with your fans, you love meeting them, but Katie keeps you penned up here, why not get up north? Look, Roni is northern based, she gets all over the place. You are working on your next Hands of Death book, and I would hope there is another book to follow Shoots of Summer, both should be promoted all over. I can work with you on the schedule, I do not think it should be as intense as the states. I must admit, I am surprised you actually did it, but honestly, you should have had breaks in between. I can pace the work to fit you, and I do not want you away for long periods, I feel it affects your ability to write, and keeping you writing, is more important than anything." She made a lot of sense.

"The US tour was too much, I was unhappy and depressed, I am not in a rush to go back alone, I really missed Birch. I would love to go north, but I will want Birch with me at times." Anita flicked back her hair, her pale green eyes were fixed on me, she smiled.

"Abby, she is about to become your wife, she should be factored into everything. I also think the fans love her; they have been captivated by you two for a while. I also think you need to use some sort of promotion from your wedding, you know, give them an insight." That surprised me a great deal.

"What are you talking about, because I would not be very comfy with a live stream. This is happening in my home, with my friends, and I would not want them in the footage?" She shook her head.

"I was thinking more of a photo album on your website, and a few carefully leaked pictures to a magazine, I can get you a very large payoff, from the right magazine. Abby, it is important exposure you have not had before, it will open you up to other markets, the three of us could sit down, and select the pictures. It would make fantastic PR and more revenue, because your fans really have taken both of you to their hearts. If you don't believe me, think about the airport meeting, the fans loved it, because it showed two people who are really in love. I mean, hell she was almost naked with her arms around you, kissing you. Yeah, it caused a stir, but your sales sky rocketed, because a lot of people asked, who is this writer? You cannot get better than that."

She made sense, I had a little internal smile, as I remembered Birch's happy face as fans wanted to talk to her, and told her how pretty she was. I could see Anita had a point, but I also knew this was a decision I could not make alone.

"I think there is a good idea in there, but I would like to talk this over with Birch. Anita this is her day as well, and I do not want to glory grab all the attention. If you are okay with it, and we plan it in advance, there could be some room to move forward with it." She leaned back on the chair.

"Okay, so we have room to work already, I can see several possibilities to help promote your work, not just within Dixon, but also at other events. I think your appeal with readers and the Curio community, could be a big advantage to getting you a broader appeal. Abby, there are other events outside of Dixon's scope, I can put you into them to greater benefits for your readers. I am really enjoying this Abby; I can feel ideas coming all the time we are talking. I have your number, and I want to keep a good contact and a good rapport, and I would ask that you stay in touch. Abby if anything happens or comes up, keep me in the loop, and if it will help publicity, I will use it."

We finished our coffee, and Anita asked if I would show her the village, so we left together, and walked up Green Street, past the Church Hall, stood level with the deli, and looked across the green. Anita appeared a little more relaxed, she stood with her hands in her pockets, and looked around.

"This really is a beautiful place; I have read a lot about it on the Curio site and your blogs. It feels almost familiar standing here, like I have always known about it, but obviously, I only drove through it the other day. I normally drive to Oxendale down the other main road, and yet I am standing here now, but your portrayal of it on your blogs is very accurate." I watched her as she looked around.

"You have read my blogs?" She smiled.

"I am a publicist, when I get a client, I read everything I can, all the good and all the bad. I am not going to jump into a pool of sharks, unless I know how many there are and how big. The more I know, the better prepared I will be if the press try to bush whack you, I don't want you left hanging by a rogue reporter." She turned to me.

"You know at the Curio live event, I told Katie to watch out for that red haired bitch, and she completely ignored me, it was almost as if she wanted her to provoke a reaction from you." It did not surprise me.

"I do not like press, they bring out my hostile side, I do not know why they cannot be more polite, if they were, they would find me more obliging." She nodded.

"I want a list of everyone you feel at ease talking to, and also a list of those who have treated you the worst, because from now on, I will be vetting all the press. I will not stack the pack though, you will need to face alternative view points, but I do know some good journalists who will stretch you, but in a good way. I understand that Katie is still the managerial organiser of all the events, but I want a free hand on the press conferences, I don't want her interfering. I hate asking, but a word from Roni would go a long way for me." I liked that she asked me, I understood, having Katie out of the way suited me fine.

"I can talk to Roni, that is not a problem." She turned to me.

"Abby, Katie is not aware of me working with you, so be prepared, the shit will hit the fan when she finds out." I had wondered if she knew yet.

"It's okay, I will handle anything she throws at me, what about you, can you handle it?" She gave a sigh, and looked a little nervous.

"I will not lie Abby, she intimidates the hell out of me, but I will stand my ground for you. My mum has always told me I need to stand up for myself, I guess I have probably the best reason ever to do so now." I frowned.

"How come?" She gave a slight chuckle.

"I really wanted this job, to be honest, I am a bit of a closet fan. I saw you at the fund raising night, but steered clear of you because I could see Katie was out of order with Jemi. You know when you look like that, the way you stared at Katie, with those eyes, you are kind of scary. I will fight for you, because I want this so badly, it is a good reason for me to toughen up and stand my ground. I aim to keep this job, no matter what, and so if Katie comes at me, which I think she will, I will hold fast for you." It sounded funny to me to hear her say it.

"You sound like me when I was walking to confront Madge over Birch, I stood my ground, but after I walked off, I pissed my pants and cried like a bitch." She gave a light giggle.

"Yeah, that could be me in a day or two."

I felt I was warming to her, she was pretty down to earth and relaxed, and if she approached everything we did with the same attitude, I could see us working well together. We walked and talked for over an hour, and when I finally left her at her car, which was pretty beat up, I felt my spirit's lift. I think I had made a good choice, and felt there were some good possibilities, and I smiled as I walked back home.

It probably sounds silly, but just knowing I would have space, and a calmer atmosphere made a lot of difference. I had hated the Curio rota and strict regime, it had felt like being in a prison, just knowing things would be easier, really helped, and obviously having some distance from Katie, felt like a massive release.

The house was still empty when I got in, I grabbed my cup, and made a coffee, grabbed some biscuits and headed upstairs to my room. I sat at my desk and opened my video call program, the tune played, and Roni's face appeared, she smiled and gave a little wave, I waved back.

"Hi Roni, do you have a minute?" I could see she was at home in her office, at her desk, she sat back.

"I have a little time; how did the meeting go?" I gave a sigh of relief, and held up the papers.

"She did not even hesitate; she scanned over the agreement and signed it straight away. I must admit, I was really happy she did, and we started to talk, and looked at what was expected of each other, so I have accepted her." Roni gave a big smile.

"Abby that is great news, I have talked with her a couple of times, and she really wanted this job. You know she has a great track record; I think she will be good for you; I am very happy about this Abby; I think it is a smart move."

"I feel a lot better today, I spent quite a bit of time talking, and it was very relaxed and less structured. If she works like that with me, we will work really well together, although I must say Roni, I am worried about Katie's reaction. I am not sure she is going to like this; Anita did ask that you talk to Katie about the press, she wants full control over that aspect of events." Roni gave a slight nod.

"You have to understand Abby, Katie is the event organiser, and she has executive power over the event. I can tell her you have requested Anita handles all the press, if that is okay?" I nodded.

"Roni, I get that Katie is the promoter of all the Dixon events, and I have no issue with that, but I sat with Anita and worked out a whole new strategy that I will be more at ease with. To be honest, I think it will really benefit publicity, all I want is to be able to work side by side with Anita on this, I am sure it will get us bigger sales."

"I will sort something out for you, let me see what I can do ab...."

"WHAT THE FUCK IS THIS SHIT RONI?"

I jumped in my seat, as I heard Katie in the background, Roni looked up at her, she was obviously stood somewhere behind the laptop. Roni stared at her, looking a little annoyed.

"Katie, I am in the middle of something, can you give me a minute?"

"Oh really, you give that cheap tart half my job, and then you fucking ask me to wait a minute? Jesus Roni, what the fuck is up now, is our little black princess having another tantrum, what have her delicate little feelings been hurt again?"

I stared at the screen and felt my stomach twist, Roni glanced at her screen and saw me staring at her, she looked at Katie.

"I was going to talk to you shortly, I have a lot on my plate, but yes, considering recent hostilities, I think it is better if we let things cool down, and Anita handles Abby. I hate to point this out Katie, but you were the one that came up with this before the Curio event. You were the one that convinced me, and we both agreed, and I am not making a change now. You are a promoter, she is a publicist, and she is representing Abby from now on, now you either deal with it, or I will bring in another promoter exclusively for Abby."

"What, so that is just fucking it, little fucking dark princess wins again and gets her own way? Wow, I never thought I would say this, but you know what Roni, she will be the ruin of Jemi, and none of you can see it. Don't let that innocent charm fool you, she can be a ruthless bitch when she needs to be, and let's be honest, Anita is very Jemi like?"

I was shocked as I listened, I could not believe she would speak to Roni like that. I mean, holy shit; Roni is her boss. It was frightening to hear it, and in a way, I was glad to hear what she was saying about me, but how could she think I would do anything to hurt Birch?

I had made Anita sign the agreement, so there would be no threat. I could see how she was trying to bend things to her point of view, I had beat myself up because I was paranoid about her, but my gut was right all along, turning her down had pissed her off, and now she had it in for me.

Roni stood up, and walked around her desk, it felt wrong to listen to any more, and to be honest, I did not want to, my stomach was squirming. I hit the end call button, I did not want to hear any more, I could not believe she thought I was bad for Birch, I felt the shock waves ripple through me, why would she even say that?

It is a terrible moment, when you see that the face a person wears in front of you is fake. The Katie I knew, was nothing like the Katie Roni was talking with, I knew she had a problem with me because Birch picked me, but I was not aware it was this bad. I had felt threatened by her at the Curio Live event, and I had seen how she tried to faun all over Birch, but even though it had pissed me off, a part of me had thought she was just getting her own back, because I called her out.

Was Birch my weak spot? Yes, did Katie know that? Yes, and she had used it to show me she was boss, but listening to her talk to Roni, it felt like her grievance with me was more sinister than even I had thought. My only consolation, was I had made a wise choice in choosing to work with Anita, which to a degree, cut a lot of my interactions with Katie out during events. Perhaps that was why she was annoyed, did she want me alone without Birch, so she could exercise her authority over me?

It felt very much like in the nine years I had known her, she had changed a great deal, and as far as I was concerned it was not for the better. I did wonder what had brought all this on, was it because I had refused to sleep with her on the US tour, or was there something more, was it because Birch had asked me to marry her?

I sat back for a moment in thought, was that what this was really about, did she feel time is running out? I suddenly remembered that day after Birch returned home from hospital, after the Martin incident, and how I had awoken to see her sat on the bed looking at Birch.

I had never forgotten the look on her face, and how upset she was, she clearly really cared, actually scratch that, she showed how in love with her she was. I think that was the first time I truly understood her, but it showed, Katie was as in love with Birch as I was, and in a way, I had not considered it threatening at the time.

At the time I understood it, I mean, how can you know her and be around her without falling in love with her? There was a time in my life when I refused to accept that I was anything but straight, but I too was in love with Birch, and put myself through hell denying it.

It is impossible to not fall for her, I am sure everyone in this house would say the same. I knew Edwina adored her, so did Chloe, and Deb' had made it more than obvious, so why would Katie be any different? I understood that and never held it against her, but she sure as hell was holding it against me. Birch once told me that love was a natural process, and it was the one thing no one had any control over.

She had counselled many who had fallen for the most inappropriate people, but she had always been able to help them, because she understood that we had no real control over our feelings. She told me, love just happens, it is a natural process of interaction with a person, you cannot choose to love or not love a person, nature was the ruler of that, which was why so many people ended up hurt.

Falling in love was easy, it was natural, the hardest part was in the hope that the other person felt the same, and in a lot of cases they did not, hence the pain of love. It made so much sense to me at the time, because she was describing my own process of falling for her. It stood to reason Katie was no different, but sadly, Birch did not feel the same, and it appeared that was going to be a big problem for Birch and myself.

Roni stared at Katie; she was starting to simmer.

"I do not know who the hell you think you are madam, but speak to me like that in front of a client again, and regardless of your usefulness, I will set K.O. Productions adrift and cut you completely out of the Dixon Group. This is my company, and don't you ever God dammed well forget that." Katie stared back at her with defiant eyes, and nodded.

"Yes, it is, but it took me to realise all your ideas and put them on the road. I made you the well known face you are, and I did the same for that dark little princess, don't you dare think for one moment you can steam roller over me Roni. When you decide to make a change that important to this company, you dammed well tell me first." Roni shook her head.

"God, you have a nerve, I taught you everything I know, and I will point out, it was all my ideas, you were just the hired muscle, and I can do that with any promotions company. I warned you that you were playing with fire, and to steer clear of Jemi, but no, you would not listen. Well now look where you are, Abby wants you out of her life, you tell me, why was it exactly you could not keep your hands off Jemi's ass? I was there right at Abby's side watching, it was inappropriate, out of order and unprofessional, and you should know better. If you want some good advice, next time your unruly vagina has an itch, go pick up one of your normal slappers to scratch it, and keep your hands off my daughter. NOW GET OUT!" Katie stared at Roni.

"You are making a big mistake Roni."

She turned, marched to the door, and stormed out of the house. Katie jumped in her red Ferrari, revved the engine, and drove off at speed. Roni took a deep breath, turned, and walked back to her desk, and looked at the ended call on the computer. She plopped into her seat, gave a long sad sigh, and put her head in her hands.

"Oh… FUCK!!"

I needed air, I shut down my computer, and headed for the kitchen. I slid open the large doors and walked into the garden, and sat on the edge of the pool's paved area. I felt panicked and shaken, holy shit, Katie was really angry. The next event was going to be horrendous, and suddenly I was right back where I started, and it felt like once again in my life, I was taking one step forward, only to be dragged ten steps back.

Chapter 13

The Hidden Sides.

I was still sat by the pool lost in thought, when Birch arrived home, she collapsed at my side, and had not changed her clothes, and was holding a drink. I looked at the glass in her hand, it was only five thirty.

"How shit was today if you need that?" She gave a long sad sigh.

"It has been a really rough day; I really need this."

She took a long swig, and stretched out her legs. Okay, so that bothered me, Birch had a routine, home, hug, change of clothes, long chat about her day, and that had not happened today.

"Is everything alright, this is not like you at all?" She gave a soft smile.

"It's okay Sweetie, I just have a rough case, and it has my head spinning. I have a young woman, and her marriage is a bloody sham, her husband is so abusive, and honestly, I want to stab him." I blinked; I had never heard her talk like this, I looked at her bag, I knew what was in there, and that bothered me.

"Birch, this is not like you, how bad is this?" She leaned forward, and shook her head, I could almost feel the bad vibes coming off her.

"The stuff I have heard, no other woman on the planet would tolerate, and it baffles me why she does." She turned and looked at me, her eyes blazed bright green.

"This guy is your typical controlling narcissist, you know the type, porn addict, locked phone full of pictures of her friends in their underwear, violent if she objects, and a sexual failure in bed?" I frowned; I had read something different somewhere.

"I thought those types were always good in bed, you know that was why the girls stayed?" She gave a chuckle.

"He is covert, he would rather get himself off to porn than screw her. She spends twenty minutes with her hand, and thirty with her mouth, and he can only manage a semi. She finally jumps on it with raging jaw ache, feeling desperate for the attention, and just as it slips in, he wilts. She gets frustrated and loses it, tells him to finish himself off, he lifts his phone, gets instantly rock hard, and she runs out of the room in tears."

I could not believe it, I was shocked, actually no, I was horrified, and felt sick to my stomach, and I really did not know what to say. I struggled for a few minutes.

"Jesus Birch, why the hell does she put up with that, it's so bloody wrong? He is sick and beyond twisted, she needs to leave him, and wow, that is so freaking abusive, and not to mention degrading and humiliating." Birch nodded.

"I know Sweetie, it has my whole head swimming around as I try to grasp some sort of rationale sense, and I cannot: and believe it or not, that is not the worst." I felt my eyes open wide as I gasped, how could anything be worse than that, I mean, holy shit, what was this guy doing?

"WHAT?" She looked so sad, it felt heart breaking, how the hell did she do this for a living? I would grab the woman, and shake her until she saw reason. Birch looked down.

"I am sorry, I needed to talk to someone and Izzy is not around. Today she told me, it has reached a point where he lies on his side, looking at his phone, and jerks himself off, and she lies at his side and moans in his ear."

She turned to look at me, looking helpless, and she had tears in her eyes, and her voice went up a pitch. It felt painful just seeing her like that, and I did not know what to do.

"He has abused her so badly that he has reduced her to nothing more than a sound effect... Deads, what the hell do I say? This is so wrong, and so abusive, you tell me, would you do that for me, because her excuse is she loves him, and made a vow to him at her wedding?" I felt my own tears, as I looked at her, and slowly shook my head, and my emotions surged up inside me.

"You would never even ask. Birch, he is an abuser, and she is the victim, she must leave him, that is not a marriage, and that certainly is not love. No woman alive would tolerate that, why the hell is she?" She shrugged, as more tears rolled onto her cheeks.

"Her whole marriage has been years of intimidation and broken promises, she is only in her early thirties, and she is tolerating such degradation and humiliation, for some out dated and over rated tradition, called a wedding vow. Now do you see why I see it as enforced monogamy; she is like his captive frigging sex toy?" I slid over to her and pulled her close, she pushed her head into my shoulder.

"I feel so utterly useless Deads, I just cannot get through to her, all the study, all the training, and yet I am useless, and it is tearing at me."

She gave a sob and just cried into me, and all I could do was just hold her close, as she shook in my arms, and released everything that was built up in her. It was horrible to see her like this, and horrible to know what that sick bastard was doing to his wife.

I could not comprehend the situation at all, none of this made sense. In my small little world, this was so vile, and my understanding of psychology was so limited, it was hard for me to give anything that would remotely comfort Birch.

The simple fact was, this is life, this is the hidden truth of society today, these things are happening behind closed doors. As to what is the motivation to stay, I could not say, because as much as I wanted to, I had no understanding at all of a situation this disgusting. I loved Birch with all my heart, and seeing her suffer like this was terrible, but I had to admit, there was nothing I could do, apart from hold her close, and just be there, and let her cry it out to release the pressure. She gave a sniffle and pulled out of my shoulder.

"I am so sorry Deads, I can normally leave this at work, but today, it has boiled up out of me. I should not burden you like this, it is not right."

She had no need to apologise, the fact she made it home without cracking, was in itself a miracle. I have no idea how people can do this; it just warps my mind to know there are people in this world that evil.

"Birch, you have no need to apologise, I really do not know what to say, but baby, I will always be here to listen. It is not much, but if you are this upset, I am here." She wiped her eyes on her jacket sleeve, and tried to smile.

"You know I really love you; I really do. I could never exploit you or hurt you like that. Deads, I have heard so many things in the therapy room, I had thought I had encountered everything there was, and then in she walks, and all this terrible stuff comes out of her. Even with all my knowledge, I just flounder like a fish out of water. I have given it everything I know to help her, but she just will not accept that even in a marriage this is wrong on so many levels, and you know what the worst thing of all is?" Holy shit, was it not bad enough already? I shook my head.

"Oh God, what is the worst thing?"

"She is so set on honouring her marriage vows, and yet she is not even a believer. She only got married in church because his family are uber religious. How frigging messed up is that, she is actually honouring something that is meaningless to her on a spiritual level?"

It was really hard to believe this was even real, knowing it had upset Birch so much, made it more than real in a strange sort of way. I was struggling to get my head around it, I looked at her.

"Birch, I am going to hate myself for asking, but you still want us to get married don't you, I mean, this is not putting you off is it?" I swallowed hard as I looked at her, and suddenly I felt afraid, she smiled and lifted her hand to my face.

"Oh Sweetie, you silly, all I want is to marry you, I cannot wait. Deads, Sweetie, I am sorry, this must all feel so weird to you, today was a rough one. I will get through it, I just need a lot longer to process this than some of the other cases." I nodded and did understand, I was relieved to know the marriage was still on.

"Birch, why don't you talk to your mum, you know she is much further ahead in the game? She may have come across something like this, and can give you some advice or pointers. I really wish I understood the therapy world better, so I could help more." She leaned forward and gave me a soft kiss, I felt the tingles run down my legs, she smiled.

"Thanks Sweetie, I actually feel better, you have helped me a lot, and I think you are right, I try not to bother mum much, but I will call her later and talk." She looked at me with those bright green eyes.

"Deads, I suddenly feel really bad."

"Why?" She gave a smile.

"You spoke with Anita today, and I was so caught up in myself, I forgot to ask how that went." I gave a sigh.

"It went really well, she was calm and relaxed, and she really understood my point of view. She signed the agreement without any worries at all, and she had some great ideas, I really think it will make a huge difference. She has a lot of ideas, and I want you to join us in a brain storming session, I also want to know what you think. Oh, and by the way, she is nothing like you, she is a very pale replacement. We have nothing to fear from her." I think she understood, I hoped she did, she gave me that shrewd look.

"Why do I feel there is more, I sense a but coming?" I giggled, there really was no hiding from her, I looked up and she smiled and her eyes twinkled.

"Just say her name Deads." I chuckled.

"She is really pissed off with me, and she is pissed off with Anita, I get the feeling she is not going to be very polite with me the next time I see her." I think she understood, I actually think she knows Katie's dark side far more than she lets on.

"I can talk to her if you want me to?" I shook my head.

"This is my problem, I created it, and I do not want you dragging in to all this, you have enough on your plate." She shrugged, and smiled at me.

"Okay Sweetie, but if it gets rough, I will be stepping in, I will not let Katie abuse you." She lifted her glass and swallowed the last bit.

"How about we fill our glasses, and then head upstairs for a while, and put an exhausted smile on each other's faces, I could really use some close private time?"

I took her hand with a smile and stood up, and together we walked hand in hand towards the house. We entered the kitchen and poured out the drinks, Edwina was stood at the island chopping veg, she gave us a grin.

"I know that look, meal time will be in an hour or so, please be done by then." Birch giggled, and she grabbed my hand.

"Quick Sweetie, we are wasting precious moments." She gave my hand a yank, and she almost dragged me out of the kitchen, Edwina chuckled as she heard us charging up the stairs.

Hot sweaty and exhausted, I pulled a baggy t shirt on, and headed smiling downstairs for our meal. We had a full table tonight, with Michael, Luke and even Terry joining us, and it was fun and lively, with a lot of wine. The meal ended and we all hung around the kitchen and mucked in with the chores, as we laughed and joked with each other, and the atmosphere was light, and very enjoyable.

Eventually we all went our separate ways, and most of us ended up in the library, Luke sat with Edwina, talking shop. Chloe and Anthony looked at hairstyles on the spare computer, and Birch messaged her mum, a full room meant no video, as it would breach confidentiality. I jumped on my com and talked with the message app, with Deb's who was at her house, I was missing her, and I filled her in about what I had seen and heard with Katie. Birch lifted her phone and dialed and walked out of the room.

"Yeah, hi mum, just give me a second."

I slid back my chair and stood up, grabbed my glass and walked towards the kitchen. Birch was stood on the lawn, talking on her phone to Roni, as her mum gave her some good advice, and I felt a little relieved. I did not like seeing Birch like this, normally she had a good handle on everything.

It was strange to think, that even with all the knowledge she had, and all the training, just like everyone else, there were the days that were so overwhelming, that even those we think have all the answers struggle.

By midnight I was lay in bed wide awake, as Birch curled round me and twitched in her dreams. I felt sorry for her, I knew she was dreaming about her client, and it worried me a little, she had not done that since the passing of Melody. I lay in the darkness staring at the wall, not really seeing it, as I had drawn the curtains and the room was pitch black.

The thing is, I am a writer, I write about the violence and cruelty of humans in my stories, but they are fictional. My current story has a priest who craves power and control, and is ruthless in the way he executes his will to take over, and yet today, I had seen two real life examples of people who will stop at nothing to get things the way they want them. I was really surprised by Katie, and even more so by a wife who would suffer such degradation, which must feel dehumanising, from a husband who rules with dominance and control.

Real life was staring me in the face, and the scary thing was, it matched with that of my fictional character. As a writer, even though my books are fantasy, and fictional, I want them to feel as real as possible, but I think there has always been a part of me, which just accepted it was fiction, and so therefore it was safe. The problem was, lying in bed in the dark, the realisation that it was not safe, and there were people in today's world that really were that cruel, was actually quite frightening.

I cannot say I fully understand why people would want to do such things, looking at Katie, I have always been grateful to her for what she has done for me, and I have shown it, and verbalised it many times to her. Yet, because I would not have sex with her in the states, it had started a war between us, and it was starting to appear that the prize was Birch.

Watching and listening to Anita today, I heard the sadness in her voice, because the simple truth was, she had really liked being with Katie, and even though I do not know her that well, I thought Katie was lucky to have her.

The sad truth was, Katie had seen her as a tool, a means to an end, just some trophy to use to try and create disharmony between Birch and myself, and Anita now knew that, and she was hurt by that. It felt so wrong to me, as I picked up on her sadness, she did not say anything directly, but I got the impression she had grown fond of Katie, and had feelings for her. I think today is the first time I really understood what happened with Marianne and Tony, Kate wanted Marianne, and she refused her, so she went out of her way, to bed Tony, just to get even.

It was cold, callous, and cruel, and the saddest thing of all, was that she did not even feel attracted to Tony. She screwed him, and took a cast of his member, just to rub it in Marianne's face, and as a result, Marianne broke off the engagement, and did not marry him. I felt really sorry for her, it must have been heart breaking for her, and yet Katie still boasts about it as her greatest joke, like it is an achievement. It was that which scared me the most, the fact she did not bat an eyelid, and made a joke out of it, I mean, how dark and cold do you have to be inside to do that?

It had never really occurred to me before, Birch thought I was worrying too much, but as I lay thinking about it, I felt like I was not worried enough. Today, I heard what she said to Roni, who is going to be my mother in law, she will be family. Katie actually faced her, and told her I was a threat to Birch. Even now, I am still trying to come to terms with that. The way I saw it, if she was prepared to say that to Roni, and had set Anita up as some sort of trap, plus the addition of what she did to Tony, it was pretty obvious, she meant business, and I should be extra vigilant.

I had not told Birch about the video call, in a way I was afraid to, I hated myself for not talking to her about it, and I felt guilty. This morning I had felt so hopeful, and Birch had loved seeing it, and I just did not want to bring her down, because she was happy I had found a way to resolve it all. I had no idea what to do, but I could not deny, I was afraid of what Katie could do.

My mind shifted, as I thought about the cruel husband, and his sick sexual ritual with his wife. I have to say at this point, I once masturbated in front of Birch. Well actually, we did it together to let each other watch, and it was sexy and arousing, and surprisingly, it made us feel closer, but this guy was different. His wife was completely excluded from any sexual experience, there was absolutely no benefit to her, it was all for his sick pleasure, and it made no sense to me that she would put herself through that. The burning question was, what did he get out of it, apart from the obvious climax?

It feels strange to me that he could not get erect for his wife, who Birch described as young and pretty, and she admitted, she thought she was quite sexy. Why was he not turned on by her, and yet when he looked at one of his pictures of a scantily dressed woman on his phone, he became instantly erect? What kind of broken mind is like that, how twisted and mentally screwed up do you have to be for that to happen?

It boggles my mind, and I cannot make any sense of it, and strangely enough, that bothers me. I cannot imagine myself, lying next to a man and moaning in his ear as he jerks off to pictures. I do not understand why a woman would do that, has she lost all of her self respect, is she so broken and damaged she would allow that, and if she is, what else will she allow?

That was actually the most terrifying part of all this, and I think the reason Birch is so upset. Like myself, I think she is aware that a man like that is capable of anything?

As a writer, I had an insight to something much deeper than a kink, I even think it goes well beyond perversion, Birch called him a covert narcissist, was this what they were really like? The thing that I did not understand was this guy apparently was well thought of by everyone, he would be worshipped in the pubs and clubs, and admired and praised by all who surrounded him.

No one knew what went on behind closed doors, they did not see the real him. From what Birch had told me, he came across as a loving husband, a dutiful son, and a loving father, his friends loved him, but the real truth was, how the hell did he hide it? Why did his wife not leave him, and show the world the truth of this guy?

It made no sense to me at all, but it made me really think, just how many people out there are like that? Birch has always told me, that I would be surprised by what went on behind closed doors, I had seen that in my own village many times as the truth was revealed. She had told me tonight, there are some very deviant and twisted people in the world, and a lot of people suffering in silence, and I suppose she should know, her team gave therapy to most of the local victims. Martin came to mind, which gave me the chills, but wasn't it also true of him?

Everyone saw him as the perfect villager, and model choir master, and yet he too was a deviant rapist, and everyone was shocked when the truth came out, it literally rocked the village. Even my own father was fooled by him, although he had also been fooled by his partner Graham, and almost ended up in prison because of it. I understood control, it was a weapon of my youth, and my father was an expert at using it. Both my own mother and myself are testament to that, but even though he was ruthless at times, I really hope he was not as sick in bed with my mother.

The truth is, even if he was, I would probably never know, and that was a scary thought. I knew my mother would never tell me anything like that, even if it was true. The thing that worried me the most, was she had always defended him, even now, she never says anything bad about him, she always tells me, he is my dad, and no matter what happened between them, I must not judge him on his treatment of her.

Was this the same mind set of this long suffering wife, did she hide her husband's sickness simply to save face, and avoid admitting something so foul and disgusting, that she would at least not have to suffer the humiliation of others?

It was an interesting thought, I understood avoiding shame, I had hidden away many times simply to avoid yet another round of derogatory comments. Was this the key to unlocking Birch's problem? I assumed Birch would have thought of that, but the question was, had she ever talked about that with her client?

There are times I think my mind is screwed up, the one thing I did know, was I needed more depth to my villain in order to really give that sense of evil to my priest. Somehow, I had to find a way to open his life and soul to the readers, and add more of the reality of life to my fiction.

Birch jerked and moaned in her sleep, and she gave little whimpers, her hand as always was on my boob, and she occasionally gently squeezed it. I put my hand on hers as she whimpered again and gave it a gentle rub, and turned my head back towards her the best I could.

"Shush Baby, it is alright, you are safe here, go to sleep."

She gave a little moan and disturbed, I smiled, and she slipped away from her nightmare and settled a little, she was so grown up, and yet in many ways, still like a little child at times.

"Sleep baby, I am here, and I am not going anywhere, you are safe here."

She nuzzled into me, and relaxed. I turned to face the curtains, and closed my eyes. Today had felt hard, and even though I was wide awake in the middle of the night, I felt weary, and my soul yearned for rest. I tried to relax, and put the day behind me, and I took a long deep breath. I had no idea how all this would pan out, I just hoped it would all calm down and go away, but somehow knowing my luck, I was pretty sure there would be a lot more drama before the wedding

"I cannot wait to get married, hopefully, that will put an end to all of this for once and all time." Birch gave a happy little moan, she was flat out, and somehow, I felt she was still listening, after all she never misses a trick, it's sort of a Birch thing you know?

I slowly drifted into nothingness, my thoughts rambled on, and at some point, they stopped without me even being aware of it. I was warm and toasty, and could hear the soft breathing of Birch behind me, as I slipped into the realm of sleeping.

My body jerked. "OH FUCK!"

My eyes were open, as I looked around alarmed in the dark, Birch was sat up on the edge of the bed, even in the darkness, her long white hair emitted a soft light. I sat up, and rubbed my eyes.

"Baby... Are you alright?"

I reached over and clicked on the small lamp, she was leaning forward resting her arms on her knees, as she sat on the edge of the bed, her long hair touched the sheet and flowed behind her. I slid over and knelt up behind her, and folded my arms around her. She was slightly trembling, and I could feel the sweat as it chilled on her skin.

"Birch this is not good, I am worried about you." She lifted her arm, and took hold of my hand.

"I will be alright Sweetie, honestly, I will be fine." I kissed her shoulder and tried to push myself as close to her as I could.

"I don't like that your work gives you nightmares, I feel useless, and I really want to be there for you." She turned and smiled, her eyes were duller than normal, and she looked so tired.

"Deads, I will be alright, just hold me, and show me your love, I feel a little insecure at the moment, I am sorry, just stay close to me, you are all the tonic I need." I stroked the hair from her face and turned her slightly, so I could see her better, and then leaned in and kissed her softly.

She responded, and brought up her arms, and pulled me in closer. The kiss intensified, as I went with it, kissing her, loving her, and a slid my hand up, and touched her. She responded as I explored her breast and played with her nipple, she gave a moan.

"Oh yes Deads."

I leaned forward pushing her down to the bed, her legs still hung over the edge, and moved onto her neck, just below her ear, and she gave a soft moan, I knew what she liked, and I needed her to feel just me, not her nightmares. My lips traced down her neck, and to the nape of her shoulder, as I softly kissed her, her head moved back a little and she gave another moan.

I moved down and kissed onto her breast, and my hand began to slide slowly down, the tips of my fingers giving her the slightest of touches as I explored her tummy, and I slid my lips onto her growing nipple. Her stomach muscles tensed, as she slightly arched her back, and my tongue swirled sending tingles through her whole body, she gave a gasp, as my hand moved over her little furry mound, I felt her legs open slightly to let me in.

It was gentle and loving, and she reacted, giving off small quiet little moans of pleasure, I wanted her to feel good, and I knew this would do that. My finger traced over her outer labia, as I teased her slightly, knowing of the sensations building inside her, I slid my hand down slightly and pushed my middle finger, and she parted, and her warm moisture oozed out, as she pushed her back up, and gave a long, breathless moan.

"Ooooooo... Oh Deads yes... Yes Sweetie."

I sucked hard on her nipple as my finger entered her, she gave a slight jerk, I knew that pulse, and the joyous feelings attached to it. My finger explored within her, as it swirled around her button, and teased her even more, her legs tensed, and started to tremble, I lifted my head and smiled, as my hand picked up speed. She lifted her head to mine, and her arm came round behind my head, and pulled me closer into a fiery passionate kiss, she was close, I could feel it building inside her.

I sped up my hand and she jerked, and then grabbed my arm, her back came up, and she went rigid as she pushed back her head, and gave a long wailing moan, and I felt the warm moisture run down my fingers. She froze locked with her back arched and her legs shook, I watched enjoying seeing her red face, I smiled at her, and she flopped back on the bed, my finger still inside her, as I felt the little pulses that were rippling through her. I leaned over her face and looked down at her.

"Was that nice Baby?" She smiled as she panted, and gave a slight nod, I leaned in and kissed her softly, as she tried to suck in more air.

"Cuddle into me now, and sleep deeper free of those nasty dreams." Her arm came up to my face, she smiled and swallowed hard, her voice was a little breathless.

"I really do love you so much Deads, I really do." I smiled and kissed her nose.

"Come on, snuggle into me, I want to feel you wrapped around me like a blanket."

I slid back across the bed, and slipped under the duvet, she slowly, with her shaking legs pulled herself back onto the bed, and snuggled into me, and the heat of her skin was hot against me. She curled around me, pushing herself into me and kissed my shoulder as she settled down, I could hear her breathing much faster than normal. Her hand cupped my boob.

"Thanks, Deads, you know, for being here."

I smiled as I pushed back into her, feeling calm, although my wrist ached a little, and just settled into my pillow, and closed my eyes. It was 4:30am and I needed sleep. The sound of Birch's soft breathing washed across me, as she slipped into a deeper sleep, this was nice, this was how life was supposed to be, and this was all I really wanted.

Chapter 14

Changes.

It was not easy getting up, both Birch and myself were tired, which meant Birch was grumpy. Anthony was running around in a flap, and asking questions, I just sat facing Chloe and ignored him, Birch on the other hand was not in the mood. She sat next to me eating the last of the muesli, and he was not happy when he saw the empty bag.

"Have we got no more muesli again? I really wanted something wholesome with a nutty taste, I suppose the grumpy blonde over there has eaten it all again?" Birch looked up as Chloe giggled. Birch stared at Anthony.

"If you really do want something with a nutty flavour, go catch a frigging squirrel, the garden is full of them." I stared at Chloe trying not to laugh, Anthony gave a huff.

"Oh, dear we are much more grumpier than normal, not getting enough are we darling?" Her eyes stared in cold annoyance through her hair.

"I get plenty, I am surprised you did not hear me last night, it felt like Abby had her whole hand inside me." I slurped and coughed, and Chloe moved quickly to the side, out of range of my spraying coffee, Anthony shook his head and cringed.

"And suddenly darlings, I am not hungry." Birch slapped me on the back, and I gave a massive cough. She smiled.

"You were good, I thoroughly enjoyed it, thank you Sweetie, I love your small petite hands." Anthony shook his head.

"Birch darling, you can be quite impossible, you will need to hurry, because if not, you will be late, and people do not like those who are not on time." Birch lifted her head, and looked at him, as he folded his arms and looked smugly at her, she lifted her spoon and pointed at him.

"Anthony, Isaac Newton, said time is absolute, Einstein said it was relative, and Karl Marx, said time was invented by clock companies to sell more clocks, so today, I am going with Marx."

Chloe sniggered, Anthony gave a dramatic huff, waved his hand across the air, and vacated the scene, and I mopped up my mess and sat back to finish my coffee. Birch slowly ate her breakfast, I was still a little worried about her, even when she is tired, she has always managed a happy 'hi Sweetie' to me, but today it was dull and lifeless.

When she finished her breakfast, she placed her bowl in the sink and headed upstairs to dress, I put my cup down and followed her, when I caught up, she was in the bathroom brushing her teeth, I leaned on the door frame.

"Birch, you are really tired, and very quiet, I am worried about you." She spat into the sink, lifted her glass and rinsed out her mouth.

"I am tired Deads, we were up late, and I am not complaining, oh god, you have no idea how much I needed that. Sweetie, I am going to be fine, I had a rough day, but I will get through this, so please, I really do not want you sitting here worrying."

She turned and came towards me and slid her arms round my waist, her eyes had rings below them, and it just felt like she had lost some of her sparkle, she smiled at me.

"I will be fine; it is just one of the many bumps in the road we all face." I gave a long sigh.

"Please do me one favour, promise me Birch, talk to Susana, she is really good with trauma, and she may shed light on this case that could help you, and Izzy could have answers. Birch, get some help with this, you know when I struggle you rush in and help me, please listen, even if it is just to make me feel better, talk with them." She gave me a nod.

"Okay Deads, I promise, I will talk to both of them, just for you, and if it helps, I will make a point of thanking you." I smiled and breathed a sigh of relief.

"It would make me so happy knowing you are not alone in this; I am so worried about you baby." I kissed her softly.

"I wish you did not have to go into work today, I would love to cuddle you all day." She smiled and a little twinkle flashed in her eyes.

"Oh, Sweetie, I would really love that, but sadly I have sessions today."

"Okay, just take care of your emotional self."

As Birch got dressed, I returned to the kitchen for a top up of coffee, I felt groggy and yawned, Chloe filled my cup, and then sat down, and looked at me, she narrowed her eyes.

"Trouble in Wonderland? Both of you have been a lot quieter than normal, and if you ask me, it is more than just tiredness from too much sex?" I turned my cup on the surface of the island.

"Birch has a really difficult case, she had nightmares last night because of it. I want to help her, but I do not understand the psychology enough, it has got me down a little." She understood.

"That is the problem with working with fucked up people, they can fuck you up at the same time. Abby she is one of the best, she will get through this, and look at the support she has at the practice. Stop worrying, she will be fine, this is Birch we are talking about." She touched my hand, and looked at me.

"Growing up and becoming adults' sucks Chloe." She gave a wide grin.

"That is the spirit, fuck them and be a child, it works for me." Birch came down the stairs, grabbed her coat and walked in, she leaned down and kissed me.

"See you later, I won't be late tonight, I want to come home at a normal time." I smiled.

"Yeah, let's snuggle up together." She smiled, and gave Chloe a small wave, a few seconds later the door banged, and I felt a little alone inside, Chloe was watching me.

"Wow, I have never ever seen her that troubled." I shrugged.

"I just feel really helpless... I think I am going to try and write today; I want to just get something positive done." I grabbed my cup and stood up.

"Sorry Chloe." I headed up to my room.

Anita Dickinson, had attended university, entered the media as a publicist, and worked her way up through the ranks. She had worked with several large publishing agencies, and had good relationships with a great many journalists, it helped that she was pretty, and always looked the part. Sadly, most of the male reporters who had offered her a helping hand, soon found out their aspirations were dashed, as she was not that interested.

The Dixon Group had head hunted her as part of an expansion program, in which Roni wanted to expand the publishing arm of the business. It was mainly due to the rise in popularity of Abby, which highlighted the potential for the business. It had been a joint project between Katie and Roni, but in the last year, Roni had taken a more active role, and had employed several people for their new roles, one of which was Anita.

In the run up to the Curio event, as Katie worked with Birch, Edwina, and Aden, Roni had begun to rethink some of her plans. The publishing arm had five reasonably successful authors, of which her and Abby were two of them, and under the guidance of a new employee, Craig Smithers, she was scouting for new and exciting writers to publish. Anita was to take charge of three, part of her remit was to find a new author. Katie would handle all events, and was in charge of locations and staging, and no longer act as a publicist for any of the authors.

The problem was, Katie wanted to keep Abby, and had not taken kindly to the news of Anita's promotion very well. Katie was often heard saying, how she had made Abby the name she was today, as without her she would have failed, and there was some truth to that. Her recent behaviour, and what appeared to Roni like an obsessive possession of Abby, had led to her losing out to Anita. Katie naturally felt Anita had stolen her away, in a bid to take over, and see her pushed out of the company. Her outbursts of late had been aggressive and loud, and Roni was not happy with her.

Abby was convinced Katie had it in for her, because Birch had asked her to marry her, and again, there was some evidence to back that up, especially in the way Katie had kept her held in her hotel room during the Curio event, whereas the rest of the group had been allowed to travel freely in pairs around the event with minders.

Katie and Anita had started dating shortly before her arrival at the company four months ago. During the Curio event, when Anita had expressed her similarity to Birch, and also Katie's wandering hands around Birch, it had all come to a head. Katie had eventually admitted, that she wanted Anita to get Abby into bed, just so she could sweep in and scoop up a recovering Birch.

Their breakup ensued, and it was loud and messy, and ended

up with Anita leaving early in the morning with her case, in tears. When Roni found out, because she was still in London, she went to visit Anita at home, and she got the full story first hand.

It was at that point, she decided on the way home to visit Abby, and suggest she work with Anita. Roni was no fool, and with her daughter's marriage on the horizon, she acted quickly to limit Katie's exposure to Abby, in hope it would cool her down. It hadn't worked, Katie was even more determined to bring down Abby, and prove to Birch she was unworthy of her.

Since that day, Roni had been at work with her legal team, to divide up the Dixon Group into smaller independent units. K.O. Production, Dixon Therapeutic, Dixon media holdings and Dixon Publishing, which would be presided over by the board, under the banner of 'The Dixon Group'. Katie was unhappy when she realised, that even though she had full control of her own company, she would lose the internal workings of the publishing arm, especially the publicity side of it.

From now on, she would organise and handle the events, but press and public relations, would be handled by Anita, a woman she had been so obnoxious with, who walked out on her. Had she not created such a big problem with Anita, she would still be dating her, and have a say in Abby's professional life. It was a shrewd move on Roni's part as she dealt with removing the tensions on her daughter and her future partner. After her confrontation with Roni, Katie jumped in her red Ferrari, and headed south.

Anita was up and enjoying her week off, she was wandering around in her knickers and a t shirt, with her hair in a pony tail, planning what she could do for Abby. She sat at her desk with a coffee and clicked open her emails, her phone pinged again for the fortieth time that morning. She lifted it up and saw yet another message from Katie, and ignored it like she had all the rest, gave a sigh and put the phone down. She took a swig of her coffee, and started to read her emails. The doorbell rang and she gave a sigh, and slid back her chair.

She got up and walked to the door without thinking, and opened it, and wished she hadn't. Katie stood there looking angry.

"I have been fucking messaging you all morning." She stepped back.

"I know, I was busy."

Katie stepped in, and looked around the place, she walked into the middle of the room and turned back to face her as she closed the door, Anita turned.

"I expected this, so just get your yelling over with, and then piss off and leave me in peace." Katie gave her a big smile, and her tone softened.

"Nita, give me some credit, I will not deny, I was not pleased to lose Abby, I made her, but that is not why I am here." Anita looked at her, not really believing her.

"It's not?" Katie shook her head, and tried to look sad.

"No, I wanted to say sorry, and hope you would take me back? I was out of order, and I have missed you." Anita was having none of it, she walked to her desk, and sat in her chair, and task barred down her emails, revealing her desk top.

"You are wasting your time, Abby is wise to your games, I signed a none fraternisation agreement with her, so I could represent her." Katie frowned at her.

"The cunning little witch... Anyway, that is beside the point, what do you say, will you give me another chance to make it up to you?" Anita swung round in her seat.

"Kate, you bloody used me to act as some sort of Jemi lure, to get Abby into bed to screw up her wedding. Do you know how shitty I felt when I saw you fawning all over Jemi, and realised I was just some token prop, to distract Abby, so you could bed her future wife? You bloody used me, and I really cared about you, I did, it was heart breaking walking away knowing I was used like that. Christ, you are a piece of work." Katie gave a sigh.

"Oh come on love, I am trying here, do you know how hard this is for me, I never apologise to anyone, and yet here I am, doing my best?" She was unbelievable, and Anita felt angry.

"Kate, I was really falling for you, I actually developed feelings for you, and I was so happy, and then we did the Curio Live event, and the real truth of why I was with you came out. Don't you get how insulting it was to me, to find out I was just some usable pale imitation of the woman you really are in love with? If you want to make amends, just bloody well admit the truth, I was just a part of your big scheme to get Jemi in your bed." She shook her head.

"It was not like that; I really care about you." Anita shook her head.

"I have not heard a word from you, and yet as soon as Abby offers me a job, you suddenly appear filled with apologies, it's all bullshit and you know it. Just so we are clear here, you never had a hope, Abby is cute and she has a good body, but her tits are way too small for me, I would rather screw Jemi, she is more my type. That being said, I wouldn't, because that ring on her finger means something, and you need to grow the hell up and accept it like the rest of us." Katie's eyes flared.

"I will never accept it, Abby is wrong for her, she has no understanding of her, she does not know her like I do. I will never accept it, not ever." Anita looked at her, and actually felt sorry for her.

"Hell, can you even hear yourself? Kate, how can you expect me to get involved with someone who will never love me, because she is too in love with a woman she can never have? Kate, Jemi was the one who asked Abby, do you get that, no matter what your crazy mind is thinking, it was Jemi who picked Abby, not the other way round?" She flicked her long red hair back, and narrowed her eyes at Anita.

"Wow you really are fucking ungrateful, when I think of everything I did for you. You had a fucking amazing time with me, first class all the fucking way, and you never complained. You just lapped it up and took everything I gave you, and yet I ask one thing of you, and you what… You stand in fucking judgement of me? Wow, I have met some arrogant dykes in my time, but you just take the fucking crown." Anita stood up, as Katie stood glaring at her, with her hands on her hips.

"Kate, you want to ruin a really good relationship, and you know what is so screwed up, if I do what you want, you will piss off with Jemi and leave me behind? Tell me, is that what our whole relationship was about, you were spoiling me to soften me up for your special task? Here Nita, have a first class hotel room, hey Nita, come Christmas I will buy you a new car, or hey, let's go on a first class no expense spared paid holiday to Crete. And now it's hey Nita, by the way you owe me for all that shit, so just go and screw up this couple, because I deserve the blonde. Have you any idea how messed up you sound right now? Katie, I fell in love with you, does that mean nothing to you at all?" She gave a snort.

"You did well enough out of it, be honest you got all the benefits, you even got my fucking job out of it." Anita shook her head slowly.

"You know what, just get the hell out, just leave Kate." Katie stared at her; her eyes narrowed as her lips pursed.

"You are a fool, I was the best thing to ever happen to you, and you are just throwing me away, is that it?" Anita gave a smirk and pointed at the door.

"Hardly the best, I was just temporary, something to do until you finally destroyed Abby and got Jemi all to yourself. Just leave Kate, this is like the hotel all over again, it is why I left, just go find another blonde, and leave me the hell alone, I have work to do." Katie shrugged and turned.

"You will regret this; I will make sure of it." Anita nodded at her.

"Probably, just do whatever it is you need to do, and I will deal with it when it happens, now please leave me alone." Katie walked towards the door, she grabbed the handle and looked back.

"You know just for the record; you were a pretty shit lay." Anita gave a snort of laughter.

"Says the girl who came here to ask me to go back to her, don't worry Kate, I am sure you will find a better screw at some point, and if not, there is always Tony."

The door slammed hard, shaking the window panes, Anita gave a long sigh, and walked back to her desk. She sat down and task barred her emails back up, she clicked Abby's message, it opened, she started to read, and she gave a small smile.

Izzy looked at Birch across the conference room table. Birch was looking uncomfortable, but standing her ground, Izzy shook her head.

"Don't play bloody innocent with me Jemi, I have known you for too long. Abby is worried, she called me, and so did your mum. Look we all have cases that are hard, and we all lose our objectivity from time to time, come on, you are skilled enough to know, you are not helping Jane. Jemi, I understand you own the practice, but you put me in here to manage because I have the skills and the experience, and as manager of this practice, I have to take you off Jane, I am sorry, but you are useless to her in this state."

Birch bit her lip, she really did not want to stop working with her, but she also knew that Izzy was right. Izzy leaned across the table.

"Look kid, you did your best for her, but you brought Susana in for these types of cases, if you have to consult on it with her, then fine. Follow the case that way, but you know deep down, this one is more her line. Jemi, this has gone beyond sexual dysfunction, Jane is now in a trauma bonded relationship, and you need to hand her over to our specialist." Birch gave a long sigh.

"We have done so much work to build trust, Jane is going to find it hard adjusting to Sue, and it is vital she keeps coming here." Izzy nodded and agreed.

"Yes it is, so sit in for the first few, let Jane see your confidence in Sue, help her adjust, and then withdraw from the case, and let Sue take over. I am sure Sue will keep you updated, I will not deny, she has become a real asset. It was a smart move on your part to get her in here, and she appears very happy in her role here. Jemi you know I am right." Birch gave a nod, she understood the way the practice ran, and she knew Izzy was right.

"God, some days I wish I had left you in Manchester, but you are right, I am over reaching, I will pass her over, but I want to supervise her. Izzy, I need to follow Jane through to a resolution, let me do that, let me see her get the help she needs." Izzy sat back in her chair and smiled at her.

"This is the right move Jemi, you have put your client before your ego, I am proud of you, if this had been Roni, I probably would have to arm wrestle her into submission." Birch gave a chuckle.

"You would lose." Izzy giggled as she stood up, and lifted the thick file off the table.

"Yeah probably, I have never won an argument with her, the bloody woman is too dammed smart for her own good. You have done the right thing here Jemi, you have acted in Jane's best interest, you are a great therapist. Chalk this one up to experience, and learn from the work Sue does with her, to be honest, everyone here would benefit with a few sit in's with her."

Birch stood up, and grabbed her coffee cup.

"Maybe we should get her to do a few presentations to the others, it might help to get an insight into her work, I must admit, I will enjoy an observation or two with her?" Izzy opened the door.

"You know that is not a bad idea, we have four very skilled specialists here, maybe we should do more detailed sharing during the debriefs, after all, it will lift everyone's game even more, especially if we have to cover for illness and days off?" Birch nodded as they walked up the corridor back towards reception.

"I think I will look into it, and bring it up next Monday, you know, see how they all feel about it." At the office door Izzy turned and looked her in the eye.

"You are alright now, aren't you, Abby is really worried and upset about this, Jemi do not hide it, if this comes back to bite you, I want to know?" She smiled and patted her arm.

"Izzy I really am fine, I am tired, it's the weekend and I want to lie in and rest up, but honestly, I feel relieved, so thanks for that." Izzy opened the office door.

"Okay I am happy to hear that, but I mean it, I do not want another Melody, we need to keep this ship afloat, and it needs you as the figure head at your best. Anything comes up, I want to be the first to know, I do not want to hear it from a worried Abby."

"I hear you, and yes I will talk to you if I need it." Izzy gave a smile.

"The rest of your day is free, I will lock up, you go when you are ready and get some sleep, tell Abby to lay off you until you are better rested." Birch giggled.

"Wow being a manager has taken all your fun away, although I will go early today, I really am that tired."

I was as tired as Birch, and lost to sleep, and yet I heard her.

"Sweetie." I opened my eyes and blinked, I was sat in my desk chair, I smiled.

"Sweetie you cannot sleep there, you will ache like hell."

I yawned and looked around, a little unsure of where I was, Birch was on her knees in front of me, I lifted my hand to her cheek.

"Hi Baby." She smiled, and took my hand.

"You are tired, come to bed for a bit and rest properly."

She gently pulled and I moved, and felt the ache in my back, I stood up and followed her to my bed, she pulled back the duvet, and turned to me.

"I am sorry, I worried you and you lost sleep over it." I shook my head.

"Birch, that is the point of being together, we share everything."

She pulled at my t shirt, and slipped it over my head, and I sat on the side of the bed as she undressed, tossing her things on the floor, and climbed over, then slid in at my side. I settled down and she curled round me.

"Birch, are you going to be alright?" She gave me a soft squeeze.

"I am fine Deads, I had a long talk with Izzy, and I have decided to pass the client over to Sue, and I will be a supervisor, but Sue will handle the trauma from now on." I was glad to hear it, and felt a little easier inside.

"I am happy to hear you won't have to keep going through that, I will not deny it Birch, it really scared me to see you like that. I felt so useless and helpless, because I wanted to help, and I did not know what to do." Her soft breathing flowed into my ear; I gave a sigh.

"Christ Birch, do you have a switch you just flick?"

I have no idea why I was surprised; I am sure I have told you; she once fell asleep feeding the bloody pigeons outside Manchester Cathedral while we sat on a bench. I closed my eyes, it was nice to feel her close and warm, her hand as always cupping my boob, I smiled, and just relaxed into the pillow.

While we slept, the rest sat down stairs at the table to eat, Chloe looked up, as she stirred her veg chow mien, with her chop sticks.

"Shouldn't we wake them up, you know Abby misses a lot of meals, it bothers me more than you realise?" Edwina lifted a large chunk of broccoli with her sticks, and gently blew it.

"Leave them to sleep, they both look really washed out." Anthony nodded.

"Well, I must admit darlings, I agree, Birch was positively moody and very off hand, the girl needs to take it easy. If you ask me, she is burning out, and that bodes ill for all of us. I prefer the happy rested Birch, plus if she does, Abby will melt down, and no one wants that car wreck." Chloe put her chop sticks down, and looked at Edwina.

"What is going on, do any of you know, because there is something happening? Do you think this has anything to do with Katie's lookalike girlfriend, because she was here a few days back, I think Abby called her Anita?" Luke looked up from his bowl.

"Want me to check her out?" Edwina shook her head as she chewed.

"No need I already have, I looked her up after the live event. She actually has an impressive working history, it is a shame she is Katie's girlfriend, she would be a much better promoter for Abby. They are in bed together asleep, so this is nothing to do with Katie, it must be something else." Izzy walked in and headed for the pan.

"It's private, she has had a rough couple of days at work, cut her some slack and let Abby heal her, they will surface when they need to." Chloe turned, and looked down the kitchen towards her.

"Can we help them, I am really worried about them, they have missed meal time, which okay is pretty normal for Abby, but Birch never misses food. Is there something we can all do to help her?" Izzy filled her bowl, grabbed some chop sticks and headed for the table, she sat down as everyone looked at her, she shrugged.

"What?" Chloe rolled her eyes.

"Izzy, you know Birch better than any of us, if she is having a hard time, we want to be there for her, so... What can we do?" She scooped her noodles out of her bowl.

"I told you, let Abby heal her. What she really needs at the moment, is her, nothing more. Abby has always been her main source of comfort, a bad case pushed her out of her comfort zone, and so let Abby remind her of who that is. Trust me, a few good sessions alone in bed and a lot of sleep and she will be right as rain." Edwina gave a nod and she watched Izzy suck in her noodles.

"I hope you have lightened her load; you are practice manager after all?" Izzy smiled.

"Yes, I am, and I have taken steps to protect her, I always have and I always will, trust me Edwina, I love her as much as you guys do." Edwina smiled and nodded.

"Should I take more of the slack off her with the Curio project, I can talk to Aden and Bradley?" Izzy shook her head.

"It is not that sort of pressure she is experiencing, trust me, try it, she will fight to the death for that project. That is Jemi's stepping stone out into the spotlight to follow in her mum's footsteps, and if you ask me, she needs to do it." Edwina gave a sigh.

"Alright Izzy, I trust your judgement, I will sit back, and keep an eye on her."

Chapter 15

New Candidates.

I woke up looking out of the window, at Birch's much larger forever tree, the bed was warm, but not Birch warm. I rolled over to empty sheets, and then saw her large white with black patched pony tail, over by the drawers, and sat up. Birch was sat on the floor with her hair tied back looking at something in front of her on the floor. I yawned, pulled back the duvet, slipped out of bed, and walked up to her.

"What Are you doing?" She turned and looked at me and smiled, I shit myself at the sight of her green face, and jumped back.

"Holy shit Birch!" I felt my heart slightly thump, her face was bright green, and had a strange texture to it, she giggled.

"Hi Sweetie, I am cleaning my pours with a mask, sorry did it scare you?" I could not really understand it, she had perfect skin.

"Birch baby, your skin is the softest and smoothest I have ever seen, you do not have a blemish, you use only natural products. Honestly, you really do not need it, I probably am the one in need, my skin is always flaring up." She gave a big smile.

"Glad you said that, look, I got you one too, I thought it would be fun to both have green faces together, and we do have that book fair thing on Saturday, so we both need to look good." My stomach turned, I had forgotten about that, Katie had arranged for us to appear at the book fair next weekend. I sat down on the floor at her side.

"Wish you had not said that, Katie is really pissed at me, it's going to be horrible." My stomach whined, we had missed our meal last night, and I was in need of food and coffee.

"Can I give it a skip; I am still foggy and need a coffee."

"Sweetie, it will only take a moment, come on, put the mask on and then we will go for coffee, I have not had one yet." I gave a sigh and nodded, she gave a little squeak of a laugh, grabbed the packet, and tore it open.

She slid it out of the packet, and gently unfolded the fine papery mask, she looked at me, and her eyes twinkled in her green face, as she lifted the mask and lined it up with my features.

"Don't move Sweetie, so I can get it on straight."

The mask felt cold as it touched my cheeks, she smoothed it slowly across my face and I closed my eyes. It felt cool and made my face tingle, and the feeling of her finger tips on my face, was so lovely, it felt close and intimate, and was something I had never really thought about. Her finger tips ran across my forehead, down the sides of my face, I gave a happy little moan, and opened my eyes, Birch was smiling at me.

"It is nice, isn't it?" I tried not to smile and wrinkle the mask.

"I like the way you touched my face, it felt intimate, no one has ever done that to me before." Her mask had tiny wrinkles in it.

"I thought we had to keep a straight face?" She nodded.

"We do, I just could not help smiling, so I guess I messed mine up, does it look bad?" I shook my head.

"No not really, can we have a coffee now, I really need one?" She stood up and offered her hand, I took it and followed her, as she headed for the door. We walked into the kitchen and Chloe looked up.

"Yikes, what the fuck is that on your face?" I tried not to smile but failed.

"It's a mask that does a deep clean, and it feels lovely." Chloe frowned.

"You look like you just landed from another planet."

I sat down and she poured us a coffee, Birch leaned on my shoulder, Chloe giggled. Edwina walked in looking at her phone, she looked up from it, she had clearly read something unsavoury.

"Guys, did you know Primula and Sophia are running for Parish Council?" I turned round and looked at her.

"Seriously, why the hell would they run for the council?" Birch leaned back.

"Yike's, bible bashers running the parish, now that is scary, will they be adopting a witch burning ritual, because we may need to move?" Chloe giggled, I turned and looked at her.

"I must admit, I really hate the idea of her in charge, my life was bad enough with Madge." Edwina sat down next to Chloe.

"It looks like Celia has decided to give up her seat, and Phillip Morrison is considering it, as his business has grown, and he wants more time at home." Birch looked at me and winked.

"Maybe we should run Sweetie, this village has really backed your mum, I am sure they would be loyal to you. I mean, let's face it, all of us have been involved with everything they have done, and we did prevent a lot of young people leaving with the Tarts program, and that is still working today?"

I was not that sure, this village had semi accepted me, and that had taken nine years, maybe four years ago when I challenged Marjorie, but I was not convinced I would have much support in the village. I looked at Birch who was looking excited, I knew that face, and it bothered me a lot.

"Birch, I really am not sure people will back us two, there are still a lot of people who are influenced by Madge?" Edwina looked at us.

"Madge is who has given her backing to her, so if we read that right, Prim will rule as proxy for Madge." Birch frowned.

"How popular is Prim, I have never seen her involved in anything, is she popular in the village?" Edwina gave a smirk.

"She is a regular at church and all their activities, so she is well known in those circles. I think from now on, she will appear everywhere. Madge will handle everything behind the scenes, that is probably why the word is out now, it will give them some time to build up a profile and get her well and truly implanted in village life." Chloe lifted the coffee pot and refilled my cup.

"If you guys are running, I will help run your campaigns, Deb's and me can work together, she will be a mum by November, so we can work together while all you lot get on with the job of getting the voters on your side." I was not sure, I looked around the island at all of them, they all looked at me hopefully, which bothered me.

"I want to talk to mum, she has a better idea of everything, she really has a finger on the pulse of things, although, I am sure Celia will endorse you Birch. She fancies you like hell, and she has been a very influential member of the council. I think I will wander round and see mum at the shop later."

Jimmy had finally released his first ever solo album entitled, 'Not Looking,' and so he was off to do a two week promotional tour of the UK, which meant Deb's was coming home, and we were all a little excited about it. I really missed her when she was at home with Jimmy, and so the air today was filled with fun. The great news was, the video download of 'Don't Look' from the Curio Live event had to date, sold over three hundred thousand copies, and it was a real thrill for him, and a great launch pad for the new album.

Deb's bed had been stripped and washed, and we needed to make it up and give her room a quick clean, although to be honest, she always left it spotless, but Birch insisted that we had to do it. Who were we to argue, we wanted her back at home with us, and so once we peeled off our masks, we all got stuck in. Chloe was really excited; she had missed her the most, I think.

We had a small crib boxed, and stored in the attic, Chloe and myself wanted to put it together and put it in her room, but Edwina threw a fit, and ranted on about how it was bad luck, and not to do it until the baby was born, she was pretty scary, so we backed down. It was probably a good thing she did not know about all the baby clothes, nappies and toys Birch and myself had stashed in our wardrobes.

We had been in Oxendale, and I was getting a little carried away in my excitement, and suddenly it kicked in, Birch got really weird and broody. I mean messed up weird, it was actually quite scary, she was like some sort of phantom winter blast breezing through the baby store snatching things off shelves. I watched her holding them up, with bright wild eyes, and making weird awe, like noises, and saying messed up stuff, like 'wouldn't little Abby look cute in this?' I will not deny, it made my uterus quiver with fear.

She spent four hundred quid, and when we got home, I worked it out, in order for Deb's kid to wear all these clothes in the first six months of her life, we would have to change the kid every three hours. When she started looking at baby walkers and cots, I dragged her out, in a mild panic.

Chloe had become just as bad, she spent a day dressed in her dungarees with a pillow stuffed inside them, just so she could empathise with Deb's. I have come to the conclusion, babies are bloody dangerous, they make women go twisted in the head, and all hyper weird and emotional. They start to stare into prams, bobbing their heads, and making weird cooing noises, like a load of mentally unstable budgies. Don't get me wrong I am happy for Deb's, she has always wanted children, but honestly, I don't.

Having lived with Birch for four years, there is one thing I have made note of to serve as future guidance, and that is, if it makes her weird and mentally unstable, avoid it, and babies have been added to that list. I have searched on the internet for a cure, but apparently if any woman alive decides to research babies, the moment they meet one, they lose all their focus and cannot concentrate long enough to do a decent study for a cure, so basically, when the thing is born, I am screwed.

It took a while, but everything was ready, so when the shop closed, Jimmy would drive her round, and we would settle her in. Birch was brimming with joy, and had a whole row of vitamins and herbal teas lined up, which she had been assured by Raven Moon, were all beneficial to women close to birth. Although, I am amazed, I have not caught her sat on her rolled up mat surrounded by candles, getting the gods of the green worlds to bless the bedroom. Mind you, this is Birch, so it could still happen.

Two hours later, and wearing clothing, t shirt, jeans, and denim jacket, I walked towards the village with Birch. She linked my arm as we walked down Manor Road, turned left onto High Street, and walked towards the shops. We had barely made it past the butcher's and Deb's bookshop, when we noticed people handing out leaflets.

Marjorie was outside the Post Office, talking to a group of women, and handing them leaflets, it did not take long to work out why. Prim came out of the Craft Shop, with a bunch in her hand, gave us both a look of disgust, flicked her head, and walked back up the street, Birch glanced at me.

"Wow, she is on the campaign trail early, it was only sent to Edwina this morning, and she has leaflets and everything. Madge is serious about putting her puppet in power."

In a strange way I was not surprised, Madge had been trying

to get back in charge for a long time, and to be honest, I had to admire her game plan. Prim was a new face who had been heavily involved with the church, and mum was an old face, she had been Chair Person for eight years. The Craft Shop had placed the flyer in the window, and the Sweet Shop, although there was no poster in the Florist Shop, it made me smile, hopefully Amanda was supporting mum.

We crossed over the road, and walked across the green towards the gallery. For two years now, mum and Ellen had built up a really great little business. I loved the gallery and how it was laid out, with the walls filled with pictures, and racks of prints available for purchase. Chloe had several pictures on the wall, as did Hatty, but what I loved most, was that mum had seven of her own pictures on display.

The shop had once been owned by Derek Werrington, and had been an antique shop, so at the back was a large warehouse space. Bradley had made some improvements, by opening up the rear shop wall, and putting an office space in.

Both mum and Ellen had desks with their own computers, and whilst Ellen focused on accounts, mum handled the online sales, which she had been taught by Edwina. In the back large open and insulated space, some of the more open and adventurous pictures were displayed, and funnily enough, a lot of them were Chloe's. The gallery featured more sculptures than I had expected, and in the furthest corner of the building, was a small enclosed space, in which was a workshop.

Gavin Sanderson was almost twenty two years old, he studied art and woodwork, and so as a struggling artist, he had turned to his woodwork to stay afloat. You will probably remember Gavin, he was once a young inexperienced painter, who came to Chloe for lessons, he learned a lot that first day. With Chloe over a year, she taught him a lot more, and his pictures were displayed pretty much in the back. His woodwork skills gave him a good little business framing, and he now worked all over Oxendale supplying frames for many artists pictures.

The best thing about the rear of the shop, was it had a coffee machine, and two old sofas', with a coffee table, from one of the houses that Bradley had leased out. Birch and I were regular crashers, and would hang out with mum and Ellen when we had some free time, so today, we walked into the gallery, and headed straight for the back. Ellen was dealing with a customer, a middle aged man, in a very expensive suit. I flopped down as Birch grabbed coffee, mum was sat on the other sofa, she smiled.

"Nice to see you two, is today boring, I normally do not see you Saturdays?" I giggled, were we really that predictable?

"I wanted to talk to you, I take it you have seen Prim has started a campaign?"

She lifted a flyer off the table, and handed it to me, I looked at the large black and white photo, with the words 'Vote for Primula' printed on it. Birch sat down and handed me a coffee, she looked at the flyer.

"God she is an ugly bitch, if that picture does not terrify the whole village into nightmares, nothing will." Mum gave a smirk, she looked at us both.

"That is probably my fault, I was talking to Hatty about possibly stepping out of my role and becoming just an officer, to make way for new blood. I have tried to talk Edwina into running for the chair, she would be so good, and would bring a new lease of life to the council, especially with Anthony as vice. Anyway, I think Phillip who also wants to step down overheard me and told Marion, and now we have Primula Wallace, the church's little goodie two shoes running. I have not even decided yet, and Madge is pushing her into my warm seat." I took a sip of my coffee, and thought for a moment.

"So, you think Edwina would win?" Mum shrugged.

"She is popular, and she has done a lot, although Anthony is also popular, but you cannot rule out the power of Madge, she still has a lot of influence around here. To be honest, Prim's youth is on her side, and Anthony and Edwina are both a little resistant, they enjoy the officer's role." Birch leaned back and relaxed as she looked round at all the erotic pictures.

"Deads and me have thought of running, the problem is, if we both run, we will split the vote, and Prim will win. She has endorsed Sophia as her vice, so the question is, who is most likely to get Chair, and who Vice out of the two of us?" Mum looked at both of us with suspicion.

"You are serious about this, I know you two, this is not a wind up, is it?" I shook my head.

"Nope, we think it is about time one of us did it, I mean, we have always thought we would, and we have been high visibility enough. We have both been involved with every event this village has done for a long time. Chloe wants to run for officer as well, so we could have a Curio council." Birch smiled.

"Be honest Flick, everyone knows what the Curio's can do if they put their minds together. Look at the Tarts program, it has kept a lot of young people here in the village, all we have to do is decide?" Mum looked impressed.

"To be honest, it may sound a little biased, but if you want my opinion, it has to be you Abby. People have a good memory, and the one thing that has cemented itself into everyone's memory, is how you faced out Madge, and confronted her, after giving Peter a rundown of the constitution from memory. You also can never forget the Tea Room incident, a lot of people saw you protect them from that maniac, it all counts. People still talk about it today, because it ousted Madge for good and you two saved lives. Abby, your face on a poster will make them all remember that. Going against Prim, I think you have the better odds of winning." Birch smiled and patted my leg.

"I agree Sweetie, you lead and I will support, I will vote for that."

I was not sure, it had crossed my mind, and I had spoken many times with my mum in the past, but with my writing and my Curio life, I had sort of let the idea go. I looked at them both staring at me.

"It is a lot of responsibility; I would need to plan it out and talk it through to be fully sure." My mum appeared to understand.

"Abby, you cannot do this half heartedly, if you are going to do this, do it with a every intention of doing it well. I cannot support you publicly, because I am sitting chair, but behind the scenes, I can do a lot to help you. Again, Birch has a good reputation, she faced a gun man and protected a lot of villagers, it counts. If you do this, and Birch backs you, I will stay on as an officer, and you will also have Hatty backing you up. But I will also say this, if you intend to run, keep it quiet and prepare behind the scenes, then come out loud and proud, and make an impact. Nominees are not normally named until late July, just before the summer events list comes out, use the time you have to get up to speed, you have Edwina and Anthony to fill you in, and bring you up to date."

It made complete sense, Birch nodded, and took my hand and squeezed it.

"We should sit at home and talk about it, Deb's will be home tonight, she will provide good input as well. Deads, you will not be alone; I will be right behind you."

Nine years ago, when we all campaigned in support of my mum, we were a very effective team, and we all believed my mum would win and Marjorie would lose, and we were right, for that was the outcome. It made huge changes to the way the village improved, and even though the outside of the buildings, and the picturesque look of the place has not changed, within, many things have changed, as modern technology has been embraced to promote this village to a greater area.

Back then, I always assumed I would follow mum, and take up a role on the council when she stepped down, I had learned everything I knew about the council specifically for that reason. As Curio's we had spent four years talking about taking a leading role in the community, so I had to really sit down and work out what exactly we were going to do about it, I leaned back as Birch and mum watched me, and smiled.

"The one thing I know for sure, Prim will want the drinking ban put back, and after three years of longer pub hours, if we promise to keep that, it will play in our favour, and go against Prim. God knows what draconian ideas she has, but if Marjorie is behind her, it will restrict a lot of people's enjoyment of this village. I have faced that alone, and I do not want anyone here to have their lives and freedoms restricted."

Ellen walked in from the shop area, she had been listening, as she finished the paperwork and delivery details of her customer, she sat down next to my mum and smiled at me.

"Abby, it is about time, I have talked to Deb's a great deal, and she has not really understood why you have not run yet. She wants to see you run, she actually thinks that you will add a lot to this community that will balance it, but she also believes you will preserve this village in a way no others will. I really think you underestimate how many people will support you, most people I know will, you should seriously consider running."

I was a little surprised by Ellen, I knew Deb's thought I should run. Every year for a good six years she has always harassed me to run, I just felt the time was not right. Sitting here thinking about it, and having seen Primula out with her mother in law promoting in May, gave me a jolt. I did not want another bigot using their platform to attack me, and if Prim did win, I somehow felt Birch and I would cop for it all. It was not hard to predict that she would focus on the sinners of the village rhetoric. Birch patted my leg; it was almost as if she was reading my mind.

"Ellen Sweetie, the only member of the Curio's that Prim will not attack, is Deb's, because she is married and by the time the election comes, will be a mother. Chloe will be attacked as a slut, for having out of marriage sex, and is a nudist, Anthony because he is a sinner in the eyes of God for his sodomy. The fact that he single handily brought back an amazing Christmas light show, that has doubled tourists to the village, will mean nothing. Edwina was unmasked for her Bi sexuality at the Curio Live event by the press, which in Prim's eyes is sinful, and then there is the soon to be married lesbians. She is going to paint all of us black." I nodded as I looked at Ellen.

"She will be armed by Madge, and she is cruel enough to use them and enjoy it. I have seen all this before, Ellen, you know how cruel they can be. If I decide to run, I will be making myself a very big target, and I will not deny, I will be walking the gauntlet in the run up to the vote." She gave a long sigh.

"I will not deny Abby, I had some rough times, but you have had it ten times harder than even I did. If you do not want to run, I will not hold it against you. If you do, my whole household will back you in any way we can, because honestly, I think you really could shape the future of the village in a way, everyone will understand. I am very sure, Prim will drag it backwards, and it will stifle all of us." Birch got up and headed toward the coffee machine.

"Well, the way I see it, if we do nothing, Prim will drag us all back into medieval hell, and if we do something, she will start a crusade to slay all the sinners. It appears to me that whatever we do we lose, so the only question I want to answer is, what will piss Prim and Madge off more?" Mum smiled, as she watched me.

"I would imagine a long table, with Abby, you, Chloe, Anthony, Edwina, Hatty and me on it, on a stage announcing the Christmas activities for this year. Let's be honest, she is pretty much certain Prim will be up there this year, but there again, she thinks Prim is going against me." She chuckled, and her eyes moved to me.

"Abby dear, her face when she finds out will be wonderful, I really hope I am there to see it."

I turned and Birch was staring at me, her bright green eyes twinkled, as she smiled, I could see the devilishness building inside her, I knew that look and started to giggle.

"You really want to do this, don't you?" Her eyes sparkled.

"We have talked about doing it since I bought the house four years ago Deads, I guess maybe we did not have a good enough reason, but come on Sweetie, we do now." I chuckled as Ellen smiled.

"Oh God girls, I really am getting excited, this could be the best thing this village has ever witnessed."

She was right, I did feel a little more than excited, I sat back and looked around the room, all of them were watching me and smiling, and they all looked eager, I gave a giggle.

"I am screwed up, you know that don't you, because she is going to make our life insane? Look, I want to get married, and get my book finished and ready, so I do not want any announcements before mid July. If we can organise in secret, and keep a lid on this, then yes, I think it is time the young stepped up to start preparing for the future of this village. Mum, promise me, you and Hatty will ride this through with us, because I will need a guide until I learn the ropes." She leaned forward in her seat and patted my leg.

"Abby, I will be at your side for the whole time if you take the chair." Birch gave a squeal, and danced on the spot spilling the coffee.

We sat with mum and Ellen for another hour, but the day was ticking on, and Deb's would be arriving after the shop closed, so we pulled on our jackets and after many hugs, and a promise for silence for now, Birch and myself headed out onto the street.

Marjorie and Prim were still at it, and a few more shops had flyers in the windows, and on their doors, showing their support,

I wondered how many of those would remain up when we made the announcement?

I linked Birch's arm as we walked past the Hunter's Arms, there was one vote we would get, Andrew Bosworth had given Hatty a double whiskey when she got the ordinance rescinded, and he was allowed to move to proper opening hours. Birch was happy and smiled, she chuckled, as we walked along talking quietly, we made it to Manor Road, when my phone rang, I saw 'Dad' on my screen and frowned.

"What does he want?" I swiped it and lifted it to my ear.

"Hello, Dad, is everything alright?"

"Abigail, I am sorry if I am disturbing you, I just wanted to know if you will still be in London next weekend?" I looked at Birch who was leaning in and trying to listen, I shrugged at her.

"I am doing the book fair, although I have a new publicist, and will not get the itinerary until sometime this weekend, but I will be there, why?"

"Well, the thing is, I would like to talk to you, but just you, alone, it is personal. Would you visit me at the flat, so we can speak privately, it is important?" Okay so this sounded weird.

"Dad you are alright aren't you, I mean nothing has happened, has it?"

"Abigail, please, do not worry, it is nothing like that, and if you must know, I have been eating much healthier, and I have reduced my drinking, and I feel much better for it. This is family business and it is important, hence I would like to talk, and it does not involve you spending any money, so relax." Okay, so now I was even more suspicious.

"What day and what time, and why do I have to come alone?" He gave a sigh.

"Abigail, I am sure you can go an evening without being attached at the hip to Jemima, please, come and see me and we will talk." I nodded into the phone which was weird.

"Alright... I will let you know when I am free as soon as I find out, and then we can arrange something."

"Wonderful, I am really looking forward to it, I will have some food arranged, and we will open a bottle of wine. Thank you, Abigail, it will be very pleasant, and I am sure you will enjoy yourself. I will look forward to hearing from you."

"Alright then, I will call you or text soon, bye."

"Good bye Abigail." He ended the call, although he actually sounded quite happy, which in itself was weird, the last time we had spoken, he was all doom and gloom, I looked at Birch.

"What do you think, is it a trap?" She gave a chuckle.

"Sweetie, he said family business, maybe a relative has died and you have inherited their poodles." She gave a snigger, she knew how much I hated poodles, oh God, that would be the worst thing ever.

"Christ that is scary, if I have, you are walking them, I would not be seen dead with one of those poncy yappy shits, they are for old ladies, whose kids have flown the coop and they need something to mother. Yikes, you can be scary." We both giggled as we turned onto Waterside Lane.

When you think about it, life is pretty weird, humanity is obsessed with age, youth and death, and staying young, and I think that is probably because no matter how hard we try to stay young, the world has this funny way of messing with you and forcing you to grow up and age.

Since coming back from Uni, I have lived the life I wanted, and although it has had lots of ups and downs, I have had a lot of fun. I love living with the girls and Anthony, every day is a reason to celebrate, but the crazy thing is, because we run the house and take good care of it, without realising, we have been pushed into being more responsible.

One minute I was nineteen with dyed hair and being shamed for it, and now I am twenty eight, and considering being an even more grown up person, by running for the Parish Council. Nine years have whizzed past, and I had not really noticed, well not in the last four at least, those years in between leaving Uni and Birch's return were not so great, but from the moment she drove into the village, and waved like a lunatic at me, life has been better, but I have shot through the years.

I work out, I eat well, I take my vitamins, and all in hope that I can freeze that nineteen year old, with a small firm butt and petite little boobs in time, so that I can hang onto my youth and not turn into my mum. It is crazy really, we blink, and hey presto, we are all adults. Hell, my best mate from school is about to be a mum, do you see what I mean?

The whole world is living in fear of aging, and running in the fear that it will catch us up too soon, whilst gazing back in the rear view mirror, and hoping youth is not that far behind. I have thought about this a lot, and I have started to realise, that I am actually happier now than I have ever been in my life. I really do feel at ease with myself, which is sort of weird, as I have always been slightly uncomfortable with myself.

I think I am ready to grow up a little more, hell, I am actually marrying Birch, and it looks like I am running for the council, maybe passing age thirty will be less traumatic for me, because I think I am actually looking forward to it.

Chapter 16

Unnatural Talent.

It was nice to have Deb's back. Jimmy dropped her off, and we all hung out in the living room, for a few hours. Later, I headed up to my room and sat at my desk to have some silence, as I went through the messages on my website, and on the Curio site. I was sat reading with a smile, as a fan wrote a wonderful passage about Sanctuary Arch. The door opened and Deb's leaned in.

"Are you busy?" I swung around in my chair and gave her a smile.

"Not very, come in and sit for a while." She gave a little giggle.

"I more wobble than walk now."

She was right, her tummy was really large and round, and she held it as she waddled into the room like a penguin, I could not help but give a snigger.

"The last time someone walked like that in front of me, it was Chloe coming out of my kitchen." She shuddered.

"Oh God, do not remind me, hell Abby, that still gives me the creeps." She waddled to the bed, sat down, and leaned back on her arms, her belly pushed up in front of her, and gave a gasp of relief.

"Oh, you have no idea how much my feet ache."

I will not deny, I have no idea how she feels, I cannot imagine what it is like to grow another human inside myself. It amazes me how her body has changed to accommodate this new growing life inside her, and I really admire her so much. I dragged my legs on the floor to pull my desk chair closer to her.

"I cannot do much, but I can massage your feet if it will help you? God Deb's I am in awe of you, I am not sure I could do this, I really am not. Is it wrong I am so happy and excited for you, but I really do not want to be a parent?" She smiled at me.

"Abby, if I have learned anything from Birch and you, it is that we can all choose how we want to live. If you do not want children, that is fine, it is up to you. Abby, having children is something you at some point, when you are married, the both of you will have to sit down, talk it through, then make a plan of what you want to do. If that does not involve children, that is fine, and right for both of you.”

I grabbed her foot and started to rub it gently, using my fingers to work their way into the soles of her feet, she gave a moan and I looked up.

“You get horny and I am stopping, just so you know.” She gave a giggle.

“You are safe Abby, it just feels nice, and helps them stop aching. Jimmy has been taking care of other needs.” I looked up from her feet.

“Can you still do that, you know with...?” She nodded her head, and rolled her eyes.

“Oh God yes, and it is really different, honestly Abby, I have orgasmed way more like this than I did before. It is really good according to the doctor, and it helps the muscles.”

I was a little surprised, and I will not deny, also a little disturbed, is it me, or does the thought of that... You know... Jimmy’s going in and out near the baby, kind of feel weird and freaky? I frowned as I watched her.

“Do you not worry about hitting it on the head or poking it in the eye?” Deb’s gave a gasp of a laugh, and the whole bed shook as she laughed.

“Abby how long do you think he is?” I did not know, hell, I did not want to. How the hell do you answer that?

“Yeah okay, that makes sense, and honestly, I really do not need to know his dimensions, that is between you two, I think I am happier not knowing.” She gave a giggle.

“I have missed this, I miss being here with you and everyone, I mean, don’t get me wrong, I am really happy Abby, honestly, I am. Since Jimmy took a break from the band, and watching him create music is amazing, I love being in the studio and listening to him play. He is so much better than the critics give him credit for, and after his video from the Curio event has hit big, Abby he is so happy.”

I watched as her face just lit up, and she smiled a huge smile, it made me feel warm inside to see her like this. I was so happy to know that things between them were so good now. A couple of years back I had my doubts, as Jimmy had gone back on his wild groupie streak. It was good to see they had worked it out, and things were better.

"I am really happy his track has done so well, I wish it did not make me cry every time I hear it, I almost crashed Petal when it came on the radio. Honestly, that was sneaky of you, those were supposed to be private emails." She gave a little chuckle.

"So, it has the same effect as your book does on Birch, where have you hid it this time?" I pointed over my shoulder.

"It is behind the pillows on the sofa bed, she always checks under the bed and in the wardrobe, so I figured it would be safe there for a while."

She sat smiling, I was still massaging her foot, so I swapped, and we chatted away happily, just like old times. Deb's slowly relaxed and lay back, I watched her eyes flutter, as she fell asleep, and I lifted the duvet over her. I figured I would let her sleep, she appeared so relaxed and calm, it seemed a shame to move her.

I left her to rest, and headed downstairs, Birch was sat in the kitchen, looking at her laptop talking to Edwina, Chloe was pouring drinks, I leaned over the island and looked down.

"Chloe, do you know your ass is bright blue?" Edwina sniggered, Chloe turned and looked down.

"Yeah, I slid back to get a good perspective again, and this time I sat on the tube of blue. I really need to stop doing it, I got some more great bum prints, I have quite a few prints now, I did think I could sell them on Ebay if I signed them?" I sat back in my seat, and she handed me a drink with a smile, and sat down.

"How is Deb's, I am so happy she is back with us, I have really missed her Abby?" I understood that, I smiled as I lifted my glass.

"I am glad she is back too; I miss her as much as you do, the house feels nicer just having her here, don't you think?" Chloe gave a big smile and nodded.

"I think she should live here with Jimmy, think about it, Luke and Michael live here too, we are like a huge family." I cannot say it was not something I considered before she was married, but she has a whole complex at Bradley's house, which he expanded and remodelled for her.

"Chloe, she has a huge house, it's so big it has its own recording studio in it, seriously you should go and visit her, and have a look, it is pretty impressive." Birch turned to look at us, she gave a big smile and her eyes sparkled.

"I have not seen the studio, when she goes back, we should go visit and help Jimmy, we could be his backing singers, like we do on the karaoke." I looked at her and frowned.

"Birch baby, we scream more than we sing, seriously it is like dying cats, I thought you wanted him to make it as a solo artist?" She blew me a kiss.

"I can sing like an angel when I want to." Chloe turned, and stared at her.

"Really, to be honest Birch, I have heard your Pat Benatar impression, and honestly, it is time to retire the mic."

Edwina burst into laughter, I must admit I could not help giggling, at the look on Birch's face. I blew her a kiss, I am quite sure she had no idea how bad she was, and I was starting to think, she thought she was good.

The living room was rowdy, it was Saturday night, and the boys had decided to have a games night, and so armed with beer and snacks, they took over the living room, plugged the consoles into the large flat screen TV, and took each other on. I was heading to the library, but stopped to lean on the doorframe and watch for a moment.

I really love the way Anthony, Michael and Luke get on. It is so nice for Anthony, and even though he has a flair for the more dramatic approach to life, I could see him as more of the boy that sat in my guest house all those years back. Around us, he was more confident, and he definitely had lost many of those ticks he had, that made him twitch and jump.

Although watching him as he tried to avoid getting shot, was hilarious, as his arms would move off to the right or left suddenly, as he made dramatic squeals. I really loved Anthony a great deal, he was sharp and witty, and maybe at times a little annoying, but he was also an amazingly good friend, and possibly one of the kindest people I have ever known.

I love how calm he was around the guys, and how he lost a little of his outside personality, he was just himself, and sadly so few got to see that side of him, he had such a lovely and infectious giggle, he made me smile.

So few at school saw that, so few in this village see that, and it is such a shame. Anthony understands bullying in ways none of us ever will. He has seen a lot of cruelty, and even though he hides it well, he still carries the pain of it all within him. Most of his ticks developed in school, as a direct result of teachers who did little to help him, I often wonder if those very teachers have ever seen his videos on the Curio site, I hope so, and I hope they feel guilty.

I gave a smile, and turned into the library, and walked slowly round to my desk, and sat down. My inbox showed I had emails on my task bar, so I clicked it open, and found a message from Anita. She wrote a quick note about how she was looking forward to the weekend, and explained how Roni, had given her full control of all press, which I was really happy about.

There was an attachment that had been sent her by Katie, and I opened it up to see the itinerary, it was going to be a busy day, but the good news was that Roni, and the other authors, would be down for the weekend. The room booked was a double, I had half expected a single, because I am very aware of Katie's feeling towards me at the moment, and deep down inside, I cannot deny, I was more than a little worried about what she could do.

Birch appeared and sat at her computer, she opened a file and started to type, and would stop occasionally to read what she had written, give a little nod and then continue. I love to watch her face as she writes, I really like the way her eyes twinkle, and how she smiles to herself, happy with what she has written. I sat back and just watched; Birch gave a little smile.

"I can feel you watching me Deads, stop it." I gave a giggle.

"I remember watching you from my bed at Uni, I would wake in the night, and just lie on my pillow watching you work late through the night, to finish your papers. I guess I just love watching you work."

She stopped typing and turned, her eyes sparkled with green fiery life, set against the background of her long white patched hair, she looked intensely beautiful, and I felt my heart give a little flutter.

"I love to watch you too, but Sweetie, I find it distracting when I should be focused on this, I start having thoughts about you." I raised my eyebrows.

"Thoughts... What kind of thoughts?" She giggled.

"Will you just stop, I cannot have those things in my head, I want to finish this?" I leaned forward in my seat, and tried to lean over the side of my chair to see her screen.

"What are you working on anyhow?" She clicked her mouse and looked at me, and went very cagey, I frowned.

"Okay, so I am really intrigued, what are you up to, I know that look, you are hiding something?" She shook her head.

"I am not up to anything, it's just a work thing." I narrowed my eyes.

"You are a terrible liar, and it does not suit you, come on, spill. I want to know what you are up to?" Was it me or was she starting to slightly unravel, and then gave a nervous giggle?

"Deads, I am not up to anything." I gave a big grin, as I moved further forward in my seat.

"Oh, you are so looking guilty at the moment, Birch, I know you, I know that face, you are definitely doing something you do not want me to see. I want to know, so come on show me, prove your innocence Dr Dixon." She started to giggle; I knew it.

"Deads, I don't want to show you, it is secret."

Oh, right, well that has really got me going, this was a person who had no secrets and often boasted about what you see is what you get, her giggling was getting faster. She was as guilty as shit, and in the process of mischief making. I had to know, there was no going back now.

"Okay, so that is a yes I am misbehaving, cough up Doc, you are well and truly busted."

I got out of my seat and she gave a wild giggle, and reached in to turn her screen off as she laughed. I grabbed her wrist and pulled it back from the button, and she gave a wild squeal.

"Deads please…. DON'T!"

I looked at the screen, still holding her wrist as the layout of hundreds of pages of a document were on the screen. I looked closely, as she giggled, and tried to pull her wrist from me.

"Birch… Is this a book… Have you written a book?" Her giggles stopped, and she looked embarrassed, and put her head down. I let go of her wrist and crouched down level with her desk.

"I have been working on it for a long time, and doing research, I am not sure it is good enough yet." I looked at her and smiled.

"I want to read it, what is it called?" She looked really nervous.

"It is not a story book, it is a study of the negative reactions to the emotional and mental cruelty inflicted through bullying and shame, by people who live a fake life, and the many different ways we can change society to heal." I was really impressed and grabbed her hand, and softly squeezed it.

"Birch, I am delighted, you finally moved forward with your plans to replicate your mum, oh wow, I am so proud of you at the moment, I thought you would never do it. What is it called?"

"The Sham of Shame." I leaned forward and kissed her softly, and then pulled back so her eyes looked really huge.

"I love that you finally wrote a book, and I am definitely going to read it." Her eyes filled with tears, and they sparkled like jewels.

"Deads, I am so nervous, what if everyone hates it, what if you and the guys hate it?" I just stared into her eyes and smiled.

"I would not worry about that; I would worry about whether or not Chloe and me will even understand it. You know, you are on a level that is way beyond us in this subject? Birch, I do not care if I understand it or not, I want to hold a book you wrote, and turn every page, and read every line, because you wrote it, that is all that matters to me." She gave a slight nod.

"Yeah, I get that, and I would really love that, I really would Deads. The truth is, I am terrified, everyone has read my mums books, what if mine are not good enough?"

I had to smile; she has no idea how much I fell apart once I had submitted my manuscript. I became instantly insecure, and went into a full blown panic, and then my sales tanked, and I went into a full on depression. Honestly, publishing is so scary, there are days when I wish I had never done it. I watched her eyes, and smiled, and I remembered a phone call long ago.

"Birch, answer me one question." She blinked.

"If I can Sweetie."

"Have you given this book everything you have got, you know, have you put your heart and soul into it?" She smiled, and tilted her head to one side.

"Why does that sound familiar?" I stroked the hair from her face.

"You asked me the same question when I sent my first book off, and I told you I had done the best I could at that time. Birch, I know you; I know you would have given this everything, and you are so good at this stuff, I think this will be the start of something wonderful for you." She swallowed hard and took a deep breath, and nodded.

"Yeah, I am just over thinking everything aren't I?" I kissed her nose, and gave her a big smile.

"Publish it, and stand proud no matter what happens, Birch, you have to believe in yourself, you have to trust your instincts, because they are really good and have guided all of us here to good things. Look at the retreat, how many people have benefited from your centre? You have to trust that this book will help many, not the critics, those who actually see a change in their lives." I stood up, and moved back to my seat.

"I want to read it, the moment it is finished."

Chloe wandered in with a stack of papers, and stood by the long table, and started to sort them out, I clicked open another email, and watched Birch. I said nothing, I could see she was a little more edgy with Chloe in the room, and got the impression she did not want to let anyone know yet, I winked, and then opened an email to read.

I began to read through each email, and respond where needed, Birch closed her file and stretched. She stood up and walked over to Chloe, who had laid out all her pile of paper, which were actually the sketches of her work for the Hand of Death books. Birch lifted one up and looked at it.

"Wow, this is so good, is this Willis?"

My ears pricked up, and I glanced over the screen, Birch was holding a picture in her hand, she saw me looking and turned the picture.

"Isn't this good Deads?"

I had never seen it and got out of my seat, and walked around the computer station to the table. The picture Birch was holding was brilliant, it was exactly like I imagined Willis, I looked at the table full of pictures, all of them relating to my stories.

"Chloe, why have you never shown me these?" She shrugged as she watched me.

"When you asked for a cover picture, I sketched loads of things, and then I picked the one I like the most and showed it you, these are all the ones I don't think are good enough for a cover." I was lost for words.

"You are kidding right, these are brilliant?"

I looked at all the pictures, with the Arch, and Gabrielle, and her evil priest father, they really were amazing. Chloe looked nervous as I picked each one up, and looked at them.

"You gave me PDF copies, and I read them all a lot of times, and these are pictures I saw in my head." I glanced up at her.

"Chloe, I love all of them, you have no idea how happy I am seeing these, you are so talented, you really have no idea how good you are. Honestly, the fact that my books inspired you to draw these, is a little overwhelming, I really love them, and I think people should see these." She frowned.

"What, like put them on your web site?" I shook my head.

"No Chloe, I think you should do an exhibition or something like that, you know, frame them and hang them on the walls of a gallery, and let the public see them." She gave a slight giggle.

"Abby you are nuts, no one wants to see pictures I have sketched, I only sell paintings because Ellen and your mum hunt down people who might buy them, honestly, I am not that well known." I gave her a big smile.

"Maybe not, but I am, and if we do it together, people will come. Chloe, I have a lot of readers, and if I rave enough on my web site about these pictures, people will want to see them."

Edwina came running down the stairs and looked into the library, she gave a gasp and looked mildly panicked.

"We have a leakage alert." At first, I did not quite understand, Birch was stood at my side, Edwina looked at me then Birch.

"It's really fucking scary; we even have a tissue circle." Birch put down the picture, and gave a sigh.

"I will deal with it, where is she?" Edwina turned and looked back up the stairs.

"In her room, I looked in when I heard her weeping, saw the book, panicked and came straight down here." Chloe nodded.

"Yeah, good move, I am telling you, that book is not to be trusted, it's cursed." Birch walked out of the library, and headed up to Deb's room. I gave a long sigh.

"It is not cursed; it is just something very deep and heartfelt from me to Birch. I knew it, I knew she would find a way to con me." Chloe was not budging.

"Abby she is pregnant, and alone with that book bawling her brains out, I am telling you, that is not a normal book, she will probably drown the baby." Edwina shook her head.

"Chloe, that is a little unlikely, her baby is growing in liquid, what do you think that huge belly she has is?" Chloe, was resolute.

"That kid is vulnerable, whatever happens to the mother has an impact on the child, I read that in one of her baby books. Just you wait, if that kid comes out Emo, I am blaming you Abby, because you wrote the fucking thing." Edwina gave a chuckle.

"Emo... Seriously Chloe, she has had the book for what, a couple of hours max, I seriously doubt that is enough exposure to turn the kid into a manically depressed goth. Look at Birch, she has read it loads of times?" Chloe looked at me.

"Yeah, she has, and she has been way weirder than when she first started. Abby, that book is cursed, and you know what, you just sent Birch up there alone, to an already bawling Deb's, they are probably planning a suicide pact about now." Edwina suddenly looked panicked.

"Oh fuck, she is right." I felt my heart lurch inside my chest.

"SHIT!"

Edwina and myself ran up the stairs at high speed, and almost collided as we cut the corner at the top of the stairs. We flew down the hallway and burst in through Deb's bedroom door. I came to an unsteady halt, as I saw Birch and Deb's, sat on her bed hugging each other with the book open between them. Both of them were bawling like babies as Birch nodded in agreement, and sobbed.

"I know... I know Deb's, it's just too beautiful." She burst into a loud wail, and buried her head in Deb's shoulder, as Deb's gave a violent sob, and patted Birch on the back.

"You are so right, it's just too beautiful." She pushed her head into Birch's shoulder and bawled her brains out just as loud, and the two of them just hugged, bawled, and sobbed, to be honest, it was pretty pathetic.

Edwina edged slowly towards the bed, and reached out her arms and spoke softly with great care. It was almost like she was approaching a wild feral animal in a trap.

"Maybe that is enough reading for tonight guys, you look like you could use a break?"

She took the book gently in her hands and closed it, and then withdrew very slowly, so as not to alert them, both of them just carried on wailing into each other, it was pretty pitiful to watch.

It probably sounds crazy, but I was starting to actually think Chloe has a point. All I had wanted was to make Birch happy, but every time she read it, it destroyed her, and now my best friend Deb's, had been hit with the curse. Was there really no one who could read this bloody book without turning to mush? I turned to Edwina.

"Hide it where they won't find it."

She gave a quick nod, and scarpered, before they noticed the book was gone. I gave a long sigh and backed away. I figured it would be best to let them cry it out, and then they could clean up the large white circle of tissue.

I came out of the room and walked to the stairs; Chloe was stood at the bottom looking up.

"Did you get it, are they safe?" I gave a frustrated sigh, and nodded.

"Chloe, it is just a fricking book, stop being so terrified of it." She shook her head vigorously.

"Laugh all you like; I am right about it. Abby, you need to take that to the church and hide it in the crypt, and then put a circle of salt round it, that is three people now affected by it." I reached the bottom of the stairs and gave her a funny look.

"Three?" She nodded at me.

"Yeah three... You watch, that kid will be drawn to black, it would not surprise me if it does not try chucking itself out of the crib. She is going to have an Emo baby, you watch, I just hope it's not a boy, because if they call it Damián, I am leaving the country." I felt a cold chill run down my spine, and goose bumps came up on my arms.

"Pack it the hell in Chloe, you are starting to freak me out, it's a love story, well actually it's a love letter to Birch, our love would never hurt a child." She just stared at me and spoke in a quiet, serious, and somewhat spooky voice.

"Well, we will see, won't we?" I swallowed hard and looked back up the stairs, she touched my arm and I jumped.

"I say the sooner that kid is christened and purified in the holy water, the better."

I actually nodded, to be honest, it was a good idea, you know, just in case?

Chapter 17

Set Up.

For most of Sunday, I sat in the garden as Birch did a little more work on her new flower bed. Deb's sat out with us and told me about how much she loved the book, and how she wanted to read it, I wasn't falling for it. The book was hidden where even I would not find it, and to be honest, I was happy about that.

It was fun being outdoors, and with all of us out there, and a happy banter between us all, I spent the day relaxing and laughing. Sunday ended and it was back to normal. The week ticked by, in a week of intense work. I pretty much lived at my computer, with Deb's wandering in and out, or sitting on my bed chatting as I wrote. I was happy to add a good stack of chapters to my new book.

I prepared behind the scenes, had several conversations with Anita and Birch, and sat around with Deb's trying to sort out what clothes I should wear. Deb's was really into the sultry sexy goth look, and had no problem picking out clothing that showed a good view of my small yet beautifully round breasts.

It was finally Saturday, and I had to get up early, to dress quickly, quaff coffee, and then with our overnight bags, jump in the limo. I was very happy to see Markus the driver, I had not seen him in over a year. The last event we did, I had a guy called Scott, and he was very dull and serious, so when I saw Markus, I gave him a huge smile, he appeared pleased to see us both too.

We jumped into the limo, poured a couple of drinks, sat back and chatted. Birch was excited because her mum would be at the event with her dad, and so for her, she got some much needed family time. We arrived before we knew it, and so it was glasses on, parasol at the ready, and the limo pulled up, and I stepped out and was steered by Birch, straight to the fans, avoiding the press.

It is odd that only a few years ago, I had never really understood the joy of meeting fans, but these days, it was one of my most favourite things to do. Stepping out to hear the screams of people who have read your book, and want to meet you. I cannot deny, I get the giggles and smile like an idiot. We had been there just a few minutes, when one fan, a woman aged about twenty five, called Julie, handed me a small wrapped gift, she had a huge smile, and was very excited.

"I hope you do not mind, I have been here five hours, and I am so happy for you both, this is a little wedding present. You guys are so wonderful, you have done so much good for us all, and my girlfriend had to work and could not be here, so I came alone. We both wish you every happiness, and hope you are happy forever." I was lost for words as I looked at Birch, she was all smiles and leaned into me, and slipped her arm round me.

"Julie that is so sweet of you and your girlfriend, we will save it and open it on the day, thank you, this means a lot to Abby and myself." I nodded to her.

"Tell your girlfriend a huge thanks, I will post a picture on the web site when we open it for you." She was so happy and bouncing on her toes.

"We all love you guys, and I love your books so much, I am so excited for the next one." I could not help giggling, these fans have no idea how happy it makes me to talk with them.

"I am almost finished, I have written a huge chunk of it this week, so not much longer, I am trying to get the book finished before our wedding."

I had to go, but I really wanted to just stand and talk to her all day. I made my way along the line of fans, signing books and having pictures taken, behind us the press shouted and screamed at us.

Finally, we made it in through the doors and were met by Anita, this was Birch's first time actually meeting her in person, she shook her hand and called her Doctor Dixon. Seeing them side by side, there was clearly no similarities, Katie must be in need of glasses, because Birch is so much more attractive than her.

We were taken to our room, it was basic, but a nice room, Anita told me we had an hour before we would be going down to the floor of the complex, to the Dixon Group stand. I was wearing flared purple pants, with a long deep purple velvet top, Birch was in all black, and we looked pretty cool. We had coffee and chatted about the fans, until it was time to move to the conference floor.

The book hall was amazing, it was like dying and going to book nerd heaven. I was in a room bigger than an aircraft hangar, filled with publishers and books. We passed a stand, and the smell, oh God, the smell of new books, it was glorious, and I was intoxicated. The Dixon stand was huge, Roni was stood smiling as she spoke to both the trade and public, Katie was not far away smiling.

Her face dropped when she noticed us walking towards the stand, I felt myself tense up, Birch took my hand and squeezed it. We stepped into the stand and Roni gave a huge smile and pulled me into a hug, Katie threw her arms round Birch.

"Howdy, you old slapper." Birch smiled.

"You know me, I am fine, how about you, slag?" I stepped back from Roni, and saw Katie holding her tight, Roni took my hand and pulled me back towards the back of the stand.

"Ignore it Abby, she wants to get a rise out of you, come on, I will show you what we are doing here."

I understood, and noticed how she completely blanked Anita, I waved her over to us. Roni and Anita explained how from the stand we could sign books, promote other Dixon Group published books and authors, and talk to the trade. It seemed simple enough, smile, chat in a friendly way, and hand out business cards. Anita stayed close to give me support, Birch teamed up with her mum.

It was a lot of fun, fans came up and asked for autographs, I sold more books and listened to fans theories about where the series would go, and I was happy that they were all wrong, what I had written was nothing like what they expected.

We took a break at lunch, other authors would be taking the stand, and in the afternoon, I was booked with Roni, on a panel for writers. Will joined us for the meal, and we all sat round and talked about the wedding, sadly Will had been sworn to secrecy about our dresses, and Birch and myself tried. We giggled as we both failed, and Will laughed at us both. That is the problem with being surrounded by psychologists, they read you way too fast, and have the road blocks built ready to put in place, and your attempts to gather facts fail.

Roni had a rule about no drinks before an event, and so at the table there was no wine, and to be honest, I could have really used one. I was a little unsettled about the oncoming panel, I have never done one before, I have not even met the other authors from the Dixon Group. I know of them, even read a few of their books, especially Juliet Samson's, because she writes great female warrior novels, Deb's has a lot in her shop. The only good part of all this was Roni would be up there with me.

With the meal over, we headed back into the arena, where Anita took us to the hall where the seats were full, and the stage was set with a row of comfy chairs, set in an arc, with small tables with bottles of water on them.

I stood in the wings with Anita and Birch, Roni would be entering from the other side of the stage. I felt a little panicked, and nervous, but that was pretty normal, I always felt this way before an appearance. I had a face mic fitted and tested, and was waiting for the moment when I was told to go on. Birch took my hand.

"It will be alright Sweetie, just go on, be yourself, smile and try to enjoy it."

I nodded as I looked into her bright green eyes, she leaned forward and kissed me softly on the lips.

"I will be right here watching, and we have a bucket, okay?"

I took a deep breath, on stage the host of the organisation who was called Brenda, was making the introductions. She called the names of all the guests.

"Please welcome to the stage, Camilla Wanton, Romance novel writer, Dr Veronica Dixon, self help and awareness writer, Henry Royce, murder novelist, Juliet Samson fantasy author, Abigail Jennifer Watson, gothic horror author." Birch patted my bum and kissed my cheek, and I walked onto the stage, Brenda continued.

"And in a slight change to our program, a very well known personality, actor and literary critic, James Deakins."

The audience were all stood on their feet applauding, I walked onto the stage, as I headed for my allotted seat, but the mention of James Deakins started my heart beating, I saw Roni turn to the wings, where Katie stood smiling and clapping. On the opposite side of the stage, a grey haired slightly balding old man walked towards the seats.

He was wearing a small deep red bow tie, a white shirt and black pants, and looked at us all over his glasses, in a posture of supremacy. I hated him pretty much from every shitty thing he had written about my books, but seeing him, I hated him even more. Birch gave a gasp, as she realised who it was.

"Oh shit!" Anita frowned.

"What is a matter?" Birch watched as I sat down trying my best to smile.

"James Deakins hates Abby's work, he has assassinated every book she has written." Anita gave a frustrated sigh, and looked right across the stage where Katie was smiling.

"What a bitch, she did that deliberately to get pay back, oh Christ Jemi, what do I do?" Birch stood watching, as all the guests sat down and settled into their seats, she could see how uncomfortable I was.

"All we can do now is hope that he pisses her off enough for that stubborn dark little beastie streak to appear. His arrogance might just be his undoing."

I felt exposed, as I sat looking out at the audience as they settled down. There were fans from all the authors present, who appeared eager to hear what we all had to say. The lights were down, but I could see at least six rows of people, to my left three seats down, Brenda was all smiles and chatting to the audience, about the high standard of the guests on stage. Camilla puffed up with pride, James Deakins scowled at me from the furthest seat opposite, and I felt my pulse rate increase. Brenda turned in her middle seat and looked at me.

"Abigail, you are our youngest author here, how does it feel to be in such well renown company?" I swallowed hard, why did she pick on me first? I could see the smirk on Deakins face, he noted my discomfort.

"Honestly... It is a little intimidating, I am a big fan of Juliet's books, and Camilla is an icon to all of us, as is Henry. I am just glad I know Roni, but I do feel really privileged to be here amongst such inspirational company." Juliet who was next to me, gave a really nice smile.

She was nothing like I expected, she had very short hair, dark eyes, and for her age, she looked a lot younger. She wore a thick heavy suede skirt, and high boots, and a thin woollen jumper. Her face was kind, and her smile soft, as was her voice, it had a gentle tone to it, and I warmed to her immediately.

"You should hold your head high Abby, I have read your books, and I love them, you know gothic horror is a difficult genre to write, and yet you have singled handily revived it, that is no mean feat."

I smiled, wow, I really love this woman's books, I am such a fan girl of hers, and she has read my books too, I was as happy as I could be. Deakins scowled at me, and scoffed, I felt a shudder run down my spine.

"Where in the hallowed halls of real writing would you say fantasy and gothic has a place? It is just popular mass market fodder, which requires little of the real craft of writing."

My moment of joy died, as I felt a pang of panic run into me, Camilla turned to him, she was very conservative looking, with her tweed jacket and matching skirt. She had a long silk scarf wrapped round her neck, below her heavily powdered face.

"Oh really James, have we not heard enough of your outdated and practically medieval jibes about modern books? I hate to point it out, but it is young people like Abigail that will carry the torch for all of us oldies into the modern age, you really need to lighten up?" Brenda looked lost for words, unsure of what to say, Deakins looked appalled.

"Are you telling me Camilla, that lewd and crude smut, Seeds of Summer, and that other drivel Shoots of Summer, is the future of writing? This is the problem with literature today, it's people like her, with that kind of garbage that is killing the book market."

I felt my heart beating, I had to say something, I could not let Camilla defend me in front of my fans. I really felt nervous and afraid, but knew that somehow, I had to find a little of the courage of my characters. I took a deep breath, and looked into his eyes, from across the stage, trying to keep my voice calm and collected.

"If my books are such garbage, why have I sold so many, and

why are there fans here today celebrating them?" Birch gave a smile and looked at Anita, as the audience erupted with applause.

"She is warming up, just wait for little miss dark beastie to come out and get all smart arse about it?" Anita looked panicked, but Birch simply smiled.

"God, she is so sexy when she is pissed off." Deakins scowled, and gave a light snigger, his contempt for me was clearly visible.

"You may have sold books young lady, but that does not mean any serious reader has read your books of lesbian and gays and their sordid antics."

Camilla gave a gasp, she looked at me as if to say are you going to put up with that? I lifted a bottle of water off the table, and felt the anger growing inside me, but in my head, I kept telling myself, don't lose it Abby, do not let him goad you. I unscrewed the cap, as I stared at him, not allowing him the pleasure of trying to rattle me. I was rattled, I was actually panicking, but I was also angry. I took a breath as Camilla watched me, she gave a nod, as if to say, you tell him girl.

"I do not just have lesbian and gays, I also have bi sexual and straight people living their lives, and yes, that includes sex. I wrote those books based on real life, about situations I know happened, they are more truthful and honest than anything you have ever written about me." Henry who to date had said nothing gave a little titter, Deakins stared at me like he despised me.

"Your crude style, and your lazy attempts at description go against every recognised style in the craft of writing, and as for the content, I find it unoriginal, uninspiring, and lacking in facts that even remotely resemble real life."

Okay, this guy was really pissing me off, he was insulting me, and everyone on the Curio site I had spoken to that had struggled. Juliet leaned forward in her seat to look him in the eye.

"That is a little below the belt James." I shook my head, and reached out and patted her arm, she turned to look at me.

"Juliet, it is alright, I am used to this from him, although I am glad to see that he could not form such an opinion, without reading each of the books cover to cover." I looked right at him, and tried to stifle my anger, I really wanted to walk across the stage and slap his smug face.

"I stand by every word I wrote as real and true to life, and I have had a lot of people in the LGBT community reach out to me and thank me for showing an honest representation of their lifestyle, and the persecutions they have faced. You know James, considering the scandal you found yourself embroiled in some years ago, I would have thought you more than most, would understand my work?"

I saw his face redden as everyone looked at him. In the wings Birch gave a happy little squeak, and bounced up and down, Anita looked gob smacked as they say up north. Deakins looked outraged.

"My private and personal life are irrelevant young lady; we are talking about your works of fictional filth."

I sat back, and gave him back a slight smirk, in my head I said to myself, 'take that you pompous shit.' I felt an inner calmness wash into me, and I breathed out, I picked my words carefully and kept my gaze fixed upon him.

"I do not agree with you, yes, my books are written from a fictional point of view, but they reflect real life, and as for personal, my work is immensely personal to me, I take it very seriously. I have addressed important issues in the LGBT community, and I support that community, as I do you. I have no issue with two consenting males having sex, I have a house mate who is a delight to live with, and he is one of the nicest people I know. Sex has no bearing on character, I really do not know why the press thought that what you did, or tried to do with your nephew, who was after all twenty two at the time, and enjoying being pleasured, so scandalous."

The whole panel gasped and looked horrified, except Roni, she just smiled facing the audience. Deakins looked like he was fit to explode, he leaned forward in his seat, and went red in the face, his voice showed his anger and outrage.

"You are a disgrace to the writing profession with the filth you write, and as for your so called gothic revival, cobbling together a genre which has been worked to death, has left you nothing even remotely original to say. I resent your accusation Miss Watson, unlike you, I have a life of morality and honourability, I have not been seen with a whore in an airport."

Oh shit... Yeah that was not the smartest thing to say, Roni snapped her head round.

"I will advise you Mr Deakins, you are talking about my daughter, and you are well within striking distance. You would be well advised to apologise to me straight away, I will not tolerate your attack on my family." Her eyes burned with malice, and he looked at me and then back to Roni.

"You are that Doctor Dixon?" She glared at him, her green eyes burning, her voice snapped back instantly.

"I am indeed." He looked worried.

"To you Doctor Dixon I will apologise, but I will not sit here and be insulted by that talentless young upstart." Juliet looked at him, and casually flicked her hand.

"Why not, it is what you have been doing to all of us for years, why can we not have a right of reply? I must admit, you have written some pretty nasty stuff about my work, and you have sat in judgement of every one of us at some point. I think you were especially insulting to all of us, and yet you do not like it when the tables are turned? Abigail is well within her right to point out known facts that are a matter of public record. As I seem to remember you pointed out a great deal about her private life in that hatchet piece you wrote in the Times, about Sanctuary Arch. May I point out, Abigail is on the best sellers list, where exactly are you?"

I heard another little squeak from behind me, and smiled, Birch was loving this, Brenda tried to regain some sort of control, as she looked round, trying to find the right words. She would make like she was going to say something, then stop, and try to think of something else. Although the audience was loving every minute of it. I felt a lot better, my nerves had completely gone, and I felt I was sat with friends, well they were defending me so that was a good thing. Roni smiled at Deakins.

"You know James, I sense a lot of pent up and repressed hostility within you. My daughter is an exceptionally talented therapist specialising in sexual therapies. I am sure her counselling specialist Colin would really help you come to terms with your sexuality, and it is not that far from where you live." He turned on her looking furious.

"MADAM, I AM NOT GAY, AND I DO NOT NEED THERAPY!" Roni smiled.

"If you say so James, but I think you may find some help there, you should consider it, it is called Sweetie's Retreat, and it is based in Wotton Dursley." Brenda looked round us all with a terrified expression, and finally plucked up the courage to speak.

"I think we need to find calmer waters to continue in." Deakins stood up, and tore at his microphone, as he ripped it out from within his shirt, and struggled, which just enraged him more.

"I find this group unpalatable, and I will not sit here and be insulted." Roni gave her head a nod.

"I do not blame you, after all that is what you have done for years, it is strange that you feel victimised, I do find that somewhat curious. I feel this has been a good moment for some personal growth James." He stormed off the stage, and the whole audience stood up and applauded, Roni sat back, looked at me and winked.

Brenda flustered, and grabbed a bottle of water, she took a large swig and tried to recompose herself, until the audience settled down. Anita watched stood at the side of Birch.

"She can be a little bit of a fire cracker, are you sure you want to marry her, she could be dangerous to be around?" Birch gave a giggle and glanced at her.

"I am far worse than Abby, she is the calm one of the two of us, I wanted to walk over there and beat the shit out of him with his chair." Anita looked at her.

"What the hell have I gotten myself into?" Birch gave a chuckle.

"She is a pussy cat most of the time, but never underestimate her." Anita looked across the stage, where in the wings on the other side, Deakins agent was giving Katie a good dressing down, Deakins was nowhere to be seen.

"I can see that Jemi, trust me, I never will."

With calm finally restored, Brenda managed to get the stage back to order, and the panel continued. Brenda started with Roni, and what the experience of writing factual books was like, and moved onto romance, then crime, it felt like she was avoiding Juliet and myself, but finally she got around to fantasy, and then the actual experience of writing.

I enjoyed this part, it was wonderful listening to the others as they described their own private writing routines, and I jumped in a few times to either agree or question aspects of the way they worked, and to be honest, I was a bit disappointed when it came to an end. Brenda stood up and thanked us all, and the audience rose to their feet with loud applause, all of us stood up and gave a bow, and then we walked off the stage. Birch was all smiles and dragged me into a hug and almost crushed me.

"You were superb, I was so proud of you Sweetie." It felt nice, as I watched Anita smiling at me, she winked.

"You did great, you stood up for your work, and defended yourself wonderfully, although I am sure, his next write up will be far worse."

Birch released me from her strangle hold, I stood back with a smile, as she took my hand, her eyes dancing with delight.

"I think we need a drink, what say we hit the bar? You too Anita, come on, the drinks are on me."

I slipped my arm around her, and with Anita at my side, all three of us headed out of the hall, and headed for the bar, where Roni was waiting sipping a large gin. She smiled and pulled me into a hug.

"I am very proud of you, Abby it is about time you had a chance to give your point of view, and you did wonderfully, you controlled yourself, and he did not, well done you." I gave a long breath out.

"My heart was pounding in my chest, I was afraid when he first spoke at me, and was not sure what to do, I am so glad Juliet was on stage with me, I must find her and thank her."

We found a table, and all sat down, Will joined us and I sat back and relaxed, I still felt shaken, and I was still angry, I had seen Katie's face, and I felt she was responsible. She knew how much I hated him; she knew the horrible things that he had said about me, and she also knew, he was the one person, who would get at me the most on stage.

Anita sat close to me and leaned in as Birch talked to her mother.

"Give me a few minutes after to talk, I really am sorry that happened, but it will not happen again, I will make sure of it. Abby, I absolutely aim to protect you and serve you to the best of my ability, I will be putting in a complaint to Roni, and asking that I screen all guests set to meet with you. I honestly did not know, if I had, I would have stopped that. And by the way, Jemi is really lovely, she really was in your corner, you should be grateful she did not walk on stage and assault him, for a moment I was getting ready to drag her back away from the stage. She really loves you Abby, ignore Katie's mind games." I nodded understanding her.

"I am glad I picked you Anita, I feel more at ease than I have in the past. I should have known better, I have worked with her long enough, and I knew she would do something to get even. I noticed when I got a down graded room, and then him slipped in at the last minute, it was a mistake to think she might just let go and walk away. I guess we all learn from our experience, but I have taken note of this." Anita smiled and lifted her glass.

"How about we chalk this one up to experience, I too have a lot to learn, so let's drink to learning together."

I lifted my glass and they chinked together, and I felt that this could be the start of something positive. I had the chance to just be me, and had Anita, who was happy to go along with me, and it felt good. Birch broke away from her mum and leaned over to me, I smiled as I looked in her eyes.

"I am so glad you are here with me, although I do feel a little guilty about my dad not inviting you. Will you be okay whilst I am gone?"

She leaned over and hugged me, and pulled me into a soft kiss, I felt her soft warm lips and just melted into her. She broke free and I opened my eyes, she was there with those gloriously green eyes, surrounded by that long snow white hair with black patches, her face soft and kind, filled with care, and I felt a little shy, my voice dropped to a soft whisper.

"I love you Birch; I love you with all my heart." Her eyes twinkled, and she smiled, revealing soft lines below her eyes.

"I love you too Sweetie, I always will, you are my Lillian." I gave a happy smile.

"I will always be your Lillian... You are going to be alright tonight aren't you, I hate having to go, I would much rather stay here and curl up with you. I will be as fast as I can be." She shook her head.

"Sweetie, you do not get much time with your dad, so go, find out what he wants, and take your time. Look, enjoy yourself take the time with your dad and be a daughter. Deads, he is trying to make up for some of his past disgraceful behaviour, so let him, he has so few opportunities to do so. Sweetie, I will be fine, I am having dinner with my dad, and I aim to make the most of it, and you should do the same."

Oh, how do I beat that, when she is so reasonable? How could I refuse to do exactly as she says, and this is why she is so unique to me? Only Birch has that way of seeing things, in a way no one else does, she considers every point and every aspect, and really does try very hard to get a full understanding of the thoughts and feelings of everyone, and it is why she stands out so much.

It is not the hair, or her crazy cackle of a laugh, or those intense green eyes, it is simply her care and consideration, and her huge heart that gives everyone the benefit of the doubt, and I do try to emulate her, I really do, because it is the reason, I fell in love with her.

After a few drinks, Anita told me to call Markus and take the limo from the underground parking garage, so as to avoid the press. We went to our room, and I had an hour with Birch, where I showered, and changed into a long black skirt and black top, I grabbed my mirror glasses and parasol just in case they were required, and when I was ready, I stood in the garage and kissed Birch.

"See you soon, stay awake, I will want some quality time with you when I get back, so we can have sex in another different hotel room, we are getting quite a collection." She gave a giggle.

"I so want that now, have fun Sweetie, and give your dad a hug for me."

I kissed her softly, and jumped in the back of the limo, and Markus closed the door. I took a deep breath and relaxed, I had no idea at all as to what my father wanted, and it bothered me a little. I suppose I would soon find out?

Chapter 18

Unexpected.

Birch sat in the restaurant alone, her father had something come up, and apologised as he had to go out, and had to take care of it. Her mother was attending a presentation for self help writers, and so she smiled as the waiter delivered her meal. She was disappointed, she had really been looking forward to a meal with her dad, she had been so busy with the Curio event, she had missed a lot of time that she could have spent with her parents.

Her phone lay on the table, as she messaged with Izzy, and explained how the day had gone for Abby. She cut into her beef and started to eat, and took a sip of her wine, she looked up as Katie slid into the seat in front of her, she sat down with a smile.

"Eating alone, is there rain in wonderland?" Birch gave a sigh.

Katie was relaxed, it was almost as if she had not even been aware that she had set up Abby. But there again, Birch was used to Katie's absolute lack of remorse, she had seen it so many times in the past. Katie had one policy, put herself first, and never worry about the casualties of others. Birch looked up at her, noting Katie's open blouse and her happy smirk, she was enjoying this.

"After today, I would think you would love that, but sorry to disappoint you. Abby has another engagement, she is out for a while, so I am eating my meal alone, as I had arranged to see dad, but something has come up." She leaned back in her chair.

"Well, if you are free and out of the grasp of your little dark princess, can I join you?" Birch looked at her as she chewed her food.

"You were going to anyhow, and I have to admit, I would like to talk to you, especially after you set Abby up today. You know what Katie, I get you have an axe to grind, but I think you are forgetting, I chose her, can you really not understand that? If you want to punish anyone, punish me." Katie gave a chuckle, and lifted her arm and the waiter appeared, she smiled.

"Two shots of tequila and a bottle of beer." He gave a nod and disappeared.

"Jemi it was not deliberate, the guest cancelled and he was next on the list, that is all, and anyhow, Abby defended herself well, I think she did a really good job." Birch looked at her.

"Katie, do not play games with me; I have known you for too long. You set the guest list and knew full well what you were doing when you invited him. Look, you need to cool it, leave Abby alone Katie. You lost her, because you could not back down, you are so stupid, because you have created a bad atmosphere between you two now. Katie you are a friend, but I am warning you, hurt Abby, and you will answer to me, so just back the hell off her, and leave her to do her own thing with Anita." Katie lifted her palms.

"Whoa slapper, I hear you, okay. Look I am bored, and you are finally free of her clutches, can we not just chill out and talk, and hey, maybe even smile, like we used to? Okay things got out of hand, so let's just call a truce, and I will back off your precious dark little princess." Birch nodded.

"Good, because I am getting really bloody tired of this shit and having to tell you to back off constantly. I mean it Katie, stop the games, I do not trust you one bit, so do me a favour and prove me wrong." The waiter arrived, and placed the cold beer and two shots on the table. Katie pushed a shot towards Birch.

"Here, a peace offering, we have not done shots in a long time, you are free, and so am I, so let's just live a memory or two." Birch sighed and lifted the glass; she held it up.

"For times long since buried." She downed the shot in one. and picked up her knife again.

Markus pulled up outside the tower that housed my father's flat, I was not really looking forward to this, but with the words of Birch still echoing in my ears, Markus opened the door, and I climbed out, he smiled and handed me a card.

"I will be here waiting, this place has a relaxation room for drivers, so just call me when you are ready, and I will be out front when you get down." I took the card, I still had one from a few years ago, I looked at the tall building of glass and steel.

"Wish me luck, I never really know what to expect from my father, this could go ten different ways." I walked in through the foyer doors, and up towards the security desk, the guard behind the counter lifted his phone and pressed the buttons.

"Good evening, Miss Watson, give me a moment, and I will let your father know you have arrived." I smiled as I looked around, I was not a huge fan of this building.

"Thanks Frank." He spoke quietly into the phone, and nodded.

"You may go up, lift four, this way please."

He walked out from behind his desk, and walked towards the long corridor, he turned right into the corridor that housed all the lifts. I followed as he took out a key, and inserted it into the lock below a key pad, the lift gave a ping, and the doors opened. I stepped in, and Frank leaned in, and pressed the penthouse button, then stepped out, I smiled as he backed away and the doors closed.

I have only been here a few times, most of the time when I meet my dad, we meet in a restaurant, and have a meal together. I have always taken Birch with me, and the fact he wanted to see me alone, bothered me a lot. I felt nervous, and really wished I could have brought her along, it felt odd being here without her. The lift shot up at high speed, I sort of hated this building, it was far too cold and sterile, not at all like my warm comfy house in Wotton.

It almost amazes me how this is the standard of the rich, everything is shiny and reflective, nothing really has warmth. Modern life and the rich, is all about the sparkle, and yet it is just fake, how it looks is far more important than how it actually is, I don't think I will ever really understand or accept that.

The lift reached the penthouse and the doors opened, my dad stood there smiling, he was dressed in brown pants, and an open collared shirt. Every time I see him, he looks older and more tired, I walked out of the lift, and he opened his arms. I loosened my coat, and let it slide off my arms, as he put his arms around me and hugged me tightly.

"Abigail, it is so nice to see you, I have missed you." My coat and parasol hit the floor, and I put my arms round him, I noticed instantly, and leaned back to look at him.

"You have lost weight." He smiled.

"I have indeed, be honest I needed to, I fear I have eaten far too many good meals in restaurants over the years, so I decided it was time I took care of my over large beer and food belly."

He smiled as he stepped back, then surprised me, he lifted his hands and took my face in them, his voice dropped.

"Abigail, I almost lost myself, and in doing so, I almost lost you. Something like that, makes a man think, and I have done a lot of thinking, and so I have decided to take better care of myself, because I have the best reason a man could, I have a daughter."

I felt a huge surge inside me, it was fear mixed with a long time desire for him to be this kind of father. There was something in his tone of voice, a look in his eyes, I am not really sure, but I suddenly felt very emotional, I felt a tear build in my eye. I cannot explain why, but I felt something come over me, almost like there was a clear and present danger around him, and I needed to protect him, it was the strangest thing.

"Dad, are you alright, did something happen?" He smiled at me, he looked so old, and dropped his hand to mine.

"Come on in, Angela is in the kitchen, say hello to her, and then we will talk."

The penthouse is lush, furnished with only the best, and exceptionally plush, dad had brought in a designer to do it when he bought it seven years ago. He had gone first class all the way, although he has been stashing cash off shore for years, so he was not short of a first class ticket for everything.

The large floor to ceiling windows looked out across the London skyline, well, more looked down, because we were forty floors up. I avoided walking too close to his windows each time I had visited, because to be honest, it freaks me out. I have no idea why anyone would want to live this high; the only great advantage is the silence. London below was busy, and bustling, and yet not a single sound rose up from it. This was not for me, I am a plain and simple solid earth sort of girl, I like the idea that when I step out of my home, I am ground level, not hundreds of feet in the air.

I followed him through the living area into the huge modern kitchen, where Angela, who was wearing a white apron, was busy, as she laid a long table ready for the meal, she looked up and smiled.

"Abby dear, how lovely, you made it. I heard you like vegetarian, but I must warn you, I am still very new at all this, so I may just poison you." I giggled; I do get on better with her these days.

"If that is the case, I would have brought Birch and made her taste it first."

She smiled, I was aware that she still worried a little about Birch, especially around ashtrays. She placed the last of the cutlery down, walked over, and pulled me into a hug, dad was behind me opening a bottle of white wine.

"I am so glad you came; this means a great deal to him."

She smiled, as she turned back to the cooker to attend to the meal, and I felt something was not being said. Angela opened the oven and took out a deep dish, she lifted it up and put it on the cooker top. All appeared well, and yet something was there hovering above us, something unsaid, and they were just ignoring it. My dad popped the cork, and I blinked and turned, he was pouring the wine into glasses, I noticed one was only half filled. He smiled as he walked to the table.

"We will talk as we eat, if that is alright?"

I shrugged, feeling more and more nervous, he pulled out a chair and offered it me, I walked over, and took the chair, and sat down, as he went around the other side and sat facing me. My mind slipped into the overthinking writer, what was not being said? I know him, and as much as I really want to build on the small amount of progress we have made, the truth is I do not trust him.

I took a sip of my drink, was this that crunch moment when his morals and principles kicked back in, was I about to be told he could not support my marriage to Birch? We had formed a sort of truce on that front, was this about to be the drawing of new lines of battle as he moved to prevent a lesbian wedding, or was there more to this?

There again, this is my dad, and I am sure the smell of money was in his nose, was I being pulled here to listen to his pitch on how my money would perform better with his company, is that what this was, yet another attempt to make money from my earnings? This was the biggest problem between us, I did not trust him, and he knew it, and so was tonight about to making me feel like a special daughter, just so he could extract cash?

I noticed his glass was half filled, and that was just too much for me, I have lived my whole life watching him drink wine, and never in half measures. The first eighteen years of my life was spent watching mum and dad open a bottle for every meal and every event, he has probably spent millions on rare wine over the years. It made me wonder, I know he took a lot of his wines from the house, did this place have a special shiny metal wine cellar, actually would it even be called a cellar, it is after all forty floors up? Angela placed a plate down in front of me.

"Do not judge me too harshly, I will get better."

I looked down, momentarily distracted, at the plate, it looked like some form of casserole, and was certainly filled with a lot of veg. There was a slightly aromatic scent of spice to it. I lifted my fork and took a taste; it was surprisingly nice.

Angela sat down with hers, and my father had a small portion, which was suspect, if there is one thing I know, it is he can eat, his whole life has been good meals. I started to chew; it was actually very tasty.

"Angela, this is really nice." I lifted my knife and started to eat, I looked at my dad.

"Okay, I am the writer around here, now we are sat with a meal, drop the pretence, what is going on dad?" Angela turned to him, he glanced at her, and she nodded at him. He chewed slowly as if in thought, and then he looked right at me, and gave a sigh.

"Abigail, I do not want to alarm you, but you should know, that I have recently had a bit of a scare." I held my fork in front of my mouth, as I felt a sudden surge run through me. My eyes moved from my fork to him.

"What kind of a scare?" Angela gave a sigh, and put her fork down.

"Oh really Edwin, you really are quite useless, I told you, relax and be loose, the way you drag things out, the poor girl will die of panic." She looked at me, my eyes moved to her, my fork still suspended before my mouth.

"Abby, Edwin had a minor heart attack, and I will tell you now, he refused to let me call you." The second jolt hit me, like a frying pan to the face, and I looked right at him.

"You had a heart attack... When?" He looked guilty, and reached out across the table.

"Please Abigail, I do not want you to worry, it was not severe, and I was only in hospital overnight." I could not believe him; I was lost for words, why was I not told, I am after all his only child?

"Overnight… Does mum know, and why did you stop Angela from calling me, I would have come straight away?" Angela looked at him and nodded.

"See, now will you listen to me?" She turned to me.

"Abby, I would not tell anyone until you had been informed, so your mother is not aware of it. You know how stubborn and bloody minded he can get? If I am completely honest, if it had been anything else, I would have informed you. I did not want him stressed out more, so I held back, but I told him he was very wrong?" My dad looked at me with sorry eyes.

"Abigail, I did not want you driving from Wotton to London like this, look at you, you're trembling, I could not take the risk of you driving whilst upset. I am sorry, but I wanted to get all the facts before I told you, and as you can see, I am fine, and taking better care of myself." Angela pointed.

"We better eat, this actually is far better than I thought it would be, I think it would be a shame to waste it."

I looked down, I had hardly touched the food, dad gave a nod and started to eat, and Angela smiled, and gave a gentle nod, I lifted my knife and fork, and suddenly the tables had turned on me, and I had so many questions, and felt five times more afraid.

Birch sat in the bar getting quite drunk, and very loud, as she pointed at Katie, and swayed in her seat.

"You did it on purpose and you know it. That was really sneaky and bloody shitty of you. I thought we were friends, you are a mean lesbian, and I am not sure I like you anymore." She downed her shot, and hiccupped, Katie sat back in her seat.

"Give me a fucking break… I was jealous, I am sorry, I have never lied to you, I have always told you how much I love you. I am sorry alright; I would have married you if you asked me." Birch swayed a little more, as Katie poured another shot, Birch leaned on the table and rested her head on her arms.

"You had that other me girl, you know the blonde, with the

small tits, she is nice, why didn't you stick with her?" She still had her finger pointing at Katie, she prodded the air.

"You know what your problem is don't you... You are a freaking greedy spiteful bitch?" Katie gave a sigh, and nodded.

"I am... I have never denied it, I have always been a greedy bitch. I find a good pussy like Nita's, and, oh God she was good, I am telling you that girl knows how to fucking play the game, but Jemi, it was not yours." Birch gave a sigh.

"Mine is taken, and booked forever, sorry slag, you need to go munch elsewhere." She started to giggle.

"I have a Sweetie only pussy and it is for Deads only, she has put a spell on it, any other woman tries, her tongue will swell and choke her, and you will die going blah blah blah blah and drown in spit."

She gave a loud cackle of a laugh, and everyone turned around to look at them, Birch smiled, looked at everyone, and put her finger to her mouth.

"Shush, don't be a noisy slapper." She was beyond drunk, and it was becoming very obvious, Katie gave a sigh.

"Wow you get pissed fast these days; I remember when you could drink treble what we have tonight. God, she really has ruined you, and made you a fucking light weight... Come on, you have had enough, you're a fucking southern pussy these days, fuck you need to get back north."

With the meal over, my dad took me into the living room, and patted the side of the sofa, I sat at his side, and he relaxed and faced me.

"Abigail, I am sorry if I worried you, but you need to know that I have changed my lifestyle completely. I have done everything the doctors have told me, I work shorter hours, I drink less, I am exercising, although it is only gently, and I have embraced a whole new diet, and I really do feel a lot better."

I was starting to calm down a little, my heart had been pounding, and I had been really terrified. I have had so many fights with him, and even hated him for a time, for hating Birch, but the truth was, I did not want him to die. In a way it was crazy, I have so many memories of crying because of him, and so many of fearing him, but here he was looking old, tired, and vulnerable.

He could see how upset I was, and smiled.

"Abigail, I am going to be fine." He reached out and took my hand in his.

"I have done some unforgivable things, and I am not asking, but the reason I wanted you to come alone, was I wanted this just between the two of us. Abigail. I regret so much, I should have believed you when you told me about Martin, I knew in my head you never lied to me, but if I am honest, I was not brave enough to face it. I was never as strong as your mother, I could not handle the thought of you being like that with him, and I rejected you, if I could take it back I would. You have no idea of the regrets I have, and I am trying so hard to make up for that." In a way hearing it really hurt, and my eyes filled with tears.

"Dad, that is done with, it no longer matters, all that came to an end two years ago. He is locked away for good, you have to stop beating yourself up about it. It happened and we cannot change that, I don't want you to die being haunted by it, my life has changed so much. Dad I am getting married, and I want you there on my arm." I wiped my eyes on my sleeve, and he was smiling.

"I will be there; of that I can assure you. I have really messed things up for you, but I am trying, you do know that I do think the world of her, don't you? I was an ass, but I could see how happy she made you, and if she is what you want, I will take pride in handing you over to her." I gave a sniffle, and smiled.

"I really want that; I want you there with me. I really want one special moment I can remember forever, where we are not fighting, something special and wonderful. Dad, I really do love her, and she does me. I know how hard it is for you to fully understand that, but trust me, this is not a phase, I want her to be with me forever." He gave my hand a soft squeeze.

"We can all see that Abigail, honestly, it has shone through everything, and both of us really do wish both of you well." I turned and looked towards the kitchen.

"What, even Angela, I thought she really hated Birch?" He gave a slight chuckle.

"Jemi does get carried away, you know I do not have to remind you, she did offer to remodel Angela a new look with an ashtray?" He gave a giggle.

"We both understand she was protecting you; I would expect no less from her, how is she?" I gave him a big smile, and sniffled, he handed me his hankie.

"She is Birch, she is older, but twice as bonkers and beautiful, you know how it is, it's a Birch thing." I nodded with a grin, and wiped my eyes.

"Oh, I most certainly do, she is alright being alone tonight, you know, I do not want her to think I am shunning her, I just wanted tonight to be between us?"

I understood now, and I was really glad in a way it was just us two, I have not had a moment like this since he had left the village.

"She will be waiting for me when I get back, and I will explain everything to her. Birch will understand."

Birch hung over Katie's shoulder like a limp doll, as Katie, tried to fumble her room card out of her pocket.

"Some things never fucking change, I have done this far too many times Jemi, fuck, you are a light weight these days."

She gave a shove, and the door to the room swung open, Katie walked in and crossed the room to the bed, she reached down and dragged the duvet back, and then with a slight lean, and a jerk of her shoulder, Birch dropped onto the bed.

She gave a sigh, and looked at her lay flat out. Katie shook her head, and then unbuttoned Birch's pants, walked to the end of the bed, slipped off Birch's shoes and then tugged at the legs. Birch's pants slipped off revealing her naked legs and sex. Katie stopped and stared at her.

"I have done this too many fucking times."

She walked back to the top of the bed, and slipped Birch's top up, she pulled her forward and tried to slip her arms out of the sleeves, she struggled, pulled hard, and finally the top came off, and Birch flopped back on the pillow. Birch lay completely naked as Katie stared at her, it was almost too tempting for her, after all, she had craved this for a long time.

Katie gave a slight smile, as her mind drifted onto something. She opened her small shoulder bag, and slipped her hand inside, and a few seconds later she slipped out her bright red lipstick.

"Let's see just how much your spoilt little dark princess really loves you shall we?"

She applied the lipstick to her lips, and then bent down, and just above Birch's right nipple, she softly kissed her, making sure her lips pressed onto the skin. She stood back and smiled as she saw the bright red kiss mark on Birch's white skin, she gave a little titter, and then walked down to the end of the bed.

Kneeling down, she leaned in, and slowly parted Birch's naked legs, and kissed the inside of her left thigh, just below her vagina. Katie gave a giggle as she stood back, she ran her finger round her lips, and then placed it just above Birch's vagina, and dragged her finger across Birch's hip, making it look like a lip smear. She nodded satisfied with her work.

"Explain that to your dark princess, and see just how much she loves you then. You will see I am right; she is not good enough for you." She pulled the duvet over Birch hiding the marks.

"Sleep well Sleeping Beauty, I will see you very soon."

She kicked Birch's top closer to the door, and then walked towards it and left the room, dropping Birch's door card on the floor just outside. Katie left with a smile, and walked down the hallway, her room was two floors lower, she pressed the button on the lift and waited.

Angela brought a stack of papers in and handed them to my dad; she smiled as she sat opposite me in a comfy chair. My dad put on his glasses and flicked through the papers, and then looked at me in a look I knew well, it was his business face.

"Abigail, due to current circumstances, I have taken a very good look at the provisions I have made in case something untoward was to happen. As you know, we have rebuilt the company, as Angela is a partner in the firm, and she will be well provided for. I always intended to build this company to ensure your future, and so we have been talking a great deal, and both of us think that certain things should stay as they are."

I looked at him, and then Angela, she gave a soft nod with a smile, my dad held up some of the papers.

"Abigail, I want you to be head of the board, Angela is more than capable of running the business on a day to day basis, and I have assembled a very competent team around her, but I have always wanted you to play a role, and you do have a degree in business, which I feel it is time you used. Your role will be to be a guiding light to my vision of the company, and keep its legacy of dealing honestly going, and as such, your share allocation will increase to ensure you have a controlling interest with Angela. So, I will need you to sign a few legal papers to seal the deal.”

He handed me the papers, all marked with tiny crosses where I had to sign, I looked at them and gave out a long breath.

“Dad, I do not understand anything to do with your business, I am sure Angela will do a better job than me.” He gave a grin.

“You will get used to it very quickly. Abigail what I am asking from you, is to use this position to support Angela, I want both of you to support each other. These shares are worth a lot of money, and they will ensure both yours and Jemi’s future, it is my legacy to you, and a means of undoing some of the damage I have done to you both, use the money it generates and live well together.”

I did not know what I could say, this was his dying wish, was it even possible to refuse it? I felt a little uncomfortable, after all, my accounts were handled by one of his competitors, it felt weird as he handed me the pen. I had no choice really but to sign them. I went through each paper and signed where it was crossed. It probably sounds daft, but I thought, I could always sign them over to Angela at a later date if I wanted to, because in a weird and twisted sort of way, she had helped rebuild the company, and I felt deserved them.

He appeared happy with the results, and shortly after he excused himself, as he was tired. It was getting late and I wanted to get back to Birch, I gave him a huge hug and said goodnight, Angela walked me out as I phoned Markus for the car.

“Thank you for coming Abby, it really did mean the world to him. He is a funny old stick, and can be set in his ways, but he really does love you. I know he does not always show it, I think it is the one thing we both share, but you are so important to him, and maybe it has taken him a long time and a heart attack for him to realise that, but he is getting there.”

I understood her, but I still felt hugely emotional. I was glad he had someone with him, in a weird way, I was glad she was there.

“I know you have played a big role in that, alone he would never have accepted Birch and me. I am grateful to you, because no matter what has happened, I want him to walk me down the aisle. He really is alright isn’t he, I think he looked very tired tonight?”

Angela gave a smile.

"He was lucky we were close to the hospital, but it was not as severe as we first thought. Abigail, I have halved his work load, and got him eating better food, and walking more, and it is helping. I am watching him very closely, so please do not worry." It was hard not to, I turned at the lift door.

"Thanks for looking after him, like him I don't often show it, but I am grateful, and do me a favour, if he tells you not to phone me again, text me, after all, it's not a phone call is it?" She gave a giggle, and nodded.

"I like the way you think, and yes, I will make sure you know straight away." She pulled me into a hug and held me tight, and it felt a little strange, I lifted my arms and hugged her back. Angela released me with a smile.

"We will see you at the wedding if not before, it is not long now, I am sure you are very excited." I was, and it showed.

"I am so excited; it is hard to keep it in, I really cannot wait, it's driving me nuts." The doors behind me opened and I stepped back.

"I will see you soon, yes?"

I pressed the button and she waved, and the metal doors closed, and I felt the floor give a slight jerk, it had been a strange night, but nowhere near as bad as I thought it would be. All I wanted now was to jump in the car, and get back to Birch as fast as I could.

Angela walked into the bedroom, and looked at him as he lay in bed.

"Right Edwin, you have seen her, now will you have the bloody operation, you are wasting time, and you need to get this done and soon. Doctor Bancroft is just waiting for your call?" He gave a sigh.

"I just needed to see her and talk that is all, I told you, as soon as I have, I will have the procedure done, and so, I will call him tomorrow and set things up."

"You better bloody had do. Edwin, no matter what has happened, that girl needs you, hell has she not been through enough, now stop playing games, I want you on her arm at that wedding? I know this is not what you wanted, but this is not just about you, it is her day, and she wants to remember the look on your face when you see her in her bridal attire for the first time." She sat on the bed and gave a long sigh, and her voice dropped.

"Edwin, I saw a very different side to her tonight, she is delicate and loving, please do everything you can to make things right between you two, for the first time in your life, stop being stubborn and be a real father to her. No matter how like Flick she is at times, she is also fragile, and loves you, and she needs it." He gave a nod and closed his eyes.

"I want that too you know; I want to undo everything and make it right, I just needed to be sure first, that is all?"

I sat in the back of the limo, and started to shake as I held the phone to my ear, it rang on the other end, I heard her voice, and my eyes filled with tears.

"Hi Abby, did everything go alright?"

"Mum... I just left dad's... Mum, he had a heart attack and he did not tell me." The tears flowed, and I started to shake.

"Mum, he looks so old and tired, Mum, I don't know what to do, I am so scared because he really does not look well. Mum, I don't want him to die."

Chapter 19

Exposed.

Markus pulled into the side of the road, the partition came down, and he turned to look at me, as the call ended, and I wiped my eyes.

"Are you going to be alright Miss Watson?" I gave a sniffle, and wiped my eyes again.

"I think so, I had some news that has really shaken me." He handed over a small flask cup of hot coffee.

"Here, take a moment and drink this, it will help, it is just coffee... If it helps, I am here, and you would be surprised at the good advice I have given in my time as I drive. Can I be of any help at all?" I tried to smile as I took the cup.

"You are really kind, thank you. My dad had a heart attack a few weeks ago, and he did not tell me, and it has taken the wind out of me a little, he could have died and I would not have been there." The tears flowed again.

"I am sorry, I hate being a miserable passenger." He gave a sad smile.

"You cry all you like Miss, that must have been quite a shock, you know if it helps, you can ride up front rather than being sat alone in the back, just don't tell the boss, she frowns on it." I gave a giggle, and sniffled.

"She wouldn't if you were female." He raised his eyebrows, and I gave a giggle.

"I would like that if it's okay with you?"

Markus got out and walked around the car, he opened the door and let me out, then opened the passenger door, and I slipped in, and sat in the front, it was much bigger than I expected. He walked back around to the road side, got in, and smiled.

"Is that better?" I gave a nod and smiled back, he handed me a tissue, my dad's hankie, which I still had, was pretty wet.

"You are really kind; I knew that the first time you drove me."

He gave a smile, and the car pulled away from the side of the road.

"Just relax and try and calm yourself, you must look nice for your lovely lady when we get back." I dabbed my eyes, I probably looked like Alice Cooper, as my mascara was all over the tissue.

Roni and Will, walked down the corridor and spotted the door card on the floor, Roni gave a sigh.

"She must have been really drunk, the bar man said she was loud." Will bent down and picked it up, he swiped the card and the door lock clicked.

Roni walked in, and saw her sprawled out under the duvet, she gave a sigh, and walked over towards the bed. Will pushed the door to close it. Roni knelt down and gave a gasp and leaned back.

"She smells like a brewery, bloody Katie, that woman is becoming a problem. Oh, well, I will deal with this first." She reached out, and gave her a shake.

"Jemi… Jemi, come on you silly fool, wake up." Birch gave a moan and stirred, she lifted her arm to her face, and groaned even louder.

"Jemi, wake up I need to talk to you." Birch opened her eyes, and looked at her mum, and then swallowed.

"I don't feel well."

Suddenly, the duvet was flung off the bed, and Birch lurched forward, slid off the bed and ran to the bathroom, Roni gave a long sigh, and Will shrugged.

"We have seen this before." Inside the bathroom Birch retched, and YERK! Will gave a titter as Roni got off her feet.

"It's not funny, she should not be getting like this, she knows better." He shrugged.

"We did worse at that age."

Roni shook her head as Birch heaved and retched, then threw up again in the toilet, between gasps and moans, she threw up again. Roni lifted the duvet off the floor, and saw the red mark, she looked at Will and held it up, he looked unsure.

"What is it?" Roni gave a sigh.

"Lipstick, and it's red." He did not understand, she looked at him.

"A very particular shade of lipstick, God Will, use your brains."

He suddenly understood, and shook his head.

"She would not do that." Roni lowered her voice, and walked closer.

"Not sober she wouldn't, but we all know what Katie is capable of, don't we?" He shook his head.

"I do not believe it, there is no way she would do that to Abby."

Roni turned to look at the bathroom door as she heard the toilet flush. The taps on the sink went on, and the sound of splashing water came out of the room, mixed with Birch's gasps. Roni stood waiting. Birch reappeared, she looked really rough, and Roni gave a loud gasp, and pointed at her daughter.

"What the hell is that... YOU STUPID, STUPID FOOL!" Birch looked down.

"What?" She saw the red marks, and her heart almost stopped, her head snapped up to look at her mother, her eyes huge and wide, looking terrified, as she shook her head.

"I didn't... I didn't mum... honestly, I wouldn't."

It had been a long and awful night, I was tired, and super emotional, and all I wanted was to curl up in bed with Birch. The lift doors opened and I stepped out, glad to see my room. I walked towards it and felt my spirit's lift. I looked a sight with my streaky mascara and red eyes, but I would be safe in bed soon with Birch. I approached the door and noticed it was open slightly, and there was shouting, it was Roni.

"HOW COULD YOU, HOW COULD YOU BE SUCH A BLOODY STUPID FOOL? HAVE YOU ANY IDEA OF THE DAMAGE THIS WILL DO!?"

I pushed the door open, and Birch was stood naked near the door with her back to me. The door swung open wider, as I saw Roni and Will, both of them were staring at Birch, and Roni looked irate. Birch was crying and shaking her head.

"I didn't... I would not do that, not ever, I did nothing, please believe me?" Roni blinked, and her eyes moved past Birch to me stood staring.

"ABBY!"

"What's going on?" Birch turned her eyes filled with tears, she looked shocked, as she saw me, and more tears streamed down her cheeks.

"It's not true, I didn't"

I saw the lipstick marks, and felt the floor fall out beneath me, as my parasol hit the floor. My heart almost stopped, as a huge waved surged up inside me followed by the tears which rushed into my eyes, as I shook my head, as my world completely crashed. Birch held out her arms.

"Sweetie, it is not true, I did not do anything, please believe me." She took a step forward, and reached for my hands.

I snapped them away from her, and stepped back out of the door, as the emotions rushed up inside me. It was horrifying, her vagina was smeared in red... Her red... That witch's red! I felt myself shake, as I took another step back, the words came out without me even thinking.

"How could you... with her...WITH HER BIRCH, HOW COULD YOU?" She shook her head, and fell to her knees shaking.

"I didn't, you have to believe me, I did nothing, I was drunk, nothing more." Roni walked forward toward me, as Birch broke down on the floor.

"Abby, come inside; we need to sort this out." I stared at her as my heart broke and the tears flowed faster. I shook my head, as I looked at her and Will, both trying to coax me inside.

"I cannot be here, I cannot do this now, I told you Birch, not with her. NOT EVER!" I turned, as Birch screamed, and I ran.

"DEADS, NO... PLEASEEE!"

I ran for all my life as my heart broke, and my whole world collapsed around me. The lift doors were closed, and I just needed to get away, just away, anywhere I could not see that red lipstick on her, not there, I could not handle that. I needed to be gone. I swerved into the door to the stairs, and grabbed the rail, and felt my legs slip as I hurtled at speed down them, going round and round, as I descended in a blur.

This could not be happening, not this, she promised me it never would. I could not handle the pain inside me, I could not take knowing that she had been there, and violated my Birch. I did not want it in my head, I did not want that picture of her covered in red. I slammed into the door and gave a squeal, as my face hit the frame, desperate and shaking, I clawed at the handle, my eyes were so filled with tears, I could barely see.

I heaved open the door, and shot through it, I had no idea where I was going, I just needed to be anywhere that was not here. I could not be here in this building; I could not be where those red marks were. I blindly ran through the foyer, and bumped into a man with cases. I stumbled, as I staggered forward and raced for the doors. Blurred shapes of people jumped out of my way, as I sobbed bitterly between gasps of air.

I needed air, I could not breathe, I felt like I was suffocating, as I gasped, but I could not stop. I saw the blurry glass doors and ran towards them; my heart was exploding inside me. I hit the door and it swung open, and I ran out into the cool air, turned sharply, and just ran. I had no idea where I was going, I just knew I had to go, I had to get away, where I could not see her, tainted with the red of that woman.

Birch wailed into the floor, pushing her face into the carpet.

"I didn't, I didn't, I didn't!" Roni crouched down at her side, and put her arms around her.

"Jemi, we have to deal with this, now come on, I need your straight game, I need to know what happened. Come on, come and sit on the bed." She turned to look at her mum, and lifted her head up, she was almost hoarse from crying.

"Mum, you have to believe me, you have to tell Abby, I would never do that to her, Mum, I love her, I could not hurt her, not ever, please Mum, I am begging you, please believe me, I did not do it." Roni gripped her under the arm.

"Alright Jemi... Talk to me, I want to make this right again, so talk to me, tell me just what exactly happened?" Birch threw her arms round her mum, and just sobbed.

"I cannot lose her, I cannot be without her mum, please help me, I need her back here, I need to tell her it is not true. I did not do anything, please help me mum, I need her." Roni held Birch tight, her temper was starting to simmer, and she was doing everything she could to hold it in.

I could not breathe, I felt like I was having a heart attack, as my chest burned. I was shaking violently, and disorientated. I gasped for air, and stopped, I had no idea where I was. I moved to the side of the path, and leaned on a wall gasping, people were looking at me, but I did not care. I felt like my chest was going to explode and I could not breathe, I leaned forward, and put my hands on my knees, my insides were swirling, and I retched.

YERK!

I threw up all over the pavement, and I shook, as I gasped in more air. I was still sobbing, and now that I was away from the hotel, I really had no idea what to do. I stood there leaning forward staring at the splattered contents of my stomach, which has slushed out in a mixture of reds, greens, yellows, and whites. It was pretty disgusting, but I needed air, so I just stared, lost, unable to think, and riddled with pain, not really caring what I would do next.

"GOT YOU…! Thank God for that, I thought I would never catch you."

I felt the strong arms fold around me, and I came out of my daze, and looked behind me to see Will panting, and gasping for air. I stood up and he pulled me closer.

"Hell, Abby you can run when you need to, I really need to visit the gym more." I felt the pain inside me again, and I turned and buried my face into his chest, and just broke down. Will held me tight, and stroked my back softly.

"It's alright sweetheart, I am here, you are not alone." I blubbered into his shirt.

"Why would she do that to me Dad, she knows how much I love her?"

He stood there as I soaked his shirt, in tears and smeared puke from my mouth, and I just wailed my pain into him, I had no idea what else to do. It just hurt so much; I thought I was going to die. Will just regulated his breathing as he held me and took long deep breaths, and allowed me to pour out my heart in the safety of his arms. His voice was soft and soothing.

"Abby, listen very carefully to me, we both know Jemi very well, but we are all emotional at the moment. Come on Abby, you know her, answer me one question?"

I gave a sniffle, my bottom lip was trembling as I breathed in, and I looked at him. His face was so kind and gentle, his eyes filled with his concern.

"What do you mean, what question?" He gave a soft smile.

"Abby, has my daughter ever lied to you or me?"

I snorted in to clear my nose, I was starting to breathe better, which I think was because of Will. I still shook as I tried to control my breathing, he has always had that sense of calm around him, I gave my head a slight shake.

"She promised she would never lie to me."

He smiled and raised his eyebrows. I understood him, a memory flashed into my mind of her sat in my bedroom at home several years ago, she was sat in front of me, and her soft words bounced through my mind.

"Be this, be this for the rest of your life Deads, this here, this honesty, this is my dark little beastie, this is who I fell in love with back in Uni. Stop doubting this, and analysing this, just accept that this is who we are. I have never lied to you and I never will, so if I tell you something, love me enough to trust it, do that and we are even, because when you look at me and doubt me, it is like being stabbed with a thousand knives, and honestly, I cannot handle it, it kills my soul."

I understood him, I loved that he had so much faith in her. He took my hands in his, and gave them a soft squeeze.

"Abby, she is wild and crazy, she has a yen for life that is strong flowing through her, but she is also clever. I admit, she has moments when she can be ditzy, but if there is one thing I know about my daughter, it is you can take her word to the bank, because she has no need to ever lie. Think about it, Abby, just think of why you want to marry her."

I nodded, as I understood him, he was right, she did not lie, she really did own up to everything good or bad. It was the one thing I have always admired about her, if people called her, she would smile and agree with them, she has never hidden anything truthful about herself.

"Birch would not lie to me, she never has, I should know better." He smiled at me and gave a long sigh.

"This was a set up if you ask me, it was the final act of a desperately jealous and selfish woman, I believe Jemi too. Not only do I believe her, I believe in her, and if there is one thing I know, it is that she would never cheat on the only person she will ever ask to marry her. Abby, she is going to be your wife, trust her more now than you ever have, and believe in her, because that is how we defeat the Katie's of this world."

Birch wiped her eyes as she sat on the bed.

"I told you mum, nothing happened, I would never do that to Deads. I was eating alone, and she just appeared, and started doing shots. I told her to quit making Deads life hard, I told her I would never sleep with her, and that I was marrying Deads because she was all I wanted. I have not drank like that in ages, we have been cleaning our act up at home, and cut down a lot, we just have the occasional night. Mum, we all have jobs and responsibilities now; we are not students anymore." Roni sat on the bed at her side and held her hand.

"What are you going to do now Jemi?" She gave a long sigh.

"I need to find her and talk to her; her phone is turned off. Mum, I have broken her heart, this is her greatest fear, it is why Katie did this. I just want to hold her and tell her I did not do anything." The tears appeared again.

"I cannot lose her mum, she is my life, she really is, I would never put that at risk."

Roni had heard the whole story, and she was satisfied, like Will, she knew if her daughter had done it, she would admit it. She lifted her phone and read the message, and gave a small smile.

"She is with your dad, and she is safe, she is upset, but he is with her and talking to her. You are really lucky Jemi, because he believes in you in a way others will never understand, and he is telling Abby that." Birch hung her head, she felt ill again, she gave a sob.

"I just want her here with me. I need a shower, I want this shit off my body, I feel dirty."

Will put his arm round my shoulder as we walked slowly back, I was surprised at how far away I had gotten from the hotel. It took us well over fifteen minutes to get back, I glanced at him.

"So you did not get your meal with Birch?" He shook his head.

"No, something very important came up, and I had to drive across London. Roni has been trying to meet up with a guy to sign some papers for over a week now, and he is down here for one night. She was tied up with the presentation, so I ran over to him for her, and sealed the deal." I could understand that, the Dixon Group was a lot bigger than most people realised.

"Was it that important?" He chuckled.

"Actually, it was far more important than any of us realised, and probably a good thing I went." We reached the glass doors of the hotel, Will smiled.

"Roni has messaged me, you caused quite the stir earlier, she has spoken to Anita, and she has cleared everything up for you." I felt a pang of guilt.

"Was I that bad, I knocked someone over, are they alright?" He gave a titter and looked at me sideways.

"You did blow through the lobby like a twister from Oklahoma, but no one was hurt, just a little shocked to see a crazy goth woman running wild like she was off to an Alice Cooper concert with the last ticket." He gave a giggle.

"I hate pointing this out, but you do look like a half crazed gothic banshee with those eyes."

I suddenly realised, I must look a right sight, and I pulled my dad's damp hankie out, and tried to wipe them. Will looked round at the street.

"It is good to see there are no press, the last thing you need is your fans seeing you looking depraved like that, although, you do have the manic vamp look going on at the moment."

We walked in, and everyone stared as we crossed the floor to the lift, I put my head down and felt horrible. The lift pinged, and I walked in, and I felt a huge surge of emotion flow up inside me, I looked at Will.

"Will she forgive me for not believing her?" He pulled me close.

"Abby, she loves you so much, trust me, once you talk it will be fine."

I felt so nervous and awkward all of a sudden, I was really scared for some reason. The lift stopped and the doors opened, I felt my heart start to thump in my chest, a part of me wanted to run to her, and another part of me was afraid to. I had no idea what I was going to say, my mind spun as I tried to think of what would be the best way. I grabbed Will's hand.

"I am scared, what if she is angry for not believing her, I screwed up once before for that?" He gave my hand a soft squeeze.

"Abby, she is my daughter, trust me, things will be fine."

We arrived at the room, and I pulled my door card out of my bag, my hand shook as I swiped and the lock clicked. I took a huge breath and swallowed, it was now or never, I still had the urge to run in fear. Will pushed the door open, and I saw Roni sat on the edge of the bed, she saw me and got up, came over, and pulled me into her arms.

"Oh Abby, I am so glad to see you are safe."

It is crazy, but I felt like a little child in my mother's arms, she squeezed me really hard, her voice was very soft.

"I once told you, she is not as tough as she makes out, talk to her Abby, no shouting, just talk, because she is so afraid at the moment, she is terrified she has lost you forever. Forget Katie and her dirty tricks, just be with her, and talk to each other... She is taking a shower to get that stuff off her, and she is extremely upset and vulnerable." I snuggled into her, it felt safe.

"Tonight, has been horrible, I just want to forget it all." Roni patted my back and released me.

"Go talk to her." I stood back and nodded at her.

"Thanks... Both of you, thanks for being here." She smiled.

"You are our daughters; we will always be here when you need us."

Will smiled as I turned to the bathroom door, I slipped off my boots, and dropped my bag, he gave a gentle nod to reassure me. I looked at the bathroom door, and walked towards it, I pushed it open and walked in.

Birch was in the shower behind the glass doors scrubbing frantically at her leg, she did not notice me straight away. I walked a little closer, and my movement got her attention, she looked up and saw me and stopped. Her hair hung wet and lank in front of her, and her bright green eyes looked dull as they filled with tears. She started to sob, and it was heart breaking to watch, I cannot stand seeing her cry, she gave a massive sob.

"I am sorry... I am so sorry Deads, honestly, I did nothing with her, I promise I did nothing."

I felt the tears fill my eyes too, it was terrible seeing her this way. She was holding a large exfoliating sponge and her leg was red raw from her rubbing so hard. I grabbed my top and pulled it up, and slid it over my head, as she stood frozen and sobbing. I pulled at my skirt, and let it fall to the floor, and stepped over it, I reached for the door to slide it back, and Birch suddenly put her arms in front of her and squealed.

"NO!"

I jumped; I felt a pang of shock run through me. She stood with her arms out in front of her, her eyes were wide, and she was shaking, she shook her head, as the tears flowed from her eyes.

"Deads, I am not clean... I need her off me, I cannot let you touch me with her on me." She looked at me with heart broken horrified eyes.

"Deads, did you see what she did to me, I am so sorry, I passed out and she did this, she has touched me where she should not have, and now I am too dirty for you."

The tears rolled down my face as she franticly rubbed at her skin, making it redder. I grabbed the door and opened it, and stepped in, and grabbed her hand, to stop her. She looked up at me, trembling.

"Birch stop, you are harming yourself, she is not worth it." She gave a sob.

"Deads, I feel like she is all over me, I am not clean enough for you." She started to shake really hard, I reached out and pulled her as close as I could, and she broke down, and wailed into my shoulder.

"Stop this Birch, she does not have that power, she is just a rancid jealous bitch, who thought she could use you. Now come on, you are better than this, you are completely clean in my eyes. Birch, you will never be unclean to me, I love you." She wrapped her arms around me.

"I would never do anything with her or anyone else, I only want you, I cannot lose you Deads, I don't want to be alone without you. Please forgive me and don't leave me, I was stupid to trust her, I will never make that mistake again. Deads, you must believe me; I did not do anything with her." I leaned into her ear.

"Birch, I do believe you, remember, I promised you I would love you enough to trust and believe in you. I hate what Katie has done to you, but I will never allow her to break us apart. I am sorry, I truly am, I am so sorry Birch." She pulled back from me and looked me in my eyes, her eyes were still filled with tears.

"I love you so much, you have no idea how much, I was so scared I had lost you; I did not know what to do." I lifted my hand and stroked back her wet hair, and I smiled.

"I am here, and I am going nowhere. Okay?"

It took a long time to calm Birch down, and once again I got to see that childlike quality within her. She constantly apologised, but there was no need. It worried me how easily Katie had managed to manipulate everything, and I was resolute that I would fight to get her as far from us as possible. One thing was for sure, if that bitch even tried coming to my wedding, I would be married with her blood on my dress.

I finally coaxed Birch out of the shower, and checked her leg, it was red raw, as was her breast, I hated seeing her this way. I sat her on the bed and dried her hair, and then pulled off the stained duvet cover, and threw it on the floor, so Birch did not see it.

I covered her with the duvet and climbed in at her side, and pulled her close to me, she snuggled up, and was clearly exhausted. I looked at her face as she rested on my shoulder, her arm across me, pulling me close, and I slid my arm up her back and inched her closer. She lay there looking at me, and I did not need words. I softly kissed her on the head, and she gave a long flow of breath.

"This is nice, this is all I want, nothing else." I smiled at her.

"We are strong, and we love each other, and we will get through this, I do not want to ever see you like that again. Birch, I know you think she is your friend, but honestly, I think you should seriously question her friendship. Chloe, Deb's and Edwina would never do something like this, they would never be jealous of you, they would stand by and support you like they do. Katie has changed, and not for the better, and I think you really need to think about that. I will never tell you who you can be friends with, but I will warn you if I think someone is dangerous." She nodded, and turned her head into my boob.

"Let's not talk about it, I want to forget tonight, it has felt like the worst night of my life."

That was fine by me, all I wanted to do was sleep, I felt drained. I lay back and stared at the ceiling, it had been one hell of a night, and my life felt so much harder than everyone else's at the moment. Birch's soft breathing rose from my chest, I glanced down, she was fast asleep, and I smiled.

"So childlike and yet so wise at times, I will never understand how you do it. Sleep peacefully Baby, we will deal with her tomorrow."

Roni sat on her bed with Will, Anita was sat in the chair, Roni looked at her.

"You say nothing Anita, this is no longer anything to do with you, I want you out of all of it. I aim to deal with this myself, this is not unexpected, but after I saw her try to hang Abby out to dry in public earlier with that shit of a critic, I realised more was to come and acted." Anita frowned.

"You acted, how?" Roni shook her head.

"It is best for now you do not know, but get ready, because things are going to change. I am going to send Abby and Jemi away from here tomorrow, we will still do the press conference, but it will not be with Abby. The other authors can talk, and then you and I will do one that will explain Abby's absence, and I will handle most of that. The press will not rattle me, and there will be a lot of questions to answer." Anita did not quite understand.

"Why will there be a lot of questions, no one knows what has happened? I mean, yes, she ran out, but no one knows why and I do not think the press saw it, because if they did, they would be all over my phone." Roni gave a naughty grin, not unlike one Birch would give.

"Trust me, the less you know the better, but there will be questions, and I am already prepared for it, just sit back and watch how I handle things; it will be a good learning curve for you." She looked worried.

"You know, I have got to say Roni, that watching Abby today, and listening to you now, I am beginning to wonder what I have got myself in to." Roni nodded and gave a slight grin.

"Anita, the one thing you should know is that we are all close in this company, we take care of each other, and if someone hurts one of us, we close ranks and protect each other. Tonight, Katie played the cruellest game of all, and she is not getting off the hook for this one, because she has hurt two people who mean everything to me. Retribution will visit her, and she is not going to like it."

Anita felt a shiver run down her spine, and she suddenly felt it was better to take Roni's advice, she intended to stay as far away from all of it as possible, it was definitely safer.

Chapter 20

Retribution.

Anita left once she was briefed, Roni grabbed her bag, Will looked at her.

"Are you sure this is wise, it has been a rough night, why not sleep on it and wait until morning?" Roni picked up her card, and slipped on her shoes.

"It is better done now. Will, if I leave this I will boil over, it is best done now, because honestly, after seeing the mess Abby was in, and seeing that level of pain come out of our daughter, if I wait till morning, I will toss her out of the fucking window." Will smirked.

"Well your foul language is expected, very few get you that mad, and I will not say, she does not deserve this, just be cautious love, you also have a reputation to maintain." Roni nodded and headed for the door.

While I snuggled into Birch and she drifted off into sleep, Roni walked down the hallway two floors below us and banged on the door. She stood back as she waited, there was no response, so she banged on the door even harder. Three doors down a guy stuck his head out of a doorway.

"Hey, keep the noise down." Roni turned, and looked at him.

"Screw you, get back in your room."

She banged again even harder. Inside the room there was a noise, and the sound of footsteps approaching the door. The door swung open, and Roni stepped forward, Katie was stood in her knickers, scratching her head.

"Fuck Roni, it is getting late and supposed to be my night off, can we not do this tomorrow?" Roni pushed her hard in the chest.

"Oh no missy, we are doing this now." Katie staggered backwards into the room.

"Steady fucking on, what the fuck has you so riled up?" Roni stared at her, her eyes blazing.

"Don't you dare play innocent with me, you know exactly what you have done. How could you do that to Abby and Jemi, just what the hell is your problem? I told you to back off, but oh no, you just had to stir it up, didn't you?" Katie gave a long snort of air and smirked.

"Roni, I was just messing around, fucking hell it was a joke, I thought it would be funny."

SMACK!

"A FUCKING JOKE, IS THAT ALL, YOU LOUSY BITCH, HAVE YOU ANY IDEA OF WHAT YOU HAVE DONE!?"

Katie went sprawling backwards over the bed, blood flooding out of her nose, and tears filling her eyes. She rolled on the carpet and sat up cradling her nose.

"YOU BROKE MY NOSE, YOU CRAZY BITCH!"

"Be glad I did not throw you out of the window, I will never forgive you for what you did, have you any idea of the trouble you caused?"

Katie leaned over and grabbed the tissue box off the side table, she grabbed a wad and held it to her face, her eyes were already showing signs of blackening, her breasts and legs were covered in blood.

"If they love each other as much as they say, this is nothing. If it is that big a problem, well then, it just proves that they should not be together, which proves I was right about Abby all along." Roni smiled.

"You will be disappointed to know, they are curled up in bed together, because both of them are smart enough to know, what a screwed up selfish cold bitch you are?"

Katie grabbed a second pile of tissue, and dropped the red soaked bunch, and pushed the new ones on, as she squeezed the bridge of her nose to try and stop the bleeding.

"I should sue you for this Roni." Roni gave a snort of derision.

"I would save your money if I were you, it will come in handy until you find more jobs." Katie looked up at her.

"And just what the fuck does that mean?" Roni looked at her with utter contempt.

"I trusted you; I thought I could rely on you, but your endless quest to bring down Abby, with your stunt earlier today, and then your sick twisted behaviour with my daughter proves I was wrong. I will not work with people I do not trust; you are fired." Katie got up off the floor still holding her nose.

"You cannot fucking do that; I am the major shareholder." Roni laughed.

"You wish… you own 35%. Will owns 5% and after buying Craig out today for a handsome profit, I now own 60% of K.O. Productions. You are out, you screw with my daughter, you screw with me. I warned you Katie, and I also told you, that you may think you are ruthless, but you have a long way to go before you catch up with me, especially when protecting my family. You are done, out, over with, now pack your shit, and get out of this hotel, I have the rest of the team handling this event." Katie stared at her with hate.

"I broke my ass to build the production company, and you do a fucking hostile takeover on me, you fucking cow!?" Roni looked at her with no mercy whatsoever.

"Like for like Katie, you tried pulling a hostile takeover of Jemi, so I schooled you yet again in how it is really done. Now get your shit, get that bony ass of yours up to Manchester, and clear out your desk. Security up there has already been alerted to your status, and HR are dealing with your paperwork, you are done with me, so stay the hell away from Abby and Jemi, or so help me God you will go off a roof somewhere. Am I clear?" Katie crumbled.

"Roni, please, let me make this right, I am sorry, I was drunk and got carried away. Give me a chance to fix this, I have given everything to this company." Roni was ice cold, as she looked at her holding her bloody nose.

"I financed you to build that company, without me you would still be printing flyers in Salford. You want the company, raise the cash and buy it back, you know where my office is. I will sell you some back, but I can promise you now, you will never get another Dixon contract easily. I mean it Katie, you have had too many warnings to leave them alone, but you just had to keep chipping away, allowing that crazy idea that Jemi would one day be yours take over you. Katie understand once and for all, if she was not with Abby, she would be with a guy, you do not have what she is looking for, now just bloody well accept it, and go lay a ton of other lookalikes." Roni turned and walked towards the door.

"All the paperwork will be sent to your home address."

She walked out, and Katie collapsed onto the bed, holding her nose, with a wad of red tissues, and burst into tears. Roni stepped through the door as a team of hotel staff hurriedly arrived, the floor manager looked at her.

"Is there a problem, we have had complaints of trouble?" Roni pointed behind her, her hand covered in blood.

"There is no trouble, just a little administering of justice, I believe medical aid is required in there, the young lady has a bad nose bleed." She smiled at them, and walked off down the hallway. The hotel Manager leaned in through the open door and asked.

"Is everything alright, do you require help?" He gave a gasp as he saw the blood all over the place, as Katie sat in her silk knickers only, crying and holding her nose.

I had a restless night, and did not sleep very well, Birch jumped and jerked in her sleep all night, and each time she did so, I woke up. Roni still had Birch's door card, and arrived just before breakfast was served, she sat on the bed and smiled, I was curled round Birch, holding her boob, with my face buried into her shoulder. She gently shook me.

"Abby... Abby, wake up."

I gave a moan as I opened my eyes, and rolled on to my back, sliding my hand off Birch's boob and down to my side. I yawned and pushed the hair out of my face and blinked to see Roni, I gave a smile.

"Hi, what is wrong?" She shook her head.

"Nothing, your breakfast will be here shortly, it is almost nine thirty." I felt exhausted, and I had a day of press to do. I rubbed my eyes, and winced, Roni leaned to the side.

"You have a bruise on the side of your face." I sat up.

"Yeah, I bumped into something last night." She looked concerned.

"Are you two alright, did you talk?" I looked at Birch fast asleep, she looked so peaceful.

"We talked a little bit, more will come, but we said what was important, we will be okay, we just need time to talk everything through." Roni gave a nod, she understood.

"It is important you understand what Katie did, Jemi did not have sex, she was passed out. Whatever went on, and I am not sure we will ever fully know, but you must remember, she was taken advantage of whilst out cold. Trust me, if she had willingly had sex with Katie, I would have got it out of her, but her story never changed. Abby, she was heartbroken, she thought you had left forever, I deal with this sort of thing every day, but seeing Jemi like that, it was so painful for me, she was devastated." I completely understood her.

"She fell apart in the shower, she was scrubbing so hard she was breaking the skin, just to remove where she touched her." I looked at Roni, and I swallowed hard as the emotion surged back up in me.

"I know that feeling, I did that when he touched me. It scared me to see Birch do it, I knew then it was all Katie and she was innocent." Roni smiled.

"You have always been very bright. Abby, I think you two need some time away, and I mean completely away. I have talked with Anita, and today I will be handling all your press conferences with her, I do not think you are in a good enough state to handle them. Will is free all day, so I want both of you to pack, and he will take you to a special place, have some time alone. Talk, relax, make love, and just restore yourselves, get yourselves well and reconnect with each other."

"I would love that Roni, but you do know I only packed enough for two days?" She gave a sigh and thought about it.

"The weather is warm, you can wash clothes, I mean neither of you wear underwear, and you are both always naked, and this place is very private, so you should make it through." She made some good points, it made sense. There was a quiet tap on the door, and it opened, a hall waiter pushed a cart into the room.

"Your late breakfast as ordered Miss." He gave me a big smile, I smiled back.

"Thanks, you can leave it, there is a tip on the table over there, we appreciate it." He picked up the twenty and gave a big smile, and left, I looked at Roni.

"He was happy, I like that, friendly staff always make the place nicer." Roni gave a resounding laugh, I frowned, she looked at me, and her eyes twinkled like Birch's did.

"Abby, he was very happy, I mean, how many times does he get to see one of the most popular authors boobs whilst delivering breakfast?" I looked down.

"Yikes... I forgot."

She giggled as she got off the bed and took the cover off the cart. She poured coffee, and lifted the covers off the food, she picked up a slice a bacon.

"Oh, I love bacon." Birch sat bolt upright in bed with her eyes closed, and sniffed the air.

"Do I smell bacon?" I giggled, she turned slowly and opened her eyes, and looked at me.

"Hi Sweetie... I had bad dreams." She burst into tears, I pulled her over to me as Roni smiled, and held her close.

"Deads, it was horrible, I dreamt you ran off and left me, and my head really bloody hurts." She erupted, and bawled her brains out. Roni shook her head.

"Some things never change, welcome to your married life."

Bacon has miraculous powers, I find its properties outstanding, as all one has to do is wave a piece under Birch's nose, and you gain complete control of her attention. Tears stop, eyes get wiped, and a smile appears as she chews, although today, there is no sudden head movements, as her head explodes at the slightest tweak.

Thirty minutes later I was back in the shower, as Birch talked to her mum, I was happy I did not have to do the press conference, to be honest I hated them. I finished my shower and walked back into the room wrapped in a towel. Birch was dressed sat on the bed, next to her mum talking, Roni was smiling.

"Look, I know you meant it for later, but Jemi this makes much more sense, you two need this. Jemi, you may think this is all done and dealt with, but be honest, you of all people know better. Deal with it now, get it all out of both your systems, and sort it out in the open, in private, and then you can both move on and get married without a care in the world. Put this all behind the both of you, and let me deal with everything else." I watched them both, not really understanding all of it.

"What are you talking about?" Birch turned and smiled.

"Nothing much Sweetie, we are just trying to work everything out. Mum wants us to take some time out and talk in a neutral place, and I do have somewhere in mind. It's a long drive, but we can stay as long as we want. Deads, we can take as long as we want, just you and me, and no one else, will that be alright, I mean if you need to not see me for a while, I will hate it but I will do it for you?" I shook my head and felt a little panicked, and it showed in my voice.

"I don't want you to leave me, I don't want to be alone, please stay with me, please Birch I want us together, I don't want to go away." She got up and walked over to me, and pulled me into her arms.

"Sweetie, I want to be at your side, I want to be your Celia."

"I want you to be my Celia too, I vowed to be your Lillian. I want us to go wherever it is together, and stay that way forever, it is kind of the point of us Birch."

It was decided, and that was our first step forward again, we packed our bags and headed down to the lobby, where Anita was waiting, she walked us to the small side café, and we sat with a coffee.

"Abby, there are going to be a lot of changes in the Dixon Group, but I will be staying on with you if that is alright?" I nodded.

"We have a contract, so yes, I have waited a long time to get someone who understands what I need, and not hang me out to dry." She smiled at me, and nodded her head.

"Good, I have a lot of ideas and things I want to talk through with you. I am tied up for a few days with Roni, but when I am free, I will drive down and we can meet up, and talk. Jemi, I would like to involve you in a lot of this as well, I would appreciate it if you would be a part of the conversations. You understand Abby in ways I never will, it will be helpful to have you on board." I sat back as she spoke to Birch, and then felt a huge shock wave hit me, I blurted without thinking.

"Holy shit Birch, what did you do to her?"

Katie was checking out at the counter, her face had a huge plastered patch across it and both her eyes were black, she looked like she had been hit by a truck. I turned to Birch. She was staring looking speechless.

"Sweetie, I did not do that, or at least I don't think so... Can you hit someone when you are passed out?" Anita gave a chuckle.

"I believe she was visited by retribution." I looked at her.

"Who did it to her?" She smiled.

"As much as I would like to tell you, it is not my place, both of you will hear more in time."

I looked back as she slipped on a pair of large sunglasses, picked up her bag and headed for the door and a waiting car. I did not know what to feel, I was angry at her, but I did not want her beating up, I won't deny it, I had wanted to beat the shit out of her a few times, but I would never have done it, I think?

Once everything was sorted and ready, I slipped on my glasses and grabbed my parasol. William was going to meet us at a different location, so we were going to leave by the front doors and jump in the limo, and Markus would drive us to meet him. It had all been planned by Anita and Roni, the odds are with the limo, the press would not follow, as the windows were heavily tinted. Roni wanted the press to see us both leave together.

As we jumped in the limo to a barrage of flash cameras, and Markus drove off, in the conference room, all the press and cameras were gathered waiting, and a thousand flashes went off. Anita walked in with Roni, they walked behind the table to the seats and sat down. Anita adjusted the table mics and smiled at the press.

"Good afternoon, ladies and gentlemen, my name is Anita Dickinson, and I am the publicist to some of the authors of the Dixon Group. I am sorry to inform you that Miss Watson, has been called away from this event, and so I will be handling any questions or queries for her today. I have no need to introduce Dr Dixon, I am sure you all know her?" Roni leaned into the mic.

"Good afternoon. I am here today as head of the group, to talk about our book publishing operation. As some of you will possibly be aware, the Dixon Group is going through a phase of being restructured, as we move each of the separate areas of our work from under the one umbrella, and place qualified managerial staff into positions that allow for more independent governance. The company needs to modernise and follow up with more of the trends in the areas of business we cover, and this will allow the new managerial teams to act faster and be more responsive. As you know, I am no spring chicken, so in order to create a little more me time, I am isolating each area of the group, and hope it will help them to create their own unique image, but fear not, they will all still answer to me."

The press looked on a little wrong footed, they had all prepared questions for Abigail, one journalist held up her pen and looked at Anita.

"How is Miss Watson, there is a rumour she ran out of here crying last night, is she alright?" Anita smiled.

"Abby is fine, she has a lot on her plate at the moment. She is almost at the end of her latest novel, her best friend is close to the birth of her child, she is also heavily involved in the work for the first Curio Centre, and she is planning her wedding. You have to admit, it is a lot of work, and she has felt the strain a little, so we advised her to take a moments pause." The journalist nodded and smiled.

"Is she excited about getting married, we noticed she was here with the doctor, I saw her at the side of the stage yesterday?"

"Abby and I have done a lot of talking; I would say she is beyond excited; she really is and it is lovely to see it, I am very happy for her, it is a wonderful time for her." A male reporter lifted his arm, and looked at Roni, she gave a nod.

"Doctor Dixon, it is well known that Miss Watson has a degree in business studies, will she be joining the group board, or publishing management when she gets married into your family?" Roni gave a big smile.

"All family members join the board, so as my daughter in law, she will naturally join. As for a managing position, that will be entirely up to her. I would love her to expand her horizons, and if she wants to talk, I will naturally be open to her ideas."

I sat in the back of Will's car, Birch decided to sit in the back with me, rather than sit up front with her dad. I grabbed her arm and snuggled up.

"Where are we going?"

She smiled, since leaving the hotel, both of us felt a lot better, it was almost as if leaving, lifted a veil off us, she gave a giggle.

"It is somewhere very special to me, and that is all I am going to tell you, but you will see."

I felt excited and I did not really know why, maybe it was because I knew we were going to be all alone, in a place with no one else. That was enough, I can be patient, well I think I can, I am feeling excited about being alone, it will be like a trial of what it will be like to be married. I looked into her eyes and gave a little giggle.

"Is it far away, or is it close by, give me a little clue at least?" She started to laugh.

"Deads, you are worse than me. Okay, it is a long drive, so settle down, we will be a little while, so just relax and enjoy the ride. Actually, snuggle into me, I am really tired."

I gave a little squeak of excitement and cuddled up to her, I was too excited to sleep, even though I was really tired as well. I thought I would talk, to try and keep my mind off things, but it was really hard to think of something, I looked at Will as he drove.

"Hey Will, have you got any idea what happened to Katie, she looked like she had been smacked in the face with a bat, her eyes are really black, please tell me it was not you; I do not think you would hit a woman... Would you?" Birch gave a snort.

"Katie is not defenceless, whoever did that is a mauler for sure." Will gave a laugh as he indicated and turned,

"Oh, it was more than a mauler, she ran into a force greater than any wrestler, and she was no match for her opponent."

Wow, I was really intrigued, I looked at Birch and she shrugged. I turned to Will, and tried to see his face in the rear view mirror, I had to know what kind of an animal did that.

"Oh wow, were they really big, I mean, she looked like she had been brutalised?"

Will started to giggle, I could see Birch was now as curious as I was, and we suddenly were not sleepy at all. We both leaned in close, and Birch spoke really low, almost as if she was afraid someone was listening.

"Holy shit Dad... Who the hell did it, what force did she tangle with, worse than a real mauler?" He chuckled.

"A very angry and pissed off mother." I turned to Birch, she frowned, and then her eyes went huge.

"Holy shit, my mum did that to her?" I gasped in shock.

"No freaking way?" We both looked through the gap in the seats as Will tittered.

"Oh my children… Yes, big freaking way."

Our jaws fell open, and we were lost for words. I could not comprehend what I was hearing, we were talking Roni, the calm controlled doctor who always found reason in everything. I was frozen staring at Birch, she was just as lost for words as I was, I had a thought.

"Jesus Birch… Your mum is like bad ass… Actually, scratch that, she is a freaking monster." Birch nodded and smiled.

"I told you she was cool, when I first met you." I smiled, and nodded in complete agreement.

"I really get why she is the boss now; how many do you think she has wiped out in the past?" Will gave a huge laugh.

"Trust me girls, there are grave yards littered with them." Birch sniggered.

"Oh Dad, don't be silly, mum is not violent, she would only fight if she had too." He looked in the mirror.

"Is that what you think, never underestimate her, you have obviously never heard of Glady's Pimpleback. I am telling you straight, she was huge. She was a big swollen beast, and your mum took her out in less than three seconds. I had endured months of trouble with her, and once your mum found out, she went straight at her. God, she was impressive, she did not even flinch, she just waded in and POW!" I blinked and jumped back in my seat.

"Holy shit Birch, your mum is really cool and awesome, but I have to say, a bit terrifying too." Birch agreed, and sat back in the seat next to me.

"I have never heard that story before, I got to say Deads, I think you might be right, I mean, she showed no fear and just waded in, that is pretty bloody scary. Was Gladys that big Dad?" He nodded as he drove.

"She was the biggest one around, everyone who saw her screamed and fled the scene." I felt really bad for Will.

"It must have been awful for you Will, I mean, having to endure months of suffering all alone? I never realised you guys had such tough times, I am really sorry to hear it, but I am really glad Roni stepped up for you, that was cool." He looked back briefly and smiled.

"Yeah, me too, it was after that, I knew I was going to marry her, I knew with her, I would never suffer the likes of Gladys again." Birch nodded with me, she smiled.

"My mum is cool, she beat up Gladys and Katie, wow, I love her so much at the moment."

William drove on with a titter, and I sat back and thought about it, I could see this huge ugly woman in my mind, and little Roni just running up to her and wham! She was floored in a single punch, God, she was totally amazing. I leaned into Birch and drifted, and before I realised, I was flat out, having dreams of Roni protecting all of us in her attempts to save us from marauding fat women, who all looked like Katie.

Roni walked out of the press conference with Anita.

"That went better than I thought, they actually had to think on their feet for once." Anita walked at her side along the corridor.

"Roni, I have to ask, Katie texted me. Is it true, you did a hostile takeover and took her company, and then you fired her?" Roni gave a nod.

"It is, does that bother you?" Anita did not really know what to say.

"To be honest, I was not with her very long, but I did grow to care for her. Roni whilst I was with her, it was all she talked about, her company was her life. It meant everything to her, she was so proud that she built it from scratch. I am not questioning what she did, I think it was despicable and wrong, but I have got to say, I feel for her a little, I do, I cannot help it." Roni stopped and turned to her.

"What are you saying Anita. Do you want to go back to her, because if you do it will have no bearing on our working relationship, you can date who you please?" Anita shook her head.

"You misunderstand me, no, she used me to try and hurt Abby, I really did care for her, in many ways I still do, but I will not take her back. Roni, she has lost everything, her whole life's work, this will be really hard on her." Roni agreed with her.

"Yes, it will. Anita, the way I see it, Katie started to take everything and everyone for granted, she abused her position, and let all the glitz go to her head, and she started to think she was untouchable. It happens to us all eventually, but when it does, we need to stop and think, she did not, and as a result, she got too big for her boots and forgot who was really in control. She deliberately put Abby on the block at the Curio event, and then again yesterday, and she failed to realise, that just because they are not married yet, does not mean that I do not see Abby as a daughter, and that was when she slipped up." Anita understood.

"Abby has been like a daughter to you for a long time, I know that, because when we were talking about you, she called you mum. It was a little confusing at first for me." Roni smiled a very beautiful smile.

"I love that about her, I remember the first time she called it me; it just came out and blew me away, honestly, I wanted to cry I was so touched. Katie should have left her alone as I asked her to, you know Anita, I gave her plenty of warnings, and to be honest, she has not lost her company, she is still a shareholder, the question is, can she raise enough to buy me out?" Anita fully understood.

"So if she can raise the cash, you will sell her back the extra shares you bought?" Roni raised her eyebrows.

"Katie needs to understand the meaning of family, she was a part of mine, a little time in the wilderness will bring her back to earth, she has been living in the clouds getting carried away for too long. She is a smart girl with a lot of drive, she earned that company the hard way, and she needs to remember who it was that backed her with hard cash and supported her. It was my stage shows that were her spring board to success, and I have taken them away for now. If she wants that company back, then she needs to find a way to get it back, she now has the motivation to do it."

"Okay, so quick question. If she does, where does that leave me?" Roni patted her shoulder.

"Let's go for a coffee and talk, I have a few ideas I want to float past you, but do not fear, Abby is really happy with you representing her, so do not screw that up, because your future lies in her hands."

Chapter 21

Happy Place.

My eyes blinked, and opened, I was staring at the base of the passenger seat. It took me a moment or two in order to get my baring's. I was lay on the back seat with a blanket over me, and my head was on the rolled up coats. I yawned and sat up, rubbing my eyes, and I blinked as I came back to life.

"Hi Sweetie, sleep well?" I leaned back on the seat and licked my lips, Birch was driving, and it looked like Will was sleeping in the passenger seat.

"Why didn't you wake me up?" I could see her eyes in the rear view mirror, she glanced at me and her eyes twinkled.

"You looked so sweet and peaceful, we let you sleep, there is a flask in the back of the seat, I got it filled up at the services, I thought you would like coffee?" I nodded at her eyes.

"Yeah, coffee would be great." I looked out of the window we were on a motorway.

"Where are we?" She gave a little giggle.

"I was not born yesterday, you will see, but it is not much further. Put your seat belt on Sweetie now you are awake." I looked at it, grabbed and pulled, after all it was good advice, Birch was driving, her eyes moved to me, and gave another sparkle.

"When we stopped at the services, I bought some vests, and shorts, because we do not have much clothing wise on us, and we do not know how long we are staying." I saw the flask, slipped in the map holder on the back of Will's seat and pulled it out. I unscrewed the top and poured it into the tiny cup.

"Do you want a coffee?" She shook her head.

"I have one Sweetie; I got a take out, and filled Dad's travel mug."

The car indicated and moved over to the slip road, the speed of the car slowed, and Birch drove skilfully up the road and onto a roundabout, and turned onto a long road lined with trees. I sat back and sipped my coffee, and looked out of the window, to try and work out where I was. We were travelling fast, but there was no sight of a town or house, most of the view between the trees was of farmland and woodland.

"We look like we are in the middle of nowhere, Birch, I have no idea where I am?"

"I know, it's exciting, isn't it? Deads, this place is very special to me; I just know you are going to love it. I came here a lot when I was a young girl, although it has been over ten years since I was last here. Wow, I must have been about fifteen when I last stayed here. I have so many special memories of this place, and I am really excited, because I can share them all with you. Oh Sweetie, this is going to be so amazing, I hope you fall as hopelessly in love with the place as I did when I first came here."

I cannot deny, I felt a twinge of excitement growing inside me, she really sounded so happy to be here, although this was Birch, she could get this excited over a cream bun, so I guess I should be wary.

I sat back, relaxed and refilled my coffee cup, it was sunny and I gazed out of the window, watching the world pass by, and let my mind drift. Will slept and Birch was focused on the road, I was trying not to, we were going really fast, but it felt like she knew this road as well as she knew the roads at home. Time drifted when she spoke.

"The air con is playing up, if you get too hot, the blue bag on the floor behind my seat has clothes in it."

I looked down and saw the bag, it was then I realised she was wearing a bright yellow vest. I grabbed the bag and opened it. My legs were sticky and my parts were really hot, I pulled out a pair of denim shorts. They were priced at £28; I pulled the tag off and undid my black jeans, and wriggled as I slid them down, it was probably a good thing we were not on the motorway.

I finally managed to get the shorts on, they were a good fit, my feet were steaming, so I slid off my socks and remained in bare feet. I slipped off my top, and the seat belt slid under my boobs and pinched. I jumped and Birch giggled, I looked up and saw her watching my in the mirror.

"Focus on the road pervert." Her eyes twinkled at me.

"You have really lovely boobs, I like looking."

I gave them a jiggle, sadly, there is not too much to wiggle, and then pulled a deep purple vest over my head, and slipped it down. I relaxed, feeling cooler, and folded my clothes neatly, and slipped them in the bag. My back ached and I stretched out my arms, Birch slowed down and indicated, and we turned onto a small parking area, set just off the side of the road. I looked out of the window at the long lawn, and the beautiful cottage with a thatched roof. The garden was glorious with shrubs, trees, and flower beds, all worked into a labyrinth of tiny path ways. Birch became really excited; she gave her dad a nudge.

"Dad, we are here." She unclipped her belt, and turned the engine off, and turned to me.

"Deads, come on, I want you to meet someone really precious and special." I frowned.

"What, is this not it, not the place?" She was very giggly, and shook her head.

"Oh no, the place we are going is much better."

Better, wow, I was already impressed, this place was stunningly beautiful. Birch opened her door and bounced out, she grabbed my door with a huge smile, and pulled it open. She bounced up and down excitedly, and waved me out of the car.

"Come on... Hurry Sweetie, I want you to meet Seth and Mable."

I slid out of the car and she grabbed my hand, and almost dragged me across the lawn, I had not even had time to put my shoes on, although the mown grass was lovely on the souls of my feet. We walked across the grass towards the house, and to our left an old man stood up, I had not seen him on his knees pulling weeds out of the flower bed.

"Excuse me my dears, but this is private property you know?" Birch turned, and her smile went massive.

"Seth!" He looked a little confused, and then it was like he understood, and gave such a lovely broad grin.

"Well, I never, is that little Jemima all grown up?"

She gave a squeal, and ran to him, her long white hair flowing behind her, with her arms outstretched, and she dragged him into a tight hug.

"Seth, I have missed you."

He wrapped his arms round her with a big smile, Birch had tears in her eyes as she let go of him, and stood smiling in front of him, he smiled with such love in his eyes.

"It has been too long little Jemi, I have missed you girl, we need your brightness round here. Why you have not changed a bit." She giggled and wiped her eyes.

"Well, I have grown bigger than you now, and hey, I grew boobs." He chuckled.

"Oh, it is so good to see you looking so well my dear." Birch took his hand.

"Seth, I want you to meet the most special person in the world to me." He frowned.

"I thought that was me?" She giggled.

"She is just a little more special."

He gave a loud laugh, and looked at me watching and smiling. Birch walked with him over towards me. Seth looked really healthy, I would say he was at least eighty, and yet he was agile and very jolly. He had thin almost white hair, and a round happy face, with a great tan, and almost bauble like round cheeks, you could tell just by looking he was a kindly person.

Birch walked up holding his hand, there was massive amounts of affection between them, she stood in front of me with a beautiful happy smile.

"Seth this is Deadly, her real name is Abigail, you can call her Abby. This is the love of my life, and the person I am going to marry."

He seemed completely unphased by the fact I was introduced as her future wife, I had expected a reaction, but he just took my hand and held it softly.

"I am so pleased to meet you, Will and Roni have told me a great deal about you. I am Seth, I was Will's dads' best friend." I smiled, he was really lovely, and obviously he still spoke with Roni which explained the acceptance.

"It really is very nice to meet you, Seth." His eyes twinkled.

"I hope you are staying for a tea, or coffee, while we sort out your supplies, Mable will be disappointed if you don't?" I looked at Birch and gave a nod.

"I am not sure Birch could be dragged away just yet. A coffee would be lovely, thank you." He smiled, and looked at Birch.

"I take it you are Birch; I like her, she is very polite?" Birch just smiled; she was so happy.

"At home they call me Birch, it is because of my hair Seth, you know, like the bark." He winked at her.

"I worked it out girl, do not forget where you are, this is country living here, none of that living on top of each other stuff round here." He was lovely, I could see why she liked him so much. She took my hand.

"Come and meet Mable."

Birch held my hand, and we followed Seth into the house, and I caught my breath, it was gorgeous inside. It was like stepping back in time, with heavy wooden ceiling beams and white walls, with a large open stone fire place, and really old but immaculate furniture. The doors were heavy slatted wood, with old fashioned latches, I was in love with the place as I looked round.

Seth led us through to the most amazing farmhouse style kitchen, with a huge heavy wooden cottage table right in the centre of the room. Birch stood in the doorway, she smiled as she saw an older lady, in a long blue dress and wearing a flowery apron. She was a small, round, woman, with a large grey bun, and the happiest of faces, filled with smile lines, and the most piercing bright blue eyes. Birch gave a cough.

"Pardon the intrusion, but is the kettle on?" She turned looking startled and stared, and then her jaw dropped and her eyes filled with tears.

"That beautiful and fully grown woman can only be my little Jemi, those lovely eyes are unforgettable?" Birch bit her lip.

"I am back Mable, well just for a visit." Mable came up, and Birch bent forward and gave her such a huge squeeze.

"Oh, my dear, I am so happy to see you, and you have grown up into a very stunning young lady, but I must admit, I still see that little lovely girl." She glanced at me.

"I know who you are, that hair gave it away as soon as I saw you."

I gave her a smile, she released Birch and turned to me, I held out my hand, and she pushed it away and stretched up to hug me.

"I am hugging the famous writer Abigail Jennifer Watson. Cissy

Benson will be envious as hell when she finds out you have been here." I had to giggle as I put my arms round her.

"In that case, I will make sure to give you a hug that counts." She chuckled in my ear.

We both sat at the table, with large mugs of coffee, and Will finally was awake enough to join us. Both of them are obviously well known to each other, I was actually the stranger in the pack, even though I was made very welcome.

Birch was on cloud nine, happily chatting away and cackling with laughter. I was happy to sit back and watch, and just listen to all the tales and stories as I sipped my coffee. The subject of the wedding came up, and Birch took my hand and held it, Mable was equally as accepting, she waved her hands around as she spoke.

"Honestly my dears, I think it is lovely. We had such a scandal a few years back with Cissy, when one of the village girls ran off with her girlfriend. I said at the time, I did not know what all the fuss was about, I mean you can buy those big black rubber willies in the post office these days, it's just as good at putting a smile on your face."

I gave a huge cough, and almost sprayed my coffee everywhere, and Mable gave a roaring laugh, as Birch slapped me hard on the back, whilst I coughed out the coffee in my lungs. Mable got up and crossed the kitchen, she grabbed an old pot cloth, and threw it across to me, whilst she laughed. I caught it and wiped up the mess. My voice was a little strained and croaky.

"So sorry about that, you caught me off guard." She sat back down and smiled at me.

"We may be out in the sticks, but we can use the internet too Abby, I am old, but not blind." I smiled and gave another cough.

"I am starting to see that, Mable."

Birch giggled at me and took the cloth off me to wipe my eyes. Apart from choking, this was such a nice place with really nice people, and I was a little disappointed when Birch informed them both we had to go. Seth went and brought in some boxes, which were packed with food, it appeared Roni had messaged them last night, and they had bought supplies, and had them delivered to the house. Seriously, is there anywhere supermarkets do not deliver to these days?

I helped Birch take them to the car, and we loaded them in
the boot next to our bags. Mable got out her mobile, and asked
William for a picture, so the three of us stood by the car and she
took a photo. I smiled at her; I really liked her.

"You know Mable, wouldn't it be wonderful to show Cissy a
picture of you with a famous author?"

Her eyes lit up with excitement, so William took her phone, and
we all lined up, with our arms around each others waist, and gave
our best smiles, and Will took the shot. She looked at it, and gave
a big grin.

"She will be so envious, thank you, I cannot wait to meet at the
guild on Thursday, I will be the envy of the whole area, she has
read all your books, even though she does not approve, I think
she really enjoyed the naughty bits in Seeds of Summer."

It was a fun break, and soon we were back in the car, and Will
took the wheel, Birch slid up to me and snuggled into my arm.

"Almost there, Deads, I am so excited."

She was right, it was a two minute drive, as Will turned off the
road onto a tree and shrub lined gravel drive, the wheels rumbled
up it, and we turned right to reveal a completely perfect house. I
opened the door and got out, Birch was already out, she stood in
front of me with a big smile, and threw out her arms.

"SURPRISE!"

I was lost for words, it was stunning. The house was a four
bedroom stone built farm house, which had Wisteria growing up
the walls and around some of the white framed windows. It had
a rich dark green painted heavy wooden door, and Birch grabbed
my hand and dragged me up to it, she turned as she held the key,
her eyes were sparkling like emeralds, and she was very excited.

"Okay, so here is the deal. Deads, this house belonged to my
grandfather, that being my dad's, dad. I used to come here
every summer with mum and dad, and I have so many happy
memories, and so when my grandparents passed away, it went
to my dad, and he has not had the heart to sell it. We let friends
come down and use it, and Seth and Mable get paid a small
allowance to take care of it." She was talking so fast she had to
take a deep breath.

"So, the thing is, mum and dad have decided to slim a few

things down, and so when my dad told me he was considering selling it, my heart broke, and so I bought it for us, this is our home from home." I stared at her.

"You bought it... For us?" She nodded with a huge grin.

"Well, I got a family discount, you know, half price. Deads, I have so many happy memories in this house, and actually, I wanted more, I wanted my happiest ever. I wanted memories of you here... Deads, that is alright isn't it, I have not gone too far again, have I?"

I smiled and pulled her into a kiss. I pulled away, and she gave a huge giggle and a squeal, and pushed the key into the lock. I had to laugh, this was the third house she had bought, well she does not own mums, she bought it for her.

"It's probably good we are no longer being investigated by the police, that copper was concerned about your wanton house buying, as I recall?" She gave a bright happy giggle, and yanked on my hand.

"Come on, see our new home, I was going to wait until after we were married, but you know, with the way things are?" She dragged me in through the door with a loud cackle. I stood inside as she beamed with love and adoration at it, her voice was soft and low.

"Wow, it has not changed a bit, I have been away for too long, I need this."

The room was not unsimilar to Seth and Mable's house, it had dark oak beams on a white ceiling, and white walls, which were plaster. At the end of the room was a huge stone fireplace, and a set of brass tools for cleaning the hearth out, the floors were deep polished wood, with scatter rugs, and there was little furniture, apart from a polished wooden cottage type set, which had a three seater, a two seater, and two single chairs, each with highly polished wooden arms, and deep red cushions.

The walls were strewn with small post card sized framed pictures, and I noticed many of a girl with huge white bunches on each side of her head. I walked over to look and smiled, it was baby Birch, and she had hardly changed a bit. There were a few of a large man in overalls, with snow white hair, many of which, had little Birch with him, I could see how Will looked like him, Birch came over and gave a sigh.

"That is my granddad Jeff, I have missed him so much, he was an engineer, and when he retired early, they bought this place and moved down here. He taught me woodwork and gardening, and we would walk for miles happily talking and laughing. He had such a cackle of a laugh, and he was always very quick to smile and giggle. I loved him so much Deads, I wish he could have stayed long enough to meet you."

I felt sad hearing her voice so soft, filled with sadness.

"Birch, he has seen me, whatever it is we have in this world, I believe it still surrounds those we love." She smiled, and a tear ran down her cheek, and she bit her lip and nodded.

"Yeah, he would never truly leave me, I really do believe that."

I lifted my hand and wiped the tear from her eye. The door banged open and Will walked in carrying a box of supplies, he walked through a latched door that was open and into the kitchen. I figured we should help unpack the car. I left Birch to open the windows and air the house out, and gave Will a lift, I grabbed the second box of supplies and took it inside.

The kitchen was bigger than Mable's, but more modern with gas appliances, and a microwave, I was a little relieved to find I did not have to build a fire, just to boil a kettle. It had a good sized fridge freezer, and another wonderful large country kitchen table, with six matching chairs round it. The house had plants everywhere, all in neat little pots and in perfect health, Seth and Mable did a first rate job of taking care of the place. Birch filled the electric kettle and put it on.

"You having a brew before you go Dad?" I looked at her.

"Is he going back, I thought he would stay overnight?" She shook her head.

"He wants to get back to mum, I think he loves room service, they have a couple of nights left to be alone together, so he wants to get back. I think mum has promised him he will get lucky tonight." I gave a giggle as he walked in, he looked round at us.

"What was that?" Birch smiled.

"I was just saying, you want to get back to mum." He nodded.

"Yeah, we have plans." Birch looked at me, and raised her eyebrows, I sniggered.

We organised the food as Will sat with his coffee, Birch just naturally knew where everything went, and I could see, this was the way her grandmother did it, and so she had to as well. My phone rang and I picked it up, it was Roni, I put her on speaker phone to talk as I stacked cans in the cupboard.

"How are you two?"

"We are fine mum, I am helping Birch put the food away, I love this place, it is so beautiful."

"I have had many happy times there Abby, you will find it a place where time slows, and you just relax. Not only that, you two have access to it any time you want it, so use it, and use it as much as possible. I am sure your little Curio group will love it too. How is Will, he is not too tired is he?" I nodded, and then giggled, he leaned over the table.

"Roni I am fine, I will be heading back shortly, I will be in London about seven."

"Alright love, but just take your time and drive carefully." I suddenly remembered.

"Roni, what the hell did you hit Katie with, it looked like you beat her with the wardrobe?" She gave a slight sigh.

"Assault should always be the last thing you use; I did give her a lot of warnings. Girls I went there to talk, things just got to me and I lost control, do not let it impress you, I was wrong to hit her." Birch turned, and looked at the table, where the phone lay.

"You just hit, like one punch?" She was a little quiet.

"Sadly yes, I punched her, and it broke her nose." I probably should not have been, but I was impressed.

"Wow. just one punch, wow Roni, when Will said you were tough, I had no idea how much." Will smirked.

"He told you that did he, and what else did he tell you Abby?"

"He told us how you were the only one tough enough to take on Gladys Pimpleback. I have to tell you, I think you are bad ass, taking her out when everyone else was terrified of her, that is pretty awesome." Birch looked at me and nodded, Roni started to laugh, I frowned at the phone.

"Why is that funny, she was huge, swollen, and bloated, and you stepped up, and wham, in less than three seconds you took her out, Roni that was as..."

Roni was almost hysterical laughing, I didn't get it, Birch

stopped what she was doing and walked to the table. Roni was howling with laughter, even Will started to giggle, I looked at Birch.

"Why is it funny, I was really impressed?" Birch shrugged. Roni calmed down a little and I could hear her trying to take deep breaths.

"Abby you are so sweet, but do not listen to Will, he is pulling a fast one. Gladys was the name he gave to the large boil that grew on his back, it was pretty disgusting to look at, and it freaked a lot of people out." She started to giggle, I gasped with shock, and looked at Will, who had his head down chuckling.

"One night we could not have any bedroom fun, because he was in so much pain, so I rolled him over, oh God it was putrid. I was almost sick just looking at it. Anyhow, I did not have a needle, so I lay him flat, and I punched it with all my strength, and it exploded. Oh God, it went everywhere, I was nearly sick, it took almost a whole loo roll to drain it."

Birch flapped her hands in front of her making strange faces, I was really grossed out, but shocked, I stared at Will.

"It was only a frigging pimple? I thought it was a big muscular beast with tits that had been bullying you, Will you are a freaking pussy." Roni screamed with hysterics; Birch flapped her hands even more.

"I want to yerk. Dad that is really gross, I have held mums hand loads of times, oh God I wish I hadn't, now I know what's been on it." Will just sat back and laughed his head off.

I was so disappointed, my admiration had soared for Roni, although she took out Katie, who admittedly scared me, so I felt she was still the top in my poll. Roni finally stopped giggling and took a huge breath.

"Girls, sleep, relax, and talk to each other, and just enjoy your alone time together, in what is your second home together. Sunny Bank is a beautiful place, so take it all in."

Saying goodbye to Will was not easy, it felt strange. He was there for me when I felt at my most alone, I still could not believe he had run all that way behind me, just to be there when I broke. He stood in front of me and smiled.

"You are going to be fine now. All your answers lie within her arms, show her what you showed me, show her how much you love her, and maybe recommit to each other. Katie did something horrible and introduced doubt, take my advice, use this place to cast it all out."

I pulled him close and gave him a huge squeeze, he wrapped his arms round me, and hugged me with love.

"Thanks, Will… Dad. I got so lost in myself, and you reached in and found me, it means everything to me." He kissed my forehead.

"I love both my daughters deeply, and I will always be there for both of you. Let go and have some fun, and come back even happier." Birch handed him a refilled flask.

"Thanks Dad, I love you." He pulled her into a hug.

"Jemi, take your time, and really lock you two solid, you know if you had kept your eye on the ball, this may not have happened. Abby is a bright girl, she spotted Katie's antics before you did, do not lose sight of each other for the sake of a friendship. If they really cannot accept you two, then they do not belong around either of you. Keep that in mind." She smiled.

"You made your point, now drive carefully, please Dad, I know you, just take it easy and get back safe." He kissed her cheek and jumped in with a wink.

Both of us stood outside the house and waved as he drove off, I slipped my arm around her waist.

"What now Birch?" She patted my butt.

"Food, I am starving, and wine, and then, well, we can do whatever we want, but I aim to screw you in at least ten places I know, and the list is growing." I gave a big smile, and we turned to walk inside.

"How long is this list going to be?" She winked at me.

"Long…. And I mean very long." I liked the idea of that.

"So we are here for some time then?" She gave a loud cackle as we walked into the kitchen, I looked down the room.

"I do hope you put that table on the list?" She turned to face me and pulled at my vest.

"It is funny you should say that, it is the first thing I put on there."

My top hit the floor, and she went down on her knees and

started to unbutton my shorts, I leaned back on the old wood, her lips started to kiss up the inside of my thigh, I looked down as I felt my heart start to beat faster.

"I thought you were hungry?" She looked up and her eyes sparkled with mischief.

"I am... First, we eat.... And then we have the food." Oh shit, I love it when she tells me the lines from my books. I pressed my palms onto the surface of the table, and slid up and back.

"Well, my darling, in my house, we only ever eat at the table."

She gave a squeal of delight, as I slid backwards and opened my legs. Birch pulled off her vest, and dropped her shorts on the floor, and stepped out of them. Birch then came crawling on all fours towards me. Her green eyes smouldered like a hunting panther, and I swallowed hard. Oh, God, I was so turned on, those eyes get me every time. She gave a sexy giggle, and then dived down into me, and I lay back and gave off a loud moan.

"Oh God... Yes!"

Chapter 22

Sunny Bank.

Naked, sexed up, and giddy, we cooked tea side by side, and then sat on the table, we had just had sex on, and we ate, and drank wine. We put the pots in the sink for later, and Birch took my hand, and led me out of the back door, and I marvelled.

Just in front of the back door was a wide patio of large natural stone slabs. Where the patio stopped, there was a sunken stream, I looked down at it as it trickled along, and bunches of small blue flowers hung down, stroking the water. Birch slipped her hands round my waist and leaned on my shoulder; I felt her warm breasts press into my back.

"When I was little, I called this the fairy stream, and it has sort of stuck. From that day onward, everyone has called it that, my mum used to make paper boats with me and sail them down the garden."

About ten feet to our left, was a small wooden bridge, that crossed the stream, and allowed passage into the rest of the garden, which I can only really describe as a field. It was a huge space of grass, with lots of trees and planters and a few scattered flower beds. There was a large gravelled area filled with stone chippings, on which was a wooden picnic table, and a glass patio set. The whole place felt natural and earthy. She took my hand, and we walked over the bridge as she told me about it all.

"I watched him make this bridge, the old one was rotten, and he made the new one in sections, and carried them out here and assembled them, and dad helped him set it in place." She gave a fond smile, and I just loved watching her face as she revealed more of who she really was.

"See the swing set over there, I helped build that, when I was seven? He drilled all the holes, and he let me hammer the long bolts through." She gave a soft chuckle.

"I kept missing the hammer was so heavy, it took forever, but I was so thrilled he let me help, and he was so patient. God Deads, I loved him so much." Her eyes welled up, and she stopped to wipe them.

"I am sorry, it just brings so much back for me, it is why it is so long since I have been here." I could understand that, although my gran was a hateful bitch, so in a way, I guess I did not completely get it.

"When was the last time you were here, was it fifteen?" She shook her head.

"No... I was here for his funeral, I was seventeen, but I stayed out in the front in the car. I did not want to stay in the house, I stayed with Seth and Mable. I just could not come in without him here."

I really could understand that, it made perfect sense to me. Four years ago Birch walked out on me, it was only for a couple of days, but I remembered coming home and not finding her. The house felt strange and alien, even though all her things were still there. I think that is what it feels like for her here.

"So this is the first time you have really been back here since he passed?" She nodded, and wiped her eyes.

"I honestly thought it would be different now." I shook my head.

"Birch, his memory will live in your heart forever, he may have gone, but the thoughts the feelings and all those happy times, they still live on inside you, and that is not a sad thing, it is a wonderful thing. I hate to point this out, but wasn't it you that told me to remember is the greatest thing you can do for a person, because as long as you remember them, they will never die?" She gave a sigh, and walked over to the swing set, and sat on one of the swings, as she regained her composure.

I followed her over, and sat on the other and gently rocked it with my feet on the floor, it gave off a slight squeak.

"Birch, my dad had a heart attack." She turned and looked at me shocked.

"How... When... Abby, why didn't you tell me?" I rocked backwards and forward, and stared at the floor.

"It happened a few weeks ago, he told Angela not to phone me, because it would worry me." I turned to her.

"Is it wrong to be upset and angry about that, is it wrong to think he was a selfish shit, because that is what I feel?" She lifted her legs and started to swing.

"He should have told you, well actually Angie should have ignored him and called you. If you ask me, it was very selfish, but be honest Deads, he has always been all about him. Is that why he did not want me there?" I started to swing, it has been years since I sat on a swing. I looked at her as she watched me.

"Yes... He wanted to talk finances and company shares. He wants to make me head of the board when he dies to keep things running as they are." She gave a nod, but she knows me better than anyone.

"Are you happy about that?" I gave a long sigh, and dug my feet in the floor and stopped.

"I really do not know how I feel. I guess it has been so long since I thought I felt something, that I no longer know what I feel at all about him. Birch, I do not feel a connection to him, well not like I do mum, or your parents, or you. Oh god, I feel so guilty because I feel nothing, it is just empty where he is supposed to be." I put my head down and stared at the floor.

"I really love your dad, last night he chased me for ages, and he never gave up, even when he was gasping for air. He caught up with me, wrapped his arms around me, and held me, and I felt so safe, so loved, so I bawled my brains out and covered his new shirt in tears and puke. My dad would never do that." Birch completely understood.

"I cannot tell you how to feel, all I can tell you is my dad has always been there when I needed him, he understands me in ways no one else does, he gets me like you do, no one else does Deads. Izzy kind of thinks she does, but she doesn't really, but my dad, he does, he believes in me. I think that is what all dads should be because of mine, I really do not understand your dad, I never have. I mean, I get his psychology, but as a person, as a man, no, I do not get him. I do not understand why he does not marvel at his uniquely amazing daughter; I just think he has lost his ability to feel anything. I think if you open him up, you will find a cold space devoid of anything. If anything, I feel sorry for him."

"I got upset in the limo when I rang mum, so I know I do not want him to die. I feel really guilty that I found it hard last night to really show love. Am I like him, because I actually felt more care for Angela, she really went out of her way to make me feel comfortable and relaxed? She was more like she used to be when I was a young teenager visiting the office. Birch, I don't think she is a bad person, and I wonder if he feels any love for her, I mean, think about it, she has been with him years, so she must care?" Birch started to swing again.

"You got upset in the limo, how upset, because I thought Markus was a lot more polite than normal today?" Wow she does not miss a trick.

"He pulled over and gave me coffee, and then he let me ride up front, and talked to me. He parked in the downstairs garage and gave me some good advice before dropping me off, he said he was worried." She turned on the swing and looked at me, and her eyes filled with tears.

"Oh God Deads, and I went and did that to you, I am so sorry... I am so, so sorry, oh my God, you came from that to see me like that, is that why you ran away?" Her shoulders started to shake, and she looked down and her tears dripped onto her legs. I got off the swing, and crouched down in front of her, as she sobbed.

"I can be such a horrible person at times, I was so stupid last night, I told Katie to leave you alone, I told her I would never want her. I told her Deads, I told her I would only ever marry you; I did not lie." I knelt down and pulled her into a hug.

"I am so sorry Sweetie, I do love you so much, I am just a bloody idiotic basket case at times." I held her close, I did not want this, I wanted this to be a happy place. I leaned back and looked at her tear filled eyes.

"Birch, I knew you did not lie; I saw the red and freaked out, but when you told me you did nothing, I believed you, but I could not handle my emotions. Hearing about my dad, and talking to my mum, and then Markus, I had reached my limit, and then I walked in on your mum screaming at you, and I hit overload. I should not have run away, but I was so freaked out, I panicked." She leaned forward and threw her arms round me, and hugged me so hard, I could hardly breathe.

"I should have taken more care, I hate what she did, Deads, she touched me where I never wanted her to touch me. Those parts of my body are meant for only you, and when you ran away and I thought I had lost you, I could not handle it. I just lost it completely, but you know what, I thought about it all day while I was driving, and I know Deads, I know for certain that I want to marry you, I know ten thousand percent, I want my life to be with you.”

I think I needed to hear that, I had been slightly emotional all day, I had thousands of thoughts going through my mind, and after arriving I had found some calmness, and suddenly I had it all back in my head, I pushed my head into the side of her head.

“I want all this to end Birch, I want a free mind, I don’t want my dad and Katie in my head. I just want you, and our home, and my writing in me, that is all. I want to put everything else behind us, can we please do that? I cannot stand seeing you cry, I live for your smile, your joy, and your crazy laugh. Birch, I want to be your wife, and wake up every day till I am older than May was with you. Can I please just have that?” Birch turned and kissed my cheek.

“Okay Sweetie, if that is what you want, then we can do that, but you know, your dad is something you need to prepare for. To be honest, I admire the way you have defended him and stood by him, even with me, because you can walk away with your head high, just because of what he did to you over Martin. I think this will come back, and when it does, face it and talk to me.” I pulled back and I gave a nod, her eyes sparkled with life, I smiled.

“Tell me where I am, because honestly, I have no frigging idea?” She looked at me and frowned.

“We are at Sunny Bank, I thought you knew that?” I gave a sigh and put my head down.

“Birch, where the hell is Sunny Bank?” She started to giggle.

“Sweetie, it’s right behind you.” She gave a giggle and leaned in and kissed my nose.

“We are right on the edge of Dartmoor.” I was shocked.

“You mean Devon, the hound of the Baskervilles country?” She gave me a huge smile.

“Oh yes Sweetie, we are in the heart of Conan Doyle country… Come and see.”

Birch jumped up, and I fell backwards, she gave an excited giggle and grabbed my hand, to pull me up. Holding her hand, we rushed back to the house, and up the narrow stairs to what would be our bedroom. She opened a cupboard and pulled out a pair of binoculars and handed them to me. Pulling back the curtain she pointed out of the window.

"It is quite far off, but if you follow that line, you will see something amazing."

I was puzzled but excited. I lifted them up to my eyes and scanned the horizon, it looked bleak, I tried to focus and moved a lot slower, and my heart skipped a beat as I caught it, and panned back.

"Oh wow, is that where he stood, holy shit, is that the actual rock, is that where they filmed it?" I turned to her looking excited, she smiled an excited smile.

"Deads, I never got tired of looking at that when I was younger, it is so cool." And suddenly, we were a pair of Sherlock Holmes geeks. I had to laugh.

"He stood there Birch... Basil Rathbone actually stood there and shot the scene, oh my god I want to go there, although, is it as dangerous up there as the books says it is?" She gave a nod and took the binoculars, and looked out of the window.

"During the boar war, Conan Doyle stayed in Devon for quite a long time, my granddad told me he visited the prison on Dartmoor, and that was when he got the idea of a convict on the moor with the large hounds tracking him. I think he must have had first hand knowledge, so he would have known all about the mires. It is so cool to know he walked up there. I read Hound of the Baskervilles in this house for the very first time, when I was eleven."

God, I was so blown away, no wonder she was such a fan, I am huge fan, but this, well, this put her ten levels of fan girl way above me.

"Deb's is going to be so jealous, when I tell her about this, she is going to freak, we must get a picture of it." Birch put down the binoculars and gave a wicked grin.

"Let's take one, and cut it into pieces, and send her a bit each day, and see if she can work it out."

Oh my God that was the coolest idea I had ever heard, my head almost exploded it was so brilliant. I nodded like a crazy person, and she gave a happy squeal, and then like a pair of mental patients, she grabbed me and we started to dance and laugh.

Yeah, we are so messed up by books, but it is wonderful, and I am not at all ashamed. We ended up lay on the bed panting, and smiling like idiots. I lay back and looked around the room, it was very floral, with lots of little bunches of flowers on the wall paper, and curtains. Birch turned her head to me.

"It is very country bumkin isn't it? I think it is a thing for rural areas, should we decorate over it, or leave it?" I turned to look round the room.

"I suppose it has sort of a quaint charm, it is up to you, if you want to decorate do so, but if you think about it, your granddad decorated all of this, and he is pretty special to you." She sat up and looked round.

"We can leave it for now, we just got this place, so we have tons of time and no need to rush." I thought that was a good idea, I rocked my hips up and down and the bed squeaked really loudly.

"If you masturbate alone, I will know." She started to laugh, and rocked her hips up and down.

"Holy shit Deads, we need to oil this bed, probably a good job we don't own a strap on." I started to laugh.

"That is probably Mable." Birch gave a really loud cackle of a laugh.

"Sweetie, your face when she talked about dildo's was so funny." I lay back on the bed as she laughed.

"Birch she is a really sweet old lady, I never expected that to come out of her mouth. I was so surprised, because she is all sweet and nice, it really shocked me." She sat up giggling.

"Dad said he replaced the shower a year ago, do you want to take a look?" I rolled over to her.

"Not yet." I slid my hand on to her, and moved it up to her boob, she looked at me, and took a deep breath.

"Deads, I am nervous."

I slid over, and moved over her, she looked really tense.

I looked down at her, where I knew the red lip stick marks had been, her normally white skin, was still red from where she had rubbed herself raw. I leaned down and started to kiss her boob where Katie had kissed her, she gave a slight gasp of shock, I slid back, and slipped my legs between hers, to part them, she gave a little jolt.

"Deads, are you really okay with this; I will understand if you are not?" I looked at her and smiled, and lowered my head.

"I baptise thee, in the name of the dark little beastie." I kissed the top of her thigh, and she tensed.

"I take thee my queen of the snow." I moved slowly along the line she had drawn on her.

"To be forever cleansed, from the red Satanic harlot, of the north."

I moved closer towards her sex, and she gave a little gasp, I kissed her passionately, and she shuddered.

"Oh god, Oh Deads."

I kissed her all around that area, and she gave a loud moan, and I had not even hit her sweet spots yet. I moved into her, and she bucked on the bed, and gave a really loud wail of a moan, her body arched, I had never known her cum so fast, I just kept motoring on as her legs began to shake. She gripped my head.

"Deads, oh god, Deads... Deads... OH MY GOD!"

She exploded into my mouth, with her hands gripping my skull like an eagle holding a baby lamb, she lay there quivering as I moved back, out of her grasp, and smiled, I sat up.

"Arise my child, in the name of the chuff, the dildo, and the really weird old lady up the road." I smiled.

"You are cleansed forever." She lay back red in the face and panting slightly, and tears filled her eyes, I leaned over her.

"No tears, she is gone. Birch, I have been here remember? I know how it feels, well, she has no power here." She gave a sniffle, and lifted her hand to my cheek.

"You are so remarkable, so beautifully wonderful, do you know that?" I smiled and leaned forward and kissed her.

"You stink of sex; do you know that? I would race you to the shower... But I do not actually know where it is." She giggled, and just held my face, I smiled.

"I love you Birch; no one will ever change that." Her eyes sparkled surrounded by a sea of white and black patched hair.

"I love you too, I really do." I took her hand, and pulled her off the bed, it was time to find the shower.

I think the thing that has bothered me the most, is that Katie deliberately targeted Birch, in a bid to destroy us. I thought about it last night in bed, and also today in the car, she saw Birch alone, honed in on her, and without even thinking about the consequences, she created a situation that left Birch doubting herself.

Anyone who knows Birch, understands how confident she can be, but the sly and devious way in which Katie set her up, I think was the cruellest thing she could have done to her. Birch passed out, and when she woke, and saw the red lipstick on her, she went into full melt down, because she simply had no memory of anything happening.

Nothing did happen, well apart from a few kisses in some pretty private places, but Birch was oblivious to that, she had no memory of doing anything herself. Such was the way she was set up, she believed she had done something. That is why this is so cruel; it is without doubt a cold emotionally traumatic thing. Did Katie screw her or not, she had no way of knowing, and so the seed was planted in her mind, and even though she is strong and intelligent, even for Birch, the self doubt germinated, how callous and evil can you get?

Jealousy is a dangerous thing, I have never had time for it, as I have always seen it as the tactic of a person to have control. I know all about control, I have grown up watching it, and also suffered from it, as I watched my father with his little digs and sly comments, try to push my mum away from the things she loved. He demanded every ounce of her attention, and never gave her a second of his, as she was forced to bend to his will. I saw his eyes and scowls whenever she was praised and he wasn't.

Sexual jealousy is even worse, because it does not matter who you are or what you feel, a jealous person will manipulate, and possess your life until it becomes unrecognisable. It is like a cancer that eats at the soul until it consumes you completely, and no example is better than that of Katie. The saddest thing in all of this is Anita, because she actually admired and grew to care for Katie, but Katie was so blinded by her jealousy, she failed to notice that she had a chance to have what we have, with Anita.

With that being said, I will never forgive her for what she has done, just seeing Birch in the shower, breaking her heart and harming herself, as she rubbed herself red raw, is something that will stay with me forever. Tonight, I knew I had to kill whatever it was that Katie did, otherwise it would haunt Birch forever. I suffered after Martin, knowing he touched my breasts, and ran his fingers over my bum, and between my legs, it made me feel unclean for a long time. I knew tonight I had to show her that she was still pure. I hope she understands that, I hope she now heals, all I can do is watch and wait.

We found the shower, and Birch found her smile again, and we had a lot of fun washing each other down. We followed that with another bottle of wine, and cheese on toast at midnight, sat on the kitchen table, which was such great fun. We jumped into bed and left the curtains open to see the stars, it is so dark here at night, I marvelled at how bright they looked. Birch snuggled into me slightly drunk and with a happy sigh.

"I like being married." I smiled, placed my hand on hers, and gave it a squeeze.

"Well at least if we have some shitty days, we now know we can overcome them, but I hope we can just have ordinary boring days of sex, cuddles and no one interfering." She giggled into my shoulder.

"That would be nice too."

I snuggled down and pushed back into her, and I felt warm and safe, as I always do when she is cuddling me. It had been one hell of a weekend, and even though I had slept in the car, I felt exhausted. I lay in bed staring out of the window and watching the stars, and as I felt Birch's breathing behind me, I gave a happy sigh, and closed my eyes, my last thought was, 'maybe the country air does make you sleepy,' but I would not really know, because by then, I was asleep.

I became aware of the sheets, and the soft pillow, and felt the heat on my face, my legs moved and I felt the yawn, I opened my eyes.

"Holy shit!"

It was blinding, and I snapped my eyes closed, and rolled over to face the other way. Note to self, stars are really pretty, blinding balls of light in the sky are not, close curtains when sleepy.

I stretched out my arm, and she was not there, I opened one eye, there was an impression in the pillow where she had slept,

I slid closer, and could smell her soft fragrant scent on it. Being in bed alone did not really feel the same, so I kicked off the duvet and sat up, and scratched my head. I needed coffee so I headed downstairs. I have decided, I definitely love latches, why did we ever give them up, and start using door knobs? That click, as you press down with your thumb, is just too wonderful, I really love it.

There really is something very special about old houses, like how the stairs have that creaking noise as you step on them, and at the bottom of the stairs there is a door, not a hall, an actual door, I just love it. I walked into the living room, and stopped to have a good look round, I have not really been alone in here so far, so it was nice to just take my time and take it all in. The mantle above the fire had a few small pot figures, mainly of elegant woman in Victorian clothing, there was a lot of brass and copper, all of which were polished to perfection, and the walls were covered in pictures.

I walked over to the wall that backed onto the kitchen, all the tiny frames filled it, and most of them were photos framed of Birch from a baby right up until being a teenager, all bar one, which was new, and was a picture of her in a cap and gown holding her doctorate from Uni. I was surprised, as I had never seen it before, and what surprised me even more, was that she had a small brooch pinned to her gown, and it was the same as the bat on my mug and door at home.

I stood staring at it, I remembered the disappointment of that day, because Katie had booked me a bookshop signing at the last minute of my book, and then on the last second had pulled out, and I had been taken care of by a guy called Richard. It suddenly hit me, she had orchestrated it in order to stop me being there. I stared at the picture, as she smiled, but that was not her smile, it was somehow duller, not quite her, and I understood why. Even back then she was working against us, I had just not realised.

I hated her so much, it is crazy, she was once classed as a friend, and yet now, I do not think I could even stand being in the same room as her. I walked into the kitchen and clicked on the kettle, my mug was already there washed and waiting I smiled as I looked at it, as I unscrewed the lid of the coffee jar, it is just the small things in life that really do mean the most.

As I waited for the kettle, I walked to the window and peeped out through the plants. Birch was sat outside at the picnic bench, her feet up along the bench. She was holding her cup close to her face, and sipping lost in thought. The sun was shining and her hair was as white as snow, as it hung down the back of her, moving softly in the light breeze, she looked so beautiful, almost mystical. The kettle clicked, and I turned to pour out my coffee.

I walked as I sipped my first taste of the day and felt my mouth come to life. I came quietly out of the back door onto the warm stones, they felt lovely under my bare feet as I padded along to the wooden bridge to cross over. The soft low cut grass was warm, and I felt my feet sink in, it was such a wonderful feeling, as I approached her, and she came out of her thoughts and looked up. She smiled and her eyes sparkled.

"Hi Sweetie." I sat down on the opposite bench, and leaned forward on the table, as I looked at her.

"You looked lost to the world; I suppose it is a lot to think about coming back here?" She took a deep breath of the air, and looked around.

"I have always thought this was a magical place, as a child my granddad talked of fairies, wizards and witches. I think he was the inspiration for my love of fantasy stories, he made this place very special for me. When dad said he was going to sell it, I knew I could not let it go. It probably sounds daft Deads, but if I sit here and close my eyes, it is almost as if he is still here, pottering around, waiting for me to walk up and ask him what he is doing, so he can show me something new. There is no way I could give this place up."

I smiled, there was an air of something about her as she spoke, nostalgia maybe, I am not sure, she looked more rested, and more peaceful than I had seen her in some time.

"You do not have to Birch, to be honest, here fits you well, it is like you are a part of it, and maybe you needed to come back here. Maybe you lost something and needed to return." She looked at me and I could see her pondering.

"What, you think this is where I am destined to be, like it is the will of the world, Sweetie we live in Wotton?" I smiled as I lifted my cup.

"You once told me we could live anywhere, I remember you saying, if it's not working, we will just sell up, grab the girls, and go where it does."

"Sweetie, we have spent four years building a life around the house in the village, it is where we both decided we would put down roots." I nodded, and I understood that.

"Birch, I have been here a day, and I can already see, this is where your true roots are. If you ask me, seeing you sat here naked in the sun, with the light streaming down on you and the house behind you, it is clear as day that this place is in some strange way the physical embodiment of everything you are." She gave a long sigh.

"Well, this place is special to me, there is no doubt of that, and I do feel very much at ease here. I love nature, and just look at this place, nature is kissing every inch of it." I took a swig of my coffee, and gave a grin, as she watched me.

"You know what I think, and you will probably think I am bonkers?" She shook her head.

"What do you think, pray tell me?"

"Looking at the walls lined with pictures in there, and actually seeing your life in full, I think this is the place where Jemi ended, and Birch began."

She sat there staring at me, contemplating what I said. I shrugged at her, moved my hand and pointed to the thick woodland that surrounded the property.

"I mean, look, look at the trees with their tall graceful trunks, lined with black, you probably know every line and mark on those trees. I honestly think the night you got that Uni girl to do your hair, you thought of this place, and it was here that inspired you to come up with something as unique as the bark of every birch tree. Think about it, your love of nature, your love of moors and plants and trees, your fascination with elves and fairies. Birch all of that is here, this is you, and you are this, it makes perfect sense to me." She looked at the trees, and her eyes followed them and their tall white trunked lines, and smiled.

"Sweetie, you have just completely mind blown me, I never saw it, but you have, holy shit, was my granddad a wizard?" I started to chuckle.

"Maybe we should ask Moon?"

Chapter 23

Secret Birch.

Birch was in a dreamy state of mind, she had a lot of memories passing through her thoughts, so we both slid on our shorts, and Birch decided she would show me around the property, which was far bigger than I had realised.

I know I am in or on Dartmoor, hell, I have seen the rocky outcrop featured in the movie, but that is about as much as I know, so as which way is north or south, I have no idea. What I can say is this, if you stand at the back door, and look over the fairy stream across the large cleared space of garden, there is a bank of huge birch, oak, and other trees I do not know the name of.

The birch trees are massive and there are a lot of them on the edge of what I am told is woodland. They are thick at the base, so they are really old, and the bark at the base is thick, lumpy, and craggy. As they sweep up, they're as white as Birch hair, with the familiar black patches I know from seeing her every day.

To the right, is a sort of meadow, come moor, the ground is soft in parts and very peaty, and there are some pretty large boulders sticking up through the grass, and lots of wild flowers, there are hardly any trees there. To the left is thick dense woodland, in the middle of which runs a river, it is actually the River Teign. Birch took me to the right of the house, and into the meadow, where there was a fine path that skirted the edge of the woodland. She packed a bag, and we walked along until the trees broke revealing a sort of oval cleared space filled with grass and flowers, here she lay down a blanket, and we had a naked picnic.

The sun was really hot, and we really enjoyed rubbing lotion on each other, which resulted in a lot more activity than planned. Hot sweaty and exhausted, we opened the chilled wine, and relaxed to eat, talk, and sleep, it was simply divine, if this is married life alone with Birch, I want more.

It was Monday, and the book fair was over. Last night, whilst Birch and myself prepared food after having sex on the table, back in Wotton, Anita arrived and asked to speak to Izzy. They sat together for a long time talking, as Anita relayed messages from Roni to her. My mum arrived midway through, hoping I would be home, I had not realised, but after talking to Roni on the phone, my battery had died, and last night I forgot to plug it in.

Izzy called a house meet, and with my mum joining in, Izzy spelled out exactly what had happened, and where we had gone to take some time out, and why it was important. Mum added the extra of explaining her call with me in the limo, so by breakfast this morning Chloe sat at the island as everyone rushed to work, worried, and missing her usual coffee buddy, Edwina noticed and sat down.

"Is everything alright?" Chloe fingered her cup handle.

"I miss Abby, mornings are not the same without her, and I am worried about her." Edwina understood, and leaned forward and took Chloe's hand off her mug and held it.

"Chloe, they are going to be fine, they need time alone, but they are strong, hell, they are so close, honestly this will actually do them so much good." Chloe gave a slight nod as she stared at the counter, her voice was quiet.

"I know... Weena, I know what it is like, I know what Birch felt when she woke up and realised what had happened." She looked up.

"I know the dark feelings you have when someone touch's you, and you do not want them to, so does Abby. It will be hard for Birch; it will put a wall between them." Edwina watched carefully as Chloe spoke.

"Chloe, are you feeling that too, I can call Susana if you want me to?" She shook her head.

"I am fine, honestly, I am just saying, I know how it feels. I scrubbed myself raw for days. It is hard, I want to talk to Abby but her phone is off, I just wanted to make sure she knows so she can help Birch... I fucking hate that red haired bitch, if I had been there, I would have pushed her out of the window."

"To be honest, if we had all been there, we probably would have dragged her to the roof and thrown her off. We will see them soon Chloe, and they will be smiling, and we should all smile with them and help them be normal. If we are weird around them, it will be hard for them." Chloe pulled her hand free, and lifted her cup.

"I have been painting them, I was going to give it as a wedding present. I might give it them early, so they can see how much they love each other." Edwina smiled, and nodded her head.

"That is a lovely idea, is it good?"

"It is the best I have ever done." Edwina looked at her.

"What, better than the one you have in your room?" Chloe smiled at her, and her eyes twinkled.

"Weena, it is so much better, as I painted it, all I did was think of all the things I have seen those two do, and all the laughter they have had. I really thought deeply about how much they mean to me, and honestly, I am so thrilled with it. I have been working on this for months to get it perfect." Edwina felt a tinge of excitement.

"Can I see it?" Chloe shook her head.

"Not yet, I want them to be the first to see it, after that, yes." She pulled out her phone and clicked it open.

"You know the picture, I mean, everyone does, I took it at Deb's wedding."

Chloe turned the phone and there was a picture of Birch and Abby, their hands together in front of their chests, as they kissed, it was the moment where they first made a commitment to each other, Edwina smiled.

"I love this picture, I remember when you first showed it me, I was so sad I missed the moment." Chloe turned the phone round to look at it.

"I painted the black eye out, you know, make her look like normal Abby, but it has turned out so good, I am so excited for them to see it." Edwina lifted her cup with a smile.

"You are a really talented artist; I am sure they will love it." Chloe gave a nod and let out a sigh.

"Thanks Weena, you know, for taking a minute and talking, I will be fine now."

Edwina headed for the library, Sam was having the morning off, so she thought she would work closer to Chloe, who headed for her studio to paint, and the day moved onward.

Today, as I lay back in the sun having had yet more great sex, followed by white wine and food, my phone was sat in the house charging up. I lay back on the blanket and stretched.

"This is glorious, I could lie here for the rest of my life." Birch smiled, as she finished making her daisy chain, she leaned over and slipped it over my head.

"I love how natural you are. Here, for you, I blend thee with nature." I lifted my head as she slipped it over, I held it up and looked at it.

"Wow, I have not seen one of these since I was a kid." Birch giggled.

"It is strange isn't it how we give up so much from our childhood to be adults. So many things are considered to be childish, but why, children are natural, they understand the simplicity of life? I love how children are not racists or sexist, they just see another kid and think, can we be friends, and off they go. You know, if you give a child a box or a stick, it becomes something, and they play with it all day, it is like they just naturally repurpose everything, when did everyone lose that?" I lay back and stared at the sky.

"School, I think... They are fine until they go there, and then in come the teachers and tell them how to be and how to act, and how not to be. I got in so much trouble for day dreaming, but I found the work too easy, so I did it, then sat back and drifted. I got so many lectures from my dad about it, but if you think about it Birch, the day dreaming was me understanding how to write." She lay back and gave a long breath out.

"When did the world get so screwed up, how did people become so cruel and spiteful? I have heard so many tales of pain in the last four years, I find some days hard to deal with, just knowing that at that moment, people are being evil to each other."

I turned and looked at her, and she was watching me as she lay on the blanket, her green eyes were clear, and wide open, and she looked so beautiful.

"I really am starting to think that some people, are just really horrible people. You know, I try to be nice with everyone, I don't like being horrible, but at times I sit back and think why am I even trying, because there is nothing good at all inside them? I saw your picture on the wall, did it hurt you that I could not be there to see you graduate?" She blinked.

"Why would you think of that Deads, you were booked in advance, you needed to be there to try and get your books off the floor. It was important Sweetie, I understood that. I will not deny, I would have loved to walk up there and looked down and seen you, but Deads, selling your books was as important to you as the retreat was to me, I get that completely?" I gave a long sigh.

"Katie was there, wasn't she?" Birch looked at me and furrowed her brow.

"She was, but why does that matter?" I played with my flower chain.

"She was supposed to be with me, but she cancelled and replaced herself with a guy to do the event. Birch, she knew it was your graduation, why did she book me a one off event, when she knew how much I wanted to be there with you? I was miserable all day, and when I got home and found out, it was crushing. Katie knew, she made out like she was a friend, but she wasn't was she, it was her way of keeping us apart because she was jealous?" Birch appeared to get a little anxious.

"Oh Deads, I just do not know anymore. I thought she was a friend, I trusted her, she has done so much to help us, and yet, I am still coming to terms with what she has done. The horrible thing is, I do not know if she went down on me, I don't know if she explored me with her tongue, or fingered me, I just do not know. All I know is if I had not drunk so much, it would never have happened. I feel so unbelievably guilty, and I do not even know if we did anything." I sat up, and turned to her.

"Then stop thinking about it, I have no idea how, but I will find out, I will put your mind at ease once and for all. Birch, I want you to treat me the same, actually, I need you to treat me the same, we have always touched each other, kissed, had random spontaneous sex. There are times I will want to jump on you, and have you there and then, and I really am worried Katie has stopped all that, and I don't want her to. I want you to be you, does this even make sense?" Birch sat up, and raised her knees up and leaned on them.

"I was afraid last night, you wanted to touch me where I think she did, but you just went down and kissed me, in all the places I had those awful red marks. Deads, it meant a huge amount to me, it actually turned me on that you were so confident, and I woke this morning feeling a lot better. I don't want to be unnatural with you, and you should be spontaneous."

I smiled at her and leaned forward, and gave her a long slow kiss, and made it linger for as long as possible. I came out of the kiss and winked.

"Is that spontaneous enough for you?" She smiled and her eyes twinkled.

"I like spontaneous Sweetie; she is very sexy indeed."

For the rest of the afternoon, we lay back and talked, and I felt like we had conquered another hurdle, in my mind I could hear Roni's words in my head. 'Talk, relax, make love, and just restore yourselves, get yourselves well and reconnect with each other.' I was trying, and I think it was working, but I do not understand this stuff the way she does. All I knew was I would never quit on her.

Chloe sat painting and humming quietly to herself, when there was a loud banging on the front door, she froze, her brush an inch from the canvass. Edwina came out of the library.

"I will get it Chloe." The brush touched the canvass and continued the stroke of colour. Edwina pulled and the door opened, she froze.

"What the fuck do you want?"

Katie stood at the door, with a wide patch of white plaster across her nose, and large very dark glasses. She fidgeted where she stood, and looked back to the gates, where the rear end of her red car was just visible. Her head turned back to Edwina, as she stroked her hair back over her shoulder.

"Look, I just need to talk to Jemi, I am not here for trouble." Edwina just stared at her with distaste.

"Jemi... Not Abby as well, because you bloody well owe her an apology as well?" Katie gave a sigh.

"Look Edwina, I have been to the retreat, so I know she is not there, and her car is parked on the drive, so please, stop stalling, and just ask her if she will see me." Edwina shook her head.

"Sorry, but she is not here, her and Abby took a few days off to recover, and talk about the really fucking shitty ass thing you did to try and break them up. It is a good thing that Abby saw your bullshit over a year ago, and she saw this coming, and as a result you failed. Honestly, you are lucky I didn't give you a mouth to match your nose when I saw you." Katie straightened up.

"Oh please, really, you want to try the alpha bitch with me, give me a small break, and just tell me where the fuck they are, I really have no time to play hostile."

"WHAT THE FUCK IS THAT FUCKING BITCH DOING HERE!?" Chloe came marching up the hallway with a brush in her hand, Edwina put out her hand to stop her.

"Leave it Chloe." Chloe barged right past, and stepped right up to Katie. She stood on her tip toes to come face to face with Katie.

"You need to get the fuck off this property BITCH!" Katie stepped back, and looked at the paint brush in her hand.

"Or what little girl, you will paint my death on the pavement, oh please, give me a fucking break?"

Chloe spun the brush in her hand as her eyes glared with hate, she held it up, looked at it, and then jabbed the pointed end of it right in her left boob with force. Katie squealed in pain, and gripped her boob.

"You fucking Bitch." Chloe leaned forward, and her anger showed in her eyes.

"What you did to Abby was fucking evil, and what you did to Birch, was fucking twisted and even more evil. I fucking hate you for what you have done, now get the fuck off this property."

Katie backed up another step, holding her boob, and looked a little afraid, Chloe lifted her brush really fast, spun it in her hand, and then poked her hard right on the plaster across the bridge of her nose. Katie squealed out in pain, turned, and ran for the gates holding her face, wailing, as Chloe stood fuming, she turned to Edwina looking really pissed off.

"Why did you even talk to her, you should have just pasted the bitch?" Edwina looked stunned.

"Jesus Chloe, did you just do that?" Outside the gates, the car revved up, and screeched away, Chloe gave a snort.

"Well, someone had to, you were fucking useless."

She spun her brush around in her hand, and walked past Edwina back into the house muttering to herself.

"Fucking bitch, bold as fucking brass, dares come here and ask for Birch, no one fucking hurts Abby, I will brick the bitch if she tries that shit again.”

She stomped down the hallway back towards her studio, Edwina just stared at her lost for words, as she closed the door. Chloe stopped at the kitchen door, and turned back, to look at Edwina.

“Why aren’t you mad as hell?” Edwina stood by the closed door and looked at Chloe.

“I am, I hate what she did to them, but honestly, do you think battering her will help Abby or Birch?” Chloe gave a sigh.

“What if she had done that to me?” Edwina started walking towards her.

“Chloe, you know the answer to that, I would fucking stab the bitch.” Chloe nodded in agreement.

“Edwina, there is no difference between me, Abby or Birch. In this house we are all sisters, you should have stood up to her like you were defending me.” Edwina stood in front of her looking upset.

“Are you mad at me Chloe?” Chloe gave a slight nod.

“A little bit, I was scared shitless, but I knew you were there, and if she hit me, you would wade in, but you know what Weena, you should have done what I did?” Edwina nodded.

“I am sorry Chloe, next time I will be more assertive. Wow, my little sis just schooled me, how the hell did that happen?” Chloe smiled.

“We are family Weena, we work, live, fight, and stand together always, that is what makes us strong.” She pulled her into a hug.

“Yeah, we are, you know, I am pretty bloody proud of you right now, that thing with the brush was pretty classy.” Chloe giggled.

“And you said martial arts and ninja movies were pants, see, they show the way.” Edwina started to chuckle as she held her sister tight.

“You are messed up; you know that right?”

It felt like a good day. We walked back towards the house holding hands, and cooked a meal side by side. Birch was more relaxed, and chatty, her spirits had really lifted, and I was happy to see it. After we ate, Birch took me into the workshop which was attached to the side of the house, she smiled as she walked around, and I stood still and simply took in everything. Down the room against the wall was a long work bench, and at the end near a window, there was a much smaller one, Birch turned to me looking happy.

"Come, see, this is where I learned woodwork." I was intrigued.

"You can do woodwork?"

I walked towards her, and there next to the bench, was a rack of tiny tools. I was amazed as I looked at them, each of them a miniature replica of the large ones all hanging above the big bench. There was even a couple a miniature hand saws. Birch gently touched each one with pure love, her voice was soft and quiet.

"My granddad made every one of these out of big tools, he filed them down, and made new handles, and when I came down in the summer, I had a bench just like his. Everything we made that summer, I used these tools at his side as he taught me correctly, it was such fun, I made the big bird house in the front." I watched her eyes move across each one of them, she glanced at me.

"You do not think I am silly, do you?" I shook my head.

"No, I think it is really lovely, the more I hear about him, the more I see where your dads love and kindness come from." She gave a soft smile.

"My dad is like him, he is really good at woodwork too, he helped make all the fencing around this property. I would hold his tin of nails, and pass them to him as he needed them."

It is lovely to see this side of her, she has pretty much seen all my life, she knows everything, and I thought I knew most things about her, but it was clear, this was a very special and private part of her life, and she wanted to share this with me. It felt special, somehow very precious, but I think she knew that. Birch looked at me with her bright sparkling eyes.

"Deads, this is a part of my life no one else knows about, not even Izzy. Apart from you, only my mum and dad know about this place and the story behind it. I was going to save this until after we were married, but you know, after what happened? Well, the truth is, I knew if I brought you here, and shared this with you, then you would see I did not cheat on you, and I was as committed to you as always. I love only you; I want only you, and I guess I need you to see that, am I making sense?" I nodded, and smiled at her, she looked almost shy and bashful.

"You know Birch, I already knew that, I did believe you, I just could not handle the fear, and the emotional overload. I should not have run from you, and I am sorry, but you know what, I am really glad you brought me here."

"Yeah, me too."

She took my hand and we walked back out in to the garden, and walked down the side of the house to where it met the trees, and there was a little bench, she gave a giggle.

"The middle plank is crooked, I was in such a rush to finish, I did not line it up right. My granddad told me, in life, it is the imperfections that make it interesting, and I think he was really spot on, I have a lot."

I was just impressed by the fact that she made it, and it was still here looking as good as ever, she sat down on it and I joined her, she took my hand in hers.

"I have read a lot of books here; I would sit out most evenings and just read until the sun set. My gran would bring me fresh pressed lemons in water, or orange juice, and a few freshly baked biscuits. It is a good place to read." I held my hand up as if reading a book, and she giggled, I gave an approving look at my hand.

"I think you are right." She giggled more as she leaned on me.

"When we get old and we have long grey hair, I want to sit here with you and read every night." I smiled.

"It could be a bit cold in winter, we would die together of hyperthermia." I felt her shake with her laughter.

"Good point, in winter we will stay inside by the log fire. I want this Deads, I want us two, side by side living alone and sharing everything."

We sat holding hands until the chill began, and I shivered. It was getting late, so we headed inside, locked the doors, and took a bottle of wine up to the bedroom. I climbed in at her side as she handed me a glass, and we watched the sun slowly turn the sky red through the window. Birch lifted her phone off the side.

"Shit, I have tons of messages, I never thought to take it with me today." I lifted mine up and slid up the screen, I had thirty notifications, I gave a sigh.

"I suppose the others are worried, but actually I am glad we had a phone free day, I am glad it was just me and you completely alone. I really loved today; it was special. Oh crap, Chloe has battered Katie." Birch looked at me looking alarmed.

"She has done what?" I turned the phone and let her see the message from Edwina. She read the message.

"She stabbed her in the tit with a paint brush, is that even possible?" I shook my head trying to draw pictures in my mind.

"It must be she did it, and Katie left, although why was she even there?" Birch looked at her messages and scrolled through them, she saw she had one from Katie. She opened it up and read it.

I watched nervously; I am not sure why, maybe it is because I did not trust her. I watched as Birch read her message, I felt nervous and unsure, Birch turned to me as she finished reading.

"She says she is sorry, it was just a joke, all she did was put on lipstick, kiss my boob and inner thigh, she said the smear she did with her finger. She did nothing sexual to me, but she is sorry." I looked at her trying to work out what she was feeling, Birch showed no signs of emotion.

"How do you feel about that, you know, she did not touch you like I would?" Birch stared at her phone.

"If that was a joke, it was not frigging funny. I am glad she did nothing sexual, but honestly, she should never have touched me, I have never wanted that." I understood, I would feel the same too. Birch lay back and gave a sigh of relief.

"I won't say it has not haunted my mind, it has Deads, we are done, she went too far." She turned to me, and looked very serious.

"Deads, I don't want her anywhere near me, I don't want her at my wedding, I never want to see her again, I really don't. You were right, Deb's, Chloe and Edwina would never do that to me, they would never risk us, and she did, and I cannot forgive her for that." All I could do was nod, what else do you do, I completely understood her?

"If that is what you honestly want, we will make sure she is not there, I promise." She nodded and then smiled.

"Holy shit, Chloe stabbed her tit." She started to giggle.

"That really bloody hurts you know, I did it once?" I looked at her and started to laugh.

"Birch, how the hell did you stab your tit?" She gave a grin.

"I was making a kebab for the barbeque, and I pushed too hard with the bamboo skewer. It shot up and got me right in the tit, look it left a mark." She looked down and lifted her boob, and sure enough, there was a little tiny scar. She looked up at me.

"I cried like a bitch for an hour it hurt so much." I started to giggle.

"What the hell were you putting on the skewer?" She looked really serious.

"Pepper, what else do you put on a skewer?" I started to laugh even harder, she looked at me.

"What... You know they have tough skin; you need to push really hard?"

I just could not help myself, I had no idea why, I just laughed and laughed, she gave a giggle.

"It really hurt, you know, tits are not meant to be stabbed."

My tummy wobbled even more, and I just could not stop, and I had no idea why, she started to laugh with me, and both of us sat in bed with a glass of wine in one hand, and a phone in the other, and we just screamed with laughter. I am sure if anyone could see us, they would have us committed.

It took us a good long while before the giggles stopped, we drank our wine, put down our phones, and curled up together, and I thought even more of Birch had returned, that sparkle in her eye was back, and that air of mischief had returned. Coming here alone was the best thing we could have done, and as I lay there looking at her, all snug and warm, I knew... I knew I wanted to do this forever.

Chapter 24

Alone Time.

Time flies when you are having fun.

Finding out, Katie had done nothing sexual to her, Birch lifted her spirits, and for the next few days she went into adventure mode. She started each day in the garden, and did some yoga for an hour, and then we would explore. Well, it was exploring for me, Birch knew this place like the back of her hand, but she got so much joy out of showing all the places she played as a child, and it was lovely to see her so happy. On Tuesday we headed down to the river, and walked along under the trees, where Birch came alive. I felt like a huge load had been lifted off me, and I found it easy to laugh and joke around her.

We did a lot of laughing as Birch showed me all the places she made dens as a child. We swam naked in the river, lay out on the banks to dry in the sun, and made love just about anywhere that we wanted to. The highlight of the week for me was when we walked onto the moors with the binoculars and looked out across the vast barren landscape, and obviously we got a closer look at what we called Sherlock's rock. It was actually one of a few tors on the moor, for us it was just great to look through the binoculars and admire it.

The most important thing we did was talk, and we appeared to do that all the time, but it felt nice. Both of us were relaxed and stress free, I would even say we were more carefree than normal. Birch has a quiet gentle side, I had seen it often at Uni, but at home in Wotton, it was not that evident. Here, alone, it came out, and I cannot deny, just like London when we went missing, it came out, and I really loved it.

Mable arranged a small garden party on Wednesday, and we were guests of honour, she was so kind and lovely, and she did clean the house in our absence so we agreed to go, and arrived to find a group of fourteen ladies, all very happy and jolly to have a famous star in the area.

Birch revelled in it, she knew one or two of them, from her childhood, and loved having a big fuss made out of her, as all of them commented on what a fine young lady she had become, nothing at all like the little wildling that had run around making such a noise.

It was nice to sit and watch her get so much attention. I was approached by a young woman with a pad, she looked a few years younger than me and worked for the local paper, they never really miss a chance to snare me, but she was very polite, and asked if it would be alright to ask a few questions for her paper.

Birch and I were completely isolated, so we knew little of what was happening in the big world. The daily papers were running with a lead story from the book fair, and it was all about my sudden absence, and the rumour I had run screaming from the hotel. The papers speculated that Birch and I had separated and the wedding was off, which was ridiculous considering the press had seen us leave together. They never miss a chance to sensationalise everything, and they were making huge capital out of a big bust up which ended in my heartbreak.

I talked to Wendy Patterson, and set the record straight, well, I told her we had both just needed some quiet time to focus on the wedding, and had visited here for a break, and a chance to rest up.

She was very respectful, and I remarked to her that if more reporters were like her, they would get more press from me. I also told her, once her article was out, she should pitch it to the dailies for more exposure. I allowed her a free hand with her camera, and she showed me her photos of Birch and I, hand in hand looking relaxed together. Both of us had bare feet, as we strolled on the soft grass, and there were one or two she got that were really beautiful pictures. One especially really caught my attention, as Birch had leaned down, and stole a secret kiss, it was beautiful, I told her to use it. I gave her my email and asked if she would forward them for my private collection, she was delighted.

Cissy was delighted to meet me, although a little envious that I had posed for pictures with Mable. That picture had become quite a sensation around the area. Mable was very good at messaging it appeared, and had gained a lot of popular capital out of sharing it.

We walked home bare foot on the hot road, hand in hand, Seth had offered to run us home in his car, we refused, but thanked him. We did not cook that night, we just snacked around midnight, to be honest at the garden party we had eaten far too much clotted cream and scones. I am sure I will gain at least five pounds, but I cannot deny, I really love the stuff.

We did have one minor problem, we had no vehicle, so as we sat in bed on Wednesday night and talked, it appeared that the best thing to do was to get Petal down to us, and first thing Thursday morning, Birch rang Edwina and talked to her. It was decided that on Friday, Chloe and Edwina would drive down, and stay the night, and then we would all head back on Saturday afternoon/evening so we could all get sorted for the new week.

I was a little disappointed, to be honest I wanted to stay longer, I had really loved being alone with her, and I had seen much more of the quieter side of Birch, and that was a side of her I really loved. She had a wonderful way of reflecting on everything, and it reminded me very much of the Birch behind closed doors at Uni, the nineteen year old I had lived with, in that tiny dorm.

For the rest of the day, we headed back to the clearing in the trees, and laid out the blanket, with a picnic and wine, and just lazed around naked. I was starting to get a really good tan, and yet Birch was still as white as snow, I don't think I will ever understand it, she should be a bronzed goddess with the amount of time she spends outside naked.

Thursday evening, as we sat in the garden eating a salad, because it was way too hot to cook, my phone vibrated on the table, it was a message from Angela, which just read, 'please call me.' I immediately dialled and put it on speaker phone, and felt a pang of fear run through me.

"Angela, is he alright?"

"Abby, he is fine, once again the old buzzard does not want me to ring, but you rang me so he cannot complain. Abby, your dad is in hospital, and is having a pacemaker fitted." I felt my heart lurch, Birch reached across the table and took my hand.

"What... Why does he need a pacemaker, is he going to be alright?"

"Abby, he is in the best hands, and actually in better condition than expected, his new diet, less drinking and lots of rest have made a huge difference. The doctor says that he is strong, and this is a very simple procedure and not as invasive as you would think. Please do not worry, he will be in and out in no time. I just think he should be more open about these things with you. He will make a fast recovery, and will feel a lot better and healthier when it is done." I gasped for breath, I hate hospitals, and I hate him being in one, Birch smiled at me.

"She is right Abby, this is a very simple procedure, and actually it does not take too long, he will be in and out in a flash, and he really will feel amazing when it is done. Listen to Angie, he will be fine." I trusted Birch, and I nodded, as I looked back at the phone.

"Will you let me know the moment he is out Angela; I am going to worry about him until I know?"

"I will let you know as soon as I know, listen to your fiancée she is right, and thank you Jemi for being with her, it puts my mind at rest, we saw the papers and it alarmed him. I made him ring Felicity, and she assured us you two are strong and fine, and I was very happy to hear that Jemi. I know we have had our disagreements, but I am actually a big supporter of you two, and I am really excited about the wedding, keep her close Jemi, you know what she is like for worrying?" She gave me a big smile and winked.

"I shall keep her very close Angie, you can bank on it."

"Good, Abby, I will phone you as soon as he is out of surgery, so please do not worry about him, he will be fine."

"Thanks Angela, I will wait for your call."

"Alright, I have to go, but I will phone soon, take care of each other... Bye for now."

The call ended, and I swallowed hard, and lifted my wine and took a swig, Birch squeezed my hand.

"He will be fine, so relax, this is a simple job. You know, I do think she has played a bigger role in your dad accepting us than I realised, it is probably best that I did not beat the shit out of her with that ashtray." She smiled a big smile. I took a deep breath.

"I have warmed to her a little, I still hate she was the other woman, but I have thought about it a lot. She was not the woman I saw in the car when I was younger, and I suppose it is always easier to blame the other woman. You know, having got to know her better, I think he is equally to blame, all my rage was at her, that was not right, some of it should have been at him." Birch winked, and lifted the bottle to top up our glasses.

"When the hell did we grow up, we used to be so unruly at Uni, how the hell did I end up owning two houses, a part of a yurt camp, and a bloody huge practice?" I giggled.

"It sort of snuck up on us didn't it? I am telling you, we blinked, and suddenly we are grownups." She frowned.

"I wanted to stay young and beautiful." I lifted my glass.

"What are you talking about, you are more beautiful now than you have ever been, I certainly think you are a lot more radiant now than when I met you." She gave me a shy smile.

"Do you really think so?" I started to giggle.

"Do not pull that shy crap with me Doctor Dixon, stop fishing, you got your compliment."

She leaned back and gave a loud cackle of a laugh, and her eyes danced with happiness, I smiled at her.

"You know once we are married and we come here, you have just got to introduce yourself as Doctor Watson, I mean, this is the perfect setting for it." She gave a chuckle.

"Well, this is home too, so I suppose, you will be at Holmes with Dr Watson." She gave another loud cackle of a laugh; I just shook my head in disbelief.

"God your humour just gets worse, you seriously need to work on it."

For the rest of the evening, I was nervous, as I waited for the call. I rang mum and told her, she was actually quite calm about it, she had known of a few people who had been fitted with them, and she assured me it was a simple procedure and not to worry, so I tried to relax. We moved indoors and curled up on the settee, and talked, Birch found a book on trees, and she showed me each of the types of trees that grew in these parts, it was really good at taking my mind off things.

Angela called at ten past ten, to tell me he was out of surgery, responding well and fine, I gave a huge sigh of relief. Birch cuddled me and was happy to see me relax a little more, we headed upstairs to shower, the bath was way too small for us to share, and she pulled me close, washed me down, and played around, which is always fun. It was late when we both collapsed sweaty and exhausted, I don't think we have ever had sex for that long. Sleep came fast, as I lay happy and calm, curled up with her.

I woke up, to the sound of Birch breathing softly in my ear, and her familiar hand on my boob, I gave a happy little moan. I liked this, as far as I am concerned, there is no other way to wake up. I just lay back, staring out of the window feeling happy and content, although this room really needs a clock, I had no idea what time it was. I saw my phone on the side, and reached out slowly so as not to disturb Birch.

My finger touched it, but I could not quite grab it without moving, I pushed down and tried to drag it. It came slowly towards me, and with a smile, I managed to get it. I pulled my arm under the covers and clicked it to open the screen, the large letters read 13:24. Shit, we had slept half of our last day away, I gave Birch a little nudge.

"Birch… Birch it's almost half one." She gave a moan.

"Who cares, this is comfy." She pulled me tighter, and I gave a sigh.

"Birch we should not really lie in bed all day; we should do something." She gave a groan.

"I am doing something, I am cuddling you, and I like it." I lay back on the pillow.

"I am wide awake now."

Her hand slid off my boob, and down on to my tummy. I gave a giggle as it tickled a little, she kept it moving, I felt a little jolt as she moved over my labia, and I breathed in. She opened her eyes and smiled.

"I am doing something else now."

Her head slid under the covers, and she started to kiss my boobs, I felt the tingles run down to my already wet vagina, her finger was exploring and my toes curled, I gripped the side of the bed, and breathed in, and then bit my lip.

"Oh god Birch, I have not even had a coffee." Her mumbles came from around my growing nipple.

"I am having dark little beastie for my breakfast, and it's way better than muesli."

I gave a little giggle, and closed my eyes, my legs separated, and she slid over me into the gap, and her warm boobs pushed into my tummy. Her tongue swirled round, and then she sucked hard, and I gripped the mattress even harder. I gave out a little pant.

"Oh God... Oh Birch, I love that." My whole body was alive and started to tingle, and I pushed my head back into the pillow and arched my back a little.

"Oh yes Baby." Her mouth slid lower on to my stomach, as she covered it with tiny little soft kisses, and I felt my skin tingle.

"Ohhh!"

Beep, Beep, Beep, Beep! Birch stopped, and I saw the duvet rise up, her muffled voice came from just above my vagina.

"Is that frigging Petal?"

I frowned, and lifted the duvet to see her bright twinkling eyes, and my huge nipples, wow, I was impressed they were massive. She smiled.

"Hi Sweetie... Boo!" I giggled.

"I thought you said they would be coming later." She gave a naughty giggle.

"I was hoping you would cum first." She sniggered.

Beep, Beep, Beep! Birch gave a sigh.

"Can you wait, or?"

She slid back and plunged her face into me and I felt her tongue hit my button and I jerked with a loud gasp. A bolt of electricity shot through me; I was still very sensitive from last night. I dropped the duvet and flopped back into the pillow, she gave a wicked giggle, and crawled up me. She smiled and licked her lips.

"Let's call that a little taste of what is to come." She leaned down and kissed me, she tasted of me, and I liked it. Birch pulled out of the kiss with a smile.

"We have guests, I suppose our alone time is over until later." I smiled.

"I like later, it gives me something to look forward to."

She shoved the duvet off us, and sat on my waist, I could not resist and ran my hands quickly up to her boobs and tweaked her nipples. I watched her shudder and smile.

"I love it when you are naughty, come on Honey, the kids are back, our fun is over for now."

She gave a giggle, and jumped off me onto the floor, and I sat up and swung my legs over the side of the bed. We made our way down the stairs towards the door, and we could hear Chloe talking.

"You are sure this is the right house?" Birch sniggered, as Edwina sounded uncertain.

"Chloe, I told you, I have the map she sent me, this is definitely the right place, I do know what I am doing you know?" She scoffed.

"Yeah, that is why we only got lost four times." Birch gave a quiet chuckle as she reached for the lock, she yanked open the door and screamed.

"SURPRISE!"

Both of them jumped back, and I started to giggle as I stood next to Birch with my arm round her waist, Chloe beamed a huge smile.

"Abby… Birch, I missed you both so much." She leaned in, and threw her arms around both of us, I let go of Birch, and pulled her into a hug. She just clung to me like a limpet.

"God it is good to see you, I was really worried about you." It felt nice, I had missed her too.

"We are both fine, this has been really good for us Chloe, but I must admit, I have missed you as well."

The following half an hour, involved a tour of the house, and Chloe and Edwina, stripping naked, it had been a long hot drive, and both of them were cooking. We sat in the garden with coffee, and we all sat on the edge of the old stone patio and dangled our feet in the cool fast flowing stream. Chloe went one better and lay down in it to cool off, which made us giggle, as she screamed it was so cold.

The bit I dreaded was all the questions, they had to come, but we had just spent several days with no mention of it, and I really did not want it bringing up again. I had Birch back as she was, actually scratch that, a whole other side of her had come out, and I really loved that part of her, I did not want it spoiling, because she was so happy, and relaxed.

They appeared to know everything, and Chloe told me how Anita had been, and how Roni had filled in Izzy, I guess we have no secrets in the Curio's. Chloe told us of the incident with Katie, I could not help giggle, as she was so funny the way she described it. I was pretty proud of Chloe, not only had she stood up for us, she had made a stand for all of us, and that impressed me, so I told her.

I had loved my break alone with Birch, it felt so special and intimate, but as I sat there listening to Chloe rattle on filling us in with every detail of the week, I smiled, I had actually missed this too.

I sat watching the water run over my feet as I swung my legs softly in the water, and I realised how lucky I was. Katie had put a huge cloud over us, but sat listening, I also understood how special my life was with such amazing and unique people. I really am not sure how Birch had worked everything out, but she had, and in her own little way, she had gathered us together all those years ago, and although we had gone a little bit wild at the time, it had blossomed into a family, because that is what we were, a really close and loving family of misfits.

I suppose you do not realise everything straight away; it has been four years since she had returned to me in Wotton, and within days all of us had been brought back together. We were nothing like that group from my summer home from Uni now, all of us had changed so much, and yet we hadn't. Again, I am reminded of how life changes, we have had so many bumps in our road, and yet here we were, still as close, still friends, and still looking out for each other, and yet nine years had passed, since that crazy first summer, when we had bonded as friends.

We were more mature, a little more grown up, and had changed inside a great deal. Life had moulded us all in different ways, but there was one thing that had not changed at all, there were no secrets, no lies, and no betrayal. We had been open and honest with each other always, and as one of us suffered, we all went through it together. I think it is something Katie never managed to learn, she had been so preoccupied with how things looked on the outside, she had missed out on what was happening on the inside, and sadly it had cost her.

The Curio's were never about that, they were about unity, support, lifting each other up, and sharing in each others success. We were a unit, a tribe with strong bonds, and we had endured everything in that manner. So few people today have what I have, so few bothered to seek it or build it, because the world today is mainly like Katie. What a shame they cannot be more like the Curio's. Oh, what a wonderful world it would be if everyone had what I had. Today, I feel like the luckiest human alive, and not very many can say that.

We all went back out front, to get their things, they had brought some cans of beer, and a few bags. As we walked out, Birch noticed a pool of water on the floor under Petal. As Chloe and I carried the things in to the house, Birch lifted the bonnet to check inside the engine, I came back out, having put the beer in the stream to cool.

Birch was bent over the front of Petal as I approached, I could see the large pool of water on the stone's underneath.

"Is everything alright, will we need a mechanic?" She popped her head up, and looked at me.

"One of the hoses has gone on the radiator, and the other one is looking a little rough, they will need to be replaced. It is an easy enough job; I will just need the hoses, and some coolant to top the engine back up."

I understood, I also found it to be a bit of a turn on that she knew her way around cars, I pictured her covered in oil, in baggy overalls. Oh God I was getting so wet, she stared at me as I day dreamed, about sliding her out from under Petal and going down on her.

"Is everything alright Sweetie?" I blinked, and gave a little shy smile, her eyes twinkled.

"Does this turn you on?"

I gave a nod, and shuffled my feet, if I got anymore carried away, I would probably make a puddle on the stones to match Petal.

"Actually, I did not realise until now, but honestly, I am so wet watching, I am even surprising myself." She gave a giggle and looked down.

"I think I will fix things around you more often." I gave a happy nod.

"Yes please." She started to chuckle, as she pulled down the bonnet.

"I will have to make some calls, if I can get the hoses and the coolant, it will not take so long, and we can head off tomorrow." I gave a sigh.

"I will be sad to leave." She understood, I could see she felt it too. She locked the hood and we walked back to the house.

"I will too, it has been really lovely being alone, you know just us, I think I really needed it, but I also will be glad to go back, we have a life there Deads, you have your writing and I have the practice. It will be nice to see Deb's and Anthony, Luke, Terry, and Michael, they are also a big part of us. I think Sunny Bank will be a good place to take those all important time outs, not just for us, but for all of us."

She made sense, but there again, she always does. Edwina had packed a cool box with some fresh steaks, and my mouth watered when I saw them, she also had a large bag of charcoal, and so we decided a barbeque was in order. As Birch went to make a few calls, which meant Seth, we crossed the bridge onto the grass and prepared the large brick built barbeque. Luckily, I had seen the cooking wires in the workshop, hung on a nail last night, so while Chloe tipped in the coals, I went and got the grills, and a couple of spare chairs I had seen.

Edwina sat watching, as Chloe attempted to get the coals lit. I sat down at her side, as Chloe lifted the lid off the cool box to waft the coals, they started to glow a fiery orange. Edwina opened a can of beer and handed me one.

"Is she really okay Abby, or is she faking for our sake?" I shook my head.

"No, she really is good, this is a special place for her, I think Roni was right to send us here, it has done her a lot of good." Edwina nodded and took a swig of her beer.

"I am glad to hear it, are you okay with what Katie did to her?" I gave a sigh.

"We have talked a lot, I frigging hate what she did, in a way the fact she did not go down on her makes it worse. I mean, if she had eaten her out, I would have hated it, but got over it, but the fact she faked it so Birch believed she had, as some sort of sick joke, that has really pissed me off." Chloe turned to look at me.

"Izzy told us what Roni described about how she just broke down, that was so cruel, making her of all people think that. I think you are right Abby; it was the most evil thing she could have done, I really hate her for what she did." Edwina gave a sigh.

"What about the wedding, those two have been friends a long time, will they patch it up, she was supposed to have a VIP pass for it?" I shook my head.

"No, Birch is really clear, she does not want her there, and I am happy to hear it, because if I even see her, I am telling you, I will hit her with something a lot bigger than a brush. As far as I am concerned, she is toxic." Chloe who was still wafting, gave a resounding nod.

"I am with you Abby." She dropped the lid and picked up a can of beer.

"I am sweating my chuff off, it's hot down here."

I gave a smile; it was nice to see them. It is odd in a way, it has only been a few days, but it feels like much longer. Birch came out with her phone, and she smiled as she crossed the bridge.

"Seth knows a place that has Land Rover parts in stock, that is probably the good thing about around here, there are a lot of owners. He will pick me up tomorrow, and we will go get what I need, I should only be an hour or so, and then I can fix her up. To be honest she has done well in the last four years, not a lot has gone wrong with her."

She sat down and grabbed a beer, Chloe fitted on the wire mesh, as the coals smoked a little, and then grabbed the steaks, and placed them carefully on the mesh to cook. We all sat round the table, and Birch answered questions about the house, and how she wanted to run things with it.

Both of them were really surprised to find she owned it, and that we would have unrestricted access to it, Chloe was especially delighted, she leaned back in her chair and looked around the place.

"I want to paint here; I feel this is a very creative space."

There is something rather wonderful about food cooked outdoors, Birch and Edwina prepared a lot of salad, as Chloe and myself took care of the steak. For most of the week we had been meat free, so a good steak had my mouth watering, and I was almost foaming at the mouth watching them cook. Chloe turned them over with skill, and just knew when they were cooked perfectly. I love having exceptional cooks in our Curio family, because we really do eat well.

When everything was cooked, rather than sit at the table, I sat crossed legged on the grass. Chloe and Birch decided to join me, and we sat in a circle eating, and I cannot deny, it tasted like nothing else. I chewed with delight and smiled at Birch, she gave a wink at me, she understood the joy I was feeling too.

After we ate, we went for a walk through the woodland down to the river. There really is something wonderful to walking naked in nature, I really cannot explain how it feels, but I find, I feel the atmosphere of a woodland in a more intimate way. I could feel the breeze on my skin, and the moisture in the atmosphere, my skin and my body respond to the feel of everything that brushes into me, and as a result, I experience a completely different view of the woodland.

At the river, after a good meal and hot day, a swim was in order, and so all four of us waded in, it was ice cold, and yet felt amazing on our bare skin. It is something we have all grown to understand, it sounds nuts, but after the last ten years of my life, I cannot understand why people would want to take off their clothes, and then put on others to get wet and swim. Since that first time, back in that crazy summer from Uni, when I dived naked into the pool, I have never wanted to wear a costume since, and to date, I haven't.

By the time we reached the house it was late, Edwina was tired, as she had done all the driving, so with a happy smile, we showed them to the spare rooms, the shower and the toilet. Birch slipped her arm round me, and we headed into the bedroom, Birch closed the door, and walked towards the bed, her arms came round my waist and she kissed me softly on the shoulder.

"Don't we have something we started and never finished?" I started to chuckle.

"I do believe, the doctor wanted to prescribe something for me." She gave a high pitched little squeal of a laugh.

"Oh yes, Deads I love role play." I turned to look at her excited eyes.

"You do?" She nodded really quickly, I figured what the hell, and took her hand, and placed it above my vagina.

"Doctor, I am not sure things here are normal, I really think you might need to thoroughly examine me." Her eyes exploded with life, and she bounced on the spot. She suddenly realised and went very serious.

"Well Miss Watson, I think you will need to lie on the bed and open your legs, and I will give you the full benefit of my expertise."

I backed up to the bed and lay back and opened my legs wide, she was way too excited, I honestly had no idea this would turn her on. I mean, technically she is a doctor, so it was not really role play. Birch leaned over me, and took a good long look at me, I kind of liked the fact that she was looking at me, and I started to get really turned on. Her eyes moved up to me, and she looked me in the eyes.

"Hmm, Miss Watson, I see you need urgent specialist attention." I giggled.

"Oh Doctor, will it hurt?" She smiled.

"It might a little, but a little pain never hurt anyone now did it?" Her head dropped and I tensed, as I felt her move straight onto me.

"Oh Doctor!"

Chloe slid into Edwina's room really fast, and closed the door quickly behind her. Edwina looked up; Chloe was looking completely freaked out.

"Is everything alright Chloe?" She leaned against the door, and shook her head.

"I wasn't listening honestly… Honestly I wasn't, but Weena, those two have been alone too long, they are doing some really fucked up shit." Edwina stared at her, and furrowed her brow.

"What do you mean?" Chloe really looked worried.

"Weena, they are playing doctors and patients, and it sounds really fucked up and perverted, you know, I think they have been traumatised?" Edwina gave a chuckle and bit her lip.

"Chloe, some couples do that, a little role play, it is quite healthy you know?" Chloe looked at her and appeared suspicious.

"I have never done it; I just fuck like normal people do." Edwina smiled.

"Honestly, it is quite normal, stop worrying so much, trust me, it is very normal." She gave a sigh of relief, and nodded. She turned to the door, and pulled it open.

"OH DOCTOR!" Chloe shut the door and turned to Edwina.

"Weena, can I stay with you tonight, this house is way too fucked up for me?"

Chapter 25

Homeward Bound.

When I woke up the bed was empty, so I headed downstairs to the kitchen. Edwina was making coffee; because she had heard me on the stairs. She smiled as she handed me my cup filled with dark rich coffee, and I revelled in the aroma.

"Birch has gone off with her friend to get what she needs for Petal, she told me to tell you, she will be as quick as she can." I took the coffee.

"Thanks Edwina, I am not properly awake yet."

I wandered outside, across the bridge, and sat at the table in the morning sun. Chloe was sat on the fence facing me with a pad, and was sketching, she smiled at me, I nodded, I was not ready for speech. Chloe looked at the house, and then down to her pad.

"This place is really beautiful, I got some sketches round the front earlier, and I have taken a zillion pictures, I really want to paint it." I sipped my coffee and yawned.

"We are lucky, Birch owns it, so in a way we have a permanent holiday home, you can come here whenever you want. I must admit, I would love all of us to come down and hang out here, we are not far from the sea, so we could have some great days out." Chloe appeared to like the idea of that, she gave me a smile.

"I would love that, I saw some great old trees last night, I would love some time here sketching, I already have loads of great ideas for pictures."

That was perfect Chloe, her whole mind worked on what she could paint, although since being here, I had taken a lot of pictures myself, especially on the moors, and they would help influence my writing in the future.

Edwina appeared and came over to sit with me, she carried a large plate of toast. Chloe slipped off the fence and grabbed a couple of slices, and headed off towards the trees, Edwina smiled.

"She missed you; it is nice to see her sketching and so relaxed."

I turned and looked round at her, happily drawing lost in thought.

"We needed this break Edwina; Katie raised a lot of issues and made me look deeply at myself. I think I needed this time, and did not realise it." Edwina understood.

"You needed to step back and take stock, I get that, I have often thought that your life as a writer is a little bit of a whirlwind at times, and you do not always have control of it, especially considering it was Katie organising it. To be honest Abby, you do look a lot better than you did." I leaned back in my chair and lifted my cup, my eyes fixed on the house.

"We needed this time, and this place, I have found it a very restful place to be, and it is a great space for thinking things through. You know, I realised we never dated, we just lived together from the moment we met, so in a way we missed out on those things people do to learn about each other. This week has sort of been a catch up." Edwina smiled.

"I am happy to hear that, I understand how hard it can be at times, trying to work everything out whilst living in a house full of other people. Luke and I take a lot of time out alone, it helps, and gives us space to talk. Birch seems very happy; I think it has really been good for her." I smiled, I was glad she had noticed, I looked at her.

"There is a side to her nobody sees Edwina, believe it or not, she can be very quiet and introverted, that is the side of her I saw at Uni alone in the dorm, and I have seen a lot more of it this week. It is the part of her that attracts me the strongest, she is so deep and intuitive when she is like that, and our conversations have real depth and meaning. I love being around her when she is like that, I think that is the hidden core of her if that makes sense, and only I get to see it." Edwina nodded as she lifted another slice of toast.

"You know, I have always thought you two were more alike than everyone realised, your quietness shows more than hers, but I have seen it in her at times as I worked with her. It showed a lot when you were on stage at the Curio event, she just stood watching you, biting her lip, and worrying if you would be alright out there on that big stage alone. You know, I really hate what Katie has done, but in a strange way, she has probably helped you." I frowned at her.

"How the hell has she helped; she almost broke us up?" Edwina gave a nod as she looked at me.

"She tried, and that is the point, look at it this way, your wedding is not that far off. Both of you are going to be nervous on the day, but because Katie tried to create problems, you have both been forced to really evaluate your relationship. Coming here allowed you both the time and space to really look at what you have, and it does appear to me, that in looking, you both found something even more valuable than before. Her attempts to break you up, have actually made you stronger."

She made sense, this week had really made me focus on what I wanted, and it was Birch. Seeing her in this setting free of the practice and the house full of crazy creative people, she had the space to recharge, and to do that. She could be her true self, and I had really enjoyed seeing that. We have had so many silly and simplistic moments, like stood side by side chopping veggies for dinner, or walking hand in hand in the woodland, and yet, they counted more than anything else.

Maybe it is the small things that make us happiest, maybe we all take for granted those daft little moments, like her face when we first lit up our Christmas tree, or those moments when I am writing and a cup of coffee appears at my side. Something as simple as holding up a plant with a happy smile to get my opinion, or share in its beauty.

Life gets busy, and hectic, and we all get dragged into the drama of others, and end up losing ourselves so easily, and that is probably the problem with modern living, we lose our connection to each other, and to what is really important.

The problem with life, is that in order to gain any understanding of it, you first have to experience it, and for all of us life had at times been cruel, these I assumed were the bumps in the road that my mum told me about. This week, I really understood what Birch had always told me, about how life does not have to be a road, it can also be like a river, and we can sit in a boat, drop the sail and go with the flow, and we had done that. Just accepting that this was life, and we really did not have much control of it, is mind altering.

I had arrived with no expectations, and just lived as the moment arose, and yet I learned more about me and about Birch in just five days, than I had in the last four years, and as a result, I felt happy and relaxed and at ease with myself for the first time in ages, and it was a really good feeling.

Birch returned an hour later, and went into the workshop, and gathered the tools she would need for the job. I had drunk plenty of coffee, so wandered around to the front, I sat on the step and watched, as she leaned over the side of Petal and worked. She flicked her hair out of the way, it kept falling into the engine.

"Do you want it tying back?" She pulled her head up from the engine.

"What is that Sweetie?" I got up and walked over.

"I can tie your hair back if you want, we have bobbles in the dash?"

She gave me a grin and wiped her cheek with the back of her hand, and left a smear. Wow, suddenly she looked so hot, and I raised my eye brows. I opened the door and grabbed a bobble, and then she leaned back and I tied her hair up.

She bent back over, and started to work on replacing the hoses. I sat, watched, and fantasized, about my sexy woman, who I was watching, in skimpy shorts and a vest, bending over the side of Petal. Is it weird I wanted to masturbate really badly, oh my God, was I becoming a stereo typical lesbian?

I needed to cool down, I was getting way too excited, and I had no idea why really, I have seen guys fix cars, and it did nothing for me, but watching her fix Petal, had me soaking wet. I looked down, and there was a wet patch on the stone, holy shit, what was wrong with me?

I decided to make drinks, I was a little embarrassed that I had made a puddle, and I figured I would remain out of sight until it evaporated. I made cold drinks and took one out for Birch, she was fastening the clips to finish the job. I put her drink down on the side of the engine. She slid back with a smile.

"Oh, thanks Sweetie, all I need to do is fill her up with water and coolant, and we can go." She looked at me and frowned.

"Sweetie, are you alright?" I grinned like a Cheshire cat.

"Can you take those tools home, you know, and pretend to fix

Petal in the garage late one night?" She gave a sudden excited giggle, and clapped her hands.

"Oh does it turn you on too, I am so happy, oh Sweetie, I am so going to fix your engine?"

Chloe got up off the floor behind Petal, where she had been sketching, and walked quickly around the back of the house, shaking her head, and muttering to herself.

"Nope, nope, nope, never going in the garage again."

We had our drinks, as she topped up the engine with water and the coolant, and then with a dirty face and dirty hands she headed for a quick shower, I followed. In the bathroom and with filth all over her hands, I helped undress her, I slid down her shorts, and looked up at her with her dirty cheek. Oh god, I am so messed up, but I could not wait another second, I had to have her, and I pushed my face into her. Chloe sat on the swing next to Edwina.

"I am not sure I can handle those two, they have changed, Abby is like a female me, she is permanently wet and horny, we really need to get her back to Wotton to calm her down. Do you think this is a result of them being alone, because she has never been this open with Birch?" Edwina swung softly, tapping her feet on the floor.

"I do not really know, but the way I see it, they have had some really good quality time alone here, and they have worked a lot of things out. If you ask me, they seem happier than they have ever been, and if that is because of a little role play, I am fine with it. I hate to say this Chloe, but some people think fucking a teddy is weird." She looked really surprised.

"They do, holy fuck, what is wrong with them?" Edwina gave a chuckle, and shook her head.

"Honestly, I have no idea, we live in a strange world."

The shower took longer than expected, but we came down with our bags smiling, and loaded up Petal. We did one more sweep, to make sure everything was safe secure and locked, and then jumped into Petal, and Birch turned the key, and Petal fired up first time.

As we drove down the driveway, and onto the road, I felt a little sad. It is strange how fast some places become so dear to your heart so quickly. I knew we would be back, but that did not make it easier. We drove down the road and pulled in outside Seth and Mable's house, to say goodbye. I got such lovely hugs, I felt quite emotional.

We hit the road again, and soon we were flying down the country lanes at high speed, and I was once again a spectator, just this time, everything felt more natural, and more normal. It was not that long before we hit the motorway, and I soon drifted off, and slept away most of the journey. When I woke up, Edwina was driving, and Birch and Chloe were asleep in the back, she noticed me jerk awake.

"Hi sleepy, wow you can really sleep, I think all that country air wiped you out, I am not sure you will sleep much tonight." I looked out of the window.

"Where are we?"

"We are about fifteen minutes from home, look there is the Oxendale turn off just ahead."

I could not believe I had slept for so long. As we approached Oxendale, I got out my phone and started to text, to let mum, Anita and Deb's know we were not far away. I also sent a text to Roni, and thanked her, I felt really revived and refreshed, and I also mentioned how great it had been for us two talking things out.

The truth was, I think we discovered even more about each other, and for that we did need space. Wotton is a busy little village, and we have been heavily involved in it, all of which takes up time, we also live in a house full of people, where there is always something to attend to, and so quiet private alone time is rare. If we are lucky, we get a couple of hours walking down the canal, but most of the time, not even that much.

This week has taught me that time is the most precious of gifts, and we had been given the greatest gift, of five days alone with no interference, and it had proven to be some of the most valuable time that we had since we first got together. I wondered if we had stopped communicating properly, I was not really sure, I just knew that a week alone had felt like a precious thing. Both of us had a chance to show more of the people we are, and it bound us together in a way that made us more solid than before Katie played her games.

We were returning home, but we had changed so much, it probably was not obvious on the outside, but I felt it deeply on the inside, and I felt more alive than I had in years. We drove onto Waterside Lane and I smiled to myself, in a way, it was also nice to be home again, to the familiar clang of the gates as they parted, and the crunch of the gravel on the drive, and the scent of the tall pines in the garden. I turned to look in the back, and Birch was sat up and smiling, she too looked happy to be home, and I wondered if she had as many things going through her mind as I had, she leaned over and put her arms round my neck and kissed me on the cheek.

"We are home Sweetie, but I loved my time alone with you, I want to go again soon, just us two, I really think I want a lot more time of just us." I turned to see her sparkling eyes watching me carefully.

"It made me very happy Birch, it is a very special place, and I will never forget this week. I think we should put Petal in the garage, and make sure she is fine." Chloe sat up and wagged her finger.

"Oh fucking no you are not, Deb's is in there waiting, and there is no way I am telling her you two weirdos are playing mechanics. You can save that for when I am in bed with my door locked."

Birch started to giggle, as Edwina pulled on the handbrake with a smirk, Chloe opened the back door and waited for Birch.

"Come on, out you get, the front door is that way." She pointed as Birch gave a cackle. I opened my door and jumped out.

"Chloe, we have not played mechanics yet, but you know what we did play?" She put her fingers in her ears and headed for the door.

"Nope, nope, nope, nope."

Birch slid her arm round my waist, and with both of us smiling, we headed in to see Deb's, Anthony, and the others.

After an hour of hugs, cuddles, and lots of questions, I finally made it up the stairs with my case, and into my room. I sat on my bed, and took a moment for myself, and felt happy to be in such a familiar place again. It is a little strange, I have absolutely loved being alone with Birch at Sunny Bank, and I felt sad leaving, but sat on my bed, I really felt happy being in what I saw as our real home.

I looked at my travel case, I had been in the same clothes for five days, and thought I should at least get some clean clothing on. I lifted my silk kimono off the chair and pulled off my sweaty vest. I stood up and dropped my pants, stepped out, and pulled the cool garment on to me, it felt soft and wonderful on my skin.

I walked over to the sofa at the side of my desk and picked up my laundry basket, then turned to my case. I emptied the whole contents into the basket, I would wash everything later. I sat in my desk chair, leaned down and hit the on button, my computer came to life. I had not looked at an email all week, and dreaded what was waiting. As I sat waiting for it to boot up, my mind drifting, as the sun warmed me through the window, and I leaned back in my seat, I heard a strange murmur, I looked around to find the source. I swung round in my chair, and stood up. My ears strained for the source, I looked at the bathroom door.

"Birch, is that you?"

I walked into the bathroom, and the murmur grew a little louder, her door was pulled too. I was curious, so I very quietly crept up to her door, and peeped through the small gap.

Birch was sat crossed legged on her bed, with her back to me, looking at the screen of her laptop. She was wearing her head set, and her face mic close to her mouth. She spoke quietly, but was really happy and giddy.

"Oh Mum, I loved it so much, she was so amazing with me, and I felt so loved, but to be honest, we talked about everything, and I found her so different from how she is here at home, and I loved every second." I smiled, and tried not to make a noise, Roni obviously responded, and she gave a quiet giggle.

"Mum seriously, I learned so much more about her, she has this secret hidden part of her, and I think I am only just seeing it, Mum I am so happy, I cannot stop smiling." I watched as Birch nodded into the camera, and gave a quiet titter.

"Okay... Yes, you were right, I get that Mum I do, you have no idea how scared I was, I would not have blamed her for leaving me, she had a right to." She shook her head.

"No Mum, I let my guard down, you know Deads warned me

and I didn't listen, I regret that, I am really lucky because she came back, and she understood that I did not lie to her."

I gave a sad sigh, I hated the fact she had been afraid, and I felt a little guilty. I do wish I had been more grown up about it, and maybe I could have dealt with things better than I had? I knew that in the future with Birch, I would stand my ground, and work things out, it frightened me that we came so close to losing each other. Birch nodded as her mum talked.

"It was good advice Mum; I am glad I did not wait and we went now. She was so relaxed and calm, it really helped me to calm myself inside, and get back to my centre. Mum she is perfect, and she was absolutely adored by Seth and Mable, and she really loves the house, I am so glad I bought it, I want to take her back a lot more, so we can have that special us time."

I stepped back from the door with a smile, I felt I should not really spy on her, but I will not deny, knowing she felt as happy about our break as I did, really lifted my spirits. I headed back to my desk with a smile, and opened my emails.

Wendy kept her promise and had sent me all the pictures she had taken over four separate emails, and I downloaded all of them, and was so happy, as they were amazing, she sent me the one of when Birch pulled me close, and gave me a sneaky kiss, in a place we thought was out of sight.

She also included a copy of her article, and also a selection of pictures of what the dailies had put out, sensationalising our breakup. I must admit, I still find it mind blowing how these papers can write such blatant lies. There was only one thing I could do, which was head to my website and update the blog there.

I opened my word processer and started to type. 'Hey all, we are back and rested after a good quiet, and reflective break. Dr Dixon and myself have had the most wonderful break, alone and isolated out in the middle of nowhere. We have relaxed, slept, and really enjoyed sunbathing with picnics, and I cannot tell you how wonderful and special it was for us.

We are back home and back on the ball, and really excited and looking forward to our wedding that is less than a month away. I think it is safe to say, that contrary to the mainstream media, we are closer, stronger and more in love than ever before, so ignore the newspapers. If you want credible information, read this article in a local paper from Devon, it is the only paper that actually got the facts right.'

I went on to add that I was writing away, and close to the end of the draft manuscript, for the next book, and also looking forward to the birth of Deb's and Jimmy's child, and seeing the first Curio centre opening.

I went through my phone, and all the pictures I had taken, I picked out a lot that did not reveal our location, and I uploaded them to the blog, and then posted it live. Within minutes it was getting hits and comments. I felt happy to know that all my readers had a scoop, and the facts were out there, I also knew, the press would be monitoring it too. I added a few pictures of us together walking on the moors, to my Insta just to make a point.

Anthony and Michael cooked a special meal for us all, and we all sat around the table laughing and joking, and I talked of the trees, the house, and the moors. We spent the rest of the night chilling out in the front room with drinks, and eventually staggered up the stairs and into Birch's bed, where we ended up falling asleep curled around each other, and drifted off into a happy dream.

I rose late Sunday, with a bit of a hangover, and after a lot of coffee, and hugs from Birch, who was happy and smiling like an idiot, which I liked, I headed to my room and sat in front of the computer. I opened it up, and looked in shock, I had pages of comments, I gave a sigh, it was going to take forever to answer all of these.

I find it weird that readers want to know everything about my life. I sit in a room alone for hours, and days upon end, and I write, and that is about it. Okay, so I live with my fiancée who just happens to be female, and I share my house with some pretty unique people, but apart from that, I am ordinary.

When I look back to my youth and the books I read, I knew nothing at all about the lives of the people who wrote them, they were just obscure people, of which, I was aware of their name. I really am not sure why in today's social media world, writers have to show every detail of who they are, and what they do. I for one am not a huge fan of sharing everything, I find it hard to understand why it matters. The story is everything, not the writer, and to be honest, if the press had not been plastering me all over the papers for years, I would give away very little.

It really is a catch twenty two, whatever I do I lose out. If I share too much, the media inflate and sensationalise it, and if I give nothing, then they make it up and lie about me, which is why yesterday, on my blog, I had to sit and explain where I have been for five days.

Looking back through the blog posts I have written, almost two thirds of them, are me explaining something to set the record straight, for a paper that made up a complete fabrication, about myself or Birch, it really is ridiculous. I sat back in my chair, and closed my eyes, and just let my thoughts drift back to the last few days of my life.

I have known Birch since I was eighteen, from that very first day at Uni, I have been learning about her. That first summer at the end of term, when I was afraid to come home, she decided to live with me, and we both ended up in the guest house. It was during that time, I really started to see who she was outside the dorm, and she was wilder, more carefree and a lot more in tune with the world than I had first thought.

I think that was the time, when I realised, most of what she told me in my first year of Uni, was not just the theory of a psychology student, but was actually her real practical life.

I shared many of my hidden thoughts and secrets with her in that summer together, as we lay in bed alone, and it still surprises me to realise how safe she made me feel back then. I suffered when I had to leave Uni, the pains of separation were brutal, because it was only then, that I truly understood myself, and started to admit, I was not quite as straight as I thought. As my life hit rock bottom, she reappeared, and once again she revealed yet more of who she was, as she struggled to come to terms with the death of Melody, a client from her mother's practice in Manchester.

Throughout that summer, both of us faced many obstacles, which revealed more of the people we were, and it bonded us together as we moved into the house, and started living as a couple, something neither of us ever expected, and we have been together for four years, surrounded by our friends, which admittedly has expanded in size.

One week ago, we arrived at the house in Devon, and just when I thought, I had learned as much as I could about her, a whole other side of her came out, and it took me completely by surprise. I guess what I am saying, or thinking is, that there is a part of me that has always asked why me, because looking at her, and knowing her, she could have any man or woman she wanted, and yet she chose me, a plain and ordinary writer.

I have always thought that we were opposites, she is loud, more creative, wilder, and very much more outgoing, whereas I am without doubt, far more introverted and very much a loner at times. The thing that has really surprised me, is that this past week alone with her, I got to see a very introverted aspect of her. The quiet calm, deeply spiritual, and very much a lonesome side of her came out, as she showed me something deep and hidden from her younger life. The side I saw was a perfect match for me, and it has left me feeling a little surprised.

I guess I should have known really, when I met her, and we spoke that first night, she did tell me she was a pagan and a naturist, who did yoga and loved woodlands. Having been to Sunny Bank, I now fully understand, why her nick name is Birch, after all, she is so like the trees that grow around that property. She is tall, slender and her skin is white, her hair which has the markings of the bark of a birch, flows with elegance and sensuality from her shoulders down her back. She really is beautiful, she got so much attention from the men at Uni, especially the rugby team, who tried everything to get her into bed, and yet she always refused them.

There is a wildness to her, a natural wildness, that is untameable and free spirited, and that shows in the depth of her bright shiny green eyes, which are the windows to a soul that feels like nature itself. There is also a source of love, deeper than any natural well. I feel so happy sat day dreaming and remembering these past few days, and just knowing that I get to share my life with her forever, is the best thing ever.

Two white arms came over my shoulders, and I smelt her perfume, I blinked and looked up, she was standing over me smiling, her voice soft and quiet.

"Hi Sweetie, it is getting late, are you coming to bed soon?" I frowned and looked at my computer, it was well past ten and I had been sat here all day. She bent down and kissed me on the head.

"I have work again tomorrow, but I would like to just enjoy some more alone time, I have kind of got used to it this week." I gave her a smile.

"Me too, I was just sat here remembering it all, I was sad to leave, I could have done at least another two weeks." She leaned down and grabbed my hands, and lifted them up.

"Come on, curl up with me and talk about it."

I slipped out of the chair, and holding my hand, she led me over to my bed. I looked at it and then her.

"Are we not sleeping in your bed?" She smiled as she slid open my robe, and it dropped to the floor.

"Not tonight Sweetie, I want to sleep in here and remember the guest house, and this room has everything from it in it, so let's sleep here tonight." She pulled back the duvet and I slid under it, she walked round the bed and slipped under, and came across to me, and pulled me into her arms.

"Hmm this is nice, now tell me all about what you thought of the house and our week."

Chapter 26

Washed Out.

I hate Mondays, and this one more than most, because for a whole week, every waking second of my life has been with Birch, and now I have to give her back to real life, and it sucks big time. Birch turned as she slipped on her jacket.

"Oh Sweetie, please don't look like that, I don't want to go either." She pulled a face, as she squatted in front of me, I looked into her huge green eyes.

"I am really going to miss you today; it will feel weird not hanging out and talking." She looked sad, and pouted her lip.

"Oh God Deads, this is killing me, I feel so wretched seeing you like this." Anthony rolled his eyes.

"Abby darling just buy a dildo, and stick a picture of her on it, and then you can feel her presence all day. Houses like this cost money, and as much as I would love to lie around, screwing all day, one has to eat and pay for the roof above us."

Birch smiled and leaned in and kissed me softly, I breathed in and enjoyed her warm lips on mine, she broke apart and smiled.

"I will see you tonight, and make it up to you." Anthony looked at his watch and rolled his eyes. I glanced up at him.

"For your information Anthony, I do not own a dildo." Every woman in the room snapped their heads around, even Deb's, Chloe stared at me from across the island in utter disbelief.

"Abby, we have a cupboard filled with them, how can you possibly not own a dildo?" Deb's nodded at me, I shrugged.

"Those are all long and fat and black, I don't like the look of them, why is it such an issue?" Birch looked at them all, Anthony gave a smirk.

"Hell, even I have four." I could not believe the way they were all looking at me, talk about judged much?

"I don't need one, I have Birch, she takes care of all my needs." Anthony gave a curious look at us both, his eyes moved to Birch.

"You two are not into fisting, are you?" Deb's gave a splutter and spat her coffee everywhere, as she coughed and choked. Chloe reached over and patted her back, I was stunned.

"Jesus Anthony, no we are not, hell, how big do you think I am down there?" Birch looked at me with a smile, Deb's continued to cough, as Edwina and Chloe mucked in to wipe her down and clean up the mess.

"To be honest Sweetie, you would be surprised what you can get in that. I know a girl who had a can of beer pushed up her by her girlfriend, she did a handstand and then pushed it back out." Anthony looked horrified, Deb's just stared as she wiped her face, and I gave a violent shudder.

"Okay, I am fine now, I will let you go to work, I am completely freaked out by that." Birch gave a little giggle, and leaned down, and kissed me softly.

"See you soon."

The next ten minutes was hustle and bustle, and with shouts of goodbye, and the bang of the door, the house fell silent, leaving Chloe and Deb's sat at the island with me, as Edwina headed into her office. Chloe refilled my cup, Deb's already had one now the mess was cleaned up, I lifted my cup enjoying the sudden silence, Chloe looked at me, I smiled at her, knowing she was going to ask something.

"Abby do you even miss it?" I could see Deb's watching me, I sipped my cup.

"Miss what?" She gestured with her cup in her hand.

"You know... Cock?"

"If I am really honest, I have not really thought about it, I am happy with what I have with Birch, and so I have not really considered sleeping with a guy. I guess I have changed a lot more than I realised, because it has been forever since Birch and I did anything in that department." Chloe appeared to understand.

"So you are all girls now, and okay with it?" Deb's turned to her.

"She is one girl Chloe, she has never been all girls, and never will be." I smiled, I looked at Chloe.

"I do not believe in the socially accepted labels Chloe. I think they are very limiting to people. Not that long ago Birch and me talked about it, and I think she best explained it to me. I think everyone's sexuality is fluid, we all change as people, and what we liked as young teenagers, we may not possibly like as adults. All of us evolve, and with that, comes our tastes and our life views, and we are free to change and adapt. You know there are girls who have sex with other girls in Uni, and never do it again after they leave?" Deb's smiled at me.

"I really get that Abby, God, that makes so much sense to me." Chloe looked at her.

"It does... Why?" Deb's gave a very naughty smile.

"Honestly, I would love nothing better at this moment in my life than for a girl to go down on me. I love Jimmy, and I love sex with him, but to be touched softly by girls just now, oh God, I would cum like crazy." Chloe shuffled nervously in her seat.

"Why are you looking at me like that, I have told you, I cannot do it?" I gave a giggle, Chloe was looking very freaked out, I figured I would join in the game.

"You know if you think about it Chloe, Percy is actually female, because he is dick-less, hence the strap on, so you technically have been screwing a female teddy for years?" Deb's gave a giggle.

"Yeah, that is no different from when we did each other with dildo's Chloe, and you really liked that." Chloe gave a shudder.

"Percy is all male, he just has a small one and feels bad about it, so I gave him something to be proud of." I started to laugh, Deb's giggled along with me, it was a good recovery there was no doubt about it. Chloe smirked at me, and I winked.

"Chloe we are all Curio's, and that is sort of the point, societies box is forever, and we do not want that, we like the idea of being open to every aspect of life. The sex with Birch is not great because we are gay, or queer, it is because we share a bond that is different to the bond we have with others, ours is closer and more intimate. The sex is good for me because it is Birch, I honestly do not think another girl could do that for me." She understood and gave a nod.

"Yeah, I get that, I really do, I could see that at the house in Devon, you looked really happy together, I liked that, I thought it was sweet." I looked at her across the island, I loved her to bits.

"You know Chloe, you make a big deal out of being straight, you should just let it go, and just go with the flow. I love the idea of being fluid, I beat myself up for years agonising over was I straight, lesbian, or bi, and I ended up lost, alone and in a really dark place. There are days I think Birch actually saved my life, just by telling me she was in love with me. I often think about it, and in that one moment I let go of everything, and decided I was just going to be Abby, and not care where it took me, and that was the day I became really happy." Deb's gave a smile.

"I remember that time, I was so glad when she came back, your messages to me got darker and darker, I was so worried about you when I was in Cambridge." I gave a giggle.

"That was then, and look at now, and hey, it gave Jimmy a top selling hit." Deb's smiled, and gave a little chuckle.

"You did good Abby." I winked.

"I have, I really have, thanks to all you guys, and sadly, I have about a zillion messages to write, so I am off to get some work done." I slid off my seat, poured another coffee, and I left Chloe and Deb's alone to talk, and made my way up to my room.

I settled into my chair, I had gotten through a lot of comments yesterday, but I still had a lot of messages on the site, and I hated not reading them all and responding. I got stuck in. I had been working for a few hours and was considering filling my cup up with fresh coffee, when my phone rang, I picked it up.

"Hi Mum, is everything alright?"

"Abby darling, I have a bit of a problem and I need a favour, you are not writing, are you?" I slouched back in my chair and pulled my legs up.

"Not really, I am going through some of my messages, and replying."

"Abby, I need a picture running over to Millington, the problem is it will not fit in my car, and Ellen is out and held up in traffic, and we promised delivery today. I wondered if you had access to Petal today?" I gave a nod, which was stupid because I was talking on a phone.

"It is okay Mum, I do not mind, I think Petal is still here, if not I will pick her up from Birch at the practice. I will see you soon."

"Abby, you are a life saver, thanks. See you in a little while darling."

Going out meant dressing, so I opened the wardrobe to see what I had, delivery girl, meant black jeans, sleeveless t shirt, with check fabric shirt. I headed downstairs and grabbed my trainers from the kitchen, I had washed and dried them, and left them overnight. I wandered into the kitchen.

"Anyone know where the keys for Petal are?" Chloe leaned round the door of the studio.

"Why do you want them?"

"I have to run into Millington for mum, and deliver a picture, it is too big for her car, so I need Petal."

"Cool, can I come too, there is a great art shop in Millington, I wouldn't mind having a look?" She threw me the keys.

"Let me grab a top and pants."

She shot past me, and headed for her room, I pocketed the keys, and made sure I had my phone and bag. Ten minutes later we jumped into Petal, and drove out of the gates, and round towards the village. It had started to rain, so I drove around the back of the shop, and reversed up to the back doors. We jumped out and entered through the back door, mum gave me a huge hug, she looked at me and smiled.

"You look really well, a few days away has done you good." Chloe gave a beaming smile.

"She had a diet of salad, sex, and sun Mrs W, we all do well on that." My mum smiled.

"Maybe I will give it a try, if I can look half as good as you Abby." She turned and walked to her desk.

"I have the delivery details here; it is not hard to find." I walked over to her as Chloe looked around. At her desk she turned with the paperwork and gave me a smile.

"You look really happy Abby, did it help you both, I will not say I was not worried when Roni rang me?" I nodded.

"Mum it was really wonderful, just being there alone with her, we talked and walked, and lay out in the sun, and both of us talked about everything we had been feeling. I think we really needed it, and I think we have come back a lot happier." She smiled and cupped my face.

"I can see the changes, oh Abby, I am so pleased for you, I really think this will stand you in good stead for your marriage. I will not deny, I am very angry with that red head, and I hope she does not come in here. I can promise you; she will be leaving by ambulance; I do not take kindly to people messing with my daughter." Chloe walked up with a big grin.

"You go Mrs W, we already booted her off our doorstep last week, she needs to know, we all have Abby's back, and we mean business."

I grabbed the picture, which was wrapped in brown paper, and then covered in shrink wrap, and carried it out, Chloe opened the door and I hurried to load it. I lay it down in the back, just to make sure it was extra safe. Mum handed me a baseball cap, she had done a few for the gallery, and I pulled my hair into a ponytail, and slipped it on, it looked very boyish.

We jumped in and set off, the rain was getting heavier, and with my lights on full, and playing Avril very loud, we headed for Millington, and the address on the paperwork. We came over the top of the hill, at the top of Manor Road, and headed down towards the town, Chloe looked at the map.

"This is on the far side of the town Abby, and this road is notorious for flooding, if this gets any harder, it might be better to head back, via Smether's Wood, and down Waterside."

I agreed as I looked out of the window, the rain was hammering down, and bouncing off the glass, I had the blowers on full, just to stop us steaming up. It had been a nice warm day, but with the rain, the temperature plummeted down. I kept my speed down, and we both leaned forward in our seats to stare at the road, I was just glad I was in a large vehicle with good tyres, that gripped the road, because the water was pooling fast.

"We have not had a summer downpour like this in years Chloe, visibility is getting insane." She nodded as she leaned forward, to stare through the glass with me.

When I saw the traffic lights at the bottom of the hill, I gave a sigh of relief. We hit the deep puddle at the bottom, which was already several inches deep, and water sprayed out from under the wheels, Chloe looked out of the side window.

"It is already pretty deep, I think we definitely need to go home the other way, the traffic here later is going to back up, why do they never clear the drains here, they know this happens?"

I was not going to argue, I was not thrilled driving on this road in this kind of weather. The lights changed, and I headed across the crossroads, as I drove through the side roads, to take me across the town to the next main road. After many turns, we finally pulled up outside a set of gates, and I leaned out and pressed the buzzer. A voice came back at me, and I leaned in front of the camera.

"I have a delivery from Waterside Galleries."

A loud buzzer sounded, and the gates clanged as they shuddered, and then opened. I waited a few moments until the gap was wide enough, and then drove through. The house was far older and bigger than I expected, I backed up to get Petal as close as I could to shorten the distance so that the painting would be carried in quickly from the rain.

A servant looking person in white gloves came to the door, I jumped out, and walked around to the back of Petal, and opened the door. The servant appeared unwilling to step out, and I was outside getting rained on already, so I lifted the painting and pulled it out of the back, then carried it in. The servant took the painting, and handed me an envelope, I slipped it in my back pocket, and handed him the sealed confirmation of sale note, it was a simple and basic operation, which suited me fine.

Apart from the drive, it was a relatively quick job, I closed up Petal, and then jumped in and slid off my wet coat, and threw it in the back, Chloe had the windows cracked to keep the condensation on the windows down. It was still raining hard as we headed back towards the gates, it was no fun driving at all, the visibility was greatly reduced. Chloe sat back in her seat, and looked up at the sky, it was almost black the clouds were so thick and heavy.

"When they said we may have rain today, they were not kidding, this is like a monsoon, you know if it gets too hard to see the road, pull in. Forget the art shop Abby, let's get across to Wotton, as fast as we can, traffic will be a nightmare later."

I was happy to hear it, to be honest, I was not happy with the driving conditions. I made my way over to the far side of town, and looked for the turning from Smether's into Waterside. The road on this side of the hill was not that well maintained, but over the Wotton end, which was where I lived, it was a pretty good road. I was glad to see the steep incline, I just wanted to get home and off the road.

The good thing about Petal, was she was designed for rough terrain, so I knew there would be no problems. The surface was rough and pot holed, so apart from the rain, it was a little bumpy, and Chloe giggled as we bounced on the seat, over a particularly large bump. Waterside Lane on this side of the hill was very steep, and I dropped gear, and pressed the accelerator to build up enough speed.

We were not going hugely fast, but the rain was pelting against the glass, and the wipers were on full speed, I strained to see the road, when Chloe leaned forward and peered through the window.

"What the fuck is that?" I leaned forward. A little way up in front was a black shape, in the middle of the road. Chloe stared with me.

"It's a car, and I think a guy, he should put some lights on, I can only just make it out."

Chloe hit the switch, and the two floodlights on the lower bumper, and the two on the roof rack illuminated. The person appeared to freeze in the road, and turned towards us. It was hard to make out what was wrong as I slowed and pulled up a few feet away, and put the hazard lights on. The person came walking down to us. I opened the window, as they walked up to the door, I was really surprised to see Nigel, he was soaked to the skin.

"Are you alright Nigel?" Realising who was driving, he suddenly looked nervous, and looked back to the car, Chloe leaned over at my side.

"Have you got a black eye?" I had not noticed at first. He touched his cheek, and looked even more nervous, I smiled.

"Do you want to jump in the back and tell us what has happened, you are getting soaked to the skin and you cannot stay here, it's dangerous?" He wanted to say something, but as he went to speak, he stopped himself.

"Nigel, are you alright, you look pretty freaked out?" He looked at the car, and then back at me, and finally he found his words. Rain was pouring down his face, and running in his eyes.

"The car just stopped and I am not sure why, I am sorry, I did not realise it was you Abby, I did not mean it to happen." I realised I was wearing a baseball cap, and probably looked more male as he walked up, although he must have recognised Petal. Chloe leaned forward.

"You really should put your hazards on Nigel, if anyone comes up from Wotton, they will not see you until the last moment in this." I nodded she had a point.

"Nigel, what are you going to do?"

He shook his head, and looked really worried. It sounds strange but I felt really sorry for him, he was soaked to the skin. It was clear he did not have a clue what to do. I turned to the back, and reached over to the back seat for my coat, Chloe gave a giggle and leaned over for her coat, she whispered in my ear.

"The naughty bugger just scoped out your ass, and he approves." I gave a sigh and grabbed my coat.

"Behave Chloe, he is in the road, and that car is a danger to anyone using this route as a short cut." I slipped on my coat and jumped out; Chloe grabbed my arm.

"Here give him this." She handed me a small plastic sheet; I took it and handed it to Nigel.

"You are pretty soaked, but this will keep you a little dryer, no point getting any wetter."

I pulled my hood up and walked to the car. I opened the door, the keys were still in, I turned on the ignition, and the dash lit up. Nigel came up behind me wrapped in his sheet, he was shivering. I leaned in and put his lights and hazards on, then jumped into his seat and tried to start it. It just clicked and drained the lights; the engine was dead. Chloe appeared on the passenger side of the car and opened the door, she leaned in.

"Abby, it's dead, he cannot stay here you know that, Petal can just about squeeze past, but anything bigger, and the road is blocked?" I looked across the seats at her.

"What do we do?" She gave a sigh.

"We have a tow rope, and floodlights, if he has recovery, it could take a while before they get here. Abby he is a mile from home, if we take it easy, we should be fine."

It made sense, but it also made me nervous, I looked at Nigel, who was looking even more nervous, he looked pitiful.

"It is alright Abby, I can walk from here, I am grateful, don't think I am not, it's just..." He did not need to explain, I climbed out of the car and shut the door, the rain was pounding, and it was deafening, I leaned in close.

"Nigel, I get it I do, Prim hates my guts. Honestly it is not a secret, but the problem is, we can just about get past, but other bigger vehicles won't, and the main Manor Road was starting to flood an hour ago. You have to move this car and soon. Look, we can tow you, it's only a mile." He looked uncertain, Chloe came around the car, and shouted through the rain.

"Nigel, stop being bloody stupid, you are blocking the road, just let us tow it, and get you out of the way." He looked at me and nodded.

"Alright Abby, but I have never done this before." Chloe came up at my side.

"Let him sit in the passenger seat, you drive Petal, and I will steer his, I have been towed loads of times, my car is crappy. Put your phone on speaker, and we can talk." I nodded, and turned to Nigel.

"Get in the passenger seat of Petal, Chloe will drive your car." He does dither, but he agreed, and headed for Petal, Chloe stood at my side.

"He is afraid of his own shadow, how the hell did he ever manage to make a kid? I will stand here and wave you through the gap, but drive slowly, it is bloody narrow here."

I jumped into Petal, and shifted into four wheel drive, and then as Chloe stood in the middle of the road. I pulled slowly forward and she waved, guiding me through the gap, Nigel was very nervous, as he sat shivering in the passenger seat. I was glad I was in Petal as I had to drive slightly on the grass verge at the side of the road. I edged through very carefully, and when I was clear, Chloe banged on the back door, and I stopped and put on the hand brake. The back door opened, and Chloe leaned in, she lifted the seat at the back, and pulled out a safety triangle and the thick heavy tow rope.

"Give me two minutes Abby and I will call you, put me on speaker." I nodded. The back door closed, and Chloe went to work, a few minutes later my phone rang, I answered, and put her on speaker.

"Abby, you are rigged up, just put it in first, and edge up slowly to take the strain, when you feel it pull, hold it there, until I say so."

"Will do Chloe." I took a deep breath.

"It will not take long Nigel, you know we are not going to do anything to hurt you, we just want to help. I know your wife, and your mum, are not my biggest fans, but I would not do anything to hurt you." He nodded.

"I know that Abby, my dad has told me about how nice you have been to him, you always were kind, especially at school." I smiled.

I followed Chloe's instructions nervously, I have never actually done this before, and was starting to wish Birch was here. The jerk on the back, as Petal took the strain scared the shit out of me, which did not help Nigel's nerves much.

I followed Chloe's advice, and kept it slow with all the front spots, and hazards on, I slowly changed up the gears, as we built up a little momentum. I gave a sigh of relief as we came over the top of the hill, Petal had very little trouble pulling the saloon behind us, Chloe talked slowly as I stared through the rain in front.

"Abby, slow down a little, this is a steep hill, and these brakes are murder with no engine running, take it real slow. I softly pressed the brakes, and Chloe did the same, and tried to keep the rope tight, we came down the hill at a very slow pace.

Half way down the hill, I saw the opening to the old Sutton's farm, I looked at my phone on the dash.

"Chloe, I see the house what do I do?"

"Abby, just go really slow, and turn really wide into it, I will use the brake to free wheel. Be ready to brake when I say so."

I took the corner as wide as I could, and pulled in very slowly, as Chloe guided me, and came to a halt on the large driveway outside the house. Nigel turned to me, and gave a smile.

"I am very grateful, thank you Abby." I smiled back at him.

"Just being good neighbours, after all we do sort of live on the same road."

I turned to face the front of the window, grabbed my phone and jumped out of my skin, I mean, seriously, Prim just appeared like a murderer in a horror film. She stood scowling with her arms folded, which pleased me, I could see at least, she was not holding a knife. Nigel opened the door and stepped out; Prim was on him in a flash.

"Why is this hunk of junk towing you, I thought I told you stay away from them?" I got out of Petal, and walked around to her, the rain was pouring, but I pulled back my hood.

"Prim, he was blocking the road, we could not leave him there." She suddenly realised who I was, and screamed at Nigel, as she pointed at me.

"YOU TOOK HELP FROM THIS WHORE?" I could not believe my eyes and ears; I felt my anger rising.

"Hey just wait a frigging minute, he was stranded, and not only was he in danger, so were other motorists. I get you do not like me, but I was helping your husband not get killed, you could be a little more frigging grateful?"

She spun around on him, and he jumped back, I saw her arm twitch, as she clenched her fist. Yeah, it was pretty clear to me where he got his black eye from. Prim turned back and looked at me, her eyes were narrowed and to be honest, she looked possessed.

"Tell me Abigail, now that slut and whore has left you, are you stealing husbands now, is that what this is?" I heard Chloe chuckle as she threw the tow rope and triangle in the back.

"Holy fuck, she has an ego bigger than Wotton, I would say that the odds are no one would want him after touching you."

She turned to look at Chloe as she closed the back door and walked around the back of Petal. Chloe stared at her; it was blatantly clear how much Chloe did not like her.

"I would be careful how you speak to me, I am not as polite as Abby, and will knock you the fuck out bitch." I raised my hand to Chloe, and looked at Prim.

"You know what Prim, we were just trying to help, you know, lose our satanic ways and try some of your so called Christian ways, you and your friends are always ramming down our throats. But as I have seen yet again, when I copy the likes of you, I get nowhere. Tell me this, who was the more Christian today? Oh, and just for the record, do not read the papers, they lie, Birch and myself are very much together, and I have no need for a husband, I prefer Birch." I looked at Nigel.

"I am glad you are alright Nigel, but looking at this, maybe I should have just run over you, and saved you years of misery? I will be on my way now, take care of yourself." I detected a slight smile on his face. I climbed in petal, and Chloe pulled on the door, and it opened, she smiled at Nigel.

"Call out your recovery Nigel, they will fix it or take it to the garage for you." She looked right at Prim, who was staring at her with hate.

"There is a word for what you are doing, it is called Spousal Abuse. I would be careful Prim, the Parish Council frowns on that, I would hate for people to find out about you." Chloe climbed in, and pulled the door closed. I put Petal in gear, and drove around the flower bed to head out, Chloe leaned back in her seat.

"God, she is horrible, how the fuck does he get in bed with her? Her face is as rancid as her manner." I nodded as I turned out of the drive and headed towards the village.

"He will probably have another black eye in the morning, I would guess he is on the sofa tonight, I actually feel really sorry for him. He is an idiot at times, but hell Chloe, no one deserves her, she is bloody horrible." Chloe unzipped her coat.

"This coat is shit, my tits are soaked, I am not sure I have ever been this wet before." I started to giggle.

"Well, that is a first, although I think that night with Zac came close." Chloe looked at me and gave a shudder.

"Jesus Abby, I told you, never say his name... I am never going to live that down; I am destined to be haunted forever by it." I smiled.

"Maybe, but even he is prettier than Prim." Chloe gave a snort and started to laugh, I laughed along with her as we cruised down Waterside Lane, and as I reached the house, I pulled in.

"Go and get dry, I need to drop off the paperwork with mum." Chloe climbed out chuckling, and ran in through the gates, and I moved on, and headed for the gallery.

I will not deny, even though he stalked me, and for a while I hated his guts, I have always known he was a soft and kind hearted boy. His only real sin, was his inability to connect with, or fully understand women, and the sad thing was, if he ever had anything like a real relationship before, he never would have married someone as foul as Prim.

I had heard a lot of things over the last few years, about her dominance and bullying, but I had also heard, that he was a great dad, and doted over his little boy, and actually, I really liked that. The sad truth was, he was never really dipped in to the alpha pool, he was destined to remain a beta male all his life, and the saddest thing of all, was academically he was brilliant.

I remember sitting with Izzy one night, and she told me, the greatest minds, make the most foolish people. What you gain in academics, you lose in social skills, because the cost of brilliance, is a life locked away in study, and looking at Nigel today, I can see how right she was. Poor sod, I would not even wish Prim on Martin Hinkley, although, thinking about it...

Chapter 27

Book Life.

Milton was sat in his study reading the paper, as he listened to the interview on Radio Four, trying to ignore the screaming and yelling coming from next door. He turned the page, and gave a sigh as he looked across the room to the wall, where he knew next door, Primula was having another tantrum. There was a loud smash, and he folded the paper down, and looked at Marjorie stood in the doorway.

"This is becoming far too regular, I have to say Marjorie, when we offered him the house, I was not expecting this kind of ruckus. It really is becoming bothersome." She clearly looked uncomfortable as she walked into the room, and sat in the spare chair.

"I promised I would not interfere; although, I do wish he would stand up for himself. People are starting to talk, his constant black eyes are noticeably showing at Church, even Gail has asked if all is well, not that I want her pushing her nose in." Milton folded his paper, and placed it neatly in his lap.

"I feel our time of silence is drawing to an end, I am a tolerant man, but I will not deny Marjorie, this is beyond a joke. I fully understand her dislike of the Watson girl, but if I am completely honest, I feel young Abigail showed a far more Christian manner than that of his wife. You know the driving conditions were awful, and she took a big risk to tow him, not to mention that her and Chloe got soaked to the skin in order to help him?" Marjorie gave a nod.

"I will not deny, I have my criticism of her lifestyle, but even I have to admit, I am grateful for what she did. He could have had a nasty accident, and her and the Pemberton girl, really did come to his rescue." There was another smash on the wall. Milton gave a sigh.

"This is ridiculous, I am seriously considering asking Isabel, if she could arrange some sort of couples counselling for them." Marjorie gave a frown.

"They do not need therapy; the problem is our son has not got the back bone to stand up to her. I have to admit, that even you with your mild manner, have been more forceful than he has, I have no idea where he gets this from." There was a very loud scream, and then a crash, and Marjorie jumped in her seat.

"You know, I honestly thought if she focused on the Parish Council she would calm down. I will not deny, if I had known she was going to turn out like this, I would never have arranged the marriage." Milton considered the point, and he tapped his foot on the carpet, something that normally irritated Marjorie.

"I hate to admit this, but I believe we need specialist help, I think I am going to take Isabel on one side and have a quiet word. I am sure she can find a solution, yes, yes, I do believe that has to be the answer, I shall see her Friday night, and just have a little chat, to see what advice she can give me." Marjorie gave a long sigh.

"I suppose it is worth a try, Prim does not listen to a thing I say, she thinks she knows better than everyone. I cannot deny, she has become a right little madam, even I am wary of her temper. I have no idea where it comes from, we need to find some way of calming the girl. I never thought I would ever say this, but I almost wish the Watson girl had said yes to his request to date. I have had my issues with Felicity and Edwin in the past, but they raised a well mannered girl, even when she is rude, she is respectful, I have always admired that about her." Milton gave a sigh.

"I have told you before Marjorie, if you would only give them both a chance, you will find they are actually very pleasant and kind people. They just want to live their life with their exotic looks and fashion style, nothing more. You know, I think they are almost thirty, and they are soon to be married, I know you do not agree with those things, but it does show commitment, and you have always admired commitment in people. I cannot deny, I have spoken with Gail, and she speaks very highly of the love and bond they feel." Marjorie gave a sigh.

"I am aware of how they feel, I saw it remember, on that awful day in the Tea Rooms? I will not deny, watching her holding that

Birch girl, was a difficult thing to see, but it really surprised me to see Abigail have such deep feelings. I have never doubted her feelings Milton, I do not understand it, but it was heart breaking to witness, it really was a terrible moment for her, and I have been true to my word, and been easier on her since." He smiled.

"The times are changing Marjorie, all these young people are the future of this place, but I am actually quite reassured that hopefully young Abigail will step up one day and fill her mother's shoes. Even you have to admit, Felicity has managed everything very well indeed? You know, I watch her at the meetings and she reminds me of a younger you, I feel she learned a great deal from you, and even you have to agree, she has continued a lot of what you started?"

"As I have told you Milton, I feel she could be more efficient with the budget, some of her purchases are a little more extravagant than I would have permitted, but all in all, I feel she has done well. I am not convinced that Primula will be as controlled at the moment, if she would just listen to reason, there may be hope."

When Birch arrived home, I was sat in her room as the bath filled, she came straight up to me, and saw me soaked through to the skin.

"Sweetie, you are shivering."

"I got wet in the rain today, I am running a bath, join me, and I will tell you all about it." I headed into the bathroom, and turned off the taps, then stripped, and threw my clothes through the door and into my own room.

I sat back relaxing when Birch came in, she was all smiles as she climbed in, sat back and leaned onto me. I slipped my arms round her waist and held her close, as both of us gave a sigh of relief, thoroughly enjoying the heat from the water.

"Oh Sweetie, this is so nice, I missed this last week, I think I need to remodel the bathroom at some point. If we are going to go there often, we really need a bigger bath." I closed my eyes and relaxed enjoying the warmth, and her soft body pressed into mine. She glanced back and smiled.

"So, are you going to tell me about today?"

My eyes blinked open, as I realised why we were here, and so I began to tell her all about my day. By the time I was finished, the water was losing its heat, and we got out, wrapped ourselves in towels, and sat on her bed facing each other. Birch considered all I had told her.

"You think it is Prim who hit him, and gave him the black eye?" I nodded at her.

"I do, I thought I saw her clench her fist, I am sure she wanted to hit him again, and to be honest, after we left, I am sure she probably has. She does not hold back, and she has no problems telling me what she thinks. She needs to control her hands, and her mouth, I honestly thought Chloe would punch her." Birch appeared to understand.

"You know, when people talk about spousal abuse, they always assume it is the guy hitting the girl, and it is not always. I know of many cases, where the guy is the one being abused, and to be honest, the number is rising, a lot more women are becoming aggressive. You are probably right; I trust your instincts." I was glad to know that Birch thought I might be right, she could see me thinking, I looked into her bright sparkling eyes.

"Birch, what she is doing is wrong, I don't hate Nigel, he is harmless. I mean, he is naïve, and really does not understand people. I hated the fact he stalked me when I was a teenager, but I know you get me, when I say, he does not deserve this kind of treatment." She smiled and leaned forward, and took my hands in hers.

"Deads Sweetie, I love the fact that you can see the injustice in this, but Sweetie, what can we do about it, it is their marriage? Honestly, considering the past, if you interfere, she will play this as you being jealous because she got him card. Deads, you will be painted the darkest, and the village will turn on you, I would say for now, sit back, and let's see what she does."

I completely understood what she was saying, and yes, she made sense, but it felt so wrong, and I have no idea why, but I felt really sorry for him. It was frustrating and I gave a sigh.

"You are right, I am the last person on earth who can do anything about this. I just hate that she walks around like she is the queen of perfection, spouting her biblical bullshit at me, as she portrays herself as the most perfect candidate for the Parish Council. She is a complete bloody fraud." Birch lay back on the bed.

"Sweetie, have you forgotten, this whole village is filled with frauds, why would Prim be any different?" I flopped back on the bed.

"Oh hell, why does everything have to be so God dammed hard? All of this sucks, I want to run back to Sunny Bank and hole up with you forever." Birch gave a giggle.

"Oh, Sweetie please don't say that, I want to do that now, I want to kidnap you and run away to Sunny Bank, and spend the rest of my life naked, having picnics, and sleeping in late." I stared at the ceiling and chuckled.

"I loved it Birch, it made me so happy, and I got to see more of you, of who you are, and I fell in love with you over and over all week, I think that place is magical." She lifted her head and looked at me.

"It's ours Sweetie, we can go every weekend if we want to, and yes, it is a magical place. I have been thinking of asking Bradley to get someone to have a look at the bathroom, and give me a quote for a bigger bath."

"Yes... I want to bathe with you at Sunny Bank too. Showers are good, but nothing beats a long soak, and I want to soak with you all over the place." Birch gave a cackle of a laugh.

"I WANT TO BUY ALL THE BATHROOMS IN BRITAIN!!" She sat up with a wild look in her eyes.

"I WANT TO RENT EVERY BATH IN BRITAIN FOR MY SWEETIE!" I started to laugh, and threw my arms up in the air.

"I REALLY WANT THAT; I WANT MY SEXY SNOW QUEEN IN EVERY BATH."

Birch gave a squeal of laughter, and lay back cackling like a mad person. I love her laughter, it is so infectious, and I lay on the bed laughing with her, and felt such joy. The door opened and Chloe popped her head round.

"Stay out of my bathroom you perverts, I will never rent it out." Birch turned her head to the side and giggled.

"You owe us a bath, we let you in ours the day we got engaged, so actually Chloe, give us your bath." She laughed out loud, and wildly, and Chloe frowned.

"Fuck!" I giggled.

"Chloe you are busted, give me your tub." She shook her head.

"Never... I am not surrendering the realm of Percy and me, so you can do perverted things in my bath." I looked at Birch as she giggled.

"Are you going to do perverted things to me in her bath?" She rolled over and looked at me.

"Absolutely... I aim to do perverted things to you in every bath I can get you in." Chloe screwed up her face.

"Ew gross, please do not violate my bath, I love my bath, it's straight." Birch rolled over and looked at her.

"Chloe Sweetie, we will spare your bath, because it's straight, we cannot be perverted in a straight bath." I laughed out loud as Chloe gave a sigh of relief.

"You know, you two have been fucking weird since you came back, I think there is something in the water down there that fucks people up?" I giggled at her.

"We have always been like this Chloe, we just hid it, but now we are back, we are flying our freak flags out of the closet." She shook her head and slipped back through the door, and Birch rolled over, her eyes danced with delight, and she cackled with laughter even more.

We spent the evening curled up in just our towels, Birch scampered downstairs, and grabbed a bottle of wine, and we chilled out together, sipping wine, and just talking about dreams and crazy things all night. We fell asleep wrapped in towels, and cuddled together.

I woke to Birch running around like a mad person, as she hurriedly dressed for work, I slipped out of bed, and dug her shoes out from underneath it, and handed them to her, she looked at them and smiled, and kissed me.

"Morning Sweetie... I am late."

I laughed as she flew out of the room and down the stairs, she was still not adjusted back to work hours, that is the problem with having a lazy week. I took my time, and had breakfast with Chloe, and then headed to the library to work. It is quieter in the library these days, now that Edwina works in her new office. I must admit I have got used to seeing her code next to me, and I missed her.

My mind was filled with the previous day's events, Birch had been right, I was the last person to interfere with Primula. I felt bad for Nigel, but I could not become embroiled with their troubles, I had to resist it. I have had so much trouble with Marjorie in the past, and Birch was right, I could not get involved. I was getting my life back together, and about to get married; I had to stop, and leave well alone.

The only way to get it all out of my head was to work, and so I got stuck in, I needed to get this book finished, as that was my priority. My ritual of writing kicked in, and I read through the last few chapters, and then started to hammer away, the words began to flow. The story had been growing in my mind whilst I was away, and now it was ready to come forth and complete itself. The day passed without me even knowing, and Birch arrived home, smiled, made me a coffee, and left it on my desk.

It was almost four in the morning when I finished the chapter, and I climbed the stairs feeling exhausted, Birch was lay on her back, spread eagled, fast asleep. I climbed into bed and curled around her, and my brain shut down to the sound of her soft breathing, and deep sleep took me. I woke the following day about mid day, and the pattern repeated, and all the days became one, as the lines formed, and the chapters came close to the end.

I had not even realised it was the weekend, and Birch was home sat at her desk next to me, as she typed away on her own project. Edwina gave a smile as she leaned on the door frame, and watched us both side by side, hammering away on the keyboards, Deb's smiled.

"If you think about it, they are a perfect match, they even type in rhythm?" Edwina gave a chuckle.

"They do look lovely side by side, married with keyboards, it's perfect for a soap opera." Deb's gave a small laugh.

"Wow, if it was about them two, I would definitely watch it."

"It will certainly be different, that's for sure." I carried on writing until late evening, when I sat back with a happy sigh, and clicked save on the file.

"One more chapter and it's done."

The room was empty, as I looked around and it was dark outside, I stretched and gave a yawn, grabbed my cup and walked to the kitchen, everywhere was dark. I opened the fridge, and the room lit up, and I noticed a flash of white. It startled me, and I turned quickly, and then frowned.

"Birch?"

Birch was sat at the table, well actually she was sat down but leaning over the table fast asleep. I gave a smile, beside her was a stack of notes, and a thick pad, she had been playing catch up. I walked over and crouched down, her eyes were closed, and her long eyelashes were illuminated in the fridge light. I stroked the hair back from her face, she looked so peaceful, although she had drooled a little, but she did look very beautiful. I gave her a gentle nudge.

"Birch... Baby, you cannot sleep here, come to bed." Her eyes flickered, and then opened, she smiled, and whispered.

"Hi Sweetie." I smiled.

"Hi Baby, you fell asleep, come to bed, it is very late." She breathed in a long drawn breath and sat up, and saw the pool on the table, and pulled a face.

"Yuk... Was that me?" I gave a little giggle and nodded at her.

"Yep, it's Birch sap." She shuddered.

Whilst she came around, I mopped it up and gathered together her papers, I knew they were confidential, so I lifted them up in one arm, and held out my other, she took it and sleepily walked with me up to bed. We slid into bed and curled round each other, and soon she was breathing softly into my shoulder, as she drifted back into sleep, and I gave a happy sigh, closed my eyes, I felt myself drift, and was gone. I was so warm and comfy when the bed bounced.

"Sweetie it's morning... Well actually it is afternoon, but not to matter, get up I am excited." I groaned into my pillow.

"Ten more minutes?" The bed jerked up and down, and I felt pressure on my bum, as it was pushed into the bed. Birch was sat on me, she leaned forward and giggled in my ear.

"I have a surprise... AND I LOVE SURPRISES!"

I screwed up my eyes as I almost went deaf, and gave a long sigh. She was excited and in child mode, I knew there would be no more sleeping. The bed bounced again, I opened my eyes and she was bent over looking at me with those wild green sexy eyes, she smiled and gave a giggle.

"Hi Sweetie, I am excited."

I was not going to get let off the hook, I knew what she wanted, and it was too soon to play this game with her, but I knew I was not going to get her to leave me alone until I asked. I had to play along, or there would be no peace at all, and I really needed coffee. She slid forward and kissed my nose.

"I made you a coffee." Now she was talking my language, so I conceded.

"Okay... Why are you excited?"

Oh God, I regret that, you see, to ask her that, is like lighting the blue touch paper of a glitter filled bomb, there is noise and sparkles and she goes bonkers. Yep, I was right.

The loud excited squeal, combined with the lifting of weight off my back, told me she was heading skyward, as her enthusiastic excitement bubbled over, why did I feel I would regret this?

I rolled over and sat up, saw my large mug of coffee on the side, and slid back into my pillows and picked up the coffee to drink. I managed a mouthful, and got the cup back on the unit just in time, as a whirlwind of white hair, flashing green eyes, and a long black robe flapping behind her white naked body came sailing through the air, and crashed down onto the bed. She knelt holding a silver box out at arms length, towards me, smiling like she was on acid.

"It's done." I frowned, I really was not awake, and if I had my own way, I wouldn't be.

"What is it?"

She sat smiling, and bit her lip, I took the box and placed it on the bed in front of me, it felt quite heavy for its size. I reached for the lid and she gave a little squeak, was she holding her breath? I looked at her as I lifted the lid, and then looked down, and I smiled.

"Oh my God, you did it, Birch that is brilliant."

I read the top sheet of her newly completed manuscript. 'The Sham of Shame. (A study in the behaviours and attitudes, of life today) By Doctor Jemima Dixon. I looked up at her with a huge smile.

"I am so proud of you at this moment Baby, I really am."

It was like watching a volcano build up to its eruption, and I swear I could see the tremors start in her core as they bubbled to the surface, her face cracked and she smiled. Then boom, she exploded in excitement, bounced around and started talking at five hundred miles an hour. I could hardly keep up with her, and just started to laugh, as her eyes blazed with life and joy and craziness.

She bounced off the bed and walked quickly up and down as she gave me a full and detailed analysis, of modern behaviour and the bad influences of the internet and social media on society, and how celebrity culture has turned people inward and created an effect of bigger better faster more, that left them competing with everyone including their family and friends, and leading to a society that pretended to be politically correct, but was indeed actually just shallow and false, and how that led to the lack of openness and honesty, and how it had morphed into deceit and shaming.

She took a deep breath as I giggled, and tried to get her breath back, she was crazy, but also a genius, I just watched her, feeling very happy for her.

"Birch, instead of telling me what it is about, can I just read it?"

She stopped walking, and stared at me, and then something very familiar happened, something I know really well, and it is a little like pulling the pin out of a grenade, as the reality of the new accomplishment sets in. Birch froze on the spot, and stared at me.

"You want to read it?" I gave a smile.

"Of course, I do, you wrote it." And boom! She fell apart.

"Oh God, I never thought anyone would read it... What if they hate it?"

I know this place well, I lived there for a while, and she looked as terrified as I do whenever a new book comes out. I could not stop giggling, she looked so funny as her eyes expanded, and she bit her lip as doubt engulfed her. It is a rite of passage all new writers have to endure, but I threw her a life raft.

"Birch Baby, I have known you since I was eighteen, and in all that time you have had your head in a book learning this stuff. Hell, you are the only one who can write this book, and honestly, I am really looking forward to reading it." She swallowed hard, as she stared at me, and gave a slight nod.

"Oh crap, I need to check it again."

There was a swish of black cloth and white hair, and she just disappeared through the door like a hurricane, I assumed heading for the library. I looked down at the thick wad of printed pages, wow, she finally did it. I had waited for this moment since we lived in the guest house, and I was so delighted, because I know her, and I know this book will really resound with a lot of people. Bless her, she is wonderful.

I got out of bed, and grabbed my coffee, and with the lid back on the box, I walked into my room and placed it on my desk. I emptied my cup, and decided a refill or two before reading, and headed downstairs.

Walking down the stairs half awake, and yawning I felt the need for coffee, I reached the lower step, and saw it on the floor. My heart gave a jolt, there was a crumpled up tissue, I glanced at the small table next to the living room door, and… Oh shit the tissue box was missing, I felt panic.

"Chloe… Edwina… Deb's?" It was silent, I swallowed hard, where were they? Chloe appeared from the kitchen; she looked up onto the staircase as she walked down the hall.

"Did you just shout Abby?" I wanted to speak, but had momentarily lost my ability, I felt a shiver run down my spine as I pointed at the base of the stairs, and my voice returned.

"Please tell me you just dropped that by accident?" Chloe walked around to the bottom of the stairs and looked down; I heard her breath run out of her lungs.

"Oh Fuck!" She looked at me with terrified eyes, and I nodded.

"It's escaped, and we need to find it." We both swallowed hard.

Chapter 28

Cursed.

With my empty mug held firmly against my chest, I followed Chloe, as we tip toed towards the living room. I was holding my breath, as I stayed just behind her shoulder, she leaned slowly round the doorframe, as I craned my neck but could not see. Her head snapped round quickly, and I jumped back with fright, her dark eyes stared at me.

"Oh fuck... There is a circle." I felt my knees tremble, as I lowered my voice to a whisper.

"Who has it... What are we going to do?" Chloe swallowed hard, and whispered back.

"It's just the circle, whoever it was, left." I nodded; okay we had cleared one room.

"It has to be Edwina; she was the one that hid it?" Chloe nodded looking panicked.

"I saw her go into her office; she probably thinks she is safe in there as it's Sunday."

"Yeah, that is smart, she would hide to read it." Chloe nodded, and we both tip toed down the hall towards the kitchen.

We quietly reached the door in the kitchen, next to the washing machine, and Chloe gripped the handle and turned it, the door opened slowly into the corridor to the new office, and it gave a squeak, my heart froze.

"Shush! Chloe, we cannot spook her."

She swallowed hard, and then very slowly opened the door, we slipped through it into the corridor. I looked at the office door and the large window further down, Chloe reached for the handle, and I panicked and snatched her wrist. Chloe jumped out of her skin and turned to me, with an alarmed whisper.

"Don't fucking do that, I am already shitting myself." I nodded.

"Sorry... Let's check the window first, we should be able to see her, then we can rush her." Chloe gave a nod.

"Yeah, good idea."

We tip toed along the corridor a little bit, and then ducked down low below the window. Our heads came up together as we spied into the room, making sure to keep our eyes to the bottom of the window.

Edwina was sat in her chair, with the head set on talking as she clicked on her computer, she appeared to be quite happy as she smiled. We turned to face each other, and Chloe frowned, as she whispered.

"She has not got it, I bet the crafty bitch has hidden it again to sneak it out when we are not looking." I agreed and gave a nod.

"We need to find it, and quick while she is busy." Chloe nodded, so we lowered ourselves down below the window, and ninja crawled back to the door. We regrouped at the washing machine, I looked at Chloe, and whispered.

"Okay, if she has hidden it, then it has to be in her room, it makes sense, because putting it anywhere else would risk it being discovered?" Chloe nodded at me as she thought.

"Good point, I know where she hides her diary, so I bet she has put it there, because she thinks it's safe, daft bitch has no idea I know where she hides her stuff. Hey Abby, she has done some pretty wild stuff with Luke, they had anal last week." I gasped

"Holy shit, really?" Chloe gave a nod and smiled a wicked smile.

"She fucking loved it." I gasped.

"I have seen him hard, how the hell did he get that in such a small hole?" Chloe shrugged.

"Lube I assume."

"What are you two planning, looking that shifty, I bet it's nothing good?"

"Argghh!"

We both squealed and jumped out of our skin, I felt my heart lurch, as I turned to see Deb's at the counter with a knife and carrots. Chloe leaned into my ear and whispered.

"Act normal, she has read half of it and wants to finish it, she must never do it, or she will dehydrate the baby." I turned and looked at Chloe.

"Normal... When the frig has anyone in this house ever been

normal?" She smiled.

"Let's just leg it then, she is too fat to catch us." I approved.

"Good plan."

I turned, smiled at Deb's, then ran for my life. I tore out of the kitchen and up the hallway, I slid at the staircase on the polished floor, grabbed the banister, and tore up the stairs. I stopped, gasping at the top, and drew in more air. Chloe came pelting up behind me, she took a deep breath.

"You bitch, you left me behind, I fucking shit myself, she had that spill the beans I am on to you look in her eyes." I looked down and saw her shadow waddling from the kitchen to the hallway, I pointed.

"Crap, she is coming; we need to hurry. Okay, we find it, you grab it, and go and hide it."

I grabbed her hand and pulled her across the landing, and into the hallway so she would not see us. I walked towards Edwina's room, and Chloe came up at my side. She gripped my hand tighter and pulled, I stopped and looked back at her.

"What?" Chloe looked really worried.

"Why the fuck do I have to hide it, Abby, I don't want to even touch it, that thing is cursed?" I looked into her large terrified brown eyes.

"Chloe, you are the only person in this house that is immune to it." She gave a gasp and swallowed hard, then shook her head.

"I am not immune, I am fucking terrified of it, that fucking book turns everyone who reads it into a watering lesbian sympathiser of mush, I am too fucking scared of it to risk my straightness. Oh, Abby I am so fucking straight it is unbelievable, and I am not fucking risking it for a fucking cursed lesbian love book." I felt offended.

"It is not a lesbian love book, I am pretty bloody straight, I just have a weakness for Birch." Chloe shook her head.

"Yeah, that is what I mean, you are like a pack of fucking pasta, you are as straight as a fucking stick, until Birch appears and gets you wet. Sorry, but I am not prepared to risk it." I gave a sigh.

"God Chloe, you are a real pussy, come on then, I will find somewhere no one will look."

We walked quickly down towards Edwina's door; Chloe grabbed

the handle and turned it. I looked back just to check we were all clear, and the door swung open, and we stepped in, and froze with shock. Chloe's eyes widened; she gasped as we looked at used tissue hell. Chloe turned to me and exploded, and pointed at the bed.

"I CANNOT BELIEVE YOU BROKE LUKE, LOOK WHAT YOU DID!"

I was lost for words, Luke was lay face down, naked on the bed hugging the book, he looked like he had cried himself to sleep. Chloe walked over to the bed, and looked back at me.

"See... Can you see what you have done, that fucking thing is cursed, you broke a straight guy. I mean it Abby, if he turns gay, I will never forgive you, because it will break Edwina's heart."

I felt my head swirling, and I had no idea what to do, I had to get the book back, I looked at her.

"I just wrote this for Birch, it was never meant for others to read, look Chloe, I am really sorry." I felt really panicked.

"A book won't turn him gay will it, I would not be able to handle that, oh God Chloe, what should I do?" She looked at me, and her face softened, she could see how distressed I was.

"Right... Abby, you grab the book, and I will try to turn him over, just yank it free, we have to limit his exposure as much as possible. No matter what, get that fucking book at all costs."

I nodded, and took a deep breath, and came a little closer to her, she bent over and tried to slide her hands under his hips, she stopped and looked at me.

"Oh fuck, we could be too late." I stared at her feeling terror surge through me.

"What the hell do you mean, too late?" She gave a gasp.

"Just grab the book and you will see."

I nodded and poised myself ready, I was sweating like hell, and my heart was pounding in my ears, I gripped the only edge of the book that was free. Chloe gave a nod, and then heaved, I pulled with all my strength, and felt the book come free as Luke rolled over onto his back, and it was then I suddenly realised what Chloe meant.

"Holy shit, did it turn him on?" I dropped the book on the floor, as I saw his huge erect penis, and I suddenly felt unclean.

"Oh god, I hope he did nothing unnatural; Birch will never

forgive me if the pages are sticky."

Chloe had a fixed grin, as she stared at his long hard member, and I suddenly had two problems, I saw her squirm and try to cross her legs. Her hand slowly moved forward, and I suddenly panicked, as I realised the mega slut in her had been unleashed. I acted as quickly as I could, stepped forward, and smacked her hand hard.

"LEAVE IT ALONE, IT IS NOT YOURS!" She blinked, and came out of her trance, Luke moaned.

I felt a shot of terror run through me, he was naked with a hard on, and had two naked girls right next to him, staring at it. I mean, Christ, he is a really good size, even I felt a little weak at the knees. I had no other choice, I bent down and grabbed the book, I stood up and faced Chloe, who was sliding her legs together as she stood staring, it was very clear the flood gates were open. I grabbed her wrist and pulled.

"Come on, go shag Percy, you have to resist that, or you never know, you could end up with it in the wrong hole, and walking like you have shit yourself."

I pulled as hard as I could, and dragged her out of Edwina's room, and up the hallway back towards my room. I panted with the effort and looked back, she already had one hand between her legs. I gasped.

"Holy shit Chloe, save it for your bedroom." She gave a slight moan, I was astounded.

"How the hell do you run and wank at the same time, my God, you are such a slut?" She just smiled. I reached her room, opened the door and pushed her in.

"Percy, come and get it."

I pulled the door hard, and it slammed in the frame, I collapsed onto the wall, hugging the book, and gave a sigh of great relief, another crisis had been averted.

"SWEETIE, YOU FOUND IT; I HAVE BEEN LOOKING EVERYWHERE FOR IT?"

I closed my eyes, I spoke too soon, as Birch came happily bounding towards me. She pulled me close and gave me a hug and big kiss, her eyes looked really wide and excited.

"Oh goodie, I can read it again, I have really missed it."

She pulled at the book, and I really wanted to hold on to it, but it was hers and I had to let go, she cradled it close to her breast and smiled.

"I love this book Sweetie, it's the best thing you have ever written." I opened my eyes and smiled.

"I wrote it just for you, please do not let the others get hold of it."

The wall behind me started to bang and thump, Chloe was going at it like crazy with Percy, Birch looked at me, and then started to squirm a little, I gave a sigh, this house was so messed up. Birch bit her lip as she looked at the wall, her eyes moved to me, as she wiggled her hips.

"Sweetie... I can always read later... Are you busy today?" I shook my head.

"This place is filled with perverts, and that one in there is the biggest." I grabbed her hand, and leaned off the wall.

"No playing with yourself while we walk." She turned, as I headed for my door.

"Wow, can you do that Deads, you know, fingers and walking?" I shook my head.

"No, but Chloe can."

We entered the room and Birch dropped her book on the sofa, she gave an excited squeal, as I let go of her hand and reached for the duvet, and before I could pull, she was on me and I fell sprawling back with her on top of me. She kissed me really passionately, and her hands were all over me, wow, she was really turned on, she grabbed my hand.

"Sweetie, I need fingers."

She pushed my hand between her legs, her eyes smouldered with lust, and suddenly I was wet and as horny as hell, as I started to play, and she moaned loudly. Her hand slid in between my legs, and she plunged her fingers deeply into me, she was wild and rough, and I felt an instant explosion within me.

A few minutes later, I lay there watching her as she approached orgasm, and felt mine building at a rapid rate, and as my back arched into an uncontrollable spasm, I could not help but wonder, was Chloe right? Birch was wild, and so sexual, and she had only held the book for a few moments, and now she was grinding down on my hand with a level of lust I had not seen for quite a while.

I felt my brain explode as I started to cum, and for a few moments my brain was completely erased. I came round to my senses lay on my bed on a large puddle of my own liquid, and just lay panting staring at the book, Birch was flopped at my side gasping for air, I shook my head.

"It cannot be the book, it is not possible, that would be silly?" Birch reached out with a floppy arm as she panted.

"What was that Sweetie?" I turned to look at her red smiling face.

"Nothing, just random thoughts, that was pretty incredible, wow, I was so turned on." She smiled and gasped in more air.

Outside the church, as was tradition on every Sunday, the congregation gathered, and talked. The main topic of conversation was Nigel, and his black eye, and cut face, which had a plaster poorly applied. Hatty viewed the scene with suspicion, and leaned into Flick's shoulder.

"Okay, so who did it, was it mummy or wifey, because someone has given him a good pasting?"

Flick was unsure, she knew what her daughter had told her, but should she tell Hatty? Patrick was still talking to Milton, so she mulled it over in her mind. Ellen walked up and smiled at them both.

"You two must be the only two not talking about him, that is suspicious?" Hatty gave a big grin.

"I was, she is being boring and diplomatic, I think it is mummy or wifey, what is your theory?" Ellen looked around at the crowd.

"It is difficult to say, Prim is just a little bit too perfect for my liking. I cannot say I believe anyone is that perfect, but as to whether or not she can inflict that sort of damage, temper is one thing, but violence?" Felicity turned to Hatty.

"We are on the Parish Council, and we both know well the damaging effects of gossip, we have all suffered one way or the other, I am just not sure we should spread unfounded rumours. You know we really do not know how he got hurt, he might have fallen or walked into something." Hatty smirked.

"Look at her Flick, she has oppression stamped all over her, I can almost sense the demons inside her, I am surprised she does not ignite in church." Ellen giggled as Felicity turned and slapped her.

"Hatty will you just stop?" Hatty smirked, until she noticed who was walking towards them, she nudged Felicity.

"Hold up, incoming assassin." Felicity looked round and smiled.

"Good morning, Madge, and how are you today?" Hatty lowered her head.

"Creep much?" Ellen looked away and smirked, Marjorie walked up with her usual fake smile.

"Felicity, ladies, good morning, nice service I thought. Felicity, I was wondering if you have a free moment today, I would very much like to talk to you?" Hatty slipped back a few feet and whispered to Ellen.

"Watch out, she is after our souls to feed to Prim." Ellen put her head down and bit her lip to not laugh. Felicity nodded.

"I am free all day, we were just going to head home and sit in the garden, and enjoy the nice weather, you and Milton are more than welcome to join us." Marjorie smiled.

"We would like that a great deal, but I would like a private conversation if that would not be too much trouble?" Felicity shook her head.

"It's no trouble at all, we could talk in the study, it is nice and private as you know?"

I had made my way through the introduction and was through the first two chapters. It is true, I like stories and I am not used to reading this kind of stuff, unless I am studying for something, or doing research for a book of my own, but I was surprisingly captivated by Birch's book. I think I had gotten into the idea that it would read like a psychology lecture, but it didn't.

Birch's book was written in layman's terms, and very easy to follow. It was simple, well thought out, and really interesting and informative. I have no idea why that surprised me, had she not spent years simplifying and explaining the workings of the mind and human behaviour to me?

The phone on my desk vibrated, I picked it up and saw it was a message from mum, it read. 'Is it possible for you and Birch to come over to the house?' I leaned back in my chair, and shouted.

"Birch, what are you doing at the moment?"

I heard a sniffle, and she came through the partition door hugging her book, she had been crying, I gave a sigh.

"Crying... Birch why do you put yourself through such agony, honestly, I am starting to wish I never wrote it?" She gave a sob.

"No, I love it, it is beautiful, it makes me happy."

"My mum wants us to go over for something, can you manage to put your book down for a minute?" She gave a nod, still hugging her book close.

"Birch, leave the book." She pulled a face.

"Deads Sweetie, I just want to hold it, nothing more, it makes me feel happy." I got out of my chair, and walked over to her.

"Baby, leave the book and put some clothes on." She pulled a face, and I smiled and gave her a soft kiss.

"We made a deal, when I read yours, you read mine, and I am not reading right now, so please Birch, go get dressed so we can see what mum wants."

It took a while, but we finally made it to mums, we walked in through the door, and I was just about to shout out to her, when the study door opened. She smiled at us both.

"Girls, we are in here."

I smiled and walked towards her, Birch followed, and as we walked into the study, we had the shock of our lives, as we were confronted with Marjorie. Mum sat down, there were two of the kitchen chairs in the room, I looked at Marjorie, and nodded.

"Mrs Wallace." Birch gave a big smile.

"Hi Madge." She sat at my side, and Marjorie gave a smile, although she looked uncomfortable.

"Good afternoon, ladies." Wow, she called us ladies, it sounded so weird, I think I prefer whore, I am used to it. Mum looked at me.

"Abby, Madge was telling me what you did for Nigel, and she wanted to ask me for some advice, and I felt, maybe you two could be more helpful." I gave a nod, I understood that. Mum smiled.

"Girls this is a delicate situation." I think we pretty much knew what was coming, Birch nodded, she was already ten steps ahead of me.

"Confidentiality is my profession, and to be honest, just listening to the rumours, I do not think it is that big a stretch to know where this is going. All I need to know is are the rumours true, is Nigel domestically abused?"

Yep, she does not piss about, and goes straight to the point. Marjorie looked very uncomfortable indeed, I smiled at her.

"He was always a nice polite lad in school. Look Mrs Wallace, I saw how afraid he was when I showed up, it is not hard to work out how Prim feels about me. The sad thing is she has nothing to fear, I like Nigel, he is a decent guy, but I am getting married soon, and I know you know, how much that means to me?" Marjorie took a deep breath; this really was hard for her.

"I cannot say I agree with your union, but I will also say, yes, I know real love when I see it." I smiled at her, which was weird in itself.

"Thanks Mrs Wallace." She looked at Birch.

"Doctor Dixon, you are right, my son is suffering. Listen, I know that you two have a lot to do with this sort of thing, you are actually doing something very good for all communities. I disagree with a lot of your ways, but I will be honest, I admire the way you have raised money to help those in need, hence, I am here as a mother, asking for advice." Birch looked her straight in the eyes.

"To be asking me for help, actually shows how bad it is, and I may add, how much you care about your son. What do you need to know, I will do everything I can to help?" Her voice cracked a little, it was shocking, the old gargoyle was showing emotion.

"I am very grateful to you both, I do want to help him."

My mum pulled a tissue out of the box, I gave a shudder, I had seen way too many tissues today. Madge graciously took it, and dabbed her eyes. Birch leaned forward in her seat, and out came her professional voice.

"Madge, the problem you have is that for anything to work, you firstly have to get Prim to admit what she is doing is wrong, and then you have to convince her to seek therapy." Madge gave a sigh.

"She is a very strong willed young woman, I am not sure she will admit to anything, is there no way other than that?" I looked at Birch, she smiled.

"How is the child's welfare, is it in the room when she hits Nigel?" Marjorie frowned.

"Why does that matter?"

"I have a friend in Social Services, a visit from her, may frighten her into thinking about things. Madge, it is devious, but I can talk to her, and get her to visit, scare her, and then it will be up to you to convince her to come to the practice. As I said, it is devious, but there again, I figure it is probably right up your street." I liked the sound of it, but had another idea, so voiced it.

"Or Nigel needs to make a stand and leave her for a while." I looked at Birch.

"If he walks out and does not come back, that might scare her too, after all, she is running for Parish Council, and how it looks is vastly important. The rumours are already around the village, if he actually leaves, it will not take long before she looks bad in public." Marjorie nodded.

"I like that idea better, I am not sure Social Services should be involved, but how will the word get out, she will go to ground?" I shrugged.

"That is easy, just tell Chloe, that girl struggles with secrets." Birch gave a giggle and agreed, even mum nodded her head as she looked at Madge.

"I love her to bits, I really do, but I only tell her what I want out there, I never tell her the good stuff." Mum smiled.

"She is a lovely girl, I cannot deny, I adore her, she is so sweet." Marjorie appeared to be a little more relaxed.

"I think I can talk to him, and convince him, the question is, how should he do it?" Birch looked at me, and her eyes flashed at me, I felt butterflies in my stomach, her mischief eyes are so sexy.

"He works over near Millington, so he can stay at the hotel there, it has a good restaurant from what I hear. He can either drive there, or if needed, we can arrange for him to be dropped off. If he needs anything Madge, drop it off with Flick, and we will get it to him. I would also suggest he does come into the practice and talks with someone; it might help, I would think he has a lot of anxiety hidden inside him, and that is not good, he needs to face and deal with that." Marjorie shook her head.

"No offence Dr Dixon, but looking the way he does, I am not sure being seen in your practice is a good thing for him." Birch understood, so did I, everything with Marjorie was about how it looked, mum nodded.

"He can come here and use the study, it will not look suspicious if he is seen entering my home, Birch, you can meet him here." Birch turned to her.

"Susana would be better; she deals in trauma therapy." Mum shook her head.

"Birch, I think I would be right in saying, Madge would prefer as little amount of people knowing about this as possible. I think to protect reputations is prudent here, don't you think?" I agreed, and it was out before I thought.

"Holy shit, if word gets out I am helping Madge, my reputation will be screwed." I suddenly realised, and looked at Madge.

"No offence Mrs Wallace?" She actually smiled.

"None taken, I was thinking the same, but less crude." I giggled with Birch, and even mum smiled. Mum gave a sigh.

"Alright ladies, we have a plan, Nigel starts therapy here, he can make an excuse he has to work late one night a week, and come home via the Manor, and Birch, you can give him therapy here, then he can stage the walk out. I think that is a good plan, and we can keep it under wraps. Thank goodness we no longer have Gwenda to worry about, if she was across the road, we would have no hope of hiding it."

Okay, that bothered me, I was avoiding any mention of the house, just in case it was still a sore point with Madge, I looked at her.

"This is as you say an unofficial truce, but we all must keep up our public personas, so in the village keep things as they are." Madge nodded.

"Have no fear, I understand the situation perfectly." Birch smiled.

"That's good, it would make the village way to weird, if you and all your hit squad, were nice to me, I would have to stay home."

With the agreement made, and considering mum and Patrick had guests, we decided to leave them to it, we both hugged mum and said our goodbyes, and headed out of the door. I linked her arm as we crossed the road, and our gates swung back as we walked in, as we reached the door I stopped, and Birch looked at me and smiled.

"What Sweetie?" I pulled her close and put my arms round her.

"Thanks for doing this Birch, I know it sounds weird, but I hate what is happening to him, and I am happy to know you will help him, he does deserve a better life than he has. You really are the most amazing person; do you know that?" She smiled and kissed me softly, and I felt all warm and fuzzy inside. Birch slipped her key in the door; I patted her soft round bum.

"I love your book by the way." We stepped through and she looked at me.

"Really, you think it is a book worth reading?" Chloe scuttled out of the library.

"What book... Where is it, did you hide it, that fucking book is dangerous. I have told you a hundred times, you need to dig a hole and bury it with salt and fire. Trust me, I watch Supernatural, those guys know how to deal with cursed shit like that?" Birch gave a giggle.

"Sweetie, we are not talking about that book, we are talking about the one I have written." Chloe looked suspicious.

"You wrote a book, holy fuck, what does yours do to people, do they like lose all sanity, and just run round naked fucking everything?" Deb's walked out of the library

"Nope, Chloe, that would be you." She smiled, as she waddled down towards the kitchen.

Our house is like a mental asylum, but I really love living here.

Chapter 29

Future Planning.

It was the twenty ninth of May, and Bank Holiday Monday, which meant Birch had a day off, and it was a scorcher. I do not know why, but I woke feeling nervous. I sat up, rubbed my eyes, blinked a few times, and noticed Birch writing on the inside of her wardrobe door. I was still a little groggy, but slipped quietly out of bed and walked quietly over to her.

"What's that?" She squealed with fright, and spun around, holding her heart, I could almost hear it hammering in her chest.

"Sweetie, do not do that, I almost peed on the carpet."

She gave me a really strange expression, turned and ran into the toilet, I looked at the inside of her door. Birch sat on the toilet peeing when I looked round the doorframe, she smiled and gave a little wave.

"Hi Sweetie." I smiled.

"Have you been ticking the days off." She gave me a huge smile.

"What, and you haven't? Deads, it's only twenty days away." She wiped, and dropped the toilet roll between her legs, and then stood up.

"I am really excited, oh Deads, I am... Oh crap, I am way too excited, I am going to pee again."

She plopped back on the toilet, and another steady stream flowed out of her, as she smiled. Wow, she was impressive; I think she expelled half her body weight in water. I shook my head in disbelief.

"I feel nervous Birch, you know what today is, it is the bridesmaid fittings at my mum's? It is silly really, because I want this more than anything, and I already live with you, and I know what I am in for, but honestly, I am so nervous, am I being irrational?" She smiled.

"No... You are being you, and I love that about you. Honestly, I am a little scared too." I frowned.

"Why, I am a freaking delight to live with?" She giggled, as she stood up, flushed, and walked to the basin.

"Sweetie, I swore I would never do this, then I swore if I did it, I would only do it once. I have lived with you for four years, and honestly, I am so happy, it has been like a dream for me, and yet, I am still nervous, and I have no idea why?"

I guess she was right, neither of us had anything to fear, or did we? I looked at her as she dried her hands.

"This will not change us will it, you know, we will still be the same?" She turned to look at me.

"Oh Sweetie, we are not capable of change, look at Sunny Bank, that was a big thing for us, be honest, it was our first real time alone, and I suppose we did change a little, but it was for the better. We came back understanding each other deeper, and I do not know about you..." She gave a shy look, and even blushed a little.

"I fell in love with you all over again, and I fell harder than before." Her smile was almost shy like, and it was such a turn on. I gave a smile.

"I did, I fell in love with you again, but this time I think I fell in love with all of you, because I saw things you have never shown before." She dropped the towel and walked over to me, and slid her arms round me.

"Oh Sweetie, I love you so much, and that will never change."

She leaned in and we kissed, and started touching, and started playing, and soon we were hard at it, and I had not even had coffee yet. If this is married life, oh boy, I can certainly live with this.

Downstairs in the kitchen Edwina looked up.

"Well, you can certainly tell Birch has a day off." Chloe looked up.

"I am telling you; they have been like that since they came back from that house. There is something in the water at that place that fucks you up. I am taking a shit load of bottled water next time we go." Deb's smiled at them both.

"I think it's lovely, you know Chloe, maybe you should take a few guys with you, I mean, you never know, one of them may turn out to be the love of your life?" Chloe lifted her cup.

"Nope, you are a soppy bitch, I'm taking no risks, I paint and I fuck, and I am keeping it that way for a long time. If I need someone to stay over, I have Terry, and that has worked fine for two years." Deb's gave a sigh.

"Is Terry okay with that, I mean, have you ever asked him?" Chloe frowned.

"Why would I do that?" She shrugged.

"Maybe he would like more, he has been a very regular visitor for two years now?" Chloe frowned at her.

"Listen to me now, miss married, pregnant, and happy, my life is fine as it is. Stop letting all this wedding talk mess with your head. I have my plans, and you have yours, just focus on your own, I am happy as I am painting, my husband is a brush and a tube of paint." Edwina turned.

"Wow, harsh much Chloe?" Chloe grabbed her coffee.

"Sorry Deb's, I didn't mean it in a nasty way, but I know what you are like, and this wedding has you all loved up, and I just do not want what you, Jimmy, Birch and Abby have, not yet, I am not ready." She walked off to her studio, and Deb's watched her. Edwina sat down and smiled.

"Ignore her Deb's, it is a touchy subject with her. Between you and me, since Martin, she has sworn never to marry. Chloe likes to be in control, and I think for her marriage is a loss of that control." Deb's gave a nod.

"I meant nothing by it, honestly?" Edwina smiled.

"She knows, let her paint for an hour, and she will be fine." Deb's nodded, and looked at the studio, where the door was closed.

I crawled out of the bathroom with trembling legs.

"Oh god, Birch, you have broken me." She lay on her back on the bathroom floor chuckling, her face red, and breathing deeply.

"Sweetie, help me my legs won't work?" I looked back and her and giggled.

"Screw you bitch, I am buggered, you broke me." She gave a loud cackle.

I dragged myself to the bed giggling, and used what little energy I had left to climb up. I sprawled across it, as my legs quivered, and closed my eyes.

"I NEED COFFEE!" Her voice came from within the bathroom.

"Yeah, you can forget that, this place has no room service, and it will be hours before I can walk again." I lay back and laughed.

Outside, cars were arriving at my mum's, as everyone arrived to have their clothing fitted. On the drive, was the large van belonging to Ella Grantham, who had designed our dresses. The doorbell rang, and Chloe in shorts and a vest, because she was getting ready to leave the house, answered, she looked at the stranger.

"Hi, can I help you?" The woman smiled.

"Is Abigail or Jemima here, I am Angela?" Chloe turned, and shouted up the stairs.

"ABBY, BIRCH, AN ANGELA IS HERE TO SEE YOU!" I sat up on the bed, Birch's face appeared round the door.

"Why is she here?" I completely understood.

"Dad... It is the fitting day, she probably feels a little weird, I mean, she is the reason mum is divorced, she will not be in a rush to go in the house."

Birch got up and staggered into the room, she grabbed her robe, I slid off the bed and grabbed my kimono. We came down the stairs, and Angela looked a little relieved, she smiled.

"I am sorry to impose, but I am not sure I am welcome over the road, and I have no wish to put a cloud on things." I understood that.

"It is alright, come in the kitchen, we can have coffees, as we are banned and not allowed to see what they are wearing." I led her down the hallway, she looked around.

"Girls, your house is really beautiful." I love that people say that, it makes me feel proud.

"As much as I would love the credit, Birch has done all the design and decoration." Angela looked at her.

"You have a talented eye for décor." Birch smiled.

"Most people find me difficult, because my mind races as I picture what can be done, and I suppose I get far too carried away, and it can come across as too much too fast. I was lucky to work with Bradley, I think he understood that about me. I am really happy with how it all turned out."

We sat down at the island and I put the kettle on, the sun was blazing through the patio doors, Angela was nervous, I sat down and smiled.

"I am really happy you came over, you know, both dad and you are always welcome." She smiled.

"That is very nice to hear, I will not deny, I was nervous of coming over. Look, I really do not want to be this wicked witch of the east figure in your lives, I genuinely want you two to be happy and successful. I wish nothing but the best for you, and I know the way your father and I got together is not as anyone would wish, but if you are truly honest Abby, your mother and him were no longer a couple, they had become friends sharing a home and a daughter. I am no fool, and I realise her commitment, and he was not interested in that, and so I guess what I am saying is, all I want is acceptance, nothing more." Birch listened to her very carefully, she took it all in and smiled.

"You played a big role in helping Ed come to terms with Abby's sexuality, didn't you?" I watched her closely as she looked at Birch.

"I pointed out a few things, like she is still his daughter, and his feelings should not be changed because of that. I had a very close friend who was a lesbian, and she killed herself because of her parents' hatred of her. I did not want that to be Abby, and so yes, I talked to him." Birch gave a nod.

"In my book, that gained you credit, it may not show, but I appreciate what you did. It was painful for me to watch Abby suffer, because of the disconnect between them. His acceptance has done a lot of good for us, and so yes Angie, I think I can accept you too, I feel I owe you that." Angela gave a sigh of relief.

Behind us in the hall, Deb's was playing sergeant major, and organising the troops, as Chloe, Edwina, Anthony, and Gill with Aden had arrived. They left to head over the road, and join the others, and we headed out into the garden to relax, and enjoy the day.

Over at mum's house, the kitchen was filling up, Patrick was there, and Edwin was his usual polite self, even if he did feel somewhat put out by the fact that mum's divorce solicitor was now sleeping with her, the idea that he had screwed both of them amused him. Ellen and Bradley were on hand as support, and Ella had her two girls, Alice and Carol, as well as a young tailor named Kenny.

Once everyone assembled in the kitchen with a white wine, Ella took control, she stood at the far end and near the dining table, and clapped her hands, everyone turned to watch her, and she gave a big smile.

"Can I just say, that as a new designer, Jemi and Abigail, have made all my dreams come true, and I am so grateful to them. I have spoken to Debbie, and when I asked her what the theme of this wedding was, for the clothing I have designed for today, she told me, take Bram Stoker, H.G. Wells, Arthur Conan Doyle, and put them in the heart of nature. I will not deny, I had to look all that up, but when I did, I was delighted." It was food for thought, Chloe sipped her wine, she looked at Felicity.

"It is ages since we sat here Mrs W, and it's nice, but I have no idea what she means, do you?" Felicity smiled at her.

"I think we will have something very grand, and beautiful; you may be surprised." Chloe shrugged.

"Deb's dressed me like a doll, if Birch gets her way, we will all be fucking fairies and sprites." Felicity chuckled.

"I am not so sure H.G. Wells would approve." Ella looked at everyone.

"I have talked to Abby and Jemi, as well as liaised with Debbie, and so I would like the boys in the spare room upstairs with Kenny, and myself and the girls will attend to you all. Bradley has volunteered to help out with the men."

With that, everyone trooped upstairs to their designated rooms, where a row of black clothing bags hung on the closet door. Ella went through the list.

"Edwina, this is you, Gill, and Chloe. Please remember you are assigned to each of the party, so Birch's ladies will be green, and Abby's in rich burgundy. Deb's as matron of honour, you have a slightly different look. Okay, breeches first, and then shirts." Chloe looked at Ella.

"What, we are not wearing dresses?" Ella shook her head, and smiled.

"We are going with a footman type feminine look, the girls have their bridal gowns, and I thought a more male focused look, would highlight your feminine charms." Chloe lifted the bag.

"Cool, I can do pants, I hate all the frills and fancy gowns shit."

Alice and Carol helped out as everyone dressed, and soon Chloe and Edwina stood side by side, looking in the full length mirror. Edwina had a dark forest green Victorian riding type jacket, of which the lace cuffs of her shirt, came out of the ends of her jacket sleeves. Around her high collar was a thick rich silk cravat in the same green. She had on cream coloured tight breeches, with knee high riding boots.

Chloe wore a same style jacket, in rich burgundy, with a burgundy cravat, and black breeches, she turned from side to side as she viewed herself.

"I love this, wow, I look pretty hot, even if it is bloke like clothing, yeah, I think this is pretty awesome."

Gill was dressed the same as Edwina, and down the hall in the other room, Anthony was very happy as he looked at himself.

"Oh yes, I look dashing and valiant, Michael will be horny all day watching this parade in front of him." He eyed himself with delight, and Edwin stared at him, looking utterly appalled.

William had been running late, so was stood in his black breeches, and white Victorian, high collar, shirt, as he slipped on his double breasted waist coat. Edwin had on a long tailed black Victorian jacket, and a cream cravat. He looked like he had just walked off the set, from a pride and prejudice stage production. He was surprised as he looked in the mirror, he really quite liked the look.

"I think this image suits me." Bradley gave a smile.

"Very Victorian country squire, I think it suits you, Edwin." He nodded.

"Honestly, I thought we would all be in rainbow suits, with sequined hats, I am quite delighted." William sniggered as he pulled on his jacket.

"I am quite sure Jemi had it on the list, thank god your daughter has good powers of persuasion, I have no wish to go to my daughter's wedding, looking like a circus clown." Edwin smirked.

"With the top hat, you may resemble the ring master." Will chuckled.

"It is still an upgrade on the clowns."

Deb's was disappointed as she looked at her clothes hung on the hanger, and Ella talked her through it.

"Don't worry about it, by then you would have had baby, and you should have your figure back to a reasonable normality. You are maid of honour for both parties, which was not easy. Look, instead of the short riding type jackets the girls have, yours is a full length one, it will cut nice at the waist, and fall down the back in tails. I like this shade of cream, it will highlight your bosom, when the jacket is buttoned." She lifted the jacket to the side.

"I love this shirt, and I am sure it will appeal to your steam punk side. Look at these lace cuffs, they are beautiful, your cravat will be red, but as you can see, it is not as deep as the other girls, you will really stand out in the group, and with the hair accessories and your hair up, you will look stunning." Deb's felt the soft thick felt of the jacket, and then the sleeves of the shirt with its lace cuffs, she smiled.

"Ella, these are so beautiful, I am really looking forward to wearing them." Roni sat in the kitchen, with Flick and Ellen.

"So, come on girls, spill the beans, what are you all wearing?" Felicity, smiled at her.

"I am not buying until I have seen everything, I want to make sure I coordinate with what everyone else is wearing. I will start looking tomorrow." Ellen gave a nod as she lifted her white wine.

"Me too." Roni pouted.

"You guys' cheat, to be honest I have a really nice suit, and a dress, but cannot make my mind up which. Jemi always gives me great advice, but she does not even know what the dresses look like, and so after seeing her dress and Abby's, I bought a dress, and then a suit, and then another two suits, I just do not know what to do." Ellen giggled.

"Three suits and a dress, seriously, you, the famous fountain of wisdom that is Doctor Veronica Dixon?" She burst out laughing, and Felicity started to giggle.

"I can see where Birch gets it from now. You should video call us and show them to us when you get back, we will help you."

The kitchen door opened and everyone trooped in, and lined up, Roni saw Will and smiled, she got up and walked over to him.

"Oh William, I like this look a great deal, oh darling, please tell me you get to keep this?" Felicity sniggered.

Ella divided everyone into groups, Gill stood with Edwina, wearing the Forest Green, and she stood Will with them. Anthony and Chloe stood in rich burgundy, and stood with Edwin. They looked amazing, Ella walked back a few paces and smiled.

"Abby wanted you all to show off your best qualities, whilst highlighting the feminine charms of her bride to be, which is why you will be their dignified escorts. Debbie quizzed both of them before we worked together to get a sense of what they would like, and Abby even noted, that Chloe hates fancy frocks. I hope all of you like the clothing, and feel at ease in them?" Chloe gave a satisfied smile.

"I love mine, pants are cool, the only thing that would beat this is a nudist wedding." Gill gave a titter, Ella looked at Anthony.

"Now you have seen the clothes, I am certain you will know what to do with the hair and accessories?" He flicked his wrist, just like he does in the salon.

"Ella darling, I think you have excelled yourself, and yes, I know exactly where I am going to go with hair now, thank you my dear." He flicked his long side fringe back.

Deb's walked up the kitchen, as everyone admired each other's clothing, she smiled at Felicity.

"Did I do alright, do you think Abby and Birch will like this?" Felicity lifted her wine glass, as she watched the others.

"I actually think that considering the dresses they will be wearing; you picked the perfect complimentary outfits. Chloe and Edwina look pretty amazing, I would never have thought of Victorian type footmen for girls. It works extremely well, Abby will love it, and Birch will find it adorable. You know them both very well, and if what Birch has in mind is as she tells me, this will be perfect." Deb's gave a frown.

"What has Birch got in mind, what do you mean Flick?" She gave a little smile.

"I am sworn to secrecy, which is what makes this wedding an exciting event, we all have a piece of the puzzle, but most of them will not be put together until the day of the wedding. It is quite different and exciting I think." She winked and Deb's gave a smile.

"I should have known she was up to something; she is always planning something extra; I take it Abby has no idea?" Felicity gave her head a shake.

"Not yet, but she will soon, what she has planned will be hard to hide."

Ella and her girls, along with Kenny, wandered around checking the fit and making adjustments, as more wine was poured, the patio doors were open, and everyone spilled out into the fresh air, there was a very distinct flavour of Victorian England to the garden, as they mingled and excitedly swapped comments.

Flick stood on the edge of the patio and lit a cigarette; she smiled as she watched Chloe admiring the cut of the pants. Edwin walked up, he looked very distinguished, she smiled.

"I think it suits you, it is very man about town. How are you, Abby was very worried about you, have you seen her yet?" He turned to look out across the garden.

"I am going to see her afterwards, I do feel significantly better, how are you doing?" She flicked her ash onto the grass.

"I survived you Edwin, I can survive anything. It is funny you know, we imagined this time very differently, to be honest, I thought we had put her off marriage for life. I am glad she found someone who makes her as happy as Birch has." He gave a nod, and smirked.

"Well, it is certainly not as we imagined, I will not deny it has taken me some time to get used to the idea, but Jemima is a lovely girl." Felicity smiled.

"I have to ask, as I won't say I am not curious, but I know you, I know how entrenched you can be in your views. So, go on, what was it Edwin, what actually changed your mind about her and Birch?" He gave a sigh, and tittered to himself.

"It was a few things, Abigail's stubbornness, her absolute belief in Jemima, and to be honest Angela, she has been quite forceful, you could say that she made life hell for a while. She told me I was far too preoccupied with the sex, and should focus on the bond and the feelings. I got quite the lecture on if a man had done half as much, and cared only half of what Jemima did for Abigail, I would be very excepting and happy for her." He gave a little titter and looked at Felicity.

"I got told in a most severe way, to stop obsessing over the vagina's and look at the facts." Felicity took a pull on her cigarette and chuckled.

"She made a good point, I commend her, where is she anyhow, I thought she may have come with you?" He gave her a shrewd look.

"Really? She is over the road with Abigail, doing damage control, she wants to make sure that Jemima, is really alright with her being at the wedding. I am not sure you know, but Jemima did once threaten to remodel her face with a pot ashtray?" Felicity gave a snort, and put her hand to her mouth, Edwin sniggered.

"She scared the living daylights out of her, it took bloody hours, and almost a full bottle of single malt to calm her down." Felicity fought her laughter down, Edwin's eyes twinkled.

"I thought you would appreciate that?" Felicity bit her lip.

"I am sorry, I did not mean to laugh, I do think she is adorable, but she does have that thread of northern hostility, when it comes to defending Abby." He raised his eyebrows and smiled.

"It may surprise you to know then, Jemima was defending you. I will give the girl her due, she is fiercely loyal to this family." Felicity gave a soft smile.

"She really is the most wonderful woman Edwin, Abby has thrived around her, and ultimately that is all I want, simply for her to be happy." He gave a nod.

"Yes, I do too. I have made a complete ass of myself, but I am trying to make up for it." Felicity patted his shoulder softly.

"You know, I actually think Angela has been good for you?" He looked very surprised.

"You do?" She gave him a nod and smiled.

"Yes, I do, you know Edwin, you could have brought her here, I would never be rude to her. Well not now, maybe a few years back, but God Edwin, we are too old for all that drama and bullshit most of the world is stuck in. I really cannot be bothered with it all. She was once a good friend of mine; I know her faults and her better qualities. Look, we have both moved on, that was then, and this is now, and honestly, it is a hell of a lot easier on Abby if we are at peace." He gave a smile, and nodded at her.

"I think you have done very well if I am honest, Patrick is a nice man, I can see the attraction, he is very fun loving with quite the twisted sense of humour, I would imagine that appeals to you rather well?" Felicity gave a smile, and shook her head, she started to laugh.

"I know you so well Edwin, and no, it is a recent thing, well a couple of years, so I was not involved with him before or during the divorce, he is far too respectful for that. I do enjoy his company; we get along fine." Edwin gave a slight nod as he glanced across at the others mingling.

"I will not deny, yes, it crossed my mind, but thank you for setting things straight. You do look good together, I do think he suits you, and I mean it when I say it, it is nice to see you smile more, I genuinely wish you both well." Felicity took it in the spirit given.

"Thank you, I appreciate that, and as you know, I am actually very relieved to see your health improving. Whatever has happened Edwin, does not change the feelings, I was always glad I married you, and look at our daughter, she is the best thing we ever did." He gave a wide smile.

"Yes... Yes, you are right, I really am very proud of her, she is a wonderful woman Felicity, and I would love to claim the credit, but to be honest, all that belongs to you. I do see a great deal of you in her." He started to chuckle.

"She certainly has your temper, and a very cutting tongue, and just like you, I do have a habit of pissing her off without realising it."

He gave an almighty chuckle, and Felicity burst out laughing, he gave a loud wheeze as he laughed, something she had not seen him do in a very long time. Ella walked out and clapped her hands.

"Everyone, can we have all of you change back now please, we have everything we need to ensure a perfect fit?" Edwin gave a smile.

"Well, it appears it is time to travel back to the modern way, so I will bid you good day Miss Watson." He gave a very courteous bow, and she smiled.

"Why sir, I thank you for your visit, it was most illuminating."

He smiled, and turned, and headed off with the others, Chloe walked at the back with a sulk on, she was really enjoying wearing the clothing. Roni walked up to Felicity.

"That was nice to see, I take it the white flags have been waved?" Felicity, gave a nod.

"It is about time don't you think?" Roni stood at her side and gave a soft smile.

"Give me a cig, I left mine in the car."

Chapter 30

Raven Moon.

When everyone returned, they were really excited, Birch was delighted to see her mum and dad, she had not realised they were coming down for the fitting, and she hugged the life out of them, Roni and Will smiled and gave a wave as Birch hung from them.

I heard dads voice and turned, and I saw him in the hallway, and moved quickly across the patio, into the kitchen, and towards him He saw me coming and smiled, Edwina who had been talking to him, side stepped, and excused herself. I walked to him with a smile.

"You are here, and Angela tells me you are feeling much better?" I pulled him into a hug.

"Dad, you cannot scare me like that, and you have to stop shutting me out, I would have been there you know?" He held me tight.

"I am sorry, I know how you worry about things, you have a lot on your plate already with the wedding, I just wanted to get it done so I could be a part of it." I slipped out of his arms and looked at him. He did look a lot better, his cheeks had good colour and he looked a lot less tired. I smiled as I looked at him.

"God, you are frustrating at times, I do not know how Angela puts up with you. I am your daughter; in future I want to know as and when if anything happens." Mum came down the hall, as he looked at me, and gave a sigh.

"I never win, you are so like your mother." She giggled as she passed by.

"Intelligent, stubborn and beautiful." She gave a loud laugh as she passed, and I shrugged as I looked at him.

"You cannot argue with that Dad?" He knows when he is beaten and he smiled, yep, he knew it. He looked at me with a smirk.

"Where is Angela, I take it she is still living?" I gave a snort of a laugh, as I took his hand.

"She is safe, I hid all the ashtrays."

We both laughed as we walked back towards the kitchen, where Angela stood smiling, as she watched us, she looked at me and I could see how happy she was. In many ways she has played a big role in the background of my life, it has been her influence that has brought dad round. There was a time I thought we would never speak again, and yet here we were, and I cannot deny, I do actually have her to thank for it.

I wandered around checking everyone had drinks and were fine, and finally headed over to one of the loungers, and grabbed my drink and sat back. It felt a little strange, because everyone now knew what they were wearing for my wedding, except Birch and I.

I have wondered if it will make the day more exciting, or will I be far too busy to notice? We had gone out of our way to make this a very different but exciting wedding, and it just made me one hundred times more nervous. I do think we are both insane, and at times like this, I wished I had planned a normal wedding. Ella came over and sat down, she looked pleased.

"Abigail, I want to tell you all about it, but I can't and it's driving me crazy. They look perfect, and the fitting is spot on, the girls look amazing, I am so excited." I was happy for her.

"I am really thrilled, Anita has got us a feature in Fashion Voice Magazine, so at some point, I will need you to do an interview with us. I really hope it helps, as we will be giving exclusive pictures to them, and all your work will be featured." She looked stunned, and she swallowed hard.

"Are you serious... really, oh God Abby, I do not know what to say, this will give me exposure that I could never access. It is possibly one of the biggest magazines for popular fashion at the moment, I do not know what to say?"

I was really happy for her, starting out is so hard, and I remember how hard it was for me, if it had not been for Roni, I would never have got off the ground. In a strange sort of way, for me, this was like paying it back, Roni helped me, and so I was going to help Ella, it helped that I loved her designs.

"I am getting married and you are the designer, I have not really done a huge amount, but my publicist is really great at what she does, and it is her you should thank really. Ella this will be so good for you, once I am married, apart from a few bits and pieces I order, the cash from me will slow down. This article I hope, will bring in more business, but you know, if it gets tough, phone me, I love your stuff and want you to do well, just know if you need financial support, I know a lot of people." She took my hand and gave it a squeeze.

"I really am so grateful, it has been fantastic working with both you, and Jemi." Roni came over and leaned over, and pulled me into a hug.

"You look like a very happy woman, wow, some time away has done you both a lot of good." I nodded.

"It was so amazing, thanks, it has made a huge difference. Roni, you have met Ella, haven't you?" Roni smiled at Ella and took her hand and shook it.

"I have, and I have been looking at your site, you do some interesting work."

I left them to talk and headed into the kitchen to get a drink, Birch was stood by the island and looked worried, I frowned as I looked at her, she was biting her lip. Her eyes moved to me.

"Deads, please tell me you have not told her?" I did not understand.

"Birch, what are you talking about?" She grabbed my hand, and almost dragged me into the hall, she turned quickly and lowered her voice.

"I do not want her to know about my book, not yet, please tell me you have said nothing?" I gave a small laugh.

"Seriously, you are afraid of telling her?" She looked terrified.

"Deads, she has sold over ten million books, she is the biggest thing since sliced bread in the British therapy community. If she even gets a whiff of a book from me, she will be all over it, and she will drive me insane, why do you think I kept it so quiet?"

I understood her, Roni was a stickler for detail, but from what I had read, her book was brilliant, I did not understand why she felt it wasn't. I gave a sigh, and nodded.

"Okay... I will say nothing, but I have to ask, how are you going to put a book out, when your mum owns the company?" She bit her lip, and screwed up her face a little.

"Yeah, about that... Sweetie, I need a really big favour." I closed my eyes and completely understood.

"Anita... You want her to sneak it through production?" She gave me a big smile.

"I know it is a lot to ask, but would you talk to her to see if it is possible?" How could I refuse her, hell, I was about to marry her?

"I will talk to her, but I am telling you now, if it goes tits up and she finds out, you are so on your own." Birch gave a happy little giggle, and pulled me into a big kiss.

"Thank you, Sweetie, I love you." Roni came in through the kitchen door and smiled, Chloe leaned over and rolled her eyes, Roni noticed and looked at her, Chloe smiled.

"Mrs D, can I ask you something weird?" Roni was interested.

"Please do." Chloe looked at her.

"You have been to the house in Devon a lot, yes?" Roni nodded at her.

"I have, is that important?" Chloe nodded at her.

"If you don't mind me asking, but when you get back, do you want more sex, and I mean all the time, you know, like wild rabbits?" Roni gave a slight giggle.

"Well, I like sex, I have a lot, I am lucky in so much as my husband still likes me enough. I suppose going away is romantic, I certainly enjoy our alone time there with no work. Is there a point to all this Chloe?" I walked in mid conversation and pretty much worked out where Chloe was going.

"Roni, she thinks the water there is spiked, and makes everyone super horny, she is convinced it has turned Birch and me into perverts." Roni raised her eye brows, and turned to Chloe.

"Really... So, Chloe, tell me, you were there, and you drunk the water, so, how many times a week do you and Percy get it on?" Chloe looked suspicious; her voice dropped a little.

"Most nights, if I am alone, I have a high sex drive." Roni pursed her lips, and tried not to smile, she leaned in close to Chloe and whispered.

"So, it's about once a day, but you tell me, it has been a lot more since you came back, hasn't it?" She moved back and winked at her; Chloe's eyes opened wide.

"HOLY FUCK!" Roni smiled, everyone in the kitchen, stopped talking and looked at us, Chloe looked shocked.

"Percy has perverted me." Roni gave a loud cackle of a laugh, as

Chloe flopped into her seat looking stunned.

Roni grabbed my arm, and pulled me away giggling, I followed to the door and went out onto the patio, dad and Angela were talking to Will. We walked onto the long lawn.

"How are things now?" She really could not resist.

"We are good, actually we are better than ever, we did a lot of talking, I really love the place, and we will be going back a lot more."

She flicked her long hair back, looked around the garden, and stopped. I stood at her side and turned to her, she glanced at me and smiled.

"I am very relieved to hear that, Jemi is very happy, she had one hell of a fright. Abby, I wanted to talk to you because Katie is fund raising to buy back her shares. Between you and me, she landed with one hell of a bang, but that was my intent, she needed the lesson." She gave a sigh.

"All this was unnecessary, if only she had listened to me in the first place, it could have been avoided. It does however, present me with a dilemma, do I restructure the publishing arm without her as the promoter, or do I give her one last chance, to correct her wrongs?" It was a big question, and I did not envy her the job of picking.

"What do you want to do Roni?" She smiled.

"What would you do?" I shook my head.

"That is an unfair question, I am not part of the company, and let's be honest, she sees me as an enemy, and I see her as a threat." She turned to me, and had that glint in her eye, that I have seen so many times in Birch's.

"I think it is a very fair question, and I also think you are the best person to give me an honest response."

God, talk about snared in a trap, I have to say, there are times in my life, where I bloody hate therapists, and it is usually when I find myself dangling on the end of their hook. I took a deep breath and thought about it.

"We both know she is the best; I will not deny she is really resourceful, and she does run a tight ship. Katie gets things done, and she is fearless when confronted with the press. She built that company, and she is on the ball, and she knows where every piece of equipment is at all times, and can pull stuff together in seconds. To be honest, she knows that company inside and out, I don't think anyone doubts she is the best hands down." Roni smiled.

"But?" I gave a slight smirk; she knows me too well, and actually, I hate it.

"Well, she hates me, wants Birch, is devious and cunning, and is the biggest lesbian slut I have ever met. I will also add I hate the way she uses people, but again, those are all parts of her personal life, and you should not consider them professionally... Oh, I have no wish to work with her as well?" Roni nodded in agreement.

"Good answer... I have another idea." I knew it, she just wanted the low down on me all along, and now for the smack to the brain.

"Okay Roni, I am listening." She smiled and reached into her pocket, she pulled out a large folded envelope, and handed it to me. I took it, held it up, and looked at it.

"What is this?" She smiled.

"Early wedding present, it is a notification of an award of a ten percent share of K.O. Productions, I have ten for Jemi as well." I stared at the envelope.

"That only leaves you forty percent shares." Roni smiled.

"She owns thirty five percent, and if I sell her ten percent, she will have a controlling interest, as long as she gets all the shareholders not to vote against her. I call it a clipped winged strategy. Be honest, she will have to put forward a bloody good business proposal, to get you and Jemi on board, especially considering I will always vote with my daughters?"

Wow, talk about turning the tables on all of us, I see why she is the top of her field, God, she is so bloody sneaky. I looked at her and she gave that happy little Birch like smile. I could not help it; I smiled back and shook my head.

"You know you are scary right, and a tad sneaky?" She giggled.

"What, just a tad... Abby this is business, she is the best, but her leash has been too long, she will respond better on a shorter one, I take it we have an agreement?"

"If I say yes, then with just you, and I voting together, Katie could not possibly vote against this, because Birch will back me, and Dad you." Roni gave a sigh.

"You suffered a great deal because of her, that is why I have given you the casting vote, I do not need Will or Jemi at this point, all I need is for you to agree. Her fate is in your hands, if you say yes, I will sell back a ten percent share, if you say no, she stays out in the cold, it is up to you Abby, show me your business skills."

Talk about a perfect trap, my God, she is brilliant. I looked at the envelope in my hand, and then back at her and right into her eyes.

"To replace her, would set your company back, if I am honest, she is still the best for the job. Others will take a long time and make a lot of mistakes before they catch her up. If it is a continuation of a smooth running company you want, you have to bring her back in, it is the only sensible thing to do."

"I agree... You made an excellent decision, based on what is right for the Dixon Group, and you did not let your personal feelings get involved, that takes a good level head Abby. Well done you, I have already informed EFG, they handled the transaction for you." I started to giggle.

"How did you know I would agree?" She winked.

"I didn't... But I know you have a good head for business, I remember that day in the court meeting room with Madge, you thought on your feet and took everything into account, then found a loop hole, and that clinched it for Jemi, I knew then you would be part of this group one day."

"That was four years ago." She gave me a smile.

"Oh Abby, I thought you knew me better, I have been watching you for a lot longer than that."

Birch came running up looking giddy, and we both turned to her, I thought her eyes were going to explode.

"Sweetie, she is almost here, I just got a text from her." I had no idea what she was talking about, I shrugged.

"Birch, what are you talking about, who is here?" She bounced on her feet, and giggled with joy.

"Moon... You know, Raven Moon? She is about an hour away, she told me she would see me in about two hours. Deads, I am so excited, I cannot wait, now she is here to marry us."

Okay, at this point, I just want to say in my own defence, I have only met her once, and that was in a crowded pub in Uppermill, where she showed Birch a video of herself stark bollock naked, rubbing her vagina on a tree and moaning in ecstasy. Birch has talked a lot about her, and she has been painted as being somewhat of a little bit of a flaky, and exuberant Wiccan priestess.

In a way, this is my gift to Birch, it was really important to her that she played a part in our ceremony, and because we will be getting married outside the church, and she is a fully ordained multi faith minister, albeit a completely bonkers one, I agreed that she could marry us, if Gail was witness to it. I have no idea why I picked Gail, I just felt it would be a good safety net, just in case, after all, I wanted to make sure we were actually legally married.

I did also stipulate that during and after the ceremony, no private parts were to be rubbed on trees, after all, we have a very large garden full of them. I have wondered if she is some sort of a Chloe to the plant world?

The time passed, and everyone started to slip away, I said goodbye to Dad and Angela, and thanked them both for being here. Angela hugged me, the fact she had not been beaten senseless, relieved her greatly, even Birch thanked her for all she had done, and gave her a hug, which I thought was really sweet of her.

Roni and Will, were going for a meal with Bradley and Ellen, Deb's hugged everyone, and they were happy to see she was fine. Ella had her truck packed up, and as we had done before, we paid her in full, which we knew would really help her new business. All her helpers got an envelope with fifty pounds in it, as a thanks from us, after all this should have been their day off, they also had a good few drinks with us so all was not lost.

Gill hugged us both, as Aden arrived back to collect her, and she scampered happily to the gates, he was taking her out on yet another date, those two were more loved up than us, and I felt pretty happy about that, as I had played a big role in helping them get together.

We were finally down to just all of us, plus Terry had arrived, and we all sat back in the garden, as Birch got more and more excited, and talked at nine hundred miles an hour about Raven Moon. I did not mention to the others about how she got a climax, I felt I was best leaving that until after they had met her, somehow, I thought once they had met her, they would probably understand better.

The time finally came, and in sawn off frayed blue jean shorts, and white vest, with my denim jacket, I headed out with Birch as she talked constantly. She was giddy and excited, I must admit, I did not understand why she did not come to the house, and as we turned onto Manor Road and then at the end, turned onto High Street in the direction of the canal, I became confused, I stopped.

"Birch, why are we walking this way?" She bounced along her long white hair jumping about all over her shoulders, her eyes bright green, and glittering with excitement, she pointed.

"She is down here Sweetie, come on, you are going to love her."

Okay, so I love Birch to bits, but as to her crazy mate, well the jury was still out on that one, and I cannot deny, if there was remotely any suggestion of rubbing my girlie bits up trees, I was legging it. Birch turned onto the canal steps, with a huge smile and a squeal, I did not get it at all. I gave a frustrated gasp.

"Birch, where are you going?" She stopped, her wild eyes looking like they would explode.

"There Sweetie, look there she is." I frowned, and looked down the canal path, and all I could see was a canal barge, there was no sign of anyone.

"Where, I don't see her?"

I was starting to worry; did Birch have an invisible friend? I mean, I would not put it past her, we have had a few moments when I questioned her grip on reality. Oh God, was I going to be married by her invisible mate, holy shit, I think I have broken her, has the strain on her been too much?

She hurried down the steps leaving me behind, I realised and hurried up, I did not want her too far ahead, especially if she was meeting an invisible entity. I walked as fast as I could along the tow path, watching her hair lift behind her back. I caught up best I could, she reached the boat and stopped and jumped on the spot, I caught her up, she pointed.

"Look Sweetie, she is here."

I turned and looked at the boat, it was painted mainly black, with stars and moons in silver on it. The name plate read. 'The River Moon.' I saw the carved wooden raven on the top of the roof, next to a long row of solar panels, and suddenly I understood, I turned back to Birch.

"She lives on a boat?" Birch smiled with pride.

"I lived on it one summer, isn't it beautiful, I painted the stars, she did the moons." Suddenly everything made sense, I looked at the gap between the boat and side of the canal.

"Should it be rocking around like that?"

It made my stomach churn a little, I am not a sailor, and just watching it move up and down in the water, made me feel really queasy. Birch climbed on board, and opened the hatch.

"Moon Sweetie... SURPRISE!"

She went down the few steps and into the boat. Trying not to throw up, I followed, and was really blown away, wow this was pretty cool. At the far end of the boat was a pair of white curtains, which gave me a sudden understanding of why the boat was moving. I could see the silhouette of a woman, who was obviously sat on top of a guy, and for want of better words, was screwing the shit out of him. I gave a gasp.

"Wow, she does not piss about; she has only been here an hour." Birch giggled.

"She is a very natural creature Sweetie, and she goes with the flow in all things." I smiled.

"Her hips certainly frigging do."

Birch giggled, and moved forward while I looked round, it was actually really nice inside the boat. She had a small table, side seats, a bookcase and wood burning stove. There were a good few cupboards, and lots of pictures painted on everything, and hundreds of bunches of drying herbs. I was impressed, it was really cosy. Birch stood just outside the curtain.

"Moon Sweetie, we are here, but carry on we will wait."

Watching the speed her hips were going, I was not sure we should be disturbing her; she was obviously on route towards cosmic bliss. Yep... There was a sudden high pitched wail, and a gasp, followed by a very happy.

"OH, BLESSED ME!"

Is it wrong that I wanted to piss my sides laughing? Some weird guy gave a moan, kind of like a child waking up in the morning, and I shuddered, I have no idea why but I found it really disturbing.

A head popped out of the curtains, and I jumped back and blinked, Birch gave an almighty squeal of joy, which sounded like a cat, whose tail had just got stepped on, and I realised in that moment as Moon squealed back, what a siren sounds like.

She had really long, sort of blonde brown hair, and it was filled with millions of tiny curls, her eyes were a really pale almost orange colour... And did she have sequinned stars on her eye lids? She smiled at me, but I could see she was still sat on the guy, and as far as I could tell, he was still buried in her tree scented cavern. Her voice was really soft, and sort of spacy, although she had just cum, so was a little breathless.

"Oh, and there you are, my brightest flower of light. Birch my angel, the stars have blessed me with your face."

Actually, she was pretty sweet, bonkers, but sweet. Her eyes moved onto me and they grew huge, as she gave a gasp, her eyes moved back to Birch as she gave a huge smile.

"Birch my child, the stars have blessed you, she is divine, and ethereal, she walks the plane of the spirits of life."

Okay, so she is pretty cool, I think I like her. Her eyes twinkled as she looked back at me.

"I seldom meet a walker of the dark and light, your past was through shadow, but your light guided you towards a saving angel."

Okay so now I am completely creeped out, I have no idea what she just said really, and Birch gave a gasp and clapped, but she sounded like one of my creepier characters from Sanctuary Arch. She suddenly gave a loud tut!

"Oh, where are my manners? I have a guest."

To be honest I was not sure I wanted to know what was behind the curtain, as long as it had not risen from the bowels of hell, I could live with it.

"What is your name again, it keeps slipping my mind you sweet flower?" I shuddered. As soon as I heard the voice, I freaked the hell completely out.

"It's Nigel."

Birch's mouth fell open, and her head snapped around to me, as the air flowed out of my entire being.

"Get dressed dear and come and join us."

She slipped through the curtain and walked to the stove, I took three paces back and she gave me a sweet smile, but I was stood rooted to the boat, Birch turned and lowered her voice.

"Er... Sweetie, do you have a minute?" Moon gave a big smile.

"Oh Birch my flower, I have many for you."

It was at that moment I saw it, and looked at her inner thigh with horror, I looked up at Birch who was watching me, as I stood behind Moon. I pointed at her leg, and Birch frowned, and then realised that moon was looking at her, as I tried to gesture. Birch smiled, and lowered her voice even more.

"Moon Sweetie, did you say Nigel?" She nodded.

"Yes my dear, to be honest, I have been moored up by the locks for a couple of weeks, I wanted to cleanse my centre completely before such a sacred ritual, and I saw him soaked through to the skin, and he was very distressed poor soul. I brought him on board and dried his clothes off, and he was so cold, well what else could I do, he needed body heat? When I undressed, well it just popped up, I mean it was obvious the cosmos required me to aid such a lost soul, and so I administered to him."

Well that is the first time I have ever heard it called that, I bet you won't get that on the NHS? I pointed at her leg, trying to get Birch to notice, it was like the bloody vicar, and my exposed vagina all over again, and Birch had no idea what I was doing.

Moon turned back to the kettle, which was starting to boil, there was movement behind the curtain and I felt panic setting in, I looked down, and Moon saw me and looked at the floor, I felt it was better to fess up.

"Moon...!" Crap, how do you actually say it? She looked at me.

"Yes Deadly, you divine child?" I had no choice, as I saw it creeping down her leg like a drowsy snail.

"You are leaking sweetheart."

I pointed, and she bent over and gave a chuckle. Birch suddenly realised and had a eureka moment as she understood, to be honest I know who the owner was, and it repulsed me, I shuddered. Birch understood, and suddenly she was freaked out too. The curtains parted, and I smiled, he went completely white.

"Hi Nigel, fancy meeting you here?"

He shut the curtains very quickly, and I could see the shape of him on the bed as he went into complete melt down. Then I heard the whimper, Birch's eyes were wider than I have ever seen them, Moon turned with a big smile.

"Oh, you all know each other, how wonderful."

It is funny, because that was not the word I had in mind. Birch looked at me, and I shrugged, I mean, if I am honest, the cat was out of the bag, and honestly, I did not care, he could screw anyone except me. I have seen his thin little stick, and the fact that Moon had cum, sort of impressed me in a weird sort of totally messed up way.

Moon smiled, and handed me a cup of some powerful smelling tea sort of thing, I smiled.

"Thanks... Do I call you Raven or Moon?" She sat down, and sipped her tea.

"You choose, and be guided by the stars that light your path." Okay I could live with that. I gave a nod.

"I will call you Moon if that is alright, I think it suits you." She gave a gasp.

"Oh, you have such insightful powers, your life will be charmed, tell me about the child I sense?" Okay, and I was completely freaked out again.

"What child? I am not having a child." Birch looked ten times more freaked out than me, she nodded rapidly.

"Moon Sweetie, we have no children planned for us." Moon stared at both of us.

"A child will arrive soon, and your lives will draw light to it, I sense it, I am not wrong."

It suddenly hit me, she was talking about Deb's child, and suddenly I gave a gasp of utter relief, although, I could see Birch had not worked it out, and so left her to hang for another minute, her sense of panic, gave me great comfort. I smiled at her, and she looked even more terrified.

"Birch... Deb's."

She pulled her hand to her chest, and gave a huge sigh of relief, I smirked, had she thought I was pregnant, because if I was, I would be watching the sky for a bloody big star, and looking for three wise men. Birch moved closer to me, as she came to sit at the table, she leaned in and whispered.

"Deads, it's freaking Nigel, what do we do, I think he is crying?" I nodded.

"Talk to your friend." Yep, I got the shit end of the stick once again, I looked at Moon.

"Moon sweetheart, could I have a quick chat with your guest, you know, old friend from school and all that?" She smiled at me.

"Oh, Deadly, please on my barge, feel free to be you and only you, let that light flow over everything."

I smiled, and thought, my frigging light is going nowhere near Nigel, he can find his own bloody light or buy a torch. Birch sat down and looked worried, I walked up the barge, apparently it is not a boat, good to know.

I separated the curtains, and looked at him. God, he is pathetic, he was curled up in the corner snivelling. Christ he is twenty eight years old, and yet he looked like a child, I gave a sigh and smiled.

"Nigel, come on, I think we should talk, walk down the path with me." He shrunk back deeper into the corner. I shook my head.

"I am just going to talk, no judgement. Nigel, you cannot hide here forever, I take it your mum has spoken to you?" He nodded.

"Right, so you know I am not your enemy, good, now come on grow a set, and let's talk." I reached out my hand, and he nervously took it. I smiled.

"Good."

Chapter 31

The Right Time.

Birch sat with Moon. "You can see his darkness, I know it. I am about to start working with him Moon, his life is not a good one." She gave a soft smile.

"I knew you would find him; you do gather all the lost hurt souls to you. Birch my dear, please show him his path, even if it is what he fears, only you can save him. You know, Deadly has a connection to him, it is fine, and has darkness woven through it, but she will aid you in this task." Birch smiled.

"Can you feel her beauty?" She gave a very large smile.

"Did I not tell you to walk in the light when we last met, I told you Kev was not your path, I told you feel for the light, and let it guide you. I am in awe of her, she is strong within, does she know it?" Birch gave a happy giggle.

"Moon I am so in love, I really am, I never thought I could love, but I am so in love with her, she is my air." Moon squeezed her hand.

"Oh Birch, my angel of light, it shows, I am honoured beyond words to be a part of joining your union."

Nigel looked at me, he looked utterly terrified.

"Abby, I am sorry, I really am, I won't do it again, please don't tell on me?" I looked at him, as I stood with my hands in my short's pockets.

"Jesus Nigel, honestly, I am not your mother or your frigging rancid wife, I don't give a shit if you are screwing a witch. To be honest, anything has got to be better than sex with that frigid bitch you married. I have no wish to sleep with you, and honestly, all I have ever cared about is you finally understanding that. Screw who you want, you don't need my approval." He looked shocked and frowned.

"You don't care at all?" I shook my head.

"Nope... Look, I helped you out at school because you were bullied. I mean, Jesus, I must have told you a million times, I did not want to date or sleep with you. Those guys who were picking on you were utter shits, and it was wrong what they did to you, that is why we stopped them. I hate to tell you this, but I have not dated that many people, I am not quite the slut I have been painted." He shook his head.

"You have never been a slut in my eyes, I would never call you that." I smiled at him, which in itself was bloody weird.

"Look Nigel, we are nothing more than friends, as you can see, in just over two weeks I am going to marry Birch, a woman, that is where I am at now, no guy has a chance with me. Really, I need you to understand that Nigel, I have no problem with being friends, but seriously stop with the worship, it's creepy." He put his head down, and I gave a sigh.

"Nigel what are you going to do, are you actually going to turn up and talk to Birch?" He looked up at me, God, he looked like a lost bloody lamb, it was pretty pitiful.

"Do you want to hear my advice?" He nodded.

"Yes please."

"Nigel, talk to her, trust me, she is brilliant at this, and when I say talk, understand that she is one of the best therapists there is, so just let go and let it all pour out, the more she knows, the more she can help you. Understand Nigel, that you will have complete confidence in her, no one will know what you say, not even me." He understood, I smiled.

"You know I have got to tell you Nigel, I am a little bit proud of you." He frowned.

"Why?" I shook my head, honestly, he has not got a clue.

"Hell, I just caught you shagging a full on Wiccan priestess, that is pretty cool you know? Hell, she had quite the orgasm, you obviously did a good job." He turned scarlet.

"Prim says sex is a sin, unless it's for children." I gave a giggle.

"I am probably the worse person to ask, but if you ask me, if she screwed more, she would probably be more stable. I think lack of sex is her problem, she needs to boot God out of your bedroom." He actually gave a giggle; it was sort of high pitched, and squeaky. I smiled at him.

"Nigel, I know things look bleak, but you know what, talk to Birch, just let it all out, and it will get better. Another thing too, when you go home, tell Prim you also have needs, actually tell her she is a spoilt bitch and you are sick of it. I mean it Nigel, find that courage you had screwing Moon, and face her, and stand proud. Drag her into the bedroom and show her what Moon has taught you, because I know you have learned a trick or to with her, so bloody well use it, get angry Nigel, hell, you need to." He just stared at me like a puppy, I shrugged.

"Nigel, a woman likes a man to be strong occasionally, so try and be strong, get your bloody head between her legs, and make her explode with joy, and maybe then the whole village will get a day off, because we all need a calmer village, and she is just a huge pain in our ass." He gave a boyish grin.

"Alright Abby, I will try." I nodded at him.

"Okay, I am going to do something I never thought I would do."

I pulled him into a hug, and he hung limp like a rag doll, and then lifted his arms around me and pulled me close.

"You smell nice Abby." And that was me done, I pulled out of his arms.

"Tell Prim that, not me, she is your wife, and do not worry, your secret is safe with both of us, we will not tell a soul about today. Now head home, and try being a man for once." He smiled, and looked all starry eyed, I must be bloody insane.

"Thanks Abby, and for the other day, I did not really thank you, so you know, thanks."

He smiled as he turned, and started to walk back up the tow path towards the locks, and the path that ran up across the meadow to Waterside Lane. I gave a sigh, honestly if you had asked me a year ago, I would have never seen today happening, but it had, and I really did not know why. I stood for a while, my hands in the pockets of my tiny shorts with my ass cheeks showing, and a vest with no bra, and honestly, I am so glad he did not get a stiffy while he hugged me.

I turned on the path, and walked back towards the barge, Birch was sat up top with Moon, she smiled as I walked towards her.

"That was nice of you Sweetie, will he be alright?" I climbed on board and shrugged as I sat beside her.

"Honestly, I really do not know, if I am honest, I am not convinced. I just know that if he does not stand up for himself soon, she will destroy him, and he does not deserve it." Moon looked at me and gave me a big smile.

"I love your light, your aura is so bright, I feel I need glasses." I looked at her.

"I like you too Moon, does this boat, barge thing lock up?" She looked at Birch and then back at me.

"Well yes, why?" I gave her a big smile.

"I want you to come for a meal, and we have a spare room, if you want a little house life, I really think you should meet our family of Curio's." Her eyes sparkled.

"I would love to meet your tribe, is their aura as bright as yours?" I shook my head and smiled.

"Honestly, I have no idea what that even means, but they are all loud, lively and pretty bloody insane, is that good enough?"

It was settled, so after a lot of gathering of herbs and charms, all of which went into a large bag, not unsimilar to Birch's bag, with Birch and Moon in tow, I walked down the canal path, and back towards our house. I was secretly dying to know what everyone thought about her.

I like the idea of us being a tribe, in truth, we did have a tribal mentality, after all we stood together, fought together, and we lived together, like a group of nomads who had found each other, and set up camp together.

Moon was met with strange looks and bright smiles of 'what the fuck, who is this weirdo? So in other words, she was a perfect fit, Izzy and her appeared to bond instantly, Chloe appeared apprehensive, and Deb's smiled a lot. Edwina was Edwina, she was calm, collected, and just went with the flow, Anthony admired her hair, and Birch was loud, excited, and cackled more than normal. Moon appeared very happy, as promised I kept her choice of bed partner quiet.

She wore beautifully embroidered clothing of many colours, sturdy work boots, and a lot of jewellery. I have never seen so many chains and charms, and it surprised me how she held up her head. Her hands were filled with rings, and she wore a hooded robe, like the one's she had made all of us, as her coat. Just like Birch, she carried a large cloth bag, which was black and covered with embroidered stars.

We all sat in the kitchen, and Moon felt very much at home, I must admit, I loved how she just knew stuff, and it was fun watching people get rattled by her. I thought Izzy was good with her ability to spot people's sexuality, but Moon was on a whole other level. We sat round the table and all ate a good meal, to which Moon added extra herbs and spices.

Once the meal was finished, we poured drinks, and made our way into the living room, and sat down. Luke and Edwina, headed upstairs, and Terry had to go, as he promised to take his mum shopping. Birch talked a lot to Moon, as they caught up, and relived a few memories, and I settled into my corner of the sofa, and relaxed. Chloe walked in eating her biscuits, and Moon was on her.

"Oh, my dear child of the ways of women, you are brimming with the powers of the Moon, I feel it strongly within the walls of your labia." Chloe stopped chewing and stared at her.

"Fuck... What...?" Moon smiled, and I stifled my giggles, even Birch looked away as Chloe stared at her.

"Chloe my dear child, your flower has such a sweet nectar, it has been tasted by many bees, such is its appeal, and yet, one day like all flowers it will wilt if it is not tended, by a most veracious gardener." Chloe looked around the room.

"Did she just tell me I am a slut?" Deb's gave a nod.

"It is not a secret Chloe; we all know it." Moon shook her head.

"Do not misunderstand me, there is great spiritual wisdom within the confines of the sated sexual. It is through the sexual release that we touch the consciousness of everything, and you my dear have such power." Chloe nodded and looked at me, I was fighting the urge to laugh, as was Deb's.

"She fucking did I know it, she called me a slut didn't she?" I shook my head.

"Not really, she said she admired your prowess." Birch elbowed me, and whispered.

"Excellent recovery Sweetie." Chloe sat on the floor and looked at Moon.

"I like to fuck, actually I fucking love it, and I am not denying it. One woman's slut, is another woman's empowerment." Moon waved her hand.

"My dear, I am not putting you down, I am accepting you as the force of feminine power you truly are, I am praising you. You see the world as it should be seen, even now you work on a piece of greatness. My dear, you have a spirit guide who is with you and guides you, as they rise from the house." Chloe looked at me, and she looked terrified, the coloured drained from her face, as her eyes opened wide.

"Abby, if she just told me that fucking Gwenda is stalking me while I paint, tell her to fuck right off, because if she is, I am moving the fuck out. That is my art, and no fucking ghost is stealing the credit for it." Deb's nodded looking terrified and lifted a cushion to hide her tummy. Chloe shook her head.

"I get totally weird, I live with Birch, but seeing fucking spooks, fuck that shit, I am going to paint... Alone!" She got up and took her biscuits with her. Birch giggled, and took Moon by the hand.

"Come and see what I have planned for Deads." She looked at me and her eyes sparkled.

"It is a secret, but you will see soon Sweetie, but I am dying to show Moon, is that okay?"

"Yeah, it's fine, Birch you do not need to ask for my permission, go show her and enjoy yourself." She smiled.

"Okay Sweetie."

She disappeared with Moon into the library, and I settled down in my corner. Deb's gave a sudden jolt, and gasped, she held her tummy, I looked across the room at her.

"Are you alright?" She winced a little.

"Baby is very active tonight, and moving around a lot." She gave a sigh, and blew out her cheeks.

"The midwife said it could be any day now." I felt a cold shudder run down my spine.

"Wait... What... Deb's what do you mean any day now, you are not due until next week?" She smiled, as she rubbed her tummy.

"Abby, I hate to point it out, but Baby does not know about dates and times, they kind of do their own thing." I nodded; I understood the biology.

"Yeah, I get that, I do, but we were under the impression baby would come somewhere between the fourth and the twelfth. When does Jimmy get back?" She gave a sad sigh.

"It was supposed to be yesterday, but they extended, he is hoping the sixth now, he has to be in London on the seventh to tenth, but he is going to commute from here for those, they know about the baby, so he will be back soon."

I must admit, watching as I have these last few months, I really admire her, it probably sounds wrong or cruel, but I do not want to do that. I think I am an utter coward, because I just do not want children. Deb's jumped again, and I blinked, and twitched, she giggled. I felt a little jumpy and my stomach twisted a little.

"Is there anything I can do for you Deb's?"

"To be honest Abby, I think I will go to my room and lie down." She got up slowly, and I got up with her.

"I will walk up with you; I am pretty tired."

She smiled, and headed for the door. I walked at the side of her, as she took the stairs one step at a time. At the top I gave her a hug.

"If you need anything, just let me know, and if you don't want to get up, phone me Deb's." She chuckled.

"Always there for me, always have been, I love you Abby."

"I will always be there Deb's, I am never further than a call away, and by the way, you have also been there when no one else was, and that means everything to me." I kissed her cheek.

"Go and rest."

I headed to my room, a little worried, in my mind everything was planned out, and yet Deb's baby could throw all of that out. My stomach squirmed a little, and I felt apprehensive, I wanted Jimmy back and soon. I slipped off my shorts, and top, and slid under the duvet, and relaxed. The bed was cool, it had been a hot day, and I lay back, and enjoyed it.

My mind wandered around, as I saw the picture of Nigel stood before me, looking bruised and blackened, and thoroughly downhearted. He was my age, and had changed, he showed a little maturity, but not much. I never thought that I would be kind to Nigel, well not like acting like a real friend, as I did today, but when I thought back, we did have a strange connection.

He has been more of a thorn in my side, and yet, I did not hate him, and I felt a need to protect him, it was so strange. Helping him in the rain, and seeing how black his eyes were, bothered me, the truth was, I did not like that he was suffering, and yet I did not really understand why. It was definitely not sexual, I hated seeing him in pain, my life is so weird at times.

I felt the bed move, and blinked awake, it was dark, and Birch was slipping into bed, she slid over to me.

"Sorry Sweetie, I was trying not to wake you." I rolled over to face her, her eyes twinkled in the darkness, I saw the light up clock, I had been in bed five hours.

"Is Moon alright?" She nodded, and I felt the pillows move.

"Yeah, she is really good, although it has started to rain, so she has gone back to the barge, she prefers to be on board in bad weather, she likes to commune with the elements." I could understand that.

"I love her barge; it must have been fun living on it?"

"Hmm, it is compact, but what I loved was sitting on the roof during the day, and reading or eating, it was a nice pace, just chugging along."

"How long did it take her to sail here, is it even sailing on a barge?" She gave a little giggle.

"I suppose so, to be honest I am not sure. It has taken her three months, but she has had many stops on route to do sightseeing, and plot lay lines, she has a bit of a thing about them, and she has visited some sacred sites."

I suddenly felt wide awake, and I sat up and turned the lamp on, Birch looked at me, she looked at my boobs and raised her eyebrows, and smiled.

"I am not sleepy, Birch I like Moon, I really do, she is a little on the out there side, but she really is kind and caring. I totally get why you love her so much, I really warmed to her today." Birch sat up, and leaned on the pillows and looked at me, I could see her eyes as they took note of me.

"Why do I feel there is a 'But' coming?" I shook my head.

"No Birch, honestly, I really like her. Birch she was shagging Nigel, I mean, I don't know how you felt, but I was pretty freaking shocked when I heard his voice, how the hell did he end up getting it good from Moon?" Birch gave a giggle.

"Hey, I pride myself on being hard to shock, but I will not deny Deads, when I realised it was him, I was absolutely mind blown. If this was one of your books, I would never have seen that coming. I asked her how he ended up there, when you went to talk to him." I waited, and she did not continue, I stared at her.

"And... Birch, what did she say?"

"She told me that day of the heavy rain, she was up near the locks, and she saw him out of the window, he was sat on the low wall crying. She called him over, and told him to get on board out of the rain, and he came over. He was soaked to the skin, and she told him to get undressed and gave him a towel. She stocked up the stove, and wrung out his clothes and hung them up to dry." I understood, and nodded as I put it all into place.

"So Prim must have exploded after I left, and hit him again, and he walked out, and went for a walk on the canal. Poor bastard, he was soaked when I left him, and he had nowhere else to go, so he went onto the canal. You know, I wonder just how long he has been doing that, because he has been married for two years. How the hell did he end up in bed with her?" Birch chuckled.

"Well we are talking Moon, she is a natural being, trust me, Chloe may find she has some competition whilst she is down here. Moon told me, he was shivering violently, so did the one thing she knows works..."

"She shagged him, yep, that would warm him up." She giggled.

"Sweetie shush, I am not finished." She gave another giggle.

"I love your humour, you know? Deads, Moon took him to the back and sat him on the bed, and she stripped so she could cuddle him under a blanket, sort of like skin on skin for body heat. Well to put it as simply as possible, the towel lifted up." I shuddered.

"Oh Jesus, I wish we did not have to contemplate his upright pole." Birch sniggered.

"It is hardly a pole." I snorted, and started to laugh, and felt guilty.

"I feel bad, I should not laugh, Birch it is what God gave him, it is not his fault."

"And there is another reason I hate Bell Twats, all that power, and he cannot even give the vicars son a sizeable dick, the mean twat."

I put my hand on my mouth, and spluttered as I tried to hold back. It took me a few minutes to calm myself. She smiled at me, and I took a deep breath.

"So he slept with her that day, and then what, he has been seeing her since?" Birch nodded at me.

"He has been seeing her every day, Moon said he was very keen and enthusiastic about it, they have done it a few times on occasion, we walked in on her third time today. Apparently, he has gotten a lot better at it." I gave another shudder.

"Honestly, I am happy he has had some sex, but I am not sure I feel comfy talking about it, it really creeps me out." I gave a sigh.

"I am not going to sleep now, I am bloody terrified I will dream about it, I need a drink, I think I will go and make one, do you want one?" She gave me a smile.

"I am excited, and it's late, and the kitchen is free, I have been staring at your boobs and thinking, and all this talk of sex is getting to me. Let's do it on the big table Sweetie, I have to have you soon." I gave a big smile.

"Race you."

I jumped out of bed and ran to the door, she gave a little squeal, and came running after me. I pulled open the door, and set off for the stairs, I looked back and saw her white hair tearing after me. I scampered down the stairs as she got closer, I swung on the banister, and she vaulted over it. I gave a squeal of surprise as she caught me, and pushed me into the hall wall giggling. She gave me a long slow passionate kiss, and I melted. She slid across my cheek and buried her face in my neck and kissed up the base of my ears and I tingled.

"Oh God, Birch, you know how much that turns me on?" She kissed slowly down my neck, and down to my breast bone and I quivered.

"Oh Birch... Oh Baby yes." There was a cough, and I turned my head, Deb's wearing a huge floral nightie, and Chloe smiled as they watched.

"Birch, we have company."

"I don't mind Sweetie; we have screwed in front of them before, and I really want you right now." Deb's stared at us and slid her hand over her big belly and lowered it, I patted Birch on the shoulder.

"Baby, we are turning Deb's on, and it's freaking me out, if she starts masturbating, that will be seriously unsettling." She gave a giggle, and stood up.

"Oh Sweetie, do you not like watching fat women play at home?" I shook my head.

"No, I frigging don't, especially when they are my best friend."

Chloe sniggered sat with her legs crossed, at the island, but that did not surprise me, just smiling at her made her horny. Birch slid her arm round my waist, and we walked into the kitchen, Deb's sat back in her seat.

"I am sorry Abby, I couldn't sleep, so I came down and made a sandwich." I looked at it.

"What the hell is on it?" She took a big bite, and chewed.

"Cream cheese, gherkins and marmalade." Birch turned at the kettle.

"Oh Sweetie, that cannot be good for baby?"

Deb's took another big bite, and Birch put her hand to her mouth, and her stomach lurched slightly, she screwed up her eyes.

"Oh dear, that is so very unsettling." She turned back to the kettle, and tried not to look.

Deb's sat back and put her hand on her chest, and gave out a really loud burp, Chloe leaned back in her seat.

"Holy fuck Deb's!" She giggled as she got up and took her plate to the sink, Birch handed me a coffee, and I sat down opposite Chloe, and lifted my cup to my lips.

Deb's waddled back towards her seat, and from nowhere an almighty flash, streaked across the front of the house, illuminating the garden in purple. Deb's gave a jump, and looked shocked. From nowhere there was an almighty explosion out of the sky, and it was deafening, it was like a bomb going off right outside the doors, Deb's froze in terror and screamed, we all jumped, I felt the shock and fear shoot through me, it was so loud.

I looked at Deb's, and her eyes were wide and she looked terrified, she was really afraid of thunder. The lightning struck again, I saw it dance across the pool outside, BOOM! An even louder rumble tore the sky apart, and the rain just blasted down. Chloe looked pale.

"Holy shit that terrified me, it's alright Deb's, I have pissed myself loads of times in fear too." I turned and looked at her, and the huge puddle on the floor, she was looking down at it, Birch leaned over the island.

"Oh crap, Sweetie, I think your waters just broke?" Deb's held her tummy and winced.

"Ow... Abby... Ow.... Ow!" I panicked.

"Holy shit, it's coming, Birch what the hell do we do, it's here?" Deb's eyes filled with tears.

"Abby, it hurts... Ow!" I felt my head spin out of control.

Chapter 32

Rain Dash.

Birch took control, she took Deb's by the hand, and guided her back to her seat.

"Sweetie, it is alright, stay calm, we need a few things." I was frozen to the spot, as Birch looked at me.

"Deads, we need clothes, Deb's bag, get Edwina up, and I need Petal outside the door." Chloe swallowed hard.

"What can I do?" I ran for the stairs, feeling panicked, and a little bit frightened.

"Sweetie, you need clothes, we have to go to the hospital." She nodded and shot off, Birch crouched down and smiled.

"Deb's count between the contractions, and breathe, it will help." Birch puffed up her cheeks, and blew.

"Like this. Fuf... Fuf... Fuf... Fuf... Fuf." Deb's copied her, and Birch smiled.

"Good, that will help you stay calm, we should have time, we will get hold of Jimmy and your mum, so do not worry."

I hurtled into Deb's room and grabbed her bag, I spun on the spot, and headed out of her room, towards mine. My heart was pounding, as I burst in through my bedroom door, and saw my clothes where I had dropped them.

Gasping for air, I pulled up my shorts, grabbed my vest, and pulled it over my head. I hardly dressed as the vest was still above my boobs, when I grabbed Birch's clothes, our phones, and snatched up our trainers with the socks stuffed inside, and headed back to the door.

Chloe zoomed past me towards her room, I headed for the top of the stairs and then remembered Edwina, I dropped the bag and tore down the hallway, and burst in through her door, trying to pull my top down over my boobs. She was in bed with Luke fast asleep curled around him.

"EDWINA GET THE HELL UP; IT IS COMING OUT, HURRY!"

Luke lurched awake.

"Fucking hell Abby?" I was sweating, panicking, and gasping for air, Edwina sat bolt upright.

"Where is Chloe?" I took a deep breath, and gasped in air, and shook my head.

"She is fine, it is Deb's, she is giving birth in the kitchen we need you." Luke looked freaked out.

"OH FUCK!"

I turned and ran for the door, up the hallway, grabbed the bag, and Birch's stuff, and then hurtled down the stairs, and came charging into the kitchen, and handed Birch her clothes. I sat down gasping and smiled at Deb's, as I pulled on my socks and trainers, I did not have time to tie them. Birch started to dress, I jumped up and headed for Petal.

I snatched the keys out of the bowl with my door keys, and unlocked the front door, and made it outside, where it was pouring down really hard. I ran to the door of Petal, unlocked it and jumped in. I was gasping for air, as I turned on the ignition, and she fired into life.

I flicked on the lights, and put her into reverse, and drove back towards the front door, and left her running with the blowers on full speed. I came back in, and grabbed her bag. Chloe was dressed and breathing with Deb's, Birch was pulling her clothes on, and talking to Edwina.

"Call the hospital first and let them know we are coming in, there is a list pinned on the fridge, then you must get hold of Jimmy. She needs him home now, and do not let that wimpy publicist guy stop him. Call Bradley and Ellen. Edwina if I am right, it is coming faster than we expect, I just hope we get to the hospital in time." She nodded and gripped her arm.

"Birch drive carefully, the rain is really bouncing, just get her there, I will handle the rest." Birch took a deep breath, and smiled, I must have looked terrified, as Birch turned towards me.

"Sweetie, get some cushions and the blanket off the sofa, I am going to put her in the back, the front seat is probably not the best place for her at this stage."

I suddenly realised, Birch had a good medical education, especially in women's studies, and she thought we would not make it to the hospital. I had to walk to the living room, I was still out of breath. I pulled the blanket off the sofa, and threw it over my shoulder, and then grabbed four big cushions. I headed to the front door. Grabbing the back door of Petal, I opened it and climbed in.

I used the smaller cushions already in Petal, to pad a row along the low partition behind the seats, and then placed the bigger cushions on top to create a comfy seating place for her. The rain was battering the roof so hard it was deafening, I looked back and saw Birch walking Deb's slowly towards me down the hallway, Chloe had her bag.

I held out my hand, and she smiled, but she looked scared. I helped pull her gently into the back of Petal, Chloe climbed in behind her, and Edwina closed the door. Birch headed towards the driver's seat. Deb's sat back and smiled at me.

"I am sorry Abby." I gave a smile.

"Deb's you're not exactly in control, that little one is, so I will let you off." She smiled; Chloe sat at her feet panting. I was not sure whether it was for hers, or Deb's benefit?

"Fuf... Fuf... Fuf... Fuf... Fuf." I climbed over into the passenger seat; Chloe suddenly panicked.

"You are not leaving me are you Abby?" I looked back as I clipped in the seat belt.

"Chloe the rain is hammering down, I will have to help watch the road." She looked as white as a ghost.

"Yeah, but what if something comes out?" Birch gave a chuckle as she slipped Petal into gear.

"Catch it Sweetie." Deb's gave a giggle, and Chloe looked petrified.

"Holy fuck... Close your legs Deb's."

Petal lurched forward, and Chloe went flying backwards into the rear door, as Petal shot through the gates onto the road, I flicked on all the switches and all the spotlights came on. I leaned forward in the seat to peer out of the window, the rain was even worse than it had been a week ago, the only good news, was it was gone two in the morning, and the roads were pretty empty, which was good, as Birch was driving.

"This is not good Birch."

She was really calm and focused, as the rain lashed against the window, in the back Chloe was holding Deb's hand and panting with her. I looked back, and she looked terrified, hell, I was terrified, but she was doing good, and really helping Deb's, I smiled and gave her a nod. We headed onto High Street, I turned back, and peered out of the window.

"Birch, go straight across and take the direct road to Oxendale, it has street lights." She gave a nod, as Petal shot across the junction at speed.

Deb's gave a yelp, and I tensed, and looked back, Chloe was doing her best, she looked at me.

"Hurry Abby, I am not sure she will make it."

I nodded, Deb's gave another yelp, her contractions were getting closer, too close for my comfort. Birch stared out of the window; the road was well floodlit by Petal.

"Chloe Sweetie, I want you to lift Deb's dress, and look at her vagina for me." Chloe stopped panting, and stared at the back of Birch's head.

"You are fucked up you know that right? Birch, I am so fucking straight it's unbelievable, if you want to see it, take a fucking photo, you pervert." I sniggered and turned round.

"Chloe, we need to know how big it is, the size will give us an idea of when the baby is coming." She looked at me suspiciously.

"I fucking mean it Birch, if this is a wind up, I will piss in your muesli."

Birch focused on the road; it was reasonably straight for a few miles. Deb's brought up her knees and opened her legs. Chloe gave a shudder, and lifted Deb's nightdress, and did a quick peek.

"She is wearing knickers... Holy fuck Deb's, your knickers are huge, they are bigger than my gran's." Birch giggled as she watched the road.

"Sweetie, you will have to take her knickers off." Chloe's head popped up from between Deb's legs.

"You can fuck off, she has been trying to get me to do that for two years, and I am not fucking having it." I looked back at her.

"Chloe, we need to know her size, just pull them off." Chloe looked over her tummy at Deb's, who gave a big smile and winked. Chloe stared at her with suspicion.

"I mean it Deb's, you even gasp or moan, and I am jumping out of the back door, and fucking leaving you." Her head dropped down, then came up again really fast.

"Why the fuck are they wet?" I giggled; I seem to remember something similar.

"Chloe, her waters broke, they must be soaking, just pull them off for God's sake." She gave a nod and disappeared, I turned to the front screen.

"Slow down a bit Birch, there is a sharp bend to the right coming up." She gave a nod, and pressed the brake. I looked out of the side window; the rain was not easing up. In the back, Chloe held up a huge pair of knickers.

"Holy shit Deb's, when you're done, you could make a hammock out of these."

Birch leaned forward to stare out of the window. There was a man in the road, he was waving a lamp, Birch slowed down as he came towards us. I opened my window, and leaned out, the rain lashed into my face. He shook his head as he walked up to the side of Petal.

"I am sorry love, the road has been washed out, the bank has collapsed, the road will have to be closed, I am waiting for a team to get here. There is nothing we can do, you will have to go back, and go the long way round through Pilkington's." I gave a nod.

"We have a pregnant woman about to give birth in the back, is there no other way?" He shook his head, and pointed behind him.

"It is going to take a day or two to clear that lot, I am sorry." I smiled.

"It is fine, we will skirt round." He wiped the rain from his eyes.

"I know you; don't you write them horror books?" I gave a nod and smiled.

"Yep, that is me, sorry love, but we are in a bit of a hurry." He nodded.

"Drive fast, but careful, and good luck." I smiled as I closed the window, and Birch went straight into gear to turn us around. I banged the dash.

"Shit!" Birch turned, and looked behind her, as she reversed.

"Stay calm Sweetie, we will get there. Chloe, I need to know the size?"

Petal spun round, and Birch floored it as she sped back towards Wotton, her one talent was scaring us with her high speed driving, but tonight, I was glad she was behind the wheel, she understood Petal in ways I never could, and she was a skilled fast four by four driver. Chloe popped her head up.

"Birch, she is fucking huge." Deb's was panting and looking worried, she lifted her hand up, and I grabbed it and gave it a squeeze. Birch stared at the window.

"How big Chloe, give me an idea, in centimetres?" She popped up, and stared at me and shrugged.

"I don't fucking know, it's big, I didn't bring a ruler, because I had no fucking idea maths would be involved?" Birch nodded at the wheel.

"Chloe Sweetie, does it look big enough to put an orange in." Deb's looked up at the same time as Chloe.

"Do what, why is she putting an orange up me?" Birch gave a giggle.

"Sweetie relax, we want what is in there out, nothing is going in, I just need an idea of size, so I know how long we have, I am going as fast as I can dare to." I smiled at her; Chloe looked at me, and shrugged.

"I suppose you might get a decent sized Jaffa in there." Birch smiled.

"Thanks Sweetie."

She gave a sigh, and I looked out of the window, up ahead a truck with orange flashing lights was in the road, they were putting up road blocked signs. Birch slowed as we approached the corner, and indicated. Birch swung Petal round the corner, and accelerated down Station Road. Deb's squeezed my hand gave a gasp, and screwed up her eyes.

"Ow! Ow!"

Chloe popped up and looked terrified. My phone beeped, and I lifted it up with my free hand and looked at it, as I felt the pain course through my other hand. I breathed in, gasped and then read the text message and smiled, it was from Edwina.

"Deb's, Edwina has spoken to Jimmy, and he has hired a helicopter, actually he has had one on standby all week. He is in Birmingham, and in the air on his way fast, so hang in there, he is coming."

I felt her hand squeeze mine, my arm was going a little numb, with constantly holding it behind me. Chloe gave a little squeal, and popped up and looked at me, she was as white as a ghost and looked terrified.

"Oh fuck... Guys... Guys... Guys we need to hurry, this thing is opening like that scary ass sand monster in Star Wars?" She took a deep breath; I could see she was panicked.

"You know, the one they tried to throw Luke in?" Deb's scowled at her.

"We get it Chloe, and by the way, for a bloody straight girl, you are pretty bloody fascinated by my vagina." I snorted, as Chloe looked scandalised.

"I am looking out for you, Deb's." Birch smirked.

"Not so sure about out, you are certainly looking in. Tell us if you see her tonsils." She stared at me in horror, as her face turned whiter.

"Holy fuck, do you think I will?"

Birch gave a cackle of a laugh as she sped onto the long winding Pilkington's Road, Deb's gave a giggle and winced, she squeezed my hand really tight, and I screwed up my eyes, she has a strong grip. Birch glanced at me, as we swept round a left hand bend.

"Are you alright Sweetie?" I gave a gasp.

"She has one hell of a grip."

To be honest the squeezes were getting more often, and I was worried we would not make it in time. My thoughts were drifting. And I whispered.

"Hurry Birch." I flinched, and I understood Birch was counting between my flinches to understand how far apart her contractions were.

"I am doing my best to keep us safe and steady, and get us there Sweetie." I smiled, I knew, I could see how serious and focused she was.

"HOLY FUCK.... FUCK... GUYS SOMETHING IS MOVING, WHAT DO I DO?"

I looked back, even Deb's lifted her head up as she panted like a steam engine.

"I am sorry Chloe I am trying not to push, I am trying honestly, but things are starting to happen and I am scared." Chloe looked at her and swallowed hard, she looked petrified.

"I am here Deb's, I am with you, don't be scared, I am here."
I smiled watching her, bless her she was so lovely. Deb's gave a
sudden lurch, and screwed up her face.

"OW!... CHLOE IT HURTS... OW... OW!" Chloe panicked.

"Abby I can see something, holy fucking hell, there is a fucking
big hairy grapefruit in there, fuck, fuck, fuck. Should I push it
back?" I shook my head and felt the panic.

"Don't freaking do that, for God's sake!" My heart was jumping
like crazy in my chest. Birch swung Petal to the right.

"Chloe if it comes out, you will have to guide it, just be gentle."
She looked at me looking terrified.

"Abby, I am really scared I do not know what to do." Birch
straightened up Petal and hit a straight, she put her foot down
and floored it. I jumped as suddenly Birch yelled, and she
sounded just like Roni.

"CHLOE, FOCUS, I NEED YOU!" Chloe blinked and swallowed
hard, she looked startled. Birch looked in the rear view mirror.

"Chloe Sweetie, do you love Deb's, is she your best friend?" She
nodded.

"Yes... Yeah she is." Birch smiled.

"Chloe, she needs you, so be there for her, and hold it together...
Help her, she needs you."

Deb's smiled, and then screwed up her face and almost broke
my hand as she squeezed it really hard, and gave a wail. We were
not going to make it, baby was coming, and it had no intention of
waiting any longer. Chloe gave a gasp.

"Holy fuck it has got a head and it is coming the fuck out."

I was finding it hard to focus on the road. Birch was leaning
up to the window as the wipers shot across the window at high
speed, these roads had hardly any lighting and we were moving
really fast. I looked back and Deb's was screwing up her face.

"I am sorry I cannot hold it; I am sorry Chloe; I am so sorry.
Grrrrrrrrrrrrrrrrrr!"

All I could do was watch, as Deb's broke my hand, and Chloe's
head appeared above her legs.

"Oh god, Deb's it has a head... You are sure it's yours aren't you,
because holy fuck it's ugly, it looks like a raisin." I could not help

but giggle. Birch looked in the rear view mirror.

"Deb's, I want you to breathe, big breaths, and on the count of three I need you to push down, alright Sweetie, are you ready?"

I hung on to her hand as Chloe breathed with her helping her. I will not deny, I was absolutely terrified, and my heart was pounding inside me. I really admired Chloe, she was really scared stiff, sweating, and as white as a ghost, but in truth, she was holding it together better than me. Birch counted slowly.

"One... Two... Three... PUSH!" Deb's clamped onto my hand, and bore down hard, I almost screamed she hurt me so much, and I felt the tears of pain in my eyes. Chloe's eyes went wide.

"We have shoulders... Guys this is amazing, there is a little person right here." Birch counted.

"Again Deb's... One... Two... Three... PUSH!"

I gave a wail as Deb's squeezed my hand even harder, and the pain shot up my arm. She screamed out as she pushed, and Chloe burst into tears, and Deb's collapsed back on the floor. I could see Chloe holding a blood covered baby crying her eyes out. She looked at me, and cried with a smile, her voice held her astonishment and awe.

"It's a girl... Guys, it's a little tiny girl."

Birch stamped on the brakes, and we came to a screeching halt, and Petal swung sideways in the road, as the wheels screamed, I screamed, as we shook to a halt, my heart was in my mouth I was so terrified. Birch looked at me, she looked panicked.

"It's not crying, Deads, you drive." She twisted in her seat, unclipped her belt, and climbed into the back.

"It must breathe." She clambered over to Chloe, as I slid across into the driver's seat, we were rolling as Birch had not even put the hand brake on. I put Petal in gear and pulled off.

Birch grabbed the baby, checked its mouth with her little finger, and holding its feet, she swung it upside down, and gave it a pat on the bum, it squealed into life and Birch gave a massive sigh of relief. Deb's was in tears. Birch looked at Chloe.

"Lend me your denim shirt."

She lay the baby between her legs, and pulled her vest over her head, and wrapped the baby up in it, and turned to Deb's with a smile, and lifted her baby to her.

"Your daughter, well done Sweetie, you were brilliant." Birch took Chloe's shirt and slipped it on over her bare chest, she smiled at Chloe.

"You were absolutely magnificent, congrats Chloe, you just birthed your best friends' daughter."

Chloe sat back against the door, and cried her eyes out, and her tears streamed down her cheeks, as Deb's smiled at her. Birch slid down by her side and pulled her into a hug, and Chloe wrapped her arms round her.

"I have never seen anything like it... Although Birch, Deb's still has bits hanging out of her, I don't want to touch those if that is oaky, they are freaking me out?" Birch chuckled.

"The hospital will take care of her now Sweetie, you did the important stuff." I smiled as I drove towards the hospital.

"Hey Deb's, your daughter was born at exactly six minutes past three, on May 30th."

She hugged her baby on her boob, and smiled. Chloe sat up and watched, as she wiped her eyes.

"All girls together." Deb's smiled.

"Always... Thanks Chloe."

The hospital came into view, and I headed for the turn off, and indicated. We came up to the ambulance bay, and Birch reached over for her pass, and permit, from the glove box.

"Screw the car park, use the staff parking spot there, I have my permits now." She placed a card on the dash, with a big NHS logo on it.

I pulled in, and Birch climbed back over into the passenger seat and opened the door. She jumped out into the pouring rain, and walked towards the porters with her badge round her neck.

"I need a chair, I have a mum with a new born, she came on route, she needs a full check up, and wash down and the cord cutting."

I was out in the pouring rain, and ran around at the back, and opened the door, as a nurse and a porter headed towards us. Chloe sat back, and I got to see my niece for the first time. Deb's gave a big smile, although she looked really tired. Deb's was taken inside, and I grabbed her bag and followed her. The nurse turned, and looked at us.

"It is staff and family only from here." Deb's looked up at the nurse.

"Those are my sisters, and she is my specialist therapist." The nurse gave a nod.

"This way then." Chloe giggled as I walked at her side, and we went down the corridor to maternity, where her midwife was waiting.

We all had to wait, whilst Deb's was cleaned up and taken care of. Luckily Birch had as always grabbed her big bag, so we had change, which meant coffee. Well, it was their idea of coffee, but I was so thirsty I drank it. I collapsed in the chair, feeling exhausted, the sliding doors opened and Ellen came rushing in with Bradley, she saw us and came straight over, Chloe gave a big smile.

"Congratulations Granny, you have a granddaughter." Ellen burst into tears, and Bradley pulled her close, Birch came over from talking at the desk.

"They are cleaning her up and admitting her, she will be ready soon." Bradley narrowed his eyes.

"Admitting her?" Birch gave a big smile.

"She gave birth in the back of Petal, Chloe delivered her, she was born at six minutes past three exactly, and at about sixty mile an hour, so her exact place of birth is a little sketchy?" Ellen crouched down and looked at Chloe, who to be honest was pretty out of it, I think she was traumatised by the whole ordeal.

"Thank you, Chloe, thank you so much, for being there for her." Chloe smiled, and her eyes filled up.

"She looks like a raisin; I hope you don't mind?" Bradley gave a laugh.

"I am sure she will smoothen up as she dries out." I giggled and nudged Chloe

"We should have brought the book; it would have dehydrated her a bit." Chloe smiled, and Ellen pulled her into a hug.

It was exhausting, and I slouched back. Outside there was a big commotion as a helicopter hovered over the car park, and Jimmy jumped out, he landed with a thud as staff ran out shouting and complained, he shrugged.

"Sorry... Look love I don't know any better, I am a fucking

rock star, what the fuck do you expect? Now if you have finished chewing my ass off, my wife is in there giving birth."

He walked up to the doors like a pro, and they slid open, the helicopter lifted back off. Honestly, the way he walked in; you would have thought he was famous.

We all sat back, and let Jimmy, Ellen, and Bradley go in to see her first, and drank more coffee, and sent out lots of text messages. Finally, we were allowed in to see her, and we all gathered around the bed. Jimmy was red eyed, but really happy, Deb's looked tired, but she smiled at me as she cradled her daughter.

"Guys, quite a while ago, we talked about names. Had she been a boy, we were going to call him Gem, after Jemi, but she is a girl, so we have named her Jennifer, or Jenny for short. You guys are the reason we found each other, and so we wanted to name our child in tribute to you both, to show you how much we love you."

I looked at her tiny little daughter, and I could not speak, I felt this huge ball in my chest. Deb's smiled at me as my eyes filled with tears, and Birch pulled me close, I gave a croaky cough.

"Deb's, Jimmy, I don't know what to say." Birch grinned like an idiot; and waved.

"Hi Jenny, little Sweetie, I am aunty Birch." I gave a laugh, Deb's looked at Chloe.

"You really are a brilliant friend, and we were not going to give her a middle name, but we both think we will call her Jennifer Chloe, so she will never forget who brought her into the world. Is that alright with you?" Chloe was already in tears, and she just nodded. Birch gave a sudden jerk.

"Oh, I have something, give me a moment?"

She opened her huge bag and rooted around inside it. I was certain it would not be a knife; I mean who the hell gets a big bloody knife out at a birth? Birch smiled, and lifted a small blue baby grow out.

"Oh nope, not that one."

She dropped it back in her bag, and continued to dig around in it. I leaned over and tried to look inside.

"What have you got blue for?" Her eyes sparkled with excitement as she glanced up at me.

"Well Sweetie, we did not know, so I prepared just in case... Oh here it is." She lifted out a tiny little pink baby grow, with a small teddy embroidered on it, she gave a huge smile.

"SURPRISE!" Deb's giggled, and Birch handed it over, Birch beamed with delight.

"It is from all of us, you know, welcome to the world, congratulations and all that." Deb's looked at me, and she gave me a big smile.

"Thank you, Auntie Birch, and Auntie Abby, and Auntie Chloe, it is lovely." Jimmy pulled us into a hug one by one, and he hugged me so tight, I almost passed out, but it was nice.

"You guys, wow, you are just the dogs' bollocks for mates, I really fucking owe you, all of you big time." He was sweet, and not good with words, just listen to any Battered Taco song, and you will understand completely.

It was really late, and we were all tired. We left the family to enjoy the moment, and headed through the hospital towards Petal. I felt dazed as we climbed in, Birch took the driver's seat, and Chloe collapsed in the back and snuggled onto the pillows, I heard her whisper to herself.

"Jennifer Chloe."

I was thrilled for her, she deserved it. Birch drove out of the hospital, and we sat silent for a while, the rain had eased a little, but we still had to watch the road. I looked back, and Chloe was fast asleep with a smile on her face. I watched the rain streak down the glass, and Birch glanced at me.

"Are you alright Sweetie?" I blinked and turned to her; my mind was swimming with thoughts.

"Moon knew, she told me today, or actually yesterday, a child would come soon, drawn by the light. It was the thunder that set her off, and sent her into birth, that first big flash, how the hell does she do that Birch?" Birch gave a giggle.

"Trust me Deads, she has done way freakier things than that. I just think it is her thing, she sees things no one else does. I am a psychologist and even I do not understand it, although I am not stupid enough to not believe in it, because I do, I have seen it. Deads, man thinks he knows it all, but when it comes to the power of the mind and perception, I think we are only just at the start of understanding, we have so much more to learn." I gave a nod and sat back.

"She named her daughter after me, I am not sure how to understand that at all." Birch reached over and gave my leg a soft squeeze.

"Deads, you were there when no one else was, you got her through the darkness, and she loves you dearly for it, I am thrilled it was a girl. To be honest I just got her laid, but you, I think you saved her life, and that really counts. I cannot think of a nicer person to name a child after." It was strange to think about it, I looked at Birch.

"It is really weird Birch, it is like she has gone full circle, we were there the night she lost her virginity. After that she went pretty bonkers, and pretty much slept with everything, and now she is back with her first guy, and has just had a child. Deb's is a mum, how screwed up is that, she is actually a mother, a parent, it blows my mind?" Birch chuckled.

"Deads Sweetie, we are about to be married, I am a doctor of psychology, and you are a famous writer. I hate to point it out, but while we were all having fun, we grew up, it happens, it is called life." She was right, we had all grown up, we were officially adults, and that scared me a little.

"Birch, I do not want to grow up."

"So don't, there is no rule to force you. I like to think that the so called rules of society, are just for the idiots, for the more awakened, they are just guide lines, to ignore if we choose to. Deads, you know, it fascinates me that people always look for someone to grow old with, but you know what? I think we should be looking for someone to stay young with. I am sure I have told you, we do not stop playing because we grow up, we grow up because we stop playing, so have fun and keep playing, that is what I am doing." I smiled; I remembered the first time she told me that at Uni.

We turned into High Street, and the village was still asleep, under the blanket of the rain. It was silent and still, with just the noise of Petal as she rumbled through. We finally pulled through the gates, and onto the drive, and I felt the weariness grow inside me.

Edwina was standing at the door, as I woke Chloe, she stirred and opened her eyes and smiled.

"Hey, we are home, go tell your big sister what you did tonight."

She sat up, and yawned, which set me off. Birch turned the engine off as Chloe jumped out of the back, and walked towards Edwina, I sat and watched as Chloe explained, and then Edwina dragged her into a big hug. I really loved how close those two were, it was nice to see. Birch patted my leg.

"Come on Sweetie, let's go cuddle."

I opened the door, and wandered to the front door, and inside the house, I heard Chloe in the kitchen talking and telling Izzy, Anthony and Edwina all about her night, she deserved the praise, so I walked straight onto the stairs, and headed to bed.

I lay back and closed my eyes, and felt Birch slide in and curl around me. I gave a happy sigh.

"I love you Birch." She snuggled in to me.

"I love you too Sweetie."

I closed my eyes and the world faded away for another night, as I drifted into dreams, of light and darkness swirling together, and pictures of a tiny little girl, called Jennifer... Hold up... You know, she was right, she does look like a raisin.

Chapter 33

Papered Windows.

Deb's gave birth in what was possibly one of the most traumatic nights of my life, last Tuesday, which was, five days ago, and I have been a little out of it, feeling all sorts of strange feelings. I will add at this point, not one of them was the desire to have one of my own. But it has made me sit up and think, about my life, my future, and also, how the hell I am going to cope for another day, with Auntie Birch?

Deb's is home now, both her and little Jenny, were given the all clear, and in front of a hospital filled with press, a very proud Jimmy, escorted his wife and new daughter, out of the hospital, and into Bradley's car. I am so happy for her, I truly am, it has reminded me of all our conversations as teenagers, as she told me her dreams of her ideal man, and her three children, and to a degree, most of it has come true.

Chloe and Edwina have gone baby bonkers, and Deb's room has been turned into a nursery/bedroom, with a crib, coloured mobiles, and light up pictures on the walls. Birch has gone wild, and keeps coming home with Teddy Bears, and pretty clothes, and she has worried me a little bit, because if I am honest, I am just not feeling the same vibe as them. Is it wrong that I just want to click my fingers, and make things normal again?

I have been sat at my desk for three days, and I have finished my last chapter, and almost read all of Birch's manuscript, and made a few foot notes on it to help her. I updated the Curio blog, and informed every one of our new family member, and that has been very well received news. Mail from our PO Box has been pouring in, and half the house is littered with new baby cards. It bothers me that Birch keeps picking them up and reading them, and making awe sort of noises.

I sat back in my desk chair and gave a long and depressed sigh. I lifted my cup, it was empty. Oh God, I have to go down to refill it, and Deb's is here for her first visit, with baby Jenny. What the hell is wrong with me, why am I not like other women? Oh crap, I have to do this, I cannot keep hiding away.

I gave another sigh, and swung slowly round in my chair, the bedroom door burst open, and I jumped with a shriek. Birch slammed her back into it closing it with a bang. She stood staring at me, with sad painful eyes, and had her hand over her mouth. I felt alarmed as her skin looked a funny colour, I got up feeling scared. I felt my heart skip a beat.

"Birch Baby, what is the matter, are you alright?" My heart beat a little faster.

She stared at me, and shook her head, I felt really worried. She took her hand her away from her mouth.

"I am so sorry Sweetie; I cannot do this." I felt a bolt of shock hit me, what did she mean, was she calling our wedding off?

"Birch... Please, you are scaring me, what is wrong?" She turned looking completely panicked, and ran for her room, I gasped, and felt really terrified, and then heard her in the bathroom.

"YERK!"

I ran after her, as she emptied the contents of her stomach into the toilet. I arrived at speed, feeling a little bit terrified, what the hell was wrong with her? She was bent over the toilet bowl, heaving and gasping.

"YERKKKK!"

I stood back, oh shit, that is unsettling, and not at all attractive! She gave a whimper, and a big gasp for air. I took a deep breath, and grabbed her hair, and pulled it back out of the way, I felt her forehead.

"Are you ill?" She gave a gasp, and took a really deep breath.

"Oh Deads... How do they do that? It was frigging green, and oh my God, the smell. Oh Sweetie, please I beg you, never want children, I can never do that again, it was..." I watched her convulse.

"YERK!"

She gasped for more air, and I did not want to laugh, honestly, I tried really hard not too? Poor Birch, she knelt on the floor gasping in massive amounts of air, I sniggered, and she turned to me, with tears in her eyes.

"Sweetie, I cannot get the smell out of my nose." Her lip trembled, she turned back fast, and faced the bowl as I saw her whole body shudder.

"YERK!"

Is it wrong that as I watched my poor pathetic wife to be, hurl her guts up, I felt a little happier? She gasped in more air. I leaned over.

"Are you alright now?" She took a deep breath.

"That is the vilest and most disgusting thing I have ever encountered, and I fell in a cow pat when I was five, and I threw up for a week. It haunted my senses for years."

Again, I really did not want to laugh, but...

"YERK!" I heard Chloe in my room.

"Abby, where are you?" I left Birch gagging, and walked into my bedroom; Chloe gave me a big grin.

"Is she alright?" I giggled, and shook my head.

"Not really." Chloe sniggered.

"I warned her, but she would not listen, I told her, all they are is little screaming shit factories, but she wanted to be an auntie, and do the little Raisin's bum. I guess she learned the hard way?" I sniggered; moans came from behind me in the bathroom.

"YERK!" Chloe giggled.

It took a lot of patience, kind words, and a reassurance that she would never have to change a nappy again in her whole life. I assured her, if needed, I would have the op to ensure I had no risk of babies. I even offered to let her rip out my uterus, and flush it, there and then, before I could finally prize her fingers off the toilet bowl, and get her out of the bathroom, and sat on the bed. Chloe did not help, as she was pissing herself laughing all the time. Chloe offered to make us a drink, and headed downstairs, and I sat at her side, and held her hand.

"Will you be alright now?" She nodded, and took a deep breath.

"I am a horrible person Sweetie, she is so lovely, but oh my god, how can she produce that fucking toxic stuff?" She retched, jumped up, and flew back to the bathroom.

"YERK!" I collapsed back onto the bed.

"Oh God, not again!?" I felt exhausted.

I try not to sound like some boring old spinster, but I have spent most of my time since Deb's gave birth thinking about her future, and also mine. The facts are, in fourteen days, Birch and I will be married, and a new chapter of our life will start, and from all our conversations to date, we want to get more time alone.

I love living here, I love house sharing, but as I have found out over the last four years, it comes at a price. The price we pay, is less time alone as a couple, because as the owners, everything that happens, overlaps on to us, and that takes us away from quality alone time.

The recent visit to the house in Devon, gave both of us a chance to be us alone. For me, it was a wonderful experience, and to my surprise, I found out, that Birch has a very private side I have never seen before. To add to my concerns, that side of her, attracts me ten times more, than the Birch I thought I knew.

Her recent behaviour of fawning over little Jenny, scared me a little, because as I have seen from watching Deb's, to have a child, will take away the lion's share of that alone time, and if we also live here, we will end with zero time alone together. I probably sound selfish, but be honest, don't we all feel that way sometimes, when all we want is to have that special time, with the one person we love?

It is Sunday, and Birch is not working, and yet we have had hardly any time together, as she has been updating the Curio site, working on the new care centre, and working on her book. It is really time consuming, and on top of everything, we are in the final stages of the wedding planning, and we are both nervous.

It is funny really, because we are no longer nervous about actually getting married, we are both nervous about actually getting all the plans for the wedding to come together on the day. Just in the last few days we have lived on phones or computers talking to the hordes of people that will be providing things.

I think Izzy has morphed into our wedding manager, bless her she has been mucking in with Edwina, and helping pull everything together with us, as we run what is starting to feel like an on site military operation.

What was a large lawn filled with shrubs, that ran up the side of the garage, has been paved, and will have two catering vans on it? Mum's patio has been commandeered and will have another marquee on it, where a kitchen prep station is to be set up, and all the food will be organised there, before being shipped across the road to us.

In our back garden, which is bigger than a football field, there will be marquees, not unsimilar to those at Deb's wedding, which is where the reception will be held, and then at the lower end of the garden, is where the ceremony will be held.

It made more sense to do it here, as I just did not want the Church Hall, which is the only building big enough. My greatest fear is rain, and my fingers are crossed in hope we have at least a little bit of sunshine. May was not that great a month, and I am living in hope, that our allotted rain fall has peaked, and that June will be nicer.

As with all things in my life, we have to prepare for press intrusion, and Luke has sub contracted a security firm to handle that on behalf of G5. There are several boxes of yellow vests with G5 Security, printed on them in Edwina's office at the moment.

I will be staying at Bradley and Ellen's the night before, where he has a small complex for overseas business guests to stay, so I will get the car ride to my own house, on the day, while Birch will use her room at home for dressing in. I think it is silly that we cannot stay together, but it appears, everyone insists.

Guests will arrive and have their cars taken up to the car park on Bradley's complex, by a valet parking service, again organised by G5, so at least the road will remain clear. We also have several drivers to collect locals and bring them to the wedding to keep the car numbers down, after all this is a private residence

Our biggest problem has been the parents, under traditional rules, the father of the bride pays a good share, hence the problem, there are two brides. Birch is a genius and she set up a special bridal account into which both parents have paid, and we have both stuck some cash in too, that way we get our own way, and as you know, Birch can get a little carried away.

As I headed to bed, I expected the coming weeks and days to fly by, Birch who was finally over her sickness, was already out cold, her bedroom floor covered with papers and plans. I crawled in at her side, and she instinctively rolled over and curled around me. I lay in the dark my head spinning with everything, why didn't we just sneak off to a remote island, and do it on the beach with a couple of hula girls as witnesses?

Beep... Beep... Beep... Beep... Beep. "Huh!" I sat up and rubbed my eyes.

"What the hell is that?" I turned to Birch; she was not there. I looked at the clock, it was seven o'clock, I gave a sigh and flopped back into my pillow.

"Oh God, what the hell is she up to now?"

In the garden a team of specialists were rolling out thick heavy mats, across the lawn, completely covering all of it. Down the side of the house, a large lifter was reversing as it carried the huge thick rolls, around to the workers on our now, hidden lawns. It was early, and it was noisy.

The door opened and Edwina appeared with a smile, and a large roll of brown paper, closely followed by a naked Chloe with two cups of coffee, she like me, looked exhausted. She said nothing and sat on the bed and handed me the cup. Edwina walked to the windows, locked the doors, and started to paper them over, I sipped my coffee, understanding none of it.

"Edwina, what the hell is going on?" She looked at me as she taped the paper over the glass. I reached over and clicked the lamp on.

"This is a Birch thing, and I am sworn to secrecy, but she insists no peeking."

Now there is irony, Birch actually demanding no peeking, she is the biggest and worst when it comes to peeking. I find it impossible to hide anything, she has the resistance of an alcoholic in a bath of gin. It was too early and I was not awake, I sat back and sipped my coffee, as Edwina slowly blocked out the light, and then headed to my room to do the same, I looked at Chloe.

"I bet you are clueless too; Birch would never trust you not to tell me?" She gave a smile.

"I am happy to be out of it, she is down there wearing a hard hat, and smiling like a lunatic, and she is very loud. I knew you would be peaceful, which is why I am here." I sipped my coffee.

"God she must be loud, you are naked, and the garden is full of men, and you are here, shit, I am dreading getting up now."

I sat in bed quiet, calm and relaxed, sipping coffee, and staying as far from everyone as possible, when she burst in through the door, in her work clothes, wearing her hair in a long pony tail, and wearing a bright yellow hard hat, which perched on her head, and wobbled as she smiled and waved.

"Hi Sweetie."

Her eyes were bright and bouncing like she was a bobblehead, oh shit, she was on that level of happy. She swept across the room and bounced down on the bed, she looked far too excited for seven in the morning. I looked over my cup at her, as she smiled, she actually looked very sweet, she rarely has her hair up, and I could see her earrings that I bought her for Christmas.

Her neck is slender, and quite long, and I will not deny, is a part of her I really love, and I focused on it, and felt a little tingle inside my lower parts. She tried to be very serious with me, but her eyes betrayed her, she was really happy.

"Deads... Sweetie, I have been working very hard behind the scenes on something I really want to do for you. Sweetie, I cannot hide this, if I could I would. Deads, will you promise me that you will not go out there until it is finished? Sweetie, this is really important to me." I took a sip of my coffee and lowered my cup.

"Okay then." She looked at me.

"Really, you promise?"

"Yeah... Birch, I just told you, if it means that much to you, I will stay out of the way." She looked at me unsure.

"This is big Deads, I really want to do this just for you, it means everything." I gave a sigh.

"Birch, I said OKAY... Would you like me to sign in blood?"

She gave me a big smile, and I put my cup down on the side, because I knew what was coming. She exploded with joy, gave a squeal, and threw her arms around me, and almost crushed me.

"Oh Sweetie, you will love it, I just know you will love it." She jumped up, and shook all over.

"I am so excited." With that, she zoomed across the room and disappeared. Chloe calmly turned to me.

"Are you really not going to look?" I nodded, as I lifted my cup back off the unit.

"If it is that important to her, I am happy to wait, why?" She shrugged.

"I would look, actually I probably will look, I am a little curious." I lifted my cup to my lips.

"And there are also a lot of builders out there too." She giggled and lifted her cup.

"You really do have all of us pegged, you are more observant than I thought." I shook my head.

"Not really Chloe, you paint, and you fuck, and you are so fucking straight it's unbelievable." I laughed at her, as she agreed with a giggle.

The rest of the day, brought sounds of laughter, and machinery, and all to the sounds of a really bad radio station, that played really tedious pop music. It all ended at five, and we ate in the living room, as all the windows in the kitchen were papered over, and it freaked us all out.

The next two days were a repeat, and as we passed through Thursday and into Friday, it was quiet, but the paper remained up, so I just continued with phone calls, emails and planning, as I followed up on leads for Birch.

I spent a lot of time face timing with Anita, she had the manuscript and was preparing it to be published after I was married. We also talked about the magazine feature of the wedding, she had arranged for a photographer and some of their writers to cover the story, and they had all access to the full wedding.

Birch and I agreed to the use of twenty pictures, and signed a waver that we would not post to my website or Curio site, until after they had done their exclusive. To be honest, we were going to get married, and then leg it off on a honeymoon, for two weeks alone in a private villa, with a private beach, and just take a moment to unwind and be us. That was all I could think about, two whole weeks alone, with my crazy and bonkers new wife.

Wow that sounded so weird! I sat back in my chair and brought my knees up, and drifted in thought.

"My New Wife"

I felt the ripples of excitement bubble inside me, and expand out, and it felt amazing. I rocked from side to side, looking at the picture on my desk top screen of Birch and me, and gave a happy little chuckle.

"Mrs Abigail Jennifer Dixon." I gave a little giggle and spun round fast with my head back, and gave a whoop, and then I noticed her leaning on the doorframe of the bathroom smiling. I was busted, and I gave a giggle, as I looked at her eyes twinkling, I gave a cheeky grin.

"So!" She chuckled, and came into the room.

"Mrs Dixon, is it?" I slid my knees down, and crossed my legs.

"Why not... I was thinking about it, everyone knows me as AJW, and I will always use that, it will just be a pen name after we are married?" She sat on the bed.

"What if I want to be Mrs Watson?" I frowned.

"Do you want to, I mean, Birch I am a writer, I can use any name I want, you are a known Doctor of Psychology, and if you think about it, you asked first? When you proposed, you asked me to be your wife, and tradition says, if I agree, I take your name. I also really want to; I want to be Mrs Dixon." She smiled and walked to me, and held out her hand.

"Well, future Mrs Dixon, I want you to follow me, for I have something for you." She gave a giggle.

"I am really trying to hide how excited I feel." I slipped out of the chair and stood up, and she walked me towards the stairs, and I suddenly felt nervous.

The kitchen windows were still papered over, and everyone was gathered looking excited, even Deb's was here, it felt weird. Birch opened the door, and I could see everyone silently staring at me, which just made me even more nervous. As we walked out into the garden, which looked untouched, at the bottom of the garden, was a line, that ran across the whole garden, and hanging from it was a huge piece of cloth.

Birch started to giggle and get excited, as she led me by the hand, and everyone behind us appeared to be really excited too. I did not know if they had been told, but I felt my heart beating a little faster, what the hell had she done? We arrived and stood in front of the cloth, Birch stood in front of it, and turned to me, with a huge smile, and did a little dance.

"Sweetie, I am so excited... This is why I want us to get married here, because what is behind that curtain, is so important to us, and who we are." I swallowed hard, I knew her, and also knew how easily she could have a mad idea and go overboard and get carried away.

"Birch, I am suddenly terrified, please do not drag this out."

Luke gave a titter and walked over to the tree on my left, where the rope was tethered, Birch gave me a huge smile.

"I really love you Sweetie, please marry me here?" She threw her arms up in the air and shouted

"SURPRISE!"

The cloth fell, and I felt a huge surge hit me like a smack in the stomach, and the air ran out of me, as tears filled my eyes. She stood looking amazingly happy and excited, and I just stared lost in a host of flooding emotions. Everyone behind me giggled, I saw Bradley, Ellen, Mum and Hatty, just smiling. I gasped the only word I could think of.

"How?" Birch came up, and slid into me, and kissed me softly, tears were rolling down my cheeks.

"Have I overdone it again? They were going to demolish it, and when I found out, I got Bradley to save it, and move it here. I could not bear the thought of you losing it forever, and I thought it would be perfect to be married under."

I was feeling so much, I did not know how to react, she took my hand and walked me to my arch, it was exactly as it had been, it was just here. Tears just kept flooding into my eyes, I had to wipe them constantly, I found it almost impossible to speak, I turned to her and just buried my face in her shoulder.

"Birch, I love you so much."

Was all I could gasp between sobs. She held me close, and smiled as her own eyes teared up, actually quite of few of the others were wiping their eyes. I took forever, before I felt my breathing coming back to normal, it was just so overwhelming, and I pulled off her shoulder, there was a huge wet patch, on her top.

I wiped my eyes, and looked around, it was mad, the whole thing was in my garden. I walked slowly towards it, and touched the walls, there was no mistake, every chip and crack was there, I turned and saw her watching me as I rubbed my hand along the stone.

"How do you do this, how do you just pick up a whole building, and just bring it here?" Bradley gave a titter.

"It is not as easy as that, it took a lot of work. Luke and Edwina did a laser scan of the whole thing, and created a computer mock up of it, and my engineers looked at the structural integrity. The water company was right, it had become unstable. We looked at the computer model, and found ways to reinforce it before we moved it. You will notice some repair work, but I insisted it was done, as your safety was paramount." Birch was all smiles.

"It is okay isn't it, I did right?" I smiled and pulled her into a hug, I still felt weepy, but I really was so very happy.

"You amaze me, I am struggling for words, but I am so blown away. Birch, you saved it for me... I cannot believe you did this, and I really want to be married here, I really do."

Mum pulled me into a huge hug, she too had cried, I think she understands how important this is to me. I have no idea how she does it, but she found out in time, and stopped them. If I had gone down the canal and seen it gone, my world would have been utterly crushed.

Everyone gathered around, this place was sort of a massive aspect of me, and yet a lot of them had not seen it. I sat on the floor in the corner, and looked up, and again I felt a huge wave of emotion wash over me. Birch knelt down in front of me, and her eyes twinkled.

"I could not let you lose it, it is such a special thing, which few will understand, but Deads, it would have broken my heart to see you lose it. I have had it aligned exactly to the sun as it was, so the shadows everything will be exactly the same as it was over there. To be honest, I am really, really excited to get married here, it just makes it all so much more special." I felt dazed, emotional, overwhelmed, and happy as I sat in my corner.

"I cannot believe you did this; it must have cost a fortune?" She gave a soft smile, and her eyes shone so brightly, her voice was soft and quiet.

"Deads, money has no value, until you give it one. It matters not what it cost, and be honest, I have more than I will ever spend. Deads, I picked you; I want you, that is all I have wanted since I returned here. This, the arch, it is the one symbol in all of this mad world that screams Abigail Jennifer Watson. I would never allow that to be silenced, because you are so unbelievably important to my life, and the lives of so many others. In a way Sweetie, this arch is your true centre, and the house is the centre of all of us, it is right I brought it here." She leaned in and kissed me so softly, and the emotions exploded out of me, and I burst yet again, into tears.

Alcohol appeared, and we all sat in the shadow of the arch, and talked and laughed, and I felt safe and secure. It is strange how random, inanimate objects become sacred to us; this was just an old broken down piece of a factory from one hundred years ago. It was broken and busted, and the water company saw it as rubbish and dangerous, and if they had got their wish, it would have been bulldozed into oblivion. To me it was sanctuary, a safe haven, a place where no one could hurt me, and I admit, I have wept many tears of anguish and pain onto these very stones, but it was also sacred, and special, and a place I loved dearly.

It was here when Martin tried to rape me, or my dad beat me, I hid. I told Birch about it all here, and that was the first time I ever talked about it, and I made love to Birch here, when she surprised me with a picnic.

These crumbling old bricks knew me, probably as well as Birch does, and as they say, one man's rubbish is another man's treasure, and I really get that. I really do, because there is nothing material in this world of a higher value than my arch, it is one of the few places I feel completely safe.

As the day progressed, everyone slowly left, but not me, I had one thing in mind, and I was prepared to wait, and as the sun turned the sky red, I saw it, the shadow of my arch surrounded by red light. That was the picture I wrote about in my books, that was my greatest memory, as I sat until sundown before heading home to bed to avoid my father. I watched the floor, and smiled, it would always be safe here now. Birch strolled down the lawn and smiled at me sat in my corner.

"Sweetie, it is late, are you going to stay there all night?" I looked at her, and she looked stunning in the last few seconds of the days light.

"I am so happy Birch, but I have one more thing to do before I go indoors." She tilted her head and looked at me.

"What is that Sweetie?"

I stood up and took her hand and pulled her into the corner under the arch.

"Just this."

I unbuttoned her jeans, and smiled at her, her eyes danced with delight. I slowly slid them down to her ankles and looked up. She was watching me framed in the background of my arch, I moved in slowly, and she gave a long low moan.

"Oh God Deads.... OH... OH!"

Chapter 34

All Girls Together.

The days that followed Birch revealing she had saved my precious arch, which was now moved, and rebuilt in the bottom of the garden, left me emotionally exhausted, as I realised just how powerful our feelings for each other were.

We made love under the arch, and it was special, and afterwards we walked back to the house happy. Birch gave me all the paperwork, that showed the announcement of the demolition, and all her correspondence, which went back eleven months. I had the computer printed map of every dimension, and the bill of sale.

For the last few days, I have spent hours, simply staring out of the window, and just viewing it. I have even moved my desk closer to the window, so I can see it when I write. Last Saturday, with just a week to go, we did the rehearsal for the wedding. Edwina and Luke mapped out the garden, by sticking tent pegs with coloured metal disks on them, to show where everything would be. Even though Moon had met mum and Gail, when she visited the church the other Sunday, she got to meet everyone involved, such as Gill and G5.

Moon lit candles, set up a small altar, and did a ritual blessing on the arch for us, she felt it should be a sacred place, and I did tell her it was, but she insisted she put protections on it. Although she did freak me out, when she told me a new child would rise up from our wedding, and play a prominent role in my future, yeah, she can be really freaky like that, and I was praying Deb's would have a second child.

The days have gone so fast, and I feel there just is not enough time to get everything done, Izzy and Luke really have been invaluable. I am not sure how we would have pulled this off without them backing up, Birch, Edwina and myself.

The subject of hen party was being banded around, and as Matron of Honour it was Deb's job, and she had organised a two day, one night sleep over event, at a retreat, and so we all packed up ready for it. Birch and Gill got the day off, Edwina briefed Samantha on what was needed to be done in the office, and we all piled into Petal. Mum, Ellen, Hatty and Roni, who was joined by newly single Bev, all jumped in Ellen's new car, which had seven seats, and followed, as we headed off in party spirit.

It was just over an hour's drive, in the middle of nowhere, when we pulled up at the Bay Leaves, spar and hotel for ladies only. I was pretty excited; Birch was positively looking to explode. We parked up, and grabbed our bags, and headed inside in our usual rowdy fashion, and stopped at reception. We were met by Camilla Denison Smythe, a very forthright late fifties health specialist, who had the manner of a drill sergeant, and I felt a little intimidated by her. Birch took an instant dislike to her, which was not good.

We signed in, and were allotted two of, as they called them, 'Party Rooms.' Our spirits lifted, and then we were guided into a large room and asked to fill in personal detail forms. It looked like a class room, and once again I had my doubts, I sat next to Birch, as Camilla gave a fake sweet smile.

"I will leave you to fill them in, and I will be back in a moment." Hatty scowled.

"Is it me, or did that sound like a threat, fuck, she is about as warm as my freezer?"

There were sniggers all around as we looked at the forms. Birch was happily filling in her form, so was Deb's, I should have known with those two, if it looks like a test, they are into it. Chloe leaned in to me, and looked at my form, she started ticking the same boxes as me. I looked at her.

"Chloe, it is not an exam, you can put your own answers, you don't have to copy mine?" She shrugged, and lowered her voice.

"This place creeps me out, I thought it would be more like loads of booze and strippers." I had to admit I was a little concerned.

"Well, we will be having spars and saunas, and getting pampered, it could be fun, let's wait and see what Deb's has got in mind." She nodded, and started ticking boxes. Two minutes later Camilla arrived back with a clip board, Chloe was instantly suspicious. Camilla looked at us.

"Good... All done? Right ladies, before you see your rooms, may I remind you, this is a high end establishment for ladies, we believe quiet corridors are the places ladies should walk. This is a healthy establishment, so we do enforce a policy of healthy behaviour, which obviously means no smoking, and no alcohol. We will serve you only the very best and healthy food, and you will be pampered until your beautiful inner woman is revealed, and you will all leave feeling like the fresh flowers you ought to be."

It is a weird thing to see the inner souls of everyone you love, be crushed and squeezed as their life dies. Chloe stared at me in shock.

"Fuck this, I am leaving." She went to stand and I grabbed her arm.

"Chloe, just wait, we do not know everything yet."

Birch, Edwina, and Gill were staring at me, I felt like Chloe had offered them hope, and I was about to steal it. Chloe shook her head at me, as I dragged her back into her seat.

"Abby, you heard her, we are going to be fucking sober and eating straw, I want to get pissed and fuck a stripper." Roni tittered; Deb's looked guilty.

"Guys, we came to be pampered." Chloe nodded.

"Yeah, by strapping blokes, not that sugar coated Nazi. Guys, listen to me, leg it now, while we still can." Birch looked disappointed, but tried to find the positive.

"I am looking forward to the sauna, and a really long massage." Chloe looked at her.

"What body rubbing with oils, well I can handle that?"

Camilla looked pleased, somehow, I felt it was because she was after our souls, and we were staying. She led us up to the third floor, and showed us to the party room, which looked like an army billet, it was just a huge room with rows of beds. I gave a sigh; this was not so much fun. A door at the end of the room opened, and Hatty appeared, at least we had an adjoining door. We looked around, and had to pick a bed, Chloe put her bag on one of the beds. Bev bounced onto the bed at the side of her, and gave her a big smile.

"Hey, Chloe love." Chloe picked up her bag.

"I think this is your bed, Abby?" Bev gave me a smile, and winked, I looked at Chloe and shook my head.

"Nope, that is Birch's bed, I followed Chloe, and hurried to the other side of the room, and grabbed a free bed quick. Deb's looked a little dejected.

"You hate it, I am sorry, I thought it would be nice, you know all girls together, having a laugh and being spoilt. When it said bar and party rooms, I thought it would be fun to have a drink after, but it is a fruit juice bar, I am sorry." I sat on my rock hard bed, Christ, wood was softer?

"Deb's it is just a day, and it is us after all, I am sure we will have some fun." Camilla stood by the door.

"Right ladies, it is twelve noon, we will all meet for your first activity at one thirty, and we will get all of you exposing your true inner beauty. There is no need for clothes, just the large towels on the rack, we are all ladies here, so get settled in, and I will see you in the recreation room." Bev sat up and rubbed her hands.

"Fuckin brill, totty in towels." Deb's looked terrified.

"Abby is it true she is single, and on the prowl again?" I looked up from my case.

"Yeah, why does it bother you?"

She looked warily across the room at Bev, who was already stripping, and showing off her bright purple pubes, Deb's shuddered. Chloe was already naked, and instead of unpacking, she was putting stuff in her bag. She looked at me.

"Grab and dash is still an option." Hatty came in and looked around.

"Has Nurse Ratchet gone?" Edwina gave a nod, and Hatty smiled.

"You guys have a balcony." She turned back to her room, and gave a whistle, and waved.

"Roni, Flick, they have one."

Hatty opened the door, and stepped out, and Roni and Flick came running in like naughty school girls, they slipped through the door, and Hatty handed out the cigarettes with a smile. Birch opened her case.

"We have a kettle and herbal tea in here, so who is up for fruit juice instead of a brew?" I turned and looked across the room at her, she smiled, and had that glint in her eye, that told me she was up to no good.

"What you got?" Birch raised her eyebrows. She lifted out a large bottle of lemonade, and grinned, and I knew straight away.

"You bloody wonder." Everyone looked at me like I was mad, Edwina smiled as Chloe scowled at her, she winked.

"Chloe, this is Birch, and she is no ordinary woman."

She was right, her case was filled with bottles and chocolate bars, and plastic cups, I grabbed a cup, and she poured me a glass of lemonade. I took a sip, smiled, and leaned in and kissed her, it was the best gin I had ever tasted. Birch looked at all the bottles in her case.

"The dandelion has rum, orange is the vodka, the diet cola is SC, and the fizzy cherry is straight red wine." Everyone instantly cheered up, and poured a cup, and we all stood around feeling a lot happier. I looked at Birch.

"To us baby." We all chinked plastic cups, and toasted us, and I felt a little warmth growing inside me, or that could have been the gin, this was Birch after all.

At one thirty, after several fruit juices from Birch's stash, we arrived at the recreation room wrapped in towels, except Chloe who had hers draped over her shoulder. Brandy was about mid forties, thin as a stick, with a fake tan, and it looked like she had drawn her eyebrows on. Edwina frowned as she walked up the room with a big smile, she nudged me.

"What's with Miss Sun Dried tomato?" I turned to look and giggled at her. She lifted her arm in a dramatic expression.

"Ladies, we are all afflicted with toxins and germs, and so we purge, purge, purge, so we become clean and healthy. Trust me ladies, no one wants bad bacteria." Bev nudged me, and whispered.

"Is it me, or did she smell like a chip butty?" Brandy was walking along a long row of running machines, I put my head down and sniggered, Birch snorted, and looked at Bev.

"Sweetie, that is the tan, it has to soak in."

Bev shrugged and followed as we were guided to a weighing machine, and handed a small slip of paper. Brandy, was in a bikini which felt unfair, although she was thin, actually a little too thin, and very dark skinned, apart from her palms, and hairline, which were white as snow.

"Ladies, weigh yourself, and make a note of it, and we will do it again before you leave, and you will see the wonders of this place. It seemed reasonable; she wandered off to assist two older ladies. Roni looked at Bev.

"You first Bev dear, this is one of them new fangled machines, if you turn up the volume, it will speak your weight."

Bev bobbed her head, she appeared un-phased, I am pretty skinny, but there is no way I want everyone knowing my weight, I figured I would turn the volume right down. Roni winked at us, as Bev dropped her towel, and stepped on. Roni leaned back, and shouted in a deep voice.

"GET THE FUCK OFF, YOU FAT FUCKING LESBIAN!" Bev jumped off, looking stunned, as we all sniggered, and she pointed at the machine.

"Did you fuckin hear that, the thing is fuckin broken, and fuckin rude, I am bi now?"

Roni and Hatty were hugging they were laughing so hard, Chloe was on the floor pissing her sides laughing, Birch had her head in my back shaking, as Bev looked at the machine.

"Fuckin IA thinks it's fuckin smarter than us."

With giggles and titters, we all took it in turn, and Bev frowned, as it said nothing. Birch smiled at her.

"I think the voice box is damaged Bev Sweetie."

Roni and Hatty sniggered. The running machines came next, which I was not that bothered about, I had been running a lot in the last year. Birch jumped on to my left, and Deb's was on my right. I turned the machine on, and started to run, as Brandy walked along the line.

"Oh, very good ladies, we all need to work up a good sweat, and open those pores, and start removing all those toxins, no one wants bad bacteria, so let's flush, flush, flush them out."

Deb's was panting, as her boobs bounced up and down, and were slapping about, as her belly wobbled. She looked at me, as she grunted and panted.

"Look at you and Birch, you run like a pair a gazelles, and I am trundling along like a hippo with heartburn." I smiled; Birch sniggered.

"Deb's considering you just had a baby, and how big you were, I am impressed how much has just gone, you do not look much bigger than you were, well except for the boobs, they are still pretty big." She looked at them bouncing about.

"Oh Abby, I would give anything for your boobs, look at them all pert and round, you have no idea how lucky you are?" I looked down at my small mounds, I had never thought about that. Bev was walking on her machine, Chloe, who was running at a fast pace, sweating, and gasping looked at her.

"What is your setting on?" Bev looked at the panel.

"Three, why?" Chloe was breathing hard.

"Mine is on three, how come yours is so slow?" Hatty was jogging, and panting like a freight train, she looked at Chloe.

"See, now you know why I told you to pay more attention in physics, and now you know why mass and velocity are so important." Flick sniggered. Brandy reappeared, and clapped her hands.

"Right ladies, now we have the process started, can we all head to the steam room?" Edwina walked down breathing hard.

"I would rather go to the pool, and fucking drown Brandy, I say we drown, drown, drown the bitch, who is with me? The fucking woman looks like a twiglet, and annoys the frigging shit out of me."

We entered the steam room, feeling glum, and sat on our towels, Brandy smiled at all of us, her chirpiness at first was quite nice, but I was starting to find it a little bit grinding on me.

"Ladies, this will do you wonders, and pull out all of those toxins that make us ill. When we are done, we will feel like we have been reborn, clean, and bacteria free, and be ready for our meal and we will shine, shine, shine with our inner radiance." Edwina scowled at her.

"Give me a flame thrower and she will glow, glow, glow, I frigging hate that bitch. She looks like a fucking pretzel; I say we drown her when we get out." All of us sniggered and put our heads down.

It was pretty hot, and the door was still open, Brandy slipped out of her bikini, hung it on a hook outside, and then pulled the door closed. We all sat on towels on the slatted bench, it was hot, but bearable. Bev was sat behind me with Hatty and Roni, on the higher bench, I felt the sweat build on my forehead, Birch slid up to me and smiled. She appeared to be enjoying herself. Brandy watched us all carefully, and grabbed a bottle of oil.

"This will open up all your senses, and purify everything, and purity is our aim." I looked at Chloe.

"Hell, if she wants to purify you, we will still be here at Christmas!" Sniggers broke out all around me. Brandy lifted the bottle, and unscrewed the top.

"Right ladies, this will be a treat, you will feel the wonder of your pores, as they finally start to breathe, breathe, breathe."

She dropped a few drops into the basin, and I could just about read the label, it was eucalyptus oil. She grabbed the ladle and poured water on it, and steam hissed out of it.

The temperature suddenly shot up, and the whole room smelt like a pot of vapour rub. I breathed in and gasped, as the eucalyptus entered my head, and honestly, I thought it had been cracked open. I patted the top of my head just to make sure, because I was sure, there was a draft on my brain, and it was breathing on its own. I looked at Birch, her face was screwed up, and her eyes were shut closed, and tight, as tears streamed down her face.

"Sweetie, I don't like this; I can feel my hair growing."

I had to force my eyes open to see, Chloe had pulled her towel to her face, Bev gave a gasp.

"Fuckin hell, open a window... It feels like a Manchester night club bog in Summer in here."

My whole body was on fire, I thought my skin would peel off, Hatty leaned forward and gave a long breath out above me, she looked at Brandy.

"I hate to point this out Brandy, but your eyebrows are heading south."

I wiped my eyes, and looked at her, and sniggered, there were black streaks, all down her nose and cheeks. I put my head down and giggled, Birch leaned forward and nudged me, as she giggled, although her eyes were still tightly closed. Brandy stood up.

"Bloody cut backs, the staff always get the cheap stuff. Right ladies, when you are done, have a dip in the pool, dry down, and leave your towels in the hamper, and get a robe each, and we will meet in the dining area at five."

She opened the door, and stepped out and closed it behind her. I leaned back and gasped, so did everyone else. Bev climbed over me.

"Fuck this, me biff is melted."

She headed for the door, and that was the signal to abandon ship. We all piled out, and jumped in the pool, I went under and came back up relieved to feel I still had skin, but oddly enough I felt really good. Birch breathed in a deep breath.

"Wow, I really feel great, I wish we could screw." I smiled.

"We will Baby... We will soon."

We larked around in the pool, which was great fun, and took our time, just relaxing and being silly until meal time. Dry, with clear sinuses, and wrapped in thick soft robes, we headed into the dining area, and sat at a long table. Camilla appeared with a row of staff, she called out our names, and we lifted our hands and got served our meal. Bev looked at her plate.

"What the fuck is this, are we eating house plants, where is the beef?" I looked at my salad, I had ticked vegetarian.

"Bev, it's healthy, and it is good for you." She looked at me.

"Deadly, I am a growing girl, it is alright for you, look at you, it doesn't take much to fill you, I need a good slab of meat to keep me happy." Edwina sniggered.

"So does Chloe."

She nodded with a smile, and we all laughed. Birch looked pissed off chewing on some water cress, she looked at me with an intense stare.

"I frigging hate Brandy, if she says germs or bacteria one more time, I am eating the bitch."

We did get pudding, I am not sure what it was exactly, it was white and had a hint of vanilla to it, Deb's looked a bit fed up.

"The price they charge for this place, and this is what we get, girls we have been robbed." We finished our meal, and headed for the relaxation room, which was part of the juice bar, I looked at Birch.

"I am starving, which one is the heaviest, I need something

filling?" She looked at me

"The chocolate bars in our room."
I was so up for that, I had a tomato juice, it lacked vodka, and then we headed back to the room. We were free until breakfast, which was at eight am. The only entertainment was a TV in the living room, and that was filled with a load of large frowning women who wanted to watch a rom com.

We all sat on our beds, and Birch handed out the drinks, I was still feeling hungry, so snacked on a chocolate bar, whilst drinking gin. I lay back and stared at the ceiling. Deb's looked really down, I smiled.
"Cheer up, I actually feel really good, and my skin is really soft, and we have had a lot of giggles. She looked miserable, so I gave her another drink. It was not long before the chat started, and as we all had a few drinks, Birch played her music on her phone, we gathered on two beds, and started to joke around.
My phone pinged; it was a message from mum. 'Balcony now, hurry.' I frowned as Birch leaned over and read it, I looked at her and shrugged. We got off the bed and wandered over, and opened the door and stepped out, I looked down to see Roni, Mum and Hatty, they were giggling like school girls. Hatty looked up.
"Catch!" She threw something yellow; Birch caught it. I looked at it confused.
"Why would she throw a washing line up here?"
Birch smiled, opened it and unravelled the plastic rope, and dropped one end over back to Hatty. Roni and Mum were both looking each way keeping look out and sniggering like naughty teenagers. Ellen was at the far end of the building waving to tell them to hurry. Hatty grabbed the rope and tied it around a bin bag, she looked up.
"We will be up in a minute."
Birch pulled quickly, and the three of them ran off laughing towards Ellen. I leaned over the rail as Birch pulled it up, it swung out and chinked, there was a bottle in there, before I grabbed it, I could smell it, and my mouth watered like crazy.
"Oh my God, is that chips?"
I grabbed it. and help lift it up, I don't think my mouth has ever

watered as much. We carried the bag into the room and carefully placed it on the table, everyone could smell the bag, and instantly gathered round. Birch undid the rope, and opened the bag, we all peered inside like it was golden treasure. Gill gave a happy sigh.

"Oh God, real food."

Birch reached in, as the excitement grew, and pulled out a rolled up paper, there was a group gasp of joy, and the smell just taunted us. She lined up all the rolls on the table, and put two bottles of gin, and four bottles of lemonade at their side. You could literally feel the energy level in the room lift. Birch looked up with excited eyes.

"Well, come on Sweetie's, grab one each."

I did not hesitate and picked one up and sat on the bed, and hurriedly unrolled it in my lap, I was starving. I grabbed a big fat chip, and slipped it into my mouth, it exploded with the tang of vinegar.

"Oh God, that is good, it is like an orgasm on my tongue." Edwina smirked.

"If that is what you think, you two are doing it wrong."

Giggles broke out. Mum arrived with her co-conspirators and gave a giggle as she walked in, and saw us all tucking in like starving orphans, I looked up and smiled.

"You guys are the best, and the maddest." Hatty smiled,

"And observant, I saw the chip shop and off licence, in that little village a mile down the road on the way in."

We stuffed ourselves on chips, drank gin, and laughed, and told funny stories, and actually we had a great night. We stuffed all the rubbish in the bin bag, weighted down with empty bottles, and let Bev launch it as far down the back of the building as possible, that way it would not be discovered under us.

Chloe sprayed the room down with deodorant to hide the chippy smell, and we collapsed into bed around midnight, drunk and happy, I lay back, and smiled at Deb's, she had been talking to Jimmy on the phone.

"Is he alright?" She smiled.

"Yeah, him and dad are doing fine, I left them plenty of bottles in the fridge."

I frowned, and then realised, she was breast feeding, she had gone to the lady's room a lot, and I worked out, the little bag she had, was to help her draw down the milk.

"Thanks Deb's, this must be hard for you, having such a little baby, I should have realised." She shook her head.

"I am fine Abby, I wanted to be here for you two."

Birch came over, and slid in at the side of me, it was a single bed, so there was not much room. I snuggled back into her, and she cupped my boob, and we settled down. In a slightly drunken haze, I slipped off to sleep.

Okay, so I love two things, coffee and bed, and it was eight am, and I was deprived of both, I looked at the woman behind the breakfast counter, and I was feeling very bloody grumpy.

"I don't want decaf, I want coffee, I am a writer, I live on it." Birch leaned into me.

"Sweetie, have the fake coffee, I have a survival kit in our room, I thought this might happen." I looked at the woman.

"Three cups." She frowned.

"Madam, it is usually only one." I gave a sigh.

"I will trade you a bowl of that sawdust she is eating, I don't eat, I drink?" She gave a sigh.

"You can have two."

I nodded, I bloody well hate healthy people, they are messed up. I got my coffees, which were minus anything significant for life, and headed to the table. I sipped what was pretty much brown piss, devoid of anything remotely enjoyable, and sulked.

Today was supposed to make me beautiful, so I had my eyebrows thinned out, and was given a facial, which was actually really nice. Chloe was disappointed, her idea of a facial was not what she got, my God, she is a slut.

Deb's needed the ladies room, and I followed, that coffee was not good and wanted to come out as fast as it had gone in. We walked along the stalls, Deb's pushed a stall door open and gave a squeak, and stepped back, I leaned around the door and instantly regretted it. A tall blonde girl stood with her arms outstretched, her eyes rolling back into her head, as the large tattooed frame of Bev squatted below her, munching away, like it was her last supper.

I leaned back on the thin wall between the two cubicles, feeling my stomach churn, I glanced at the horrified look on Deb's face.

"Avert your eyes, or it will curdle your milk."

I really needed to pee, but as sat there in the furthest cubical from Bev, listening to her slurping noises, nothing would flow, my river had been temporally dammed by trauma. Needless to say, I made a sharp exit and went looking for the rest of the group, I found Gill with Birch, she looked at me and frowned.

"Sweetie, you look pale, are you alright?" I was finding speech hard; Deb's walked up and looked at Birch.

"We found Bev, she got her meat, she was gnawing at a kebab in the ladies." I shuddered violently, and Birch pulled me close.

"Oh Sweetie, twice in one life time, you poor sweet beastie."

Next came the massage, now I must mention, I have never actually had one before. I had avoided meeting with Katie on our return to Uni, as it had been my time of the month, and I had bad cramps and a cold, so Birch had gone alone. Gill assured me, it was incredible, so I got a little excited. After the trauma of seeing Bev a second time, I knew I had a lot of stress to get worked out of me.

There was a room with fifteen tables in a row, why is everything here done in groups? We walked in, and there was a huge woman lay on her face, covered in oil, being rubbed all over by a woman with the smallest hands I have ever seen. I felt for her, I did, man she had her work cut out for her, she had a lot of area to cover.

I lay down, and was attended to straight away, Birch was at my side. The woman I got was oriental, and she was really sweet, she talked to me in broken English, I think. She told me how nice my skin was, and how she loved my hair, I lay face down watching Birch, I got aroused watching as the woman rubbed her thighs, and calves, which bothered me. My masseur chatted happily, and I rolled over and she smiled.

"You all same group, you want hair taken away?" I nodded; I hated shaving my legs.

"Yeah, that will be nice."

She smiled, and signalled to the other girls, and carried on rubbing my leg muscles, I closed my eyes and just relaxed, it was heavenly. She opened my legs a little and kneaded my inner thighs, and I just lost myself in thoughts, I felt so calm, although the oil was a little warmer than I expected.

I drifted away, until I came back to reality with a blood curdling scream. My eyes snapped open and I lifted my head.

"YOU FUCKING SPITEFUL BITCH, THAT COST ME THIRTY QUID!"

A small masseur was backing away from Bev, holding what looked like a sheet of paper filled with purple fluff. She dropped it, and ran away from the fuming Bev. I felt a jolt and looked down; the girl was looking at me very nervously. I realised what she was about to do, I took a deep breath, and lay back, and clenched my teeth then nodded.

The ripping noise is bad enough, the fire that shot up my vagina was worse, I started breathing like Deb's on her delivery night, Birch screwed up her eyes.

"Oh Sweetie, that looked very unsettling." I looked at her, and gasped through clenched teeth.

"No shit Doctor, see what I go through to have it smooth for you?"

The girl gestured for me to roll over, and being the absolutely frigging idiot I am, I did. I felt the warmth in my bum crack and suddenly realised, and started to panic. Birch squealed, and hid behind her hands.

"Oh Sweetie, no."

I gripped the table, there was a loud ripping sound, as my legs went stiff, and I pushed my face into the bed, Birch shrieked, and looked terrified. Chloe on the next bed chuckled.

"Wow Abby, that is a lot of hair, but yep, you are a true blonde." I was panting, it hurt like hell. Birch looked at me, shaking her head slowly, looking panicked.

"Please, don't make me do it Sweetie." I smiled.

"If am this freaking smooth, you better bloody had be when I get you in bed." She whimpered, I looked at the girl at my side.

"Do her next."

Birch covered her eyes and dithered on the bed. I have decided, all beauticians are secretly sadists. I lay back, as I remembered, the fuss she made over chopping onions, am I cruel, as I lie here waiting for the rip?

The rip was followed by a high pitched squeal, like that of a baby pig, which announced the event. I smiled as she shook her legs, and held her hands over her face.

"Fuck... Fuck... Fuck... Fuck!" I looked at her, and smiled.

"Roll over sweetie." She shook her head really fast, looking in pain and terrified, with tears in her eyes.

"Sweetie, I don't want to." I lifted my hand and twirled my finger, she whimpered, as I grinned an evil smile.

"Sweetie, I am scared, I don't like pain, please Sweetie, save me?"

I nodded to the girl, and Birch felt the hot warm wax, she grabbed the table and pushed her face into it, and wailed, before they even did anything. The rip was fast, and she kicked her legs up and down fast as she screamed into the bed. Chloe pissed her sides laughing.

When we walked out towards the spars, Birch walked slowly, with her toes pointed inwards. We entered the spar room and we saw Brandy sat in a whirlpool, she smiled.

"Oh ladies, looking nice and tidy, and radiant, I always say, clean is best, I cannot stand unclean or untidy, hygiene is everything. Clean, clean, clean, that is what I love." Birch stared at her with hate. She leaned into me and whispered.

"I am getting in the twiglets pool." I looked at her.

"What the hell for, there are two free over there?" Her eyes twinkled.

"I frigging hate her and her freaking weird ass eyebrows, and I really need a piss, and my hooch is burning like a God dam lava flow, so I am getting in with that bitch." I sniggered.

"Cool, I could use one, I am dying for a piss, let's go share our beauty with her." Birch gave an evil smile.

We slipped into the warm swirling water, and got comfy. Birch leaned back and smiled a big smile.

"Tell me Brandy, don't you worry people will piss in the pools?" She gave a frown.

"Well, I have never thought of it, why do you ask?"

Chloe walked down the corridor with Edwina, Gill, and Deb's, having been made hair free.

"I am sure I saw them come this way."

A little way down, the doors burst open, and Brandy came screaming out of the room, and ran naked and dripping down the corridor yelling.

"Filthy, disgusting, germs, it's perverse." Chloe nodded.

"Yep, that will be them."

Half an hour later, we were all dressed and stood in our room, looking at the floor, and trying not to laugh. Camilla looked very stern.

"This is no laughing matter, Brandy has been traumatised, she is very concerned about bodily germs, so, I am sorry, but I have no other choice but to ask you to leave." Chloe nudged me and I sniggered, and saw Birch shake.

We grabbed our things as we walked out in shame, closely followed by Hatty, Ellen Roni, Gill and mum, who were all openly giggling. We reached Petal, and Hatty smiled as she opened the door.

"That was ace fun girls, what are we doing next?" Birch looked around at us.

"Well, it's really early, and we are still on girl's time, so I say send out those text messages. The Hunters is open, and we still want our brides to be party, so we will meet there, and gather the women of Wotton." Chloe punched the air

"Fuck yeah... Where do I hire a stripper?"

Wotton was about to have its loudest Thursday night ever.

Chapter 35

Wedding Tears.

I woke around one, very hung over, Birch was still asleep. I raised my arm to my head, and covered my eyes.

"Oh God, kill me now."

Last night can only be described as the night the vagina party took over Wotton. We rolled into Wotton playing Avril full blast in Petal, having finished off Birch's survival kit on route. Deb's drove, and we sang and laughed, to find out Bev had the paper filled with her purple pubic hair.

Sat in the back, she pulled her pants down, to reveal two thin strips of purple down the insides of her thighs, and a long straight smooth bare patch down the centre.

"Look at that, it cost thirty fuckin quid, and they just left a quid's worth." And that is how our night began.

We invaded the Hunters, where Birch ordered a round on the house for everyone, and a free bar for all females in the celebration of our wedding to come. We took over the whole back room, loaded the juke box, and the party started.

Alex, Denise, Megan, and Samantha, arrived first, closely followed by Moon, and Izzy. Celia, Lillian, Stacy, and Louise turned up, as did Susana, and Pat from the practice. Mary from the post office, Angela from the bakery brought food, and even Amanda the florist showed up, and Gail. I called Anita, and Birch called Daisy, and a few random women we did not know, who the others texted arrived, and the place was packed with wild women, and the men vacated early.

Chloe managed to get a couple of strippers, I will never ask how, and they showed up to great cheers, it was the craziest night Wotton had ever seen. We spent three thousand quid on drinks and snacks, so it was worth it for Andrew Bosworth. This morning, scratch that, this afternoon, I want to die, although sex and freshly shaved vagina's I highly recommend, God, what a night.

I walked very slowly down the stairs, Chloe was sat with her head on the cold marble island surface, when I walked in, Edwina laughed, and put a coffee, and two pain killers in front of me. I forced a smile, but did not nod, and gave a sad sigh, Edwina shook her head.

"Bloody light weights, you let yourself go, you two used to lead the pack, and look at you now, it's pitiful?" I moved my eyes to look at her, it was less painful.

"Was it a dream or did we really do that?" Edwina poured another coffee for herself, and chuckled.

"Well Birch got Deb's so pissed, she turned her into a human milk pistol, that was funny as fuck, I filmed it." I groaned, and put my head on the cool island surface, I faced Chloe.

"You Okay?" She lifted a thumb. Movement was good, she was still alive, I was happy.

"Good chat." She lifted her thumb, I closed my eyes, and wished the paper was back up on the windows.

"Edwina, please tell me that was all we did?" Edwina chuckled.

"Hell no, that was just the start. Let's see now, Bev auctioned off her purple pubes and made fifty quid, the strippers got the best blow jobs they have ever had, not by you guys, but one of them was your mum, egged on by Roni and Hatty. Bev is still asleep in the wheelbarrow you brought her home in, at the front door. I have no idea even where you got that from?" I gave another groan; Edwina was enjoying this.

"The police were called by some moaning old woman, and they sent a female cop, it was her last call, so Moon talked her down, bought her a drink, got her pissed, and took her to bed on her barge. You and Birch had a smoothest vagina competition in the lady's toilet, and Gill was judge and very embarrassed, so Lillian and Celia presided, and they ended up having sex in a cubicle, with the door open, and Hatty was passed out on your mum's lawn when I last saw her."

"Oh Christ, please tell me that is it?" Edwina thought.

"Oh yeah, the other stripper was blown off by Gail, who got expert instruction from Chloe, oh, and Paula that nudist mate of yours, took one of the stripper's home, the other is still asleep in

Chloe's bed. And finally, Andrew Bosworth locked all the doors so we could continue, got pissed, and snogged a lot of the women, until he tried it with Birch, and she was a little bit sick in his mouth, which put him right off, I filmed that too, it was a riot. He did however end up taking a very drunk twenty seven year old to bed, so he was thrilled. I am telling you; it was the best hen night I have ever been too." Chloe turned her head, and looked at me with bleary eyes.

"I wondered who that was when I woke up, and why he was wearing a coppers helmet?"

I did not want to know any more, the newspaper headline flashed in my head, debauchery with writer, doctor, witch, and local vicar in Wotton. I wanted to die. I felt the warmth of Birch drape over my back.

"Sweetie, I was sick in the toilet." I tried to nod and failed.

"My head is exploding Baby, please don't shout."

It was a slow, dark glasses sort of day, and we had a wedding to organise tomorrow. It took a lot of coffee before I felt the slightest bit alive, and movement could be achieved. I unpacked my case; Luke was good enough to go to the Hunters, and collect Petal. Outside was noisy as G5 organised the Marquees and the chairs. And Terry handled the catering vans, as they set up at the side of the house.

Michael took Creamy over the road, to help my mum, who was not feeling at all well, and they organised the catering Marquees in mum's garden. The retreat was closed today, as was the gallery, but everywhere else in Wotton was open, and as I was not aware at the moment, all the women had sworn a pact of secrecy, and Andrew Boswell had got laid, and three grand in cash, for booze and food, so he was not saying anything either.

I looked at my case, and just packed what I needed, which was nothing clothing wise, because all my wedding clothing was at Bradley and Ellen's. Deb's texted me, she was not good, and Jimmy thought it was hilarious that Bradley had walked in with her hung over his shoulder, and then gone back for Ellen.

Ella was at her house getting organised, and would be here shortly. Everything was to be put in my room overnight, she had put locks on all the clothing bags, with a combination only she knew, just in case. The day appeared to whizz past, as I cleaned my room and organised my desk.

I spent an hour with Birch alone in her room, as it felt strange to know I would not be sleeping with her tonight. We were both recovering slowly, having drank plenty of coffee, and filtered water to rehydrate. I sat on the bed and took hold of her hand.

"I will really miss you tonight, promise you will video call with me?" She smiled, and her eyes shone brightly.

"I will, how could I not, I will be here alone thinking of you? Deads, this time tomorrow, we will be married, we will be together forever. I am trying to hide it, but I am so excited and happy, and I am a little bit nervous." I swallowed and took a breath.

"Me too, but not because I am marrying you, I just want everything to go well, I want our day to be perfect." She gave me a big smile.

"It will... We have come a long way together Deads, it has been quite the adventure, but tomorrow we start an even bigger one, a special one, just for you and me."

I pulled her into a hug, and held her tight, this felt like our last time together, and in a strange way it was, because after tomorrow, we would be different people, we will actually be an officially recognised married couple.

"Birch, you are the love of my life, I know it took me a long time to face it, but since the day I met you, I have been so happy. I love you so deeply and dearly, I want you to know that." She squeezed me tight.

"I know my dark little beastie, my Sweetie, my beautifully dark Deadly. I love you equally as much, and more, and I always will, my Lillian." I slipped back and smiled.

"I have to go; I will talk to you in a while." She nodded.

"See you Miss Watson." She gave a smile.

"I wanted to say it one last time."

I kissed her softly, and picked up my case. I stopped at the door and looked back at her sat on the bed, surrounded by the light of the window, and with her bright white hair, she looked like an angel, she was, she had saved me from the darkness.

"See you soon."

I walked out of the house with my case, and jumped in Bradley's car, the press were already there, and Morty and Bongo had them behind steel barriers. I noticed the no parking cones outside mum's and our house, as I looked back, and the cameras flashed. I was right, this event was going to be a big thing for the press, and I was glad Luke was in charge of security. He knew better than any, of the intrusions we had suffered. Edwina and Luke wore headsets as they communicated, and all G5 had ear pieces, they were like our own private secret service. Luke even had teams of security in the manor grounds to ensure no one tried to get above the fence.

Vans arrived all day at the house. Edwina's office, was a collection point, for parcels, and wedding gifts, which would be moved to the library later. Petal and Edwina's car were parked with Chloe's in the garage, which was locked, as it also had all the flowers in there to stay cool. People were everywhere setting things up, and on the gates of mum's and our house, there were two large security guards checking passes, and ID badges.

The large wide marquee in the garden had a hardwood floor, and millions of lights. The tables were laid out with long white table cloths, and seating decorated, as an army of waiting on staff, were supervised and watched by a vigilant Chloe, in paint covered dungarees and a vest. In my room, next to my desk, two travel cases were ready and packed, so we could grab them, and leave to fly off to our private villa in the Bahamas, and start our life together.

There really was little else for me to do, I had done everything. I just had to sit at Deb's and wait, which for me was not good, because I hate having to wait for anything, and I was suddenly really nervous. I arrived at Bradley's and was shown to my room, Chloe, and Anthony would be here later, as would dad and Angela, Deb's smiled as I sat on the bed feeling utterly lost.

"It's weird, isn't it?" I nodded, as she sat at my side and took my hand.

"You know, Abby, I did not think I would ever be able to say this, but I am so thrilled to be here at your side, the night before your wedding. I never thought you would ever marry, which just shows how very special Birch is."

"Deb's, I am terrified, and I have no idea why, because I really want this, but I am shitting myself." She giggled.

"Come over to my place and chill with Jimmy and the band, they are mucking about, but it will help calm you."

I nodded, I needed to get out of this room, there was no Birch in it, and I felt strange. Deb's took me downstairs, and across the yard to her complex, the band were in the studio strumming around. It was actually pretty fascinating to see them all back together again, Jimmy waved through the glass window. I smiled and waved back.

Deb's put the speaker on so I could hear them, a guy called Baz was working the console. Floyd was messing with a riff, trying to make it work, and Jimmy plugged in, and within a few minutes, they were playing a harmony, and nodding with smiles on their faces at each other. Zac got on his kit, and started to drum along, and then in came keys and bass, and Battered Taco were playing a brand new song, and I was blown away, it was awesome, and my nerves faded away.

Deb's ordered pizza and beer, and we all sat in the studio, eating and chatting, when Doug Collins looked at me.

"So, what tune have you picked to walk down the aisle to?" I gave a wide smile.

"I will be, by Avril. I love it, as it sort of tells the story of the ups and downs behind Birch and me." He nodded.

"I have seen pictures of you at school with Deb's, long blonde hair, blue eyes, black eye liner, yeah, it makes sense. Do you know the lyrics?" I nodded, he smiled.

"Well, we know the tune, we have covered a few of her tracks, in the early days. How about it guys, give her a mic, and let her pretend she is a rock star?" Jimmy grabbed my hand.

"Up here Abby girl, just stand here, and sing your little heart out, the place is sound proof so you won't frighten the neighbours." I panicked a little.

"Jimmy I am not that good." He smiled.

"Neither are we doll, but we sold a few albums. I hear you were a choir girl, so just think of your lady, and pretend she is here." Deb's stood at my side and handed me a beer.

"I will sing back up."

The guys got ready, and Jimmy counted them in, I closed my eyes and focused on the tune, and then imagined Birch was there. I could see her in my head, sat on the bed with the light behind her, and her hair illuminated like she had shimmering light flowing out of her.

I felt my feelings surge inside me, and I started to sing, as all my happy memories flooded into my thoughts. My mind filled with her sat on the bed at Uni, dancing naked in the woodland at the sun club, smiling as she sat at the window in the guest house, the light illuminating her bright white hair, and those gorgeous green eyes close to my face and filled with life. I felt my heart filled with love for her soar, as I sang my love out for her.

Floyd looked at Jimmy and smiled, and I felt happy as I thought of Birch, and our story together, and sang my heart out as if I was Avril, singing to Birch in the crowd. It was great fun, and I loved it, the tune faded out, and Jimmy winked. The band stopped and I felt really happy and warm inside. Baz looked at me from behind the window and gave me a thumbs up. Floyd turned to me.

"That was pretty amazing, you got good pipes Abby, you really surprised me, can we use it?" I frowned.

"How do you mean use it?" Jimmy winked.

"On the album, it was a bloody good take, and Deb's sounded great behind you, I am serious, we can use it?" I looked at Deb's, and she smiled and gave a nod.

"Abby, that was bloody brilliant." I felt a little panicked, I was not a vocalist.

"I am not sure, I am a writer, you guys are the band, I was just messing about." Baz came over the speaker.

"Let me mix it, and throw a couple of overdubs on it, and I will let you hear it back, I will even burn it to a CD if you want?"

I did not know what to say, but felt, I was not singing anything else tonight, these guys were serious professionals, and in a league of their own. Chloe and Anthony arrived, my dad had also arrived, so avoiding any coaxing for another song, I left the studio and I legged it quick, and went to see him.

I sat on his bed next to him, and we talked for a long time. It felt so different and wonderful, and I wondered why we could never have done this sooner, he took hold of my hand.

"How are you doing, nervous?" I nodded, and gave him a smile.

"I am a little, not because I am getting married, I really want that, but I just want it all to go smoothly."

"It will, just you watch... Abigail, I have been a shitty dad, and I regret that. I regret some of the things I have said, I really do. I just want you to be happy, to live as you choose and enjoy your life. We only get one, so don't waste it, make the most of every moment with Jemima, and thrive off it." I felt a tear run down my cheek.

"I am so happy you will be at my side, for a long time I thought you wouldn't be. It means something dad, it means something to me, and I am so happy you will be there, I don't care anymore about the past." He smiled and gave my hand a squeeze.

"Believe it or not, it means a great deal to me too, nothing will stop me walking down that aisle. I am so proud to stand at your side as your father. You have become an amazing woman, and exceeded every expectation I had for you. Abigail, I made a lot of mistakes, but never think I never loved you, I do, very deeply." I smiled as he squeezed my hand, and wiped my eyes, on my sleeve.

"I am sorry, I am really tired and very emotional, I think I am going to go to bed, I promised Birch I would talk to her." He leaned in and kissed my cheek.

"Go talk to her, you will feel better, then get a good night's sleep."

I gave him a hug, and kissed his cheek back, and walked to my room, feeling a little lost. I set up my laptop on the pillow, and slid into bed, right on time she called me, and I lay on my pillow with her at my side on screen. She was in bed too.

"Hi Sweetie, I am hugging your pillow, because it smells like you."

"I wish I had brought your pillow; I am missing you. I talked to dad and he sends his love." She yawned, and I yawned with her and smiled.

"You are sleepy Baby." She nodded and looked dreamy.

"I am not used to parties like that one anymore, I had a glass of wine, and I am even more sleepy now. I want to stay awake and talk though; it is lonely here without you to cuddle, but this is nice."

"I know, but I will be there tomorrow, and then we can sleep together every day for the rest of our lives... Birch.... Birch?"

I gave a sigh; she frigging fell asleep on me. I have never known anyone like her, I once sat on a bench with her feeding the pigeons, I am sure I have told you this before, but she actually fell asleep.

I lay back and watched her sleep, she is so beautiful, and although she was not here, I could see her, and that helped. I yawned; God I was so tired. I smiled as I watched her and my eyelids fluttered.

"Night Baby, I love you." My eyes flickered, and I closed them just for a second to rest them, and was gone.

Baz sat back as the track ended. Chloe stared at him.

"That was Abby, no shit?" He smiled.

"It certainly was." He looked at Jimmy.

"You would be fools not to use that, she is bloody good, and it's her, think about it. Battered Taco, featuring Abby Watson, I am telling you guys, that is a hit." Floyd shrugged.

"I love it, and think she did a great job, well better than bloody you Jim." Chloe burst out laughing.

"If you guys don't use that, you are mad, what do you think Deb's?" She turned, and Deb's was fast asleep in the chair. Baz pulled out a CD, and handed it Chloe.

"There you go, that is the first ever copy, you can have that for backing me up." He smiled at her, and she winked.

"Abby... Abby, I have coffee."

"What, Birch we have coffee." I blinked and saw Deb's, she smiled at me.

"It is your big day, I brought you breakfast in bed." I sat up and yawned.

"Where is everyone?" I looked around, not quite awake. She gave a little giggle.

"Anthony, your dad and Angela, are having breakfast with my mum and dad, and Chloe was lay naked on top of Baz when I took her coffee. Your mum and Ella are on their way." She hesitated.

"We do have one tiny little problem." I felt my heart lurch, suddenly, I was wide awake.

"Problem, what bloody problem?" Deb's gave a sigh.

"Birch made a circle." She handed me the phone. I panicked, and snatched the phone out of her hand, and held it to my ear.

"Birch, Baby?" It was not Birch, it was Roni, and she sounded stressed out.

"Abby, I need your help, she is sat on the bed surrounded by fucking thousands of tissues, sobbing her heart out, hugging a fucking big book, and telling everyone it's so ruddy beautiful, and I cannot console her. Her eyes look like pickles on forks, please help me?" I gave a sigh as I looked at Deb's.

"I wish I had never written that bleeding book." I held the phone back to my ear.

"Roni, give her the phone." I heard her try to coax Birch, and then heard her voice.

"Hi Sweetie, I love your words, I love you so much... hep... hep... hep." I gave a sigh and tried to calm down.

"Birch Baby... You have to put the book away for a while, otherwise you will miss your wedding, and I will be upset. Please Baby, give your mum the book. I am going to make myself the prettiest you have ever seen me; will you do the same for me?" She gave a loud snort.

"Okay Sweetie, I will try." I smiled.

"I am coming soon Birch; I love you Baby." She gave a huge sob.

"I love you too Deads, I will put the book away for now."

"Okay Baby, give the book and the phone to your mum now." I heard Roni as she gave a sigh of relief, Deb's leaned into the phone to listen.

"Thank you, Abby, I was at my wits end, what is this book anyhow?" Deb's and me screamed together.

"DON'T FUCKING READ IT!"

"Alright... Chill out girls, I am putting it in your room Abby." We both looked at each other and gave a sigh of relief, the call ended, and I flopped back on the pillows.

"I am not going to survive today."

My wedding day began after four very large cups of coffee. First up was Anthony, he smiled at me.

"Oh Abby Darling, I am choked up, never in my life have I wanted to do so much, to make you the most beautiful woman on the planet. Alas, I know, it will be hair down and fringe as always, my dreams have been cast into the waste bin of life." I sat in the chair and smiled.

"Have I ever told you how much I love you Anthony? Just for today, knock yourself out." His eyes opened wide, and he fanned himself with his hands.

"Do not toy with me Abby, I really want to do this, my heart could not take a jest." I giggled.

"Jesus Anthony, drop the drama, this is me, but please, make me look as beautiful as you can, I want Birch to see me at my best." He teared up, and his voice went squeaky, Deb's giggled.

"I cannot believe I get to style the holy grail; my life is complete." Deb's rolled her eyes.

"Drama much?"

I giggled, and Anthony looked at my hair, as he rested his hand on his cheek, and then went to work. He muttered as he swept my hair up, and back, leaving the fringe, and creating a little tuft of red at the back, above where he pinned my hair, he even had a pin with dark feathers and a little sparkling bat.

I sat for twenty minutes, as Deb's fed me coffee through a straw, Anthony smiled, and gave little squeaks of happiness, and as he finished, he reached into a small black box, and kept his hand there. He looked at me, and twitched, I frowned, he had not twitched around me in years.

"Abby... You have been so much to me in my life, my protector at school, a sister in the village, at times you have been like a wife or a mother. Oh, dear, I feel all emotional." He wafted his free hand in front of him, and twitched again.

"Abby, I love you so much, and I am so happy for you today, so I want to give you something, something special, and just for you. It is my heartfelt thanks for everything you have done for me."

I did not know what to say, I already felt so emotional, I hated seeing him upset. He lifted out an elegant choker, and stood behind me, and draped it round my neck, Deb's gave a gasp.

"This is special, I had it made just for you Abby, it is black cubic zirconia, and it is perfect for this hairstyle, and showing off the elegance of your neck."

I looked in the mirror, it was stunningly beautiful, almost like lace, and it sparkled as the light bounced off it, the tears filled my eyes.

"Oh Anthony, you have set me off."

The tears ran down my cheeks, he came around the front of me and crouched down as I cried, he was already crying.

"I love you so much Anthony, thank you, for always taking care of me, and my hair." He leaned in, and kissed me gently on the cheek, as he smiled, with tears in his eyes.

"I am not hugging you, that hair is too perfect. You are what I call a true beauty Abigail, because your beauty goes beyond the skin, and flows from your heart."

"Guys stop it you are worse than that bleeding book." Deb's wiped her red eyes, and tried to smile.

"Honestly, you two are killing me." We chuckled, and the door banged open, and Chloe staggered in, her hair was everywhere, Anthony freaked completely out, and stood up and pointed at her.

"WHAT THE HELL IS THAT THATCH?" Chloe scratched her head, and shrugged.

"I don't know, stop shouting my head is banging."

She looked up and pulled a knotted lump out in front of her, and smiled as if remembering something, she looked at Anthony.

"I think it is cum?" His arm stayed straight, and moved swiftly to point at the bathroom.

"YOU SLUT, GET IT FUCKING WASHED NOW!" She smiled, and walked towards the bathroom.

"Just because you have never done it, jealous much?"

I wiped my eyes, next was makeup. Anthony had found me yet another makeup artist, Birch and I had a bit of a reputation for being difficult. I sat in the chair with yet another coffee, and opened my phone.

"Birch does my eyes in dark red, and I love it, but I can never get it right myself, she really loves it like this, can you do that?" I showed her the picture on the phone. She was called April, and was really sweet, she looked at it, and smiled.

"I can do way better than that, trust me, if that is what she likes, that is what I will give, but with a lot more pop, you have amazing eyes, so let's really see them. This stuff is water proof, so tears are fine." She smiled at me, as she worked.

"I have got to say Abby, I have seen your face a lot in the media, and I have wanted a crack at these eyes for a long time, I was thrilled when Antonio asked me to do it. I will leave you a card, so if you need me again, I will be available."

It is strange how fame has its effects, and how everyone sees me differently, I think that is why I have such a small group around me, they are in a sense my normal people, and through them I stay grounded, and just me.

April finished, after twenty minutes of matching shades, and I was stunned, wow, my eyes looked incredible, Chloe sat rubbing her hair with a towel.

"Fuck Abby, I am straight, and I think even I am a little bit wet." She looked down.

"Nope, that is Baz, fuck!" Anthony shuddered, as he did Deb's hair.

"Chloe darling, I love you, but your sluttery has no end."

I loved my eyes, they looked so amazing as I looked at them closely in the mirror, that was the true dark little beastie she loved. I thanked April, and took her card, and slipped it in my phone case. Anita arrived with a smile.

"Wow, I really love the hair and eyes, are you ready for today?" I took a deep breath; my heart was beating faster than normal.

"Yes, I am ready, nervous as hell, but I am ready." She took my hand, and led me outside into the hall, where two people stood waiting.

"These are the people from Fashion Voice. There are two with Birch now, this is Francesca and Benito, they are from the Italian office, and will be the ones writing the full length feature up."

I looked at them both, and took their hands and shook them. Both of them were tall, dark complexioned, and very feminine and masculine, I thought they made a nice couple. They introduced themselves, and then followed me to the fitting room. Francesca spoke very good English, Benito was a little broken, but fluent enough to understand him. He had a black bag on his shoulder, and two cameras hanging from his neck.

I explained how I had not seen my dress yet, and neither had Birch, as we both had worked with Ella, and designed something we thought fitted each others personality, and had been blindfolded during the fitting. She pulled out a voice recorder as I spoke and recorded everything I said, as she asked me questions.

I told them about Ella, and how I felt she was going to be a new star of fashion, and how I adored her designs. I wanted to plug her as much as possible. When we reached the room, Ella was waiting outside, she looked beautiful, in a black dress, which was stylish and creative, she had dark red accents on it which I loved. I looked at the reporters.

"Would you like to go in, I just want a quick word in private with Ella?" They nodded and went in, and I smiled at Ella.

"I just want a moment, to say a huge thank you. Those people are from Fashion Voice Magazine, they will be doing an exclusive on the wedding, and I have plugged you the best I can. Talk to them, they are paying a lot of money for this feature, as no one else will have pictures of the dress until they print." I looked at Anita and smiled.

"You tell her, this is your work." Anita gave a happy giggle, she looked at Ella.

"Fashion Voice are paying us three million for this exclusive. I get my cut, and obviously so do the Dixon Group, and Abby and Jemi, have decided that the rest of the payment should be split three ways, there will be about seven hundred thousand each. They feel it will set you up properly, and you deserve it for all you have done." Ella gasped, and then swallowed hard, she looked at me and her eyes filled with tears.

"I don't know what to say, I cannot believe your kindness, it is just too much, Abby I am happy with the pictures." I smiled at her.

"Oh, please don't cry, I am as emotional as hell already. Ella, you deserve this, you are so good, you have no idea of your talent. This will give you better equipment, more people, and a better chance of making it. Ella, we do not need all the money, we are doing really well, I want you to last, I will be ordering more stuff." She wiped her eyes, and shook her head.

"You guys just blow me away, you know when Hailee told me to work with you, I had no idea my life would change so much, I am the one that should be thanking you." I could feel my excitement building and I giggled.

"Come on, I want to finally see my dress." She gave a small giggle. I took her hand and we walked into the room, as she dried her eyes.

Birch jumped up and down and waved her hands.

"I want to see, I want to see, hurry, I cannot wait anymore…. I want to pee, hold up."

She ran into the bathroom, as Alice and Carol giggled, and Roni shook her head in disbelief. Alice waited, the toilet flushed, and Birch came hurtling back in, and stood jigging on the spot. Alice pulled down the zip on the dress bag.

The front of the bag fell away, and Birch gasped as the shock hit her, Roni smiled as she watched Birch walk up to it, and carefully reach out and touched it. She softly ran her hand down the fabric, and as she touched the sequins, they sparkled casting rainbows on her hand. Her voice was quiet, and soft, as she stared at the dress in awe, her head turned to her mother.

"It's a snow queen, she made me a snow queen. Mum, she really loves me." Her eyes filled with tears.

Deb's handed me the phone; it was Roni.

"Abby, first the book, and now the fucking dress, she is on the bed bawling her brains out, and I cannot console her. You need to fucking sort her out, or it will be midnight before we are ready. Does your mum want to swap, because I can fucking deal with you?" I gave a sigh, and waited until I heard her sobbing.

"Baby, you need to get your dress on, time is ticking, and you have to be ready for me at four." She gave a massive sob.

"Deads, it's the Snow Queen, you really love me, Bwa Waa Haa!"

"Baby please don't cry, it makes me sad, and I don't want to be sad on my wedding day. Please stop, and go put your dress on, I want to see you sparkle like rainbows in it." She stopped crying.

"I love rainbows." I smiled.

"I know Baby, when you spin in that dress, you will light up the room with rainbows, go on, try it on and see."

"I want to make rainbows Deads."

"Put the dress on Baby, and look at them all."

"Okay... Bye...." I giggled.

"Roni has not got a clue."

Deb's sniggered. Ella gave a sigh, and walked over to the dress bag. She looked back and smiled, and then pulled the zip down, and the front of the bag fell off, and I saw it for the first time. I felt the air run out of me, I turned and looked at my mum.

"It's stunning. It's the dark little beastie." My eyes filled with tears.

Mum sat on the bed and held my hand, as Deb's handed me another tissue.

"Mum, she really loves me, I mean, look at it, it is gothic vampire, Victorian, and so feminine, it is everything and perfect. Bwa Waa Haa!" Deb's sat down with a thump.

"I seldom swear Felicity, but fucking hell, this day is just getting harder and fucking harder!"

Chapter 36

Abigail's Wedding.

Both of us were finally ready, Birch was very dizzy, and had to be held up by Edwina and Gill, as Roni sniggered. Seeing Deb's, Chloe and Anthony in their clothes had me in tears again. Oh God, it has been so emotional and traumatic, I felt exhausted, and the wedding had not even started. I took a deep breath, flanked by Chloe and Deb's. My dad and Anthony were waiting downstairs, with Mum, Ellen and Angela.

Chloe and Deb's went first, to flashes from the camera, and Ella made me wait, she gave the nod, and Anita smiled at me, I felt nervous and a little shy. I looked at my bracelet and turned it over, and read her name on the back of it, and smiled. I walked to the top of the staircase, and stopped as I had been instructed to, and I looked down and smiled. The camera flashed.

"Dad, do I look alright?" He looked up at me and smiled, and his eyes filled with tears.

"Perfect Abigail, simply perfect and so incredibly beautiful."

I smiled, Anthony blew his nose and sounded like a trumpet. I stepped onto the stairs, and walked down slowly; I was terrified of falling. The camera flashed and it felt like I was royalty, it was such an odd feeling. Anita and Ella followed holding the long flowing back up slightly.

My dad wiped his eyes, Anthony and Deb's were bawling their brains out. Deb's wiped her eyes.

"I am sorry, I am trying not to." She blew her nose; it was not attractive.

Dad took my arm with a large proud smile. Mum, Ellen and Angela patted their eyes, and I walked towards the door sniffling. Deb's guided the back of my dress, which was really full, and pulled me back a little it was so heavy. Bradley and Anthony held the doors open, and I stepped out into the bright sunlight.

By the limo stood Markus, he looked at me and smiled, I was so delighted to see him.

"Markus, I am really happy it is you." He gave a big smile, and opened the door.

"I wanted the honour of driving Miss Abigail Jennifer Watson one more time, tomorrow you will be Mrs Dixon I believe?" I gave a big smile and nodded.

"I will... Markus, thank you, you are my most favourite person in the world to drive me." Anthony smirked.

"Well, that is hardly surprising, we have all seen how your future wife drives."

Markus looked amazing, he was wearing his chauffeurs' hat, and had on white gloves, and the limo had long white ribbons on the front, and I noticed, there were bows on the doors, that were the same red as my dress. He opened the door with a smile.

Getting in wearing such a long dress was not easy. Ella organised me, and straightened the dress, and my dad got in, and sat at my side. Behind me was a line of black cars, that all the others got in. Markus sat in his seat, and smiled, and the car started, and suddenly I felt really nervous, as we followed the other cars out of Bradleys complex, and onto Waterside Lane.

"Dad, I am shaking, I think I am terrified." He took my hand and gave it a squeeze.

"Good, that proves you made the right choice."

Birch stood at the top of the stairs and gave a twirl, she staggered, and Edwina and Gill snatched her quickly. The cameras flashed and her dress sparkled.

"Dad, I make rainbows." He stood at the bottom of the stairs, and swallowed hard, Roni smiled as she watched him.

"Oh God, Jemi... You look like an angel." She gave a big smile.

"I am not wearing knickers, can you tell?" Roni chuckled, and Will gave a big smile.

"I think you might just get away with it at a pinch." She smiled.

"Dad, I really love you, and you too mum, I am getting married, SURPRISE!"

She threw her arms in the air, and Will smiled, the love in his eyes was unlimited, and Roni loved seeing it, and lifted her tissue to her eyes.

It was only a short drive, but it felt like forever, as the other cars entered the drive and emptied out, and Markus held back a little waiting for the all clear. Outside the house the road was closed, and security stood in a row as hundreds of cameras pointed at the car. The metal railings ran all the way along mum's front wall, and across the road which was blocked off for my arrival, it was packed with press. The flashes exploded as we approached, even I was amazed at how many there were. Dad gave a sigh.

"Bloody blood sucking vampires, sorry no disrespect to your books, but they are. They call you, and humiliate you, and now look at them, fighting for scraps, I hate what they do to you."

I was really surprised, and yet so happy he felt that way, I had never really thought he had cared that much. I smiled.

"I love you dad."

He looked so much older, but his smile was young and full of life. The car swung in through the gates, and I felt my heart beat quicken, I swallowed hard as we pulled up outside the door. A large frame had been erected covered in black cloth, to screen the whole of the porch and doorway from view, I smiled, the press would get nothing, God I loved G5 they were amazing.

It took a few minutes to get out, and we headed into the library, where last minute adjustments were made, and we all got our flowers. I held mine close, they were red with green and white mixed in, and tied with a beautiful bow. They vibrated as my hands shook, Deb's was close and attentive, she took my hands and pressed hers against them to stop the flowers shaking. She smiled and spoke quietly to me.

"You will be wonderful." I nodded, and tried to breathe.

Outside in the back, people had been arriving for over an hour. Everyone was dressed in their best, and there were two hundred guests. Madge and Milton looked around the garden, it had changed a great deal since Gwenda had owned it, and Madge felt it was actually quite stylish.

Peter and Mary, sat with the naturists club, all dressed of course. Celia and Lillian were up front with Bev, and the blonde girl from the spar. The band, the Peter's from the bakery,

Amanda who had done all the flowers, the Jessops, and Norman and Daisy and their children, and everyone from the retreat, as well as all the people I have worked with on the road, or at the Curio events, the garden was packed.

The library doors were closed, as we prepared to take our positions. Across the hall in the living room, Birch amused herself, twisting her hips, making little rainbows on the carpet. At the arch, Moon had set up a little altar, and stood with Gail, as they prepared. Bongo, dressed in a black suit, tested the boom mic, which hung above them, and was relayed into the speakers so everyone could hear clearly, and it was almost time.

Mum, Roni, and Angela sat in their seats, with Ella, Anita and my cousin with her husband, and turned to smile at everyone, and Bongo pressed his ear piece on his head set.

"Luke, we are good to go."

In the kitchen, Luke gave a nod, and Samantha in her head set, walked up the hall, and opened the door to the living room. Birch stopped mid twist and looked up with a smile, she looked stunning. Samantha opened the doors wide.

"It is time Jemi."

The way it had been set up by Edwina, we would both take up our positions, on the ends of the large marquee out of sight. The chairs were placed in a huge semi circle around the arch, in the centre of which was a triangle of seats, that marked an open aisle where we would each walk, and slowly come together. There was a thin corridor down the centre, in which Deb's would carry a besom, or broom, which had been decorated by Moon.

Deb's also had the rings, she would walk to the front, and as she reached the halfway point, Birch and myself, would walk out from the ends of the marquee, and come together at the arch. White curtains hung across from the end of the Marquee, to shield both Birch and myself from view, until the last second. Samantha led Birch and her party to her place, where Terry was waiting, and he pulled another curtain behind them to ensure Birch did not see me, until I walked out. Birch stood taking deep breaths.

"Dad, hold my hand, I am shaking like a leaf."

When the Library door opened, my heart almost stopped, Dad

smiled, as he offered his arm.

"Could I have the pleasure, Miss Watson?" It made me feel calmer, and I took a deep breath. Chloe stood in front of me and looked back.

"Don't sweat it Abby, this is meant to be, but just so you know, if you try running, I will drag you by your hair to that altar if I have to." She winked.

"I am straight, and even I fancy you a little bit today."

"Wow Chloe, such high praise, and I think I just got really wet for you." She shuddered.

"Oh God, I am so straight Abby, you have no idea how straight I am." I giggled and she gave me one of her huge big smiles, God, I loved her, she was wonderful. Samantha looked at me, and gave a big smile.

"It is time Abby, follow me."

It was happening, it was finally happening, I am not sure I ever thought it would. Holding my dad's arm, I walked through to the kitchen, where Luke stood smiling.

"Wow, you look stunning, if I was not with Edwina... I."

"You would be with Chloe... I have always been Birch's girl." He gave a chuckle.

"That you have, which is why men for miles are heartbroken today." He raised his arm to the patio doors.

"If you would care to follow me, Miss Watson?"

I took a huge breath, and stepped out onto the patio, in the marquee there was a lot of activity, Deb's gave a nod, carrying the broom, with a black velvet bag on her wrist.

"See you up there, I will be waiting... Oh God Abby, I think I am going to bawl my brains out, I love you so much."

She stepped into the marquee and made her way to the middle and the centre corridor through the seats. I took a deep breath, trying not to burst into tears, and walked with dad, Chloe and Anthony to my waiting position. I swallowed hard and felt my heart beating really fast, Chloe turned, and looked at me.

"If you need tissues, Anthony has them, but grab them quick, he is going through them faster than a book reader." I giggled, and she winked. Luke gave a nod and talked into his mic.

"We are set and ready. Sam prepare Deb's, Terry stand by, and cue music."

The music began, I will be, by Avril Lavigne, or was it? Chloe sniggered in front of me.

"Baz did a great remix." I gasped, she sniggered.

"You sound great." I was shocked, Birch stopped fidgeting.

"That's Deads!" She gave a massive smile.

"Deads is singing to me Dad, I love this tune."

Deb's walked slowly, holding the broom, like a guard of honour. Luke pulled a string and the curtain opened, and I saw the garden for the first time and it was packed. Birch panicked.

"Dad there are too many, I will pee." He pattered her hand.

"It's alright darling, we are on grass, and you are not wearing knickers, go for it, no one will know." Luke watched Deb's; he spoke to Terry.

"And we go on three... two... one."

He stepped back, and Anthony and Chloe, side by side stepped out, as across the other side, Edwina and Gill stepped out smiling. I thought I was going to have a heart attack. Luke nodded, and Dad patted my hand.

"Let's go and get her."

I took my first step, and walked out into full view, there were gasps as people watched and smiled, I looked across and saw her, we were level and walking together, and she looked unbelievably beautiful, I felt butterflies in my tummy and smiled at her. She gave a big smile and gave a quick wave, all those watching her turned and looked across at me.

The music played, and it was my voice singing the story of how we came together, and I felt a huge lump in my throat. Birch got closer and closer, and I could see her dress flashing with tiny rainbows, I felt so unbelievably happy. Deb's stood in the centre, in front of my arch, holding the broom as we passed, and Chloe and Anthony stepped to one side and stood back, as I came face to face with Birch, she gave me a huge smile.

"Hi Sweetie." Her voice came out of the speaker, and she jumped.

"Jesus, that is loud, it scared me... Oops... Shit!" I giggled, and everyone laughed. We turned to face Gail, who was all smiles.

"You two look stunning."

Behind us Deb's laid the broom on the floor, and moved into her position. Gail looked around at everyone. I glanced at the side towards Birch, God, she looked so unbelievably beautiful, her dress sparkled and cast rainbows everywhere. She noticed me looking, and smiled a shy smile. Gail held her prayer book.

"Today we gather, to join two very special and wonderful people, and I am delighted to be able to share in this privilege. We also share in faiths with my good friend, Raven Moon, who is a Wiccan of high standing in her faith. It is refreshing to see, another wonderful tradition established in our village, that has embraced two faiths and a greater understanding of the many kinds of love that exist in this world. I am truly honoured to be here."

I knew her bishop had outright refused the church for us to marry in, and that she had argued on our behalf, but I was glad to see her here, with her rainbow coloured stole round her neck, and hanging down in front of her. She looked at us and her eyes were sparkling with happiness.

"Abigail, Jemima. Who gives you away on this day?" Will took Birch's hand, and my dad took mine. Both of them lifted them, and placed them together, and Birch's hand rested on mine, it felt warm, and soft.

"We do." My dad gave me a huge smile, and I felt so happy, as I smiled at him, he had no idea of how much this meant, just to have him do this for me.

Gail gave a nod, and they both took a step back, bowed, turned and walked to their seats, and I stood looking into her dancing green eyes, and smiled, her hand trembled. Gail stepped back.

"Priestess Moon, if you please."

Moon was dressed in all white, and had pale blues stars and moons all over her robes, she had her hood up, and her long curly hair hung out of it, she smiled at both of us as she lifted a ribbon of red, black, green and white, and wrapped it around our joined hands.

"My children, I bring you together as one, and I bind thee with life and love, here in the temple of nature where all can see. As one with this earth, bind yourselves to each other, honour each other, bless each other, and join as one, so you may be united in this real world, and all others. Take the spirits of your line, and weave them as I have the ribbon that connects you."

I took a huge breath as I watched Birch silently say the words, I did not even know she knew them. My body was filled with emotion. Deb's and Anthony were already weeping, and it was getting me going. Moon smiled, and stepped back, and Gail came forward, and looked at me, she smiled.

"Abigail Jennifer Watson, will you take this woman, Jemima Dixon, to be your wife. Will you honour her, love her, cherish her in all you do, and remain at her side as her life long companion?" I looked in those eyes, those bright green beautiful eyes, and I felt the tears fill mine, and I smiled, I gave a gasp.

"I will, yes." Birch smiled, and her eyes filled up.

"Oh Sweetie, you are setting me off." Everyone laughed in their seats, Gail gave a titter.

"Jemima Dixon, will you take this woman, Abigail Jennifer Watson, to be your wife. Will you honour her, love her, cherish her in all you do, and remain at her side as her life long companion?" She gave a sniffle, and her eyes intensified.

"Oh yes, I most definitely will." I giggled.

"Stick to the script Baby." She gave a giggle, and there were chuckles behind me. Moon came up at the side of Gail.

"May we have the rings please?"

Deb's wiped her eyes, and stepped up, she handed one to Chloe, and one to Edwina, both of them stepped forward with their palms flat. I smiled at Chloe, she had tears in her eyes, and I looked down at the golden band. Gail nodded.

"Abigail, your vow please." I felt my knees shaking, as I took the ring. I looked at her as I placed the ring on the top of her finger.

"Jemi, Birch, My Snow Queen. I am yours; I think I always have been. From the moment I met you, I have lived in your wonder. I have never met anyone so filled with love and life, and I love you so deeply, I cannot find the words to fully and adequately express it. I want you with me always, I want you at my side no matter how bad or how good it gets, I promise here, before all the people we love that I will never leave you, I will always be yours." I slid on the ring, and leaned in and whispered. "My Celia forever."

Birch smiled, as her tears streamed down her face, Chloe handed her a tissue, and stepped back. Birch wiped her eyes, and looked at the ring on her finger. Moon gave her a moment, and then touched her shoulder.

"Jemima my child, make your commitment to Abigail."

Birch nodded; I was doing my best to keep breathing. I felt so hot, as everyone watched. Birch lifted the ring and looked at me as she slipped it just on the tip of my finger.

"Sweetie, I have forgotten what I was going to say, I got so excited and overwhelmed, so I am going to make something up. Is that alright?" Everyone started to laugh, I giggled.

"Go for it." She gave me a huge grin.

"Deads... Abigail, Sweetie, my dark little beastie, I really love those eyes by the way." I snorted, and laughed, everyone in the seats laughed with us. She took a deep breath.

"Oh Abby, I love you, I really do, I love our life, I love who you are, especially that quiet shy side not many see. I love that I am the one who sees it the most. I love talking to you, and you know, the other things we do." I smiled.

"I want you so badly, I want us to never be apart, last night was torture. I want to wake every day at your side, and curl against you every night, I want you and only you, because you are so special and unique, and If I could not have you, I would stay alone. Please stay with me always, never leave me, and if you can do that, I will love you deeper every day for the rest of my life and beyond." She looked at Moon.

"Is that good enough or do we need more?" Moon smiled.

"That was perfect." She turned and smiled.

"I love you Deadly, I always will." She slid the ring down my finger, and whispered very quietly. "My Lillian." Moon smiled, and looked out into the rows of guests.

"You have heard their vows, and so I say unto you, the world, and all the spirits that have walked before us, embrace them, and take them as one into your hearts, and into your lives, for they are now one, bound in their love, and the joining of tribes." Moon stepped back, and gave us both a big smile. Gail came forward.

"This union is sacred in the eyes of the law, and in the eyes of your god. And we have seen here this day, your commitment spoken before your witnesses. Through this union, we bless you, and all surrounding you. Priestess Moon if you would prepare, please."

Moon came back, reached in and took one end of the ribbon in her hand, Gail looked at us.

"What we have brought together, let no other try to separate, as we both pronounce you to be married as wife and wife."

Moon pulled, and the ribbon shot around my wrist and came free. She handed the ribbon to Birch. We both turned to face the guests, and Gail spoke up loudly.

"And now the blessing." Birch slid her hand into mine, and I gave it a squeeze. Moon raised her arms behind us, and her voiced echoed all around the garden.

"May the nourishment of the earth be yours. May the clarity of light be yours.

May the fluency of the ocean be yours. May the protection of the ancestors be yours. Go in peace, love, and light, with eternal blessings."

Gail tapped our shoulders.

"You may kiss, and jump over the broom stick, congratulations you are now officially married."

Birch spun around and grabbed me, and pulled me into a long kiss, and oh God, I really needed that. Flashes exploded everywhere, as everyone rose up in their seats and applauded, I was so happy, I just wanted to laugh and scream and dance. Birch was all over the place dancing on the spot, she grabbed my hand.

"Are you ready, one... Two.... Three."

I grabbed my dress, and with her hand in mine, jumped the best I could, and we just about made it laughing wildly over the broomstick. I pulled her round to me and hugged her as hard as I could, behind us Luke and Terry carried a table under the arch, and the county court official placed a large book on it.

We were far too excited, as Deb's hugged us and Chloe dived in with Gill and Edwina, and Anthony pulled me into his arms.

"I have never kissed a girl, but it is customary to kiss the bride." He gave me a very soft kiss on the lips, and pulled out with a smile, I raised my eyebrows, and he gave a chuckle.

"Trust me, that is most definitely my first, and last."

God, I love him so much. Mum and dad appeared and dragged me in the their arms, and they squeezed me so hard I could hardly breathe. Just as they released me Roni snatched me into her arms, with tears in her eyes.

"Oh Abby, I have never been happier." I was fighting back my own tears as she stepped back, and Will lunged in and pulled me into his embrace.

"Never in my life have I felt such a deep privilege as this moment, where I can welcome you in to my family Abby, I am so delightfully happy."

He stood back and smiled as Birch took my hand, and he was just lost in the moment as we stood side by side, and found himself unable to speak. I smiled at him, and he just smiled at us both with his eyes filled with such love, it was a perfect moment, and one I will never forget.

Next comes the boring bit. We had to sit and sign the register, and then pose for pictures, which involved being dragged into all areas of the garden, to stand with family and friends for endless shots. I even had a shot taken with my cousin and her husband, who dad had flown over from the states. All I wanted to do was hug Birch, and grab a drink, I was parched.

The best part was when all the Curio's stood under the arch, with huge smiles, and yet again we had another picture taken of us all together.

It felt like it took forever, the garden was roasting under the first real day of sunshine in over a week. We finally got to walk down the central aisle together, surrounded by happy smiling people, and we made it to the table in the marquee, and were sat side by side as everyone trooped in. It had taken over an hour of hugs and pictures, and I was utterly knackered. It was hot, and the dress was heavy, but I had a bottle of white wine under the table, I knew Birch hated champagne, so I filled our glasses and we chinked to us.

In front of us, to one side, was a huge cake, half white with green Birch leaves, and half black, decorated with deep red roses, and a few tiny little bats, I really loved it, this was all Deb's work, and it was perfect.

Once everyone was seated, I got a chance to relax and take it all in. I could not fault Chloe, she had played a huge role in setting up, and organising the marquee, and it was beautiful. The tables were laid out impeccably, and had tall vases of flowers, which would be donated to the hospital and the care home afterwards. The ceilings were filled with small twinkling lights, and little bats and snowflakes, it just looked so amazing, and I found it overwhelming.

Masses of waiters and waitresses descended, and food was served, which was a full roast beef dinner. Wine flowed, as each course was delivered, and by the time we were served, I wished my dress was a slacker fit. Birch leaned into me and we giggled and laughed, and I was so unbelievably happy, I have never in all my life felt this amazingly wonderful, as I looked at my finger, and the ring, this was without doubt, the happiest day of my life.

With the meal finally over, as the staff cleared away all our plates. Anthony stood up, and with smiles, and a few tears, he read out all the letters and emails of congratulations. His humour was wonderful as we laughed and giggled, and he looked at both of us as we snuggled together, with such strong love in his eyes. He wiped his eyes as he finished, and raised a glass to us and took a sip, then sat down. I love him so much, he was there for me at my loneliest time, and I will never forget that.

Will stood and tapped his glass, he looked around the room for silence.

"Ladies and gentlemen. I am sure all of you agree, when Jemi and Abby, decided to marry each other, it posed the problem of who gives the speeches, and so after a little chat from the parents, we decided that we would share the task, as technically father of both brides now, I shall present a speech, and then as mother of both brides, Felicity will present one." I leaned into Birch as we giggled at dad. Will looked around the room.

"I just want to say how lucky Edwin and myself are, because both of us thought our daughters would never marry." Everyone giggled.

"They are both so unique and special, I am sure all of you know that. When I first met Abby, I thought what a kind caring and such a calm girl, I did think, what the hell is she doing with my daughter?" Everyone chuckled.

"I did hope she would calm Jemi down, but sadly, Abby is secretly as bonkers." I giggled and grabbed Birch's hand.

"In all seriousness, she is simply perfect as a match, they meld together in such a way, that they enhance each other, and what flows out, is a form of beauty and love, that has left me breathless at times, as I stood in awe of both of them. They certainly are a force to be reckoned with, especially when they put their heads together, and I cannot deny, as parents, all four of us are so proud of their work with the Curio Life project. I am exceptionally happy today to welcome Abby into our family, and all I want is to see her and Jemi live a long, happy, and wonderful life together. Ladies and gentlemen, please raise your glasses to two kind, caring and very deserving people. To Abby and Jemi."

It is so weird to see two hundred people raise a glass, and say your name in unison, we snuggled together and giggled.

"Sweetie, this is really freaking weird, they are talking about us."

"I know, how screwed up is this?" She giggled, as my mum got up and looked at us both.

"I am very emotional today, because I did not lose a daughter, I gained another one, she is not like us, but she is so lovely." I gave a snort of a laugh and looked at Birch.

"It's true, Baby, you are as weird as hell." Everyone was laughing. Mum looked at us.

"I am, and I know Roni is also, so thrilled and so proud, Jemi, or Birch as I know her is a beautiful girl, oh Birch you have no idea how happy I am to know you are with my Abby, she really loves you so deeply, I am so really happy. I know you two have had your tests, and boy have you faced such discrimination, but you know what, you two are a shining example for all of us? Your love is how all of us should love. Ladies and gentlemen, I am so proud of my daughters, please wish them well together."

I felt my eyes tear up, as I looked at my mum, and saw Roni smile and raise her glass, everyone toasted us, and all I could do was snuggle into Birch. Deb's stood up, and giggled.

"I have never given a speech, but we all talked, and I got the short straw, because Edwina would bang on for hours, Chloe cannot be trusted with our secrets, and Anthony would just bawl like an idiot."

I laughed; she was so right. She turned and looked at us, I loved her so much, she was my oldest and best friend, she gave us both such a loving smile.

"Oh guys, what can I say? You two just came back into our lives, and you changed them forever, with your crazy kindness and love. All of us owe you so much, how can we ever repay you? We all wished for such a long time you two would get together, and just when we had all given up, you saw what we have always seen, you guys love each other in a way that puts all of us to shame. I never thought today would happen, but oh, I am so glad it finally has. I think all the Curio's will join me in agreeing, you two have taught us how to live, how to love, how to fight, and stand together, but most importantly, you taught us how to fuck."

She screamed with laughter, and held her glass up, as the room gave a gasp, she looked at Edwina, and giggled.

"Edwina, that will teach you for shoving me up here." The Curio's all stood up and held up their glasses, and shouted out.

"We fight, we stand, we live, and we love together."

I stood up with Birch and lifted my glass, and saluted them all, and took a drink. They banged on the table.

"SPEECH!"

I shook my head, Birch dropped down and tried to hide, and they banged even harder on the table. I felt panicked and looked down at Birch, she was slipping down in her seat. I gave a sigh, and nodded at them, they stopped banging, Birch grabbed my hand, and gave it a squeeze.

"Well, I am up now... You guys know I hate this, but I will get revenge." They all giggled at me, I looked around at everyone, my legs shook like crazy.

"I went to Uni, and I shared a room with this loony, but she was so cute with it, how could I not end up falling in love with her? To be honest, both of us fought this for a long time, and four years ago we finally stopped fighting it, I mean, how can you go against nature? In this room is a lot of people, and all of you have loved us, or hated us, or just been captivated. I really do not know what to say. Today two hundred people came to share this with us, and that has made us both so very happy. But the one thing I do really want to say, is that Birch and I have been blessed by knowing a really special group of people, all of them are so very precious, and special, and creative, you call them Curio's, but we call them family. They really are our brothers and sisters, and just look what they have done for us, because this is all their doing. We are so lucky, because we start a new life today, and just look at the support we have. Guys, you have no idea how much we love you; you are our rock, you are the reason we made it. Thanks." I lifted my glass.

"FAMILY!"

Everyone raised their glasses as I looked at each of them in turn, and smiled. Birch stood and saluted each of them. Chloe shouted out.

"CAKE!"

Roni stood up, and handed me a long silver knife, I looked at Birch as she stood up, and we moved to the cake, and she snuggled in. The photographers came up close and zoomed in, and with both of us holding the knife, and giggling, we pushed down, and made the first cut. Birch smiled.

"I love cake!"

I giggled as the camera flashed, she stood holding my hand with the knife, and softly kissed me, everyone cheered, and cameras went off everywhere.

With that, the music came on, and Birch took my hand, and led me out onto the floor, I felt a bit weird about dancing alone. She pulled me close, and looked deeply into my eyes. I picked this for you, she nodded at the DJ.

Avril exploded out of the speakers, and it was 'I am with you.' She knows how much I love this tune, and as we danced, she quietly sung it me, as everyone watched us together. I smiled as the song came to an end.

"I can kiss you in public now."

I pulled her close, and gave her a long slow kiss. Cameras flashed, as everyone flooded onto the dance floor, and danced all around us. I was gloriously happy, as I looked into her eyes with that amazing white hair. I never expected this when I was just eighteen, my life had a whole different plan, but it just goes to show, how none of us can really plan our lives and should relax and go with it, just go with the flow.

It was hot in the marquee, after an hour of dancing and hugging people. I had danced with dad, and my other dad, danced with Anthony, Bradley, Jimmy, and Luke, and I was so hot.

I stepped out for a second, and was surprised to find all the chairs had gone, so I walked slowly down to my arch, the sun was lowering as I looked at it. It had seen some moments of my life, it really was my sanctuary arch, and Birch knew that, and she saved it, and brought it to me. I have no idea how to repay that, I just don't.

I suppose my arch will now see more of me, and more of my life, it holds so many secrets of who I am, and is the only thing that knows as much, as Birch, and I suppose that really says everything. I walked up to the gothic window, and turned around and was faced with Hatty with her camera, it clicked.

"Got ya... I have waited all day for that, because that is the one I will paint." She looked at me and smiled.

"You did it kid, you broke her curse, and you followed your heart, I am so proud of you." I looked down at the floor.

"Did I really, I swore I would never marry, but I could not help myself, I want Birch more than anything else in my life." Hatty walked onto the stone, and leaned on the wall at my side, and pulled out a cigarette and lit it.

"That is why you broke the curse Abby. She wanted something far more than Edwin, but she stepped back at the last second, and married him instead. You married your hearts desire, she didn't, because she was not strong enough, you did, and that is so very important. Abby, you did what you wanted, and you did it your way, she backed out with cold feet." I looked up at her.

"You are pretty happy now with Clive, yes, you must have finally got over her?" Hatty blew out a smoke ring.

"Clive is a wonderful man, but he will always be second to her. Abby, I will never get over her, you almost made the same mistake, and I am so fucking glad you did not."

I understood that, twice I have almost lost her, and I never want to even come close to that again.

"I really want this marriage to work, I never want to lose her Hatty." She smiled.

"You won't Abby, there is absolutely no chance of that."

"How can you be so sure Hatty, people change?" She turned on the wall, and looked at me, her eyes were bright and full of life.

"Abby, I never had kids, I didn't need to, she had you. You are as much a daughter to me as you could get. I changed your bum as a baby, pushed your pram, saw your first steps, heard your first words. You are my daughter, and I love you so very much, now ask yourself this, when you came within an inch of losing her, who was it that pulled you back together?" I felt so close to her, I always have, and I felt this huge wave of emotion boil up inside me, and my eyes filled with yet more tears.

"You were always there, when they weren't, you were, I love you too Hatty, you have always been my second mum, you know that?" She smiled.

"I won't let you fail kid, not ever, I will never let my daughter fail." I gave a huge sob and she pulled me into her arms, and hugged me closely, and spoke softly.

"Abby, go and live, be you with Birch, and be happy."

She was right, she has always been there like a shadow watching over me. She stood by me with Martin, kept her word when I told her about my dad's affair, defended me in the village, and was there to help when I screwed up with Kyle. Without her I would never have made it through. When my parents shunned me, she loved me even more, I could never thank her enough. She let me go, and I stepped back and smiled, she handed me a tissue.

"You will have to leave soon Mrs Dixon." I looked up and gasped a smile.

"Oh Hatty, you are the very first person to call me that." I wiped my eyes, and she smiled.

"I know, it was deliberate. Go on, go and get ready, you have a whole new life of adventure waiting with that insanely beautiful woman." I nodded and smiled.

"I love you Hatty, thanks for everything, without you, I would never have made it." I gave her another huge hug, and then she pushed me back with a smile.

"Go live."

I headed to find Birch, and prepare for our departure. Inside the marquee, the music was playing and everyone was happy. Hatty leaned on the wall, and took a long pull of her cigarette, and looked around.

"I have always liked this arch; I am glad they saved it; I am glad it saved them."

Chapter 37

New Adventures.

I found Ella, and she came up to the room with us, and helped us unlace our dresses, and she repacked them for us. She helped undo my hair and brushed it for me. All my things from Deb's had been brought back to my room, and I slipped my laptop, phone charger, eBook reader, and a few other things into my black carry on bag. I had the passports, and flight tickets, I did not trust Birch as she was so forgetful.

I dressed in new black velvet flares, with my high wedged heel boots, and a tight fitting black top. I pulled on my long black, woollen crochet coat, and I was ready. I looked down at my hand, and the golden band, and smiled, Birch came over dressed in dark green, and pulled me into a hug.

"Time alone Sweetie... Finally."

I lifted my arm to her head, and pulled her into a loving kiss, and just enjoyed melting into her, the door opened and Chloe walked in with a large flat wrapped present, she looked at us.

"Sorry guys... I really want you to open this before you go, I know you are not opening anything till you get back, but would you... You know, just for me?" Birch released me.

"I love presents." I giggled as she took it, and tore the paper off, I looked at the painting, and it took my breath away, Chloe fidgeted.

"If there is something wrong, I can work on it while you are away." I shook my head as I looked at the picture of us kissing at Deb's wedding. I felt close to tears again as I looked at us in her painting, she had Birch perfectly.

"Wow Chloe, you did it again, it lives, holy shit, it lives completely, I absolutely love it." She broke out into a huge smile.

"Honestly... You are not just saying that because it is me, you really mean it?" Birch placed it on the bed, and stood back.

"Chloe... This is the best picture you have ever painted, I am so glad I do not have to buy it, because I would not be able to afford it, because this is master class, I am blown away." Chloe gave a huge sigh of relief.

"Guys I have worked my ass off on this, actually it is one of my first bum prints, I painted over it." Birch approved.

"You have a great ass, it is a brilliant painting, you got the truth of Abby perfectly." Chloe walked up and threw her arms around Birch.

"From you, that really means a lot." I smiled, she is so lovely, and so talented. She stood back and wiped her eyes.

"I love you guys, today will always stay with me, it was an honour to help you two with your day." I pulled her into a hug.

"You are our sister Chloe, a frigging straight one, but still a sister." She giggled.

"Abby, I am so fucking straight, it's unbelievable." I giggled, and kissed her cheek.

"I love you Chloe, even though you are straight." She smiled.

"I really love you guys too."

Chloe helped, as we carried our things down to the hall, and headed downstairs, back into the marquee. The DJ stopped the music.

"Ladies and Gentlemen, our happy couple are off, would you make your way to the front of the house, as they leave to start their new life." My dad came up to me and smiled, Angela, and my cousin were at his side smiling.

"I will not come round the front; I will say goodbye here." He pulled me into a hug.

"I found the service quite inspirational, you both looked beautiful. It was a lovely day, and very special for me, Angela has taken a lot of pictures, and I am going to sit and look at all of them tonight." I hugged him hard, and looked up at him, from his chest.

"You were here, that made it special for me, it was all I wanted." He smiled and kissed my head. Angela dragged me into her arms as dad hugged Birch. Angela held me tight.

"I am so happy for you Abby; it was a beautiful wedding. Go and be happy." I pulled back a little.

"I know what you did to make him see the light, and I will

always be grateful to you for that. Having him give me away, is all I have ever wanted." She smiled at me.

"You deserved more from him, I am happy to see him and you on better terms, the old bugger has no idea how much he needs you." She smiled, my cousin pulled me into a hug, and squeezed me hard.

"I wish you were here longer, so we could get to know each other better, but when I am in the states, I will look you up." She smiled, with her dark hair and blue eyes, she really did look like a younger me. Angela smiled and turned me to Birch.

"Go live."

I took Birch by the hand, and we walked into the kitchen, the place was packed, and it took forever to get to the door as we got hugged and mobbed. Even Madge smiled and told us what a beautiful service it was, and commented on how stylish the house was. We finally got outside, and it was no better. Mum handed us our bouquets.

"It is tradition, when you get to the gate you know what to do. Markus has packed all your things in the car." She handed Birch her huge bag.

"The knife is under your pillow; you know metal detectors and all that?" I giggled, and was a bit jealous she got to go through the contents of her big bag.

I hugged all my favourite people, as I walked along the line, Jimmy, Roni, Anita, Ella, William, Ellen, Bradley, Gill, Aden, Izzy, Hatty, Celia, Lillian, Chloe, Terry, Anthony, Michael, Deb's with little Jenny, Luke and Bev. She gave me a big smile.

"That was blinding, I balled me fuckin brains out I did. You are right for her Deadly, I know, because I have seen her, and no one was right, but you... Well, I knew the day I met you; you were always the one, and I am well chuffed for her."

I threw my arms round her and pulled her so tightly, as tears filled my eyes.

"Thanks Bev, I love you to bits, we will always be here, and you are always welcome, you are family to us you know that?" I released her and she smiled, and she had tears in her eyes, she gave me a big smile and swallowed hard, she knew. Birch dragged her into her arms.

"Sweetie, I love you, you are my best mate you know that?" Bev pulled her really tight, and almost squeezed her to death. Birch stepped back and wiped her eyes, and Bev smiled.

"If you get a cat, call me." I giggled, and she winked.

"Bought you a strap on, figured it was the right gift." Birch gave a loud cackle.

"Oh Sweetie, that is perfect."

We stood in the drive, and Luke lifted his arm and pressed a button in his hand, there was a massive explosion, and Birch jumped out of her skin and squealed, and then looked up, as thousands of pieces of confetti fell from the sky.

Birch squealed with delight, she spread out her arms, and threw her head back, and stuck out her tongue, like it was snow. Everyone laughed, as she spun on the spot.

"IT'S BEAUTIFUL SWEETIE." She was covered, and it stuck to her hair. I looked at Edwina, she had done so much for this wedding, and I smiled.

"We both owe you so much, you really pulled out all the stops, it was the greatest day of my life, thanks." She pulled me into her arms.

"You two saved Chloe, what I did was nothing compared to that, but it was fun, and you two deserve all of this, you really have no idea how remarkable you are?" She let me go, as Birch slipped her arm round me. I looked at Luke, and then back to Edwina.

"You kept a lot of secrets Edwina, I admire that, but there was one you missed in all of this." She frowned, and shook her head.

"No fucking way, I even gave Chloe loads of red herrings to throw you off, nothing got past me." I giggled and looked at Birch.

"She just completely missed it Birch." She nodded.

"Not as bright as I thought, I am a bit disappointed Deads." I agreed, she stared at me.

"No... I am having none of this, I did it all by the book and missed nothing." I shrugged, and pointed.

"So how come you missed that?" She frowned, turned and Luke went down on one knee and held up a ring. She looked shocked.

"Edwina Pemberton, will you marry me?" I gave a huge laugh, as Chloe saw the ring, screamed, and jumped up and down with Deb's, which woke baby up. She looked terrified, I leaned in.

"You are supposed to say something like, yes." She looked at me, with terrified eyes and then back at Luke.

"YES... YES!" I handed her my bouquet.

"Congratulations WEENA!" Birch laughed wildly.

"See, I told you she was not that on the ball Deads."

Birch turned her back to everyone, bent low, and then heaved her bouquet backwards, and it sailed through the air. I watched as it came hurtling down, Chloe dodged and ran away from it, and Gill snatched it just before Alex could get it. I looked at Aden and smiled.

"Now there is fate?" He smiled at me.

We walked to the car and left Edwina crying and hugging Luke. Markus opened the door, as we walked out of the gates, holding hands and smiling, the flashes of the press exploded. Everyone behind us piled out into the road, as I stood lost for words.

There were hundreds of fans in the crowd behind the barriers, and I stopped and smiled. We both walked around the car and into the road, held up our joined hands, and waved with our free ones to the fans, who screamed with delight and took pictures. The press went wild, finally they had clear shots of us.

I waved and smiled, turned and pulled Birch into a kiss, and the roar of the fans was unbelievable. The press loved it, so did Birch, she did not want to stop.

We jumped into the car, and Markus closed the door. We drove slowly as the barriers were pulled back by the security, and all the fans held up signs wishing us congratulations, I could not believe how many there were, if I had known, I would have come out sooner, and talked to them.

We got to the end of Waterside Lane, and Markus sped up, the long white ribbons flapped on the front of the car, as we headed for the airport. Birch snuggled into me and we laughed and hugged, and kissed.

The airport was just as crazy, as hundreds of photographers waited for us. Markus pulled up, and looked back into the car.

"Remember Mrs Dixon, keep your head down, and get through to check in as fast as possible. I have a porter to take your luggage, so just wait while I unload." I gave him a grin.

"I like how you say Mrs Dixon." He giggled and opened the door, Birch pulled me into a kiss, and had to stop because she started laughing.

"Deads, I am so excited, I am Mrs Dixon too." I nodded.

"Wow we have the same name; how did that happen?" She smiled.

"Sweetie, I am so happy, today was the best ever."

It was, there was no doubt, I don't think I have ever been this happy. The door opened, and we climbed out smiling, I was glad I had my hair down again, it does make a good shield. The cameras went off, and they all shouted at us.

'What is it like to be married Abigail?' I stopped and looked at the reporter. I held up my hand, that was holding Birch's with a huge smile.

"IT IS FRIGGING WONDERFUL!"

The cameras exploded, and he smiled at me and nodded. We broke out in giggles, and hurried inside, where the porter stood with our luggage. Birch thanked him and gave him ten quid, and we pushed our way towards departures. This was day one of our new adventures.

We have been married almost a week now, we have not been out in the sun much, actually we have not been out of bed much. We have made love, talked, eaten, played music, and just been naked and very lazy, and I feel like a million dollars. Today we headed down to the private beach, and the sand is white and fine, and really hot. I had to laugh, as I watched Birch scream and squeal, as she ran to the water to cool her bare feet off, I did tell her to wear her flip flops.

I lay back on my lounger and just felt the joy of the sun on my skin, being naked in the sun is glorious. Birch came over and handed me an ice cold rum and cola, and straddled my waist, she smiled.

"Watch the sun, you do not want sun burned boobs." I shook my head and smiled.

"Birch, I am your wife, if you put any more oil on my boobs, I will be permanently water proof. If you want to play with them, just play, they are yours forever." She bit her lip.

"I love your boobs Sweetie… I actually want to kiss them; I love how horny it gets you." I looked over my glasses at her.

"So, just kiss them."

She gave a big smile, and moved down, I lay back a bit, I love her kissing my boobs too. She pushed her mouth onto my left nipple and gave it a hard suck, and swirled her tongue on, and then sat up really fast, and screwed her face up.

"YUK!" She spat into the sand, and then smacked her lips and dragged her tongue across her teeth.

"Ew, Sweetie sun oil tastes horrible. I don't like it."

She spat in the sand, and stuck her tongue out, I just sat back and laughed at her, as her face stayed screwed up, and she held her tongue out looking miserable.

"Sweetie it's horrible, help me."

I handed her the glass of rum, she took a huge gulp, and swirled it round her mouth, and spat it out, and sat on my waist smacking her lips.

"Sweetie, go for a swim, and wash will you, I prefer your tits salty compared to oily?"

As we lay basking in the sun, in the Bahamas, back home the garden was clear, and was lush green lawns, with the arch stood at the bottom. We were so lucky, the day after our wedding, it threw it down, and the poor workers taking everything down, got soaked.

Normality returned to Waterside Lane, although all the papers were splashed with pictures of us leaving the house, and most of it was great press. Fashion Voice put an amazing article together, with some stunning pictures of us, it became their biggest selling copy, which they were very happy about, they also got to sell their pictures worldwide, and made a lot of money out of the deal. The papers finally got hold of pictures of the actual service, and they were everywhere, although I did not see that many myself, I was busy enjoying my relaxed life.

Edwina was gloriously happy, and has messaged me every day, and I would read them to Birch as we ate our evening meal, but because of the time difference, at home in Wotton as it drizzled, and we baked, everyone was gathered in the Church Hall, listening to Primula, who was giving her pitch of why she should lead the Parish Council. It was all about tradition, she intended to undo pretty much everything my mum had done to improve the village, including, controlling the pubs drinking hours.

Hatty sat at the back with Clive, Debs, and Chloe, she had arrived late, so rather than join the Council on stage, she sat at the back like old times.

"Jesus, why not make us all wear biblical clothing and chastity belts?" Primula was coming to her end of speech, and she smiled smugly.

"That is why I want all of you to vote for me as Parish Chair, and Sophia Banbury as Vice Chair. Thank you for your time." About half the gathering applauded. It was not the best reception; Hatty gave a sigh.

"If that little prick gets the chair, I am quitting, God if we need new blood, we need something with a pulse, not that dried up old maid. My God, Nigel needs to tie her to a bed, and at least attempt to fuck her, she might just lighten up." Felicity applauded as Primula left the stage, and stood in front of the mic.

"Thank you, Primula, that was a very informative pitch. Ladies and gentlemen, as many of you know I have decided to step down from my role, and work as just an ordinary member, and Celia, who has been invaluable to us, has decided to retire, as has Phillip. It is time for new eyes and new blood, and it was nice to see youth in the form of Primula come forward."

She sat in her chair looking smug, with a smirk on her face. Felicity smiled, and leaned into the mic.

"I am pleased now to welcome Mrs Debbie Ford Battersby, to the stage to make another announcement for all your attention." Hatty turned and looked at her as she got up.

"You sneaky bitch, what are you up too?" Deb's walked towards the stage, Hatty turned on Chloe.

"Do you know anything about this?"

Chloe shut her mouth tight and shook her head, looking terrified. Hatty smiled.

"You lying Bitch, it's alright I will wait."

Chloe let out a long breath, and gasped air in relief. Deb's approached the mic. She took a deep breath as she arranged her papers, and then looked out across the rest of the hall.

"Good evening, everyone. I would like with your permission

to read out a statement that has been prepared for me, so I can address you all." She unfolded a piece of paper, and gave a slight cough to clear her throat.

"Dear villagers of Wotton Dursley, I would very much like to be with you tonight, and would like to publicly thank two of Wotton's hardest working council members, for their loyal and dedicated service. Sadly, I cannot be there in person, because I am currently enjoying my honeymoon, but even so, you are all in my thoughts."

Deb's took a breath.

"I am not sure that such great shoes can be filled, and I am greatly relieved to see that Mrs Felicity Watson, will be staying on as a guiding hand for all new candidates, and so it is with that factor in mind, that I feel it is time for many of us, who have spent a great deal of our life working behind the scenes, to step up, and provide an opposition candidate to Primula Wallace."

Murmurs rose in the audience, and Hatty sat back and smiled, Deb's continued to read.

"I feel it would be wrong to field only one candidate, and it is in that spirit, that I have finally decided to throw my hat into the ring, and make known my intention to run for the position of Parish Council Chair. So, I, Abigail Jennifer Dixon, formally Watson, announce my intention to run, and I nominate Doctor Jemima Dixon as my intended Vice Chair. It is my hope, this provides a fair competition, to give you all a chance for a balanced election. I also feel that to undo such great work, as done by the current council and its predecessors, would be detrimental to the future prospects of this village and its surrounding area." Deb's took a breath and licked her lips.

"I intend to present my case in the form of a full presentation in person at the next public meeting in July. If you see Miss Chloe Pemberton, she does have some printed materials already available at the back. Thank you for your time, and I look forward to seeing you all soon. My regards to you all. Abigail Jennifer Dixon."

Deb's turned and pulled a black cloth off a large board, revealing a huge poster of Abby and Birch, with Dixon and Dixon printed on it. A loud round of applause rose up that completely engulfed Prim's. Deb's smiled, and walked off stage as the applause continued, Hatty smiled as she leaned against the wall.

"Oh you wonderful girl... You bloody marvellous girl."

Marjorie sat looking ahead, with hardly an expression on her face, as Prim turned on Nigel.

"How can she do that, she has no right, it is my turn, I want that seat?" Nigel just stared at her looking terrified, but Marjorie just for a second smirked.

I lay on the bed, it was warm, even being naked. Birch came in and put a tray on the bed filled with bowls of chopped salad and fruit, we had really got into finger food while we were here. I chewed a piece of cucumber.

"They should be making the announcement about now, Prim is going to be pissed off, I hope she does not take it out on Nigel. How was he at the last meeting?"

Birch gave a nod as she snacked on a large chunk of mango.

"He is talking, but we are only a few sessions in, and he has a lot to talk about, it will take time, but I am feeling positive. He hardly said a word at the first meeting, so he is getting there, just slowly, He bloody loves your ass." I shuddered.

"Jesus Birch I am eating." She giggled.

"He did tell me he sees you as a really good friend, so you are safe for now from his pencil dick." I picked up a baby sweet corn, looked at it, and dropped it back in the bowl with a shudder. Birch gave a cackle of a laugh. I looked at her as she laughed at me.

"I am going to tell him; you have wet dreams about him." Her face went instantly straight.

"Sweetie, please don't do that." I cracked out laughing.

"Bloody scary, isn't it?" She smiled, and lifted her glass, and took a swig.

"It is funny really if you think about it, for such a long time we have had to fight to be treated fairly, and I would imagine tonight, most of the village is really relieved that we are in the running. They have finally found something more unacceptable than us, Primula!"

It was strange, we have fought so hard against name calling, bullying and intimidation, even sexual discrimination and homophobia. We have faced so much, and gone through the fires several times, and how times have changed. There have been so many bumps in the road for us, and it has been tough at times to overcome them.

I will never forget that day, at the bottom of Manor Road, as I buried my face in Birch's shoulder and wept out of fear, because I was so afraid to face my mum, and the village. Those years were rough, they almost broke me, I almost did something so stupid, that I cannot believe it now.

The day after that awful night, she came back, and never left, and I am so grateful. The Curio's had splintered, and we had drifted apart, and all faced tough times, and she just popped up with that crazy smile, and a head full of crazy ideas, and glued us all back together again.

I watched her pick up another mango piece, she examined it and then popped it in her mouth, looked at me and smiled, she had no idea at all of how amazing she actually is, she is just her, and we all just flocked to her. She is like a happy magnet, and we are all attracted to her like opposing poles, we just get drawn into her.

"Birch, do you remember when you told me, you did not use the road of life. You were sat in a boat, with the sail down just drifting along, going with the flow?" She nodded as she swallowed.

"Yeah, that is how I see my life, why?"

"Are we still doing that now?" She picked up a small cherry tomato, and popped it in her mouth, and chewed, she nodded.

"I think the boat is bigger now, it is more of a house boat, as we have the whole village on board, and we are tied up to the bank."

"So, we are no longer drifting with the flow?" She shook her head.

"Sweetie, we are at the start of something new. We need to organise, you know, take on supplies, and expand the crew, which is what we have been doing. When that is done, we just untie and drift, and see where we go from there."

"Okay, so how do we untie the boat?" She swallowed and grabbed her glass.

"You win the council and take over, and boy, then we will really be in for a ride, think about what we did with the house. Holy shit Deads, what can we do with a whole village?" She smiled.

"It won't be boring that is for sure." She pointed at the food.

"Eat something, I don't want you to lose weight, your boobs are the perfect size for me, here rub this mango on them, I want a tasty snack later." She winked.

I took the chunk of mango and started to rub it round my nipples, it was cold, and they started to grow, I glanced at her, as she excitedly watched.

"You know you're a pervert, right?" She smirked.

"Says the girl rubbing mango into her nipples, like a frigging weirdo." She giggled at me, and I burst out laughing. Oh God, I love being married.

Voice over, Curio Intro.

Instrumental

Don't look at me that way.
Don't say those things you say.
Why don't you treat me right?
You won't see me cry tonight.

Someone take this pain away.
Stop saying the things you say.
Can't you see that I am in pain.
Stood here crying in the rain

I keep asking myself why, am I living a big lie.
I just cannot take this pain; I need to just be me again.
Tell me why, let me go, give me a reason, so I know.
Understand it's now too late, I cannot handle much more hate.

Tonight, I am sat here on my own.
No one sees how much I feel alone.
Trying so hard to not lose sight
I have thought of ending all tonight

She does not know I feel this way.
Or how much I wished I'd stayed.
I just want to have her near.
Cause I am afraid she'll Disaster.

I keep asking myself why, am I living a big lie.
I just cannot take this pain; I need to just be me again.
Tell me why, let me go, give me a reason, so I know.
Understand it's now too late, I cannot handle much more hate.

Don't look at me that way.
Don't say those things you say.
Why don't you treat me right?
You won't see me cry tonight.

Instrumental fade…

More Author's
From
Violet Circle Publishing

Mike Beale. (Children's Book)

Crumble's Adventures.
ISBN: 978-1-910299-06-7
Digital ISBN: 978-1-910299-08-1

Colin Smith (Play)

Heaven knows I'm Miserable Now
ISBN: 978-1-910299-16-6
Digital ISBN: 978-1-910299-23-4

Ted Morgan. (Poetry and verse)

Wordsmith's Wanderings.
ISBN: 978-1-910299-04-3
Digital ISBN: 978-1-910299-09-8
Peregrinations of the Wordsmith
ISBN: 978-1-910299-18-0
Digital ISBN: 978-1-910299-21-0
Silhouette Soldiers
ISBN: 978-1-910299-19-7
Digital ISBN: 978-1-910299-22-7
A Menu of Memories
Digital ISBN: 978-1-910299-32-6
Digital ISBN: 978-1-910299-33-3

Robin John Morgan. (Fiction/Fantasy/Slice of Life)

Heirs to the Kingdom.

Book One, The Bowman of Loxley.
ISBN: 978-1-910299-00-5
Digital ISBN: 978-1-910299-10-4
Book Two, The Lost Sword of Carnac.
ISBN: 978-1-910299-01-2
Digital ISBN: 978-1-910299-11-1
Book Three, The Darkness of Dunnottar.
ISBN: 978-1-910299-02-9
Digital ISBN: 978-1-910299-12-8
Book Four, Queen of the Violet Isle.
ISBN: 978-1-910299-03-6
Digital ISBN: 978-1-910299-13-5
Book Five, Crystals of the Mirrored Waters.
ISBN: 978-1-910299-05-0
Digital ISBN: 978-1-910299-14-2
Book Six, Last Arrow of the Woodland Realm.
ISBN: 978-1-910299-07-4
Digital ISBN: 978-1-910299-15-9
Book Seven, Bridge Of Sequana.
ISBN: 978-1-910299-17-3
Digital ISBN: 978-1-910299-20-3
Book Eight, The Circle of Darkness.
ISBN: 978-1-910299-26-5
Digital ISBN: 978-1-910299-29-6

The Curio Chronicles.

Part One, Abigail's Summer.
ISBN: 978-1-910299-27-2
Digital ISBN: 978-1-910299-28-9
Part Two, Curio's Summer.
ISBN: 978-1-910299-34-0
Digital ISBN: 978-1-910299-35-7
Part Three, Curio's Christmas.
ISBN: 978-1-910299-38-8
Digital ISBN: 978-1-910299-39-5

Part Four, Abigail's Wedding
ISBN: 978-1-910299-42-5
Digital ISBN: 978-1-910299-43-2

Other Works.

Rise Of The Raven
ISBN: 978-1-910299-30-2
Digital ISBN: 978-1-910299-31-9
The Countess Of Darkness
ISBN: 978-1-910299-40-1
Digital ISBN: 978-1-910299-41-8

Han's Cottage.
ISBN: 978-1-910299-36-4
Digital ISBN: 978-1-910299-37-1

Find out more about our authors and their books at
www.violetcirclepublishing.co.uk

Violet Circle Publishing Manchester UK